Pride & Prejudice:

Behind the Scenes

Edited by
Susan Mason-Milks, Maria Grace,
Abigail Reynolds and Mary Simonsen

Introduction

It is a truth universally acknowledged that writers obsessed with Jane Austen must be in want of new ways to show their devotion to the peerless authoress. This book is the product of 15 authors of Austen-inspired fiction who shared the vision of an homage to Jane Austen by imagining scenes she never wrote. We knew our scenes could never match the original, but who could?

In 2011 we conceived the idea of celebrating the 200th anniversary of the publication of *Pride & Prejudice* by writing new scenes based on the original book and posting them on Austen Variations, our group blog, in real time exactly 200 years after the events of the original book. The project took on a life of its own, and at the end we decided to publish a collection of our scenes as *Pride & Prejudice: The Scenes Jane Austen Never Wrote* (now out of print), with all royalties to be donated to Austen-related charities. In 2015 we had the honor of presenting a check for over $9000 to the Jane Austen House Museum in Chawton.

After changes in our group, we decided a revised, more complete edition was in order. This book includes many of the best scenes from the first book, but more than half of it is new material. Some are scenes mentioned in *Pride & Prejudice* but never shown, like Lady Catherine de Bourgh telling Mr. Collins to take a wife or Darcy dining with the Gardiners, and others are re-imaginings of Austen's existing scenes from a different point of view, such as Darcy's impressions of the Netherfield Ball. Once again, all royalties will be donated to charities honoring Jane Austen.

What you will read in these pages is not a novel. It is a collection of scenes imagined and created as complements to the original story. You can read it from start to finish or just dip in to the scenes that sound interesting to you. Along the way, you may notice inconsistencies between scenes or find slightly different versions of events. This is not a mistake or careless editing. We made a conscious decision to let the scenes stand as each author was inspired to write them.

We hope you enjoy our loving tribute to the genius of Jane Austen.

The Table of Contents begins on page 717.

Netherfield Park is Let at Last!

by Abigail Reynolds

September 18, 1811

Mr. Anderson reined in his horse at the top of a hill. "And there you have it, Mr. Bingley," the solicitor said. "Netherfield Park!"

"So this is Netherfield!" Bingley shaded his eyes for a better view. "It looks delightful."

"The proportions are indeed excellent, as you will see as we approach the house. Come, the drive is just ahead."

Bingley had rarely seen such pleasant countryside. He turned his head from one side to another as they rode, trying to take in every detail to report later to Darcy.

They trotted past an orchard where a gnarled old man clung precariously to a ladder as he plucked apples from an equally gnarled old tree. Mr. Anderson said, "As you can see, the land here is rich and productive. And the hunting! You have surely heard of Lord Pryce-Wellington's famous hunting parties, Mr. Bingley."

Bingley could not recall anything of the sort, but he nodded obligingly. "My sister will love this house. She has always wished for a country estate." He doubted Caroline would wish to have hunting parties in any case; she would be more concerned with hosting house parties for her well-bred friends. Darcy would enjoy the hunting, though, and if Darcy liked it, Caroline would adore it.

"Will Miss Bingley wish to view it as well?"

Bingley smiled broadly. "No, it is to be a surprise for her." Just a few weeks past, Caroline had praised Darcy's habit of purchasing surprise gifts for his sister. Bingley had immediately decided to take a page from Darcy's book, and there was nothing Caroline wished for more than a fashionable country estate. She would be delighted!

Mr. Anderson cleared his throat. "Perhaps your sister might prefer to see the house before you sign the contract," he said delicately. "There is no accounting for a lady's taste in these matters."

Bingley waved away the suggestion. "Unless the interior disappoints, I see no cause for concern." He paused with a frown. "It does not have a parterre, does it? Caroline despises parterres. She says they are ridiculously old-fashioned."

"I do not recall any mention of parterre gardens, but we shall see for ourselves. Come, the housekeeper is expecting us and will give us a tour of the house."

Lady Catherine Interviews Mr. Collins

by Diana Birchall

September 19, 1811

Mr. Whitaker, the clergyman of Hunsford, was dead. Lady Catherine, however, could not bring herself to regret it. "Certainly," she said, "I shall mourn as much as is proper; that is, I shall wish him every mercy at the seat of Judgment, but that, of course, is no more than what is due to us all. In my own judgment however, his life on earth was peculiarly dissatisfying."

"He was a good clergyman, was he not, ma'am?" Mrs. Jenkinson ventured timidly.

Lady Catherine made a contemptuous tut-tutting sound. "Speak only of what you are qualified to assess, Mrs. Jenkinson," she said. "You know I have often told you that your opinions are all too weak-minded. I would not wish the person who is companion to my daughter to be otherwise; to hold strong, decided opinions would be a drawback in your position. Biddibility, and gentility, are what I ask, and I make no complaint of you. But you are unable to discern a good sermon from a bad, and therefore I must inform you that Mr. Whitaker was very wanting in his abilities in that capacity."

Her visitor, Lady Metcalfe, a lady of a similar time of life and equal dignity as Lady Catherine, put down her teacup. "Is that so, Lady Catherine? I never heard Mr. Whitaker, but if he was such an inferior practitioner of his duties, it is most fortunate that you now have the opportunity to replace him."

Lady Catherine nodded vigorously, and the lace on her headdress shook. "To be sure. I confess, however, Lady Metcalfe, that in this instance I am quite at a loss. Mr. Whitaker died suddenly, having been so foolish as to catch a cold, and most unjustifiably leaving me unprepared with a suitable successor."

"A cold? Did he?" commented Lady Metcalfe. "He cannot have been of very stout constitution. We have had dry weather this summer, and it is only the first of September."

"Mr. Whitaker was so kind as to visit me every day," spoke up Miss de Bourgh, "in my most recent illness."

"But I question if his fatal cold was caught by visiting you, Anne. Hers was only a very slight catarrh," she turned to Lady Metcalfe, "always a matter for the very greatest care, with delicacy like Anne's, and she was confined in bed for some weeks, but it ought not to have been anything a man like Mr. Whitaker could not counter."

"Do you not think it may have been our summoning him four and five times each day?" asked Mrs. Jenkinson hesitatingly. "He could not have had a full night's sleep for at least a month, because of his extreme exertions."

"Bah! That was no more than his duty, and it was the dirty Hambly family in the village, all down with scarlet fever, that did the mischief, I am sure. I told them to keep their farm animals out of the cottage and to wash themselves with lye soap, but did they? They did not. I have no patience with such people."

"And so now you are in the position of finding a new clergyman," said Lady Metcalfe meditatively. "I should think you the very last person to be without resources. You have always supplied your circle with suitable governesses, and servants."

"And my own four nieces," said Mrs. Jenkinson, "are so happily settled, and all because of Lady Catherine's wonderful cleverness and benevolence."

Lady Catherine looked graciously. "Those are the qualities for what I am famed," she admitted simply.

"Mama, is it not the usual thing, in such cases, to inquire at the universities?" asked Anne languidly.

"You are right, my dear, and I have written to the Master of Balliol. He is my cousin," she told Lady Metcalfe, "but I do not like the tone of the letters I have received in return. Young men of the present day show no suitable deference. Do you know, one young man has written to demand a curate, not paid for out of the living, but presumably from my own pocket! As if the stipend were not of almost unheard-of liberality! And another candidate, a Mr. Blaylock, who seemed a more modest kind of young man, refused to submit his sermons to me for approval, or confine himself to less than half-an-hour."

"Shocking!" said Lady Metcalfe.

"Is not it? And a third, a very respectable young man or so I thought, wishes the family's cottage-visiting, and other charitable works, to be entirely under his own direction. Heaven and earth! I do not know what will become of the Church at this rate, if its servitors are all to be of this stamp."

"There is a young man I have heard of," Lady Metcalfe said thoughtfully, "our new governess, Miss Harrison, was telling us of a friend of her brother's, who was lately ordained with him. I believe he was at Oxford with Mr. Pope. I will make inquiries if you like."

"I would be most obliged, Lady Metcalfe. Do write. Find out how old the gentleman is—he must be under thirty, so that he is ductile enough to get used to my ways. He need not be a remarkable genius; I should prefer obedience, and a young man who would be sensible that to hold the living of Hunsford is a great privilege. Only think! He will be able to see Rosings from his very doorway."

"To be sure," replied Lady Metcalfe, "not many young clergymen in the kingdom could expect to be as fortunate as your new rector."

"And he must not be bred too high. I do not require a high-and-mighty gentleman, but naturally he must be a gentleman. Find out what his family are and be sure he is of a docile, agreeable temper, but without inconvenient prejudices, or set in his ways. We will want him to make up a card table and not be overly censorious about such practices as Sunday visiting."

"I will inquire of Miss Pope at once and have her write to her brother. I believe the young man's name is Mr. Collins."

* * *

Since his ordination, Mr. Collins had kept his lodgings at Oxford, in hopes of maintaining himself by tutoring while waiting for a more remunerative preferment; but there had been no pupils so desperate as to seek out the ministrations of a man who had little reputation for cleverness or learning, and no valuable appointments had been offered. On receiving Lady Catherine's letter, which followed Miss Pope's inquiry, Mr. Collins did not hesitate. With such speed and dispatch as his slowness to form long sentences required, he wrote a return letter full of obsequious professions of gratitude and eagerness to demean himself. Lady Catherine thought his alacrity to perform any duty she might wish, most promising, and wrote a condescending answer; and so it was fixed that he would wait upon her at Rosings, only a sennight after his receiving the first communication.

Mr. Collins arrived promptly as expected, and Lady Catherine was disposed from the first to be pleased with him.

"So you are Mr. Collins. What is your age?"

"Five and twenty, Your Ladyship."

"And what was your father?"

"He was a farmer, Your Ladyship."

"A farrrmer!" Lady Catherine trilled, and lifted her heavily marked eyebrows. "Then you are not the son of a gentleman. How did you come to be a clergyman? There is some mystery here. I do not like mysteries."

"Madam, my father was certainly not a very great gentleman by your standards; he was not rich, and did not frequent the court or move in genteel society, as you and your noble daughter are entitled to do." Mr. Collins made a clumsy bow and a scrape, simultaneously. "Yet he was of good blood, of the Hertfordshire Collinses; and my mother was own sister to the late Mr. Bennet of Longbourn of whom you may, perhaps, have heard. Mr. Bennet disapproved of her marriage, and after my mother's death, quarreled with my father, so that there was a breach; but I have reason to believe that Mr. Bennet's son is of a more amiable disposition. And by a fortunate circumstance, whenever the present Mr. Bennet, my cousin, dies, I am the heir by entail to the valuable property of Longbourn."

"Are you indeed? Well! And is it a large property, Mr. Collins? What do you suppose Mr. Bennet's income to be?"

"Longbourn is nothing compared to the unrivalled magnificence and beauty of Rosings, of course, your Ladyship. You would think nothing of it. It is, however, a good sized, modern-built house, in the village of Meryton, and Mr. Bennet is said to have a thousand pounds a year. He is not an economical man, I have heard, but he has so far managed to keep the property together, so that I can expect to inherit a respectable estate."

"You do not take possession until his death," pursued Lady Catherine, "and how old a man do you suppose him to be?"

"Mr. Bennet is between forty and fifty and has five daughters."

"Indeed! And no son. That is well for you, but I must be assured that if you come to Hunsford, we will not be in danger of your abandoning us in the space of a twelvemonth for Meryton."

"I do not think there is the remotest danger of that. Mr. Bennet is in good health, and I would rank my duties at Hunsford as far above any other earthly ones, should I be so unspeakably fortunate as to be granted your Ladyship's patronage."

"That is well. And you are versed in all the duties that will attach to your station?"

"Indeed, I have made good use of my time at Oxford, and have learnt about tithes, and sermon-writing, and visiting the poor."

"About writing sermons," Lady Catherine fixed him with a suspicious eye, "how long do you consider the proper Sunday sermon to be?"

"Not more than five and twenty minutes, my lady, and I assure you I would always submit to direction from my benefactress with the most extreme obligingness."

Lady Catherine seemed pleased. "Hm. Very good. And you will not object to being at Rosings often, to fill in at the dinner table, and make a fourth at cards, whenever it is desired? You will be available day and night at a moment's notice?"

Mr. Collins took a deep breath. "Lady Catherine," he said feelingly, "I should consider my being admitted to visit Rosings as the very greatest honor I have ever had in my life."

She nodded. "A most appropriate sentiment. And you will not interfere with my decisions as magistrate of the village?"

"I should never presume to do such a thing, madam!"

"The living is five hundred a year, but it is capable of improvement and has a very good house attached to it. I will take you to see it—it is time for Anne's walk, and we will take it together. The house is in need of some repairs, and I will undertake these for you before you take possession, on one condition."

"Anything you desire, Lady Catherine!"

"You must marry and bring a wife hither." She made an emphatic rap on the floor with her silver walking-stick.

Mr. Collins looked all acquiescence. "I would be only too happy to gratify you in such a way," he bleated. "I think it right that a clergyman like myself should have a wife, to serve as a praiseworthy example to the parish; and I assure you that to marry is my object."

"That is well. We are too retired a society here and require a neighbor. Someone who is not too proud, and will be very attentive to Miss de Bourgh and me, yet always know her station."

"That is exactly what I should look for in a wife. I confess I had thought—" He stopped.

"Well? What is it?"

"The five Miss Bennets have all a reputation for great gentility, economy, amiability, and—and beauty, ma'am."

"Have they now? But you are not on terms with your cousin, their father."

"No, but if I should be so unspeakably fortunate, beyond all men, as to accede to the Hunsford living, I would, by your Ladyship's leave, take a journey into Hertfordshire, to offer an olive branch to the family and to see for myself if the Miss Bennets are as respectable and fair as reputed."

"That's well thought of." She looked at Mr. Collins with condescension and approval. "Only be sure that the Miss Bennet you choose is the right sort of girl, mind."

"I would by no means wish to marry anyone who would be in any degree offensive to my patroness."

"You show a most suitable spirit. Yes, Mr. Collins, I believe, on mature consideration, that we are of like mind, and that you are the very man to whom I wish to give my patronage and raise to all the privileges of the Rector of Hunsford."

"Oh, Lady Catherine, I cannot speak my infinite gratitude," he said, with the very lowest bow of which he was capable, and a tremble in his voice. "I can only promise you that I will fulfill every one of the duties I owe to your gracious Ladyship, and of course to the Church of England."

"Then it is settled," said Lady Catherine, satisfied. "You will preach your first sermon the last week in September or the first of October—whichever you prefer."

"The sooner the better, dear madam. You may expect me on the earliest date."

Bingley Takes Possession of Netherfield

by Abigail Reynolds

September 25, 1811

Caroline Bingley glared at her brother as their carriage rattled over the cobblestones of a little country town. "Charles," she said in a deceptively honeyed voice, "you know I do not like surprises."

Bingley rubbed his hands together gleefully. "You will like this one." She had been trying to wheedle the information out of him since they had left London, but he was determined not to tell her until the last minute. He could not wait to see the look on her face when she realized that Netherfield was theirs! "We are almost there, in any case."

"Good. I have had more than enough of being gawked at by the locals. One would think they had never seen people of fashion before. That woman—her dress must be at least five seasons old, and she has the audacity to actually point at us!"

Bingley glanced out the window and smiled at a particularly pretty girl. "I am given to understand that there are a number of excellent families in the area, but strangers must be something of a novelty."

Caroline's lips twisted, but she did not trouble herself to reply.

Ten minutes later the carriage pulled up in front of Netherfield. Caroline barely glanced at the house. "What is this place?" she asked scornfully.

"It is called Netherfield Park." Bingley tried to suppress a grin of anticipation.

"My surprise is here? Charles, don't tell me you have purchased another horse!" She curled her lip as the footman opened the carriage door for her.

Bingley hurried around the carriage to hand her out. "No, my dear. It is not that your surprise is here, but rather that here is your surprise!"

"What on earth do you mean, Charles? I see nothing but the house."

"How many times have you said we must find a country estate? Well, here it is. I have signed the lease, and it is ours."

She turned an ominous stare on him. "You leased an estate without discussing it with me first? Charles, what in God's name were you thinking? This is in the middle of nowhere, and heaven alone knows what condition it is in!"

Bingley's shoulders sagged. This was not at all how Georgiana Darcy reacted to surprises from her brother. Perhaps it was just the shock of the moment. "I showed the drawings and the estate books to Darcy, and he said it was a good idea."

"One can hardly trust the word of two men in the matter of a household!" she snapped.

"Come, let me show you the interior before you say anything further," he said, then played his trump card. "Darcy says he will come for a long visit once we are settled in."

"Hmmph," she snorted, but with a thoughtful look. "A long visit, you say?"

"Yes. Look, there is the housekeeper waiting for us." He bounded up the steps, leaving her to trail behind him. "Mrs. Johnson, it is a pleasure to see you again! Allow me to introduce my sister, Miss Bingley, who will be acting as my hostess here."

The housekeeper curtsied deeply, but Caroline barely spared her a glance. Instead, she looked around slowly, examining the hall. "I suppose this will do, although it could be larger, and the furnishings are hardly to the latest fashion."

Bingley's spirits brightened. From Caroline, that was practically praise. "The library is to our left, and a ladies' sitting room on the right. But come through here—you must see the grand staircase and the drawing room. It is in the shape of an octagon, and I immediately thought of you when I saw it."

Caroline rolled her eyes, but proceeded through the gilded doorway with him. He had hoped for a better response to the grand staircase, which was indeed of the caliber of anything seen at Pemberley, but she said nothing until they reached the drawing room. There she stopped in the center of the room and pivoted around, slowly nodding her head. "I suppose you could have done worse," she said grudgingly, then turned to the housekeeper. "It will take a great deal of work to make this presentable."

Mr. Bennet Calls on Mr. Bingley

by Mary Simonsen

October 3, 1811

Mr. Bennet was among the earliest of those who waited on Mr. Bingley…though to the last always assuring his wife that he should not go; and till the evening after the visit was paid, she had no knowledge of it. - Pride and Prejudice - Chapter 1

Despite his insistence that he would *not* call on the newest member of the Meryton neighborhood, Mr. Bennet had always intended to visit with Mr. Bingley. After all, they were near neighbors, and if his cows were to wander onto the man's property, he hoped to encounter a friendly face when he arrived at Netherfield Park with an apology for any inconvenience as a result of bovine trespass.

From intelligence he had gleaned in the village, Mr. Bennet knew that each morning, before breakfast, Mr. Bingley enjoyed a ride in the park on an excellent stallion that was sparking as much comment in the village as its rider—at least from the male population. He knew that if he arrived at Netherfield Park at approximately 9:30, Mr. Bingley would still be in the park on his mount, and he would have sufficient time to make his own inquiries about Netherfield's newest master.

As hoped, it was Buttons, who had served the previous owners of the manor house as its butler, who opened the door. Following an exchange of knowing looks, Buttons directed Mr. Bennet to the study, explaining that Mr. Bingley was expected within the half hour.

Mr. Bennet began by paying Meryton's newest resident a compliment. "If Mr. Bingley has opted to retain the services of the Darlingtons' servants, then I already know him to be a man of good sense."

"Mr. Bingley *is* a man of sense," Buttons agreed, "but as for how long I'll have this position, there's no telling."

"Why is that, Buttons?"

"When Mr. Morrow, the agent, told me that Mr. Bingley wanted to retain my services, as well as the missus as his cook, I reckoned all the servants would get called back." Buttons shook his head. "But that didn't happen. The gentleman, Mr. Bingley that is, told me only this morning that he's off to London to fetch his sisters and that one of them will keep house for him, nothing being said about any additional servants or even keeping the present ones on. All that will depend on the sister—a Miss Caroline Bingley as were. But for the time, I'm serving a kind man, and I'm content with that."

After commiserating with Buttons over the vagaries of service, Thomas Bennet got to the reason for his visit. "So, tell me, Buttons, what is this Mr. Bingley like?"

"I knew that was why you come whilst Mr. Bingley is out in the park riding," Buttons said with a smile. "There ain't a family in the parish what isn't curious about every particular pertaining to Mr. Bingley right down to the blacking he uses on his boots."

"No surprise there—what with the imbalance in the resident population."

"What imbalance would that be?"

"Too many unmarried daughters and not enough gentlemen. I can account for five of them myself."

With a knowing nod, as Buttons had two daughters of his own, the butler shared with Mr. Bennet that Mr. Bingley was of a most amiable disposition but seemed unsure of his position as lord of the manor.

"Word about the village is that he inherited a large fortune from his father's businesses in the North and has never had a house of his own. For guidance, he looks to his friend, Mr. Darcy of Derbyshire, the grandson of an earl. Night and day, those two are—Mr. Bingley being rather informal in the way he goes about things whilst Mr. Darcy looks as if he sleeps standing up—stiff as a post that one is. But rumor has it that he is one of the richest men in England."

"I am happy to hear that Mr. Bingley has a mentor—and a rich one at that—but a man of wealth and rank will have no interest in my daughters. Besides, I was charged by Mrs. Bennet to find out everything I could about Mr. Bingley. My girls are very keen to know if the man dances."

Buttons again nodded. "Only this morning, the gentleman specifically mentioned that he enjoyed dancing and that it was his intention to attend every dance whilst in the country."

"Well, then my business is done here!" Mr. Bennet said, pretending to rise. "If Mr. Bingley attends the assembly, he will most certainly fall in love with one of my daughters—most likely Jane. That will make Mrs. Bennet happy, and peace will reign at Longbourn."

"Mr. B., I wouldn't count my chickens before they're hatched. As determined as your missus is to have her daughters married, Mrs. Bennet isn't the only one looking to have a daughter take up residence at Netherfield. I'm thinking of Lady Lucas and…"

Any additional information would have to wait as the sound of hooves on gravel could be heard on the drive, signaling the return of Mr. Bingley.

* * *

"I hope you have not been waiting too long. I have no wish to inconvenience anyone," Mr. Bingley said after introductions had been made. "Of course, there was no way for you to know that I ride every morning."

"Mr. Bingley, there is very little about you that is not published abroad for the perusal of all and sundry. I can assure you that whatever home you enter in the shire, you will find your favorite wine stocked in the wine cupboard."

Bingley laughed at the comment. "And why is that?"

"It is a truth universally acknowledged that a single man must be in want of a wife. The truth is so well fixed in the minds of the surrounding families that he is considered as the rightful property of one or other of their daughters."

Bingley scratched his head. "This comes as news to me."

"Then you are fortunate that I called so that I could enlighten you—or warn you—whichever way you choose to view the matter."

Bingley looked perplexed.

"Allow me to explain. In the country, there are fewer entertainments than in Town, and you, sir, are a much needed diversion for all those families with daughters of a certain age, one of whom you will most certainly wish to marry."

"I do confess that I take much pleasure in the country, and I have it on good authority that there are many attractive ladies hereabouts with a fondness for dancing, an amusement I greatly enjoy. As to the matter of marriage, I cannot say."

"You need not say or do anything, Mr. Bingley. It will all be said and done for you."

"Mr. Bennet, you are possessed of an extraordinary wit—"

"...and five daughters."

Bingley laughed out loud. "I am happy to call you neighbor, sir."

"I hope you feel the same way after the assembly. Now, as to the matter of bovine trespass. On occasion..."

Mr. Bingley Returns Mr. Bennet's Call

by Mary Simonsen

October 7, 1811

In a few days Mr. Bingley returned Mr. Bennet's visit, and sat about ten minutes with him in his library. - Chapter 3

Five days had passed since Mr. Bennet had called on Mr. Bingley at Netherfield Park. The delay in returning the gentleman's call was a result of the number of visits the gentleman had received from his neighbors. It appeared that there was not a man in the county who had not traveled down Bingley's drive for the purpose of welcoming him to the neighborhood. In fact, there were so many callers that it had necessitated a postponement of his journey to London.

In deference to rank, Bingley had first to pay a call on Sir William Lucas. It was at Lucas Lodge, where he was graciously received by the recently knighted gentleman and his wife that Bingley understood the truth of Mr. Bennet's assertion that every mother with an eligible daughter was already sizing him up for his wedding suit. The Lucas's undiluted determination to have him as a son-in-law prompted several awkward exchanges. By listing every talent possessed by Miss Charlotte Lucas, Lady Lucas had succeeded in embarrassing her eldest daughter as there was a hint of desperation in the recitation of her accomplishments. It was an exercise repeated at the homes of Mr. Long, who had two nieces, and Mr. Eaton, who had two daughters *and* a niece. Although Mr. Garvey had neither daughter nor niece, he did have a female cousin who would be eager to come to Hertfordshire. Mr. Bingley need only ask.

After several visits with neighboring families, Bingley was looking forward to calling on Mr. Bennet at Longbourn as it would make for a nice change. During visits with his neighbors, people deferred to him with a reverence usually reserved for members of the aristocracy—a display he found discomfiting. There would be no need to stand on ceremony with Mr. Bennet.

There was another reason for the visit to Longbourn. Due to the absence of family and friends, Bingley found Netherfield Park as dull as the king's speech to Parliament. Of course, things would improve once his sisters and Darcy arrived from London. In the meantime, he would enjoy the company of a man who dropped *bon mots* as readily as a tree shedding autumn leaves.

Once seated in Longbourn's library, Bingley was not disappointed. Disarmed by Bennet's wit and charm, Bingley admitted that he had hoped to catch sight of the Bennet daughters as he had been told by his butler that the Bennet sisters were particularly handsome, possibly the most handsome ladies in the shire. Bingley was not averse to being surrounded by a bevy of pretty faces.

"Indeed, they are," Mr. Bennet answered without embarrassment, and when he saw Bingley's smile, he continued, "You think I am bragging, Mr. Bingley, but I am not. My Bible compels me not to hide my lamp under a bushel."

"I am happy to hear that the reports are accurate."

"Yes, it is common knowledge that my wife presented me with five handsome daughters. And as such, you have my permission to marry whichever one of the girls you choose. However, I should point out that Jane, as the eldest and the prettiest, merits your attention, but my second daughter, Elizabeth, has something more of quickness than her sisters."

"Apparently, with regard to your daughter Elizabeth, the apple does not fall far from the tree."

Mr. Bennet acknowledged the compliment with a smile. "As for the three youngest sisters, Mary, Kitty, and Lydia, to continue the apple metaphor, they need to stay on the tree a little longer—a little maturing will hurt none of them. As for catching a glimpse of my daughters, when you mount your horse, all you need do is look to the upper windows, and you will see five faces pressed against the glass. They are as curious about you as you are about them."

Before taking his leave, Bingley explained that business would take him to London for several days, but when he returned, he would be accompanied by two of his sisters, his brother-in-law, and his friend, Mr. Darcy of Derbyshire.

"Is Mr. Darcy married?"

"No, sir, and he gives no indication of wishing to trade the title of bachelor for that of husband. As he is the son of a noted member of the gentry and the grandson of an earl, if he were to look for a wife, it would be amongst ladies of his own rank."

"Of course," Mr. Bennet said, acknowledging the obvious. "After all, this is England. We cannot have mingling of classes, although I daresay it would produce a more intelligent upper class if it did happen."

Not knowing how to respond, Bingley quickly added, "Darcy is of a taciturn nature and can be awkward amongst unfamiliar company. I shall warn you that he can appear aloof."

"Then let him come to the assembly. We shall make him welcome."

"Sir William Lucas has already extended the invitation. It will be my job to see that Darcy actually attends the dance. No easy chore there."

"See that you do, Mr. Bingley. At every dance, there are ladies in need of partners, and if he can keep time to the music, he will be a welcomed addition to our little community."

Outside, Mr. Bingley mounted his horse, and in doing so, stole a glance at the upper window. As predicted, there were at least four faces framed in its panes, including one fair-haired beauty, and this brought a smile to his face. He had a weakness for golden-haired maidens.

She must be the eldest Miss Bennet, Bingley thought and remembered that Buttons had been particularly generous in his praise of Jane Bennet's beauty and temperament. *It seems the butler did not exaggerate.*

As he turned his mount in the direction of the gate, Bingley touched the brim of his hat to acknowledge that he had seen the daughters. The ladies, now giggling, hurried away from the window.

"An excellent start to my time in the country. There will be no shortage of dance partners," Bingley mused. As he made his way toward Netherfield Park, another thought occurred to him: *If Darcy had seen the ladies at the window, he would not have approved.*

Mr. Bingley Goes to London

by C. Allyn Pierson

October 9, 1811

By the time he reached London, his horse was lathered and faltering, but his enthusiasm was unimpaired. He could hardly wait to reach the Hurst's townhouse to tell his sisters about the wonderful opportunity to meet the people of Meryton. The Hurst's butler bowed deeply when he opened the door to the scion of the Bingley family and allowed himself a dignified smile while he greeted him.

"Come in, sir! Mrs. Hurst and Miss Bingley are in the drawing-room, and I am sure they will be happy to see you!"

"Thanks, Bledsoe, I will show myself up." Charles ran up the stairs three at a time and entered the drawing-room. "Caroline! Louisa! I have the best news!"

Both ladies dropped their needlework onto their laps and stared at their brother. Finally, Caroline spoke. "What *can* you be talking about, Charles?"

"I have just returned from Hertfordshire to gather you all up and take you to Meryton. They have an assembly tomorrow night! It will be a wonderful opportunity to meet the local gentry!"

Caroline glanced at her sister and back to Charles. "I cannot imagine why you are so in alt about this, Charles. Or why you leased this manor in such a backwards place in the first place."

"Oh come, Caroline! Netherfield is a very comfortable manor and the people are friendly. The hunting season is starting soon and it looks like the coverts are well stocked." He turned to his friend Darcy, who was leaning silently against the mantel, his face a mask.

Charles tried again. "Darcy, don't you think a few weeks in the country doing some hunting and some visiting sounds pleasant?"

Darcy's lip lifted in a brief sneer, which was quickly suppressed. "You will find the society something savage, Charles. If you want some country air we should go to Pemberley."

Caroline sat up straighter in her chair. "Oh yes, Mr. Darcy! Pemberley must be lovely at this time of year! I long to visit!"

Charles's pleasant face hardened slightly. "Caroline, you have been to Pemberley, and now that I have a manor of my own to visit, I was under the impression you were to take charge of the house for me."

"Of course Charles, of course, but I am not particularly thrilled about the wilds of Hertfordshire. I cannot imagine that there is society of any kind there. I think you should drop this lease and we can stay in London until Mr. Darcy leaves for Christmas at Pemberley. We might even see Miss Darcy. Did you not say that she was to spend a few days in London soon, Mr. Darcy?"

Darcy had been watching this family squabble and suddenly felt a pang for his friend and his enthusiasm for his new home. He stood up suddenly. "Well, I think I must go home and pack my things, Charles. What time do you want me to be ready in the morning?"

Miss Bingley and Mrs. Hurst both pursed their lips and glared at Darcy as he traitorously gave in to Charles's ridiculous whim. When Darcy caught and held her eyes, his lips compressed, Caroline squirmed in her chair. When she could not tolerate it any longer, she broke out, "Very well, Charles. I suppose we must go if it means that much to you."

Bingley grinned at the two of them, knowing Louisa would give in if the two dominant personalities had ceded.

They spent the rest of the evening packing and preparing for their sojourn in Hertfordshire, while Mr. Hurst had his postprandial nap on the drawing-room settee.

Louisa and Edward Hurst at the Meryton Assembly

by Mary Simonsen

October 15, 1811

"Edward, you look so handsome tonight," Louisa Hurst said to her husband of six years.

Although short, portly, and balding, Mr. Hurst was the apple of Louisa's eye. Others might criticize his appearance or misinterpret his silence as a lack of wit or vocabulary or intelligence, but that was because his company misunderstood him. Unlike Darcy, who rarely spoke without saying something that would amaze the whole room, or Charles, who hated pregnant pauses and would rattle on endlessly, Edward engaged others in conversation only when he had something substantive to say. His darling wife knew there were few who appreciated Edward's sardonic wit or who guessed at the fun they had behind closed doors. After a half dozen years of marriage, there were few married couples who could make such a claim for contentment.

"Do you really think so, my dear? The buttons on my waistcoat are popping," Edward said while looking at his bulging vest.

"That is true, my love. But do you not think a flat stomach is a sign of poverty? Besides, it takes effort and fine dining for one to burst one's buttons," his wife said, tickling his middle.

"I am so glad you think so. I know Caroline does not approve of my expanding girth."

"Please give me one example of anyone, other than Mr. Darcy and Miss Darcy, who meets with my sister's approval?" Louisa asked, her mood immediately souring.

"No one comes to mind, except, as you say, the Darcys. Will you allow Caroline to lead you around by the nose tonight?"

"Of course I shall. If I do not, she will whine and pout and stamp her foot, and if that does not work, she will say something unkind about you and that is something I cannot bear."

"Your sister is in need of a set-down. I wonder if anyone is up to the task."

"If such a thing were to happen, it must come from Mr. Darcy as Caroline does not give a brass farthing about anyone else's opinion."

"I wish it would happen sooner rather than later. Even though I do enjoy annoying your sister with my snoring, I am tired of pretending to fall asleep on the sofa every night."

"Well, you shan't have to pretend tonight as we have an assembly to attend, and while I am dancing, you will visit the card room and win lots of money for us as you always do."

"That certainly is my intention." Edward gave his wife a quick kiss.

* * *

"Oh my, Louisa!" Caroline said, covering her mouth with her fan. "This assembly is worse than anything I could have imagined. There is not one person here whom I would consider to be fashionable. And the smells! The finest perfume from Paris could not conceal them."

"I could not agree more," Louisa answered. *But considering we are in the country, not Grosvenor Square, really, what did you expect?*

"Other than Miss Jane Bennet, who is presently dancing with Charles, there is not a pretty face in the room. I am sure Mr. Darcy agrees. Did you see how he walked away from Miss Bennet's sister?"

"Yes, he did turn up his nose at her," *before turning around and staring at her for ten minutes.*

"He refused to even consider dancing with her."

"Yes, I noticed that as well." *I am sure it had nothing to do with the fact that she had walked away from him because she had found him to be above his company.*

"I think Mr. Darcy has decided that Miss Elizabeth Bennet is beneath his notice. Even at a country assembly, he will not lower his standards by dancing with her."

"Yes, Caroline," *which is why he keeps staring at her. He absolutely, positively wants to make sure he has no interest in her whatsoever.*

"Here comes Mr. Hurst. As he is smiling, I shall assume he won at cards," Caroline said. "Your husband is incredibly lucky."

"Yes, he is." *His "luck" paid for all the finely-carved French furniture in the townhouse you share with us.*

"Edward, your pants are bulging. Are they laden with newly-won coins, or are you just happy to see me?" Louisa whispered.

"Behave yourself, Louisa, that is, until I do not want you to," Edward whispered in her ear.

"Will the two of you please stop?" Caroline protested. "It is indecent."

Although Caroline had been a proponent of Louisa marrying Edward Hurst, it had never occurred to her that Louisa would actually fall in love with her husband. In order to get away from the cooing lovers, Caroline moved toward Mr. Darcy.

"I can hardly believe Caroline is still in pursuit of Mr. Darcy," Edward said as soon as his sister-in-law was out of earshot. "Does she not realize Mr. Darcy is a snob and would never marry the daughter of a merchant?"

"What about a farmer's daughter?"

"Whatever do you mean, Louisa?"

"See that dark-haired lady in the yellow frock," Louisa said, pointing her fan at Elizabeth Bennet who was talking to Miss Lucas.

"Mr. Darcy has been stealing glances at her ever since our arrival. She is the daughter of Mr. Bennet, a gentleman farmer, and because her father is a gentleman, she and Mr. Darcy are equals."

"But some people are more equal than others," he said with a laugh. "I cannot imagine the grandson of an earl being interested in a farmer's daughter."

"Shall we test my theory?"

Edward eagerly agreed.

"Mr. Darcy has asked me to dance the next with him. While I am dancing, you will watch Mr. Darcy and then tell me what you think."

Louisa, who found Mr. Darcy to be of a taciturn nature on the best of occasions, made little attempt to engage him in conversation, and he was perfectly content to have it so. After the conclusion of the dance, Mr. Darcy offered to get Louisa a glass of punch. During his absence, she hurried to Edward's side.

"Well, what do you think, my love?"

"By Jove, Louisa, you have got it right. The man is smitten. While dancing, it was as if he had an owl's head. No matter which way you turned, he was looking at Miss Elizabeth. I declare him to be a lost cause."

"I agree. While you were in the card room, I was busy eavesdropping on Miss Elizabeth's conversations, and I can tell you that she will humble him."

"Mr. Darcy! Humbled?"

"Yes, Fitzwilliam Darcy of Pemberley will have to climb down from his perch if he wishes to engage that particular lady."

"Well, Louisa, I thought it was going to be rather dull in the country," Edward said, chuckling. "It looks as if it will be anything but. Who would have guessed that the staid Mr. Darcy would provide the entertainment!"

Charlotte Lucas at the Meryton Assembly

by Abigail Reynolds

October 15, 1811

Not so many years ago, Charlotte had hated attending assemblies. Now they were among her chief pleasures, as she enjoyed the music and the opportunity to visit with her friends, but when she had been younger, she had been agonizingly aware that she might as well have been invisible to the young gentlemen in attendance. Their eyes would always slide past her to the prettier girls, and while any of them would have described her as a good sort, she had rarely been sought out as a partner.

As her pretty friends became wives one after another, Charlotte grew somewhat resigned to her lot. She had always wished to marry and have her own establishment, but spinsterhood was not so bad, after all, not when she had three brothers who would support her after her father passed away. She was grateful not to be in the precarious position of her particular friend Elizabeth Bennet; without any brothers, Elizabeth would eventually face a life of genteel poverty if she did not marry, and although Elizabeth possessed the beauty Charlotte herself lacked, her liveliness tended to frighten off potential suitors.

This particular assembly had begun auspiciously. Mr. Bingley, their charming and wealthy new neighbor, had asked her for the first set of dances, and proved to be an excellent dancer. Charlotte was sensible enough to take pleasure in the act of dancing rather than to waste her time dreaming of anything more, knowing that a gentleman of Mr. Bingley's caliber would have no real interest in her. True to form, early in the first dance Mr. Bingley spotted the lovely Jane Bennet. He was apparently quite struck by her, immediately asking Charlotte who she was and angling transparently for an introduction. It would make a fine story for her to tell Lizzy later on.

It was no surprise when Mr. Bingley asked Jane Bennet to dance the next set with him, while Charlotte, as usual, was without a partner. Her father took the opportunity to introduce her to Mr. Robinson, a gentleman of about her own years who was paying an extended visit to their nearest neighbor, Mr. Willoughby. She had seen him on several previous occasions, but he had never paid her the slightest bit of attention. Now Sir William's maneuverings practically obliged Mr. Robinson to ask her for the next set. The poor man; she was sure he wanted to do nothing of the sort. Her father's well-meaning but pointless attempts to find her a husband had put many an innocent young man in an embarrassing position, but Mr. Robinson proved to be not only amiable, but seemed to find her company diverting, asking her about her interests. If she had been anyone else, she would have thought he was actually flirting with her, but no one ever flirted with Charlotte, so that was impossible. Still, it was a delightful half hour.

Afterwards Mr. Robinson returned her to Sir William who was in conversation with Mr. Bingley. Although reluctant to lose Mr. Robinson's company, Charlotte decided to slip away before her father tried to embarrass Mr. Bingley into dancing with her again. She was only a few paces away when she heard Mr. Robinson ask, "So, Mr. Bingley, how do you like the assembly?"

"I like it very well indeed!" said Mr. Bingley stoutly.

"Are we not fortunate to have so many pretty women in the room? Which do you think to be the prettiest?"

"Oh! The eldest Miss Bennet beyond a doubt, there cannot be two opinions on that point," replied Mr. Bingley immediately and with great enthusiasm.

This intelligence gave Charlotte an excellent reason to seek out Lizzy Bennet, to whom she repeated the story.

Elizabeth agreed heartily. "Mr. Bingley must be half in love with her already. I heard him tell that dreadful Mr. Darcy that she was the most beautiful creature he had ever beheld. Then he encouraged Mr. Darcy to ask me to dance, even though he had been refusing to acknowledge the existence of any ladies besides those of his own party. Fortunately for me, Mr. Darcy announced that I was tolerable, but not handsome enough to tempt him." She laughed. "As if I would ever want to tempt such a proud and unpleasant man! It would be a punishment to have to dance with him."

"It is fortunate Mr. Bingley did not try to make him dance with me, then, since if you are only tolerable, I hate to think of how Mr. Darcy would describe me!" said Charlotte.

Elizabeth said, "I think you may have made a different conquest. Mr. Robinson seems unable to take his eyes off of you."

Charlotte laughed at Elizabeth's foolishness. "If he is looking this way, it is you he must be looking at." She glanced over her shoulder only to discover her friend had been correct. As Mr. Robinson's eyes met hers, he gave a slow smile that made her feel a little odd inside.

She smiled back, which he seemed to take to be enough an invitation to join them. As he spoke to her warmly, Charlotte found herself blushing, something she had thought to have left behind her years ago. Then, instead of asking Elizabeth to dance as Charlotte had expected, Mr. Robinson said, "Miss Lucas, would you permit me—or do I ask too much—to request the honor of the next set with you?"

Charlotte could not remember ever having been asked to dance twice by the same man at an assembly, but she managed to keep a calm demeanor as she accepted, ignoring Elizabeth's amused glance.

After another enjoyable set, Mr. Robinson, noting that she was slightly out of breath, offered to bring her some lemonade. Charlotte acquiesced, enjoying the novelty of having a gentleman fetch her refreshments. Jane Bennet always had a cluster of admirers eager to serve her, but Charlotte, like Elizabeth, was usually left to her own devices.

Mr. Robinson returned carrying two glasses of lemonade. Charlotte revised her opinion of him upward; the men of Meryton were all drinking something much stronger. She made room for him to sit on the bench beside her. He sat closer to her than she expected, enough so that she once again found herself blushing under his scrutiny. She was grateful that the crowd around them hid her from general view; she did not wish to be subject to the inevitable teasing merely because a man had danced with her twice.

She struggled to find a subject of conversation to distract herself from improper thoughts. "How did you come to meet Mr. Willoughby?" she asked.

"Willoughby? Oh, we were acquainted at Cambridge, but then I lost track of him until last year when we met again in London. A capital fellow, Willoughby."

"Indeed," Charlotte said non-committally. She wondered how well Mr. Robinson actually knew Mr. Willoughby, who was considered to be quite a rake. He had cut a swath through the local female population, even turning his eye on Charlotte at one point. Fortunately, she had been too sensible to fall for Willoughby's wiles; she knew he only wanted one thing from her. It surprised her that such a respectable man as Mr. Robinson would be his friend, but perhaps there was more to the story than she knew.

"I cannot tell you how grateful I am for your company, Miss Lucas. I feel quite a stranger here," Mr. Robinson said. "I had not hoped to discover a lady who was so easy to talk to and an excellent dancer as well."

Had he made the usual compliments about her beauty, Charlotte would have dismissed him completely as a flatterer who wanted something from her, but it was a novelty to discover a gentleman who cared about something besides a lady's appearance. Nothing would ever come of it, but she told herself there could be no harm in enjoying a man's company for a few minutes.

Elizabeth Bennet's Reflections on the Assembly

by Shannon Winslow

October 15, 1811

Chapter 3 of *Pride and Prejudice* describes the night of the Meryton assembly, where we (and Elizabeth) first meet Mr. Darcy as a member of the Bingley party from Netherfield. But what was Elizabeth thinking and feeling afterward, especially concerning Mr. Darcy, who had insulted her?

The Bennet ladies had only just settled into their carriage to commence their short journey home from the assembly when Lydia, obviously very well pleased with herself, burst forth with, "What a ball! I declare, it was as if the whole affair was organized specifically for *my* enjoyment. Did you notice? I was never without a partner, not for a single dance!"

"Nor was I!" said Kitty, not wanting to be left behind. "Poor Mary, though. How could you bear it? Not to be asked even once! How mortifying I should have found it." Kitty looked round at Lydia, who then joined her in laughing at Mary's expense.

Mary, sitting on the opposite seat between Jane and Elizabeth, was not unused to enduring this sort of treatment at the hands of her younger sisters. And yet she found it impossible in this case to turn a deaf ear. "This is one more proof of how unlike we are," she rejoined with considerable distain. "Not being asked merely saved me the inconvenience of declining, for I am sure I saw no one there whom I cared to stand up with. Rollicking about with such frivolous young men as you two found to dance with, partners with no grace and nothing intelligent to say for themselves—well, it would have been a punishment to me to spend even five minutes in so irrational a manner. I had much rather sit quietly by, listening to the music."

Kitty and Lydia began to loudly remonstrate against these remarks until their mother, even more loudly, put an end to it saying, "Girls, girls, enough of that! Your high spirits are understandable for you both spent the evening doing exactly as you wished. And we must give Mary her due, you know, for tonight she was mentioned with favor to Miss Bingley as being quite 'the most accomplished young lady in the neighborhood.' So, you see, she has her claims as well. But Jane's being so admired by Mr. Bingley; now that is the real triumph!" Mrs. Bennet then turned to her eldest. "I daresay the man is half in love with you already, and who could blame him? Anybody could see that you were by far the prettiest girl in the room."

"Mama!" Jane protested. "You embarrass me."

"I know you are too modest to say so, but it was as plain as the nose on his face how he admired you. A very fine beginning! Yes, on the whole, I am well satisfied with tonight's success. Well satisfied indeed!"

Elizabeth kept her thoughts to herself. She trusted there would be time later for a private conference with Jane, where they could both give uninhibited voice to their ideas about the amiable Mr. Bingley... and about his less-than-amiable friend and sisters. Jane liked Mr. Bingley a good deal. That much was already clear from how she behaved at the assembly and from the shy smile that even now remained on her lips. With her reserve, the clues were subtle, but very little escaped Elizabeth's notice, especially where her dearest sister's happiness was concerned.

As for herself, Elizabeth was surprised to find that she concurred with her mother for once; the evening had been entirely satisfactory. Although she could not boast, as Jane might, of being almost in love by what had passed that night, she had other sources of pleasure. She had seen Jane sincerely admired. She had enjoyed the agreeable exercise of dancing with several good-natured young men. And she had talked and laughed to her heart's content, much of it thanks to the odious Mr. Darcy.

His slighting of herself in her hearing had stung for a moment; that could not be denied. Only *tolerable* indeed! But it cost her no more than that one moment's distress. Elizabeth, who was not formed for discontent, quickly turned the incident to her favor, deciding it had been a matter of good fortune instead, one which had begun paying handsome dividends almost immediately. Had not it already proved a fine source of humor and a spur for her lively wit as she told the story with great spirit to her friends? Moreover, she intended to make the most of it for as long as possible. After all, one did not every day stumble across such a perfect cause for jesting, such a fine example of the ridiculous as Mr. Darcy had kindly provided her.

She should be sorry to insult an innocent person for the sake of a joke, but Mr. Darcy was hardly innocent. His own words and actions had condemned him in everybody's eyes, and, at the same time, made excellent fodder for Elizabeth's sportive tongue. Likewise, the gentleman had saved her the effort of ever being civil to him, and she could henceforth abuse him as much as she liked without any temptation to regret.

As the carriage started up the gravel sweep to Longbourn House, Elizabeth reflected that it was a mercy her mother had been equally put off by Mr. Darcy's disagreeable manners. Else, with her eldest daughter firmly in Mr. Bingley's sights, Mrs. Bennet would surely be throwing her second eldest at his very eligible friend every chance she got. In fact, Mr. Darcy's rudeness may have been the only thing to have saved him from being likewise accosted by every enterprising mother of an unmarried girl in the vicinity, once the size of his fortune had been generally circulated.

Mr. Darcy might be rich and even *tolerably* good looking, which Elizabeth would allow only if pressed, but she flattered herself that she would never be taken in by such superficial attractions. A handsome face could not hide a heart of stone, after all, nor could any amount of money excuse bad behavior. No, Mr. Darcy was almost certainly the last man on earth who could ever interest her in a romantic way. As a source of amusement, however, he might be worth knowing.

Once they were all inside, Mrs. Bennet took great satisfaction in regaling her husband with a detailed description of all that had transpired at the assembly, finishing with an account of Mr. Darcy's insolence, slightly exaggerated for dramatic effect.

"But I assure you," she added in closing, "that Lizzy does not lose much by not suiting *his* fancy; for he is a most disagreeable, horrid man, not at all worth pleasing. So high and so conceited that there was no enduring him! He walked here, and he walked there, fancying himself so very great! Not handsome enough to dance with! I wish you had been there, my dear, to have given him one of your set downs. I quite detest the man."

Elizabeth deemed her mother's assessment of Mr. Darcy's character remarkably accurate, especially coming from one whom she did not ordinarily consider an astute judge of such things. Of course, it stood to reason that even a person usually wrong must be accidentally right on occasion. The law of averages would insist it was so. That must be the explanation. Still, Elizabeth felt a vague uneasiness that her mother's and her own opinions should so perfectly coincide—and twice in one day, too! How very odd. Such a thing had not happened last in a month of Sundays. What could it all mean?

A Party at Lucas Lodge

by Jack Caldwell

November 1, 1811

It was a capital night at Lucas Lodge.

Sir William Lucas was hosting a gathering in honor of the _____ Militia Regiment, and the lodge was filled with the principal families of the district: The Longs, the Gouldings, the Philipses, and the Bennets.

The Lucases had been successful in trade, so much so that William Lucas was able to sell his interests and establish himself as a gentleman farmer. He bought a fine house, renaming it Lucas Lodge. He became mayor soon afterwards, and when King George III visited Meryton, it was his august duty to welcome his sovereign.

Truly, the speech he delivered was inspired by Provenance herself! The old man had nodded, smiled, and showed great benevolence with his appreciation. How proud Mr. Lucas was when his name appeared on the honors list on the king's birthday next! The day of his investiture at the Court of St. James's was burned in his memory.

True, it was but an *honorary* title, not hereditary. Just as the office of mayor was honorary and held no power. And the king *was* mad. Still, Mr. William Lucas was now *Sir* William, and his wife was *Lady* Lucas. Capital, capital!

Sir William realized with his new title came new expectations from his neighbors. He strove to be worthy of his position and their respect. He considered his family and the Bennets, owners of the largest estate by acreage in the area, the principal figures in the district. By conscious effort, Sir William changed his manner of comportment. Since his every word was important, he learned to choose them with great care. His friend, Thomas Bennet, was a great help in this endeavor. Bennet advised Sir William to use words of at least four syllables whenever possible. Sir William knew he was on the right track every time Bennet smiled or chuckled.

What did not change was Sir William's natural benevolence and liberality. Indeed, he was sometimes too generous for his own good. Thank goodness for Lady Lucas! Her pains at economy allowed them to live in a finer manner than their income usually afforded.

Lady Lucas's frantic efforts resulted in a most pleasant evening for friends, neighbors, and guests. The gentlemen were in their Sunday best, the soldiers resplendent in scarlet and buff, and the ladies wore a rainbow of lace and taffeta. Wine and punch were in abundance. The pianoforte stood ready to provide entertainment.

The militia officers were the usual types—men trying to act the gentleman while stuffing themselves with food and drink. It was of little consequence. Their dashing uniforms gave the setting a dignified air, and their presence made the ladies happy. As a knight, Sir William knew it was his duty to provide for those charged with protecting the kingdom and keeping the peace. What were a few pounds compared to upholding their station, he explained to his wife.

The militia was not the only guest of honor. Sir William was happy Mr. Bingley's party was in attendance as well. The new resident of Netherfield Hall was a most amiable gentleman, wealthy and sociable. He was a very fine figure of a man, and he hoped Charlotte would catch his eye.

Ah, Charlotte! Quiet, cleaver Charlotte! Sir William loved all his children, but none more than his eldest. It was a shame no one worthy of her had yet approached him for her hand, and Lady Lucas was concerned. Sir William was not. All things in their time, he thought. Besides, Charlotte's recent preoccupation could be a sign someone had caught her eye.

Perhaps it was Mr. Bingley's august companion, Mr. Darcy! The gentleman's dress, carriage, and demeanor screamed of money and position. Sir William had met his like before at Court. They were not rude, he explained to his wife, but displayed the reserve expected for their class. It was best to speak politely to one's betters.

Mr. Bingley's sisters were elegance itself. They moved and conversed with the economy of their station. The Bennet ladies were quite the opposite. They were an explosion of liveliness and loveliness, brightening the room as they entered. Jolly Miss Lydia and giggling Miss Kitty were as thick as thieves with his daughter Maria. Miss Jane Bennet and Miss Elizabeth sought the company of Charlotte.

Ah, there it was—Mrs. Bennet and Lady Lucas, smiling and nodding and fighting again. Sir William had grown up with the former Fanny Gardiner, and at one time had been attracted to the pretty tradesman's daughter. Miss Charlotte Wigglesworth soon made him forget all about Miss Gardiner, though. She made him a capital wife, running his household, an affectionate mother to their splendid children, and neatly ascending to their elevated situation. He lamented Miss Gardiner not for an instant. It was his one regret he could never convince his dear Lettie of that.

He eyed his son John. Oh, bother! He was at the punch table. There was no telling what he had added to the punch. That he *had* was not in doubt; his self-satisfied smirk was an admission of guilt. Sir William could be discreet when it suited his purposes. A quiet word to a servant, and the punch was soon diluted.

The crisis averted, Sir William could return his attention to his guests. He took pains to share words with each and every one. Bennet was his usual amusing self, though sometimes his humor quite escaped Sir William's understanding. Mr. Bingley was easy and affable, a man after his heart. Mr. Hurst, on the other hand, was not, but the host felt no insult. Hurst was from London, and their ways were more confined than gentlemen of the country. Philips was boisterous, and Goulding was a bore. Poor Goulding was *always* a bore, but as there was nothing for it, the good knight nodded, smiled, and pitied him.

Music now filled the air, which sent Sir William's toe to tapping. Miss Elizabeth Bennet was at the pianoforte, and her easy and unaffected performance was all that was charming. Several were the entreaties she would sing again, but she was eagerly succeeded at the instrument by Miss Mary.

Her talents tended towards more serious, challenging pieces, and even Sir William had to grant that she was not quite mistress of them. At the end of a long concerto, the young lady was glad to purchase praise and gratitude by Scotch and Irish airs at the request of the younger Bennet sisters. They, with some of the Lucases and two or three officers, joined eagerly in dancing at one end of the room. What capital entertainment!

Mr. Darcy stood near him. Sir William had yet to greet him personally, so he thus began.

"What a charming amusement for young people this is, Mr. Darcy! There is nothing like dancing, after all. I consider it as one of the first refinements of polished societies."

Mr. Darcy's voice was level. "Certainly, sir, and it has the advantage also of being in vogue amongst the less polished societies of the world. Every savage can dance."

Sir William only smiled. He had heard that tone of voice many times at Court. It was an indication of Mr. Darcy's great importance.

Upon seeing Bingley join the group, Sir William continued after a pause. "Your friend performs delightfully, and I doubt not that you are an adept in the science yourself, Mr. Darcy."

"You saw me dance at Meryton, I believe, sir."

"Yes, indeed, and received no inconsiderable pleasure from the sight. Do you often dance at St. James's?"

"Never, sir."

"Do you not think it would be a proper compliment to the place?"

"It is a compliment which I never pay to any place, if I can avoid it."

What an amusing man! He quite reminded him of Bennet. "You have a house in Town, I conclude?" Mr. Darcy bowed. "I had once some thoughts of fixing in Town myself, for I am fond of superior society. But I did not feel quite certain that the air of London would agree with Lady Lucas."

Sir William paused in hopes of an answer, but his companion made none. Miss Elizabeth was at that instant moving towards them, and he was struck with the notion of doing a very gallant thing.

"My dear Miss Eliza, why are not you dancing?" He turned to the gentleman with a smile. "Mr. Darcy, you must allow me to present this young lady to you as a very desirable partner. You cannot refuse to dance, I am sure, when so much beauty is before you."

Taking her hand with the intention of giving it to Mr. Darcy, who, though he seemed surprised, was not unwilling to receive it. Miss Elizabeth instantly drew back and spoke with some discomposure.

"Indeed, sir, I have not the least intention of dancing. I entreat you not to suppose that I moved this way in order to beg for a partner."

Mr. Darcy, with grave propriety, requested to be allowed the honor of her hand, but in vain.

Sir William tried to shake her purpose with an attempt at persuasion. "You excel so much in the dance, Miss Eliza, that it is cruel to deny me the happiness of seeing you! And though this gentleman dislikes the amusement in general," he indicated Mr. Darcy, "he can have no objection, I am sure, to oblige us for one half-hour."

"Mr. Darcy is all politeness," said Miss Elizabeth, smiling.

"He is indeed, but considering the inducement, my dear Miss Eliza, we cannot wonder at his complaisance. For who would object to such a partner?"

Miss Elizabeth looked archly and turned away.

Sir William sensed a cut and eyed the gentleman with some discomposure. But he was relieved by what he saw. Mr. Darcy was far from injured; indeed he took the entire episode with some complacency. Why, there was almost a smile dancing on his lips!

Sir William wondered if he had been saved by Miss Elizabeth and Mr. Darcy from committing some great *faux pas*. That would never do! He would have to remember to ask Bennet about it.

He gave a short bow to his guest, taking his leave of him. He had yet to greet Colonel Forster. By the time he found the officer, he had forgotten his intention of talking with Bennet. Instead, he lost himself in the laughter and music which filled his house.

What a capital evening!

Charlotte Lucas on Guy Fawkes Day

by Abigail Reynolds

November 5, 1811

Elizabeth said, "It is evident whenever they meet, that he does admire her; and to me it is equally evident that Jane is yielding to the preference which she began to entertain for him from the first, and is in a way to be very much in love. I am pleased, however, that her feelings are not likely to be discovered by the world in general, since Jane unites with great strength of feeling a composure of temper and a uniform cheerfulness of manner, which should guard her from the suspicions of the impertinent."

"It may perhaps be pleasant," replied Charlotte, "to be able to impose on the public in such a case; but it is sometimes a disadvantage to be so very guarded. If a woman conceals her affection with the same skill from the object of it, she may lose the opportunity of fixing him; and it will then be but poor consolation to believe the world equally in the dark." Besides, there were other ways a lady could guard the privacy of her affections. She and Mr. Robinson had silently conspired not to be overly attentive to each other; when they conversed, it was often in a dark alcove or in the shadows poorly lit by candles. Even Elizabeth had not guessed at her interest, but Mr. Robinson understood her well enough.

Charlotte could see Elizabeth was not convinced, so she continued, "There is so much of gratitude or vanity in almost every attachment, that it is not safe to leave any to itself. We can all begin freely—a slight preference is natural enough; but there are very few of us who have heart enough to be really in love without

41

encouragement. In nine cases out of ten, a woman had better show more affection than she feels. Bingley likes your sister undoubtedly; but he may never do more than like her, if she does not help him on."

"But she does help him on, as much as her nature will allow. If I can perceive her regard for him, he must be a simpleton indeed not to discover it too."

"Remember, Eliza, that he does not know Jane's disposition as you do."

"But if a woman is partial to a man, and does not endeavor to conceal it, he must find it out."

"Perhaps he must, if he sees enough of her. But though Bingley and Jane meet tolerably often, it is never for many hours together; and as they always see each other in large mixed parties, it is impossible that every moment should be employed in conversing together. Jane should therefore make the most of every half hour in which she can command his attention. When she is secure of him, there will be leisure for falling in love as much as she chooses." Charlotte had been following her own advice in this matter. She had seen Mr. Robinson on three occasions since the assembly, and each time she made sure to single him out. He was responding beautifully, and she herself was happier than she had ever been.

"Your plan is a good one," replied Elizabeth, "where nothing is in question but the desire of being well married; and if I were determined to get a rich husband, or any husband, I daresay I should adopt it. But these are not Jane's feelings; she is not acting by design. As yet, she cannot even be certain of the degree of her own regard, nor of its reasonableness. She has known him only a fortnight. She danced four dances with him at Meryton; she saw him one morning at his own house and has since dined in company with him four times. This is not quite enough to make her understand his character."

"Not as you represent it. Had she merely dined with him, she might only have discovered whether he had a good appetite; but you must remember that four evenings have been also spent together—

and four evenings may do a great deal." It had sufficed for her to reach the point where she could communicate with Mr. Robinson by a mere look across a crowded room.

"Yes; these four evenings have enabled them to ascertain that they both like Vingt-un better than Commerce; but with respect to any other leading characteristic, I do not imagine that much has been unfolded."

"Well," said Charlotte, shaking her head over Elizabeth's *un*romantic nonsense, "I wish Jane success with all my heart; and if she were married to him to-morrow, I should think she had as good a chance of happiness as if she were to be studying his character for a twelvemonth. Happiness in marriage is entirely a matter of chance. If the dispositions of the parties are ever so well known to each other, or ever so similar before-hand, it does not advance their felicity in the least. They always contrive to grow sufficiently unlike afterwards to have their share of vexation; and it is better to know as little as possible of the defects of the person with whom you are to pass your life."

"You make me laugh, Charlotte; but it is not sound. You know it is not sound, and that you would never act in this way yourself."

Charlotte knew better than to argue with her strong-minded friend, but she was already acting on her opinion. Mr. Robinson was amiable, presentable in company, and he admired her; and she felt a sharp tug of attraction when he looked at her in that certain way. Only last week he had found the opportunity to surreptitiously rest his hand on her lower back after they had danced together, making shivers run through her. He had leaned his head close to her when speaking to her alone so that the warmth of his breath tingled her ear, and the first time his lips had brushed against her ear she had thought it an accident, but by the second time she knew better. She did not think it would be a hardship to share his bed, and she saw no reason to examine any other flaws he might have. She would discover them soon enough if he made the offer she was hoping for. What a surprise it would be to everyone, include Elizabeth who was so certain of her own perspicacity!

43

***

Sir William Lucas prided himself on his status as the sponsor of various civic activities in Meryton, including hosting the celebration of Gunpowder Treason Day. All traces of hay had been removed from the field behind Lucas Lodge. Sir William had donated the traditional two cartloads of coal, which, when added to sticks of wood collected by the local youngsters, created a bonfire impressive enough that Sir William was noted to say on more than one occasion that it was as fine as any he had seen near St. James' Court. A few of the local gentry saw fit to attend, though they mostly remained inside Lucas Lodge except during the fireworks.

Charlotte had her own plans for the evening based on an earlier whispered communication from Mr. Robinson. She made a point of supervising the outdoor activities, wrapped in a dark, heavy shawl for warmth. Once darkness had fallen, Sir William with all due pomp, thrust a lighted torch into the pile of combustibles. Cheers rang out as flames rose into the air, sending out a welcome pulse of heat. Children jostled to be as close as they dared, shouting to be heard over the crackling of the fire.

Charlotte allowed herself to drift toward the back of the crowd furthest from Lucas Lodge. She had not seen Mr. Robinson that evening. Perhaps he had been unable to come after all. Disappointed by his absence, she was disinclined to join the conversation inside and so remained on the periphery of the festivities. As the first fireworks shot into the sky creating a cloud of sparkling lights, she felt hands descend on her hips and a familiar voice whispering her name in her ear, this time accompanied not by a brush of the lips but by a shocking nibble on her earlobe. "Will you walk with me?"

She understood now why he had not shown himself earlier. She would not have been allowed to walk out with him in the darkness, but this way she was free to go with him. All eyes were on the bonfire, though she knew other couples would be stealing away. There were always several hurried marriages after Bonfire Night.

He did not offer her his arm but rather laced his fingers through hers, which had the effect of making them look like the more ordinary peasant couples. He had also dressed in dark colors and simple clothes. Charlotte smiled to herself at the success of her plan. Finally, after all these years, she would have her own moment with an admirer.

As they ambled toward the small woods bordering the field, Mr. Robinson said, "I was hoping to speak to you privately tonight. Miss Lucas...Charlotte, we have not been acquainted long, but I feel as if I have known you for years. I will be going to visit my parents tomorrow, and I would like to seek my father's approval on asking a certain question, but I would not wish to make free with your name when addressing him without your permission. Would you, or do I ask too much, allow me to name you when speaking to my father?"

It was not precisely what she wished to hear, but she had to admire his delicacy in discussing the matter with his family prior to making an offer, and it was thrilling simply to know that he wished to. "I would have no objection," she said demurely. "Will you be away long?"

"I will return within a fortnight," he said with certainty, "and then I will speak to your father."

They reached the edge of the woods and he was still urging her on. Charlotte hesitated a moment, then followed him. After all, a few stolen kisses would only bind him to her more.

Caroline Invites Jane to Netherfield

by Kara Louise

November 12, 1811

Caroline Bingley marched with strident steps back and forth, her arms folded tightly in front of her. She was quite perturbed that Charles had accepted an invitation to dine with some officers in Meryton. She was perturbed not so much that he was going, but that Mr. Darcy agreed to accompany him, commenting that he hoped to find intelligent conversation amongst them. She shook her head and let out a huff. What would it take for the man to realize he could readily find that with her? And so much more?

When it was settled that the two gentlemen and Mr. Hurst would go, Charles approached his sister with a suggestion.

"Caroline, since we will be away, this would be a perfect opportunity to invite Miss Bennet to tea so you and Louisa can further your acquaintance with her." He smiled eagerly, waiting for her to respond in hearty agreement.

Her mouth opened, but she could not formulate words to express what she truly thought of his suggestion. She could have readily explained to him how little she wished to do this, that she thought Miss Bennet a sweet girl, but certainly not the right one for him. However, Caroline determined to display nothing but polite acquiescence to him, especially with Mr. Darcy seated nearby. She returned a smile and told him she thought that was a splendid idea. She reluctantly sent an invitation to Miss Bennet to join her and Louisa at Netherfield.

On the morning of the concurrent visits, a dreary chill invaded the county, very much like what Caroline felt, despite the warmth inside Netherfield. Thick clouds settled over Meryton, and Caroline was fairly certain a storm was imminent. She wondered whether Miss Bennet might be forced to abandon the plan if it began to rain. In truth, she ardently hoped she would!

Caroline was determined to make some good out of this situation, and when Mr. Darcy joined her in the sitting room as he waited for the other two men, she summoned the housekeeper.

In a rather loud voice she said, "Mrs. Lewis, I want to make sure everything is ready for our guest later today. She is to be received with the utmost hospitality, and I will spare nothing for her comfort."

The housekeeper nodded. "Yes, Miss Bingley. We have everything prepared for her visit as you requested."

"Good! I am so glad to hear that!" She stole a glance at Mr. Darcy, hoping he had overheard and would be impressed with how well she performed her duties as Mistress of Netherfield. For her greatest wish was to be Mistress of Pemberley!

As the men prepared to leave, Caroline watched Mr. Darcy don his heavy overcoat. Such a fine specimen of a man! She let out a soft sigh as she considered that not many of Charles's friends were much of a benefit to him, let alone to her. Mr. Darcy certainly had changed all that.

When the men took their leave, Louisa and Caroline sat in front of the blazing fire in the sitting room. As they waited for Miss Bennet, each silently hoped that the time spent with her would pass quickly. Caroline gazed out the window, noticing how dark it had become, and soon after, they heard the sound of rain pelting the windows.

"Oh, Louisa! It is a torrent out there. I daresay Miss Bennet will most likely not venture out in this! I would imagine we will spend our afternoon by ourselves!" She settled back comfortably into her chair and let out a long, drawn-out sigh, followed by a satisfied smile.

"Such a pity!" laughed Louisa.

"Yes," Caroline said softly. Then turning to Louisa, she added, "For Charles!"

At the sound of the bell a short while later, the two ladies looked at each other in surprise. Neither said a word, but it was apparent they were both thinking the same thing. Certainly it could not be Miss Bennet!

When Mrs. Lewis appeared at the door and announced Miss Bennet, Caroline could do little to conceal a gasp. Their guest was soaking wet, water was dripping onto the floor, and her appearance was completely deplorable.

"My dear Miss Bennet!" Caroline exclaimed, forcing herself to rise to her feet. "Whatever has happened? You are positively drenched from head to toe!"

Louisa and Caroline quickly attended to Miss Bennet as she explained that she had ridden over on a horse in the hopes of escaping the storm, but it had begun to rain much earlier than she had anticipated. Dry clothes were ordered for her and they had their lady's' maid escort her upstairs to assist her in changing into them.

When she left the room, they could not hold their tongues about the foolishness she had exhibited in riding from Longbourn to Netherfield on horseback instead of taking a carriage. In a rain storm! She should not have ventured out at all!

"Upon my word, Louisa! I can hardly believe it! Such reckless actions!"

"I quite agree, Caroline. What could she have been thinking?"

"It shows an ill-bred thoughtlessness, if you ask me."

The two ladies agreed that someone established in good society would never have exhibited such behavior.

While Miss Bennet was still upstairs, Caroline tugged at her sister's sleeve. "Louisa, I am becoming more and more convinced of Miss Bennet's unsuitability. While she is here today, we shall have the perfect opportunity to determine exactly what her family connections are."

Louisa gave her a quizzical look. "Do you have any doubt they shall prove to be deficient, Caroline?"

Caroline let out a cackle. "Of course not, but it shall be fun prying the information out of her!" The two ladies laughed in conspiratorial accord.

When Miss Bennet returned, she expressed her gratitude to the ladies, and they repaired to the dining room.

Caroline and Louisa questioned Miss Bennet politely about her family, her accomplishments, and a variety of other carefully picked subjects. She was most forthright in her answers, but it was her admission that she had an uncle in trade in Cheapside that prompted Louisa and Caroline to exchange pointed glances with each other. This was abominable!

At first, Miss Bennet acquitted herself reasonably well to the interrogation. However, Caroline soon began to notice that her face was ashen and she did not have the serene countenance that she normally displayed. At length it became apparent that she was feeling quite ill, and they thought it best to adjourn to the sitting room where she could be settled in front of the warm fire.

As the rain continued to pour down in torrents throughout the rest of the afternoon, Caroline and Louisa became resigned to the fact that Miss Bennet would be forced to remain with them at Netherfield. It would be uncivil to send her home in this tempest when she was feeling so poorly.

As Caroline attempted to make Miss Bennet comfortable, she inwardly hoped the gentlemen would return directly or that the rain would let up. Unfortunately, her hopes were in vain; Miss Bennet continued to exhibit increasing distress, the men were absent the whole of the afternoon, and the rain continued without intermission.

Caroline and Louisa saw to it that Miss Bennet was taken to a room and settled comfortably in bed, and then Caroline sent a missive to Longbourn informing her parents of her illness.

The two ladies returned to the sitting room and Caroline heaved a sigh as she sat down in a plush chair. "This has certainly been an interesting day, Louisa. I did not think anything could surpass Miss Bennet's grand arrival, but then to hear her talk about her uncle in trade…"

"In Cheapside, no less!" added Louisa with an air of disgust. "And she volunteered that information so readily! It appears she feels no shame in admitting it!"

"I daresay she does not." Caroline slowly clasped her hands together.

"We would never mention our…"

"No, we would not!" Caroline cut her off directly.

Louisa cast a side glance at her sister. "Will Charles feel the same repugnance we feel in this matter?"

"Oh, Louisa, I fear our brother may not." Caroline's voice trailed off.

A sly smile appeared as she thought of something—Mr. Darcy! He would have influence over her brother and would certainly show him how inferior Miss Bennet is… if he does not realize it on his own.

And having Miss Bennet here for her to care for would allow Mr. Darcy to see just how compassionate she could be toward someone in ill health. She nodded her head slowly and a devious gleam appeared in her eyes. Yes, she would go out of her way to ensure Miss Bennet's comfort and see to her every need. Mr. Darcy would have every reason to be impressed!

She settled back into her chair and began to hum.

"You seem quite content, Caroline," Louisa said. "Whatever are you plotting?"

"Plotting? Me?" She waved a hand at her sister. "I am merely thinking that things may work out much better than what I ever expected."

Jane's Thoughts on Riding to Netherfield

by Kara Louise

November 11, 1811

With a final tug to secure the ribbons of her bonnet, Jane glanced at her reflection in the hall mirror, catching the eye of Lizzy who approached from behind with an expression of worry and censure. "Please do not say it, Lizzy."

A sigh escaped her sister's lips and Jane cringed at the disapproval in her younger sister's steady gaze.

Returning her gaze to her own reflection, Jane turned and adjusted her riding habit. "I am not as outspoken as you, and I could never defy my mother. Besides, the rain may not begin until after I have arrived at Netherfield."

"Speak to Papa," implored Lizzy. "I am certain he could be made to see reason."

She shook her head. "All will be well. You will see." Lizzy's shoulders dropped; her dearest sister was disappointed, but it could not be helped. Jane did not have her younger sister's confident, outgoing manner.

"Jane!"

She gave an involuntary flinch at her name being screeched as her mother entered the hall from the sitting room.

"Hurry, child! You must not leave Miss Bingley and Mrs. Hurst waiting!"

Her mother's frenzied fingers began adjusting her collar and the bow of her bonnet. "You look very well. I am certain you are not so beautiful for nothing. Just be sure to remain long enough to see Mr. Bingley and for him to see you!"

"Mama!" she cried in tandem with Lizzy.

"Do not 'Mama' me! You will be the next mistress of Netherfield. You mark my words!" A quick glance of the clock prompted her mother to begin waving her handkerchief. "Oh! We do not have time for your nonsense, Lizzy!"

Jane bit back a giggle as Lizzy's expression morphed to one of incredulity, yet she did not have much time to savor the humor of the moment since her mother grasped her arm and steered her towards the door.

"Let us pray it rains. Then you will not have to delay until Mr. Bingley returns from dining with the officers."

"Mama—"

"Look! Mr. Hill has Nelly saddled and ready. Make haste! Miss Bingley and Mrs. Hurst may enjoy being fashionably late to a ball, but they will not be so appreciative of the practice when it is an invitation to tea."

With the help of a mounting block, Jane ascended to the saddle but found her mother had already bustled everyone except Lizzy into the house before she could bid them farewell.

Lizzy peered at the sky. "You must make haste—if for no other reason, than to avoid the rain. Miss Bingley and Mrs. Hurst will look upon you with disdain if you arrive soaked through."

"They are not so mean-spirited, Lizzy." Why did Lizzy always insist Mr. Bingley's sisters were so uncharitable? They had been everything affable and kind at the assembly.

Her sister shrugged a shoulder with a knowing smile. "I beg to differ, but I will not argue with you. Please do be careful. I expect you to tell me all when you return."

Jane grinned at her sister's now insistent gaze. "Of course." She gave a small wave and turned the old mare in the direction of Netherfield, giving one last turn at the top of the hill and lifting her hand to Lizzy before the house could no longer be seen.

With a nervous glance to the sky, Jane studied the grey clouds overhead. Her mother was correct; it did look like rain, yet she fervently hoped the ill weather would not occur until after she arrived at Netherfield. A soaked gown and undergarments was a disagreeable thought indeed!

A heavy exhale left her lips as she turned her thoughts to the gentleman at the heart of her mother's machinations. Mama was determined her eldest daughter would wed Mr. Bingley when they were still nothing more than acquaintances.

He was certainly gentlemanly and quite good-looking. He was pleasant company for the time they spoke at the assembly and an accomplished dancer. She enjoyed his conversation, but was not of a mind to accept a proposal on such a slight knowledge of his character.

Maybe, once she was more certain of her feelings as well as his regard for her, she would be honored by a proposal of marriage from that gentleman; however, what would happen if she decided Mr. Bingley was not the gentleman for her? How would her mother react?

After all, Mama insisted she ride, possibly in the rain, to Netherfield! Not only that, but her mother's words prior to her departure! She was determined to have her eldest daughter become the next mistress of Netherfield, yet Jane cared naught for the material considerations her mother coveted. She wished to marry for love, not situation. A small voice to the back of her mind voiced its displeasure in her present circumstances, riding to Netherfield to ensnare a man she knew little of in regards to demeanor, when the clouds appeared about to burst!

Those were not her only complaints either! Her mother's crowing as to her beauty—how tiring that had become! Mama never failed to mention Jane's handsome features. To be certain, Jane did not bemoan her appearance, but if Mr. Bingley did favor her, she hoped he would do so for reasons other than her looks. Most men of the local area did not attempt to hold a meaningful conversation with her, and either stared at her face or her décolletage as they danced. She had no wish to wed someone who would treat her thus for the remainder of their lives.

She could not claim to have Lizzy's wit or vivacity, but she had a steady and true heart, one that sought the best in people. Caring for others came with little effort, and Mr. Bingley appeared to have a similar demeanor, a quality that made him an attractive partner for her future life.

A drop of cold struck her face, and with a gentle hand, she brushed the raindrop away, knowing it would be the first of many. Perhaps it would be no more than a slight rain, and she could arrive at Netherfield merely damp.

Her heart sank when the drops became more frequent and increased in size until it was showering at a steady pace in every direction. She had no shelter nearby to take refuge from the storm, and her mother would be furious should she return to Longbourn. No choice lay before her except to forge ahead, and pray Miss Bingley and Mrs. Hurst would be gracious when she appeared at their door waterlogged.

Her mother was sure to be crowing about the success of her scheme. She prayed Lizzy would not be too impertinent in her response to Mama's exclamations of delight, though it was a pleasurable thought to have her dearest sister come to her defence in such a manner. At the moment, Jane was not certain she could be her usual temperate self if she was in the presence of her mother. Her present situation was not conducive to such behavior!

She brushed the sodden curls of her fringe from her eyes as Netherfield came into view in the distance and pressed a leg into Nelly's side so she might come to a slow trot. The older horse resisted, but Jane continued to cue her for the faster gait until the animal grudgingly capitulated.

A gust of wind arose and caused a chill that prompted her to shiver. The rain had permeated through her habit, her gown, her petticoats, her stays, and her chemise; she was soaked through and becoming cold, making it necessary for her to reach Netherfield soon.

The next mile or so was not a comfortable ride as Nelly's trot was not in the least bit a smooth one, but Jane endured the rough ride as best she could. A desire to weep in relief assailed her as she approached the front of the house, yet she restrained her tears as a groom approached to take the horse.

Once her feet were back upon the ground, she took in her bedraggled appearance, mortified to appear at Netherfield in such a state. She had so hoped to make a good impression upon Mr. Bingley's closest relations, yet she would not appear at her best.

Since there was naught she could do, Jane climbed the steps as the butler opened the door. Her new friends had been so kind at the assembly. They would be considerate now, would they not?

Lydia Goes to Meryton

by Diana Birchall

November 13, 1811

At Meryton, Lizzy left her younger sisters near the lodgings of one of the officer's wives, Mrs. Pratt, and crossed the road to walk through the fields leading toward Netherfield, where Jane lay ill.

"Isn't she a silly to go," said Lydia, "slopping through the mud just to see Jane with a cold, which she might see any day at home, if any of us had colds."

"Yes," Kitty agreed, "and to go to Netherfield, where it is so dull. There are no officers at Netherfield."

"No; nobody but that horrid prune, Miss Bingley. I would not talk to her for the world."

"Well, but Jane is obliged, Lydia, if she wants to marry Mr. Bingley!"

"I don't think there would be any fun in that, he has no spirit, or he'd join the militia and wear a red coat," Lydia declared. "Here is Mrs. Pratt's door. Now for a good time!"

Mrs. Pratt was a gay young wife of no more than Kitty's age, and she pulled them inside the house, her eyes sparkling with delight.

"Oh, I am glad you are come! And in good time too. What do you think, girls, Captain Carter is here!"

Lydia and Kitty exchanged significant glances and went inside, where half a dozen red-coated officers were having some talk and a slight libation.

"Ah, there's my Miss Lydia," cried Captain Carter, a very handsome young man of two and twenty, "come and sit on my knee, and you shall have a sip of my cider, now."

Lydia screamed long and loud with delight. "La! Captain Carter! You are mighty absurd. I won't sit upon your knee unless you promise me you won't go to London."

"You know I can't do that, duty calls," he protested, "But I will be back soon enough, I'm only carrying some messages for the colonel, and then we'll see if you'll sit on my knee—or give me a kiss."

"Oh I'll do that any time," Lydia answered coolly, "there's not a bit of harm in kissing."

This raised a howl. "Hark at her!" cried another officer, Ensign Chamberlayne. "That's a bold lass. A health to Miss Liddy!"

"Now, I prefer a quiet girl," observed a young, plain-faced Mr. Willis, "like this one. Won't you sit by me, Miss Kitty?"

"Not on your knee," she said, trying to sound roguish like Lydia.

"Pish! Tush! Girls," cried a young lady who was enthroned upon the knees of Colonel Forster himself. "There is no harm in knees, I'll be bound. And if you persist on sitting on the same ones, you may find yourself with a husband."

"Or a spanking!" said Colonel Forster hilariously.

"For shame!" she exclaimed, and much more of that nature, and the two began to pummel each other and disarrange their clothing.

"Oh! Look at Harriet, she is so fortunate," sighed Lydia enviously. "What do you bet she catches the colonel?"

"She would seem to have caught him already," answered Kitty, her eyes critically on the tumbling pair.

"That is the way to have fun. Look here, I am going to sit with Captain Carter, you sit with Mr. Willis, and we can stuff on plenty of this nice fruit the officers will give us, won't we?"

Captain Carter pulled Lydia onto his lap. "Yes, you sit here and I will give you a banana!"

The hilarity was immense. Lydia pulled back and looked coyly into his face. "For shame, Captain Carter, you must tell me what a banana is?"

"Oh, a new-discovered fruit, from the Indies. A botanical print was in the Quarterly—did you not read about it?"

"Lydia doesn't read anything," Kitty told him.

Lydia tossed her head. "I have better things to do."

Captain Carter continued. "The natives eat them. They are long —and yellow."

The officers roared. "Perhaps they grow them in Chiny," cried Chamberlayne. "But we have British courage and don't need any long yellow fruit, do we lads?"

The landlady appeared, a faded woman with an anxious expression. She needed the money from the officers and their ladies who were billeted upon her, but she was in continual terror lest their carousing make trouble, and lose her their custom.

"Officers, sirs, won't you please not get a poor old woman in difficulties with your noise, I beg you?"

"That's all right, Mother Barnes, we're just having a little fun. When we tumble the girls you'll have quiet enough."

"Oh no—oh no, my house must not lose its reputation," she began.

"Don't worry, ma'am, they are only joking, and I will make them keep quiet," Mrs. Pratt reassured her. "Now, fellows, we must not torment the life out of our good landlady. How would you like to pass the afternoon?

"We might go call upon Miss Lydia's Uncle, Mr. Philips," said Forster, "always good cheer at his house."

"Yes, and I'll answer for it they'll give us a good supper," Lydia announced.

"But Lydia, we cannot stay, Mama will be wondering about us."

"Pooh, Kitty! As long as we are with the officers she will not mind. She likes us to be with them. And you know they'll be glad to see us. But where is Mr. Denny, he should be here to make up the party."

"Denny's in London, but will be back and then I'll take his place with the dispatches," Captain Carter told her.

"But what are they about?"

"Ah my dear young lady, I cannot tell you regiment business, you must know," he laughed.

Lydia pouted. "I'm sure I don't care. What I want to see is if there are any new hats at the milliner's, and we can walk past on our way to Uncle Philips."

"Very well, then. Give me a kiss to keep up my strength for the walk."

Lydia complied enthusiastically, and then squealed, "Oh! Captain Carter, I swear you are the best kisser in the regiment."

"Hear that, men?" he cried. "And have you tried them all, then, Miss?"

"Good Lord no! What a story." She whispered in his ear, "I am sure I would never kiss a dog-faced little man like that Mr. Willis sitting by my sister. I hope you don't think as ill of me as that."

He caught her by the hand and pulled her up from the sofa. "Well, then let's rescue Kitty, and repair to the Philips'. They do set an uncommonly good table."

"Come on, fellows, we march!" Col. Forster declared, and the gay party went frolicking through the streets of Meryton, their hallooing and laughter resounding from one end of the village to the other. Mrs. Philips had the window open and was leaning out before they were halfway down the street.

"Lydia! Kitty! Do you bring up Col. Forster and all the officers, we have got some very nice ragout and ale, and you might have a little dancing after."

"We're coming, aunt!" called back Lydia, and capered on her way, Kitty scuttling after her.

"Oh, Kitty, what better times we have without Jane and Lizzy, don't we," she tossed over her shoulder.

"To be sure we do!"

"Why, are they not very handsome, and very good-tempered young ladies? I thought they were," inquired Col. Forster.

"Oh! No. They hate anything that's the least bit fun going on. We call them Miss Prim and Miss Priss. Always scolding and lecturing, you would think they were old maids of thirty. You wouldn't like them at all if you knew them better, Col. Forster."

"Perhaps not. I do like my girls young and silly," he said, looking down at pretty Miss Harriet, hanging from his arm.

"Yes, yes, Aunt, don't worry—I said we're coming!" shouted Lydia at the top of her voice.

Caroline Plans for the Netherfield Ball – Part 1

by Maria Grace

November 14, 1811

The garish Bennet women finally trundled out of Netherfield's parlor. Not a moment too soon. Caroline pressed her eyes with thumb and forefinger. They had already overstayed their allotted quarter hour by that much again.

How much trouble had that wrought? What disaster might ensue if they stayed any longer? Pray they not choose to call again.

Had it not been enough to play hostess to two of the Bennet women, the two least offensive to be sure, but still—this latest affront was too much to be borne.

"Charles, a word if you please." Caroline beckoned him to follow, nodded to Mr. Darcy, and strode from the parlor.

She led him to the morning room and shut the door firmly behind them. *One, two, three, four.* She must control her temper. A proper lady did not give voice to the vitriol that bubbled within. That did not mean she would not struggle in the effort. Perhaps if she kept her back to him, hands firmly knotted together, that would help.

"Caroline? Caro, are you well? Is there something wrong?" Heavy, booted footfalls approached.

She drew a deep breath and turned very slowly to face him. An open palm stopped his advance. "Is there something wrong? Is that all you can say?"

Charles pinched the bridge of his nose. 'What is not to your liking now?"

"You do not know? Oh, Charles!" She stalked away. Was he truly that uninformed or did he just take some perverse pleasure in vexing her just because he could?

He pulled a chair from under the table and sat down, bracing elbows on knees. "Pray, just tell me, what have I done?"

"The ball!"

He winced.

He was right, her voice had become more of a shriek. She must master that. It would not do to have the rest of the household hear her use such an unladylike tone.

"Did you not tell me you wished to host a ball once we settled in?" He picked at the tablecloth, refusing to meet her gaze.

"Yes I did."

"Then pray tell me, what is the problem?"

"Problem, brother? Problems!" She paced along the windows. If he did not know, how was she to begin?

"Just tell me, do not keep me here like a child to be scolded or I shall leave directly."

She whirled and took two steps toward him. "Why did you allow that little Bennet chit to choose the date of the ball?"

"Is that all?" He shook his head and rolled his eyes.

"How can you say such a thing?"

"It is only a date. Is not one as good as the next?"

"I am mistress of your house, Charles. You should have given me the task." She folded her arms across her chest and pulled herself up to her full height.

"Why does it matter? Are you truly so small minded you would begrudge—"

"Did you take note of the date she selected?"

"November twenty-six."

"What date is it now?"

"November fourteen."

"Do you not see the problem?"

He pressed his temples. "Just tell me. I have no desire to play guessing games with you."

"How long have I to plan and execute this ball?"

"A fortnight."

"Exactly."

"I still do not see the fuss. You have an entire fortnight to accomplish what you need to do."

She pulled out a chair and placed it facing his. *Five, six, seven, eight.* She sat down across from him, knees nearly touching his. *Nine, ten.*

"When should we send invitations out?"

"I do not know." He twitched his hands between them. "When ample white soup has been made?"

She covered half her face with her hand, pressing her fingertips into her forehead. "Let me start at another point. What exactly do you think needs to be done to carry off this event we are committed to?"

"Hire a few musicians, invite the neighbors…"

At least he had the good sense to stop talking before he made a complete fool of himself.

"Consider, just for a moment the invitations. To begin with, a proper ball invitation is sent a month, and better six weeks in advance, after having been professionally printed by a copper plate. How long do you think it takes to get invitations printed for an event?"

His eyes widened and jaw dropped. "I…I…I…"

"The best I can hope for now is that the printer will have some sort of general invitations available that require the specific details to be handwritten in. And if those are available, do you have any idea how long it will take to see them all written?"

"I…I can assist—"

"With your handwriting? You must be joking. Bad enough they should not be printed. If you wrote them, who knows what day our guests would arrive!"

"I am sorry…"

"If I leave to consult with the printer this very moment, I would count myself very fortunate to have the task finished by tomorrow evening. So, at very best, the invitations cannot go out less than ten days before the event. Ten days! Can you imagine what the neighbors will say?"

"I had no idea."

"Clearly. Have you any idea of what else must be done—no—do not bother to answer. I already know you do not."

He sprang to his feet and took her place pacing in the sunbeam. "What is to be done? Shall I call upon the Bennets and explain?"

"Certainly not. The very notion. I have no doubt Miss Lydia will have told the entire population of Hertfordshire by now. To revoke the invitation or even change the date would be a stain upon our reputation."

"Surely you exaggerate."

"Indeed I do not. This ball will be the singular social event of the year. Our standing in this dreary patch of country will be made or broken by the ball. I will not have you ruin it before we have even begun."

"Then what would you have me do?"

"Open your wallet, close your mouth, ask no questions, and stay out of my way. I have a ball to arrange."

Charles stared at her and gulped.

"And thank me when it is all over and I have made you the talk of the county."

"Yes, Caro." He jumped back as she swept out of the room.

Caroline Sees the Dangers of Elizabeth

by Shannon Winslow

November 15, 1811

While she had been playing the Italian tunes, which she knew by memory, Caroline had also been watching Mr. Darcy—normally one of her favorite occupations. On this occasion, however, she had derived little enough pleasure from it. For it seemed to her that the gentleman in question, rather than listening to the music she skillfully performed for him, had been paying far more attention to Miss Bennet. He had tried to be inconspicuous—pretending to look beyond her and averting his eyes if Elizabeth should turn his way. But Caroline was not deceived; she knew him too well.

The situation had gone from bad to worse when she had next launched into a Scotch air, hoping to redirect Darcy's attention to herself by the liveliness of the tune. It seemed to have only driven him closer to Elizabeth, though. Now he was actually taking the trouble of speaking to her! Caroline could not hear the content of their conversation, but she could see the lady's sportive manner, although it was not quite clear if this was meant to provoke or flirt. She could also see Darcy's bemused countenance. The poor man looked positively bewitched!

Caroline stumbled uncharacteristically in her performance, sounding a discordant collection of notes too loudly to go unnoticed. Mr. Darcy did then, at last, render her his full attention, as did the others.

"Sorry," she said to the room in general. "I cannot imagine how that happened. I must have played this piece a hundred times without once making such a mistake."

Caroline resumed her playing, trying to be more attentive to her task. But the distraction of Darcy conversing with Elizabeth — by choice, this time, and not by necessity—persisted.

There was danger here. Mr. Darcy might not yet see it, but it should be plain enough to his true friends. How earnestly then did Miss Bingley wish for the invalid's immediate recovery. Parting with Jane would be a small price to pay for also getting rid of Elizabeth!

In the meantime, the presumptuous female's mesmerizing effects must be counteracted as much as possible, before things were allowed to progress too far. Surely the man was not yet slipped beyond the influence of reason. Perhaps a few well placed words about Elizabeth's low connections, a few well drawn portraits of what life married into such a family would look like, might wake Darcy from whatever delusions he currently suffered. It would be risky, but Caroline saw no alternative.

And it was for his own good, after all. Darcy might be irritated with her for a time, but he would thank her in the end, once the danger had passed and he saw how she had saved him from it. Caroline could picture it now. He would take her into his arms, just as she had imagined a thousand times, and he would say,

"My darling Caroline, can you ever forgive me for looking at another woman? You have been as patient as a saint, you noble creature. I am so grateful that you showed me the error of my ways in time. There never could be anyone for me but you. Will you marry me?"

"Yes! Oh, yes!" she cried, closing her eyes to receive her beloved's kiss.

"What was that, Caroline?" said Mr. Bingley, unpleasantly drawing her back to reality. "Do you have a headache or is the light too bright?"

Realizing that all eyes were once again trained on her, and not necessarily with the admiration she could desire, Miss Bingley grasped at the offered excuse. "Yes, a headache," she said, abandoning the pianoforte and rising, one hand held to her forehead. "Perhaps I will go to bed now."

Her campaign to undermine Miss Elizabeth Bennet would have to wait until morning.

Darcy Adheres to His Book

by Abigail Reynolds

November 16, 1811

To Mr. Darcy it was welcome intelligence—Elizabeth had been at Netherfield long enough. She attracted him more than he liked—and Miss Bingley was uncivil to her, and more teasing than usual to himself. He wisely resolved to be particularly careful that no sign of admiration should now escape him, nothing that could elevate her with the hope of influencing his felicity; sensible that if such an idea had been suggested, his behavior during the last day must have material weight in confirming or crushing it. Steady to his purpose, he scarcely spoke ten words to her through the whole of Saturday, and though they were at one time left by themselves for half an hour, he adhered most conscientiously to his book, and would not even look at her. – Pride & Prejudice

"I will leave you to your book, then." With those words, Bingley departed the room, leaving Darcy and Elizabeth in sole possession of it.

Good God! Had it not been struggle enough to avoid engaging Elizabeth in conversation all morning, saying nothing beyond the very least required for civility? How could Bingley have actually left him alone with Elizabeth? Darcy was not prepared for such an eventuality, having been certain that Miss Bingley would not permit such a tête-à-tête, but she was off somewhere, no doubt haranguing the housekeeper for some imagined fault. And here he was, at last alone with the woman who had so bewitched him, with nothing but his own determination to stand between them.

He had to forcibly remind himself of the importance of demonstrating to Elizabeth that she should have no expectations of him; it was bad enough that Bingley was constantly dangling after her sister. Beautiful and well-mannered as Miss Jane Bennet might be, she would not do as a wife for him. Bingley needed a bride of higher breeding to improve his status in the *ton*; Georgiana, when she came of age, would be a far better choice for him, and it would solve Darcy's own dilemma of finding a husband for her who would not intimidate her or take advantage of her gentle nature. And Elizabeth Bennet would be an even less suitable bride for the Master of Pemberley.

No! He could not afford to even consider such a thing; it brought visions of Elizabeth more suitable for his private nocturnal imaginings of her. He needed to focus on his book and on appearing completely indifferent to her presence. How much easier that was said than done! He had already quite forgotten what he had been reading about, although the page was still open in front of him.

The sound of turning pages alerted him that Elizabeth must have picked up a book as well, and he mentally breathed a sigh of relief. He could not look at her; that would defeat his entire purpose, but surely it would not hurt to steal one brief glance in her direction when she was engaged in reading.

He immediately regretted his decision. Another woman might appear uninteresting when reading, but not Elizabeth. Her lips were half-parted in a smile at whatever she was reading, and with her free hand, she was unconsciously toying with one of the dark curls that lay against the soft skin of her face. That was the damnable thing about Elizabeth; her hands were so often in motion, seeming enamored of exploring every tactile sensation in her vicinity, so that a man could think of nothing but how she might touch him with the same sensual curiosity. It was a subtle betrayal of the passionate nature so clearly within her. She might be unaware of it now, but the right man would be able to awaken it, and all that suppressed passion would pour forth onto that fortunate soul. God, but he hated to think of her with any man but himself! That she could turn those fine eyes on anyone else or that such incredible fire might burn for another man! But she was not for him. She could not be for him. He had duties and responsibilities, and he must remember that at all cost.

It was better to think that she would never marry and that she would pass her lifetime in the enchanting unawakened state he witnessed now. Or perhaps her husband might be one of those with little interest in his wife, and never see the sensual possibilities in Elizabeth's bearing and even the way she breathed. What sort of man was he to be wishing an indifferent husband on this bewitching woman? He knew the answer to that too well: he was the sort who would do almost anything to possess her himself. *Almost* anything. His family honor and duty must take precedence even over his near-desperate physical need.

Perhaps he should speak to her after all—her sparkling repartee could be no more dangerous to his self-control than his private thoughts, and at least in those moments of conversation, he could imagine he was the only man in her world. But no, he must protect *her* as well from expectations of him; it was the only honorable thing to do. Damn honor! Why must it stand in the way of him taking for his own the one woman in all of creation that he wanted above all others?

He heard another page turning, and realized with a shock that he himself had been staring blindly at the same page for a quarter hour now. Quickly he flipped to the next page and forced his eyes to scan the lines, though for the life of him he could not take in a word of it. It might as well have been in Chinese for all the sense it made to him. How could he think of anything else when Elizabeth was but a few feet from him? Good God, how her mere *breathing* lit up the entire room on this cloudy, dismal day?

Elizabeth's soft, musical laugh filled the air, and he risked another glance in her direction, just to reassure himself that it was her book and not himself that gave her amusement. At least that was his excuse; the truth was that he could not resist. The ladies of the *ton* would never lower themselves so far as to laugh; it would not fit the bored, languid persona demanded by high style. Elizabeth showed her amusement frequently, as suited so lively a woman, and it did not matter how much he knew she would be scorned in the London ballrooms for it. His body reacted viscerally every time she laughed, wanting to hear that lovely sound again at the same time as he longed to stop it with his own lips. Not for the first time during her stay at Netherfield, he thanked merciful heaven for the fashion in trousers. If gentlemen were still required to wear tight breeches, he would have had to spend half his time hiding behind furniture.

He was starting to lose the battle with himself. He was too desperate for her, too desperate for her to turn those laughing fine eyes on him, to awaken that part of his soul that had remained dormant these many years during which he had been unmoved by the most beautiful ladies of the *ton*. He needed to gaze his fill of her —as if that could ever happen!—and to cross verbal swords with her once more before she left Netherfield. What if he never saw her again, or only across a crowded room, never close enough to share a conversation with her? It was untenable, just as untenable as the idea that he, Fitzwilliam Darcy, Master of Pemberley, would lose his vaunted self-control to any woman, much less one as unsuitable and hauntingly tempting as Elizabeth Bennet.

Just then Miss Bingley entered the room, saving him from himself. If only he could manage to be grateful for the interruption, and not feel like he had lost something precious because he could no longer sit in silence alone in a room with his own Elizabeth!

Elizabeth and Jane Leave Netherfield

by L. L. Diamond

November 17, 1811

On Sunday, after morning service, the separation, so agreeable to almost all, took place. Miss Bingley's civility to Elizabeth increased at last very rapidly, as well as her affection for Jane; and when they parted, after assuring the latter of the pleasure it would always give her to see her either at Longbourn or Netherfield, and embracing her most tenderly, she even shook hands with the former. Elizabeth took leave of the whole party in the liveliest spirits.

Elizabeth followed Jane as she entered the carriage, giving a blissful sigh as she took her seat. While Jane would, no doubt, miss the company of Mr. Bingley and his sisters, Elizabeth could not feel the same. She was pleased to depart Netherfield and its disagreeable inhabitants—well, with the exception of Mr. Bingley, that is.

Over the past week, she had endured enough of Miss Bingley's incivility, Mrs. Hurst's titters, Mr. Hurst's boorish snoring from across the drawing room, and Mr. Darcy's proud and pompous manner. If her dearest sister had been well enough, she would have rushed Jane back to Longbourn upon her arrival, yet the past days in their company had been a necessity despite the unpleasantness of the situation!

Her elder sister waved with a peaceful smile to Miss Bingley and Mr. Bingley, who stood to his sister's side. Elizabeth had reason to believe her elder sister's feelings for the brother had increased during her convalescence; however, she did not envy her such sisters if she did in fact wed Mr. Bingley. Of course, her mother would not

72

be content until such a happy event occurred.

Elizabeth started when the carriage lurched forward and relaxed into the comfortable seat, pleased beyond measure to be travelling home.

"The week was not so terrible, was it?" asked Jane with a tilt of her head.

"Forgive me if I do not enjoy the company of many of the party. I will not include Mr. Bingley in that statement as he is an amiable gentleman, but I cannot appreciate the manner of his sisters or his friend."

Her beloved sister's face became scolding. "Lizzy! Miss Bingley and Mrs. Hurst were very agreeable, and I am certain his friend must be just as kind. Mr. Darcy strikes me as one who is not comfortable amongst strangers and not one to rattle on as some young men do."

Elizabeth bristled. Mr. Darcy was insufferable! How could Jane not see how proud and disagreeable he was! "He is a man of wealth and education, and his behaviour since entering the has illustrated his insufferable pride and contempt for those beneath his notice."

"Yet, he is friends with Mr. Bingley, who has yet to purchase his own estate. I believe there is more to the man than an ill-spoken insult at the assembly."

"You always seek the good in people, Jane, and never wish to acknowledge when one is ungenerous."

"I prefer to believe there is some kindness in all and sundry whether it be to the fullest measure of the individual or whether it be in a small amount in one corner of their heart."

A lift of Elizabeth's lips could not be helped. Her sister's unswerving devotion in the goodness of all was part of why she adored her elder sister; however, one day, Jane's heart would be broken by her inability to see the ill of the world.

Her view of Mr. Darcy was certainly not a fair assessment of his character. The wealthy gentleman from Derbyshire had been taciturn, rude, and unfriendly for the entirety of his residence in Hertfordshire; his manner during their stay at Netherfield did not improve her opinion of him one jot!

Mr. Darcy had been intent on arguing with her based on their conversations after dinner each evening. The accomplishments of women, indeed! He looked upon her to find fault, so now he also found deficiency in her abilities—not that he was aware of her accomplishments. He had scarcely spoken to her much less inquired as to any talents she might possess!

She would not even contemplate the scandalous remark he made about her and Miss Bingley's figures!

"Lizzy, Are you well?"

She snapped from her reverie. "Yes, I am exceedingly well."

"I am grateful to you for coming to Netherfield. I am only sorry you did not find associating with the Netherfield party more agreeable."

Her sister's weary and worried expression weighed upon her heart. "Your company made it worth the trial, dearest."

Jane's face transformed with a sweet smile as she took Elizabeth's hand, and gave it a gentle squeeze. "I believe you are too good to me."

A loud shriek caused both Jane and Elizabeth to startle and peer out of the carriage at their mother, who stood before the open doors of Longbourn, her hands upon her hips.

"I expressly instructed you to remain for another day, Miss Elizabeth Bennet! I am certain Mr. Bingley would have declared himself had you waited!"

The carriage came to a stop and Elizabeth followed Jane from Mr. Bingley's fine equipage. "Jane is well, as you can see, Mama. It would have been rude to impose for another night."

"Rude?" exclaimed her mother. "The party at Netherfield should have no reason to perceive you as rude! Jane was so very ill!" Her eyes narrowed as she stared at Elizabeth. "It was you who was so mad to return home, dashing all of Jane's hopes in the process! How you try my nerves!" She gave an indignant huff and returned indoors.

"I have no hopes to be dashed—none as of yet anyway," explained Jane.

With a slight shrug to the shoulders, Elizabeth levelled her elder sister with a stern expression, which likely was not severe in the least. "I do not believe your falsehood for a second, Jane Bennet."

Jane's smile was serene, as always, but there was something more in her eyes. Her eldest sister's heart was touched! She was certain of it!

Reflections on Jane and Elizabeth's Visit at Netherfield

by Kara Louise

November 18, 1811

On Sunday, after morning service, the separation, so agreeable to almost all, took place... Elizabeth took leave of the whole party in the liveliest of spirits. - Chapter 12

Darcy and Bingley stood quietly side by side as they watched the carriage conveying Jane and Elizabeth Bennet drive away. The Hursts and Miss Bingley had quickly returned to the house after bidding the ladies farewell. The men's eyes remained fixed on the swirl of dirt kicked up by the wheels from the carriage as it made a turn and soon disappeared from view. They turned and slowly walked back towards the house. Bingley let out a long sigh. Darcy kept his to himself.

The men joined the others in the drawing room where Bingley collapsed into a chair with a wistful smile. His head fell back and he folded his hands onto his lap.

Miss Bingley looked from her brother to Darcy. She lifted a brow. "I certainly hope we can endure the absence of those two ladies." She directed a forced smile at Mr. Darcy. "Mr. Darcy, you shall no longer have the benefit of a pair of *fine eyes*. Shall you miss them? Perhaps you have etched them in your memory? Are they truly so fine that they have erased every trace of her objectionable family?"

Darcy let out a low grumble, but clenched his jaw so he would say nothing. For the past few days, Miss Bingley's spiteful remarks had continued unabated, and Darcy regretted ever admitting to her that he found Miss Bennet's eyes fine. But oh, how fine they are!

There was more to her than just her fine eyes, however. With each passing minute in her presence, he found it more and more difficult not to take great delight in her spark of liveliness and intelligence, her warm and frequent smiles, her musical laugh, and in his repartees with her. The mere thought of her made his pulse race. He stifled another sigh.

Darcy's silence seemed to subdue Miss Bingley's criticisms, for which he was most grateful. He had heard enough from her since the first day Elizabeth arrived.

He picked up his book; one he had started before the Bennet sisters arrived at Netherfield. He normally would have finished it by now, but his mind had been so filled with Elizabeth's presence, he could barely concentrate on a single sentence. He hoped picking up the book would indicate to Miss Bingley his preference not to engage in conversation at the present.

Fortunately, Darcy was left to himself. Bingley was inclined to speak about Jane to anyone who would listen. Miss Bingley listened politely as her brother accounted for the days Miss Bennet had been there, starting with his concern over her illness, to being so delighted that he could offer her exceptional care, and finally, that she had improved in health.

As Darcy surreptitiously listened, he believed he had never seen his friend display such intensity of affection for a lady. He had seen him in love several times, but this was different. Very different.

That night, Darcy retired early to his chambers. He dismissed his valet and sat down in a chair, letting his head drop back. "So she is finally gone!" he gruffly whispered. "So be it! Perhaps this will finally allow me some peace of mind again!"

In the darkness of the room, lit by a single candle, he suddenly felt an emptiness grip him. He closed his eyes and fisted his hands, attempting to rid himself of this most inexplicable feeling. He blew out a puff of air. She was entirely wrong for him!

He began to slowly shake his head. "Miss Bennet, your relative situation is considerably beneath mine! This is merely a misplaced affection on my part. I shall no longer dwell on those things I find so..." Darcy drew in a breath and whispered, "...that I find so irresistible."

He suddenly sat upright and grasped the arms of the chair. "You displayed your impudent country manners, Miss Elizabeth Bennet, by walking through muddy fields and along waterlogged roads. You mocked me, claiming I was without those follies and nonsense that allow for teasing! Examine me, Miss Elizabeth, and proclaim all my defects! Then challenge my every thought and opinion, even when I am extending a compliment your way!"

His rigid and erect comportment began to gradually collapse as he slumped into his chair. "Refuse my offer to dance a reel. Laugh at my attempt to placate the incivility directed at you by Bingley's sisters."

He swayed, as if every fibre of his being was in a swirl of conflicting thought and emotion. "Dare to weaken my defences and my resolve with your sparkling eyes and delightful smile, even as you confront me! Then astonish me by defending me to your mother when she misconstrues my meaning. How am I to remain collected in your presence when one moment you defend me and the next you pronounce judgment?"

His head dropped back and his eyes stared vacantly at the ceiling above. The single candle sputtered, sending muted flickers of light about the room. "Disappoint me by remaining silent when I wished so much to hear your lively voice and your clever and thought-provoking opinions."

He let out a huff and roughly ran his hand through his hair. "Torture me with your relations! How can one be so suitable for me in so many ways whilst at the same time be so completely unsuitable because of her family connections?"

"When you arrived with mud on the hem of your dress, why did you have such a glowing countenance? Did you suspect the effect that would have on me? Was that a deliberate employment of your arts to entrap me?"

The flame of the candle finally extinguished, cloaking his chambers in darkness. He felt a surge of determination consume him. In a whisper, he declared to himself, "Now that you are gone, Elizabeth, I shall finally have some peace!"

Caroline Plans for the Netherfield Ball– Part II

by Maria Grace

November 18, 1811

With the Bennet sisters gone from Netherfield, perhaps Caroline might now get on with her business. There was no time to be lost in frivolous chattering and gadding about. She pulled her housekeeping journal from her reticule. At least she had an ally in her efforts.

Nicholls had proven herself a treasure. Not only was she able to suggest where qualified additional help might be hired—at least two scullery maids, two kitchen maids, and an additional man to help polish the silver and attend the men's retiring room, and a pair of maids for everything else—Nicholls also crafted a very suitable menu for the evening—all sixty-three dishes of it. What was more, she identified the best local resources for everything the ball required. And the list of requirements was long.

To think Charles had initially balked at the salary the housekeeper demanded. To be sure he was willing to pay handsomely for his valet when he could honestly make do with a far less expensive man, but one never, ever, skimped on a housekeeper.

And this one was worth her weight in sugar, beeswax candles and the ice she knew remained in the ice house. Without her help and better, her experience, the event would be entirely impossible. Nicholls was, without a doubt, to date the best housekeeper they had ever enjoyed.

She even kept the guest list from the ball thrown by Netherfield's last tenants. To be sure it was two years old, but it was a place to start. That foresight saved Caroline at least two hours' time in her efforts, two hours she desperately needed.

It would take at least that long to engage the musicians Nicholls recommended and the artist to chalk the floors. Caroline flipped to the back of her book. Thank heavens, the sketch she had made of tall ships and starry skies remained tucked in place. Done by a proper artist, it would be the perfect complement to a candlelit ball room. Not to mention it would help cover those scratches and stains on the floorboards that no one had bothered to notice until she checked under the carpeting. Ah well, Nicholls could not be perfect, could she?

Oh the chandler! Botheration, she nearly forgot. That shop was on the way to the musician's. She really ought to stop there first. Best insure sufficient six hour candles were available. It was entirely possible she might have to enlist the services of a second chandler in this sleepy little village. Who could predict what kind of stock would be available here? Surely it would be unusual for them to fill very large orders. Balls like this one could not happen more than once a season, if that often.

If only she had time to go to London—

She pinched the bridge of her nose. That conversation had not gone well. Charles had been so agreeable until that point. Why would he balk at a perfectly reasonable suggestion?

Capitulating had been mortifying, but permitting him to cancel the ball would have been far worse. Their reputation might never recover were that to happen.

At least Mr. Darcy had calmed Charles when the wine-seller's bill arrived. What did he expect her to make punch and negus from? What would a ball be without iced punch served to cool the dancers between each set?

Dear Mr. Darcy had agreed with her and convinced Charles to give her her head with everything else. What would this ball be without him to convince Charles of the desperate need to make this

81

the event of the season?

Why it would be little different than that dreadful assembly attended by every shopkeeper and apprentice in the country where one could not always tell them from the gentlemen. To think whom she had agreed to dance with that night! Poor clerks should not be permitted to wear excellent suits and pass themselves off as more genteel than their occupation renders them.

And Charles thought it such a fine joke, even going so far as to suggest she might wish to invite him so that she might dance with him again.

Perish the thought. The Netherfield ball would be everything a proper, private, ball should be. Excellent company, excellent music, excellent victuals. All the height of fashion and refinement.

Well, perhaps not all the guests. The Bennets and the utterly garish Sir William Lucas and family had to be invited after all.

Nonetheless, this would be her opportunity to show Hertfordshire—and Mr. Darcy—what a proper mistress could do for Netherfield Park.

She paused and drew a deep breath. That was a far more agreeable thought to dwell upon. Mr. Darcy, with his fine figure, his excellent manners and extensive grounds. If she could impress him, show him she had all the qualities necessary for the mistress of a grand estate, perhaps then he would pursue her more seriously.

Clearly that was his intent. The conversations they shared, the snide remarks he offered for her enjoyment alone, he must be considering her. Surely concern for her fitness to manage his home had been the reason he hesitated. As cakey as Charles could be, Mr. Darcy must need concrete assurances that she would reflect well upon him in society.

And he would have it. The Netherfield ball would be every bit as grand as if it were held in London. She would prove herself a credit to her brother...and to any man who would make her mistress of his estate.

Yes, that would make all this inconvenience and bother entirely and completely worthwhile.

She tucked her journal back into her basket and turned into the chandler's shop. About three hundred candles would do very nicely.

Mr. Collins at Longbourn

by Mary Simonsen

November 18, 1811

Mr. Collins was punctual to his time, and was received with great politeness by the whole family. Mr. Bennet indeed said little; but the ladies were ready enough to talk, and Mr. Collins seemed neither in need of encouragement, nor inclined to be silent himself. - Chapter 13

After re-reading the letter from Mr. Collins, the son of her father's estranged cousin, Lizzy was uneasy. She agreed with Papa when he described the man as a mixture of servility and self-importance—an unusual combination if ever there was one—but that description was their only point of agreement. Although her father was prepared to be entertained by his cousin, this was the same man who held the future of the Bennet women in his hands. After Papa's death, and with little notice, William Collins could turn the whole family out on the road and take possession of Longbourn and its contents. His visit should not be taken lightly.

When she had learned of the parson's impending visit, Lizzy had hoped that Mr. Collins would be sensible, but if his letter was any indication, that was not the case. At the very least, he was an oddity. And what did he mean when he wrote that he was offering the Bennet family an olive branch? What form would such a gesture take?

Upon arrival, the newly ordained Mr. Collins was greeted with great civility by all, including Mrs. Bennet, especially after he had complimented her on the beauty of her daughters: "I have heard much of their beauty, but that, in this instance, fame had fallen short of the truth." In Lizzy's mind, the praise was excessive and puzzling. From whom would he have heard such a report? As far as Lizzy knew, the parson had never before visited Hertfordshire. If anything fell short of the truth, it was Mr. Collins's acclamation. During dinner, whilst listening to Mr. Collins pontificate on various subjects, most particularly his esteemed patroness, Lady Catherine de Bourgh, Lizzy stifled a laugh as she thought about various travelers discussing the beauty of the Bennet sisters on the roads between Hertfordshire and Kent. With the absurdity of that notion in mind, she decided to take her father's advice and enjoy the parson's visit.

On that first evening, as the two eldest Bennet daughters prepared for bed, Lizzy asked her sister what she thought of Mr. Collins. She found that Jane, too, was puzzled. "I wonder what he means when he says that it is his intention to admire us? In what way will he accomplish that?"

"Perhaps he will treat us with the same deference he employs when in the company of Lady Catherine de Bourgh. He will flatter us with delicacy by suggesting elegant compliments sprinkled about at appropriate times."

"For example?"

"'Why Miss Bennet, I noticed how daintily you walk. You practically glide.'"

"Lizzy, do be serious."

"'Miss Elizabeth, I could not help but notice how you cut your meat into tiny morsels so that they fit perfectly on your fork and slide so elegantly into your mouth.'"

Although Jane laughed, she chided her sister for being unkind.

"Chastise me if you will, but I find the man ridiculous. Although Papa is pleased by the absurdity of his pronouncements, Mr. Collins is actually quite tedious. He does not even read novels."

"He certainly would not be the only person to look down on those who do."

"I think his lack of interest in anything other than religious treatises indicates an absence of imagination and intelligence."

In nodding, Jane acknowledged that she did as well. "However, we must be considerate. Not only is he our father's cousin, but he is also heir to Longbourn. I would like to think that when Papa dies, he will be kind to us by allowing us to stay in our home."

Lizzy could see that tolerance was the best approach to a man with a good education but little understanding. "You are wiser than I am, Jane. I am too quick to speak my mind without taking into consideration the effects of what I say. I should hold my breath to cool my porridge."

"I do not think you have to worry too much about saying the wrong thing as Mr. Collins rarely stops talking, and when he does, he does not listen to what is being said."

"Now it is *you* who is being unkind."

"Not unkind, just truthful," Jane said as she placed the hairbrush on the table. But then a look of alarm crossed her face. "Lizzy, please tell me that Mr. Collins did not come to Longbourn with the intention of finding a wife."

The concern on Lizzy's face matched that of Jane's, but then she smiled. "Fortunately, being the second eldest and less blessed as far as beauty is concerned, *I* have nothing to worry about. However, *you*—"

"Do not even think about finishing that sentence," Jane warned.

"I wonder if Mr. Bingley knew he had competition for your affections if he would immediately propose marriage."

"And I wonder when you are going to hold your breath to cool your porridge," Jane said before snuffing out the candle. As she climbed into bed, she warned her bed companion, "Not another word about Mr. Collins and *me*, Lizzy, or you will be the one to be teased. I shall tell Mr. Collins that I suffer from an incurable disease and that he should make *you* the object of his attention."

"What is that you are saying, Jane? I cannot understand you. I am already half asleep."

Wickham and Denny in Meryton

by Jack Caldwell

November 19, 1811

Lydia's intention of walking to Meryton was not forgotten; every sister except Mary agreed to go with her; and Mr. Collins was to attend them (...) In pompous nothings on his side, and civil assents on that of his cousins, their time passed till they entered Meryton. The attention of the younger ones was then no longer to be gained by him. Their eyes were immediately wandering up in the street in quest of the officers, and nothing less than a very smart bonnet indeed, or a really new muslin in a shop window, could recall them. - Pride & Prejudice

The return from London by post was not unpleasant for Archibald Denny, lieutenant of militia, but his good humor was not only due to his traveling companion. George Wickham was an engaging sort of rascal much like himself, always ready to enjoy a drink or a barmaid. Their lively conversation made the hours in the crowded coach fly by, and before he knew it, Denny was back in Meryton.

No, Denny's happy mood was due to two different reasons. First, his contacts in Town had finally borne fruit, and there was at last the opportunity to acquire the funds he needed to buy a lieutenancy in the Regulars. Second, with his return to Hertfordshire, Denny hoped to further his acquaintance with Miss Lydia Bennet, the pretty and lively daughter of a local gentleman.

"To what sort of place have you brought me, Denny?" said Wickham, looking out the window as the carriage came to a stop.

"A most delightful country town," Denny assured him. "The fellows in the regiment are a jolly bunch, and the local girls are comely and friendly."

Wickham grinned. "Jolly and comely—my favorite sort of people! Lead on, my friend!"

Upon exiting the post carriage, Denny arranged for their trunks to be delivered to the militia's camp, but instead of reporting directly to Colonel Forster and finalizing Wickham's commission in the regiment, Denny agreed to Wickham's request to see more of Meryton first. They had not walked five minutes before Denny was glad he agreed to Wickham's suggestion. There, on the other side of the street, was Miss Lydia with three of her sisters and a tall, stocky man dressed in the clothes of a clergyman.

Denny bowed at Miss Lydia's wave, and he heard Wickham's light whistle of approval. "Well, you were right about the comely ladies, Denny," his friend said in a low voice.

Denny smiled. "Come, I will introduce you."

They crossed the street, Denny unconsciously straightening his uniform jacket. He addressed the company directly and entreated permission to introduce his companion. Mr. Wickham. Wickham began conversing with Miss Bennet and Miss Elizabeth, which gave Denny the opportunity to talk with Miss Kitty and Miss Lydia. Both officers ignored the ladies' cousin, a Mr. Collins of Kent, as blustery a fool as Denny had ever met.

Miss Kitty was nervous and coughing as usual, but to Denny's disappointment, Miss Lydia was more interested in Wickham than himself.

"And where did you meet the gentleman?" she asked for the second time. Denny was about to answer her when two gentlemen rode up. At a glance, Denny recognized Mr. Bingley and his guest, Mr. Darcy.

The gentlemen began the usual civilities; Mr. Bingley was the principal spokesman and Miss Bennet the principal object. He had been, he said, on his way to Longbourn on purpose to inquire after her, a statement Mr. Darcy corroborated with a bow.

At that moment, Wickham, who was facing Miss Elizabeth, his back to the newcomers, turned, and something extraordinary happened. Wickham locked eyes with Mr. Darcy and both changed color; Wickham paled, while the gentleman on horseback grew red. Wickham, after a few moments, touched his hat—a salutation which Mr. Darcy barely deigned to return.

Denny was shocked. *Why was George afraid of Mr. Darcy?*

Mr. Bingley continued to speak with Miss Bennet for another minute, without noticing what had passed between the two men. Then seeming to sense his friend's unease, he took leave and rode on with Mr. Darcy.

There was no opportunity for Denny to inquire about the incident for the ladies announced their intention of walking to Mrs. Philips' house, and the two men accompanied them.

"Will you not come in with us?" cried Miss Lydia at the door of the house, her eyes more on Wickham than Denny.

"Lydia," Miss Bennet gently admonished the girl.

"We would not want to intrude," said Wickham.

"Oh, you will not!" returned the girl. "Our aunt loves company, especially that of handsome officers!"

"Lydia!" It was now Miss Elizabeth's turn to correct her sister.

At that moment, the window was thrown open and a matronly lady stuck her head out. "Oh, there you are, girls! I have been waiting an age, I am sure!" Mrs. Philips took in the gentlemen with a glance. "Oh, sirs, you are well met! Please come in! You must come in!"

Denny was tempted, but duty came first. "I thank you, madam, but we must report to headquarters. Pray forgive us." The entreaties were pressed and refused one last time before the officers took their leave of the party, but only after promising Miss Lydia more firmly that they should all meet again soon.

After Denny and Wickham were a distance away from the house, Wickham glanced at him. "Do you know that tall, dark-haired man we met just now?"

"On horseback? That was Mr. Bingley's guest, Mr. Darcy, a gentleman from the north. Do you know him?"

Wickham smiled tightly. "I do. Tell me, what do the people hereabouts think of him?"

"Not very much—only that he is grave and quiet—and many say his pride sets him above the common folk in the country."

"Pride!" cried Wickham. "Yes, I should say that man is very proud indeed!"

"You sound as though you know him."

"I do, very well. I daresay there is no one who knows him better." Wickham grinned. "We grew up together at his family's estate in Derbyshire. His father was my godfather."

"I am surprised at that, for it looked to me that he all but gave you the cut direct in the middle of the street!"

"That is no surprise, for he hates me."

"His father's godson? You cannot be serious!"

"I am." Wickham looked around. "Too many ears about. Let us find a tavern, and I will tell you my tale of woe."

Denny was tempted, but he knew this was not the time. "Later, George. We must hurry to Colonel Forster. We have to get you sworn in and fitted out with your kit. You are in the king's service now, and your time is not your own."

Wickham rolled his eyes. "You are right, I suppose. Damn that Darcy! I was meant for better things, but that is all behind me now. I am a soldier, as you said. Let us to the colonel's tent!"

Wickham Makes a Plan

by Abigail Reynolds

November 19, 1811

Wickham appreciatively eyed the assets Miss Lydia Bennet purposely flaunted in front of him. If the flirtatious and forward Miss Lydia was an example of the pleasures Meryton had to offer, perhaps he would enjoy his time in this godforsaken market town more than he had anticipated.

His sole reason for joining the militia had been to hide from angry creditors in London, but he might as well find some amusement while he was in uniform. And here he was, only an hour in town, and already four pretty girls were hanging on his every word. Well, perhaps the eldest Miss Bennet could not be described that way. She was a true beauty, one he would definitely not mind bedding, but she was also reticent and proper. It would not be worth the effort it would require to seduce her. Miss Elizabeth was pretty enough, but she had a clever, impertinent wit, and Wickham preferred his women very young and foolish. The other sister, whose name he had already forgotten, was a bit drab, but Miss Lydia showed great promise—just out of the schoolroom by all appearances, completely lacking in wit, propriety and restraint. Just the way he liked them. Too bad his new friend Denny was already scowling at him. He must have already set his cap for Miss Lydia, but why should Denny's sentiments stand in the way of his pleasures?

He gave Denny a practiced smile. He still needed him to make introductions to the other officers. It would be much easier to fleece them at the card table if they saw him as Denny's dear friend. Maybe this time he would win for once.

Miss Elizabeth asked, "Mr. Wickham, is this your first visit to Hertfordshire?"

He made a slight bow. "I have passed through it before, while travelling from my home in Derbyshire to London." Was that a slight frown that passed over her face when he mentioned Derbyshire? He hurried to add, "Of course, I have lived in London for some years now." That seemed to please her. How curious! What could she dislike about Derbyshire?

Two gentlemen whose coats showed the fine fit only the best London tailors could achieve approached on horseback. Wickham observed them with a sidelong glance; he always liked to know where the deep pockets were, just waiting to be fleeced. But wait—no, it could not possibly be! But it was.

Of all the devilish luck! Why did Darcy have to appear here of all places? Perhaps joining the militia in Meryton had not been not such a good idea after all.

At least Darcy had not seen him yet. His attention seemed to be fixed on Miss Elizabeth Bennet, and he was watching her with an expression Wickham had never seen him wear before, a look of mingled longing and desire. His former friend shifted in the saddle as if he could hardly bear to stay astride.

Could it be? Had the arrogant Fitzwilliam Darcy fallen for the charms of a country miss? If so, Miss Elizabeth seemed oblivious of the important conquest she had made. Her eyes were on Darcy's friend who was inquiring about her sister's health.

Darcy could not possibly be thinking of marrying the chit, could he? He would never consider anything but fortune and breeding in his wife, and Miss Elizabeth Bennet could not hold a candle to Miss Anne de Bourgh in those regards. Did he want to make her his mistress? That was even more difficult to believe; it was beneath Darcy's moralistic dignity to conceive of seducing a gentleman's daughter. So what *did* he want?

Just then Darcy tore his eyes away from Miss Elizabeth, and Wickham felt that piercing stare burning into his face. Now Darcy's expression was one of distaste, perhaps remembering the sight of his precious sister in Wickham's arms. Oh, how he hoped that memory haunted him. Damn him for interfering! Without Darcy, Wickham would now be in possession of Georgiana's thirty thousand pounds, rather than hiding in this insipid town from debt collectors.

Darcy, white-faced, made the most perfunctory nod possible toward Wickham, who shifted from one foot to the other. Would his old friend expose him? But of course he would not dare, not when he knew Wickham had the power to ruin his sister with a word. What a pleasant thought! There was nothing Wickham liked better than making Darcy squirm.

With just a hint of a mocking smile, Wickham touched his hat, a salutation which Darcy barely deigned to return. After Darcy's friend asked a last question of the eldest Miss Bennet, the two gentlemen rode off, but not before Darcy subjected Wickham to his best cold stare.

So, Darcy was in Meryton, and at least half in love with Miss Elizabeth Bennet. Wickham's smile grew. How could he resist the opportunity to charm a lady Darcy so admired, and perhaps plant a little poison about Darcy in her ear? Oh, yes. It would be a great pleasure. Miss Elizabeth might not be the kind of young lady he preferred, but he was willing to overlook her cleverness if it gave him the chance to put a spoke in Darcy's wheel.

Yes, it would be most satisfactory to make Miss Elizabeth fall in love with him instead of Darcy. With a warm smile, he turned to her and said in his most charming manner, "I hope you often brighten our day by visiting Meryton, Miss Elizabeth."

A Party at the Philips'

by Maria Grace

November 20, 1811

"Thank you so much for inviting us." Lady Lucas kissed Mrs. Philips' cheeks.

Charlotte turned away. It was always uncomfortable watching Mama express more warmth than she actually felt.

"It is always a pleasure to host your distinguished husband and your lovely daughters." Mrs. Philips stepped back and gestured to a tall, heavy looking young man. He could not be less than five and twenty, but his grave, stately manner lent him a very mature air. He bowed, a stiff, precise movement that had surely been rehearsed to perfection.

"Permit me to introduce a new member of our acquaintance, Mr. Bennet's cousin, Mr. Collins. He is vicar to Lady Catherine de Bourgh of Rosings Park."

"We are pleased to make your acquaintance, sir." Lady Lucas tapped Charlotte with her elbow and they curtsied. "Has Mrs. Collins come with you?"

Charlotte winced. Yes, it was an innocent, appropriate question, but when one knew the answer already, was it necessary?

"There is currently no Mrs. Collins, madam, though my esteemed patroness has instructed me that I should find a bride soon."

"Well you have come to an excellent place to find one, sir. There are many lovely eligible girls here in Meryton, including my dear Charlotte."

94

Mrs. Philips pressed her lips and gave Mama a decidedly sour look.

Why did she say such a thing? Charlotte's face burned hotter than the many candles in the drawing room. With essentially no dowry, she was hardly eligible and none but the dearest, most generous of her friends would call her lovely. No, she was at best plain and practical. All Mama had managed to convey was a sense of desperation.

Mr. Collins smiled at her, that same conciliatory smile offered her by the matrons of Meryton and her elderly relations. "It is a pleasure to meet you in person. My fair cousins have told me about their most amiable friend."

"My nieces are indeed very dear, kind girls, are they not?" Mrs. Philips turned up her nose just a mite. With no daughters of her own she was every bit as attentive to promote the fortunes of the Bennet girls as their own mother.

Charlotte could hardly begrudge her friends their supporters. It was not their fault that there were not enough men for all the single young ladies. No, they all might thank Napoleon for that favor.

More guests pushed through the front door. Mrs. Philips excused herself and dragged Mr. Collins away for more introductions.

Mama pulled out her fan and drew Charlotte into the drawing room. "He would be a very suitable match for you."

"You well know his intentions. It could hardly be suitable to throw myself at him under the circumstances."

"I am not so certain the opinions he states are his own. I suspect they are ones given him by his patroness, his desires for ease and comfort, and the artful hints and suggestions of Mrs. Bennet herself."

Charlotte's eyes bulged. Pray, no one was looking her way now! "How can you say such things? You have only just met the man."

"I may have only just met *this* man. But I have known a great many men. Have you forgotten I have nine brothers? Trust me, I know a simple, easily governed man when I see one. Mr. Collins is exactly one of that sort. You would do very well with him, indeed."

"But he is not—"

Mama grasped Charlotte's wrist hard. "I know what he says, but I also know what he will do. Jane is all but spoken for; he will not have the spleen to challenge for her and can you see him with Eliza? She would not have him even if he had the bollocks to ask."

"Mama!"

"Forgive me dear. You are quite right." She sucked in a deep breath and straightened her shoulders. "Still though, I do not think even Mrs. Bennet and the threat of destitution could bring Mr. Collins and Eliza together. Which brings us to Mary." Mama glanced about the room. She need not have bothered. A quick listen located Mary at the pianoforte.

"Mary is your true rival for him. It is to your disadvantage that she plays and studies Fordyce. Gah! She is a dreadful bore, while you have a charming disposition and practicality that any man would value."

"You make us sound like goods on a market shelf."

Mama glared. She probably would have pinched Charlotte's arm had they not been in a crowded room.

"Our one hope is that Mrs. Bennet ignores Mary, as she usually does, so Mr. Collins does not turn to her when Eliza refuses him."

"I cannot believe you would be planning his choice of bride within minutes of meeting him, much less instructing me on how to steal a prospect from my best friend."

Mama clenched her hand and fluttered her fan a little faster. "Go watch your friend and you will see clear as I do. You will do her a favor diverting his attentions from her. It is obvious she does not want them. Go, go." She shooed Charlotte away. "Mrs. Goulding, how lovely to see you this evening..."

Charlotte slipped away and hugged the edge of the room, not an entirely unfamiliar position. People clustered in groups around the drawing room, making small talk and sharing pleasantries. Eliza was engaged with several of the officers and Lydia and Kitty. Probably just as well, all things considered. It was not as if she could walk up to Eliza and ask her opinions. In that, Mama was correct. The best she could do was carefully observe and draw her own conclusions.

Mr. Collins approached the group, apparently eager to engage them in conversation. Eliza's countenance lost its bloom. She really must learn not to roll her eyes so. Perhaps she considered herself discreet, but at least to a dedicated observer, she was not.

Mr. Collins, though, appeared oblivious to the amused reactions he garnered, not just from Eliza, but from all within earshot. Was it good manners or a level of unawareness rarely seen outside the very young? Both were certainly a possibility.

Miss Long took Mary's place at the pianoforte, and the entire company paused briefly to take note.

Eliza approached her, hands extended. "Oh, Charlotte, how I have missed your company."

"Indeed? You seemed to enjoy at least some of your conversation a great deal."

Eliza glanced over her shoulder toward the corner where Mr. Wickham chatted with Lydia and Kitty. "Some of it has been quite pleasing. Have you been introduced to my cousin, Mr. Collins yet?"

"We were introduced when we arrived." Charlotte tipped her head toward the fireplace.

Mr. Collins, Mrs. Bennet and Mrs. Philips gathered there, speaking far too loudly.

So, that particular mannerism was not confined to the Gardiner branch of the family. For all his propensity to judge failures of propriety, Mr. Bennet's family was not without its transgressors.

"So then you have heard a great deal about the wonders of Lady Catherin de Bourgh and Rosings Park in Kent." Eliza rolled her eyes.

"I believe he made mention of his pleasing circumstances."

"You are too kind, Charlotte, far too kind."

"I cannot think it a good thing to so quickly form a prejudice against one I have only just met."

"After a full two days in his company—and I do mean two *full* days. I believe I have sufficient grounds to declare him a unique and peculiar man."

"But would not his patroness's approbation suggest—"

"Yes, I suppose you make an excellent case. I will allow him to be a tolerably good fellow, quite, unlikely to cause harm to anyone." Eliza's cheek dimpled and she cast about the room. "It seems Maria has wasted no time becoming acquainted with the officers."

"I think few young ladies are immune to their charms."

"Unfortunately my mother is among those still." Eliza fluttered her hand before her face in an amazing imitation of Mrs. Bennet. "I had quite a fondness for a red coat in my day."

Charlotte giggled.

"I know, I know, I should not speak so. Forgive me. I am not quite myself."

Mrs. Philips bustled up to them. "We are short a player for a hand of whist. Can I persuade you to join us, Lizzy?"

Eliza's eyes widened and she glanced about the room like an animal trapped.

"I think I should very much enjoy a hand of cards." Charlotte dipped her head at Eliza and made her way to the card table where Papa and Mr. Collins already chatted amiably.

Eliza mouthed a tiny 'thank you' and scurried off whilst Mrs. Philips sputtered.

"Are you going to join us at cards, Charlotte, dear?" Papa asked. "I did not think you would prefer cards to a conversation with your friends."

"Mrs. Philips suggested you might be in need of another player to fill out the table." She sat down. Best not to acknowledge the tension that radiated from her hostess in waves like heat from a hob.

"Indeed we are." Mrs. Philips sat across from Mr. Collins and handed him a deck of cards. Their white backs were stained in places and some of the edges were worn. Mr. Collins shuffled awkwardly, but at least he did not drop the cards.

"My patroness, Lady Catherine de Bourgh, makes it a point to open a new deck of cards for every card table she hosts. She is the soul of generosity."

Mrs. Philips smiled a tightly strained expression that seemed to reflect her patience more than her good humor. Eliza wore that same expression at times.

"Rosings Park, we are given to understand is a very fine place indeed," Mrs. Philips muttered.

"I am sure it is, very sure." Papa said.

"I do not mean to draw ill comparisons to your very fine establishment. By no means. I feel quite as if I have been welcomed to the small and intimate breakfast parlor at Rosings. Lady Catherine favors that room in the spring and summer."

Mrs. Philips feathers ruffled and she twitched like an angry hen.

"Please, madam, you must understand the chimney-piece alone in her favorite drawing room cost eight-hundred pounds. Her taste is the most refined and elegant in all of England, to be sure. It is indeed the highest compliment I might offer to compare anything favorably with Rosings. I indeed regard it the highest of condescension that she herself has planned all the improvements in my own humble abode."

"Oh, now I see. I believe I had misunderstood your intent, but I do understand there was no slight intended at all." The tension in Mrs. Philips' shoulders eased.

So, Mr. Collins was not entirely insensitive to the feelings of others. Had Eliza recognized that?

Mrs. Philips tapped the table. "Perhaps we should play Mr. Collins?"

"Perhaps so, but I should like to hear more about Rosings and your establishment there." Charlotte leaned forward a little.

Mrs. Philips brows rose. "Miss Lucas, you are all politeness and curiosity."

"Charlotte certainly knows how to make people feel welcome, the spit and image of her mother, the consummate hostess."

"Please, Papa, it is not seemly to offer such compliments, particularly in public." Charlotte's cheeks burned but at least Papa was all kindness and affability. Unlike Mr. Bennet.

"Your humility does you credit, Miss Lucas. It is after all one of the chief of virtues in a young woman." Mr. Collins handed the shuffled deck to Mrs. Philips.

A warm little place filled within her heart. Compliments like his were so rare—was this the way one normally responded?

"Lady Catherine has been so generous and solicitous to my wellbeing—she is so attentive to such things you know. No detail in the Parsonage is below her notice. She even saw to the fitting of the closet with shelves. Everything is arranged with all proper attention to my station, neither too high nor too low. Imagine my relief—for I am a bachelor and know little of keeping an establishment— to know everything is in right and proper order." Mr. Collins's chest puffed up a little and he picked up his hand.

As they played, he continued his glowing descriptions of the work done on his home and the generosity of his patroness.

To be sure, abundant elements of the ridiculous surrounded every word he said. But through that, his undertone of satisfaction, even joy in the situation of his life spoke as well. How very agreeable to be so satisfied so early in one's life. He was fortunate to be so young and already so settled, and in such a pleasant sounding situation.

"Mr. Collins, the suit is hearts." Mrs. Philips rapped the card on the table.

"Forgive me, madam." Tiny beads of sweat dotted his upper lip. "I know little of the game at present, but I shall be glad to improve myself to learn more if you will but instruct me."

Charlotte folded her hand and placed it on the table. "Perhaps we should begin again and change partners. Papa is an excellent player, and I am not at all opposed to assisting a less certain player through the finer parts of the game."

Mrs. Philips bristled, eyes glittering like a hen about to peck. "There is no need—"

"What a very generous and thoughtful offer. I should hate to be a strain upon our generous hostess's good graces." He rose.

Papa did like-wise and changed places with him. Mrs. Philips muttered protests but Papa gathered the old hand up, shuffled and re-dealt the game.

Charlotte picked up her cards and smiled at Mr. Collins.

Some of the tension in his face eased and he settled more comfortably in his seat.

She played her first card, along with a mild comment about the rules of play.

Mrs. Philips huffed under her breath, but Mr. Collins nodded, granted a bit too vigorously, and on his next turn, played very well indeed.

A little congratulation, a reminder of rules now and then, and an occasional raised eyebrow or tap on the table rendered him a tolerable player.

Was he naturally observant and pliable, or was he hungry to be given an example of right conduct. Not that it particularly mattered, both were agreeable qualities.

At the end of the rubber, Mary Bennet moved to the piano in the corner. Lydia and Maria demanded she play a tune for dancing.

"I think dancing, in a private home, such as this, in so agreeable a company, to be a very appropriate occupation for young persons."

"I find dancing quite agreeable." Charlotte stood.

Mr. Collins scanned the room. Eliza was already lining up with one of the officers and Jane with Charlotte's brother.

The corner of Mr. Collins' eyes drooped just a mite.

Rejection was hard, even when you never actually asked.

Jane looked toward them. "We need another couple for the set."

"Would you care to dance, Miss Lucas?" he asked, still staring at Eliza and Jane.

Yes, Eliza and Jane were the prettiest, most eligible girls in the neighborhood, and they were his cousins who would suffer when he inherited Longbourn. It was entirely right and proper that he should look to them first.

But they did not seem to like him and she…well she just might. She took his arm on the way to the impromptu dance floor. Eliza and Jane certainly had first claims on Mr. Collin's interests, but if they relinquished them…it might be a very pleasing possibility.

Darcy's Resolution

by Susan Mason-Milks

November 23, 1811

Darcy cleared an opening on the desk in the study at Netherfield, marveling at how Bingley could find anything, let alone get work done with papers and correspondence stacked everywhere in such a careless manner. Clutter and disorder always inhibited Darcy's ability to think clearly. His hope in retreating to the study was to find a few minutes of peace in which to write a letter to Georgiana. Taking quill in hand, he paused, uncertain what he wanted to say. What was foremost in his mind was probably not something his sister should read. Pouring himself some of Bingley's excellent brandy, he moved to look out the window hoping it would clear his head. As he watched the dark clouds making their way across the sky, his thoughts returned to how nothing had been the same since Miss Elizabeth and her sister had left Netherfield. All conversation bored him, and even the usual pleasures of reading did little to fill the space she left when she departed.

Worst of all, Miss Bingley had sensed something, awakening a primal reaction in her. Like a predator following the scent of its prey, she had begun tracking him around the house. If he went to the library to quietly read, she found that she, too, was in need of a new book. Since she was never sure what to read, she always asked for his suggestions. By the time he helped her chose a book and returned to his own, he had usually forgotten what he had been reading. It made no difference anyway, because she continually interrupted asking a question every few minutes. When her ceaseless chatter became too much to tolerate, he would get up and move to another room. Inevitably, she followed after a few minutes, and thus the cycle repeated. What a contrast to Elizabeth who had once sat in the library with him for more than half an hour without saying a single word!

After a week of her relentless pursuit, Darcy, fortunately, remembered Miss Bingley did not like horses. Since that time, riding had become his favorite occupation. As his friend Bingley was not an early riser, Darcy often went out in the morning alone. The exercise seemed to renew his spirit and help him think more clearly. Usually after an energetic ride, he walked his horse, Hector, slowly along the lanes in the neighborhood. At first, he told himself he was just exploring, when in truth, he had to admit he was secretly hoping to discover where Miss Elizabeth went on her morning walks. Once as he ambled along, he almost crossed paths with her. A noise nearby alerted him just in time to see her coming out of a small wooded area. Quickly turning Hector down a path to his right, he was able to disappear before she saw him.

Darcy generally used the pleasant silence on his rides to recall and analyze every word that had passed between them during Elizabeth's stay at Netherfield. As he reviewed their interactions, he frequently thought of something he should have said that was far cleverer than his actual response. Other times, he found himself caught up with imagining entirely new conversations. In these scenarios, instead of being tongue-tied, he knew exactly the right thing to say to amuse her. It was all so clear in his mind that it was almost as if he could hear her voice as they engaged in verbal sparring. When Darcy imagined making such a witty comment as to amuse her, he was certain he could hear her laughter. As he closed his eyes to listen to that sweet music, just the thought of her brought warmth to his core, and when that heat began moving downward in his body, he bent over in the saddle and groaned aloud. Cursing, he quickly looked around to see if anyone had heard him, but fortunately no one was nearby. To keep himself from thinking about her, he took an extra long ride that day so that he and Hector were both exhausted by the time they returned to the stables.

At first, Darcy considered these daily imaginary conversations with Elizabeth as harmless amusement. He could talk to her as much as he wished as long as no one knew. He was not harming her reputation or putting himself in danger, but as he became more and more preoccupied with thoughts of her, he began to realize he was playing with fire. It was not right to let this continue, and one day out on a solitary ride, he vowed to banish Elizabeth from his mind forever.

Once back at the house after his ride that morning, Darcy found he was out of sorts and irritated with the world. He was short with Jennings, his valet, over the way his cravat was tied. He complained that the temperature of the water for his bath was too cold and then found something wanting with the polish on his boots. Later, he felt guilty for being so abrupt. Since an outright apology would only embarrass them both, he tried to let Jennings know he was sorry by sending him to Meryton for the afternoon on an errand they both knew to be invented. Darcy thought the man might enjoy getting outside in the lovely fall weather for a change and even gave him some extra coin so he could stop for hot cider along the way.

When he realized trying to banish Elizabeth completely from his mind had only resulted in making him uncivil, he decided he would allow himself the pleasure of thinking about her, but only when he was out riding alone. This strategy worked at first, but soon Darcy found his preoccupation spilling over into other parts of his day. There was no escape. The rooms at Netherfield were alive with memories of her. The drawing room made him recall the mischievous look on her face as they discussed the accomplishments of a lady. In the dining room, he thought about the grace of her slender hand as she reached for her wine glass. Whenever they repaired to the music room, he remembered how his eyes had followed the curve of her shoulder to the hollow at the base of her neck and how he longed to touch that place with his lips. And how could he forget the swell of her...Oh, Lord, what was it about this woman that seemed to drive all rational thought from his head!

Once when he was thus occupied, Miss Bingley had asked him a question. To avoid having to admit he was not attending, he mumbled agreement and much to his displeasure found she had been asking if he would like to join them at cards. He was forced to spend a miserable hour at the table until he could politely extract himself from the game and retreat to his rooms.

When Darcy realized that for some time he had been calling Elizabeth by her first name in his thoughts, he knew he could not let this continue. What if he slipped and actually said it aloud? Leaving Netherfield as soon as possible was his only choice. Unfortunately, there was the upcoming ball to consider. It was a major event for Bingley and would firmly establish his friend's place in the neighborhood. As Darcy knew he must lend his support, he was forced to stay until after the ball. Upon forming this plan, he rationalized that since he was leaving soon, there was nothing wrong with letting himself continue to think about Elizabeth for just a few more days. After that, he would be safely in London where their paths would most certainly never cross.

As his thoughts returned to the present, the rain slowed, and off in the distance he could see a small patch of blue that promised better weather to come. Just at that moment, he resolved to ask Elizabeth to dance at the ball. He had no idea where this impulse came from, and although he knew he should resist, something inside him cried out for one more opportunity to look into her fine eyes and touch her hand, even if it was only through her glove. Darcy decided he would allow himself to admire her, to drink in her sweet charms just one more time, and then he would be gone. He only hoped that indulging himself in this way would allow him to exorcise her from his mind once and for all.

Brandy finished and his thoughts arranged in a more orderly fashion, he returned to the desk. Picking up the quill, he dashed off a short note to Georgiana informing her of his plans to return to London within the week.

Darcy Prepares for the Ball at Netherfield

by C. Allyn Pierson

November 26, 1811

Darcy awoke early on the 26th and immediately realized that the day of the ball had arrived. He tried to ignore his excitement over another chance to see Miss Elizabeth Bennet. And...to ask her to dance. Yes, he was still determined to dance with the lovely Miss Elizabeth and what could be more natural? Of course he would dance all night, helping to entertain his friend's company at this, Bingley's first ball. No one would even notice when he asked *her* to dance.

His resolute calm was dented as soon as he entered the breakfast parlor and found the entire Bingley clan at table.

"My! Aren't we all early risers today?" Bingley quizzed his friend.

Darcy kept his face unmoved, and answered, "I would not know, Bingley. I am usually back from my morning ride before your face appears in the breakfast parlor."

Bingley laughed, and Darcy could tell that his friend was excited about his ball and would be twitting him mercilessly all day. He took a place at the far end of the table, which unfortunately put him next to Miss Bingley and across from Mr. Hurst.

"So, Mr. Darcy," Miss Bingley purred, "are you prepared to gallop around the ballroom with the Meryton maids tonight?" She turned to her brother. "Charles! You are going to order the orchestra to play a few waltzes, aren't you?"

Charles considered. "I had thought not. The waltz is not yet accepted in polite society in Hertfordshire, and I would not like to offend anyone. Also, I don't know if the local ladies and gentlemen have yet learned the steps."

"Don't be absurd, Charles, of course they have. Just because some old tabbies won't allow it at the local dances does not mean others might not like it! And I shudder to hear you describe the gentry of Hertfordshire as 'polite society'. What a joke that is!"

Darcy tuned out the bickering and concentrated on his eggs and gammon. What would Elizabeth wear to the ball? The gown she wore to the assembly at Meryton was simple and not particularly notable...except for the way if fit her form and emphasized her graceful movement. And the way it clung to her shape!

His daydreaming was suddenly severed by Miss Bingley's voice, sounding a bit impatient, as if she had spoken his name more than once. He turned to her.

"Yes, Miss Bingley? I am sorry, I did not hear you as I was wondering if the last book I ordered would come in today's post." (Whew. Lame, but at least a comprehensible sentence!)

"I was asking, Mr. Darcy, what your opinion was of the waltz. Do you think Charles should ask the orchestra to play 2 or 3 during the course of the evening? I despise letting narrow-minded provincials determine what music we should play."

Darcy swallowed convulsively as he thought of waltzing with Elizabeth, her right hand held in his left for the entire dance, while his right hand touched her waist, feeling the warmth of her body as they whirled through the ballroom, the others blending into a swirl of color that left the two of them alone in their own private space. He swallowed again, trying to pretend a bit of gammon needed to go down, then spoke, "I do not think it would be a good idea to shock the locals at Charles's first ball. I would wait until the next before trying to set fashion forward. But, it is entirely up to Charles, after all."

Miss Bingley turned petulantly from him to harangue her brother.

Darcy escaped from the table as soon as he decently could and went up to his room to make sure his valet was prepared for tonight. His black coat and black satin knee-breeches were already hanging up, fresh from the iron, and it was clear he could not hide in his room while his valet spun from task to task like a dervish. He sighed and decided to go for a walk… No, he would be obliged to ask his hosts if they would like to join him, and he was in no mood for idle chatter or petulant complaining. A sudden thought caused him to smile. Billiards! He would ask Hurst for a couple of games, effectively banishing Miss Bingley from that bastion of masculine entertainment!

Eventually, the long day drew towards evening and the Netherfield gentry gathered for a substantial tea to fortify them for the ball. When he finished his second cup, Darcy firmly put it away from him and marched up the stairs to his dressing room. He felt like a knight girding his loins for battle…for such was his usual intercourse with Miss Elizabeth Bennet.

As Jennings primped and polished him for the evening he tried to put himself into a trance…thinking about how beautiful the fall leaves were at Pemberley, and how soon he would see Georgiana. Finally, he heard, "There you are, sir. All finished."

He looked into the mirror and carefully examined his hair, his cravat, and his clothes. His face looked a bit pale, but the heat of the ballroom would soon remedy that. He heard the first carriage draw up to the door and swallowed the lump in his throat, pulling the cravat just a fraction looser in hopes he could breathe. Even now she might be here, in a silk gown and pearls…simple adornments to emphasize, but never overshadow her loveliness. He heard a throat clear.

"Is everything all right, sir?"

Darcy turned to the anxious valet. "Yes, everything is quite all right." And he turned to the door.

Mr. Darcy's Valet Has his Doubts

by C. Allyn Pierson

November 26, 1811

"Mr. Jennings, is there something amiss with your dinner?"

Jennings came to an awareness of his setting with an almost audible thump.

"Ah...not at all Mrs. Nicholls, quite to the contrary, the dinner is delicious. I was merely contemplating which waistcoats I should lay out for my master. With all the work you have done for the ball, I would want the master to be an ornament to honor your efforts, but I am not sure of my choice...I don't know why I should worry, for the master will make his own choices, and very elegant they will be, but, as you know, I may be able to influence him by my selection of several from which he can choose." He gave her a simpering smile and was relieved when she smiled graciously upon his compliments.

What he had, in truth, been contemplating was the very odd behavior of his master. He had never known Mr. Darcy to fuss over his toilette...to the contrary (as he had commented to Mrs. Nicholls.) Darcy's clothes were all of the first style of elegance, tailored by Weston to fit his form like a second skin. The master insisted on quality, made sure his cravat was perfectly tied...then he forgot about his clothes. He did not check his appearance in every mirror he passed like the Bond Street Beaux, nor did he try to skimp by with flashy but inferior goods. But never—not in his entire eight years of service—had Jennings ever seen Mr. Darcy in such a state as he now was.

Naturally, he had not said anything to the master, since he did not seem to want to discuss it, but he had been as resty the past two days as a three-legged dog in a butcher shop. Pacing, unable to sit down for more than a few moments, and trying very hard to avoid the Bingleys...not that he could blame him for that since Miss Bingley had been excoriating the staff mercilessly all week to make sure the ball was up to her standards. He was sure Hertfordshire had never seen such an entertainment before, but she had been a sore trial to her servants and, undoubtedly, to her family and friends.

Still, he did not think Miss Bingley's ill-humor was to blame for his master's mood. He seemed to be thinking about something which absorbed all his attention and made it impossible for him to concentrate long enough to even choose a waistcoat in the morning, veering from intense particularity over his choice to sudden insensibility within seconds.

Now that he thought about it, the master had been a bit out of sorts since Miss Bennet went home after her unfortunate illness. Wait a minute...surely his master could not be falling for Miss Bennet himself? He would never perform such a turn on his friend...would not even look at Miss Bennet after Mr. Bingley had chosen her as his favorite in Hertfordshire. No...no, it was not possible...but it would certainly explain Mr. Darcy's mood if he had developed a tendre for Miss Bennet.

Miss Elizabeth Bennet he set aside. She, while a lively and attractive young lady, was in no way up to the master's standards for female pulchritude. The servants, every one, felt both Misses Bennet were Quality, in spite of their appalling mother and sisters, all of whom had invaded Netherfield while Miss Bennet was ill, giving the servants a great deal to talk about below stairs. The local servants had much to say about the Bennet family, but the plain truth was they were bad *ton*, barely scraping by as gentry and in the unfortunate position of being too poor to overcome their low connections when it came to the Marriage Mart.

Still and yet, the two eldest Bennets were the beauties of the county and the heart did not always listen to the head. He was stricken with a sudden chill as he thought of the possibility of Mr. Darcy developing a tendre for a country miss. How could he hold up his head in the servants' hall if his master was taken in by a pretty face attached to vastly inferior birth? It was not to be thought of.

He must try to observe the guests during the ball. Once this accursed meal was over he would find a discreet position from where he could spy on—perhaps he would stick with the word "observe"—his master and see if he could determine his thoughts.

Mr. Bennet at the Netherfield Ball

by L. L. Diamond

November 26, 1811

The night had begun as most tedious social affairs for Mr. Bennet: his wife's shrill panics that Jane's gown would not be fine enough to attract a man of five thousand a year, her proclamations that Lydia would be a favorite of all the officers, and of course, her concession that his Lizzy "looked well enough."

Yet, here he stood to one side of the ballroom. How he despised the ridiculousness of the activity! Of course, balls were a necessary evil for a gentleman who boasted of five daughters and an entailed estate, especially one whose wife lacked economy, but he would much prefer the solitude of his treasured book room and a nice glass of port!

As he observed Mr. Bingley's guests, his gaze was drawn to the dancers where Mr. Collins, exuding an air of pretentious self-importance, led Lizzy to the start of the first set. She caught his eye and rolled hers just before the music began. He pressed his lips together hard. Smirking from the side of the room never served him well.

Mrs. Bennet's latest scheme to match Lizzy with their ridiculous cousin was not at all his preference, yet it provided an amusement he was loath to part with as of yet. It was not as if his most intelligent daughter would ever become betrothed to someone as imbecilic as Mr. Collins. He had no reason to worry, so he would find humor in the farce whilst it lasted.

Mr. Collins trod upon her toes, and he chuckled. The thin line of Lizzy's lips and the glint in her eye indicated she was not best pleased by her cousin as a partner. Of course, Mr. Collins was as much a dancer as the king was sane!

With a groaning exhale, he glanced to the side of the room where his wife revelled in the attention of the other ladies of the neighborhood, wearing a smug smile as she exclaimed her good fortune for all to hear. During a lull in the music, Mrs. Bennet's voice carried across the room.

"Mr. Bingley is so charming and rich! What a fine thing for my Jane!"

"Mr. Collins may not be as rich as Mr. Bingley, but he will do for Lizzy very well!"

With a shake of his head, he made to depart the ballroom intent on some male company; he could abide no more of his wife's effusions. He had borne them since Mr. Bingley's arrival at Michaelmas and could bear it no more!

One last glance at the dancers revealed Lydia and Kitty giggling and flirting inappropriately with the soldiers they partnered. His foot stepped in their direction. Should he check their behavior? Lydia might cause a scene if he interceded. His two youngest were the silliest girls in all of England; no one would expect them to behave with propriety, would they? His shoulders dropped as he pulled his foot back. Sorting those two could take the entire evening. Who had time for such a tedious chore? Certainly not him!

He turned his back to the dancers and entered the card room. Sir William Lucas and Mr. Goulding, who often amused him, were seated at a table in the far corner, so he headed in their direction.

"Bennet!" cried Sir William Lucas, as he approached. "You are joining us so soon?" Sir William passed a few crowns to Mr. Goulding who grinned.

"Of course, he is." Mr. Goulding looked up from his winnings to Mr. Bennet. "We are all well aware he does not dance, and I was certain Mr. Bennet would seek respite from his wife sooner rather than later. She has too much to crow about tonight."

As Sir William watched Mr. Goulding retrieve the coins from the table, he sighed. "You could not have waited another quarter hour, Bennet?"

"No," Mr. Bennet responded with a chuckle. "Goulding always wins these wagers, so why do you continue to accept such bets?"

"I hope to win back my losses." Sir William's voice was a grumble.

Mr. Goulding laughed. "Do not persuade him to relinquish the habit. I enjoy surprising my wife with a little trinket or gift from my winnings."

Mr. Bennet shook his head. "Let us not speak of wives. I have had enough of mine for the evening."

Sir William laughed and stood. "As I have no further money to wager, I shall return to the ballroom. I have yet to compliment Mr. Bingley on such a grand evening!" He glanced about the room with a jovial grin. "Capital!"

Mr. Goulding held up the cards when Sir William departed. "Would you care for a game?"

He nodded and wasted an hour, at least, at cards before returning to the ballroom where upon a survey of the guests, his attention was garnered once again by Lizzy who stood up with none other than Mr. Darcy!

The disagreeable man who had refused to even request a set from her at the assembly must now find her tolerable enough to tempt him at the very least. A gleeful chuckle escaped his lips. How diverting it would be tease Lizzy on the morrow!

A study of the pair was interesting indeed! Mr. Darcy wore his usual serious, haughty air, yet he stared at Lizzy with such an intent gaze. Lizzy frowned, whether offended by a statement made by the gentleman or just by dancing with him was anyone's guess.

At the end of the set, the pair went their separate ways—Lizzy to join Charlotte Lucas and Mr. Darcy to stand near the wall to the opposite side of the ballroom. The wealthy gentleman's gaze found Lizzy through the crowd and remained fixed upon her, but naught changed—Lizzy remained with Charlotte or dancing with the officers and gentleman of the neighborhood whilst Mr. Darcy's eyes bored through her. How dull!

He continued to observe those around him as the night wore on, but the evening progressed as a snail up a stone wall until supper was served. What a welcome respite from the tedious evening!

Part of his humour was restored as he savored the wine and the meal before him until a familiar shrill tone jarred him from his agreeable occupation.

"And Jane, being so well-married, will throw the girls in the paths of other rich men!"

His vision darted to his wife, but his eyes set upon Lizzy, who sat nearby, her beetroot red complexion a testament to her mortification. Her brow lifted in his direction. What did she believe he could do? He could not contain his wife! She had let slip the dogs of war and could not be stopped!

Lizzy leaned forward and whispered to her mother, who waved her daughter off with a frown.

"What is Mr. Darcy to me, pray, that I should be afraid of him? I am sure we owe him no such particular civility as to be obliged to say nothing he may not like to hear."

Lizzy dropped back down in her seat, still red-faced, but stiff in her seat. She widened her eyes at him, but he gave a shrug as a loud cackle from his youngest daughter drew his attention to the side of the room.

Lydia and Kitty each held a glass of wine in their hand, but by their louder than usual tones, they had already imbibed more than was their wont. His youngest leant forward with her free hand upon her hip whilst the officer with whom she was flirting stared down her bodice.

He moaned and glanced back to Lizzy, who now held her face in her hands. A throbbing began in his temple, and he took a gulp of wine. Perhaps it might relieve the tension before a megrim plagued him as much as this insipid evening!

His eyes avoided Lizzy and his wife, though he could hear the latter, until the discordant tones of a pianoforte rattled his brain. With an abrupt jerk of the head, which did nothing to improve the pounding within, he turned to Lizzy. Her eyes were again wide, and she sat forward in her chair, gripping the arm with one hand until her knuckles were white.

Mary's weak voice joined the ill sounds she made on the instrument as his brain threatened to hammer through his skull. He needed to escape, but Lizzy would never give him any peace when they returned to Longbourn if he did not intercede!

His slow rise from the chair was accompanied by a weary sigh. With a steady step, he moved to the instrument, placing his hand near the keys to garner Mary's attention.

"That will do extremely well, child. You have delighted us long enough. Let the other young ladies have time to exhibit."

There! It was done! Lizzy was, no doubt, content that he had handled the situation, and he could escape to the terrace for a bit of peace and solitude. He exited the nearest door as he rubbed his temples. The musicians began tuning for the second half of the ball; a low groan escaped from his lips.

He glanced to the sky as a star streaked through the heavens. He had not wished upon a star since Lizzy was a small child, even then, it was more for her benefit than his own that he took the matter so seriously. With a deep breath, he closed his eyes tight and prayed the evening would come to a swift conclusion.

As he gradually opened his eyes, he turned towards the house and the light pouring from the ballroom windows. Had God heard his prayer? His wife's ear-piercing screech ripped the hope from his breast as swift as that star had flown through the sky.

His wife would ensure they were the last to leave. What had he done for God to curse him with such a fate?

Charlotte Lucas at the Netherfield Ball

by Abigail Reynolds

November 26, 1811

Charlotte had dressed with unusual care for the Netherfield Ball. Her dress was one she had worn only once before. The deep blue of the bodice brought out the color of her eyes, which were perhaps her best feature. At the last minute, she had torn out the lace along the neckline, making it more revealing than anything she had worn before. She wanted to see admiration in Mr. Robinson's eyes.

More than anything, though, she wanted to see *him*. He had promised to return in a fortnight, and he was already a week past his time. The delay had caused her more anxiety than she cared to admit. If his father refused to give his blessing to the match, would that be enough to change his mind? She could not believe it, not after he had been so touchingly tender to her during their encounter in the woods. But thinking of that made her even more uncommonly anxious when she considered his tardy arrival.

She was counting on the Netherfield ball to reunite them. All the neighborhood would be there, and even if Mr. Robinson had found it difficult to separate himself from his host, Mr. Willoughby, neither of them would miss this occasion. She had played through the possibilities for their meeting in her head. She would not chide him; nothing would make a man flee faster than the possibility of a shrewish wife. She would greet him warmly and welcome him back, making no mention of the delay.

A quick glance around the ballroom revealed that he had not yet arrived. To distract herself, she sought out Eliza Bennet, whom she had not seen in a week. She hardly needed to say anything, since Lizzy was quite ready to pour out the tale of her own woes over the absence of her Lieutenant Wickham. It made Charlotte grateful that she had not said anything to Lizzy about her interest in Mr. Robinson; she did not want anyone watching her reunion with him. She listened with half an ear as Lizzy, her good humor finally restored, told her of the odd cousin who was visiting the family at Longbourn. When she pointed him out, Charlotte could not see anything so odd about him, but Lizzy's standards were always impossibly high. A woman of little beauty could not afford to be so choosy.

No one asked her for the first dance, the one she had hoped to dance with Mr. Robinson, so she retired to the side of the room where she could observe without interruption while she tried to control her own anxiety. Lizzy was dancing with her cousin, and apparently an inability to dance must be added to any deficiencies of that gentleman, for he showed no grace. Charlotte winced in sympathy when she saw him step on Lizzy's toes for the third time. Still, even a poor dance partner was better than none.

Charlotte had some relief when one of the officers asked her for the next set. He was a homely fellow with spots, but he danced well enough and laughed easily, and more importantly he took her mind off Mr. Robinson's absence for a few minutes. Whenever they reached the end of the line, though, she could not stop herself from scanning the room. She bade her partner adieu at the end of the second dance with no regrets. Almost immediately Lizzy appeared beside her, asking about her new beau, which gave Charlotte quite a jolt until she realized her friend was referring to the officer who had partnered her.

Mr. Darcy came over to them and asked Elizabeth to dance— quite a surprise since he had once found Lizzy not handsome enough to tempt him, but then again Lizzy did tempt most gentlemen. After accepting him, Lizzy began to bemoan her fate anew. Charlotte had no patience for her, though, for she had just spotted Mr. Willoughby across the room, and his friend Mr.

Robinson was still nowhere to be seen. For the first time, she admitted to herself the possibility he might not come to the ball at all. With a sick feeling at the pit of her stomach, Charlotte could muster no sympathy for Lizzy for having to dance with a handsome and rich gentleman, and so she said only, "I daresay you will find Mr. Darcy very agreeable."

That was enough to set Lizzy off again. Shaking her head, Charlotte told her impractical friend in a whisper, "Do not allow your fancy for Wickham to make you appear unpleasant in the eyes of a man of ten times his consequence!" She doubted her words would make any difference, given Lizzy's impulsive ways.

As her friend went off with Mr. Darcy, Mr. Willoughby approached Charlotte and requested that she honor him in the next set. Normally she would refuse, knowing that a dance to him was but an excuse for an attempt at seduction, but tonight she was too eager for news of Mr. Robinson to avoid his friend. She had fended Willoughby off often enough in the past. It was odd, though, that he should ask her to dance, when in general he wanted nothing to do with her since the time she had exposed his behavior to her family and friends. Perhaps he had a message from Mr. Robinson to deliver.

Mr. Willoughby's stare was as insolent as ever when they lined up for the first dance of the set. Charlotte calmly chatted about the weather, getting very little reply from him. The music started and they began to dance their way down the set. Charlotte said, "I do not see your friend Mr. Robinson here tonight. Is he still visiting you?"

"He left a fortnight ago after settling a certain wager with me." Willoughby bared his teeth in the approximation of a smile. "I had wagered him, you see, that he could not succeed at enjoying the favors of a certain oh-so-proper lady without the benefit of marriage. Under normal circumstances, I do hate to lose a wager, but in this case, it was well worth two hundred pounds just to know how the mighty are fallen." He slowly raked his eyes down her body as if stripping her naked. Then he released her hand as they separated to walk down the outside of the dance set.

It was marvelous, Charlotte thought, how she could continue to dance and smile as if nothing had happened when there was a knife twisting in her gut. Worse than that; there was no knife spilling her life-blood, and therefore no hope of a merciful death. She did not waste her time wondering if it was true; experience had taught her that the cruelest interpretation of a man's behavior was most likely the correct one. It had been too good to be true, that a man would care for plain, long on the shelf Charlotte Lucas. At that moment, she hated every man in the world, even her own brothers and father.

She had no intention of giving this particular man the satisfaction of thinking her hurt. When they came back together at the head of the line, she raised her chin and said, "Is that what Mr. Robinson told you? Even I know better than to believe a man's boast about a woman, especially when there is money at stake."

"But I have my proof," he said softly in her ear. "I watched you go into the woods with him, and again when you walked out over an hour later, with twigs in your hair and your skirt wrinkled."

Charlotte resorted to an old game of pretending she was somewhere else as he continued to take advantage of the dance to whisper ever more vulgar insinuations. She focused on keeping her head up and smiling as if her world were not crumbling. She ignored Willoughby when the dance ended, instead chatting with another dancer for a few minutes before making her way to the safety of Lizzy, whose sharp tongue would keep even Willoughby at bay. Fortunately, Lizzy's preoccupation with Mr. Bingley's fascination with Jane seemed to keep her from noticing anything was amiss with Charlotte, and soon they were interrupted by Lizzy's cousin, Mr. Collins, who had the remarkable ability to carry a conversation without very little input from anyone else.

The ball seemed to last an eternity as Charlotte labored to keep her composure. She could hardly eat a bite of supper. All the gossip around her about the presumed future happiness of Jane Bennet with Mr. Bingley only rubbed salt in her wounds.

Oh, how could she have been foolish enough to get into this predicament? Usually she was so sensible, but this time her feelings had led her further astray than she would have believed possible. And what if there were consequences of that night in the woods? She would have no defense, and she would disgrace her entire family. As it was, she could be the target of humiliating gossip if Willoughby chose to spread his poison. He seemed to be taking great pleasure in smirking at her whenever she looked his way.

In self-defense, she began to talk more to Mr. Collins and to distract his attention from Lizzy. His conversation might be silly, but he was presentable enough, and the world would only see a tall fellow with grave and stately manners talking intently to her. At least this way Willoughby would see that she could still engage a man's interest without the incentive of a large sum of money. It was little enough consolation when she considered her now-blighted future, the degradation of having believed like a fool that Mr. Robinson actually cared for her, and the strong possibility that Willoughby was not yet done humiliating her. If she proved to be with child, or if Willoughby went to her father with his claims, it could be even worse. If only she could somehow escape from Meryton ... but there was nowhere for her to go.

Caroline Bingley's Generous Appraisal of the Evening

by Marilyn Brant

November 26, 1811

Insupportable! Really, there was no other word for it.

Caroline Bingley had done her level best to point out to her brother how unnecessary and ridiculous it would be to have such an event in their home—*and for what? to appease some silly Bennet girls?* — but it was futile. Charles, the fool, would not be dissuaded. "I made a promise," he argued back. "I am a gentleman of my word."

So, here she was, not only in the midst of an evening that would have been beneath her to attend, and sheer punishment at that, but indeed, she was now one of the hosts of it. She took a steadying breath, adjusted the trim on her sleeve and caught sight of Mr. Darcy. He, at least, had the decency to look appropriately displeased by the goings on.

And what was going on? Good heavens, what was *not* going on! Those younger Bennet girls were racing around the ballroom and giggling like peasant children who'd just seen their first Red Coat. Their mother was gossiping to that Lucas woman in tones that could drown out the voice of a commanding officer. And that middle Bennet girl—that horribly unmusical one—was fingering her piano music, just biding her time until she could unleash her immorally bad taste on the party. Caroline sniffed. If desperation had an odor, this would be it.

But, as annoying as they all were, these people were of little consequence to Caroline. No, she had far larger issues to contemplate. Her very own brother was staring at the eldest Bennet daughter as if he'd just seen Aphrodite personified. It was revolting. And Jane Bennet herself could hardly keep from smiling in her sweet but, clearly, simpleminded little way at everybody. Nobody was that good all the time, unless they were lacking in sense and sophistication.

Nothing, however, inspired the nausea deep in Caroline's belly quite like having to look at Miss Elizabeth Bennet for any sustainable length of time. She watched her on numerous occasions throughout the course of the evening: Dancing with that odd, uncoordinated man at the start of the night (something-or-other Collins, she'd overheard the Bennet mother say). Laughing with Miss Charlotte Lucas, though over what topic Caroline would hardly chance a guess. In the company of her mother or one of her many sisters, always eyeing the world with her particular brand of impertinent regard. But it was her dance with Mr. Darcy that distressed Caroline most of all. She was positively mystified as to why he would have committed himself to Miss Elizabeth for so many precious minutes while she—*Caroline herself!*—was available for both dancing and conversation.

She was quite sure it must have been an act of pure graciousness on his part. He, too, must be doing his best to be the type of generous host that she knew herself to be, making sure each guest had at least one bright moment in their otherwise dreary little lives. That was why she'd insisted to the head cook that the punch be sufficiently spiked with rum. The locals might not have appreciated the more delicate flavors in the drink, but they would be aware of the absence of their favorite element. See how she was thinking of others? How anxious she was to please the common people? Mr. Darcy must be doing the same although, in Caroline's opinion, he was, perhaps, taking his kindness to an extreme in this case.

Fortunately, during the course of that particular dance, Louisa came bustling up to her with news of Jane Bennet, who'd been asking questions about Mr. George Wickham, an officer Caroline knew was most repugnant to Mr. Darcy. Caroline soon gathered that Miss Bennet's interest was, without a doubt, inspired by Miss Elizabeth's personal curiosity. She smiled to herself. At last, she had something helpful to impart to that obnoxious second Bennet daughter. Knowledge that *she* had—that Miss Elizabeth *did not*—which would prove just how much higher in esteem Mr. Darcy held Caroline's company over hers…despite the other's supposedly "fine eyes." What utter nonsense that was.

Caroline needed only to wait until the dance was over, and then she would seek out Miss Elizabeth and kindly—*so very kindly*—enlighten the silly girl on how things really stood. That would knock down a few of Elizabeth Bennet's undeserved airs! And she would be doing a great service to Mr. Darcy in the process, as well as to everyone who had the misfortune of being socially connected with the Bennet family.

The very thought of her own generosity made Caroline almost blush with a rare sense of delight. And this made the insupportability of the evening just a bit more tolerable. For a brief moment, the Netherfield Ball was almost enjoyable.

Denny at the Netherfield Ball

by Jack Caldwell

November 26, 1811

Lieutenant Denny, immaculate in his Number One uniform, paid his respects to his hosts, Mr. and Miss Bingley, before following Captain Carter into the main room of Netherfield. At his shoulder were his comrades, Pratt and Chamberlayne. His friends were looking for diversion, something that Denny sought as well, but he had a task to perform.

"Ah," said Pratt, "Carter is making for the card room."

"All the better to avoid Miss Watson," drawled Chamberlayne. "You know she has set her cap for him."

"At her age? I do not believe it."

"Stranger things have happened. I say, who is that? The young lady with the freckles?"

"Her?" Pratt looked over. "That is Miss Mary King. The word is that she has expectations of an ill grandfather and ten thousand pounds."

"Ten thousand? That might make up for her *atrocious* fashion sense," Chamberlayne sniffed.

For not the first time, Denny wondered about Chamberlayne. At that moment, the Bennet family arrived and Denny smiled. Miss Lydia was particularly fetching tonight, and Wickham was not there to get into his way. As his two companions made their way to the

126

punch table, Denny slowly approached the Bennet ladies, wishing to accomplish his mission as soon as possible.

"Ah, Mr. Denny!" cried Miss Lydia. "Is he not handsome, Kitty? So fine in his uniform and sword! I believe I shall swoon!"

"I shall swoon as well," parroted Miss Kitty.

"Girls, that is enough," Miss Elizabeth said quietly. "Good evening, Mr. Denny. I hope I find you well." As she spoke, her eyes were scanning the room, obviously looking for someone.

As was Miss Lydia. "But where is Mr. Wickham?"

"I bear unfortunate news," said Denny. "My friend is not in attendance. Wickham was obliged to go to Town on business yesterday and will not return until tomorrow. He sends his regrets."

Lydia and Kitty were vociferous in their displeasure at this pronouncement, and Miss Elizabeth was clearly disappointed, particularly when Denny, with a significant smile, added in a low voice meant only for Miss Elizabeth's ears, "I do not imagine his business would have called him away just now if he had not wished to avoid a certain gentleman here." He gestured with his head at Mr. Darcy, who was standing in a corner across the room.

Wickham had told Denny of the shameful treatment he had received from his godfather's son, and a shocked Denny felt sympathy for his friend. The rich had their own rules, he had reflected, and a poor man could do nothing but make his own way in the world. Opportunity was scarce in the militia, which was why Denny was determined to join the Regulars and rise in his chosen profession.

Lydia, who had heard nothing of Denny's last comment, stamped her little foot. "Well, pooh! If Mr. Wickham thinks that business is more important that dancing with ladies, then I say he is a dull fellow! As for me, I shall dance the night away!"

Denny extended his arm. "If you are not otherwise obligated, may I request the first set? And Miss Kitty, the second?"

Lydia took his right arm and flashed her eyes coquettishly. "Why, Mr. Denny, that would be very agreeable."

Kitty took his left. "I should dance first! (*cough*) I am almost two years older!"

Denny knew he had to defuse this potentially explosive situation. "Ah, but Pratt would never forgive me, Miss Kitty, as he has spoken of claiming your first."

"Oh!" Kitty was exceptionally pleased.

Denny turned to make his excuses to Miss Elizabeth, only to see she was in conversation with Sir William Lucas's plain daughter. He walked away towards his comrades as Miss Lydia asked whether the rumors were true that Colonel Forster would marry soon.

The ball was like any other ball as far as Denny was concerned. After the first sets with Miss Lydia and Miss Kitty, he danced with several of the other ladies of the district. Denny was amused that Captain Carter stood up with Miss King. Not that there was anything wrong with Mary King—if one's tastes ran towards the uninformed and insipid. But a potential ten thousand pounds was an attractive inducement for attention in some men. Men not like Archibald Denny. He liked lively people.

There were interesting moments during the ball. Denny was surprised at first that Miss Elizabeth danced with Mr. Darcy, knowing that Miss Elizabeth was distressed over the man's treatment of Wickham. Amazement turned to amusement when he noticed two things. First, Miss Elizabeth was clearly scolding Mr. Darcy during the set. Second, Mr. Darcy seemed to be unaware of it, and Denny thought he caught flashes of admiration in the rich man's eye.

The proud and unpleasant Mr. Darcy is attracted to a lady who hates him! he thought. *I know a man of his stature would never offer for her, but I wonder what would happen if he did? Would Miss Elizabeth flatly refuse him, puncturing his pride, or would she do the prudent thing and accept him and make the rest of his life miserable?*

* * *

Denny was enjoying Miss Lydia's company at dinner when Miss Mary Bennet began her concert at the pianoforte. Her playing was

128

truly appalling, but he was embarrassed at the way Lydia and Kitty openly laughed at her. It was not his place to correct her, but he suspected that for all her loveliness and high spirits, Miss Lydia needed a firm hand to guide her to better behavior. He had not the right to do that, but he could stop those who were abetting her conduct.

"Pratt," he hissed, "pray stop providing punch to Miss Lydia and Miss Kitty. Can you not see they have had enough?"

"And very good punch it is" laughed Chamberlayne, "especially with all the whisky *someone* added to it!" He winked at Pratt.

"*What?*" Denny was outraged. Officers were meant to act as gentlemen, and this was not the action of a gentleman! "Pratt, this is insupportable!"

"Aw, shut your gob, Denny," drawled Pratt, half-way into his cups. "Just having a bit of fun. Besides, I don't have to listen to you. You're not my commanding officer."

"True, but I am your brother officer, and I tell you this is wrong."

Pratt, bleary-eyed, leaned over and belched. "You ain't in the Regulars yet, Denny, so hold your bloody tongue. Or are you going to be a damnable scrub and report me to Carter?"

Denny pulled his lips tight. There was a code in the ranks—*stand by your comrades*—and Denny was not going to break it. At least, not over this. But it went against the grain. "I think it best that the ladies receive no more punch. Can I depend on you?"

Pratt raised his hand in defeat. "As you wish. Besides, it leaves more for me and Chamberlayne."

Chamberlayne laughed again. "I thank you for my share, Pratt!"

"Denny?" asked an inebriated Lydia. "Are you arguing with Pratt?"

"Not at all, Miss Lydia. May I get you some punch?" He glanced at his chuckling comrades. "There is a different batch that I highly recommend."

Lydia grinned. "Lord, you are so sweet! Is not Denny sweet, Kitty?"

"Yes." Kitty blinked happily.

Denny moved over to a different punch table, one that was halfway across the room, bemoaning the fact that it would still take almost nine months before his uncle's shipment arrived from India and provide the last of the promised funds he needed to purchase his commission in the Regulars. Ah, to leave this collection of militia misfits behind! September of '12 could not come fast enough!

The Hursts Discuss the Netherfield Ball

by Mary Simonsen

November 26, 1811

"Louisa, you absolutely outdid yourself tonight," Robert Hurst said in praise of his wife's efforts. "The musicians played brilliantly, our guests stepped lively, and most of the young ladies who exhibited were truly talented. The wine selection was excellent and the food superb. However did you manage it?"

Knowing she had done little, Louisa smiled at her husband's compliments. After all, the musicians had been recommended by Robert's sister-in-law, Lady Banfield. As for the refreshments, under the direction of Caroline, the Bingleys' butler and cook had seen to everything, and it was Robert who had selected the wines. But she understood the reason for his excessive praise: Her spirits were low, and he knew it.

"Thank you, my darling. Everything was exactly as it should have been—at least on our part," Louisa said, thinking of Mary Bennet's unfortunate exhibition on the pianoforte and Mrs. Bennet spilling sherry on one of the officer's trousers. There was also some excessive drinking amongst the younger officers, but that was to be expected. On the other hand, no one got sick—or none whom she knew about. Louisa admitted, all in all, the ball had been a great success.

"Then why are you sailing in the doldrums?"

Louisa, who had been sitting at her dressing table brushing her hair, put down the brush. "Did you see how happy Charles looked tonight?"

"Yes, I did. It was as if his smile was painted on his face. And how could he not be happy? He is in love with Jane Bennet, and every minute he could spare from his duties as host was spent with her. I expect we shall hear news of an engagement shortly."

After completing her toilette and dismissing her maid, Louisa told her husband that there would be no news of a betrothal. To the contrary, she believed they would be leaving Netherfield Park within the week.

"Because you were in the card room, you did not see Mr. Darcy and Miss Elizabeth Bennet dancing," Louisa explained. "It was obvious to me that Miss Elizabeth did not want to dance with Mr. Darcy. Her jaw was clenched so tightly, I could practically hear her teeth cracking. But Mr. Darcy, being so enamored of the lady, did not notice and attempted to engage her in conversation. Miss Elizabeth responded with those tired platitudes one always hears in a ballroom before introducing the subject of Mr. Wickham. Once the subject was broached, Mr. Darcy's whole demeanor changed. Barely a civil word passed between them from that point on. When the dance was over, they could not get away from each other fast enough."

"Yes, I understand Wickham is a sore spot with Darcy, but Miss Elizabeth could hardly be expected to know of their mutual dislike. Surely Darcy must know that."

"Although we do not know the particulars of their quarrel, Caroline and I are convinced that Mr. Darcy's sister was somehow involved. If that is the case, then anyone who is a friend of Mr. Wickham is not a friend of Mr. Darcy."

"But we were speaking of your brother. What do Charles and Miss Bennet have to do with Darcy and Miss Elizabeth?"

"Caroline is well aware of Mr. Darcy's interest in Miss Elizabeth, and from the time she saw the first spark ignite, she has been looking for a way to get Charles to leave the country. Up to this point, she was alone in her efforts, but now she will have an ally in Mr. Darcy. He, too, will want to leave Hertfordshire."

"But that does not change the fact that Charles is in love with Miss Bennet. You cannot convince a man who is so in love that he is not."

"Oh, that is not how they will pursue the matter." Louisa tsked at her husband's naiveté. "Caroline and Mr. Darcy will try to convince my brother that Miss Bennet does not love *him*."

"But how?"

"Miss Bennet is a placid creature and gives nothing away with her looks. Although I personally believe she is in love with Charles, only the most acute observer would be able to discern any particular regard on her part. Because of that, I believe Mr. Darcy and my sister will succeed in convincing Charles that Miss Bennet is not in love with him. If they are successful, then there is no reason for us to remain in the country, and we shall all return to London."

Robert shook his head. "Your predictions are so dark because you are tired from your exertions this evening. You look perfectly done in."

"This is not merely guesswork on my part, Robert," Louisa said, patting her husband's hand. "Caroline told me that it is her intention to speak to Mr. Darcy tomorrow about Charles and Miss Bennet. She is quite determined to separate them."

"It is possible you may be wrong, my dear."

"Knowing my sister as I do, I know that I am right."

Mr. Collins Proposes

by Susan Mason-Milks

November 27, 1811

After the ball, Mrs. Bennet lay awake delighting in thoughts of Jane's wedding to Mr. Bingley. He had not yet proposed, but after making his preference for Jane so clear at the ball tonight, it was surely only a matter of time before he declared himself. What fun it would be to shop for new wedding clothes in London, and of course, her eldest daughter must have the very best! Although Netherfield was a grand house, the furniture and draperies were quite another story. They would definitely have to be replaced, and Jane would need her advice on the colors, the fabrics, and style. The prospect excited her more and more. It was all she could do to keep from clapping her hands together with joy. The idea of having a daughter settled so close by was delightful. She would be able to visit nearly every day!

When Mrs. Bennet awoke late the next morning, her head throbbed from lack of sleep and possibly that final glass of punch at the ball last night. As she lay abed absently pondering her plans for Jane's wedding, she noticed some enticing smells coming from downstairs, and following her nose, made her way to the breakfast room. Yes, a little coffee was just the thing she needed to clear her head this morning.

As she sipped, she did a mental inventory of the family. Mr. Bennet had already retreated to his library and would probably not emerge for the rest of the day. Jane and Lydia were still in bed, while Elizabeth and Kitty lingered in the breakfast room talking softly—

thank goodness—about the ball. And Mary? Oh, no one cared where she was as long as she refrained from practicing the pianoforte today. The noise would simply be intolerable.

Having finished her first cup of coffee, Mrs. Bennet was just spreading butter and jam on a thick piece of bread when Mr. Collins appeared and addressed her, asking for a private interview with Miss Elizabeth. Suddenly, all her senses were alert! She had been hoping for this for the past several days but had not expected Mr. Collins to approach her this morning!

"Oh, dear! Yes, certainly. I am sure Lizzy will be very happy— I am sure she can have no objection. Come, Kitty, I want you upstairs."

As surprised as Mrs. Bennet was at his application, she was even more surprised by her second daughter's reaction. Lizzy, looking startled and confused, begged her mother and Kitty not to leave her. To Mrs. Bennet, this seemed like a strange response. Surely, after Mr. Collins's attentions the last few days, her daughter must have been expecting his proposal. She should be happy to hear he had requested a "private interview." When Lizzy's eyes narrowed in one of her defiant looks, and she appeared ready to bolt from the room, Mrs. Bennet glared at her and firmly insisted she stay and listen to what Mr. Collins had to say. Taking Kitty by the arm, she pulled her toward the door.

"Mama, please," Kitty whined. "You are hurting my arm!"

Mrs. Bennet silenced Kitty with a withering look, and then quickly directed her best reassuring smile at Mr. Collins. Exiting the room, daughter in tow, she was careful to leave the door slightly ajar. After shooing Kitty off to rouse her other sisters, she moved back to the breakfast room doorway. At first, all she could hear was the throbbing of her head.

Then she heard Mr. Collins nervously clear his throat several times and begin his speech. His proposal started off with promise. He generously complimented Elizabeth on her modesty and enumerated her other admirable traits. *Thank goodness, he does not yet know what a trial the girl can be,* Mrs. Bennet thought to herself. Then he went on for some time explaining how he had singled her out as the companion of his life almost from the first moment he entered the house. Mrs. Bennet frowned. She knew this was not exactly true. His first interest had been in Jane, but after a few hints about Jane's anticipated engagement, he had quickly redirected his attentions to Lizzy.

As Mr. Collins began a rather long-winded recitation of his reasons for marrying, Mrs. Bennet nearly stomped her foot in irritation. She could not understand why he did not just get on with it! No one cared why he wanted to marry. It was only important that he did. But the self-absorbed parson was not to be hurried. Droning on, he complimented himself on his generosity in choosing his bride from among his cousins, as this would ensure the security of the rest of the family once he inherited Longbourn. The comfort of knowing that if Mr. Bennet died they would not be put out into the hedgerows made the pounding in Mrs. Bennet's head begin to subside.

As Lizzy started to speak, her voice was so soft her mother had to strain to hear. What was she saying? Why was she disagreeing with him? It took all of Mrs. Bennet's self-control not to push the door open and rush into the room so she could shake some sense into her foolish daughter. How could she do this to her family? Although Mrs. Bennet tried to calm herself, the pounding intensified in her head again. It began to feel as if it might explode. Of course, Lizzy would come to her senses and accept him. She simply must! The conversation went back and forth for several minutes with Lizzy remaining firm in her refusal, and Mr. Collins refusing to accept her protestations. She had to give Mr. Collins credit. He might not be a very exciting man, but he was persistent.

Feeling secure that Lizzy would see reason and do the right thing, Mrs. Bennet retreated into the vestibule, took a few deep breaths, and waited for the appropriate time to rush in and express her surprise and happiness at their engagement. After a few minutes, her daughter emerged, and without even a glance in her mother's direction, retreated up the stairs towards her bedchamber. "Lizzy, dear, where are you going?" Mrs. Bennet waved her hands wildly and called after her, "You must come back. Lizzy! Lizzy?"

Mrs. Bennet pressed a hand to her throbbing head. Then shrugging her shoulders, she sighed and rushed into the breakfast room to congratulate Mr. Collins in the warmest terms and express her joy that they would soon be more closely related. He happily received her felicitations.

"Her modest refusals of my proposal only show what a bashful, delicate creature she truly is. Certainly, her purpose is to increase my love by suspense, and that she most assuredly has accomplished. I am now more eager than ever to call her my wife," he said, brushing back an oily lock of hair that was stuck to his forehead.

Although Mr. Collins did not seem disturbed by his ladylove's reluctance, Mrs. Bennet quickly became concerned. Something was not right. "Depend upon it, Mr. Collins!" she assured him. "Lizzy shall be brought to reason. I will speak to her about it directly. She is a very headstrong, foolish girl and does not know her own interests, but I will make her see reason."

At this, the smile on Mr. Collins's face faded a bit. "Pardon me for interrupting you, madam, but if she is really headstrong and foolish, I wonder if she would be a very desirable wife for a man in my situation. I am one who naturally looks for happiness in the marital state. If she persists in rejecting my suit, perhaps it would be better not to force her into accepting me. Such defects of temper would not be conducive to marital felicity."

Suddenly, Mrs. Bennet felt faint and wavered on her feet. Oh, no, he could not be allowed to change his mind! To keep from toppling over, she grabbed the back of a chair for support and began reassuring him that Lizzy was only headstrong in matters such as this—whatever that meant. She told him again of her daughter's gentle nature even though she knew in her heart Lizzy could be just like her father—very stubborn indeed! Mr. Collins would find that out for himself once they were married, but by then, it would be too late, and Lizzy would be securely established at Hunsford.

"I will go directly to Mr. Bennet, and I am sure we shall have it all settled very soon," she said. Without giving Mr. Collins a chance to reply, Mrs. Bennet left and flew directly to the library where she knew she would find Mr. Bennet ensconced among his books. Although she was certain the sound of her excited breathing should have alerted him to her arrival, he did not seem to notice her standing there for at least a minute. When her husband finally did look up, he appeared disinterested.

"Yes, what is it, Mrs. Bennet?"

While trying to keep her voice from becoming too shrill, she begged for his help in making Lizzy accept Mr. Collins. As sweat popped out on her forehead from the exertion, she began dabbing at it with her hankie. In spite of the urgency she tried to convey, Mr. Bennet continued to look at her blankly as if she were a fly buzzing around the room. Why did he not offer to help? After all, he was not doing anything important—only reading a book. Mrs. Bennet's agitation rose in direct proportion to his refusal to understand her. How could he not support her in this? Certainly, he understood the importance of finding suitable husbands for their five daughters? She had discussed this with him repeatedly although she often suspected he was only pretending to listen.

Finally, much to her relief, Mr. Bennet seemed to grasp the situation and agreed to speak with Lizzy. Confident her husband would take her side, she waited for him to take charge.

After asking Lizzy a few questions, Mr. Bennet cleared his throat. "Very well. We now come to the point. Your mother insists upon your accepting Mr. Collins. Is it not so, Mrs. Bennet?"

"Yes, or I will never see her again," she declared firmly crossing her arms across her chest. Certain he was about to tell Lizzy she must comply, Mrs. Bennet stopped listening for a moment and began congratulating herself on her success. Then, suddenly, Lizzy was smiling. Mrs. Bennet looked at them both in confusion. Something had gone horribly wrong! What had she missed? Surely, he would never allow his daughter to refuse a perfectly good proposal? The pounding in her ears increased until it sounded like an entire drum corps marching through her head.

"What do you mean, Mr. Bennet, in talking this way? You promised to insist upon her marrying him."

"Mrs. Bennet, I promised no such thing. I said I would speak with her about it, and that I have done. The matter is settled." When she did not move, he added, "I would appreciate having my library to myself again—as soon as possible." And with that, he returned to his book.

At first Mrs. Bennet was not certain she had heard him correctly, but as she watched her daughter leaving the room looking happy, she fully realized what had just happened. He had taken Lizzy's side, and she was being thrown out of his library—in her own house! This was not to be tolerated! "Oh, Mr. Bennet!" she cried and ran from the room.

Since her husband had once again proved to be of no help, she knew it was entirely up to her to salvage the situation. With that in mind, Mrs. Bennet burst into Lizzy's room and began trying to wear her down, urging her again and again to accept Mr. Collins before he changed his mind and would not have her. She coaxed, cajoled, pleaded, and tearfully called for Lizzy to have mercy on her poor nerves. Finally, she resorted to threats in a desperate effort to convince her disobedient daughter.

When she was exhausted and her head began to pound, Mrs. Bennet gave up and returned to the breakfast room, sitting down with a loud sigh. Just as she was pouring another cup of coffee and wondering if she should add a bit of Mr. Bennet's brandy—medicinally, of course—she was startled by the appearance of Charlotte Lucas. Without considering that news of Lizzy's refusal might become fodder for neighborhood gossip, she took up her case with Charlotte. As Mrs. Bennet continued to fan herself with her handkerchief, she bemoaned to her new audience that no one seemed to be taking her part in the dispute.

"I have only the best interests of my daughters at heart. Surely, you understand that, Charlotte. Perhaps you could explain it to

Lizzy for me," she said, directing a scowl in the direction of her second daughter who had just entered. Waving a handkerchief in front of her face, she moaned, "No one is concerned for me! Oh, the flutterings, the spasms of my poor nerves! What did I do to deserve such a disobedient daughter?"

"I am certain everything will work out for the best," Charlotte said giving her a reassuring look. As Mrs. Bennet felt Charlotte put a comforting hand on her arm, she wondered why her Lizzy could not be more like her sweet friend.

Glancing up, Mrs. Bennet saw Lizzy looking unconcerned and very satisfied with herself. At times like this, Mrs. Bennet could see her daughter's resemblance—both in temperament and in expression—to her father, and it was infuriating!

When Mr. Collins arrived and basically withdrew his offer, Mrs. Bennet completely lost heart. Unable to think of another strategy, she succumbed to her headache and retreated to her bedchamber. Jane, her good, kind daughter, who would never betray her the way Lizzy had, came and laid a cool compress on her mother's head. "You must not worry, Mama. All will be well," Jane said softly.

Mrs. Bennet took her eldest daughter's hand in hers, "Oh, Jane, I was so certain today when Mr. Collins asked for a private interview that I would have at least one of my daughters engaged before the morning was over. I do not understand what went wrong! Now it is all up to you to secure Mr. Bingley, my dear."

Mr. Collins Talks to Sir William

by Shannon Winslow

November 27, 1811

Mr. Collins could be no less satisfied with his own eloquence than with its effect. He had obtained his object and, there in the garden, the amiable Charlotte had promised to be his.

The more he had thought about it, the more certain he became that his second choice had been the right one all along, for surely Miss Lucas more closely matched his noble patroness's description of the proper wife for him—an active, useful sort of person, able to make a small income go a good way. Yes, Lady Catherine would be well pleased.

"When is to be the day that you make me the happiest of men?" he entreated his intended as they reentered the house. "Do say it will be soon, my dear Charlotte!"

Charlotte could not help being flattered by her lover's impatience. In truth, however, Mr. Collins was thinking as much of Lady Catherine at that moment as of herself and of his triumph to come when he presented his very appropriate bride to that lady.

"Really, Mr. Collins," Charlotte said in a low voice. "I have said I will be your wife and I will, but first you must do two things to satisfy what is right on the occasion."

"Only name them, my beloved."

"You must promise to keep our understanding a secret at Longbourn until I can break the news to the family myself." Though it would cost him dearly to do so, Mr. Collins dutifully agreed. "And, of course, you must speak to my father. I am persuaded that he will make no difficulty whatsoever, but the formality must be observed."

"Naturally!" Mr. Collins enthused, relieved to know that this second stipulation was more in keeping with his taste. "I would not slight your honored father for the world. I hope I do not merely flatter myself in saying that I know how it should be done, too. You can trust me, my dear Charlotte, to show him the respect and deference which are his due."

"Very well. Do step into the library here, and I will tell my father that you are waiting to speak to him."

Charlotte disappeared, and Mr. Collins used the next few minutes alone to arrange in his mind the fine compliments and ceremonial words he would use when Sir William Lucas appeared. It was the sort of thing a person could expect to do only once and, therefore, it must be done correctly the first time.

"Mr. Collins," said Sir William, smiling magnanimously as he entered. "How delightful to see you again so soon! My daughter tells me it is a matter of some importance that brings you this morning. Pray, do be seated," he invited, gesturing to the nearest chair.

Mr. Collins steadfastly declined the offer, thereby obliging his host to continue on his feet as well. "It is a matter of too much import for me to take my ease prematurely," he said by way of explanation. "In truth, my dear sir, it is nothing less than the making of my future happiness and, if I may be so bold," he said with an exaggerated bow meant to portray just the opposite impression, "that of your amiable daughter's as well."

"Indeed? How so?" asked Sir William, feigning more ignorance than what was rightfully his at that moment.

"Well may you ask. Allow me to enlighten you, sir. It is simply this. I rejoice to say that I have been so fortunate as to procure the honor of Miss Lucas's favor, and now I humbly beseech the honor of your blessing on our union as well."

"Dear me! This *is* a surprise, although not an unpleasant one, I assure you, Mr. Collins. I had thought your interest tended in a different direction. That is all."

"How perceptive you are. While it is true that conscience compelled me to attempt some reparation to my fair cousins…"

Here, Mr. Collins was briefly interrupted by an eager Sir William, saying, "Naturally, naturally. A man of your high moral tone could do no less."

"…I am relieved to say that I have satisfied that obligation without loss of either my dignity *or* my liberty."

"Elizabeth?" guessed Sir William. A sober nod from his companion confirmed it. "Perhaps too headstrong for her own good."

"So she had proven to be. But I harbor no ill will towards her— no, indeed I do not—for she has done me a great service in the end by freeing me to find a more affable partner elsewhere."

Mr. Collins allowed a suspenseful pause. Having ably set the stage, he instinctively felt the time was right to begin building toward the final climax. Presently, he undertook his most stately manner and proceeded.

"My dear Sir William, a gentleman in your position—a knight of the realm and a man once distinguished by the king himself— perhaps has every right to expect more than a humble country parson for your daughter. Still, I beg leave to point out that although my suit may appear modest at first, it is not completely without merit. You know my happy connection with the noble family de Bourgh and, of course, my future prospects as regards the Longbourn estate." Here he dropped his voice by way of an aside. "Understanding the man is a friend of yours, I will say no more about that. Still, I trust that a woman who can count these blessings among the benefits of marriage can on the whole have very little reason to repine."

"I should think not, my dear Mr. Collins. I should think not! Indeed, I must say that I am very well pleased with the idea, and if Charlotte has agreed, I certainly will not stand in your way. Let us share the happy news with Lady Lucas at once, shall we? I think I can promise she will be as delighted as I am at the prospect. Capital, capital!"

Sir William hurried to call his wife and daughter, who had been, fortuitously, waiting not far down the corridor for just such an eventuality. Lady Lucas, having already taken a hint from Charlotte, began expounding on her joy at once and of her sanguine expectation that it would prove a most fortunate alliance on both sides.

Soon the entire Lucas household was taken into the celebration, each member quickly perceiving how having the weight of Charlotte's impending spinsterhood off their hands would go a fair way to improving their own prospects. Charlotte herself was perhaps the most composed of the lot. Giddy excitement escaped her, but on the whole she was satisfied with her day's work.

Darcy and Caroline Conspire

by Kara Louise

November 27, 1811

Mr. Darcy walked into the breakfast room eager for a cup of coffee and some solitude to allow him to think more about the events at the Netherfield Ball. Particularly regarding Miss Elizabeth. Despite his less than amicable dance with her, he could not dismiss her from his mind. But he knew he must.

He was surprised and more than a little disappointed to discover Miss Bingley already there. He greeted her politely and asked the servant for a cup of coffee, seating himself at the table.

He took a sip of the freshly poured drink, thanking the servant with a nod of his head. Turning to Miss Bingley, he asked, "Do you know what time Bingley is departing today for London?"

"I believe as early as possible," she answered with a smile, which quickly faded. "You are still planning to go with him?"

"I am not inclined to remain here any longer." His fingers gripped the cup tightly.

Miss Bingley waited until the servant left the room and closed the door behind him. She looked back at Darcy and quite unexpectedly uttered a commanding, "Mr. Darcy, you cannot leave!"

He turned toward her, astonished at her exacting demand. "I beg your pardon, Miss Bingley?"

"Mr. Darcy," she said, as a smooth smile replaced her previously disturbed countenance. "Please accept my apologies for my outburst. I see we are both of like minds; neither am I inclined to remain here even one day more! The society here is intolerable!" She leaned forward and in a conspiratorial whisper said, "However, I have something of the utmost import to discuss with you and it can only be done whilst Charles is away. I see no other alternative but to request that you remain at Netherfield!"

Darcy's brows pinched in curiosity. "What is so urgent that I remain behind, Miss Bingley?"

"We must discuss this Miss Bennet disaster directly!" Her voice rose to a fevered pitch. "You must agree with me after what we witnessed at the ball last night that Charles should be made to see the imprudence of this affection. Naturally, we cannot discuss it whilst he is in our midst, and I am relying on your counsel, for I know he will listen to you. I fear it may prove to be too late if we delay discussion of this until you both return!" She shook her head vehemently. "We must formulate a plan to separate him from her!"

Darcy slowly lifted his coffee cup and gazed into the swirling liquid as if it might hold the answers to all his unanswered questions. He pondered Miss Bingley's words silently and then took another sip.

Miss Bingley continued, "Mr. Darcy, you beheld her family. Have you ever witnessed such undignified behavior? Each member of that family is objectionable!"

Darcy glanced up to see Miss Bingley eyeing him. He wondered if his tightening jaw betrayed to her any sign that he was still drawn to Miss Elizabeth's fine eyes, sparkling wit, uncommon intelligence. He shook his head to remove her from his thoughts.

"Certainly you were appalled at the lack of breeding displayed. It would be insupportable for Charles to marry into that family!" She continued in a softer, yet more determined manner, "Please, I beg you to consider remaining at Netherfield so that we may discuss what we shall do without fear of Charles overhearing!"

Mr. Darcy lifted his eyes to her and was about to reply when Miss Bingley added, "You heard her mother, did you not? Miss Bennet is a dear, sweet girl, but her mother! Is it not quite clear that her sole purpose in promoting a marriage between her eldest and my brother is to elevate their family in society?"

Miss Bingley's pleading was halted by the entrance of Bingley himself, and they both turned in surprise towards him, fearful he may have heard her last comment. It was apparent he had not, for he entered the room in a buoyant manner and with a most jovial greeting.

"Good morning, Caroline! Good morning, Darcy! Beautiful day, is it not?"

Miss Bingley's eyes darted to Mr. Darcy as she answered, "I suppose it is."

Bingley looked to his friend, who merely took a sip from his cup of coffee. "I simply hate to quit Netherfield today," he continued. "I have had such a pleasant time here... especially at the ball. I do believe everyone enjoyed themselves. I know I did."

A smile beamed from his face as Miss Bingley looked down and rolled her eyes. "Yes, Brother, but I believe *some* enjoyed themselves more than *others!*"

"Tell me, Darcy, do you still wish to accompany me to Town? I should thoroughly enjoy your company on that tedious journey thither!"

Miss Bingley looked at Mr. Darcy, biting her lip as she awaited his answer.

Darcy paused, rubbing his chin as he contemplated what to say. "I know I told you I was considering it, Bingley, but I fear I cannot. I regret that I have news from my steward of pressing business at Pemberley, and I do not think I have the time for a London visit. If you anticipate being in Town any length of time, I shall endeavor to join you at a later date."

Bingley accepted his friend's words good-naturedly and without question. Miss Bingley, upon hearing his comment, looked well-pleased.

* * *

Later that day after Bingley took his leave, Mr. Darcy sat with Miss

Bingley and Mr. and Mrs. Hurst in the sitting room. The two sisters were of like mind in their plotting and scheming as they attributed a most disheartening account of the Bennet family's behavior at the ball.

Miss Bingley's eyes pleaded with Mr. Darcy as did her argument. "Certainly you agree with me that Mrs. Bennet is a most presumptuous woman! How dare she speak so openly and freely about her expectations for Charles and Miss Bennet to become engaged directly? I am quite sure she has the whole of Meryton prepared to offer felicitations."

"Quite imprudent," agreed her sister.

"Now exactly how did Mrs. Bennet phrase it as she was enumerating the many advantages of the match?" Miss Bingley pointedly asked. "I believe it was something to the effect, 'Their marriage will be such a promising thing for my younger daughters, as Jane's marrying so greatly must throw them in the way of other rich men!'"

Upon hearing those words, Mr. Darcy grimaced and took a final gulp from the cup of coffee he gripped in his hand. He had to admit he had been appalled when he overheard Mrs. Bennet speaking so loudly and in such a tasteless manner.

"And the youngest sister; you observed her, I am sure, displaying such unrestrained manners! Is there a redcoat in Hertfordshire unworthy of her flirtations? I could barely keep my countenance!"

Her eyes locked onto those of Mr. Darcy. "We cannot allow any sort of attachment between Charles and Jane Bennet. He is far too guileless to withstand the arts of a family looking to elevate their status. And if they succeed in their scheme, what will become of Charles then? Left to care for an ambitious mother-in-law, obliged to entertain soldiers for the sake of flirtatious, ill-bred sisters? It is not sound!"

Darcy took in a deep breath as he deliberated on her words carefully. But before he could reply, Miss Bingley offered up one more observation from the night of the ball.

"It must have come as quite a shock to you, Mr. Darcy, to learn of Miss Elizabeth Bennet's admiration for Mr. Wickham. I could not understand myself how she had come to be so enamored of him." She cast a glance at Mr. Darcy and appeared pleased at the effect of her words.

Darcy took in a breath to steel himself for what he was about to say. He stood up and walked to the sideboard, setting down his empty cup. "You are correct, Miss Bingley. What you have said about separating Bingley and Miss Bennet is something upon which I wholeheartedly agree."

Darcy turned to his co-conspirator. "I will concede that Miss Bennet is pleasing of countenance and manner, but it is more than that. In all the times, I have had the opportunity to observe her, she displayed no outward regard for Bingley. I believe you may be correct in that she is receiving his attentions to secure a husband of fortune so as to benefit her family, and that is solely due to her mother's encouragement. I would be doing a disservice to Bingley to allow him to ask for Miss Bennet's hand in marriage."

"Yes, you are so correct, Mr. Darcy," Miss Bingley agreed. "She shows no affection toward him. None at all. It is as though she cares nothing for him! What can be done about this?"

Very slowly and deliberately Darcy replied, "We must keep him from returning to Netherfield."

Miss Bingley looked to her sister and then back to Mr. Darcy. "Yes! We shall all depart on the morrow for London and I shall instruct the servants to close up Netherfield for the remainder of the winter. We shall inform them that it is very unlikely that any from our party will return any time soon." A smile came to her face. "And once we are on our way, I shall have a polite little missive sent to Miss Bennet to inform her of our plans and not to expect us back."

"This will hardly please Bingley," Darcy countered.

"He will be displeased for but a short while. You know how easily he falls in and out of love. Once he has been away from Miss Bennet, she will soon be forgotten, as will any attachment for Netherfield. He listens to *you*, Mr. Darcy. He regards *your* opinion most highly." She let out a breath and a smile appeared. "And perhaps there is a pleasant, young lady in Town, someone of excellent breeding and disposition, who will soon come to take Miss Bennet's place in his heart."

"Perhaps," Darcy said, not really hearing her words. "I believe it *would* be prudent for *him* to be separated from Miss Bennet to discourage any sort of admiration to continue." Darcy let out a raspy breath. "I heartily concur. We must leave on the morrow! This unsound attachment must be obliterated in its entirety!" Darcy spoke with such force and command that Miss Bingley appeared surprised.

Once these words were out, Darcy felt an odd sense of hopelessness and regret, as he struggled with the fact that Miss Elizabeth's family was completely unsuitable—for Bingley perhaps—and for himself unquestionably. With pinched brows, Darcy slowly sat back down, realizing that the weight of his argument was directed chiefly towards himself. He needed to distance himself from Miss Elizabeth and he was going to destroy his good friend's prospect for love and marital felicity, as well as his own, by doing so.

Swaying Bingley's Opinion of Jane

by Kara Louise

December 8, 1811

Darcy paced back and forth in the sitting room awaiting his guests. He knew this meeting was not going to be easy, but it must be done. Promptly at two o'clock, the Bingley party was announced. Charles Bingley walked in jubilantly ahead of the others and greeted Darcy with a firm handshake and a broad smile upon his face.

"Goodness, Darcy! I can understand my sisters following me into Town, but your arrival has certainly taken me by surprise! But do not take me wrong, I am pleased to see you!"

"Thank you, Bingley. It was unfortunate you had already left when I received word from my steward that the issue at Pemberley had been resolved and there was no need for me to make the trip there."

Darcy greeted the others, and Miss Bingley swept into the room. "Good afternoon, Mr. Darcy. It is so good to see you again! Is your sister here? How we would so enjoy seeing her!"

"No, I regret she is not."

Miss Bingley looked to her brother. "Oh, is that not a shame, Charles? She is such a sweet girl. We must make plans to see her soon!" She turned back to Darcy with an enthusiastic smile.

Darcy simply gave a nod of his head and extended his hand toward the chairs and sofa. "Please, come in and sit down."

Bingley settled himself into a chair, sitting on the edge and leaning forward. "So how did you decide to come to Town?"

"We began talking about how envious we were of you, Charles, in such superior society and…" Miss Bingley looked over to Darcy for confirmation, "…the next thing we knew, it was decided that we would all quit Netherfield the following day and set out for London."

Bingley gave his sister and friend a brief smile. "But Netherfield … I had hoped to return in a day or two."

"There is no need to rush back, Charles," Miss Bingley began. "We all concurred how much we missed the excellent society here that was so lacking in Hertfordshire. It has been far too long."

"When do you think we might return to Netherfield?" Bingley asked, turning from his sister to Mr. Darcy.

"I see no reason to hurry back at all." Darcy took in a deep breath. "Bingley, in all honesty, Netherfield was a decent house in the country, but I fear it would not prove to be a wise purchase. I must agree with Miss Bingley that the neighborhood lacked any sort of good society."

"Just what are you saying, Darcy? I found everyone to be most friendly!" Bingley looked squarely at his friend.

"Perhaps that is true, but unfortunately I found them to be simple country folk. No one of any great esteem lived in the vicinity. You must begin to think about those with whom you associate; mere amiability cannot be your only standard."

A flicker of concern crossed Bingley's face. "They were all good people," he protested.

"They were, Charles," added Miss Bingley. "But therein lays the problem. They were merely good. They lacked the connections, the breeding, the status to which we are accustomed…to which we are entitled."

Bingley turned back to Darcy. "Are you of the opinion, then, that I should not make an offer to purchase Netherfield?"

"I do not believe you should."

Bingley suddenly stood up and shook his head violently." But what of Miss Bennet? I must go back so I can further our acquaintance!"

Darcy walked over to him. He normally stood a few inches taller than his friend, but the distance seemed greater now, as Bingley's posture was slightly slumped and Darcy's very erect.

"For what purpose, man?" Darcy asked, his mouth suddenly dry.

"What purpose? She is an angel! She is everything I have longed for! I intend to offer her—"

"Bingley." Darcy subdued him by placing both hands firmly on his shoulders and looked him squarely in the eye. "Certainly you viewed Miss Bennet as nothing more than a delightful distraction."

"Delightful distraction! Good Lord, Darcy! She was much more to me than that! Could you not see how taken I was by her?"

"But was she as taken with you?"

Bingley's eyes narrowed as he looked from his friend to his sister and then back to his friend. "Yes, I believe she was."

Miss Bingley stepped forward and with a cunning, condescending smile said, "Indeed, she is a very sweet, amiable girl, Charles, the most delightful person in all of Hertfordshire, but..." She looked beseechingly at Darcy for assistance.

"But what?" Bingley demanded.

Darcy spoke softly, but forcefully, to his friend. "Bingley, it pains me to say this, but she exhibited no outward regard for you. She received your attentions very politely..."

"Politely?" Bingley interrupted, his countenance reddening and his whole demeanor shaking. "You are all quite mistaken!"

"Bingley, consider this. You came to Hertfordshire and singled her out. Without taking into consideration her family connections, you deemed her worthy of your undivided esteem. With the pressure from her mother to secure a husband of at least moderate fortune as their home is entailed away, she had no choice but to accept your attentions."

153

"No! It is much more than that!" Bingley directed his attention to Louisa and her husband, who had been sitting quietly, observing the machinations of Darcy and Miss Bingley. "Certainly you beheld her admiration for me!"

Louisa raised her eyebrow and shook her head. "No, my dear brother, I honestly cannot say I did."

In a fit of frustration, Bingley pounded his fist against the wall. "You did not make her acquaintance as deeply as I, nor did you apprehend the admiration in her eyes as she spoke, the tenderness of her voice, or the warmth in her smile. She loves me! I am convinced of it! And I love her!"

"Bingley, I am willing to allow that she has a most serene nature, but there is more to consider than merely that and her angelic beauty." Darcy fortified himself with a deep breath and continued. "She is continually pressured by her mother to marry a man of fortune, her family connections are nothing, their behavior time and again points toward their ill-breeding, and she challenges every word you say!" His eyes flashed with anger.

Every eye turned in astonishment to Darcy, who closed his own as he realized his blunder.

"Challenges my every word?" gasped Bingley. "How could you accuse her of such a thing?" He sat down, completely spent. Shaking his head, he softly uttered, "You just do not know her. None of you. You do not know her!"

Miss Bingley interjected while Darcy made an attempt to gain back his composure. "Charles, Miss Bennet may have appeared to be everything you have ever wished for in a woman, but is it worth taking the risk of going into a marriage where love is not returned?"

Bingley's face lost all expression, paled, and he looked down at the ground. "I... I..." He shook his head and raked his fingers through his hair. "I really thought she returned my affection. How could I have been so mistaken?"

Miss Bingley threw a triumphant smile at Darcy and then drew near to her brother, placing a hand lightly upon his shoulder. "Love can sometimes blind us, Charles, and we need those who love and care for us to point these things out when we cannot see them ourselves."

Darcy stepped back and leaned against the wall for support. The fire in his eyes was suddenly displaced by a searing pain and anguish. Despite the apparent victory, a sense of defeat and resignation swept over him as he realized he felt as much grief in losing Miss Elizabeth as his friend felt in losing Miss Bennet.

Charlotte Waits at Lucas Lodge

by Abigail Reynolds

November 29, 1811

Charlotte wrapped herself in a second shawl and returned to the window seat in the upstairs sitting room. The windowpanes were still edged with early morning frost. It was too cold for sitting so far from the fire, but it served the purpose of keeping her family at a distance. Her younger sisters were sitting as close to the hearth as possible, and it was too much trouble for them to call over to her every time they wanted to include her in the conversation.

After spending three days listening to Mr. Collins's excess verbiage, she was not in a mood to converse with anyone. She prayed that all her attentiveness had not been for naught. After dinner last night, she had thought him on the verge of making her an offer when he rambled on about his hopes for the companion of his life. At the last moment he had changed the subject, despite all the encouragement she had given him, telling him how fortunate he was in his position, how anyone would envy his proximity to Rosings Park, and even expressing a desire to hear one of his sermons some day. She could understand how the set-downs Lizzy had given him would give him pause, but he was due to leave Hertfordshire the following day, which meant she had only one more chance to bring him to the point of proposing. As soon as the hour was late enough, she would pay a visit to Longbourn for a final effort.

She did not know what she would do if she failed, despite all the sleepless hours she had spent trying to resolve the issue. Her courses should have begun last week, and while it was not unusual for the time to differ for her from month to month, she feared the worst. Mr. Collins's arrival in search of a wife was providential. She could not like or respect him, but she could tolerate him, and he would take her away from Meryton and Willoughby's mocking eyes. He did not seem to care much that she was plain-featured as long as she flattered him. And he was safe—he was not clever enough to pull the wool over her eyes the way Mr. Robinson had. He was also dull enough that she could most likely fool him into believing her a virgin if she was careful to make sure he drank a few glasses of wedding brandy first. She could cry out as if in pain at the appropriate moment, and a pin secreted in the bed would serve to help her produce a few drops of blood for the sheets. But first he had to be brought to propose.

Just then she spotted a dim figure coming down the lane. A moment of blowing on the windowpane to clear the frost revealed it to be Mr. Collins himself, despite the early hour. An overwhelming wave of relief surged through her. She would not be disgraced; her family would not cast her off, leaving her to a life on the streets. Instead, she would be respectably married to a man of good prospects, and when she returned to Meryton someday, her position as mistress of Longbourn would put her above worries about what Willoughby might say or do. It was the perfect solution to her dilemma.

She would make it as easy for him as possible. Snatching up her bonnet, she hurried out the door, and set out to meet him accidentally in the lane.

Caroline's Letter to Jane

by Monica Fairview

December 18, 1811

Caroline was in the parlor instructing her housekeeper on household matters when the front doorbell rang.

The time for morning calls was over. Who could this be?

The unmistakable voice of Mr. Darcy reached her. She dismissed the housekeeper and looked to the doorway in anticipation.

"Mr. Darcy," announced the butler.

"Mr. Darcy?" said Caroline with a tinge of concern as he entered, for he looked pale and slightly disheveled. His cravat was askew and his perfectly combed hair was ruffled.

"Nothing has happened to Charles?" she said in alarm.

"No," said Mr. Darcy. "Charles was well when I last saw him."

She searched in her mind for a reason for his perturbance, but could find none.

"And dear Miss Darcy?"

"Georgiana is well."

"Won't you sit down, Mr. Darcy? I will ring for some tea."

Mr. Darcy sat down, but scarcely had she time to tug at the bell-pull when he was up again. He began to pace the room.

A sudden glimmer of hope rose up in Miss Bingley's heart. Her pulse quickened. She could only account for his strange behavior with one thing. Surely not? Could it be? Did he intend to...?

"Miss Bingley," he said.

Caroline pressed trembling hands together. This was it, the moment she had been aspiring to for so long.

"Miss Bingley," he said again.

Say it, willed Caroline. Say it.

"I have determined that you must write them a letter."

"A letter?" she gawked at him, though she never gawked, trying to make sense of his words. Her heart plummeted. She controlled her sense of disappointment with difficulty. Foolish, foolish girl, she told herself.

"Write a letter to whom, sir?" she asked. "You mock me surely? It is you who are the more experienced correspondent. You write such charming letters."

She was beginning to have an inkling what this was about. Bitter disappointment rose up in her.

"I cannot write to them with any propriety," said Mr. Darcy. "It would be unseemly."

She schooled herself to show no expression, but inside her heart was like lead.

"I am afraid you have lost me, Mr. Darcy. I do not understand you."

He put a hand to his brow and approached the armchair.

"You must write Miss Bennet a letter," he said urgently. "She will surely be expecting your brother to return to Netherfield. You must make matters entirely clear. You must remove from her mind any expectancy or desire for such a possibility."

Surely such a letter did not call for such turmoil. Was that the way of it, then? A woman's instinct does not fail her and she knew then that the message was not for Miss Jane Bennet at all but for Elizabeth Bennet.

Even as pain lanced through her, she felt a kind of fierce joy. He was denying himself then. He was bidding Elizabeth Bennet farewell.

159

"I shall write the letter, Mr. Darcy," she said. "You are perfectly correct, as always. We cannot give Miss Bennet false hope regarding my brother. It will not do at all. Tell me what I must say, and I will be happy to do so. I am always at your service, as you know, Mr. Darcy."

Charlotte Confesses Her Engagement to Elizabeth

by Abigail Reynolds

November 30, 1811

One dreaded task remained for Charlotte, and that was telling Lizzy about her engagement. Her dearest friend could not have made it clearer that she thought Mr. Collins barely worthy of acknowledgment, and this news would come as a blow to her. Charlotte's anxiety over the event was mixed with annoyance; after all, marrying Mr. Collins would be prudential even if she had no other incentive than a desire for independence, but Lizzy would not see it that way, and she had no intention of humiliating herself by telling her friend the whole truth.

Indeed, Lizzy's reaction was all that Charlotte had feared. "Engaged to Mr. Collins! My dear Charlotte—impossible!"

This reproach was so strong that for a moment Charlotte could not help biting her lip, wondering if she should tell her friend everything. She only regained her composure as she contemplated the unfairness of Lizzy's reaction. After all their years of friendship, apparently Lizzy still had no faith in her judgment.

Charlotte raised her chin slightly. "Why should you be surprised, my dear Eliza? Do you think it incredible that Mr. Collins should be able to procure any woman's good opinion, because he was not so happy as to succeed with you?"

Apparently Lizzy heard the reproach in her voice, for she sat quietly and took a deep breath before saying, "Of course not, my dear—it was merely that you took me by surprise. Of course I am pleased for you, and I wish you all imaginable happiness."

"I see what you are feeling," replied Charlotte. "You must be surprised, very much surprised, so lately as Mr. Collins was wishing to marry you. But when you have had time to think it all over, I hope you will be satisfied with what I have done. I am not romantic you know. I never was, I ask only a comfortable home; and considering Mr. Collins's character, connections, and situation in life, I am convinced that my chance of happiness with him is as fair as most people can boast on entering the marriage state." Lizzy was too young and innocent to realize that, compared to men like Mr. Willoughby and Mr. Robinson, Mr. Collins was a candidate for sainthood—or perhaps Lizzy was just fortunate enough never to have been mistreated by a man.

Elizabeth quietly answered, "Undoubtedly."

In the awkward silence that followed, Charlotte knew that Lizzy would never understand, and most likely would hold this decision against her forever. Would she lose her dearest friend as one more consequence of a night's indiscretion? But a still voice inside her reminded her that her intimate friend truly ought to have more faith that she knew what she was doing.

Mr. Collins and His Successful Love

by Diana Birchall

December 1, 1811

Mr. Collins was not left long to the silent contemplation of his successful love.
~Pride and Prejudice

Mrs. Bennet, on learning the result of the interview between Mr. Collins and her daughter, hurried to her husband's library, to remonstrate with him, and to insist on his making Lizzy marry Mr. Collins. While the three were talking over the matter, Mr. Collins, left alone in the breakfast room, had some time to consider his suit. It was true, he thought, that if Elizabeth continued to refuse, the question being put to her a second, and perhaps even a third time, he would be obliged to concede that she was, indeed, a headstrong, obstinate girl, who did not know her own good fortune in being selected by him from so many other young ladies, including her own sisters. He could not, however, admit the possibility of her being so foolish, for more than a moment. In the first place, his observation, by no means very acute, was at least tolerable enough to collect that Elizabeth was by far the wittiest and the brightest of the sisters. He had some doubt if her cleverness was quite necessary, or would please Lady Catherine; but surely, once married, she would submit, as a good wife ought, to her husband's will, and become quiet and obedient. Then, her mother had assured him that she was only foolish and headstrong in such matters as these, and he was perfectly willing to attribute her reluctance to maiden modesty and to take her real good-nature on faith.

163

Mr. Collins had studied Logic at Oxford, and by such like reasonings and deducings, he came, as quickly as the slow workings of his mind would permit, to the logical conclusion: Elizabeth would not persist in refusing him. At this very moment, her respected father must be having the word with her that would bring her to reason and compliance. Assured of a happy ending and a pretty and vivacious bride, Mr. Collins called for the servant to bring him writing-materials, and there, in the breakfast room, he happily composed a letter to his Patroness, Lady Catherine de Bourgh. Signing with a flourish and sealing it, he handed it to the servant with instructions to carry it to the post at once, and gave him, in the overflowing pride of his heart, an extra sixpence to speed it along.

This important letter was written, and sent, on the morning of Wednesday, the twenty-seventh of November; and as the servant put it into the morning post, the letter was received at Rosings, no later than Friday, and placed into Lady Catherine's hands. In the parson's absence, that lady had considered it highly praiseworthy and sensible to spend the morning looking into cottages, to make sure that everything inside them was going rightly. Her daughter was not strong enough for such an expedition, and Mrs. Jenkinson remained with her, but Lady Catherine sallied out in a party that included her great friend Lady Metcalfe, her two daughters, Annabella and Isabella, and their governess, Miss Pope.

Word had spread in the village that the ladies were abroad and on the prowl, and the people were in a panic. Some shut the doors tightly and pretended not to be home. Some housewives had the thought of jumping back into bed, pulling the covers up over their heads, and pretending to be sick. Others collected their children and fled to the market in haste. Lady Catherine and Lady Metcalfe, therefore, were quite shocked to find one cottage abandoned, with the fire still blazing merrily in the hearth; another with overturned footstools, children playing, and no housewife in sight; and in a third cottage, a woman apparently expiring of a chest complaint, for she could hardly breathe.

Lady Catherine flung open the door. "My good woman! Lady Metcalfe, have you ever heard such sterterous gasps? She must surely be dying. Fling water upon her, Annabella, will you?"

"Who can she be?" asked Lady Metcalfe, who was very short-sighted. "Poor woman! This is very dreadful."

"It is the Swansons' cottage, is not it, Harrison?" Lady Catherine addressed the governess. "Yes, I believe it is; Swanson is the carpenter, and will be in his shop, or out on some job of work. My good woman, are you able to speak? Where is your husband?"

"He has gone," came the faint whisper. "He has left me—and all my babies."

"Left you; has he? He had no business to do that. I will have a word with him, and he will behave better in future, if he ever wishes to be employed at Rosings again. But why, in his absence, have you kept this cottage so untidy? That floor has not been swept in a week." Lady Catherine ran a silken-gloved finger along the rough wooden mantelpiece. "Pah! I thought so. Soot, as black as night. A disgrace! No wonder you are having trouble breathing. Illness is no excuse for slovenliness. You must get up and dress immediately, Mrs. Swanson, upon my orders, and set about your tasks at once."

"She already is dressed, Lady Catherine," Isabella pointed out.

"Bless me, so she is! What can be the meaning of this? Is the wretched creature shamming?" Lady Catherine moved close to the bed and peered into the heap of blankets. With a swift movement, she pulled them away, revealing a fully clad countrywoman, apron, boots, and all. Leaping out of bed, the woman fell to her knees before her.

"Begging your pardon ma'am," she pleaded, "I was only a-lying down because—because I was took so bad. Jem—that is my husband—left before first light saying as he had a job over three miles past Hunsford, and I have a terrible suspicion he is taken with a woman over there."

"He has, has he," said Lady Catherine grimly. "I will settle that, quickly enough. Harrison, when we get back to Rosings, you will send a man after this recalcitrant workman. Mrs. Swanson, this is no time to be malingering. Your children are hungry, and I see here some potatoes. You ought to boil them, but don't serve them plain; the infants require some more nourishing food. Have you some meat handy?"

"No ma'am, nothing, my man hasn't left me with any money this last ten days you see," she protested sullenly.

"Never mind. Send your oldest boy—you there, run to the butcher's, at once, and tell him to bring your mother a pound of beef, with Lady Catherine's compliments." She turned swiftly to the lamenting woman. "You can pay for it by sewing for me later. Now, come along, Lady Metcalfe, I want to get to the bottom of the strange appearance of some of these other cottages."

Scarcely were they three feet from Mrs. Swanson's door, when a servant from Rosings came running up, a letter in his hand.

"What is that, Morton? What is the matter?"

"A letter come express, ma'am, from the minister, it is, and housekeeper said I was to run and find you," he panted.

"A letter? From Mr. Collins?" She turned it over, frowning. "Surely that might have waited. What can Mr. Collins have to say? He is expected back here tomorrow. I hope he has not written to put off his return."

"Open it and see," pursued Lady Metcalfe. "I confess myself to be curious."

"Very well." Lady Catherine opened the fine seal, and after perusing the letter for a moment, exclaimed. "Gracious Heaven! He has found a wife already."

"Mr. Collins, married?" Lady Metcalfe exclaimed.

"No, no. I will read it to you."

Longbourn House, near Meryton.

To the Right Honorable Lady Catherine de Bourgh,

Your Ladyship will forgive me for addressing you in so unexpected and forward a manner, as may not entirely become one of my station, but that it seems to me the office of clergyman in the Church of England is equal to the highest in the land, always supposing his duties are carried out in the spirit of humble self-effacement that I am always wont to practice. I believe I do not presume too highly, in supposing that you will evince all the gracious kindness I have already met with from you, in receiving the news which I am about to relate. I have found the young woman whom I have nominated to be my wife; and when I return into Kent on Saturday, I expect to be in the happy profession of an affianced man. The young lady has not quite accepted my overtures as yet, which is natural, in her modesty and timidity; but she is with her father at this moment, and I have no doubt that she will emerge from his sanctum carrying the orders that will make her consent to be my wife.

This young lady, who is to be united with me as soon as may be, is the second daughter of my cousin Mr. Bennet, whose heir by entail you know I have the honor to be; and although her fortune is negligible, yet it is a highly estimable connection. And Miss Elizabeth makes up for her lack of wealth, by all the qualities that make a true lady and worthy helpmeet. She has wit, and vivacity, to charm me and to brighten our fireside circle at Rosings if I may presume so far; but she also possesses the virtues of economy, prudence, and obedience, as well as youth, good health, and a capacity for hard work that will perfectly suit the situation of a clergyman's wife. I therefore apply for your approval for my seeking her hand, and hope for a speedy acquiescence from the young lady, on which you may depend I shall bring you the happy tidings on Saturday.

I remain, your devoted, honored, and obedient servant, William Collins.

"Well! That is remarkable," finished Lady Catherine dryly.

"Hm! Very suitable, I suppose," said Lady Metcalfe.

Lady Catherine noticed the same, and putting the letter into her reticule, she climbed into the carriage and directed the coachman to take them home forthwith. They talked of the remarkable letter all the rest of the wet afternoon.

Mr. Collins returned to Hunsford late on Saturday, and the ladies did not see him until church on Sunday morning. There was no opportunity to speak to him, therefore, until they shook his hand after the service, which might not have seemed the best moment to speak of secular matters, but Lady Catherine thought marriage a sacrament, and therefore a subject perfectly suitable for Sunday. As he bowed low over her hand, she condescended to allow a sly smile to linger on her strong features.

"I believe, if I am not mistaken, that we may have occasion, today, to congratulate you, Mr. Collins?"

He looked up, turned violently red, and stammered as he nodded. "Oh! Yes, yes. That is true. I am indeed the happiest of men, in securing to myself the hand and heart of my most beloved Charlotte."

Lady Catherine looked puzzled. "Charlotte? Excuse me, but I thought your affianced was called Elizabeth. Miss Bennet, is not she?"

"No, no, she is Miss Charlotte Lucas, of Lucas Lodge. The daughter of Sir William Lucas, the neighbor of—of my cousin, Mr. Bennet."

"Here is some mistake. You wrote to me that you were engaged to Mr. Bennet's daughter. I am sure of it. I have the letter here." She lifted her heavily marked eyebrows in some surprise, and indicated her reticule.

"Yes, yes I know I did, but—I must explain—confidentially, that is — Miss Bennet did not accept—and Miss Lucas was—"

He stopped, in confusion, as a hearty man of fifty came up with his wife and train of children, extending his hand.

"A fine sermon, Collins, 'pon my word! My compliments, Lady Catherine," with a bow.

"Good morning, Sir Basil," said Lady Catherine distractedly. "Mr. Collins, we will speak of this later. Come to tea this afternoon, if you will," she nodded at him with firm finality, gathered her skirts, her daughter and her companion, and moved toward her carriage.

"Yes—certainly, Lady Catherine," he called after her forlornly. For Mr. Collins yet dreaded making known to her the circumstances of his engagement, undoubtedly happy though he was in his successful love.

Mrs. Bennet Consoles Jane

by Kara Louise

December 10, 1811

Jane has received the letter from Miss Bingley declaring they will not be returning to Netherfield and that she has every hope that her brother will soon marry Miss Darcy.

Mrs. Bennet hurried through the hallway to Mr. Bennet's study. Without thinking, she pushed open the door and came to an abrupt halt in front of her husband's desk.

Mr. Bennet slowly lifted his head. His bushy eyebrows lowered, partially covering the eyes that looked up to her. "Mrs. Bennet, have I not requested that you knock before you come bursting into my study? Have I not asked that you not disturb my peace unless it is of utmost importance?"

She waved her hands in agitation. "Oh, but Mr. Bennet, I assure you, it is! This is most distressing! I do not know what can be done about it!"

Mr. Bennet lifted a brow and tilted his head. "Distressing?" He put down his book and leaned back in his chair. Folding his arms across him, he said, "What is it, my dear?"

"It is Jane! And Mr. Bingley! He is not to return to Netherfield! She has received a letter from his sister. It is all for naught! These past few months with all our high hopes and expectations have been in vain! I do not think he intends to marry our Jane! What can be done?"

Mr. Bennet looked down and shook his head. He fingered some papers on his desk in silence, while Mrs. Bennet waited fretfully.

When he looked back up, he asked, "What am I to do about it? If that is his decision, there is nothing that can be done!"

Mrs. Bennet leaned towards her husband. "What do you suppose our Jane did? He must have some reason for not returning. Do you suppose she said something he found unseemly? Could her behaviour have been unbecoming?" She suddenly turned, pounding her fists through the air. "Oh, I do not know what to do!"

He folded his hands, pressed his lips together, and then finally answered, "I do not believe Jane would ever do or say anything improper, but I would suggest you go to Jane to console and reassure her. She must be bitterly grieved and disappointed."

"Yes! That is what I will do. And I will try to find out what she did to bring about this unexpected predicament!"

Mr. Bennet lifted his hand to voice his objection, but his wife quickly departed the room before he could say anything.

Mrs. Bennet went in search of Jane and found her with Elizabeth, both sitting on Jane's bed. Elizabeth's head leaned against Jane's, and her arm was wrapped about her sister's shoulder, which shook as she silently sobbed.

Mrs. Bennet entered the room with her arms braced on her hips. Elizabeth looked up, and her brows quickly lowered.

"Lizzy, I must talk with Jane. Run along."

Elizabeth was not certain she wanted to leave her sister alone with her mother.

"Please, I need to be here for Jane."

"As do I!" insisted Mrs. Bennet, who then looked at Jane. "A mother always wants to console her child!"

Elizabeth could readily see the look on their mother's face, and her posture displayed more irritation than a desire to console. She knew Jane did not need to have their mother question her about what may have happened.

Jane slowly glanced up and looked at her mother through reddened eyes. "Thank you, Mama, but I want Lizzy to stay with me." She clutched a handkerchief and brought it up to wipe away a tear that trailed down her cheek.

"If you insist, but I ask that you remain silent, Lizzy, while I speak with... console Jane." Mrs. Bennet forced a smile and sat down on the bed on the other side of Jane. "We want you to know, dearest Jane, that we are as upset as you are about this news." She reached over and took one of Jane's hands. As she stroked it lightly, she said, "We all liked Mr. Bingley quite well. He was always so polite and amiable."

Jane drew in a shaky breath and mumbled, "He was."

Mrs. Bennet continued to stroke Jane's hand and soon began to pat it lightly. "I am deeply grieved over this, as I am certain you are. I do not think you will find a finer man than Mr. Bingley."

Jane silently nodded, while Elizabeth clenched her jaw to help her remain silent as her mother requested.

Mrs. Bennet's pats on Jane's hand became quicker. "But, what could have prompted this decision not to return?"

Jane's fingers trembled as she fingered the handkerchief. "I do not know. He seemed most attentive to me at the Netherfield Ball," she said in a quaking voice.

Elizabeth could hold her tongue no longer. "Mother, we do not know why he has chosen not to return. We can only hope this is a misunderstanding on Miss Bingley's part."

Mrs. Bennet pulled a handkerchief out of the bodice of her dress and began fanning herself with it. "You must tell me if there was anything you did that may have upset him." The pats she gave to Jane's hand now were sharp and in cadence with her words.

"Mother!" Elizabeth cried out. "Jane would do nothing—"

Jane put up her hand to silence her sister. "No, it is an honest request." She glanced at her mother. "I have asked myself that same question, but I fear I cannot think of anything I said or might have done that would have prompted this decision of his."

"There was nothing you *ever* could have done to warrant such an action!" Elizabeth assured her sister.

Mrs. Bennet frowned and she abruptly moved both her hands onto her lap. As she took in a deep breath, her shoulders raised and then lowered as she let the breath out. "Something *must* have occurred to cause him to leave Netherfield so abruptly." She looked sternly at Jane. "Think on it, Jane, for you cannot allow such a thing ever to happen again!"

She rose to leave and then stopped. "Oh, dearest Jane. I would have you know that I suffered a great heartache when I was younger, and like me, you will soon forget him. I hope that gives you some consolation."

Jane and Elizabeth watched silently as their mother walked out the door.

Jane turned to her sister. "Oh, Lizzy, Mama may be correct that it was my fault, but I cannot imagine what I may have done to bring this about!"

Elizabeth glanced over at the empty doorway. "Oh, dearest Jane. Do not fret that it was anything *you* said or did."

She felt a tight knot growing inside as she recollected the behaviour of her younger sisters, her father, and more particularly, her mother, at the Netherfield Ball. She had seen the expressions of disapproval on the faces of both Mr. Darcy and Miss Bingley, although she had not witnessed any look of displeasure or censure from Mr. Bingley. She was fairly certain this decision was due more in part to Mr. Bingley's friend and sister than with him.

No, she was certain Mr. Bingley's abrupt change of plans could not be attributed to Jane, but she doubted that other members of the Bennet family could be considered as blameless as her favorite sister was.

Lady Catherine's Christmas

by Diana Birchall

December 25, 1811

Christmas makes the strongest demands of any sacred day upon a clergyman, but one might particularly feel for Mr. Collins, whose maiden Christmas sermon he must preach before his formidable patroness, Lady Catherine de Bourgh. All went off well, however, and he was gratified to be invited, after his efforts, to take his Christmas dinner at Rosings. To him this was the crown of his ambitions, and he took his seat at the foot of the table, and followed Lady Catherine's minute directions for carving the roast of beef, with such alacrity and compliance that her ladyship actually smiled upon him.

"I must say, Mr. Collins, you make a better job of carving than our previous clergyman, Mr. Horner, ever did. I never could persuade him attend to my instructions properly. He would always carve the meat against the grain, and it ended, as it must, in strings. Strings, Mr. Collins!" Her Ladyship told him.

"Strings! Very sad, upon my word," he answered, looking complacently at the platefuls he was filling rapidly with nice thick rosy slabs.

"Yes; and he never would listen to my directions about his sermons, either. Quite indecent, they were. Why, once he preached a sermon about how the sin of pride would keep one out of Heaven, and he looked most meaningly at me for its entire length. Insufferable man!"

"And I do believe," put in Mrs. Jenkinson, Miss de Bourgh's companion, "that he had designs in matrimony—above his station." She nodded and winked vigorously, so the lace on her specially fashioned Christmas headdress swung, as she cast her eyes on Miss de Bourgh, who blushed and simpered.

"That is never to be spoken of, Miss Jenkinson," said Lady Catherine severely. "Never. What the man's presumptions might be is no concern of ours."

"Shocking, shocking," chimed in Mr. Collins, starting to attack his beef and parsnips with a good will. "A clergyman, of all people, ought to know the meaning of the hymn, 'The rich man in his castle, the poor man at his gate, God made them high and lowly, and ordered their estate.'"

"That might be the subject of your next sermon," ventured Miss de Bourgh with the air of saying something very daring.

"Indeed it might," nodded Lady Catherine, "those fine sentiments cannot be too widely promulgated."

"I hope," asserted Mr. Collins, "that I know my place. A clergyman such as myself, should be very certain to know it. A man of the cloth, educated at Oxford as I was, is of course a gentleman, equal in some ways to any in the land; yet in his calling, he must ever show a proper humility. That is exactly what I did when I cogitated upon the important matter of selecting a companion for my future life."

"And you seem to have done it very well," said Lady Catherine approvingly. "Mrs. Collins, that is to be, has no ideas or airs above her station, I collect, but is a modest country woman, who knows how to mend and make do."

"Indeed, that she is; my Charlotte is a very model for prudence and economy. I will warrant, Lady Catherine, that you will find nothing at all in her to disapprove."

"I am sure of that. I know, in fact, that you have chosen where you should, and as you should. It will be well to have a clergyman who is wisely married, and not subject to any preposterous ideas."

"Oh, I hope I never have any ideas at all, Lady Catherine," he assured her earnestly. "That would be most inappropriate—most unfit. To think of your daughter, who might marry anyone!"

Lady Catherine drank a glass of French wine reflectively, and swirled it in its crystal. "Yes—that is the question. Now that you are so soon to be married yourself, Mr. Collins, and as you are a man of the cloth, after all, I believe I may confide in you."

"Confide—in me?" he almost stammered, and lay down his knife lest he drop it in his excitement. "It would be the greatest honor of my life, and be very sure that you may count upon me, in my sacred office, to keep anything you say, perfectly confidential."

"I am sure you would," she nodded, and fixing him with her penetrating dark eye, she proceeded. "You are an uncommonly intelligent young man, Mr. Collins, with more than ordinary perception, and I suppose it has occurred to you to wonder about my daughter's marriage, has not it?"

"It is not my place, madam," he began, but she continued.

"What you may not be aware is that my late sister, Lady Anne Darcy, and myself, destined her to be the bride of her son and my nephew, Mr. Darcy. You have met that gentleman, I believe?"

"Why yes, I have indeed. I told you he was at Netherfield, the home of some neighbors of my cousins at Longbourn. They—the Bingleys, I mean—perhaps had hopes that he would become attached to Mr. Bingley's sister, but I never saw any sign of it."

"Naturally not. His hand and heart are both intentioned to be the property of my daughter."

"Oh!" Mr. Collins clasped his hands together with an ecstatic smack. "That will be a marriage such as has never been seen before between Kent and Derbyshire. What an alliance of family and fortune, to say nothing of the abundant personal qualities of gentleman and lady!"

"They will be a most handsome couple," added Mrs. Jenkinson, tipping her head affectedly.

"When is the wedding to be?" asked Mr. Collins. "You know I am engaged to bring my Charlotte into Kent only a scant few days after these Christmas festivities. I hope we will be in our little nest at Hunsford before the middle of January. As I will be traveling to bring her to her new home, I probably ought not to offer to be available for the ceremony before the fifteenth, or perhaps the twentieth, of that month. But I need hardly tell you how honored, how gratified, I would be, to perform these distinguished nuptials. Unless," a thought distracted him, "you mean her to be married in Derbyshire?"

"No, no, Mr. Collins, you mistake me." Lady Catherine's dark brows beetled together and she looked thunderous, so that Mr. Collins quailed.

"Have I said anything—" he said with compunction, trembling a little.

"Certainly not. It is only that I have not made myself clear. There is no engagement as yet."

"No engagement? But I thought the match was planned, between you and Mrs. Anne Darcy.

"So it was, and Anne is docile and obedient in this matter, just as she ought to be. The difficulty is the gentleman himself. He is more than of age, and yet he has never come forward to fulfill the pledge made by his mother."

"That is bad—very bad," commented Mr. Collins. "What do you suppose is the reason for this hesitation?"

"I am afraid," said Lady Catherine grimly, "that he has a spark of self-will, my nephew. It is difficult for us to conceive, but he may consider that a promise made by his mother, and not by himself, is not a necessary one to keep."

"Oh, surely that could never be!" Mr. Collins drew back in horror. "That would hardly be possible. Mr. Darcy is a byword for proper thinking and behavior, he is a very fine gentleman, from all I have ever heard, and seen with my own eyes. I have had quite a bit of conversation with him, too. You know I consider myself a judge of gentlemanly behavior, as is only proper and becoming to my position."

"Have you conversed with him, indeed? Then you may have seen something of his pride and self-will."

"He was all graciousness and condescension to me, I assure you, Lady Catherine. My cousin Elizabeth—" He pronounced her name with a little embarrassment that his patroness did not miss, "she wanted to check me from speaking to him; but I told her I must know better than a young lady like herself, and I was right."

"Miss Elizabeth," said Lady Catherine suspiciously. "Is she one of your cousin's daughters?"

"Yes, she is. The second," he said shortly.

"Is she a pretty girl?"

"Some might say so. I prefer, I confess, the looks of my own dear Charlotte."

"As is very proper. But this Miss Elizabeth—she is acquainted with Mr. Darcy?"

"She is indeed. They danced together at Netherfield, and it was the talk of the neighborhood."

Lady Catherine was silent for a moment. "So!" she exclaimed, in a tone of extreme anger. "This is where the mischief lies!" She pondered a little longer. "Wait—that letter you wrote to me, announcing your engagement to one of your cousin's daughters. This girl is the one?"

Mr. Collins was beet red in his confusion. "Yes—no—it was all a mistake. I never had any serious thought but for anyone but my Charlotte," he stammered.

"So, this girl is a minx and a vixen, and she is causing trouble." Lady Catherine nodded emphatically to herself. "I knew there was something amiss somewhere. It is well. I thought things were awry when we were not invited to Pemberley this Christmas."

She drummed her thick fingers on the lace-covered mahogany table. Everyone was silent as she considered. "I know what I must do," she said at last.

"Wh —what?" asked Mr. Collins, awed.

"I will go to Pemberley this minute. Yes, and take Anne, and you may accompany us, Mrs. Jenkinson. Summon the maids to pack, and tell Harris to inform the coachman to make ready for a long trip with the best horses. If we leave immediately after breakfast tomorrow, we will be only one night on the road, and be at Pemberley by this time the following night."

"What will you do there, madam, if I may ask? Am I to remain here?" asked Mr. Collins nervously.

"Certainly you are to remain here," she said impatiently. "You are not going into Hertfordshire yet, and we will return well before it is time for your own wedding-journey. No, I am going to see Mr. Darcy," she stood and rapped her mahogany stick sharply on the shining floor, "and make him see what is his duty."

Christmas Dinner at Longbourn

by Maria Grace

December 25, 1811

Later that night, Elizabeth paced the very clean drawing room, waiting for their guests to arrive. Fresh evergreen and holly filled the room with the season's fragrances, tied with cheery red bows. It should have been a very pleasing scene, but the tension in the room threatened to suffocate her.

"Why do you not take a seat, Lizzy?" Aunt Gardiner asked.

"I should surely run mad if I did." It was quite possible that she might do so even if she wore a track in the carpets.

"It seems like they are so long in arriving tonight. I cannot wait for the officers to get here." Lydia peered out the window, wrapping the curtain around her shoulders.

"They are such agreeable company, so gallant and always in search of a spot of fun." Kitty bounced in her seat

"Do sit still. It is unbecoming to twitch about like a hound waiting to be fed." Mary folded her hands in her lap and adjusted her posture to something entirely stiff and proper. "And unwind yourself from the curtains before you tear them off the wall entirely."

"You need not be so disagreeable. It is not as if you are anticipating anyone special to arrive." Lydia sniffed and rolled her eyes.

"Lydia!" Aunt Gardiner slapped the sofa cushion beside her.

180

"Well, it is true. None of the officers like her, for she is so very dull."

Mary's cheeks colored, and her lips pressed tight into something not quite a frown, but nearly.

"Your opinions are not helpful, nor are they kind."

"But they are true," Lydia whispered.

"Lydia!" Jane's eyes bulged the way they usually did when someone said something distasteful.

Lydia huffed and tossed her head.

The front door creaked and voices drifted upstairs.

"Oh, oh, someone is here! I think I recognize Sanderson's voice." Kitty clapped softly.

Lydia and Kitty pinched their cheeks and checked their bodices. Mary moved to the pianoforte.

"Would you favor us with a light welcoming piece?" Aunt Gardiner asked, but it was more of a directive than a question.

At least Mary did not seem too disgruntled by it. If anything, she looked pleased to have her accomplishments recognized.

Mama swept in with several officers in her wake.

"Sister, may I introduce Lieutenants Wickham, Denny and Sanderson."

Aunt Gardiner rose and curtsied. "Pleased to make your acquaintance, I am sure."

"Thank you for admitting us to your acquaintance, madam." Wickham bowed, his eyes shining. He always seemed to know the right thing to say.

Lydia and Kitty drew Denny and Sanderson away as Hill ushered Aunt and Uncle Philips in. Jane excused herself to attend them.

Aunt Gardiner cocked her head and lifted her eyebrow at Elizabeth. "My niece tells me you are from Derbyshire, sir."

"Indeed, I am, madam. Are you familiar with the county?"

"I spent my girlhood there, in the area of Lambton."

Wickham's eyes brightened and his face softened with a smile so compelling even a French officer would have been drawn in. "I lived on an estate very near there, Pemberley, if you know it."

"I do indeed. One of the loveliest places I have ever seen. We were by no means in such a way to keep company with the family there, but we heard much of their good name whilst we lived there." Aunt Gardiner's eyes always shone when she spoke of her girlhood home.

"I was privileged to live on Pemberley, my father was steward there."

"Then you were well-favored indeed. Have you been there recently?"

"Very little since the death of old Mr. Darcy. While old Darcy was a very good and kind man, and very well disposed toward myself, I am afraid his son did not inherit his father's noble traits." He glanced at Elizabeth, such suffering in his eyes, her own misted.

She nodded for him to continue. Surely Aunt Gardiner would be interested to hear his account in all its fullness.

"I have no desire to burden you with such tales as would dampen your spirits on this very fine occasion. Let us talk of acquaintances we may share in common. Did you know the old apothecary there, Mr. Burris, I believe his name was."

"He was a great favorite of my father."

"Of mine, as well." Though Wickham had been little there since five years before, it was yet in his power to give her fresher intelligence of her former friends than she had been in the way of procuring.

It did not take too long for their recollection of shared society to turn to a discussion of old Mr. Darcy's character, whom both liberally praised. The conversation then moved on to the current Mr. Darcy and his treatment of Wickham.

"I grant you, that I recall the younger Mr. Darcy spoken of as a very proud, ill-natured boy, but the charges you lay at his feet are quite alarming sir. I am surprised you have not been able to bring some kind of influence to bear against him."

"Would that were possible, madam, I would probably be the better for it. In truth, though, I still hold his father in far too high a regard to be able to take action against his son. The thought of bringing old Mr. Darcy pain is far too disturbing to brook."

"But surely you must consider how his own son's behavior would distress him. He might have been very pleased to see its improvement. I know that to be the case if it were one of my own children charged with such heartlessness."

"You might be very right, but surely you can see I am not the one suited by station or inclination to bring correction to such a man. So I shall continue on as I have been, grateful to such friends as I still have around me. I am truly blessed to have some very staunch supporters."

"I imagine so." Aunt's eyebrow raised into an elegant arch. "You demonstrate very great forbearance, quite the model of a gentleman."

There was something in Aunt's tone, the faintest bit sharp. Elizabeth tried to catch her eye, but she looked over Elizabeth's shoulder. Elizabeth glanced back. Jane and Aunt Philips approached.

"How are you enjoying your visit, sister? Is not the company tonight delightful?" Aunt Philips extended her hands toward Aunt Gardiner, but glowered at Elizabeth.

Aunt Gardiner took Aunt Philips' hands and kissed her cheeks. "Indeed it is. But we always appreciate the hospitality at Longbourn; I should hardly expect anything else."

"Mr. Wickham, it is especially nice to see you and the other officers here tonight as well. We have missed your company of late."

"I regret any discomfiture I might have caused, but I am honored my absence might have been noticed." Wickham bowed from his shoulders.

"Of course, it was, of course it was. I am very pleased to see *you*, Miss Lizzy, are not above keeping such very plain company with us tonight." Aunt Phillips's lip curled just the way Mama's did when she was angry.

Elizabeth had been seeing a great deal of that expression lately.

"Whatever do you mean?" Aunt Gardiner's honeyed tone had been known to placate tired children and churlish adults alike. "Elizabeth is always a sparkling companion."

"In company she deigns to keep, of course she is. It is just possible her opinion of herself has grown a mite higher than it should."

Elizabeth's face grew cold, but her cheeks burned.

Mama burst into the room. "Shall we all to dinner?"

"Might I escort you, Miss Elizabeth?" Mr. Wickham offered his arm.

Elizabeth muttered something, curtsied to her aunts and took Mr. Wickham's arm.

"Thank you." The words barely slipped past her tight throat. "Pray excuse my Aunt's indelicate choice of conversation."

"What indelicate choice, Miss Elizabeth? You do not think her conversation reflected in any way upon you, do you? I have found when people resort to dialogue, which some may consider disagreeable, it is most often attributable to indigestion."

Elizabeth snickered under her breath.

"Perhaps it would be wise to suggest she have a few words with her cook. A change in diet might be the very thing to relieve her discomfort and improve her general disposition. See there, how her husband is red in the face and his hand is pressed so obviously to his belly? I would venture to say he may be suffering from indigestion, too, and it is his cook and no one else to blame."

It would seem Mr. Wickham did not, or chose not to, see Mama at Uncle Philips' side, speaking with great animation and casting sidelong glances toward Elizabeth.

"I shall suggest that to her." The words came easier now. She forced her lips up into something resembling a smile.

"Ah, that is a far better expression for you, Miss Elizabeth. Unhappiness does not suit you at all."

"It appears it is difficult to be unhappy in your presence sir. Do you make it your business to drive away such specters wherever they might appear?"

"I certainly do. What better occupation in life than to bring happiness where ever I wander?"

How very true, and how very different than Mr. Darcy. To maintain such a disposition despite the very great unfairness and trials he had faced. Mr. Wickham was truly too kind.

For all Mama's fussing and fluttering, she did set one of the finest tables in the county. Candlelight glittered off mirrors and crystal, filling every corner of the dining room with sparkling warmth. The table and sideboards groaned under the weight of the dishes heaped with fragrant offerings. The huge goose lay near Papa's place, waiting for him to carve it. Elizabeth's mouth watered. Nothing tasted like a Christmas goose.

Wickham held the chair for her and sat beside her, politely ignoring Lydia's cross look. What did she have to be cross about though? With Denny on one side and Sanderson on the other, it was not as if she would be in want of company and conversation herself.

Mama sat up very straight and rang a little silver bell. The door swung open and Hill appeared, holding a platter of roasted boar's head high. Her arms quivered under the massive offering.

Denny and Sanderson jumped to their feet, nearly knocking their chairs to the floor, and rushed to her aid. Together they made a lovely show of bringing the final dish to the table. Though Mama glared at Hill, she seemed very pleased at the officers' efforts and settled into her comfortable role, presiding over the table.

Wickham leaned toward her. "It has been quite some time since I have enjoyed such a Christmas feast."

"I hope then, you take every opportunity to enjoy this one."

He served her from the platter of roast potatoes nearby. "I will certainly do just that and lock it into my memory to treasure against times which may be far less agreeable."

"I am sure it is difficult to spend Christmastide away from one's home and family. The militia requires a great deal from you."

"I find that it gives back as much as it demands. It is not at all disagreeable for one in my state. The hardships do not at all compare to those I suffered the first Christmastide of my banishment from Pemberley."

"Banishment?"

"Perhaps that is too strong a word, you are right. It does not serve to be so melodramatic." He bowed his head. "You must forgive me, for it is the subject of some trying remembrances. Christmastide at Pemberley was a most wondrous season, filled with warmth and generosity. My family was invited to dine at Christmas dinner with the Master. A complete roast boar would be carried in by two footmen. A goose, venison, and roast beef would be on the table besides. I am sure it was a month's worth of food for my little family at least, all brought to table at once." He closed his eyes and licked his lips.

"I can imagine one might miss such extravagance."

"Pray, do not think I intended to belittle the wonderful hospitality Longbourn offers. Not at all. It has reminded me of much happier days and I am most grateful."

Mama's silver bell rang again and Hill, the maid, and two girls employed for just this evening hurried in to clear the first course. Platters and used dishes disappeared along with the table cloth. The second course dishes filled the empty table and fresh china appeared before them. Amidst the staff's efforts, Aunt Gardiner caught her eye, tipped her head toward Wickham and raised her eyebrows.

Elizabeth allowed a hint of a smile and shrugged. He was very pleasant company. What did she expect?

Mama announced the dishes, but the platter of minced pies needed no introduction.

Wickham placed a small pie on her plate, along with black butter and spiced apples. The first minced pie of Christmastide was always agreeable, but somehow it would be nothing to the ones that would later be made from the leavings of the Christmas feast.

Mama's bell rang again, and she slipped out of the dining room. Hill circled the room, snuffing candles until only one in each corner remained.

Although Mama repeated this ritual every year, somehow the flaming pudding entering on the silver platter, held high in Mama's arms never lost its thrill. Blue brandy flames, glinting and multiplying in the mirrors and crystal, cast dancing shadows along the wall turning the dining room, for those brief moments, into a magical fairyland.

Too soon, the flames died down. Hill and the maid scurried about relighting candles and the normal world reappeared with Mama standing over a great cannon ball of plum pudding. She broke into it and served generous slices.

"Mind the charms!" Mama's smile looked forced, and she averted her gaze from Elizabeth.

What better way to remind Mama of Elizabeth's transgressions than the pudding stirred up whilst she still had hopes of Mr. Collins. Pray let her not discover the ring, or better still, any charm in her pudding. Further notice from Mama could not be a good thing.

Elizabeth held her breath as the company partook in the pudding. Heavy, sweet, spicy and saturated with brandy, this was the taste of Christmas and family.

Uncle Gardiner laughed heartily. "What ho, what shall I do with this?" He held aloft a tiny thimble.

"Consider it for thrift, my dear." Aunt Gardiner winked at him.

Thank Providence that Mary was spared that omen!

Lydia squealed. "I have the coin! I shall come into a fortune."

Papa muttered something, but Elizabeth could not make it out. Probably best that way.

Wickham neatly pulled his slice apart with knife and fork. He dug in with his knife and lifted it to reveal a shining ring hanging on the blade.

"Now you've done it, Wickham!" Sanderson pointed at him, laughing.

"I would not go about showing that off, if I were you." Denny leaned back and held up open hands. "But whatever you do, keep it well away from me."

"So you shall be married this year, Mr. Wickham." Mama looked far too pleased.

Had there been any way to have achieved that end intentionally, Elizabeth would have though Mama manufactured this result. But such a thing was not possible. Still, the smug way she settled into her seat and dug into her own pudding begged the question.

"You may threaten all you like." Wickham slid the ring off the knife and held it up in the candlelight. "But I have no fear of this innocent little ring."

Did he just wink? At her?

Heat crept over the crest of her cheeks, but Aunt Gardiner's brows drew a little lower over her eyes and her forehead creased.

Darcy and the Harlequin

by Maria Grace

December 30, 1811

Darcy laid his newspaper aside. Miss Bingley should not have worried; her little dinner party hardly garnered any notice at all. A few brief words of Sir Andrew's and Lady Elizabeth's attendance and little more. Would she be gratified at the mention of her event or offended that it garnered no more notice than a few brief sentences? It was difficult to predict. No doubt he would find out soon.

The mantle clock chimed. Had he been traveling with his parents, they would have left by now. Mother was always determined to arrive early when they went to Drury Lane. The crush of people seemed less that way. She knew he found crowds unsettling.

Some things had changed very little, even decades later. Years of practice made it no easier for him. He could wear a mask of civility longer now, but that was all.

Mother had always been comfortable in a crowd, much like Bingley...or Miss Elizabeth. She seemed to know what to say and what to do to make people around her at ease. How did she do that?

The clock chimed the passing of another quarter hour. Procrastination would not make things any easier. He called for his carriage to be brought around.

The ride to the theater passed quickly, too quickly. He scanned the crowd for Hurst and Bingley's sisters. Several ladies turned toward him with inquiring glances. They followed his gaze into the crowd, as if trying to discern who he sought. He winced and pinched the bridge of his nose.

No, not her!

The woman in the outlandish purple hat with far too many feathers contributed to the society pages. The hat was new, but the abundance of feathers was the shrew's trademark, appearing in far too many of Darcy's nightmares. No doubt his innocent outing to the panto would be the subject of her pen, probably even tonight.

A white plume bobbed in the crowd and approached. Beneath it, Miss Bingley, with the Hursts tagging behind, approached.

"Good afternoon, Mr. Darcy." She and her feather dipped in a small curtsey. "How kind of you to join us."

"I appreciate Bingley's invitation."

He did not like to lie, but sometimes it was unavoidable.

"Shall we find our box before any more children arrive?" Hurst cast about the milling crowd, his upper lip pulled back. "Dashed inconvenient thing that these performances draw so many children who should be in the nursery."

Children who often behaved better than their parents once the performance whipped spirits into a frenzy. Young ones rarely incited a riot.

"At least we shall have none in our box." Miss Bingley tapped her fan on her palm.

"You do not like children?" Darcy asked.

"What is to like or not like? They are necessary. That is why nurses and governesses and boarding schools are employed." Miss Bingley shared a knowing glance with her sister.

"Hear, hear," Hurst waved his hand, ducked his chin and waded into the crowd.

Darcy ushered the ladies to follow Hurst and stepped behind to bring up the rear.

It should not bother him that Miss Bingley did not like children.

A woman of her rank had little need to. She was entirely correct. Nurses and governesses and tutors could relieve her of all need to interact with any offspring.

His mother had not felt that way about her children, though. How many times had she stolen away into the nursery for the opportunity to read to him from his favorite book?

The nurse used to assure her there was no need for the mistress to trouble herself. Still, Mother would not be gainsaid. Sometimes, Father would join her. He would fold himself in a tiny nursery chair to sit with them as she read.

Some of the servants thought the arrangement peculiar, but Mrs. Reynolds would not permit that sort of talk below stairs. He had once overheard her scolding a maid who dared criticize his parents for paying far too much attention to the goings on in the nursery.

What man did such a thing?

The kind of man Darcy wanted to be.

But that would require a wife. And more importantly, one who wanted to do more than merely birth her children.

Miss Elizabeth drew children to her. Walking on the streets of Meryton, nursery maids brought their charges to her. Miss Elizabeth would drop to a knee to address them eye to eye.

He had never been close enough to hear what they said to her or how she replied. But their laughter and looks of delight said enough. She was not the kind of woman to become a disinterested mother.

"What say you, Mr. Darcy?" Miss Bingley settled herself into the seat beside her sister.

What was she talking about?

"For heaven's sake, Miss Bingley, do not bother the man so. I have no doubt he does not care about the state of Mrs. What's-her-name's daughter's hat." Hurst flipped the tails of his coat out of the way and sat behind his wife. He gestured to the chair beside him.

A flash of purple in the next box over twisted his guts. Did Hurst recognize her, too? Not sitting next to Miss Bingley was a very good idea. He settled himself on the velvet covered chair.

The theater filled and soon the curtain parted. The crowd hushed, ready to be transported by the magic of the players.

He leaned forward, studying the stage. Mother had a remarkable eye for detail. She would whisper in his ear about this bit or that. It had been a game they played, who could discover the most about the details of the stage before the first player came out.

Miss Bingley preferred noticing the details of the other ladies who attended.

Masked characters entered the stage, Cinderella and her father. The masks and costumes were excellent and different to what he had seen before. Definitely distinct from a Drury Lane production.

Miss Bingley pressed her shoulder to her sister's and whispered something. "There, in the second rate seats, the fourth row," she gestured with her chin. "Do you see?"

Were they paying any attention to the production at all?

"I believe I do. In the pink dress? Sitting between the children?"

"Yes, yes. Do you think...?"

Darcy shifted, leaning on his elbow. Who were they looking at? He peered into the crowd, following their directions.

"Why yes, I think you are right. Oh, Caroline, what are we to do?"

How could they recognize someone by the back of her head, and why ever would it be so significant? Stuff and nonsense!

Darcy leaned back and returned his attention to the pantomime. Harlequin waved the slapstick and the Fairy Queen appeared to change the characters and the setting.

The corner of his lips rose just a mite. As a boy, this was his favorite part of the entire show. There was something innately appealing about such change being so easy and effortless, even if it was just a stage illusion.

Masks and outer robes fell away, set pieces turned and tipped and transformed. The world of the harlequinade appeared.

"Here we are again!" Clown cried from the stage and vaulted from one set piece to another.

The children in the audience, especially the youngest ones, jumped to their feel squealing and pointing. The young woman sitting in the fourth row below them turned to speak to the little girls beside her.

Darcy gasped.

Jane Bennet. What was she doing in London?

When had she come and how long was she to be here? More important, was her sister with her?

Darcy leaned as far forward as he could and peered into the crowd for any sign of Miss Elizabeth.

Not that he had any intention of speaking to her, no that would surely appear in the society pages. No, any public meeting with her would be impossible. But it would be pleasing to see her, to simply know she was in Town.

"She said she had an uncle in Cheapside."

Did Mrs. Hurst realize she sounded just like a hissing cat?

Perhaps she was merely capturing the spirit of the merry chase scene below them.

"No doubt she is staying with them. I can only guess her intentions are toward continuing her pursuit."

Perhaps not.

Cheapside? That was not very far. He could perhaps contrive to walk in that direction...regularly. No matter if she were in the city, Miss Elizabeth would arrange to take a morning walk, somehow. She was a creature of habit.

But she would not go out alone, a maid, or perhaps her sister, or even the children would accompany her. She might walk out with the nursery maid, or she even take the task from the maid altogether and entertain the children entirely on her own. Perhaps she would walk with them all the way to the tower green. The little boys would no doubt enjoy the opportunity to stretch their legs there in a good run.

Mother had sometimes taken him there when they stayed in town. How invigorating it had been to stretch his legs then with a good solid run. The confinement indoors had been one of the things he least liked about their visits to Town.

The tower green was the kind of place where one might accidentally encounter any number of persons. One might even have a brief conversation, an entirely unremarkable conversation. What might one say in such an encounter?

A contented murmur rippled through the crowd. Pantaloon placed Columbine's hand in Harlequin's. Cheers rose, all was now as it should be.

Darcy stood with Hurst and applauded, still searching the crowd for signs of Miss Elizabeth.

After a rousing chorus, to which the audience sang far too many repetitions, the players disappeared back behind stage. The crowd trickled out of the theater.

Miss Bingley pled a dislike of the crush, and insisted they remain in their box until much of the theater cleared. Mrs Hurst agreed, so there was little to be done but wait for their leisure.

Perhaps, though, it would be best for him to be seen leaving alone. That could go far in clearing up misunderstandings about the company he kept today. He rose.

"Pray, Mr. Darcy, do not leave us yet." Miss Bingley looked up at him, batting her eyes.

He knew that look far, far too well. Bingley was definitely wrong about his sister's intentions.

"Forgive me, but I definitely must go." He probably should not have come in the first place.

"Wait, I beg of you. There is a matter of very great import which we must discuss."

He took half a step back. "I have no idea to what you refer."

"Did you not see what we did, there in the audience below us? Jane Bennet."

"I observed a young woman who looked much like Miss Bennet."

"She did not look like Miss Bennet, she was Jane Bennet. I have no doubt whatsoever. Have you already forgotten why we insisted Charles keep to London and eschew his country house?"

In truth, for a moment, he had.

"I fear this is a most serious situation, very serious indeed. You were so integral to convincing Charles to remain in Town. I beg your assistance again. We must ensure that he does not become reacquainted with Miss Bennet here in Town. I am entirely certain he will not agree to yet another change of venue."

Darcy returned to his seat. "I understand your concern, but I hardly think it likely they should meet by some chance encounter. As I understood, her aunt and uncle are not often in company, and he is in trade. How many opportunities do you have to rub shoulders with tradesmen? No, I think it quite unlikely indeed. You have no reason for concern."

"You underestimate Charles's attachment to Miss Bennet. I have no doubt that should he learn of her being in the city, he will make every attempt to renew his acquaintance."

Was Bingley so very attached? It had not seemed so. But if he was, did that change anything about the situation?

"He well knows the danger such connections might pose to your family's standing. Surely he could not wish for Mrs. Bennet as a mother-in-law."

A shudder snaked down Darcy's spine. That would truly be an awful fate. That possibility alone should be enough to render any Bennet woman entirely undesirable. And yet...

The Darcy name and connections were recognized, well able to withstand a ridiculous connection or two. Not at all like the fragility of the Bingley line, so newly established amongst good society.

Miss Bingley fanned her face with her handkerchief. "One would think he had the sense to realize, but I am not entirely sure. We must agree to keep this news amongst ourselves. Charles must not suspect that *she* might be anywhere nearby."

"I abhor disguise—"

"I understand that, sir, and I hold your character in the greatest of respect. Consider what is at stake, though. Moreover, there is no deception being practiced here. We are merely choosing not to speak, not speaking falsehoods." A thin smile crept over her face, and she blinked a little faster.

The line between the two was very, very fine, perhaps too fine to truly distinguish between. Deception, active or passive, was deception, and as such was an affront to the Darcy character.

So then what was he to do? Should he go out of his way to mention that he had seen Miss Bennet? No, that would not do either.

"So long as he does not specifically ask if I have encountered Miss Bennet at the theater, I will hold my peace."

It was an uncomfortable compromise, but it was tolerable.

And necessary.

"I admire your principles, Mr. Darcy. I cannot imagine asking more of you. You are a good friend to my brother. We appreciate the way you are guiding him into society." She batted her eyes again.

"If that is all, then, pray excuse me. Good day." He bowed.

Her features drooped just a mite. "Good day, sir."

He turned and strode out as quickly as he could without breaking into a run. The sooner he left Miss Bingley's presence, and the longer he stayed out of it, the better it would be.

The long staircase was relatively empty. A definite blessing, given his frame of mind. Having to pick through a crowd might have left him running entirely mad.

Outside, he gulped the cooler, crisp air, exactly the balm he needed for Miss Bingley's attentions. Now, to find the coach.

Good man! His coachman had the coach waiting exactly where it should be, and he climbed in. Purple hat and feathers had observed his hasty exit from the theater and followed him at a discreet distance. She kept looking over her shoulder, as though she expected to find Miss Bingley trailing after him, or even more dramatic, left somewhere, crying bitter tears in the wake of his rejection. What a truly vile creature!

Even the possibility of seeing or meeting with Miss Elizabeth hardly outweighed the risk of being subject to that harpy. He needed to return to Pemberley soon, before the surveillance of the gossips drove him barmy.

But to do so without seeing Miss Elizabeth? That was hardly more acceptable.

He had several more social engagements demanding his presence. Leaving before those would cause more problems than it would solve. Surely he could find out whether Miss Elizabeth was in Town during that time.

He would; and then he would leave and be done with the intrigues of the *ton*.

First Footer

by Maria Grace

December 31, 1811

The Scene: Mr. Bingley and his party have left Netherfield. Jane has gone to London with the Gardiners.

"Hurry along now, hurry along." Papa ushered Kitty and Lydia ahead of him as he trudged down the stairs and into the parlor, exactly the same as he had done last year and the year before and the one before that.

Elizabeth turned aside and bit the inside of her cheek. Mama would scold if she sniggered aloud. *Proper young ladies do not laugh in company.*

Still, Jane would have shared a private laugh with her when they finally tucked into bed had she not already left with the Gardiners for London. Gone only a day and already she was sorely missed.

"You have had the maid remove all the ashes?" Papa pulled chairs toward the center of the room into a rough circle.

Mama flipped her skirts and settled into a seat. "Yes, yes, and Hill has given all the kitchen scraps away as well. I dare say your pointers are very happy tonight."

"Capital, capital." Papa nudged a final chair into place.

He asked the same questions every year. There was something quite comforting in his predictability.

"Truly Mr. Bennet, I do not understand why you insist upon this—"

"Do not say foolishness, Mrs. Bennet," he raised a warning finger.

She arranged the fringe on her shawl. "It is naught but superstition and nonsense."

"I endure your endless talk of lace and frippery. One evening of the year, it is not too much to ask of you—"

Mama harrumphed. "When you put it in those terms—"

"It is very nearly midnight," Kitty cried, clapping softly.

They all turned toward the venerable long-case clock in the corner, its hands nearly overlapping below the '12'.

Papa rose and hurried to the front door. The clock struck the first chime of midnight and he opened the door. "Welcome to eighteen twelve. Now to usher out eighteen eleven." He tromped through the hall to the back door. It creaked in protest and thumped against the wall like it always did when fully opened.

A sharp breeze whistled through the front door. Elizabeth rubbed her hands up and down her upper arms. Somehow, it always seemed to be windy on New Year's Eve.

"Do hurry along Mr. Bennet or we shall catch our deaths." Mama drew her shawl more tightly around her shoulders.

Papa waved her down as he passed through the parlor.

"Halloo there—is a first footer wanted here?"

Surely that could not be… Elizabeth rose, but Lydia and Kitty preceded her to the front door.

"Mr. Wickham!" Lydia squealed and shouldered Kitty out of her way.

How did he know Papa's custom? Surely Lydia must have suggested it! Did she know no propriety?

"Come in, come in." Papa ushered Mr. Wickham in and shut the door.

"A tall, dark and handsome man is the best first footer." Lydia clung to Mr. Wickham's right arm.

"But only if water will run under his foot." Kitty clutched his left.

They half escorted, half dragged him to the parlor.

He glanced at Elizabeth, who remained several steps behind them. It was difficult to determine whether he simply tolerated her sisters' attention with good humor, or he actually enjoyed them. In either case, he was jolly company.

"Sit down, Mr. Wickham, and let us see your feet." Lydia shoved a chair at him.

"You will find them very acceptable, Miss Lydia," he stammered.

Kitty pulled his arm and he stumbled into the seat.

"I believe we can take one of His Majesty's officers at his word regarding the shape of his feet." Papa folded his arms over his chest.

"Besides, I believe it equally significant that he does not arrive empty-handed." Elizabeth cocked her head and quirked her brow.

Mama glared and Mary rolled her eyes. But Mary had an excuse. She had hoped for Mr. Collins' attentions when Elizabeth had declined them. Since he turned them to Charlotte, Mary had been taciturn and broody.

Mama leaned toward her. "Do not be so rude. Mr. Wickham is welcome regardless—"

"No, Lizzy is right. It is a bad omen indeed for a first footer to arrive empty handed." Papa wagged his finger at Mr. Wickham.

"Never fear, my gracious hosts! I have come well prepared for the evening." He reached into the market bag slung over his shoulder. "Let me see now. Here is a coin." He handed it to Mama with a bow.

She giggled as she took it.

"And a bit of whiskey." He passed a flask to Papa. "Sweets for two sweet young ladies." He handed Lydia a piece of shortbread and Kitty a small black bun.

He must have visited Papa's favorite baker in town. That was the only place one could acquire a black bun in Meryton.

Elizabeth ran her knuckles along her lips. What could such diligence mean?

"And Miss Mary," he handed her a small paper packet, "for you, salt, replete with symbolism you best appreciate."

She took it, a little light returning to her eyes.

He turned to Elizabeth. "I fear all I have left for you is this." He held up a lump of coal.

"Lead him through the house and demonstrate the excellent work of your mother's staff. Then we may warm his welcome by putting the coal on the fire."

"Mr. Wickham does not need to see that the house is clean." Mama sniffed.

"And I am sure he would much rather a toast than to put coal on the fire." Lydia donned a well-practiced pout.

"At the right time, my girl." Papa twitched his head toward the door. "There is an order to these things that must not be forsaken."

"Indeed." Mr. Wickham offered his arm and Elizabeth slipped her hand into the crook of his elbow. They headed for the kitchen.

What had motivated him to choose her to accompany him? "You are very good to be so attentive to my father's traditions."

"It is a pleasure to offer service in whatever way I can." He bowed from his shoulders. "A man in my situation has so very few true joys in life I must indulge in the ones available to me whenever possible."

"Surely you exaggerate, sir."

"Perhaps I do, but can you blame me for taking every opportunity to call upon a family of so many fair sisters."

But was there one he wished to call upon more than the others? "That is a reason I can much more readily believe."

"No one can doubt your powers of perception," He paused and stared deep into her eyes.

Oh! His gazed reached in and plucked the strings of her heart. Surely he could not mean...

"Have you found the house to your discerning standards?" Papa asked, suddenly behind them.

"Cleaner than even my grandmother could desire."

How was it, Mr. Wickham seemed able to respond to any unexpected remark with such aplomb? His wit was even quicker than hers, and there were few about whom she could say such a thing.

"I have poured a toast in the parlor then." Papa pressed the dull steel flask into Wickham's hand. "Your gift is most appreciated, but my ladies are not accustomed to the rigors of whiskey. You and I may so indulge, but wine is far more to their sensibilities."

Wickham tucked the flask into his coat. "Of course you are right, and very gracious of you to make it so."

They followed Papa back to the parlor. On the way, Wickham placed his hand over hers in his arm and pressed it. Though he did not look at her, the corner of his lips lifted just a mite.

Why was he paying such attentions to her? What did they mean?

No sooner did they step into the parlor than Papa pressed a glass into her hand. "Add the coal to the fire and we shall have a toast."

"Hurry, Lizzy, must you always take so long at everything?" Lydia edged her out of the way and looped her arm in Wickham's.

Elizabeth tossed the coal into the fire. "And so we shall have warmth in the coming year."

"To Longbourn and all who dwell within." Wickham raised his glass. "May the welcomes continue to be warm, the table full and filled with flavor and prosperity."

They all sipped their glasses.

"If I may have the privilege, sir?" Wickham placed his glass on the mantle.

"It is your right." Papa gestured at Mama.

She offered her hand. Wickham took it and brought it to his lips as she tittered.

Lydia edged closer, but he turned toward Mary and extended his hand.

Mary's cheeks flushed and she muttered sounds that resembled protests, but she extended her hand toward him. He kissed it with the same ceremony he had Mama's, and she flushed deep crimson.

Lydia and Kitty jostled for position nearest him and presented their cheeks.

Wickham smiled, eyes twinkling, and placed a kiss on each of their cheeks. As one they sighed and pressed a hand to their cheeks.

Such silly girls. Perhaps, Papa had not exaggerated when he called them the silliest girls in all England.

Elizabeth fought not to roll her eyes. She turned aside and into Mr. Wickham's shoulder.

"Would you deny me my kiss?' he whispered, far closer than he should have been.

"Of...of course not." She raised her hand, but he leaned in very close.

How warm were his lips on her burning cheek. It was very pleasant indeed to be kissed by such a handsome man. Even more pleasant, the lingering of his gaze on her face and he slowly retreated.

"Will you stay a little longer, sir, or do you care to usher out last year's troubles and sorrows with you?" Papa gestured toward the back of the house.

"I would not overstay my welcome. Lead the way, sir. Ladies." Mr. Wickham bowed and followed Papa out.

The backdoor swung shut and Elizabeth sank into a chair. No doubt he would be off in search of another house in want of a first footer. Preferably one with pretty young ladies to kiss. It had been presumptuous to think he could be partial to her. But it was a pleasant thought for the moment that it lasted.

What would it be like to be the object of attention of a desirable young man? Surely it would be quite agreeable. But would she ever know that for herself?

Charlotte Lucas on New Year's Day

by Abigail Reynolds

January 1, 1812

Lady Lucas was all aflutter at their first visitor in the year of Our Lord 1812. "A happy new year to you, Judge Braxton! This is an unexpected pleasure. I cannot recall the last time our home was honored with your presence. Please sit down and allow me to order some refreshments."

Charlotte was paralyzed for a moment until she realized the judge was alone. Even then, after a polite greeting, she attended to her work with more than her usual diligence. She had no reason to suspect this was anything more than a social call, but it seemed odd that Willoughby's uncle would make a rare appearance just at this moment.

The judge was slightly more stooped than she recalled, but his pride of bearing was still evident. "The pleasure is mine, and please accept my good wishes for the new year. I spend most of my time in London these days, but even I can wish to see my own home at Christmas, and if it affords an opportunity to renew my acquaintance with my neighbors, so much the better. I am hoping to persuade you to attend a Twelfth Night dinner at Ixton Place. Not a ball, just a friendly gathering."

Lady Lucas clasped her hands together as if this were the most delightful news she had ever heard. "We would be honored to attend. Would we not, Charlotte?"

Charlotte forced a smile. "It would be a pleasure." She would run away from home before she would go willingly to Willoughby's home.

"Splendid!" He nodded at Charlotte. "And I hear there is to be a wedding soon. I hope you will forgive me if I still half expect you to be a young girl rather than a lady on the brink of matrimony."

After a visit of perhaps half an hour, the judge announced that he must be going. When Lady Lucas, all attentiveness, would have seen him out, he instead requested the company of the bride-to-be.

Charlotte, her stomach clenched in knots, walked beside him until he stopped just short of his carriage.

"Miss Lucas, as much as I respect your parents, the main purpose of my visit was to speak to you."

"To me, sir?" said Charlotte faintly.

"Yes. A rather disturbing report regarding my nephew has come to my attention, and I hope you can assist me in determining whether it is true." His keen eyes drilled into her.

"I do not know him well." How had he learned of the wager? Had Willoughby bragged about it so freely?

"Still, perhaps you have heard of this business. Apparently he made a wager that required another young buck to seduce and abandon a certain young woman of his acquaintance, a young lady against whom he held some past grudge. Do you know anything of this?"

"Your nephew mentioned as much to me when we met last," Charlotte said tightly.

"Are you aware of the nature of the grudge?" His tone demanded a response.

She hesitated, feeling sympathy for barristers forced to plead their cases before him. "I can only surmise that it may have related to a time years ago when he approached the lady without any intentions which could be called honorable. The lady reported it to her brothers, who took some sort of action against him, but I cannot say what it was." It was the truth. They had taken great pleasure in refusing to tell her what they had done.

"I see." The judge nodded. "Is it your impression that his

intention was to injure the lady in question?"

"To injure and humiliate her, and perhaps to blackmail her," she said bitterly. "He made that much clear."

He frowned. "I am very sorry to hear it. However, I will make certain that he does not trouble you again."

"I would appreciate that." Charlotte heard her voice trembling.

"I would also be particularly grateful if you would attend my Twelfth Night gathering rather than indulging in a headache or whatever else it is that young ladies do these days. I can promise you that my nephew will *not* be in attendance."

"In that case, I will do my best."

"Nor will he escape unscathed from this sordid affair. My apologies, Miss Lucas, that you were affected by it." He inclined his head in what was obviously a farewell.

"Judge Braxton?" She spoke to his retreating back.

"Yes?"

"May I ask how this matter came to your attention?"

He gave her a long, thoughtful look. "I received a visit from the man— I cannot call him a gentleman—who had accepted the wager. To his credit, he apparently now regrets it, and was concerned that you might come to further harm from my nephew. Under the circumstances, I did not consider his word to be reliable, hence my visit today."

"I understand. Thank you."

"Please accept my best wishes for your marriage, and my sincere hope that your husband will be more worthy of your faith than these men who are best forgotten."

"I hope so as well." She curtsied as he stepped into the carriage.

"I will look forward to seeing you on Twelfth Night, Miss Lucas," he called through the window as the carriage began to move.

Charlotte bit her lip as she waved with a smile that belied her feelings of humiliation.

Her mother was waiting for her just inside Lucas Lodge. "What did the judge say to you, Charlotte? He sounded very serious."

"Nothing of great import," said Charlotte, practical and calm as ever. "He wanted to be sure I would be able to attend Twelfth Night with my wedding so soon."

"What condescension!" Lady Lucas said admiringly. "Then again, he did seem particularly fond of you when you were a child. Mr. Collins will be delighted!"

Elizabeth Discovers Wickham's Interest in Mary King

by Abigail Reynolds

January 3, 1812

"You are keeping the warm brick to yourself, Lydia, and my toes are turning numb!" complained Kitty Bennet.

Mrs. Bennet elbowed her. "You are sitting in the middle, and that should be enough to keep you warm. Why does your father not have the carriage window fixed? It lets in the cold so terribly. If I die from a chill, it shall be his fault."

Kitty shoved Lydia to the edge of the carriage bench, receiving a sideways kick in response.

Elizabeth shook her head with amusement. True, it was an unusually cold day, even for January, but nothing could interfere with her pleasure today. Soon she would be dancing with Mr. Wickham, and she had no doubt he would be as attentive to her as always. That thought was enough to keep her warm.

She had dressed with great care so she would look her best for the festivities—or more particularly, for *him*. It had been ten days since she had seen him last—not that she was counting—and she had missed his amiable company. Even then he had seemed more interested in speaking to her aunt about Derbyshire than in talking to Elizabeth. No doubt it was simply because he missed his home there. Another thing to blame Mr. Darcy for!

The carriage rolled to a stop in front of Lucas Lodge, the windows already ablaze with light even though it was barely dusk. How typical! Sir William liked everyone to know how rich he was, and wasting expensive candles was an effective way to show it. But candles were the least of her cares tonight; she planned to enjoy Mr. Wickham's company to the fullest, even if her aunt had reminded her at Christmas not to fall in love with him. She could still find pleasure in being with him, could she not?

Lydia pushed her way out of the carriage first, followed by a fluttering Mrs. Bennet. Elizabeth waited until last, wanting to make a poised entry just in case a certain someone was watching for her. But it turned out she had no audience except the ostentatiously dressed footmen.

Inside it was a crush of people. Charlotte had warned her most of the neighborhood was invited, since her father saw this also as a celebration of her upcoming wedding. Of course, that also meant Mr. Collins would be there, but with luck Elizabeth could avoid dancing with him this time. The humiliation of their last clumsy dance at the Netherfield Ball still stung.

Elizabeth stood up on tiptoe and craned her neck to see over Lydia's shoulder. A year ago, she could have done it easily, but now her youngest sister was taller than she, as she never missed a chance of pointing out. As if height determined maturity! But none of the red-coated officers in the room had Wickham's golden curls. He must be further in the crowd.

A little disappointed not to find him waiting for her, she shouldered her way past a variety of neighbors, but of course that meant stopping to converse with some of them, since she could hardly admit she was looking for a gentleman. She was able to excuse herself from several conversations, but then she was accosted by Miss Penelope Harrington and her sister, Harriet. They greeted her extravagantly, each taking one of her arms.

What mischief were they up to? Neither were particular friends of hers, and she had not forgiven them for mocking her sister Jane for failing to secure Mr. Bingley. "You both look lovely tonight," she said. That was inoffensive.

"As do you," giggled Penelope. "Is that not new lace you have sewn on your dress? It looks almost like this year's styles."

"And new shoe roses," added Harriet. "You do not usually go to such efforts for an occasion like this. Is there someone in particular you are trying to impress?"

As if they did not know she had been keeping company with Mr. Wickham! She had heard enough of their jealous whispers about what he could possibly see in her. "Just to give honor to Sir William and Lady Lucas for inviting us. Have you seen Charlotte Lucas? I must give her my best wishes on her engagement." And that might let her escape them.

"Oh, she is in the sitting room with all the dull people. You should go to the saloon where the dancing is. Have you seen Miss King tonight?" Harriet placed great weight on the name.

They were definitely up to mischief. Elizabeth said, "Not yet. I have only just arrived."

The two girls exchanged a smirk. Penelope said, "You must make a point to find her. She is in particularly good looks tonight."

Why in the world did they want her to see Mary King? She barely knew the shy, retiring girl. "I will tell her you said so. Now, if you will be so kind as to excuse me?"

"Oh, we could not possibly desert you in this crush! Do let us go into the saloon. Perhaps one of the officers will ask us to dance."

Since she wished to go there in any case, she saw no point in resisting their efforts. She allowed them to lead her through the throng of people to the saloon. Most of the furniture had been moved out and the rugs rolled up to make room for dancing. Mariah Lucas was playing a reel on the piano as half a dozen couples circled each other in a country dance.

There he was! Wickham was among the dancers, his golden hair shining in the candlelight. He was facing away from her, but once he reached the top of the set, he would turn and walk right by her. Then he would give her that wonderful warm look that made her insides seem to turn upside down.

"Oh, look!" cried Harriet. "Mary King is dancing with Mr. Wickham!"

Did she suppose Elizabeth would be jealous because Wickham was dancing with another woman? He always did seek out other partners after the two dances he could properly dance with her. He always asked her teasingly for a third, but he knew as well as she that it would cause gossip. "I imagine she is enjoying it, then. He is a good dancer."

"And you would know, wouldn't you?" said Penelope archly.

Elizabeth ignored her. Wickham and Mary King had reached the top of the set and turned to walk down the outside of the set. Her heart beat faster as he approached, a welcoming smile suffusing her face.

He did not catch her eye. In fact, he looked straight through her as he passed, as if she were not even there, though he nodded to another acquaintance further down the line.

A heavy stone seemed to have taken up residence in Elizabeth's stomach. Why was he cutting her? Had she done something to upset him? She could not imagine what it would be, though he had been a bit cool when he called at Christmas. And why were Harriet and Penelope watching her with such avid expressions? They must have known what was coming, and attached themselves to gloat over her response.

Could it perhaps be a joke? Had Wickham set this up with them as a jest, or to see how she would respond? She would not give them the satisfaction of showing distress. "How much more pleasant dances are since the militia arrived in town! I think all the officers must be here," she said coolly.

Surely Wickham would come to her when the dance ended.

But he did not. Instead, he offered his arm to Mary King and took her to the far end of the room where a few chairs lined the wall. He sat down beside her, a little closer than was proper, and turned towards her. Elizabeth could not see his face, but Mary King was gazing up at him with adoring eyes. She felt sick.

A man in a red coat approached her and bowed. "Miss Elizabeth, might I have the honor of this dance?"

In her shock, it took her a moment to recognize Mr. Chamberlayne. She pasted a smile to her face. "I would be delighted, sir."

He led her to the head of the line, just a few feet away from Wickham and Mary King. She refused to look in their direction, but she could not avoid their voices. Wickham's familiar tones came first "…the next dance?"

"You know we cannot, Mr. Wickham! People would talk."

He gave a rumbly laugh. "I do not care if people know how I feel about you."

The room was overheated, but Elizabeth felt suddenly cold. To her everlasting gratitude, the music started. Numbly, she took the hand Mr. Chamberlayne offered her.

He leaned towards her. "Smile," he said quietly. "People are watching. Do not give them the satisfaction."

So he knew. Everyone knew. Everyone but her.

At least Mr. Chamberlayne was being kind, rather than glorying in her distress. Fluttering her eyelashes, she gave him the most brilliant smile she could manage. "Mr. Chamberlayne, you do say the loveliest things!"

He patted her hand proprietarily. "It is easy to pay compliments to so charming a partner."

They took hands across with the couple beneath them, precluding any further discussion. Elizabeth kept the smile fixed to her face as they cast down the line, most especially when she had to pass Wickham and Mary King.

So Wickham had thrown her over without a word, and Mary King was her replacement. But why? They had not quarreled, and she would not have thought Mary would hold any particular attraction for him. She was far from a beauty, and could certainly not be called clever. Wickham and Mary King. The image of the two of them together seemed burned on the inside of her eyelids. It was too painful to contemplate when she had to keep her composure.

Somehow she made it through the first dance of the set. During

213

the pause before the music began again, Mr. Chamberlayne said, "Well done. *You* have nothing to be ashamed of."

His sympathy threatened her composure. Lightly she said, "Mr. Wickham does not owe me anything. If he prefers the company of Miss King, it is nothing to me."

He smiled understandingly, and then said in her ear, "I believe it is not so much her *company* he prefers as her *fortune*."

"Her fortune? You must be mistaken. She has no particular prospects."

"Have you not heard? She recently inherited ten thousand pounds, and Wickham has debts of honor. He is not the only officer to have suddenly noticed her appeal, but he found her first."

Suddenly it was less painful to swallow. To be thrown over for money was more tolerable than if he had done it out of preference for Mary King; still painful, but not as personal. "No, I had not heard. Thank you for enlightening me. It explains a great many things." But she still had no desire to watch him pay court to another woman while he ignored her.

It was going to be a very long evening.

A Ball to Forget – Part I
by Maria Grace

January 5, 1812

The Scene: Mr. Darcy has left the company of Charles Bingley and contemplates the approach of Twelfth Night in his London townhouse.

The afternoon sunlight tumbled through the windows, laying a neatly ordered path of light through his study, illuminating everything the way he best liked. Even the well-arranged room could not soothe his soul. Darcy paced across the front of his desk, eyes never leaving the taunting bit of stationary. Lady Matlock's elegant hand tormented him with an invitation to her Twelfth Night ball.

The day the dreadful missive arrived, he sent his promise to attend. The act had been automatic, a reflex of politeness, bred into him by a long line of proper, well-mannered Darcys. Had he but taken a few moments to consider his actions, he might not be in this current dilemma.

He dreaded balls, this one in particular—loathed it with a fire reserved for all things pretentious and social. He did not perform well to strangers, and this ball would be naught but an extended performance to many strangers. He might as well be a circus animal —a wise pig or a counting horse—put through his paces for the peeresses and heiresses by ring master Lady Matlock.

The port decanter caught a glint of sunlight and tipped its hat at him from across the room. What an excellent notion.

The housekeeper's knock stopped him mid-step.

Botheration. He squeezed his eyes shut. It was too early in the day to seek solace from port in any case. "Come."

She peeked in and dropped a small curtsey. "Colonel Fitzwilliam to see you, sir. Are you home to him?" At least she recognized he did not appreciate the interruption.

Fitzwilliam? "Show him in."

How could Fitzwilliam have known how little he wanted company at present? His timing was remarkable that way. Darcy tugged his coat straight and hurried into a chair near the fire. No point in giving Fitzwilliam the satisfaction of seeing evidence of his discomfiture.

"Good afternoon, Darcy." Fitzwilliam sauntered in, relaxed and informal, as though this were his own home. How did he do it? Fitzwilliam seemed at home where ever he went.

"Good afternoon." Darcy rose and offered a small bow. Still probably too formal for the occasion, but it was the most comfortable greeting he knew. "To what do I own the pleasure of your company?"

Fitzwilliam extended his hand and would not withdraw it until Darcy shook it. Yes, their relationship did permit such familiar gestures, but was it necessary to exercise them at every encounter?

"Do try to relax, Darcy. We are family after all." Fitzwilliam sunk into his favorite chair and balanced one foot upon the other.

Had he any idea of his appalling posture? What a dreadful picture he painted of one of His Majesty's officers.

"You may thank my mother for the call."

Darcy clutched his temples. "Dare I ask her purposes?"

"Probably not, but I will tell you all the same." Fitzwilliam laced his hands behind his head and sniggered. "She instructs me to ensure your attendance at her ball."

"I already sent—"

"I know—I saw the response myself—she showed it to me to scold my penmanship. Excellent hand you have, by the bye, most elegant."

"And that is not enough for her?"

"You know how fastidious she is, and she knows how you would rather break your own leg than attend."

"You think I would manufacture a fall down the stairs to avoid the ball?"

"Not I." Fitzwilliam touched his chest and shook his head.

"Thank you."

"But my mother is an entirely different matter." He punctuated the pronouncement with his characteristic wry half-smile.

Darcy stared at the ceiling and muttered under his breath.

"Truly, I do not understand your aversion to—"

"Donning a costume—worse yet, one not of my own choosing?" Darcy stalked to Fitzwilliam and towered over him.

"Must you always make the worst of everything? I will have you know, Mother selected your character very carefully. Brooded over it for days, lest it keep you from attending. I am instructed to inform you that there will be no random draw out of a hat for you. Father has strict directions as to the sleight of hand necessary to ensure you receive her choice for you."

Such thoughtfulness. He had done Lady Matlock a great disservice expecting so little from her. Assuming the best from people, even his own people, was clearly not his strong suit.

"I can see you are surprised."

"Aunt Matlock is indeed most gracious." He rubbed the back of his neck. "Whilst I appreciate the consideration, it does little to change the material fact that I am expected to perform!"

"She assures me that your character will require no performance on your part, merely act like yourself and you will be 'in character' as it were. She has probably crafted Christopher Curmudgeon in your honor." Fitzwilliam swallowed back a laugh.

Best ignore that remark all together. Darcy stalked across the room, following the faint track worn into the carpet. "I do appreciate her efforts, but still, I am denied my choice of partners

217

for the evening. I must spend my time with whomever she draws from that ridiculous bag of hers."

"As to that, she wishes me to assure you that if you but indicate a preference to her, she will contrive to ensure you have the partner you desire."

Darcy stopped at the window and pressed his forehead against the cool glass. There in lay the problem. The partner he desired was not in London and even if she were, her name would be completely unknown to any lofty personages. He pinched the bridge of his nose.

Rot and nonsense! He must regulate his thoughts, not allow them to wander to *her*. She was most unsuitable in every way— fortune, breeding, connections, even her manners were barely adequate. And her family—truly appalling nearly every one of them! That was what he must focus on…not her fine eyes and informed, if pert, opinions. Not the exhilaration he found in conversation with her or the compelling way she challenged him to consider his own opinions. He ran a finger along the inside of his cravat.

"Darcy?"

"I… I do not wish to be forced to spend the entire evening with any one young lady. People—including her family will get ideas, conveniently forgetting it was an act of chance alone that led to being with her the first place." He threw his hands in the air.

"What about my sister? Letty is engaged, but her betrothed is on the continent right now. She has no need to use the opportunity to seek out an eligible man, so will miss nothing by being your companion. Not to mention, Lord Blake is known for his jealous streak. You he will not perceive as a rival for Letty's attentions."

"But she has accepted his offer—"

Fitzwilliam shrugged. "I know. You need not convince me of the unseemliness of his attitude. Speak to Blake yourself. All I can say is that you would be doing Letty a favor as much as yourself."

"I suppose that would be acceptable." But only barely. Letty was not unintelligent, but her interests extended only so far as the *ton*.

He would be forced to listen to her prattle on all evening about the latest *on-dit*. At least she would not be coy or flirtatious—and she would not expect him to call upon her the day after the ball.

"So then I may assure mother you will come tonight?"

"I can tolerate an evening in your sister's company, but I will not—"

"Play any games, except a dignified rubber of whist. Yes, yes, be assured, we all know that. I did not expect this would be the year we would see your face deep in a bullet pudding or silently gesticulating a clue in charades."

Darcy shuddered. How did anyone find such pastimes amusing?

"You are fortunate Letty prefers cards to other games. Though you may have to lower yourself and compromise to play commerce with her. She is notoriously bad at whist."

He had forgotten that. Darcy grunted. "I can accept that."

"Very well then, I shall bring my mother the news she most desires to hear." Fitzwilliam rose. "I do not understand why she works so hard to see you come or why you say you will attend an event that you so clearly dread."

"Aunt Matlock wishes to see me married and will take any opportunity to present me on the marriage mart, even if it is with your sister on my arm. I have no doubt she still hopes I might dance with some other young ladies and give her the credit of bringing me together with the partner of my future life." Darcy pressed his eyes with thumb and forefinger. What would she think, seeing him dance with the young lady he truly wished to partner?

Fitzwilliam sniggered. "Why do you put yourself through this when you could so easily decline?"

"It would be improper, impolite, and ill-received to decline her invitation."

"As you will." Fitzwilliam tipped his head and left.

Darcy returned to his desk and cradled his face in his hands. How fortunate Fitzwilliam had left before extracting the full truth from him. Politeness aside, Lady Matlock's invitation might help him forget, even if for an evening. Any distraction from the intruding memories of a charming Elizabeth Bennet was a welcome one, even if it was a Twelfth Night ball.

A Ball to Forget – Part II

by Maria Grace

January 5, 1812

Darcy blinked rheumy eyes, head throbbing, stomach protesting like a rioting mob in the streets. A mob would have been easier to quell. He pressed his belly and smacked his lips. Drinking so much had been a poor choice, even if it has been in the privacy of his study after the ball. His study—he glanced about—he had slept in his study!

He squeezed his eyes and groaned. He had intended to return to his chambers, but the port had called to him, one glass after another, until his best intentions faded away into an alcohol muddled haze. Port after several generous glasses of Aunt Matlock's famed punch was a very bad idea indeed.

The housekeeper pounded on the door. Why did she feel the need to do that, today especially? A polite tap was all that had ever been needed to garner his attention. He would have to speak to her about that … later.

The door squealed like a dying animal as she opened it. "Sir."

"What?" He clutched his temples and bit back the harsh words dancing on his tongue.

"I brought you something to help your ill-ease, some coffee, and a bite to eat if you wish it."

He flicked his hand toward a small table. Was it possible to make more noise setting a tray down? It would be a miracle if she did not crack every piece of porcelain on the tray with all the rattling and clattering.

She shuffled out and slammed the door. The woman had never been so ungainly before—why now? He would have sharp words for her when—

His stomach roiled and he reached for the glass, full of a slightly opaque liquid, sparkling in the too bright afternoon—afternoon?—light. He shaded his eyes against the glare. How could it become afternoon so quickly?

Gah! With any good fortune, the drink would work better than it tasted—that would not be difficult. Would it have been too difficult to provide him with something less foul than his temper?

What a fool he had been, trusting Aunt Matlock's judgment in choosing a character to suit his temperament. So clever of her to assign him and Letty the bard's Benedict and Beatrice, so, in her words "their debates and disagreeable remarks would be entirely in character."

He gulped down another mouthful of the housekeeper's foul tonic.

At least the costumes had been tolerable, an officer's coat for him and a wreath of flowers for her. Acceptable enough.

The evening began to unravel after his second cup of punch, happily provided by Letty herself. She had been pleased enough with her part, disagreeing with him at every turn and doing nearly all the talking for both the entire evening. She knew the bards work too well and precisely how to draw him in. He had politely remarked upon the weather—the weather!—only to receive her response:

"I wonder that you will still be talking, Signor Benedick: nobody marks you."

"What, my dear Lady Disdain! Are you yet living?" The words slipped out before he could control them, and the game, for Letty was on.

"Is it possible disdain should die while she hath such meet food to feed it as Signor Benedick? Courtesy itself must convert to disdain, if you come in her presence."

Heat rose along his jaw—or perhaps it was the punch. How dare she insult his deportment! It was not to be born. "Then is courtesy a turncoat. But it is certain I am loved of all ladies, only you excepted: and I would I could find in my heart that I had not a hard heart; for, truly, I love none."

Why had he permitted himself those words? Letty took far too much delight in them.

The look she had given him as she said, "A dear happiness to women: they would else have been troubled with a pernicious suitor. I thank God and my cold blood, I am of your humor for that: I had rather hear my dog bark at a crow than a man swear he loves me."

Her betrothed would be pleased with that public declaration. "God keep Your Ladyship still in that mind! So some gentleman or other shall 'scape a predestinate scratched face."

"Scratching could not make it worse, an 'twere such a face as yours were."

That was uncalled for. He gulped the remainder of his punch. In retrospect, perhaps not the wisest choice. "Well, you are a rare parrot-teacher."

"A bird of my tongue is better than a beast of yours." She laughed, a shrill, ear splitting sound on the best of days which had clearly not improved with drink.

"I would my horse had the speed of your tongue, and so good a continuer. But keep your way, i' God's name; I have done."

Oh she had not liked that, given the face she made at him. "You always end with a jade's trick: I know you of old."

Had she but a modicum of restraint, it might have been bearable. She shrieked and carried on as though those words were meant personally, not written for the public's entertainment. He scrubbed his face with his hands. Great heavens, even the Bennet family had checked themselves better! Was it possible that family demonstrated greater decorum than his own?

223

That was not possible. What would Lydia Bennet have done with the character of Beatrice? He shuddered. No, that thought must have been the result of far too much port.

He leaned back in his chair and threw his arm over his eyes. Even with Letty's outrageous behavior, his plan for the ball had largely been a success, at least until this moment. He had not thought about Elizabeth Bennet during the entire evening. Not when the young Miss Blake, wearing the gown that would have better suited Miss Elizabeth, sauntered past. Not when the musicians played the same music they had danced to at Netherfield. Not when he caught a glimpse of the library on the way to the card room and the same book Miss Elizabeth read while she stayed at Netherfield caught his gaze. Not when Letty attempted to involve him in conversation with her shallow chatter and gossip that bored him senseless instead of endeavoring to engage him in sensible discourse. None of those moments made him consider Miss Elizabeth at all.

It was only now in the solitude of his study that thoughts of that maddening woman invaded his consciousness, refusing to give way in the face of his stalwart defenses.

Why was it no young lady, regardless of fortune, connections, or beauty, seemed to measure up to the standard set by the impertinent Hertfordshire miss? There had to be something for this untoward distraction—something other than a stay in Bedlam.

Perhaps if he could escape the company of ladies all together. There was a thought...his club, fencing, boxing, horseracing. Sequestering himself away from the fairer sex—he had not tried that yet. He pressed his eyes. Beginning immediately...no tomorrow, he would withdraw to the company of men and at last escape the distraction of one Miss Elizabeth Bennet.

Charlotte's Last Day as a Single Woman

by Abigail Reynolds

January 8, 1812

Charlotte's farewell visit to the Bennet ladies was not one she would remember with pleasure. Mrs. Bennet, who had always been kind to her until she became engaged, was ungracious throughout it. Lizzy had the courtesy to walk her downstairs afterwards, which Charlotte particularly appreciated since she wanted to invite her to visit in Kent. She had not forgotten the judge's words about finding her companionship elsewhere than her husband, and Lizzy had been her closest friend for years.

Lizzy at first tried to dodge the invitation—hardly surprising given her dislike of Mr. Collins—but finally agreed, to Charlotte's great relief. It meant a great deal to know that she would have a friend still, even if Lizzy still couldn't hide her disapproval of Charlotte's marriage. Sometimes she forgot just how young Lizzy was, and the difference between the ages of twenty and eight-and-twenty. Lizzy's world was so simple; she lived in the present and did not think of the future. People had few shades of grey in her mind. Charlotte wondered what Lizzy would think if she knew the truth of her situation.

Apparently feeling some guilt over her reluctance to visit, Lizzy offered to walk back to Lucas Lodge with her, but Charlotte declined graciously. "I need a little time alone to think. Once I am home, I will be inundated with wedding preparations."

Lizzy, who loved solitary walks, apparently saw nothing odd in this, and waved to Charlotte as she set off down the drive. But Charlotte had no intention of taking the usual road back to Lucas Lodge, and soon veered off on a narrow path into the woods. Her pulse raced, but not from the exercise, and anxiety gnawed away at her insides. Would he be there, or had he already left Hertfordshire?

She hitched up her skirts for the final climb to the ruined chapel on the hilltop. Overgrown by trees, no one ever visited it, but it had been a favorite childhood retreat of hers. Now it was something else entirely. It was where they had gone on Guy Fawkes Night.

He was standing in the doorway waiting for her. She had planned to keep her distance from him, but the urge to be close to him was more powerful than she had anticipated, and she permitted him to draw her into his arms. Permitted was perhaps the wrong word when she had practically fallen into his arms, finding herself awash with sensations and feelings as soon as she had. Desire was only part of it; rather it was knowing *he* desired *her* and cared for her for who she was, not merely to satisfy a demanding patroness. But it made her happy, and grateful she was not yet married and could justify these liberties to herself—almost. How would she live without this?

She would find a way. It was sweet to be wanted, but she was in the habit of finding contentment where she could. Who would have thought it would be in the arms of her former lover on the day before her wedding to another man? How shocked all her friends and family would be to see practical, dependable Charlotte right now! That thought made her even happier.

"Thank you for agreeing to see today," he murmured in her ear. "You cannot imagine what it means to me that, even if we have no future together, that we part with happier memories. And I will do my best to wish you happy in your future."

Charlotte did not want to think about that future, or the man she was to marry who was waiting for her at Lucas Lodge. She wanted to treasure this moment and the sensation of being held by the man she cared for. She did not question her decision to marry Mr. Collins, at least not seriously. She was happy to be with her lover, happy to hear his voice and to rest in his embrace, but she also recognized that fundamentally he was a weak man who was too easily swayed by what he desired at any given moment. If they married, that trait would eventually kill her affection for him. She would rather have the memories of today to carry with her through the years ahead.

Reluctantly she drew back from him. "Shall we walk?" If they remained at the chapel, it would be too easy to go farther than an embrace.

"If you wish." He offered her his arm

As they began down the path into the woods, she said, "You said before that there were things you still wanted to tell me."

"And you expect me to remember them when you are with me?" He placed his hand over hers where it rested on his forearm, his gaze intent.

"You mentioned something about telling me why you were so angry at women."

"Oh, yes." He sighed before launching into his tale. It was the usual story; a bored heiress who had led him on for her own entertainment, and then humiliated him with a very public refusal. "I do not claim it as an excuse for my behavior; still, I wanted you to know. But there is one thing I would ask you."

"Yes?"

He hesitated. "Were there any consequences of that night in November?"

She did not pretend to misunderstand him. "I cannot say. I have had no proof that I am not in that condition, but it is not unusual for me to lack proof on a regular basis."

"I do not know whether I wish for it or not, but it will be hard never to know."

"If you wish, I could try to send a message through Judge Braxton, although it might be some time before I have the opportunity to do so. I do not know how often I will return here, and he is frequently in London."

"I would appreciate some word, and it will be...good to know I will hear from you again, at least that once, even if you are far away. Where does he live, your Mr. Collins?" he said with an edge to his voice.

"In the village of Hunsford in Kent, not far from Tunbridge Wells."

He looked away for a moment with a sharp, indrawn breath. "I know where it is. It is just over ten miles from my father's house. I visit there occasionally. Someday it will be mine."

Her eyes widened. "You do?"

"Tell me that you will allow me to see you again, at least from time to time. I will find a way to make it work. Please, Charlotte. I will not ask for anything improper. I give you my word."

And this from the man who had embraced her as soon as she was close enough to touch! "Will you not want more than friendship?"

His expression grew determined. "Of course I will *want* more, but I will settle for friendship."

The tightness in her chest, the fear of finality, lessened. "I am willing to make the attempt."

They walked on, without knowing in what direction. There was too much to be thought, and felt, and said, for attention to any other objects. Finally she realized the shadows were getting longer. She had been gone from Lucas Lodge too long, and would have to think of a good excuse for why she had lingered at her farewell call to the Bennets, but she did not care. This was not a final goodbye, and that made all the difference.

He took her hand and lifted it to his lips. It was not the polite hand-kiss of a friend. "Do not forget me, I beg you."

Charlotte's stomach lurched as she re-tied her bonnet strings. "Do you think I could?"

"I hope not."

"These last months have been quite unforgettable, and you may depend on me to remember. After all, I am practical, dependable Charlotte Lucas."

He caught her hand once more. "You are practical and dependable—but there is much more to you than *that*. Remember that when you remember me."

She looked into his eyes and nodded slowly. "I will remember."

Charlotte's Wedding

by Abigail Reynolds

January 9, 1812

Charlotte had never been one to have romantic dreams about a perfect wedding. She knew she would never be a beautiful bride that women would cry over, and there was not even to be a wedding breakfast, since she and Mr. Collins were to leave for Kent from the church door. Lady Catherine apparently felt he had been absent from his post a bit too often in these last months, so naturally Mr. Collins was determined to return at the earliest possible moment. It was going to be a very long day, especially with a wedding night at the end where she would need to have all of her acting skills at their best.

The ceremony went smoothly, which was all Charlotte had hoped for. The only shock came when she walked back down the aisle with her new husband and saw some unexpected faces in the pews. Judge Braxton sat between his young nephew and Mr. Robinson.

She allowed her eyes to rest on Mr. Robinson for just a moment. He gave her a slight smile—not a happy one, but neither was it completely false—and then she was past his pew. She wondered at his presence, but he could not be planning to cause difficulties if he was with the judge.

The newlyweds were surrounded by well-wishers at the church door. Charlotte could hear Mr. Collins droning on to someone or other in his usual manner with frequent references to Lady Catherine de Bourgh and Rosings Park while she was bidding her final farewells to her family and friends. She could not keep herself from glancing around every few minutes in search of Mr. Robinson, oddly embarrassed at what he would think of her new husband.

When she saw him, it was a worse shock. He was actually being introduced to Mr. Collins. Her social smile firmly plastered in place, she hurried to Mr. Collins's side, hoping that her interest looked like nothing more than the eagerness of a devoted bride to be with her new husband.

"Yes, of course, near Rosings Park," said Mr. Robinson smoothly. "I remember it well. My father was a great friend of Sir Lewis de Bourgh, and during that gentleman's lifetime, we often called at Rosings. He and my father were both devotees of chess and whiled away many an afternoon with one match after another."

"If you have met the family, then you comprehend the great honor I feel in having the opportunity to be Lady Catherine's most humble servant." Mr. Collins showed the same eagerness to impress that he had when meeting Mr. Darcy at the Netherfield Ball.

"Indeed I do. I recall standing quite in awe of Lady Catherine. Rosings Park is, of course, among the finest houses in the county. I am sure there are many who are envious of your position." His eyes momentarily slid toward Charlotte with a very different message about his envy.

As Mr. Collins thanked him at length for his great condescension, Charlotte wondered what on earth he was about. It certainly had not taken him long to take the measure of Mr. Collins's nature, and he was playing to it beautifully.

"I was delighted to hear that Miss Lucas—Mrs. Collins—would be taking up residence in Hunsford. She is just the sort of practical, dependable lady to be a perfect clergyman's wife. In fact, I was hoping you would not object if I introduced my younger sister to her acquaintance. This was to have been Mary's first Season until my father became ill, and she is disappointed to be spending it in the country instead. I believe Mrs. Collins would be an excellent steadying influence on her, with your permission, of course."

Mr. Collins turned to Charlotte, rubbing his hands together with every evidence of pleasure. "We would be delighted, would we not, Mrs. Collins?"

Charlotte curtsied slightly. "I would be very happy to meet a new friend in Kent." She was not certain whether she was more amused or horrified at his initiative in asking her husband for permission to call on her.

He bowed. "In that case, I will look forward to seeing you again very soon, Mrs. Collins, but I will not keep you from your other guests any longer."

She offered him her hand, and he bowed over it deeply, giving her fingers a little squeeze as he did so. It was as if a little spark passed from him to her, but she felt no urge for anything more. Today was not the day to be thinking of him.

She was relieved when the hired carriage pulled away from the church and she was alone with Mr. Collins. She listened absently as he talked on at length about what a success the day had been and how pleased Lady Catherine would be that Judge Braxton himself had condescended to attend the ceremony. "She will be glad to hear that you are already acquainted with one of our neighbors, but I must admit I did not quite catch his name—was it Rogers, my dear?"

"You refer to Mr. Robinson?"

"Ah, yes, Robinson, that was it. And to think his father had the honor of knowing Sir Lewis de Bourgh! I will have to tell Lady Catherine about him. How did you come to meet him?"

"Judge Braxton is a friend of Mr. Robinson's father, and is acting as a mentor of sorts to the son. Mr. Robinson attended many of the social occasions in Meryton during his visit to the judge." She was pleased by the apparent detachment in her voice. "But I hope you will tell me more about what I should expect to find in Hunsford and at Rosings Park. One can never be too prepared, after all."

As she hoped, that sent him off into a long monologue of praise, waxing eloquent about every detail of Rosings. It was rather soothing, actually, since he required so little from her apart from the appearance of attention. She was used to this sort of effusive behavior from her father, so it did not trouble her greatly.

She folded her hands in her lap and made herself as comfortable as one could be in a coach with fewer springs than might be wished for. She had no complaints, though. Today was evidence enough for her that she had made the correct decision. She might feel an attraction to Mr. Robinson that she did not for Mr. Collins, and she would certainly enjoy his company more, but her pleasure in their time together did not prevent her from noticing that today he had shown himself once again to be a skilled liar with a talent for manipulation. His willingness to involve his sister in the situation did not speak well for him, either. If she were married to him, she would always have doubts about his motives and his veracity, and if he could lie so easily and disguise what must be serious dislike for his rival, it was quite possible he could fool her about other things.

No, Mr. Robinson would not have made the kind of husband she could depend on. She remembered him with pleasure, and looked forward more than she might like to admit to their next meeting, but she knew where she stood with Mr. Collins. If his effusiveness bordered on embarrassing, she could learn to ignore it. She would finally have an establishment of her own, a comfortable income, and hopefully children to raise.

"Is something the matter, my dearest Charlotte? Is the motion of the carriage too much for you?"

"I am a little tired, perhaps, but quite well," she said, patting his hand. "I do hope Lady Catherine will approve of me."

That was enough to distract him, and he was off again on his monologue, leaving her with the quite satisfactory thought that Mr. Willoughby would be most distressed if he knew how much she had benefited from his attempt at revenge. Without him she would not have made the desperate attempt to attract Mr. Collins's attention when he hoped to marry one of the Bennet sisters, and she would still be an aging spinster destined to be dependent on her brothers forever. Instead, thanks to Willoughby, she had a new home, the prospect of someday being mistress of Longbourn, a husband to provide for her, and an admirer to remind her that there was more to her than the practical, dependable Charlotte everyone else knew. Yes, she had a great deal for which to be thankful.

Jane Calls on Caroline and Louisa

by Susan Mason-Milks

January 10, 1812

Jane found herself sitting in the parlor at the Hurst's home on Grosvenor Street waiting for Caroline Bingley and Louisa Hurst to appear. Perched on a velvet covered chair, she felt a little uncomfortable and out of place. The house was not large, but almost everything about it was pretentious, as if designed to impress visitors with the financial standing of its owner. Jane deemed the decoration of this particular room much too formal and stuffy for her taste. The only personal touch was a small grouping of miniatures on a nearby table.

Examining the tiny portraits more closely, Jane recognized Caroline and Louisa. Both appeared to have been painted when they were about fifteen or sixteen years of age. The artist had generously rounded out some of the sharp angles of Caroline's features making her appearance softer than it was in person. Jane smiled to herself noting how he had also considerably reduced the size of her nose.

The miniature that interested Jane the most, however, was of Charles Bingley. As she picked up the tiny portrait to examine it more closely, she involuntarily took a quick deep breath, exhaling it slowly with a quiet sigh. She had spent many weeks denying how much she felt for this man, but seeing his likeness brought it all back in full force causing that now familiar empty feeling to return. Jane lightly touched her finger to the painting as if she could actually stroke his face. All the pain of loss she had been holding inside now threatened to rush out. She would not allow herself to cry. It would not do to let anyone, especially his sisters, see how much she was hurt.

Mr. Bingley was everything she had ever hoped for in a suitor, and that made his loss all the more difficult to bear. It was not his fault his friendliness and charm had caused her to misinterpret his attentions. He was, after all, known for his good manners and friendly mien. Jane had been so certain he was developing an attachment to her and that his affection equaled hers. When he did not return to Netherfield, she had been forced to awaken from the delightful dream of becoming his wife that she had created for herself. She knew in the future any man who sought her attentions would be compared with him—her first love. The sad truth was Charles would marry someone like Georgiana Darcy and forget he had ever known Jane Bennet of Longbourn. She had just been an amusing diversion during his stay in the country. Jane thought she had no one to blame but herself for thinking it was more than just a flirtation. If his heart had been truly engaged, he would never have left without a word. In spite of what happened, Jane still hoped she would be able to continue her friendship with his sisters that had begun so promisingly in Hertfordshire.

Before Jane left for London, she had written to Caroline and Louisa informing them of her arrival in Town, and also giving her Aunt and Uncle Gardiner's direction so they could write in return or come to call. More than a week had passed, but she had heard nothing from her friends. Jane was certain if Caroline had received her most recent message, she would have replied. The silence could only mean the letter had somehow been lost. That thought was what had prompted Jane to take the initiative of calling on them first.

"I cannot believe she has actually called upon us!" moaned Caroline. She and Louisa were still in her dressing room freshening up to meet their guest. "I thought my letter made it clear she should not hope for more from Charles." Caroline was very unhappy she would be forced to be pleasant to Jane Bennet. Whatever would she say to that country bumpkin? Caroline intentionally had not answered Jane's last letter with the hope of avoiding just this very situation, but she had come to call on them rather than taking the hint. Caroline was certain she had done everything she could to imply that Charles's affections were otherwise engaged.

"Should I send word I am indisposed with a headache?" Caroline asked her sister.

"Do not be silly. We cannot both claim a headache, and I am not meeting with her alone," Louisa replied. "Caroline, she is a sweet girl. I believe we must see her."

Caroline let out a snort of disgust.

"You know it would be unforgivably rude not to at least spend a few minutes with her," Louisa counseled.

"Then we must have a plan for cutting her visit short. What should we say?"

"I have no idea. You are the one who excels at making up excuses," said Louisa absently as she checked her hair once more in the mirror.

"I shall instruct Graves if we have not emerged in ten minutes, he should come to the door to remind us we must leave almost immediately for our appointment." Caroline frowned as she smoothed imaginary wrinkles from her dress.

"Oh, stop fussing," said Louisa slapping at her sister's hand.

Caroline jumped back and threw Louisa a nasty look. "Do not do that! You are not Mama!"

Louisa rolled her eyes, and then focused her attention on their problem again. "You could also inform her Miss Darcy is dining with us this evening," she said slyly.

"Perhaps that will provide sufficient discouragement," Caroline replied.

Just as they were ready to exit the dressing room, Caroline put a hand on her sister's arm. "Oh, dear! Louisa," she said with a look of horror on her face, "courtesy will require us to make a return call. I am not sure I can bear the thought of going to...to..."

"Cheapside!" they moaned simultaneously as if the very word was disgusting to pronounce.

"If you recall, I warned you this might happen! Next time Charles gets an idea in his head to pay attention to someone as unsuitable as she is, we must put a stop to it much sooner," said Caroline as she linked arms with her sister.

Just before they entered the room where Jane waited, Caroline took a deep breath and set a bright smile on her face.

"Oh, Jane, dear! How very lovely to see you!" she cooed in her sweetest voice as she floated into the parlor. "Why did you not let us know you were coming to Town?"

"I sent a letter a few weeks ago just before leaving Hertfordshire. Perhaps it was lost," Jane offered.

Caroline thought it was so very like Jane to conveniently offer her own explanation. It saved Caroline the trouble of making something up on the spot.

"And is your family all in health?" Louisa inquired politely settling into a nearby chair.

"Oh, yes, thank you. Everyone is very well. And your family?"

"Yes, they are all well," Louisa responded.

Jane looked down at her hands. "Is your brother also in health?" she asked tentatively.

Louisa and Caroline exchanged looks. "Oh, yes, of course, but we rarely see him these days. He has been spending so much time at the Darcys' we are beginning to think he lives there," Caroline responded with a forced laugh.

"And how are the Darcys?" Jane asked more out of politeness than actual interest.

"Mr. Darcy was somewhat out of sorts upon his return from Hertfordshire, but I believe he is feeling well enough by now," said Caroline. After all, it was perfectly understandable. Being forced to endure the company of so many unpleasant people in Hertfordshire had made her feel ill, too.

"Miss Darcy is also in excellent health," Louisa added. "She is such a lovely young lady. Who would not be taken with her beauty and accomplishments?"

Caroline brightened. Louisa had created the perfect opening. "Yes, we are looking forward to Miss Darcy dining with us this evening!" She did not add that Charles would be out with Mr. Darcy at the home of an old school friend. It would not hurt if Jane assumed the gentlemen would be joining them as it would further the idea there might possibly be more than one union between the two families. Caroline still seethed with hatred for Eliza Bennet because of Darcy's marked preference for her. She thought it would not hurt a bit if Jane wrote to that impertinent sister of hers that two of the Bingleys were on very intimate terms with the Darcys. Fine eyes, indeed! Let her be the one who was jealous!

An uncomfortable silence fell in the room. They really had so little in common other than their brief acquaintance in Hertfordshire.

"Have you been to any assemblies or balls since we left?" asked Caroline, stifling a smirk behind her hand.

Jane looked confused for a moment. "Oh, yes, we attended a wonderful ball on New Year's Eve, and during December there were many parties and dinners in the neighborhood."

"How lovely for you," said Caroline. Louisa launched into a lengthy discourse about all the balls and dinners they had attended since returning to London. By describing in great detail some of the fabulous gowns and jewels they had seen at these events, she hoped to impress Jane and further emphasize the gap between the Bingleys and the Bennets.

As Louisa rambled on, Caroline frantically tried to think of another topic. Since nothing came to mind, it seemed as good a time as any to mention they must be leaving soon. A sudden inspiration hit, and she jumped into the conversation interrupting her sister.

"Mr. Darcy has been gracious enough to send his carriage for us so we may call on Miss Darcy this afternoon. I am afraid we only have a few minutes before it will arrive to whisk us away," Caroline

239

said with an artful swish of her hand. She thought it was especially clever of her to invent this little tale, as it was yet another example of the close relationship between the two families.

Just at that moment, Graves appeared in the doorway. Caroline rose immediately from her chair indicating the call was over, and Jane followed her lead.

"It is so unfortunate we will not return to Netherfield and will be robbed of the pleasure of seeing your dear family again. You must send them our regards," said Caroline sweetly as they ushered Jane to the front door.

Even though she had already given her card to the butler when she arrived, Jane reached into her reticule and pulled out another card with the Gardiners' direction. "I would love to have you call at my aunt and uncle's home while I am in Town. Please come any time."

Both Caroline and Louisa assured their guest that she would see them very soon. Once the door closed behind Jane, the Bingley sisters looked at each other and fell into fits of laughter right there in the hallway.

When Jane reached the sidewalk, she turned to look back at the house. Something did not seem quite right, but she just could not put her finger on what it was. Their promise of a return call sounded hollow and forced. They had not even offered her the courtesy of refreshments. Suddenly, it hit her. Why were the Bingley sisters going to call on Miss Darcy this afternoon if she was coming to their house for dinner that very evening? It did not make sense.

Although Jane puzzled over this all the way back to Cheapside and debated about seeking her aunt's opinion, in the end she decided she must have misunderstood. Caroline and Louisa were her friends. Assuring herself that they would return her call very soon, just as they promised, she began to arrange her schedule so she would be at home to receive them when they came.

Darcy and Georgiana Attend Bingley's Party

by Kara Louise

January 11, 1812

Darcy walked slowly while people hurried past him as they sought shelter from the sudden winter storm that had descended upon the busy streets of London. Icy pellets hit his face, which he tried to bury within the folds of the dark green scarf Georgiana had knitted for him for Christmas. He pulled his hat down further and wrapped his coat more tightly about him. He shivered, and the cold took hold of him down to his toes.

He reached up and fingered the scarf, realizing his neck was the only thing that felt any warmth. A rueful smile touched his lips as he thought of his sister. He had attempted to join her in the joyful spirit she exhibited over the holidays, but it had been in vain. She knew something was not right with him. Despite assuring her that nothing was wrong, she could readily discern otherwise.

As he slipped his gloved hands into his pockets, he fingered the invitation to a ball he had just received. The first of many, he supposed, as the season in London was about to commence. He drew in a deep breath and felt the cold sear his insides, and then quickly let it out in a huff. His expelled breath was transformed before him in a frosty wisp.

He usually received more invitations than he was inclined to accept, and this year, especially, he wished to forego them all. He preferred smaller dinner parties or an evening at the theatre or a concert, but only with his closest acquaintances. This year, however, he felt very disinclined to do much of anything.

He stopped at the corner of the street and gave his head a shake, as he still had two blocks before he reached his home. A pressing need to get outside and walk had impelled him to do so before the weather worsened. He had been walking aimlessly for the past hour, his thoughts in turmoil.

Part of the reason for his restlessness—despite thoughts of Elizabeth invading at the slightest memory—was that he and Georgiana had been invited to a small dinner party given by Mr. and Mrs. Hurst. While he did not always enjoy the company of all, Bingley's presence would do much to cheer him. At least he hoped as much.

He wondered how his friend was faring. If he were to judge Bingley's condition by his own, he surmised his friend was likely not faring well at all. He was certain Bingley was still pining for Miss Jane Bennet, as much as he was for Elizabeth. He shook his head. Pining did not seem a strong enough word. His heart literally ached at the thought of never seeing her again.

Darcy took long, hurried steps up to his house. The wind picked up even more, but the icy rain had stopped. He hoped that would be the end of the frozen moisture. The last thing he needed was a treacherous drive the three miles to the Hursts.

Darcy stepped into his house and handed off his hat, coat, and gloves. He moved to the fireplace, blazing with warmth, and stood before it, rubbing his hands briskly. His walk, which he had hoped would clear his thoughts, served only to chill him to his bones.

"You are home!" Georgiana hurried to his side. "I was beginning to worry about you. I feared everything would turn to ice."

Darcy turned and smiled at his sister. "I appreciate your concern. I took care as I walked."

She pinched her brows and a look of apprehension crossed her face. "Do you think we still ought to go? It could get worse."

Darcy smiled. His sister was so like him. If it were anyone but Bingley's relatives, he would choose to remain at home. "The sleet has stopped. I think we ought to be fine."

Georgiana offered her brother a brief smile. "I should get ready."

Darcy nodded. "We should depart by six o'clock." He attempted to give her a reassuring smile, but he doubted he had been successful in easing his sister's discomfiture.

* * *

Darcy and his sister were brought into the Hursts' drawing room, and they found themselves in the midst of almost two dozen people. He tensed as he realized this was not what he had been expecting. He knew Georgiana felt the same, as he noticed her steps falter.

He wished to remain by her side, to assist her in conversing with others, but Miss Bingley seemed intent on taking that responsibility. Georgiana was soon whisked away, and he watched as Miss Bingley introduced her to others in the room, initiating the conversation. Throughout the evening, he often sought his sister out, raising his brows in question, and she would reply with a smile. It appeared, at least, that Miss Bingley was carrying on the conversations quite well, and Georgiana nodded or smiled as needed.

Darcy was rather surprised at the people who were invited. He did not claim to know all of the Hursts' acquaintances, but it was all married couples, save for an elderly gentleman, Mr. Hogan, who had been widowed for several years. Darcy found him quite interesting. Apart from Bingley, this gentleman's company was preferred.

As the two conversed, the gentleman began to talk about his wife. His sunken blue eyes seemed to light up when Darcy asked about her. "Oh, she was lovely. She could make me smile and laugh with just a look. She was intelligent and we could talk for hours." He winked his eye. "And sometimes all night."

Darcy smiled and suddenly could not get images of Elizabeth out of his thoughts. As Mr. Hogan spoke, he realized just how much he wanted to love his wife as much as this man had loved his. He

243

continued to speak about his wife, and Darcy could not imagine anyone other than Elizabeth in that role.

When dinner was served, Darcy was even more dismayed that he and Georgiana were placed at opposite ends of the dining room table. She was seated between Bingley and the wife of a friend of the Hursts. He was seated next to Miss Bingley and this same friend's husband.

Again, he watched to see how Georgiana fared. He was actually surprised that Miss Bingley had not taken the seat next to his sister, but was beside him. As the meal was served and conversations commenced, the gentleman at his side began speaking to the person on the other side of him. Miss Bingley tapped him on the arm to secure his attention.

"You must be so proud of your sister, Mr. Darcy," Miss Bingley said, as she nodded her head in the young girl's direction. "She has become a delightful young lady and has been so affable this evening. Everyone seems to have a high regard for her. "She seemed quite pleased with herself.

He looked at her and forced a smile. "I am glad to hear that."

"And just look at her and Charles. I believe they are alike in so many ways and have so much in common." She tilted her head. "I do believe they are enjoying each other's company."

Darcy could not necessarily agree with Miss Bingley's estimation of his sister's enjoyment, and Bingley enjoyed nearly everyone's company. It appeared that Bingley was not conversing with his sister, but was speaking to the woman on the other side of her. Georgiana appeared to be merely looking from one to the other, with a sweet, but nervous smile on her face.

It was after dinner that concerned Darcy, for the men would go off by themselves and Georgiana would be left to fend for herself with the ladies. He told himself not to fret, but when it came to his sister, it was difficult not to do so.

As Darcy left with the other men for Mr. Hurst's study, he sent Georgiana an encouraging look. He was grateful—in a way—that

Miss Bingley immediately went to her side. Her fondness for his sister would this one time be appreciated.

When the men joined the ladies later, Mrs. Hurst and Miss Bingley performed for the guests on the pianoforte. But when games were then announced, Darcy expressed his regrets that he and Georgiana had to take their leave. They thanked the Hursts for a pleasant evening.

Miss Bingley looked at her sister and told her she would see them out. Turning to Georgiana, she said, "We must do this again." She walked by Georgiana's side, taking her hand. "This has been simply delightful."

Georgiana nodded meekly and spoke softly with her eyes cast down. "Yes, thank you."

"Thank you, again, Miss Bingley," Darcy said as the carriage approached. "And express our appreciation to your sister and Mr. Hurst."

They stepped into the carriage and Darcy looked at Georgiana. He could barely see her in the dark, but he could discern that she was looking down.

"You did well tonight, Georgiana. I am quite proud of you."

She let out a shaky breath and murmured a soft, "Thank you."

He heard the catch in her voice. "Has anything happened to upset you?" He reached over and took her hand. "If so, please tell me."

She turned her head away, and her words faltered. "I… it is just that…"

"Pray, tell me what is troubling you."

She turned back and grasped his hand tightly. "Is this something that you truly want for me? You have never said anything, and I did not know what to say."

Darcy shook his head, trying to make sense of his sister's words. "Georgiana, I am at a loss to know of what you are speaking. What is it I am supposed to want? All I have ever wanted is for you to be happy."

"Miss Bingley told me about the hopes you share that Mr. Bingley and I will marry."

Darcy's eyes widened, and his chest tightened. "Heavens, Georgiana! She is obviously under a great misapprehension." Darcy shook his head and drew in a breath to calm his rising ire. Finally, in a mellow voice, he said, "Indeed, Bingley is a good friend, and I thought you would enjoy spending the evening with him and a few friends, but Georgiana, I would never enter into a scheme with her regarding you and her brother."

Georgiana looked down. "Miss Bingley kept talking about how delighted you and she would be if he and I would join our families together in matrimony."

Darcy fisted his hands. He could not believe that Miss Bingley would say such a thing. He did not trust himself to speak for a few moments. "She made you believe that I felt this way?"

Georgiana silently nodded and wiped a tear from her eye.

He squeezed her hand, regretting the discomfiture Miss Bingley put her through. "Trust me; I have never entertained such thoughts." He let out a long sigh. "I know that due to my friendship with her brother, you will likely be in company with Miss Bingley at some point in the future. I shall speak with her and insist she not speak of this again. If she does, please know that it is not my wish."

"Thank you," Georgiana replied softly.

Darcy turned away. His stomach was in knots, not just because of what Miss Bingley said to his sister, but because it also made him wonder if her sole motive for separating Bingley from Miss Jane Bennet was because she wanted him to marry Georgiana.

As he thought about it, she had been very vocal about the need to separate the two, and when he mentioned that he had seen little affection on Miss Jane's part, she agreed wholeheartedly. He had taken her agreement as an affirmation of his assessment of his friend's latest venture into love.

Now he wondered whether Miss Bingley had her own purposes in wanting them apart.

Darcy grumbled and shook his head. No, he was not wrong in separating them. It did not make what Miss Bingley had done then or this evening right and proper, but he felt completely justified and it gave him a great deal of satisfaction that he had been looking out for his friend. He rubbed his jaw as he turned to gaze out the window into the darkness. At least he thought it did.

In Which Charlotte Collins Faces the Inquisition

by Diana Birchall

January 13, 1812

?a week

Charlotte had now been married a month and was quite as satisfied with her situation as she had ever dared hope to be. If her husband was not the pleasantest of companions, there was only one of him, and any man, not vicious, might easily be managed by a clever woman. In the case of Mr. Collins, it was only needful for Charlotte to be willing to adapt her expressions to the flattering sort he plainly needed for his contentment. This was but a small sacrifice, for Charlotte, though ordinarily a plain spoken woman, felt it a gratifying improvement to have only him to please, by such simple and expedient means. At Lucas Lodge, she had been required all through her young womanhood to assist her mother with the care of her many younger brothers and sisters, a slavery that had reduced her to little more than a bonne or nursemaid. How much, therefore, she now delighted in having her own house, may be imagined; and with her intelligence and tact she was quite equal to the business of keeping Mr. Collins happy, occupied, and not too much in her own way. In the intervals when Mr. Collins was silent, or away from the house, as did happen for several hours of each day, she could enjoy her own peaceful occupations, to her heart's content.

February was too early a month for gardening, but Charlotte discerned that Mr. Collins was all eagerness to be planning and planting, and she encouraged him to draw up handsome schemes for laying out the vegetable and flower gardens, and set him to pore over seed catalogues. Then he must spend a good deal of time surveying his parish, and visiting those parishioners who were in difficulties. In this he was frequently joined by his patroness Lady Catherine de Bourgh, who had the greatest delight in cottage visiting, and considered Mr. Collins to be her adjunct, rather than the other way round, as might have been supposed. They were often busy for several hours together, in the happy occupation of looking into their villagers' affairs, and no one would disturb Charlotte, although on her husband's return she must pay the tax of listening to the whole story of what Lady Catherine had done, and said, and decreed, to every person in and around Hunsford. Charlotte generally took out her sewing then, and while Mr. Collins talked, need not give more than half an ear to him, with an occasional interjection of, "That was very well done, my dear, upon my word."

Fortunately, he was as a man about the house not unamiable, nor difficult to please for one who was such an efficient housekeeper and judicious manager as Charlotte, and she had only to accept his compliments on her contrivances, which was no severe hardship. From the start, he violently approved of her disposition of cupboards and cabinets, and of her pleasant but firm manner with their domestics. And as the cooking in the establishment improved immeasurably, under Charlotte's direction, from the bachelor meals he had ordered, he really did not know how to be grateful enough, or more pleased with his own acuity and genius for selecting such a paragon of a wife. In moments, he shuddered at the narrow escape he had from his cousin Elizabeth, whom he was now certain would never have suited him at all.

As for more intimate matters between husband and wife, Charlotte had always known she must accept them as a matter of course, and there was nothing about the person of her young and healthy husband to disgust; especially after she had given him a little tactful and delicate instruction. Mr. Collins often rewarded her with expressions of assurance that she pleased him, more than any other woman in the world could have done; and in being very conscious of his blessings, he did much to reconcile Charlotte to hers.

So the marriage prospered from its earliest days; but Charlotte was also fully aware that there was a second person, not in her household, whom she must conciliate. This was Lady Catherine de Bourgh. Charlotte had come to Hunsford prepared to endure much interference in her business, and she resolved ahead of time to meet every attack with patience. That Lady Catherine should approve of Mr. Collins's wife was of the most extreme importance. Charlotte could scarcely be more cognizant of this than Mr. Collins himself. Lady Catherine had nothing less than the power to make or to ruin her happiness; and so she deliberately set out to please, and to promote the most harmonious intercourse possible between Hunsford and Rosings. Charlotte well knew that the benefit of Lady Catherine's patronage was inestimable; she might help her brothers find places, her sisters husbands. Elizabeth might have found it disagreeable to dance attendance upon Lady Catherine, but Charlotte sensibly accepted it as part of the price of her happiness, and she welcomed the most outrageous impositions willingly, or at least quietly. This was greatly, be it noted, to the relief of her husband, who had been anxious that nothing like conflict should arise between the two women most important to him.

Lady Catherine allowed one week to elapse, from the arrival of Mrs. Collins in Hunsford, until she set about making an inspection of her methods. There had been one dinner already, and her Ladyship declared herself perfectly pleased by the quiet, neat appearance of the parson's new wife, and of the deference with which she addressed her superiors. She seemed a modest, proper, sensible sort of young woman—not too young, but all the better for that. A sennight was enough to allow for Mrs. Collins to put herself in order. Lady Catherine was impatient, but at last the seven days were passed, and she sallied forth, curious to see with what economy the new bride managed her household.

Lady Catherine came therefore when least expected, resolved to give Mrs. Collins no warning, no chance to clear up any disorder or to give her house a better appearance than it might have in the ordinary way. At eleven o'clock on the Tuesday forenoon, as soon as she knew that Mr. Collins had gone out in his gig, to make his regular circuit of the parish, Lady Catherine ordered one of her own carriages, and presented herself at Charlotte's door.

Charlotte, discerning her from the window, came out to welcome and invite her into the house.

"I came," announced Lady Catherine, "to satisfy myself as to the state of your arrangements."

"I hope you will be pleased," Charlotte answered calmly, "will your Ladyship have some tea?"

"Tea! I am not one of those ladies who require tea at this hour. But stay—what sort of tea do you purchase, Mrs. Collins?" she asked suspiciously. "Fine India tea is a luxury that does not become a clergyman's household, you must know. Where do you order yours, say?"

"It is some I have brought from home," replied Charlotte. "I mean to keep it only for company, indeed, for distinguished guests; and as we expect to have few visitors, my supply will last for some years."

"Is that so? That is well thought of. Well, now, let me penetrate into your kitchen quarters."

"Certainly," said Charlotte. "If Your Ladyship will step this way. I have had the maids hard at work scrubbing the cook-stove, which I am sorry to say was quite black with crocks and smuts; Mr. Collins as a single man seldom ventured himself into these quarters, and the cooking regions have had to be thoroughly cleaned from top to bottom."

Lady Catherine nodded approvingly, at two kitchen maids deedily down on their knees, and the sparkling stove. "That is satisfactory, most. And here is the pantry, I declare. Let me look inside."

"Dry goods are here, you see, and I am using this little room for a creamery for it is quite cool, and we can use it as an ice-house in summer."

"Cleverly thought of, upon my word. And I see you have used these canisters for—what? Flour?"

251

"Yes; and barley is here—and nuts—and cream of tartar…"

"I have no fault to find," Lady Catherine said, in a tone of mild surprise. "But tell me now—what did you and Mr. Collins eat last night, pray?"

"Why, the Sunday joint of beef, we had warmed over yesterday; and today we shall have hash."

"Most economical," nodded her Ladyship. "Well: let us go down the corridor, and look into this room—and this—" she ran her finger along a mantelpiece, and looked out the window to judge of its cleanliness and clarity. "But what is this? Why are your writing-things and books in this dark little back drawing room? Surely the lady of the house ought to use the handsomer apartment in the front? Would that not be more proper?"

For the first time Charlotte blushed. "I thought it best," she said, "for Mr. Collins to retain his own book room—he is happy in it, and that way, I can have my own privacy, that is," she floundered, lost for words, "a room of my own…"

"Hum! I should have thought it inconvenient, but you know your own interest, Mrs. Collins, I see," said Lady Catherine shrewdly.

"I hope I am putting my husband's interests first, as is my duty," she hastened to answer, with modesty.

"It was not thought necessary in Sir Lewis de Bourgh's family. But then as a bride I had a fortune of my own, which you are unhappily without."

"I hope to be a useful helpmate to Mr. Collins, and by economy ensure that he makes the most of his money," Charlotte said earnestly.

"Aye, no doubt; and I begin to suspect you will succeed, Mrs. Collins," said Lady Catherine with a small and grudging smile of approval. "Now. Show me your bed-chamber. It this where you keep your under garments?"

Elizabeth Hears from the New Mrs. Collins

by Shannon Winslow

January 16, 1812

The wedding took place; the bride and bridegroom set off for Kent from the church door, and every body had as much to say or to hear on the subject as usual. Elizabeth soon heard from her friend; and their correspondence was as regular and frequent as it had ever been; that is should be equally unreserved was impossible. Elizabeth could never address her without feeling that all the comfort of intimacy was over, and, though determined not to slacken as a correspondent, it was for the sake of what had been, rather than what was. - Chapter 20

When Elizabeth had said goodbye to the former Miss Lucas at the church door, it had been with a heavy heart. The previous years of unreserved friendship, of easy intimacy were over. The fact that one was now married and the other not, would have formed somewhat of a barrier in any case. But the manner of Charlotte's marrying—whom she had accepted and why—was an obstacle Elizabeth feared could never be overcome. Henceforth, the specter of Mr. Collins would always divide them.

Nevertheless, out of respect for what had been, she was determined to preserve at least a remnant of their past friendship. Charlotte had asked her to visit Hunsford in March, and Elizabeth had agreed, though she foresaw little pleasure in the scheme. In the meantime, there would be letters exchanged.

Elizabeth anticipated the first missive from Kent with a sort of morbid curiosity. Not that she hoped her friend would be unhappy. Certainly not! It was simply impossible for her to imagine the situation as being otherwise, to envision Charlotte's state of mind without her own feelings creeping in. *"You were right, my dear Lizzy!"* she would surely say. *"I have made the biggest mistake of my life in marrying Mr. Collins, and it is one from which I fear I will never recover. Why, oh, why did I not listen to your advice?"*

But instead, Charlotte wrote the following:

My dearest friend,

I know you will have been wondering how we are getting on here in Kent. So I will jot down a few lines for you, while I have a half-hour's leisure, to assure you that Mr. Collins and I are very well. We experienced no difficulty with our travel from Hertfordshire after the wedding, arriving in good time. And my impressions upon first setting eyes on Hunsford were most agreeable as well.

The Parsonage, while not grand by any means, is as neat and tidy as any reasonable person could well wish for. I already feel quite at home and have been allowed to claim a pretty little parlor at the back of the house for my own particular use. I find the furnishings throughout exactly suited for a clergyman's family. This should come as no surprise since Lady Catherine has done it all according to her own discriminating taste and judgment, as she informed me herself when she condescended to visit me the very day after my arrival. Was not that considerate? I anticipate that she will be just as generous with these civil attentions as my husband has always given her the credit of.

As for more about our distinguished neighbor, her daughter, and the splendors of Rosings Park, I must defer to another occasion the detailed descriptions Mr. Collins has encouraged me to make to you. I simply have not time or room on the page to do them justice now. In any case, you will see all these things for yourself when you come in March. For the present, be satisfied to know that everything here— house, furniture, gardens, neighborhood, etc.—is to my liking, and I am well satisfied with my situation.

Please write soon, Lizzy. I long to hear all the news from Meryton

—all your little comings, goings, and doings—and none of my own family has yet proved to be a very satisfactory correspondent.

With loving regards from Hunsford,

Charlotte Collins

P.S. – Mr. Collins sends his greetings to you and to your family as well. He asks that you would be so kind as to apologize to your father on his behalf, for his not having written more promptly himself. This is a circumstance he promises to remedy very soon, at which time he will beg Mr. Bennet's pardon in proper form.

Oh, my. *Well satisfied*. It was precisely what she should have expected to hear from her friend—all cheerful practicality and no complaints. Elizabeth could accept that much. She could even respect such a statement, whereas she would never have believed a claim of Charlotte's being deliriously happy with Mr. Collins. Impossible! Very well. Elizabeth supposed she must be satisfied too. She could not quite understand it, but she owed it to Charlotte to be glad for her, to be glad she could be content with the life she had chosen for herself. There was clearly nothing else to be done.

Well, there *was* one more thing. Elizabeth drew two sheets of paper from the desk and took up her pen to write an answer.

My dear Charlotte,

Thank you for your letter. I was so pleased to hear that you are well, and that you find everything at Hunsford so consistent with your taste and expectations. Here at Longbourn, we continue on much as you left us...

Jane's Dreams

by Susan Mason-Milks

January 25, 1812

Jane moved slowly back and forth in the rocking chair in an attempt to soothe herself as she might an unhappy child. Four weeks in Town had passed, and she had neither seen nor heard from Mr. Bingley. Jane was persuaded by something Caroline had let slip that her brother knew she was in Town, but still he did not come. Even as sanguine as she usually was about such things, she finally knew she had to accept he was gone forever from her life.

Her call at Grosvenor Street earlier in the month to see Caroline Bingley and Louisa Hurst had been awkward and uncomfortable, but it was nothing compared to what had transpired when Caroline finally called on her here at Gracechurch Street. From the moment she arrived, Caroline had looked bored and indifferent. Although Aunt Gardiner tried to be helpful, attempting to smooth over the awkward pauses, the conversation lagged as Jane had no heart to try and Caroline no interest. Mercifully, the call was short.

Jane never liked to think ill of people, but at last, she knew she must. Miss Bingley had been wrong, very wrong to be so duplicitous in pretending to be her friend. In the beginning, Jane was certain Miss Bingley's efforts to form a friendship had been sincere, but now she even doubted that. Had Caroline's attentions been just a way to pass the time while in the country? Or had she only wanted to know Jane better because her brother had taken an interest in her? If that were true, then it made sense Miss Bingley's interest had faded just as her brother's had.

In spite of the hurt she felt, Jane did not regret having known Charles Bingley for those wonderful weeks. They were some of the happiest of her life. If only she could let go of the vision she had created of Mr. Bingley as her gentle and attentive husband, their comfortable home, and most importantly, the children they would have together. She had been so certain he was forming an attachment to her, but then he had just disappeared.

In her darkest moments, she despaired of ever again meeting someone as amiable as Mr. Bingley. What would happen to her now? As the eldest of five girls, Jane felt a responsibility to marry well in order to provide for her mother and sisters in the event of her father's death. Several gentlemen in the neighborhood had shown an interest in her recently including Mr. Wyatt, a very nice widower with two small children. Jane did not mind the idea of becoming mother to his children. Caring for and nurturing children came naturally to her. Mr. Wyatt had a small estate about the size of Longbourn, but he was a much more attentive landlord than her father. As a result, the estate prospered, and she knew her life would be a pleasant and easy one. Surely, it would not be such a terrible thing to be married to a man like that. At least she respected him and knew he would treat her respectfully as well. Maybe love would even grow between them. Perhaps, when she returned to Longbourn in the spring, if he were still unattached, she would make more of an effort to talk with him.

Jane continued to rock to soothe herself. Several times, she cried silently, salty tears rolling down her cheeks. She would allow herself this moment of self-pity, and then she would go on with her life and not look back. At least that was what she told herself. In truth, she knew she would never forget Charles Bingley who had been so perfectly suited to her. How she had loved it when his eyes came alive and sparkled when he saw her. She had felt as if it made her come to life, too. Her mother always told her how beautiful she was, but Jane did not believe it until she saw herself reflected in his eyes. He had called her his angel.

Jane dreaded writing to Lizzy about recent events because she would have to acknowledge how wrong she had been about Caroline. It would be difficult to admit to Lizzy that she had been right all along, but Jane knew if circumstances repeated themselves, she would most likely be deceived again. She had nothing to reproach herself for. Her behavior had been sincere and true. Caroline Bingley would have to live with the unkind way she had acted. In her heart, she felt pity for Caroline whose happiness seemed to depend so much on things outside herself—her social connections, her clothes, her money. Jane knew that she herself was rich in the things that really mattered.

So, Jane rocked. First, she began to feel calmer and finally, she grew sleepy. Abandoning the rocking chair, she crawled into the bed she shared with her eldest niece who was her namesake. Sensing her aunt's presence in the bed, Janie moved to cuddle up against her. In turn, Jane was comforted by the little girl's warmth. Kissing her niece, Jane smoothed her tangled curls on the pillow and soon fell into a deep sleep.

Mr. Darcy and Colonel Fitzwilliam Take a Trip to Cheapside

by L. L. Diamond

January 25, 1812

The bustling streets of London passed outside the carriage, and a foul-tempered Darcy turned away from the happy faces of the passersby to his cousin who sat opposite him.

An hour prior, Colonel Fitzwilliam had appeared at his home, insisting they had to venture out to a shop in Cheapside. Cheapside! Of course, he refused, if for no other reason, but to avoid yet another reminder of Elizabeth Bennet. Was there nothing that would spare him the torment of her memory? Unfortunately, his cousin would not leave him to the solitude of his library.

"I must insist you finally tell me where we are going," he demanded in a surly tone.

Fitzwilliam lifted his eyebrows. "My but you are ill-tempered this morning. What has you in such a mood these days?"

"You are aware how much I dislike the balls and dinner parties of the season? I have had to endure your mother's Twelfth Night ball as well as a dinner party given by none other than Miss Bingley. I should think those two events alone would be enough to sour anyone's disposition." Darcy steered his attention to the view outside the window as he attempted to avoid any further discourse on the subject.

A hearty chuckle came from across the carriage. "The only teeth set on edge by Miss Bingley belong to you, cousin, and I daresay it is

259

your own fault."

His head jerked back. "My fault?"

"You are too concerned with offending Bingley, so you do not treat her in the curt manner you do most women."

Aggravation with his cousin's observation and the situation welled within him. "I may not enjoy speaking with the ladies as you do, but I am not curt."

The colonel gave a small snort. "I beg to differ. I have seen many a lady who was offended by your method of keeping them at bay."

"I have no wish to be ensnared by any of them, so I ensure I do nothing to encourage their hopes." With a heavy exhale, Darcy grimaced. "But I am afraid my latest endeavor to be of aid to Bingley has not helped the matter with Miss Bingley."

His cousin's expression reflected his curiosity as he leaned forward in his seat. "So, you have saved Bingley from himself once again? What was it this time? Another bad investment opportunity?"

Darcy shook his head. "Bingley became enamored of a local girl while in Hertfordshire."

"That does not sound too dire," responded the colonel. "He is always fancying himself in love; it passes soon enough."

Again, he shook his head. "No, this time was different. Bingley showed a decided preference for the young lady from the first of their acquaintance, and by the time of the ball at Netherfield, it became apparent he had raised the expectations of the neighborhood. They all believed him soon to propose."

His cousin furrowed his brows. "You felt a marriage to this lady to be imprudent?"

Darcy closed his eyes as he envisioned the deplorable behavior of Mrs. Bennet and the three youngest Bennet daughters. "It would have been a most imprudent match. She had little dowry, no connections, and the behavior of her family was objectionable, to say the least."

"You must consider it a triumph to have successfully separated the two."

"You can be certain," he stated with conviction. "My only regret is that by being in collusion with Miss Bingley, she seems more assured I will one day propose to her. She is intolerable.

Colonel Fitzwilliam regarded Darcy with a critical eye, prompting him to shift in his seat. "Come to think of it, your insufferable mood was not present until your return with Bingley." A smirk lit his cousin's face. "Did you make the acquaintance of a woman in Hertfordshire? Would you be pining for someone as unsuitable as Bingley's new angel?"

He scoffed as he adjusted his cuffs. Elizabeth Bennet? Unsuitable? If not for her family and connections, she would be eminently suitable. "You are ridiculous. I would never be so imprudent."

The colonel sighed. "No, I suppose you would not."

"What is so special about this wine and brandy merchant?" asked Darcy with the intention of changing the subject.

"As I told you earlier, he boasts of a particularly fine assortment of port, claret, and brandy. My father was impressed by their selection when he placed his order for the ball. I thought you might wish to meet the proprietor."

He suppressed a smile at the success of his maneuver. "I do not see the urgency of such a matter. I have a perfectly adequate supplier on Piccadilly Street, who I have used since my father passed."

With an irritated huff, his cousin sat back against the squabs. "I would wager this man's prices to be more reasonable. He will also deliver to Grosvenor Square and Belgravia, which means you should not have to return once you have set up an account."

The two gentlemen stared at one another for a few seconds until Colonel Fitzwilliam shook his head and turned to watch the buildings pass through the window.

A row of houses along Gracechurch Street drew Darcy's particular interest while he avoided further conversation with his cousin. Did one of them belong to the uncle of Elizabeth Bennet? He had never taken the time to study the neighborhood in the past, and he had to admit some of these homes were actually pleasant and well tended. Of course, the appearances did not necessarily correspond to the personalities of the owners. After all, Longbourn was not objectionable from all outward appearances.

A small park ahead caught his eye. Had Miss Elizabeth ever walked in that park? With her love for the activity, she must have during one of her visits to her family. He could almost envision her strolling through the trees, her hair windswept and the hem of her dress stained with grass and dirt—much as she had appeared upon her arrival at Netherfield to care for her sister.

They drew closer, and a young lady at the front gates came into focus, revealing her to be none other than Jane Bennet. Darcy leaned back from the window, while he watched her walk into the park hand in hand with a small child, a servant trailing behind.

He would have to ensure Bingley remained away from Cheapside for the near future. They had struggled so to prevent his return to Hertfordshire and to conceal Miss Bennet's presence in London; it would not do for him to happen upon her now.

"There is a handsome young lady," said his cousin, interrupting his thoughts. "Who is she?"

With a shrug of his shoulders, Darcy donned a mask of feigned indifference. "How am I to know? I would imagine a tradesman's daughter, one of good means by her dress."

"You appeared to have recognized her, or at least, taken interest?"

"No, I am not acquainted with her, and as for her being of interest..." His last view as they passed was of Jane Bennet smiling to the child at her side. "She smiles too much."

Colonel Fitzwilliam gave a bark of laughter. "That has to be the most preposterous notion I have ever heard you utter. What man has not been bewitched by the smile of a beautiful woman?"

Miss Elizabeth again came to mind and Darcy gave a wry grin.

"Perhaps a pair of fine eyes might one day garner my notice."

His cousin chuckled. "I pity you when they do. You are so accustomed to maintaining your distance, you will be at a loss as to how to win her favor." He turned serious and held Darcy's eye. "But she will be a lucky woman—a lucky woman.

The Impressions of Anne de Bourgh

by Diana Birchall

January 26, 1812

"My dear Anne," Lady Catherine de Bourgh said to her daughter, "I do hope you will be taking your drive today. You need an airing."

"Is is so cold," Anne replied fretfully, "I do not see how a constitutional drive can be expected to do any one good in the month of January."

"You know what Dr. Shaw said," Lady Catherine put down her eggshell-thin teacup deliberately. "Your health requires a great deal of fresh air, and today it is sunny."

"A pale sunshine, and I do not believe it is going to last. There are several black clouds. And it is so dreary sitting up in the pony phaeton alone."

"Take Mrs. Jenkinson," urged Lady Catherine, "Upon my word, I would go with you myself, only I have an immense deal of correspondence. There are important matters occurring in the nation, and I, as a magistrate, must inform the Prime Minister of my views. And then I must do some sick-visiting. There is a laborer in the village who is refusing to labor, and I am certain he is just shamming."

"I could come with you there," said Anne, brightening up a little.

"No; if he is ill, we could not run the risk. You are not strong, Anne, and would be liable to catch cold, in those chilly cottages. Besides, I wish that you would call at the Parsonage."

"The Parsonage?" Anne frowned. "Oh, Mama, have we not paid sufficient attentions—and more—to those odious people?"

"My dear! Mr. Collins is our clergyman, and a very good sort of young man, I think. Certainly he has shown himself properly deferential to me, as is very right, and treats me as he ought, considering that I am his patroness, squiress, and superior, in every way. Besides, it is to Mrs. Collins that I wish you to speak."

"Me!" Anne drew back with horror. "What have I done that you must inflict her upon me?"

"Why Anne! She is a harmless creature enough. Where is your objection?" Lady Catherine poured some more tea, and urged it upon her.

"No, I won't have more tea, Mama. I am too upset. The whole trouble with that Mrs. Collins is that she is common. And you know it."

Lady Catherine's heavily marked black brows drew together. "I cannot say that you are not right—but then, I myself urged Mr. Collins not to marry any one high born, or with pretensions. Mrs. Collins appears to me to be a very good sort of housekeeping body."

"She is not a lady. And her husband is a clown."

Seldom, very seldom, had Lady Catherine been so at a loss for a reply. After a moment's consideration she said, "So, this is why you never speak to them at dinner, and are so silent. I had observed that."

"You are correct. And if I may dare to say so, Mama, it is my opinion that you have been inviting them here to Rosings far too often. I know precisely what sort of pushing, presuming people they are, and if you give them an inch they will take an ell! They have been here seven times in their month of married life, and will soon begin to believe twice weekly visits to Rosings are theirs by right. You are altogether too soft hearted and susceptible to inferiors, Mama."

"I have ever been celebrated for my kindness of heart, it is true," Lady Catherine agreed complacently, "but if I may contradict you, my dear, I do believe them to be quite harmless, and agreeable enough. And you know how little company we can have here in these dark winter nights. It is well that a tame clergyman and his wife can be called over at any time for a game of cassino or quadrille."

"Pah! I would much rather sit with a book, than listen to the pratings of Mr. Collins, or the flatteries of his wife."

"So that is why you never open your lips from one end of a card game to another, either," her mother mused. "I see."

"Exactly so. And may I remind you, Mama, that we need not be so desperately craven for society, as that. When I am married to Darcy, the society at Pemberley will be quite another thing. And you shall spend the whole of every winter with us, I am determined on that."

"Ah, Anne, your sweetness is fabled. I know Darcy will never be able to resist it, when he sees you. He must be quite ready to settle down by now, and I do hope that another season will see you the happy mistress of Pemberley, as your dear aunt and I always planned. Surely this will be the year."

"Of course it will," murmured Anne, who had always seen this fate before her, and in her pride and self-satisfaction, it had never occurred to her to doubt it. "When I am Mrs. Darcy, you know, I will never have to converse with such common women as that Mrs. Collins. Did you see her at dinner the other night? Her gown so very drab and plain, and she could not even eat her soup delicately. That shows her to be so very ill bred."

"Her father, Sir William Lucas, is a knight," Lady Catherine pointed out doubtfully. "A recent creation, it is true, but they say he was presented at court."

"Well, it did nothing for his daughter's manners," said Anne tartly. "You know she was nothing but a baby nurse to that dreadful brood of brothers and sisters she talks about, and she has no elegance, no refinement, no air about her at all. And is that the sort of person you want me to associate with, so soon before my elevation to be Darcy's wife, and chatelaine of Pemberley?"

"I only wanted you to give her the receipt for beef tea that old Nanny wrote out for me," said Lady Catherine, in a tone of unwonted meekness. "Mrs. Collins believes her husband's voice is strained, owing to the rigors of his last sermon, and a chill upon his throat. It would be a kindness, my dear."

"Oh, very well," said Anne crossly. "I'll call for the phaeton." She pulled irritably at the bell-rope, and Mrs. Jenkinson came hastily into the room.

"I am sorry, my dear Anne," she said breathlessly, "but I was only talking to Nanny about that receipt your mother wanted, at her request. Shall you drive over to the Parsonage now?"

"Apparently so," Anne replied ungraciously. "I must be a ministering angel to the lowly. Pretty preferment, upon my word, is it not?"

"May I come and keep you company?" asked Mrs. Jenkinson humbly. "I could carry your cashmere shawl, so you will not catch a chill when you get out of the carriage."

"No; to be sure not. If I am alone, I will say that it is not a regular call, and then I need not get out of the carriage at all. They can come to the gate. I will not give them even one quarter of an hour." And she swept out of the room, her small, thin figure upright, to put on her driving costume.

Lady Catherine and Mrs. Jenkinson, left alone, met each other's eyes.

"It is true that the Collinses are common, very common," said Lady Catherine, "but I do wish Anne could try to be a little more engaging. She thinks she will have nobody to do with at Pemberley but the high born, but managing a great house like that, makes many demands."

"Oh, but she was born to the task," said Mrs. Jenkinson, rolling up her eyes and looking at the heavens earnestly. "Was it not Mr. Collins who said that she would be an ornament to the rank of duchess? He never spoke more truly."

"To be sure," said Lady Catherine, pleased. "Her grace and condescension are such as are not often seen. Oh, I know Darcy will be very taken with her, when he comes. This must and shall be the year."

Mr. Bingley Regrets

by Susan Mason-Milks

February 2, 1812

Charles Bingley lingered at the breakfast table over a cup of coffee that had grown cold long ago. Although the newspaper from London was open in front of him, he had not read a word. His heart and mind were engaged elsewhere. Closing his eyes, he could see Jane Bennet's face looking up at him serenely as they danced. Just one glance from her was enough to leave him completely speechless. Charles Bingley, speechless? That was something new! Her eyes were so bright and completely without pretense; her gloved hand in his, light as a feather. She had no idea how alluringly beautiful she was. Jane truly was an angel.

He knew he had a tendency to be too impetuous, to speak before thinking, and her sweet, gentle nature was the perfect counterbalance. Once when she was sitting beside him, he had started to open his mouth to make some rash pronouncement, but she had placed her hand ever so gently on his arm for just a second. Although her touch had been so light, as if a small bird had perched there briefly and then flown away, it was still enough to slow him down, to make him think before he spoke. In all the time they spent together, he had never heard her say a derogatory word about anyone or pass on gossip, an activity his sisters seemed to delight in. His Jane always believed the best of everyone. His Jane. He liked the sound of that. Taking a deep breath, he let it out slowly. She *could* have been his Jane, but he had thrown it all away.

Bingley had been so certain Jane returned his affections that it had come as a complete shock when Caroline and Darcy told him they believed she was indifferent and just paying attention to him to please her mother. How could he have read the signs so incorrectly? At first he listened only to his heart, which told him they must be wrong. Jane was not a coy, sophisticated woman like so many he had met. There was no artifice about her. The Jane he knew had more true sweetness than any other woman of his acquaintance. Although Caroline had insisted the Bennets had no connections, no status in society, and had implied Jane was not good enough for him, Bingley felt exactly the opposite—he was not good enough for her.

But what if it were true she did not care for him? Perhaps, she had already begun to favor some other gentleman as soon as he had departed. Bingley did not know what to trust—the pull of his own heart or the warnings from his sister and Darcy. His friend had never steered him wrong before, but then Darcy did not know Jane the way he did. No, he had not been wrong. She did care for him just as he cared for her.

Jane Bennet was a treasure, but he had given her up. He knew there was a distinct possibility he would regret her forever. Why did I listen to them instead of my heart? Perhaps, he should defy them all, return to Netherfield, and pay court to his angel again. He shook his head. No, he could never return. If he was right and Jane had harbored true feelings for him, she must hate him by now for abandoning her with no word. Caroline had said she would write to Jane and break it to her that they would not be returning. If his sister believed Jane did not care for him, then why had she told him she would try to let her friend down gently? Then it occurred to him —Caroline's reasons for not wanting him to return to Netherfield could be more in her own self interest than out of concern for him.

After a few minutes of contemplation, Bingley's head began to hurt. Putting his fingers to his temples, he closed his eyes and rubbed in a circular motion hoping to relieve the pain.

Just then, he heard a rustling of silk and detected the scent of Caroline's perfume as she crossed the room. Bingley knew it was rude of him not to acknowledge her or stand as she entered, but he was too irritated with her to be polite. Instead, he pretended he was studying the paper so intently that he had not heard her approach.

"Louisa and I are going shopping this afternoon. You did not have other plans for the carriage, did you?" Caroline asked, as if daring him to deny her request. As her fingers drummed on the table, each tap felt like a blow to his already sensitive head.

Bingley remained silent. He was not sure with whom he was more angry—Caroline for trying to influence him or himself for believing her. *Why do I still put up with her antics?* In the past when he had tried to rein her in, she always pouted or did something else to make his life miserable.

"Charles, are you listening to me?" Her voice had that sharp edge to it he always took as a warning not to cross her, but this time, he ignored it.

"Caroline, have you had a letter from Miss Bennet recently?" he asked suddenly. As he waited for her answer, Bingley noticed that the only sound in the room was the ticking of the mantle clock.

"I believe I received a letter in December," she responded slowly, examining her perfectly manicured hands.

"I remember she mentioned the possibility of visiting her aunt and uncle in Town during the winter. Did she say she was coming to London?"

Caroline looked off and to the left as if searching for an answer. "Let me see now. Hmm… No, I do not believe she mentioned any visits to Town." She followed this with a smile that stopped short of her eyes.

When he did not respond, she continued, "Then you have no objection to our taking the carriage for the afternoon? And one of the footmen to carry our parcels." He noticed how smoothly she had changed the subject.

Bingley was about to protest as he had planned to meet Darcy at the fencing club for a little sparring. They had both been engaging in that vigorous activity with some frequency of late. It would be

271

inconvenient, but he could make other arrangements. Perhaps that would be easier than telling Caroline "no." Denying her would only result in much unpleasantness. He knew at some point he would have to begin standing up to Caroline, but this was a relatively small matter. He thought it wiser to pick his battles carefully.

Caroline took his silence as assent. She nodded and stood to leave. Looking down at her dress as she smoothed out the tiny wrinkles, she said distractedly, "You must go with us to the Chadwicks' dinner party on Tuesday. We cannot have you at home moping about."

From the doorway, she added, "I understand their eldest daughter is very accomplished."

"Mmm...accomplished," he replied, but his thoughts were already back in Hertfordshire.

Caroline Bingley Schemes to Catch Mr. Darcy

by C. Allyn Pierson

February 17, 1812

Caroline tapped her quill against her tightly pursed lips as she contemplated the dilemma before her. So far, her plans to dazzle Mr. Darcy with her wit and elegance had not yielded the matrimonial fruit which she had hoped to cultivate. But...all was not yet lost. Now that their party had retreated to London and the abominable Bennets were no longer flaunting their milkmaid prettiness in front of Bingley and Darcy, perhaps she could divert Darcy's mind enough from her brother's stupid infatuation to focus on her availability (and eligibility).

Perhaps Georgiana could help her...oh, not knowingly, of course. The dear girl would not say boo to a goose, let alone try to manipulate her revered elder brother. But...Charles was spending most of his free hours with Darcy, hanging around at their stupid club, shooting at Mantons, or riding in Hyde Park. Certainly, she could shake out her riding habit and start showing her face in the park, but it would probably be more effective to arrange some outings with Georgiana.

She turned to her daybook and perused the next two weeks. They were already engaged to dine with the Darcys in two days. Perhaps Georgiana would enjoy a visit to the British Museum. It would be devastatingly boring, but would likely impress Darcy with her affection for his sister and show him what a good sister-in-law she would be. Of course, any time spent with Georgiana would also allow her a closer relationship with Charles...surely he would forget Miss Bennet with such a superior young lady in his company!

She felt an urge to write down a list of her plans, but knew that would give too much appearance of planning if it fell into the wrong hands, so she just wrote a quick invitation to Georgiana and sent it off with a footman.

He soon came back with an acceptance, and the next day she stopped at the Darcy townhouse and picked up Georgiana.

"How delightful you look this morning, Miss Darcy! Are you ready for our outing?"

"Yes Miss Bingley. I am looking forward to visiting the museum. Do you suppose there is any chance Lord Elgin's marbles will be purchased by the museum so we can see them whenever we want?"

"We can only hope, my dear Miss Darcy"

They spent two hours in the museum, most of it in the Egyptian Hall. Georgiana showed a quite gruesome interest in the disgusting mummies.

"Ugh! How *can* you bear to look at those hideous things, my dear Miss Darcy? They are nasty!"

"Oh, Miss Bingley! How can you say that! Just think...these are the mortal remains of real people from one of the greatest ancient civilizations! Does it not give you the chills to think about what grandeur and history these people saw?"

Miss Bingley shuddered. "All I can think about is their disgusting current appearance, which does, indeed, give me chills."

"Oh."

Miss Darcy's shoulders slumped a little and she moved on to the next room, giving a glance back at the mummies before she did so. Miss Bingley thought she should put this outing on a more interesting level.

"My dear Miss Darcy, shall we find a cup of tea to refresh us before we go home? My brother tells me we will be seeing you tomorrow evening for the theatre."

"Yes, my brother told me about it. I am looking forward to it."

Later, when Caroline reached home, she gave a sigh of relief. What an exhausting day! Hopefully, the opera would be more stimulating. Perhaps she should go to the lending library and find out more about the opera and the composer. She had no interest in such things, but Darcy certainly had an ear for music and she must convince him she was worthy of his interest.

Her hopes were destined to be dashed. Darcy and Georgiana both kept their eyes on the stage for the entire performance and had their heads together talking about it during the interval. Miss Bingley tried to enter their discussion, but found herself overwhelmed by their talk of the staging, the sets and the costumes, as well as the story and music. Who in the world cared about such things! Their late supper was no better. Caroline managed to seat herself next to Georgiana, but Darcy, whom she thought was directly behind her, somehow ended up across the table between Charles and Louisa. Damn his over developed courtesy! Georgiana was still taken up with the opera, which she talked about *ad nauseum*, and Caroline was stymied.

Later that night, she sat up in bed, contemplating her hunt for Darcy, but she was too exhausted to come up with another plan of attack. Tomorrow she would begin anew, she resolved as she blew out the candle.

Darcy Reflects on Elizabeth

by Kara Louise

February 18, 1812

Very unlikely Feb in Derbysh.

A few weeks before Darcy sets out for Rosings

Darcy looked out at the grounds from the window of his room at Pemberley. The countryside, which had been a palette of muted browns since autumn, was at last bursting forth with new life, evidenced by the greens that dotted the trees, shrubs, and lawn.

He drew in a deep breath. It was always in these first few weeks of spring that he appreciated Pemberley most. Winter had been particularly cold this year, especially those months he had spent in London. For some reason, it seemed colder than he had ever recollected. He shuddered just thinking about it.

He rubbed his jaw and looked back at his valet, who was readying his clothes for the day. "Do you think it will warm up today?"

"Oh, I do, sir. I stepped out earlier and it was quite pleasant." The valet gave him a reassuring nod. "There is nothing like the first hint of spring to wipe away the icy frost that has built up over the past several months."

Darcy nodded to himself and then replied, "Yes, that is so very true." He turned back to the window and clenched his jaw as he considered how the bitter cold perfectly described how he had felt the past few months. He had entered London with a glacial demeanor, intent on separating Bingley from Miss Jane Bennet, but more than that, fighting within himself the attraction he had developed for Elizabeth.

Darcy pressed his lips tightly together. The more he fought the temptation to think about Elizabeth, to dwell on those things that he found so irresistible, the colder he felt inside. He had tried to convince himself that she was not at all suitable. He fisted his hands tightly as he considered her connections and station in life were decidedly beneath his own! The behavior of most of her family members was undeniably most unbecoming. No! She would not do for him!

Despite having made several attempts to join in the festivities of the Season in Town, he had found it increasingly dull and tiresome. Elizabeth invaded his thoughts and he could not help but wonder how much more pleasant it would have been if she were accompanying him. He found himself comparing other ladies to her, and to his chagrin, they always came up wanting.

Her sparkling eyes followed him wherever he went. He often heard her lively laugh in the silence of a wintry night. Her face, although unfashionably tan, was silky and smooth. The mere thought of her smile warmed him. Her dark hair had often glistened as it reflected the sun or candlelight, practically beckoning him to caress a curl, pull out the pins that held her hair up, and run his fingers through her long tresses.

He slowly shook his head as the image of her was so vivid and real, it was as if he had just seen her yesterday.

"Foolish heart!"

"Pardon me, sir?"

Darcy tensed. Had he really spoken aloud? He turned to his valet. "I merely said... I would like an early start." He winced at the thought that it made absolutely no sense. None of it did!

"Today, sir? I was not aware of any pressing need."

"No, I was referring to my departure for London. I would like an early start when I set out."

His valet nodded, and it was followed by silence, giving Darcy hope that his valet was satisfied with his answer. He turned back to gaze out the window. As he looked at the grounds, it took every ounce of resolve to keep Eliz..., no *Miss Elizabeth Bennet*, from invading his thoughts.

After a few moments, his valet said, "When you are ready, sir."

His words stirred Darcy out of his reverie and he walked over to him. As the valet helped him out of his nightclothes, Darcy made a determination. Just as he shed his clothes for the new day—for the new season—so he would shed whatever remnant of attraction he harbored for Miss Bennet. Just as the cold days of winter were transforming into days of warmth and new life, so would he transform his heart and mind and set them on a new course.

No longer would he live in this cold shell that had shrouded him the past few months, but he would step into the warmth of spring with nary another thought of *her*! It appeared as though Bingley had done whatever needed to be done to put thoughts of Jane Bennet aside. Certainly *he* could put aside any and all feelings for Miss Bennet, as well!

He would depart for Town in a few days. He would see Georgiana and then meet his cousin and spend time with him in London before the two set out for Rosings. He would focus on that. Yes! He was greatly looking forward to seeing Georgiana and Fitzwilliam again!

A small smile touched his lips. This was what he needed. Spring was here and he was already beginning to feel its warmth, new life, and a new determination grow within him. There would be nothing in Kent to remind him of Eliz... her!

Darcy Anticipates a Trip to Rosings

by L. L. Diamond

February 20, 1812

A knock at the door roused Darcy from the ledgers before him. "Enter," he called.

The door opened to reveal none other than Georgiana, who remained in the doorway until he gestured her inside.

"Did you wish to speak to me?" Her voice was little more than a whisper, but such a tone was not unusual since Ramsgate. Blast George Wickham for hurting her as he had!

With a nod to the footman in the corridor, the door was closed behind her as he rose to escort her to a chair. Once she was settled, he sat upon the corner of his desk.

"I received a letter from Lady Catherine."

Georgiana's eyes bulged. She never had dealt well with his aunt's overbearing nature and her present state would only make matters worse.

"Do not fret. She merely wished to inform me that she expects us for Easter. Colonel Fitzwilliam will join me as he does every year, but would you care to make the trip with us?"

Her head began to shake. "Please do not make me. I could not bear Lady Catherine—not since…"

His hand grasped hers. "I have no intention of forcing you, Georgie. My intention was to know your wishes, remember?"

She gulped as she glanced at the portrait of their parents that graced the spot above the mantle. "Will she be angry, do you think?"

"Nothing I cannot manage." He gave a gentle squeeze of her hand, and she turned back to him. "I am certain she will use your absence to press me to finalise a betrothal to Anne, so she will be distracted soon enough."

With a gasp, she leaned forward. "But you said you would not wed Anne! You have not changed your mind, have you?"

"No, I have not changed my mind." He released her hand, stood, and resumed his place at his desk. No, he had not altered his opinions on that subject. He would never marry Anne! His quandary was the image of the lady he now envisioned in the role!

"I shall never marry Anne, despite her mother's proclamations of us being destined from the cradle."

How could he wed his cousin when Elizabeth Bennet possessed his heart and mind? Images of her now haunted him as he wandered the rooms of his London home. She sat at his mother's dressing table, grinning mischievously at him in the looking glass and penned letters at the escritoire in the mistress' sitting room. The worst, however, was the evenings, when he would inevitably find her lying upon her side in his bed! She painted an irresistible picture with her chestnut curls trailing down her arm to the mattress below.

He required a distraction from the memory of Elizabeth Bennet! He needed to depart London!

After a shake of his head, he cleared his throat. "Do not worry yourself. I desire more from marriage than an estate, regardless of who deems me a fool."

"I am relieved," she responded. "I may have never said as much, but you are the best of brothers. Anne is too much like her mother, and I fear she would never develop the regard you deserve. You should not have to settle for such a marriage."

Darcy's eyes burned, and he blinked hard as he cleared his throat. His sister was too good a creature!

"I am flattered."

Her cheeks pinked, and after a quick look around the room, she rose. "I should return to Mrs. Annesley. I have not yet finished practicing the pianoforte and the master comes tomorrow for my lesson."

He stood. "Of course, though I am sure you will impress him."

"I hope so." Georgiana stepped forward and embraced him, her arms squeezing his chest. After a moment, she withdrew with a small smile and departed.

The sound of a sigh joined the ticking of the clock on the mantle as he glanced to the sofa. Elizabeth looked up from where she was seated at the end, reading a letter, her feet tucked under her as she relaxed against the back of the furniture. She glanced up at him and lifted one eyebrow with an impish grin.

His hands flew to his face and he rubbed his eyes hard with the heels. When he peered back in the direction of the sofa, she was gone.

This madness had to stop! He could not continue on in this manner!

With a huff, he dropped into his chair and lifted his pen. He would immerse himself in work, so he could no longer dwell on Elizabeth Bennet!

After twenty minutes of sitting in such an attitude, he thrust the pen back into its place. "Blast!"

The chair scraped discordantly against the floor as he stood and strode from his study. He required a diversion! He peeked into several rooms, but to no avail. A low growl resonated through the corridor. He would go out! There was sure to be something! After all, this was London!

An hour later, he returned. How could Elizabeth follow him to Hyde Park? And the booksellers on Bond Street?

His walking stick and greatcoat were thrust into the hands of the footman before Darcy stomped up the stairs. Once in the privacy of his bedchamber, he poured himself a large glass of brandy, which was brought with haste to his lips. After a searing gulp, he dropped into the closest chair and stared into the fire.

281

He could not continue in such a fashion. He would go mad! The trip to Rosings was propitious, as it would keep him occupied and free of the spectre of Elizabeth Bennet. At Rosings, he would conquer this infuriating infatuation!

Miss de Bourgh's Expectations

by Diana Birchall

March 1, 1812

Lady Catherine prided herself on her deportment, which consisted in a magnificently upright carriage, and a way of moving that might be called an arrogant glide. To display a need for haste, would be deserving of contempt; a lady did not hurry-skurry like a schoolgirl. Yet on this morning, Lady Catherine did enter the small summer breakfast-parlor at Rosings with such unwonted rapidity that Miss de Bourgh and Mrs. Jenkinson looked up startled from their work.

It was only March, yet the ladies liked to sit in this room of a morning because it had good light for stitching, and was in its way more comfortable than many of the grander rooms. Anne, who hated to walk before noon, liked to sit and sew, and look out the window. She was engaged in making yet another garment for her trousseau, which had been her self-assigned daily task for many years. Almost since she was a little girl sewing her sampler, had she worked on the embroidered linens and night-dresses for her marriage to Mr. Darcy. She seldom accomplished more than one or perhaps two stitches a minute, but fortunately Mrs. Jenkinson had worked more steadily and great piles of fine Irish cloth and delicate laced muslins were put up in lavender in the massive cedar-lined chests, waiting in the great store-rooms of Rosings for the happy day.

"My dear!" trumpeted Lady Catherine. "Here is news, tremendous news."

"Oh!" Mrs. Jenkinson exclaimed, "Is it something that must be broke to her in stages, Lady Catherine? Anne is delicate. You know we are always saying that she is not at all strong. Shall I fetch some water?"

"No, no," impatiently returned Lady Catherine, "it is good news—the very best."

Anne's eyes grew wide and a pink color mounted in her sallow face as she sat forward in her seat. In no other way did she betray her expectations, but they were no less than that the letter her mother so excitedly flapped, should contain a proposal from Mr. Darcy.

"Only think!" Lady Catherine cried. "Darcy is coming! He will soon be here!"

Anne made an impatient gesture with her needle and a satin flounce. "Why, yes, Mama. We know that. He always said he would come in the spring—perhaps with Fitzwilliam, to make their yearly tour of inspection. But is that all the news?"

"No, it is not all. Stay and you shall hear. Darcy will be here as early as next week. Yes! He will be at Rosings for Easter. And you know what that means, Anne!"

Anne rose to her feet, her face scarlet. "Has it come? So soon!"

"Soon, you call it!" Lady Catherine made a "tsk" noise of impatience. "My dear girl, you are eight and twenty years old. Darcy has not been at all forward in settling your marriage. Indeed I have at times been almost cross with him for being so—not reluctant precisely, but... Naturally I could never be truly cross with dear Darcy, but you will allow that he has not been expeditious."

"Oh, but Lady Catherine," protested Mrs. Jenkinson. "So much as Mr. Darcy has to do! With running the Pemberley estate, and the house in Town, and overseeing Miss Georgiana's education—he never meant to marry until his sister was a young lady in society herself, I am sure. Now she is out, and will be a perfect companion for Miss Anne, when Mr. Darcy brings her home to Pemberley."

"Does he—does he say anything about that, Mama?" Anne ventured.

"Well, no, not directly. He would hardly do so in a letter. Darcy was always the very soul of delicacy and discretion. But, depend upon it, he will make his declaration in form when he is here. A springtime engagement! Only think! That is what he has been waiting for, I know."

"So romantic!" simpered Mrs. Jenkinson. "All the little sheep and lambs, and the primroses too."

"But we are hardly prepared," Lady Catherine bethought herself, drawing her heavy eyebrows together.

Mrs. Jenkinson lifted her hands with a wordless sigh. "Oh, Lady Catherine! Not prepared! Why, we have been sewing Miss Anne's trousseau for these twenty years at least! The bed-sheets alone—the Mechlin lace—oh! She will be the envy of many a Duchess."

"That is not what I mean," said Lady Catherine, frowning. "I am talking of Anne's own person, her own tout ensemble."

"Why, she has as many pretty gowns as any young lady in the kingdom, surely, Madam. Anyone would be sufficient to invite the proposal."

"Her clothes are well enough," returned Lady Catherine shortly.

"Mama, you don't mean—do you not think Mr. Darcy will be pleased with me? Will he not think me handsome enough? Perhaps there are other young women of his acquaintance who are—showier."

"Certainly not, Anne," snapped Lady Catherine, in a manner that betrayed it was exactly what she meant. "You are handsomer than the very handsomest girls, because you have so decidedly the aristocrat in your lineage. No, no, the lines of your nose, the bearing of your head…"

Anne felt comfortable again. "That is true," she said complacently, "I don't suppose Darcy can have been associating

285

with any girls of such antecedents as mine. Our own family is the noblest of all, even more than those of higher rank. And what sort of people can he have met in traveling lately, in Hertfordshire, with his friend Bingley?"

"Yes, very common people there," Lady Catherine sniffed agreement. "Assembly balls and things of that sort, where you might meet anyone. And Darcy has not lost his sense of what he owes the family. He has the proper Darcy pride, and would never forget himself."

"Oh, Lady Catherine!" sighed Mrs. Jenkinson. "I am sure he would be the very last young man to do that."

"Very true. Still, he has been seeing a great deal of the world, and so I think it expedient—that is, it cannot do any harm, for Anne to look her very best for the meeting."

"Why, what more can I do?" asked Anne perplexed. "I did think I would wear my green sarsanet—it is my best gown this season, and cost seventeen pounds, you know. And Helene is well schooled in all the best Parisian ways of curling my hair. Ringlets, you know, are all the style, and you see they become me so well." She shook her curls so they bounced, like a dozen brown mice.

"Green!" Lady Catherine fell back in her chair, momentarily lost for words. "My child, no woman ever received a proposal in that unfortunate color. And your figure—" She looked her daughter up and down, and her expression grew grave.

Anne regarded her parent with astonishment. "Why, mother, you have always said my figure was the perfect size for true elegance! It is not fleshy, but rather more aerial."

"The truth is, I am afraid you may be too thin," muttered Lady Catherine. "What if Darcy's taste is for a fleshpot, a tall, full-figured woman."

"Not in a wife, surely!" ejaculated Mrs. Jenkinson with horror.

Anne had regained her poise. "Really, Mama, where did you get such an extraordinary notion? Mr. Darcy could not wish his wife to

286

look like a milkmaid. He will want her to be a person of refinement, and ton, and of course, related to him in an advantageous way."

"And the promise was made when the children were still in their cradles, do not forget that," reminded Mrs. Jenkinson.

"Yes. Why, you have always promised me that I would marry Mr. Darcy. Mama, how can you forget?"

"It ought to be so," said Lady Catherine, troubled.

"And I will take your advice in one thing, and wear my pink India muslin. That will give my complexion a rosy hue."

"You will look like an angel on a cloud," enthused Mrs. Jenkinson breathlessly, "a pink cloud."

"Perhaps you are right," said Lady Catherine, still with some air of doubt.

"Of course I am right, Mama. Never fear." Anne got up and went to the beveled mirror above the sideboard, and regarded herself with her head on one side, again shaking her new-fangled ringlets, a style which in truth did little for her mouse-colored hair and pallid skin. "I think I am most uncommon looking, with all the tints of real refinement."

"She is like a painting, an oil painting," nodded Mrs. Jenkinson in ecstasy. "I have always said so. Or perhaps a really elegant watercolor."

"And Mr. Darcy will assuredly honor his obligations in the course of this visit. He has the reputation of being the very pattern of honor. And it is high time! He must know that I do not want to be a bride at thirty."

"I only hope he has not been forming any new attachment, that is all," said Lady Catherine thoughtfully. "It would explain his dilatoriness. But no, no, I know that to be impossible. Darcy is far too proud to lower himself to such nonsense."

"Proud! Of course he is. And I have a very good pride of my own," cried Anne. "We are so alike, it is quite ridiculous. I laugh about it to myself all the time."

"And," Mrs. Jenkinson reminded them, turning back to her stitchery, "remember, no matter how many girls he has known, he has remained single-minded, and pure. He has been saving his heart for no one but Anne."

"So sweet a notion," Anne sighed. "But you will say, Mama, that we are being too romantic. Even in a prudential sense, then, remember all that Darcy gains in marrying me."

"True," Lady Catherine agreed. "Not many girls have such a fortune." Then she remembered something. "Girls—yes. I had forgot that the Collinses are here almost every night. We must put a stop to that."

"Why ever bother?" asked Anne. "Darcy surely will not pay any attentions to Mr. and Mrs. Collins, so common and dull as they are. He will converse with us, and on the first night I will say—" She swirled the satin material about her and did a little dance in her thin slippers. "Shall we not take a turn, I will ask him?"

Lady Catherine and Mrs. Jenkinson's eyes met and there was apprehension in each. They were both thinking about the contrast the pretty Miss Bennet might make with Anne, and they acknowledged their mutual thought, without any words.

"Oh, no," said Lady Catherine decidedly, "we won't want them here."

"Certainly not. Do you wish me to write a note, Lady Catherine?"

"That won't be necessary. The invitations shall simply cease, until, of course, everything is settled—or not."

"It will be settled," Anne assured her complacently, fluffing up her ringlets. "Don't worry, Mama. Have not you always said that Darcy and I are the perfect match?"

Mr. Collins's Cucumber

by Mary Simonsen

March 5, 1812

Engaged to Mr. Collins? Impossible! — Pride and Prejudice

Lizzy winced at the memory of her reaction to Charlotte's engagement to her cousin. Without thinking highly either of men or matrimony, for Charlotte, marriage had always been her object. Once Lizzy accepted the fact of the engagement, she understood the reason: It was the only honorable option for a young woman of small fortune, and now here she was in Kent to observe in close quarters the union of these two dissimilar souls.

Weary from a day of traveling, Lizzy was eager for her bed, but before saying good night, the parson had extracted a promise that his cousin tour the gardens the next morning.

After a hearty breakfast, Lizzy followed Charlotte and Mr. Collins into a large plot, handsomely fenced, adjacent to the Parsonage. To Lizzy's mind, it looked very much like the vegetable garden at Longbourn and Lucas Lodge and every other house in the Meryton neighborhood, but that was before Mr. Collins mentioned his cucumber.

"Have you ever seen a cucumber of such size, Cousin Elizabeth?" he asked, pointing to the lengthy gourd at her feet, and Lizzy admitted that she had not.

"Her Ladyship has encouraged Mr. Collins to tend to his garden so that we might have sufficient vegetables for our table," Charlotte explained.

Mr. Collins had happily adhered to Her Ladyship's decree. "Lady Catherine visits regularly. She has been as captivated by this plant as I have, watching it grow, inch by inch by inch, until reaching its current length. If stood erect, I am sure it would reach a length of nine inches."

"Mr. Collins, I am speechless!" Lizzy said, trying to suppress the urge to laugh. She very nearly lost the fight when Charlotte mentioned the enormous oblong vegetable was planted next to her husband's radishes, also of a goodly size.

After Mr. Collins retreated to his study, Lizzy asked her friend how she had kept a straight face throughout the exchange.

"Because he shows me his cucumber at least twice a week, usually on Wednesdays and Saturdays."

And, finally, with Mr. Collins out of earshot, the two ladies had their laugh.

Mr. Collins's Cucumber Goes Missing

by Mary Simonsen

March 6, 1812

Charlotte and Elizabeth were returning from the village when they saw Mr. Collins coming down the lane. As he was frantically waving his black parson's hat as if hailing a London cab, it was apparent the man was in distress.

"Charlotte, you must come! Come quickly!"

"What is the matter, dear," Charlotte said, quickening her pace.

"My cucumber has gone missing."

After a quick glance at his breeches, Mrs. Collins informed her husband that his cucumber was still there. Lizzy, stifling a giggle, whispered that Mr. Collins was referring to the gourd in his garden.

"Of course," Charlotte said, blushing."

The two ladies hurriedly made their way to the garden where the theft of the nine-inch cucumber, pinched off at its root, was confirmed. After Mr. Collins informed Charlotte and Lizzy that he had already interrogated the staff to make sure they had not pilfered his plant, he asked if they knew of its whereabouts. Both shook their heads in unison. But then Lizzy pointed to footprints embedded in the path, revealing the culprit to be female. After following the bandit's path, they arrived at the gate that fronted the road to the village. It was there that they discovered tracks made by a carriage, the get-away conveyance of the thief.

After careful study, it became apparent the carriage was of a goodly size and drawn by four horses. Obviously, the person who had nicked the gourd was someone of considerable means and not some hungry passerby.

"Dare I say it, Mr. Collins," Charlotte said in a gentle voice, "the only person in the neighborhood who owns such a conveyance is Lady Catherine."

"Lady Catherine!" the parson croaked. "Impossible! She has her own garden. Why would she want to take hold of my cucumber?"

"I suspect it is cucumber envy," Elizabeth said. "Did you not say just a few evenings ago you imagined no one could look upon your cucumber with anything less than admiration? I suspect Lady Catherine was envious of your accomplishment in growing such a lengthy vegetable."

"But, but…" he sputtered.

"My dear, I must agree with Elizabeth," Charlotte added. "I think when Lady Catherine was on her way into the village, a vision of your cucumber appeared, and being a wee bit jealous of its size, she stopped her carriage and grabbed the gourd."

"But that would be stealing!" a shocked Mr. Collins answered.

Charlotte shook her head and explained that because Lady Catherine actually owned the Parsonage and the acres surrounding it, including the garden, she probably saw it merely as taking possession of something that already belonged to her. "I am sure, by this time, your cucumber has been sliced, diced, and served up on a platter for supper."

In an attempt to comfort her grieving husband, who compared the loss of his cucumber to losing a vital organ, Charlotte mentioned his huge radishes. Unfortunately, it was then discovered that those, too, had gone missing. But was it not to be expected? In order to have a satisfying salad, the one was as necessary as the other in achieving the desired result.

A Fortnight at Hunsford

by C. Allyn Pierson

March 19, 1812

Elizabeth sighed and folded away her embroidery. Charlotte and Maria had gone to town to visit an ailing parishioner and take her soup and tea, and Elizabeth had decided to stay at the Parsonage and enjoy the peace and quiet for a short while. Mr. Collins was at Rosings Park visiting Lady Catherine and the morning chores were done, so the house was silent except for the faint buzzing of the bees coming through the open window at her elbow. Early as it was in the spring, Mr. Collins's efforts in the garden gave her a fragrant and soothing background to her stitching.

Two weeks she had been at Hunsford. Sir William Lucas was already home, and Elizabeth and Maria had settled into a quiet routine of walks and domestic concerns between long talks with Charlotte. Her friend, unlikely though it might be, seemed to be happy in her marriage, and Mr. Collins was proving to be a conformable husband. The park at Rosings was lovely and had many pleasant walks, and she went out and enjoyed them daily when the weather allowed her.

Still, life was a bit dull in Hunsford. Lady Catherine had informed them that Mr. Darcy and his cousin would be coming for Easter, and Elizabeth was not quite sure how she felt about that. The gentlemen would certainly add interest to their evenings at Rosings, but she could not think of anyone she would not prefer to Mr. Darcy as company. Well...perhaps Mr. Collins would be of less interest. She hoped Darcy's cousin, who was called Colonel Fitzwilliam, would have better manners and more interesting conversation than Mr. Darcy.

What was wrong with the man, anyway? She had never met a man so difficult to understand as Mr. Darcy, or so severe in countenance. Still, she would be in Hunsford for a number of weeks and even a reserved and rude man was an improvement on Lady Catherine's "conversations," which bore a great resemblance to lectures. Only last evening she had criticized Maria's gown as dowdy and poorly tailored, reducing her nearly to tears when she had to admit her sewing skills were not adequate to correct the flaws. Unfortunately, she had also acquired just a bit of mud on her hem on the walk from the Parsonage and this, too, was cause for criticism. Poor Maria was trembling with fear and completely inarticulate by the time Lady Catherine had finished. Fortunately, Mr. Collins asked Lady Catherine about a problem with one of his parishioners and deflected her "helpful" lecture away from his sister-in-law. Bless the man. Stupid Mr. Collins might be, but he was not an evil man.

Ah well. Perhaps the early rain had dried enough for her to take a walk now. She gathered her pelisse and bonnet and pulled on her gloves, then set out towards Rosings Park.

Fitzwilliam and Darcy on the Road to Rosings

by Jack Caldwell

March 23, 1812

Colonel the Honorable Richard Fitzwilliam of the ___rd Light Dragoons was trying to make himself as comfortable as possible in the rocking carriage—a mighty task, for the fineness of the Darcy coach could not make up for the ruts in the road through Kent. The other gentleman in the carriage had more success.

The colonel was just thirty years of age. Other than that, he was most unlike his companion. Fitzwilliam was of moderate height with a ruddy complexion and sandy-reddish hair. His lean body sported broad shoulders due to his profession. He was not particularly handsome, but his character was friendly and open. He liked people very much. Usually easy-going, his patience was stretched to its limits that day.

"Blast!" Colonel Fitzwilliam cried as he cracked his head against the side of the carriage. "I knew I should have ridden my horse! I knew it!"

His cousin and great friend, Fitzwilliam Darcy, rapped on the roof with his walking stick. "A more moderate speed, if you please, Edwards," he said. He did not shout, but his forceful tone carried over the noise of the road. There was a muffled affirmative answer and the vehicle slowed. Now it simply rolled alarmingly from side to side.

"Oh, that is so much better! Thank you, Cuz."

"No need to be sarcastic, Fitz. The winter was beastly. It is no wonder the roads are in such a condition."

"The weather was just as bad in Derby, but you will not find the roads to be like this; my father would not stand for it."

"My uncle takes a prodigious interest in his roads."

Colonel Fitzwilliam laughed. "All because the old man likes his feet warm and bum comfortable!"

Darcy glanced at him, trying to hide a smile. "I have missed you, Fitz. I am happy you are back from Spain."

The colonel stretched. "For a time. Wellington does not need much in the way of cavalry to lay siege. After our *coup de main* at Ciudad Rodrigo in January*, I am allowed a few months leave in the loving bosom of my family." Darcy frowned, and Fitzwilliam noticed. "Do not glare at me, Darcy! You know of what I speak!"

Darcy's chin rose. "It is our duty to visit Lady Catherine at Easter."

"It is *your* duty to review Lady Catherine's accounts and meet with the steward at Easter," Fitzwilliam returned. "It falls to me to play court jester for the amusement of my aunt and cousin. By the way, could you condescend to spend some time with Anne this year? The way you ignore her is disgraceful."

Darcy looked away, his face flushed. "You know why I cannot."

Fitzwilliam grew a little angry. "You choose not! That poor girl suffers and not just from her ailments. Cooped up at that overdone mausoleum of a house with only Aunt Catherine and her companion to keep her company, no wonder she is ill! I know well our aunt's wishes. Lord, the whole family does! No one supports her in this. If you and Anne choose not to marry, the family would stand by you."

Darcy was unfazed. "I must act as I see best, Fitz. Anne understands."

Fitzwilliam grimaced at his friend. *Oh, Cuz—one day that famous Darcy pride will get you in trouble!* He changed the subject. "How is Georgiana getting on? Truly?"

Pain flashed over Darcy's features. "Not as well as I had hoped. She has not yet recovered from Ramsgate."

Fitzwilliam cursed. "If only I had been there instead of in Spain! There would be one less rascal in the world, I can assure you!"

"Then it is well you were not, for there would then be one less reckless colonel serving the king," Darcy shot back. "You would do Georgiana no good being hung for the murder of George Wickham."

Fitzwilliam crossed his arms. "It is better to pay him off?"

"I only covered his debts—he got nothing more from me."

"*This* time."

Darcy shook his head. "There will not be a next time. Wickham has shot his bolt. He cannot talk of Georgiana, for he still thinks to make his way in the world by marrying into society. Should word of Ramsgate get abroad, he would be shunned."

"It would not do Georgiana any good, either."

"Do you not think I know that?" Darcy shouted.

Fitzwilliam grew alarmed. Darcy never lost his temper. "Of course, of course. Easy, old man—"

Darcy's face fell into his hands. "You have no idea, Fitz! No idea at all how this whole affair haunts me! I failed her—I failed the person I love best in the world."

Fitzwilliam placed a hand on his cousin's shoulder. "Come now, none of that. You did nothing wrong. The blame must be borne by those responsible: Wickham and that Younge woman—"

"I should have investigated her references more thoroughly."

You are crying over spilled milk, old friend, Fitzwilliam thought. Aloud he said, "You did the best you could. I am sure her references

297

were of the highest quality. They usually are. Deceitful people are expert at obtaining such things."

"I should have done better."

Fitzwilliam shook his head. *What will bring you low first, Darcy—your pride or your habit of taking too much upon yourself? You cannot yet deal with the whole truth—that Georgiana bears some of the responsibility for this near-debacle.* He had to change the subject again.

"Tell me of Town. I understand our friend, Bingley, is moving up in the world."

Darcy looked up. "Yes. I spent the bulk of last summer with him, after... well, after that. He leased a place in Herefordshire and wanted my opinion of the place. I think he will give it up when the lease runs out."

"Something wrong with it?"

"No. Netherfield is a fair prospect, and with improvement should prove to be profitable."

"Then, why? Gentleman farming not up to snuff for Bingley? Or should I say Miss Bingley?"

"It is Hertfordshire and the folk who reside there that Miss Bingley finds lacking." Darcy paused. "I was relieved to return to London before December." He looked out the window.

"Missed Georgiana, I daresay. Did you enjoy the Season?"

Darcy turned and gave his cousin a look. "Have I ever enjoyed the Season?"

Fitzwilliam laughed at Darcy's incredulous expression. "I see— just the same! Still fighting off mercenary mamas and their insipid daughters."

"Not me this time, but I had to help an acquaintance of ours."

"Really? Who was it? Knightley? I have never understood why he has not married by now."

"Fitz—"

"Or maybe Bingley? He falls in love at the drop of a hat."

Darcy held up his hands. "I shall not reveal names. But I must congratulate myself for saving a friend from a most imprudent marriage."

"When was this? You said you have not been in Town long this year."

"Oh, it was last year. There were very strong objections to the lady, particularly her family."

"It must have been bad."

"Bad enough. But pray keep this to yourself. It would be unpleasant indeed if this became known to the family involved."

Fitzwilliam raised his hands in protest. "I shall be discretion itself."

"That would be the first time."

"Darcy, you wound me! Am I likely to meet with this unnamed family in any case?"

An unreadable look came over Darcy's face. "No—it is not likely at all."

Fitzwilliam had no time to contemplate Darcy's countenance. "Ah! Rosings! We are here!"

Darcy Discovers that Elizabeth Is at the Parsonage

by Kara Louise

March 23, 1812

Jane Austen does not tell us when and how Darcy discovered that Elizabeth was next door at Hunsford in Kent. We only know that he and his cousin pay a call soon after arriving at Rosings.

As the carriage turned onto the drive that led to Rosings, Darcy looked out the window and let out a gruff laugh. "I do not believe it!"

"What is it?" Colonel Fitzwilliam asked as he leaned forward to see what had his cousin's attention. He saw someone peer across the lane, give a quick bow, and then turn to walk with brisk, but rather laborious steps towards the parsonage. "Who was that?"

"That," Mr. Darcy began slowly, "was Mr. Collins, our aunt's clergyman."

"You have met him?" the colonel asked as the carriage came to a halt.

"Unfortunately, I have."

"I do not like the sound of that. You do not approve of him? Have you heard him deliver a rather blasphemous sermon? Have you witnessed him exhibit improper behavior?" Eyebrows raised, he gave his cousin a pointed look. "I must hear it all!"

Darcy casually shrugged his shoulders. At least he hoped it was a casual shrug. He now wished he had not said anything. "I met him while in Hertfordshire. There is nothing wrong with him other than some oddities that I found annoying." He hoped that would be the end of it.

"How did you come to meet him in Hertfordshire?"

Darcy felt himself tense. He was about to reply when the carriage door opened. "Ah, our aunt awaits." He extended his hand. "Shall we?"

The two men stepped out and stretched their arms and legs. "Oh, to be on the ground again! That ride was unbearable!" Colonel Fitzwilliam had never been one to endure a bumpy carriage ride.

Darcy patted him on the back. "I am quite surprised by your lack of backbone, Fitzwilliam. I cannot imagine how you tolerate the discomforts of being on the battle-field."

"Ha!" the colonel exclaimed. "You are one to talk about tolerating the discomforts of a battle-field! You have yet to face head on the one battle that presents itself every Easter!"

Darcy clenched his jaw, but said nothing.

"And being silent will not suit, with me or with Anne! You must propose… to someone! That is all there is to it! If you do not want to offer for Anne, at least offer for someone else!"

Darcy stopped and turned towards his cousin. "There will be no proposal—to Anne or anyone else— in the near future!"

Fitzwilliam shook his head. "I do not understand, Darcy. Do you not realize that the longer you go without finding a suitable and eligible match, the more Anne will believe you will one day marry her?"

Darcy turned sharply and began walking towards the front door. "I have nothing more to say on the matter!"

As he marched away from his cousin, he now wished he had answered his cousin's question about Mr. Collins. He clenched his jaw as he contemplated that both conversations had at their very core one Elizabeth Bennet, and that was what had him so disconcerted. He had tried for months to forget her, but now he was faced with being both in company with her cousin, as well with his cousin, whom he was promised to marry.

Their arrival was usually the most trying time for Darcy, as he attempted to be civil to Anne, but not give her too much reason to suspect he had any intention of asking for her hand. It was always easy for Colonel Fitzwilliam, who had no claims on her. He was also naturally ebullient, and had her smiling and chuckling in no time.

After the initial greeting, the men sat down with the ladies. The drawing room had the window coverings drawn, which always angered Darcy, who believed the sun would improve Anne's spirits, while her mother believed they would have a detrimental effect on her.

After talking about the unpleasant journey, they began to discuss the neighborhood.

It was then that Colonel Fitzwilliam, who apparently had not forgotten about Mr. Collins, said, "I believe we noticed your clergyman across the lane. I understand he is new since we were here last."

"Yes, Mr. Collins has been here less than a year."

The colonel leaned forward with his hands clasped. "And are you pleased with him?"

"I am. He gladly receives my generously given advice and correction, and his wife certainly knows her place." A satisfied smile curved Lady Catherine's lips.

"His wife?" Darcy asked.

"Yes, he married a few months back. He met her in Hertfordshire." Suddenly Lady Catherine frowned and glared at her nephew. "Oh, that is right. They did claim some such acquaintance with you. I was most seriously displeased!"

Colonel Fitzwilliam's eyes widened. "Displeased that they claimed an acquaintance with Darcy?"

Lady Catherine's fingers trailed across the neckline of her dress, and she sent Darcy a pointed look. "I found it quite objectionable that they were in your company much of the autumn while I must settle for a short visit in the spring."

Darcy schooled his features as he attempted to determine who Mr. Collins might have married. A wave of dread passed through him that it possibly could be Elizabeth! And if not Elizabeth, one of her sisters.

"I had no idea when I left Hertfordshire in November that he had a partiality for any of the ladies." He found it difficult to breathe as he waited for his aunt to reveal the name of Mr. Collins's bride.

Colonel Fitzwilliam leaned over and whispered, "Perhaps he married the young lady you felt was unsuited for your friend. Then you would no longer need to worry about him!"

Darcy did not feel that discovering Mr. Collins had married Miss Jane Bennet would ease his mind.

"What is the name of the young lady who was so honored to become Mrs. Collins?" Fitzwilliam asked.

"Her name is Charlotte, and she is the daughter of Sir William Lucas. A good match, I believe, for Mr. Collins."

Colonel Fitzwilliam glanced at Darcy with a raised brow as if to ask whether this might be the lady in question. Darcy gave his head a slight shake.

Darcy felt a great sense of relief at the news, but he readily recollected the close friendship Miss Lucas had with Elizabeth. He wondered what he would have done if it had been Elizabeth who had married Mr. Collins. The thought appalled him, yet he reprimanded himself for those feelings which still seemed as strong as they had ever been.

"Was Mr. Collins walking this way?" Lady Catherine asked.

Colonel Fitzwilliam leaned back in the chair. "No. He appeared to notice the carriage and then hurried back to the parsonage."

"Most likely to inform his wife and guests. You ought to pay them a call in the next day or two."

"Guests?" Darcy asked.

Lady Catherine waved her hand. "The sister of Mrs. Collins and her friend from Hertfordshire. No one of any consequence."

Could that be Elizabeth? Darcy felt his chest tighten, and he stood up abruptly and walked to the window. He knew all the color had drained from his face and he attempted to calm any and all outward signs of unease and impatience. His head and heart seemed to be engaged in a great battle. He was not certain whether he wanted his head to triumph and find out it was not her, or his heart to triumph and discover that she was right next door at the parsonage.

He turned to face his aunt. "And what is... what is her friend's name?" He held his breath once he posed the question, but he need not have asked, for somehow he knew, deep down inside, what she was going to say.

"Miss Elizabeth Bennet."

Darcy Appears at Church on Good Friday

by Mary Simonsen

March 27, 1812

"Darcy, you are grinding your teeth," Colonel Fitzwilliam muttered to his pew mate.

"You are mistaken, Fitzwilliam. I was attempting to swallow what the parson is serving."

"You have a tendency to grind your teeth when you are displeased. I take it that Mr. Collins's sermon is not resonating with you."

"Or *you* or we would not be having this conversation."

Before the colonel could respond, Lady Catherine gave both a cold stare, and the whispering ended. Darcy's thoughts now returned to the true reason for his grinding his teeth: Elizabeth Bennet.

I thought I had left all thoughts of Elizabeth behind in London. If I had known that she would be here exactly at this time, I would have postponed my visit until after Easter.

After returning to London following the Netherfield ball, Darcy had made a determined effort to put Elizabeth Bennet out of his mind. The behavior of Mrs. Bennet and her three youngest daughters at the ball had served to illuminate how impossible it was for him to form any serious design on the lady. If Mrs. Bennet were not talking too loudly, it was Kitty and Lydia Bennet, literally, chasing after officers, begging for a partner. And Mary! Her performance had proved the middle Bennet daughter incapable of embarrassment.

These inappropriate displays were followed by Sir William Lucas's proclamation that there were expectations in the neighborhood that the engagement of Miss Jane Bennet and Bingley would shortly be announced. From that moment, Darcy was determined to do everything in his power to remove his friend from Hertfordshire and the grasp of the Bennet family. As Bingley relied heavily on Darcy's opinion, convincing him that Miss Jane Bennet had no particular interest in him was easily done. With the support of Caroline and Louisa, it was the work of a moment. He, on the other hand, was finding it difficult to erase Elizabeth Bennet from his memory.

It is her smile that makes it so difficult. No. It is her laugh. Yes, her laugh. It floats in the air before disappearing into the ether. And then there is her handsome figure and her beautiful face framed by an avalanche of curls. Oh blast! She is in my head again!

"Darcy, seriously," the colonel mumbled under his breath so as not to invite a rebuke from his aunt, "you are grinding your teeth so loudly that I am sure Miss Elizabeth, sitting over there," he said, nodding with his chin in her direction, "can hear you. She must be wondering what on earth you are thinking."

I am thinking of her—again. Darcy shook his head. *I do not understand it. Yes, Elizabeth is lovely, but so are a dozen women of my acquaintance. It is true that she dances divinely and has the voice of an angel, but there are many others who are equally accomplished. Why is it that I am preoccupied with her?*

"Darcy, excuse me for interrupting your thoughts, but you are staring at Miss Elizabeth, and she is looking at you with a very odd expression."

Darcy looked across the aisle, and when he did, Elizabeth looked right at him with a quizzical look and a tilt of her head that was very nearly adorable. It was at that moment that he understood the reason he could not dismiss her from his mind was because he was in love with her. As he held her gaze, he imagined he looked like a lamb in search of its mother—because he was lost—lost in a love that could never be.

After the service, the congregants gathered outside the church, complimenting the Reverend Collins on the excellence of his sermon. Darcy could only nod as he had not heard one word of it. Instead, he made his way over to Elizabeth Bennet who was standing alone.

"Miss Elizabeth, how very good it is to see you again."

Lizzy doubted the sincerity of Mr. Darcy's statement. When the gentleman had paid a courtesy call at the Parsonage, he had barely said a word to her—or anyone else for that matter.

"Mr. Darcy, you seemed lost in thought during the service. I imagine you were thinking of the solemnity of the commemoration of Our Savior's sacrifice. After all, it is Good Friday."

"I wish it were so, Miss Elizabeth. The truth of the matter is that when in church, I have a tendency to let my mind wander."

"And where does your mind take you?"

"To a forbidden land."

Lizzy laughed at the notion that a "forbidden land" existed for a man of his station and position in life. "Be honest, Mr. Darcy, for a man such as yourself, is there any place where you cannot go or anything you cannot do if you have a mind to do it?"

"Even for a man such as I, there are prohibitions, societal restraints."

"In that case, I imagine you must decide if this forbidden land that beckons you is more important than the possible censure of your peers for visiting it."

Darcy had no ready response, and the sound of his aunt's voice saved him from an awkward silence. "I am summoned, Miss Elizabeth. Perhaps, we may continue this conversation at another time."

"As you wish, sir," she said with a slight bow of her head.

"You make it sound as if my wish is your command. It is not.

Every heart sings a song, incomplete, until another heart whispers back."

"Sir?" a confused Elizabeth asked.

Darcy was as confused as she. He had not anticipated a quote from Plato welling up inside him. Embarrassed, he repeated that he must go. "My aunt will be displeased if I tarry. I wish you a joyous Easter, Miss Bennet."

Lizzy's gaze followed Mr. Darcy as he joined Lady Catherine de Bourgh in her carriage and continued to do so until the conveyance disappeared from sight.

"What on earth did Mr. Darcy mean by a 'heart that whispers back'? He speaks in riddles."

"And you are talking to yourself," Charlotte said, teasing her friend.

Lizzy nodded, realizing that was often the case following a conversation with Mr. Darcy.

Easter Sunday at Rosings

by Abigail Reynolds

March 29, 1812

It had started at church, which had been the usual affair of attempting to disguise the fact that he could not stop stealing glances at Elizabeth combined with utter disdain for Mr. Collins's foolish sermon. Easter and rebirth—he had that much right, but the ridiculous ramblings that followed would have been laughable had they not been so dreadfully dull. Darcy had already steeled himself to the knowledge that he would not have the acute, painful delight of seeing Elizabeth again until the next week's service when he heard Lady Catherine invite Mr. Collins and his party to join them at Rosings that evening.

He wanted to be dismayed by the news. It was better to limit his exposure to Elizabeth to once a week at church, where he could remember why he could not have her as his own, but no matter how well he knew he should stay away from her, he could not find the least trace of regret in his heart that he would have another hour in her company, another hour of feeling alive, that evening.

Anticipation of her visit haunted him throughout the day, making him unusually restless. Colonel Fitzwilliam even commented on his preoccupation, which brought Darcy back to the present for a few minutes, but the colonel could not compete with the bewitching Elizabeth who filled his thoughts.

After all his agitation, her arrival was anticlimactic. Since Lady Catherine insisted upon monopolizing his attention with her incessant demands, he could only watch her from across the room while his cousin was fortunate enough to seat himself by Elizabeth and enjoy her lively smiles. Darcy could only make out fragments of their conversation, but they conversed with such spirit and flow that he could not deny to himself that she seemed to be enjoying Colonel Fitzwilliam's company more than she ever had his. It did not matter, though. Neither of them could ever have her, so there was no point thinking about it—and certainly no call for obsessing constantly about it.

It would be beneath him to feel jealous of his landless, often fundless cousin. He tore his gaze away from them and tried to focus on his conversation with his aunt, monotonous as it was, until out of the corner of his eye, he noticed his cousin leading Elizabeth into the next room, presumably to the pianoforte. The sound of their laughter floated through the opening between the rooms.

He was certainly not jealous, but he did not choose to be deprived of the opportunity to rest his eyes on Elizabeth's loveliness, so he excused himself and stationed himself where even the colonel would realize that he commanded a full view of them.

Elizabeth must have noticed as well, since at the first convenient pause, she turned to him with an arch smile, and said, "You mean to frighten me, Mr. Darcy, by coming in all this state to hear me? But I will not be alarmed though your sister does play so well. There is a stubbornness about me that never can bear to be frightened at the will of others. My courage always rises with every attempt to intimidate me."

What was it about her teasing that intoxicated him so and sent the blood racing through his body? He smiled slowly before offering his rejoinder. "I shall not say that you are mistaken because you could not really believe me to entertain any design of alarming you; and I have had the pleasure of your acquaintance long enough to know, that you find great enjoyment in occasionally professing opinions which in fact are not your own."

Elizabeth laughed heartily at this picture of herself, and said to Colonel Fitzwilliam, "Your cousin will give you a very pretty notion of me, and teach you not to believe a word I say. I am particularly unlucky in meeting with a person so well able to expose my real character, in a part of the world where I had hoped to pass myself off with some degree of credit. Indeed, Mr. Darcy, it is very ungenerous in you to mention all that you knew to my disadvantage in Hertfordshire—and, give me leave to say, very impolitic too—for it is provoking me to retaliate, and such things may come out, as will shock your relations to hear."

He smiled, confident that her teasing could have no malice. "I am not afraid of you."

"Pray let me hear what you have to accuse him of," cried Colonel Fitzwilliam. "I should like to know how he behaves among strangers."

"You shall hear then—but prepare yourself for something very dreadful. The first time of my ever seeing him in Hertfordshire, you must know, was at a ball—and at this ball, what do you think he did? He danced only four dances! I am sorry to pain you—but so it was. He danced only four dances, though gentlemen were scarce; and, to my certain knowledge, more than one young lady was sitting down in want of a partner. Mr. Darcy, you cannot deny the fact."

Why should he deny it? "I had not at that time the honor of knowing any lady in the assembly beyond my own party."

"True; and nobody can ever be introduced in a ball room." This time her tone had some bite. "Well, Colonel Fitzwilliam, what do I play next? My fingers wait your orders."

His mind whirled. Why was Elizabeth taking aim at him? Perhaps she had misunderstood what he meant. "Perhaps I should have judged better, had I sought an introduction, but I am ill qualified to recommend myself to strangers."

"Shall we ask your cousin the reason of this?" said Elizabeth to Colonel Fitzwilliam. "Shall we ask him why a man of sense and education, and who has lived in the world, is ill qualified to recommend himself to strangers?"

"I can answer your question," said Fitzwilliam, "without applying to him. It is because he will not give himself the trouble."

311

They had both turned on him, and in the most painful way. His cousin knew how he had failed to achieve acceptance in certain circles, that same success that came so easily to the colonel. "I certainly have not the talent which some people possess, of conversing easily with those I have never seen before. I cannot catch their tone of conversation, or appear interested in their concerns, as I often see done," he said stiffly.

"My fingers," said Elizabeth, "do not move over this instrument in the masterly manner which I see so many women's do. They have not the same force or rapidity, and do not produce the same expression. But then I have always supposed it to be my own fault—because I would not take the trouble of practicing. It is not that I do not believe my fingers as capable as any other woman's of superior execution."

Relief flooded him. She understood, more than he had ever imagined she would understand, how he struggled to avoid giving offense, yet failed again and again—and she was showing him in the best possible way that it was not necessary to be perfect to be appreciated. He smiled and said, "You are perfectly right. You have employed your time much better. No one admitted to the privilege of hearing you, can think anything wanting. We, neither of us, perform to strangers."

Here they were interrupted by Lady Catherine, who called out to know what they were talking of. Elizabeth immediately began playing again. Darcy watched her in a daze, his world shifting under his feet. He had seen Elizabeth as witty, amusing, attractive—oh, so attractive!—and temptation personified, but this was a side he had never known existed. How had she known so perfectly what he needed to hear just at that moment?

He had forced himself to ignore his desire for her, but this new realization showed him she was more than just a bewitching woman. She was vital to him.

Family and duty be damned. He was going to marry Elizabeth Bennet.

Lady Catherine's Easter

by Diana Birchall

March 29, 1812

The wished-for proposal did not come. The green sarsanet, the primrose silk, the floral printed gown with the fichu, were all cunningly constructed so to give Miss de Bourgh's figure consequence, and accordingly worn with her best French ringlets and hair decorations. None of these things, nor all of them, brought Mr. Darcy to a declaration. To Lady Catherine's mortification, Darcy was invariably polite, and listened to her deliver strictures and dictates with commendable patience, but he seldom seemed to even notice that Miss de Bourgh was in the room at all.

Darcy and Fitzwilliam had arrived with promptitude, just when they were expected, in the week before Easter; and they were welcomed with all the festivity that was at the command of Lady Catherine in doing the honors of her own house. She had hoped that Anne might be equal to charming and entertaining at least one of her cousins, but Anne said very little, and whether from embarrassment or from pique, remained a silent stick in the corner each evening, despite Lady Catherine's grossest and most urgent attempts to bring her forward.

"I do wish Anne could play for you. She has such taste! Mr. Collins the other day said that never did he see a young lady with more real musical ability, who did not know how to play, and that her preference for Mozart over Haydn showed her taste to be very nearly divine."

There was nothing to say to that. Mr. Darcy and Colonel Fitzwilliam looked at each other, and Fitzwilliam consulted his pocket-watch. It still lacked an hour to supper.

"We do miss hearing some good music," Fitzwilliam finally offered. "Do you know, Lady Catherine, today we walked over to the Parsonage, and the young lady guest there, Miss Bennet, is said to play rather well. Perhaps," he hinted, "the family there might make up an evening party."

That was not to Lady Catherine's purpose. She could not wish the tame vicar and his female entourage to be the prime entertainment offered to the young men, or for the prettyish Miss Bennet to perhaps be a distraction to prevent Darcy from making the proposal so ardently desired by mother and daughter. Yet to her chagrin, she had to confess to herself that the visit was not going altogether as she would wish. Both Darcy and Fitzwilliam loved Rosings immensely, she knew, and had nothing but the greatest respect for herself and her daughter; but still, they were young men, and in this bleak, not-quite-spring weather, there was not much for them to be doing outdoors, no hunting, no field sports. They liked their walks, and she had already observed that nearly every day one or both walked through the park of Rosings and past the palings to the Vicarage, and generally spent all the afternoon there, not returning until nearly time for the evening meal. Dull, plain Mrs. Collins could not be the attraction, nor yet her insipid sister who was as silent as Lady Catherine's own daughter. No, it was with some displeasure that she suspected it was that Miss Bennet they crossed the park to see; and as this must be discouraged, she took the step of planning a very fine supper and inviting some of her grander neighbors of the county.

On the whole this was the worst failure of all. Lady Metcalfe and her red-nosed old husband, who fell asleep over the fire with his port, and the Lassiters of Saddlefield Place, who liked to quarrel as soon as they picked up a set of cards, and the Munnings, with their three spinster daughters in their forties, giantesses who liked to talk about their ailments, were not the most enlivening society. The talk and the food were heavy alike, and both Darcy and Fitzwilliam, though their manners were perfectly proper, were anything but animated. Fitzwilliam found less to say than usual, and Darcy never opened his lips except to eat the oysters and the ragout.

After the guests rolled away in their carriages, and the two young men went to their rooms, Darcy pleading a headache and Fitzwilliam fatigue, Lady Catherine hopefully tried to assure Anne and Miss Jenkinson that all had gone well.

"Well! I must say that was a delightful occasion. One of our successful soirees. Rosings is a house made for hospitality. That is what Mr. Collins always says, and it is true."

"Mr. Collins was not here," Anne pointed out dryly.

"No, I thought that he and the ladies of his household would have felt rather out of their element, in such a noble society as this. Sir George Metcalfe a baronet, and the Munnings related to the Duke of Beaufort."

"Mrs. Collins's father is a knight," said Anne.

"Pah! A creation within memory, and only as a reward for civic duties, at that. He is quite vulgar, Anne, quite, though there is no real harm in the man. No; they were not to be made uncomfortable. Our guests tonight were more in Darcy's rank of life."

"He did not seem to enjoy their company so very much, Mama. He barely spoke."

"That was the head-ache, to be sure, nothing more. I sent him to bed with a posset. He was most grateful for the attention. 'Lady Catherine,' he said, 'thank you.'"

"I thought he did not eat his dinner very well, either," put in Mrs. Jenkinson. "He only ate three oysters, and did not touch the salad."

"He asked to be helped to the ragout twice," began Lady Catherine repressively.

"Oh, Mama! You make the best of it, but the evening was not a success. Such company as the Lassiters and the Munnings are no pleasure for two such young men. They are all so old."

Lady Catherine was thoughtful for a moment, and adjusted her purple satin bandeau over her forehead in an absent way. "They do go to the vicarage daily," she admitted. "I cannot presume to conjecture what merit they find in the society there, but perhaps we ought not to avoid giving the invitation to the Collinses any longer, after all. I did hope…"

"That I would get a proposal?" demanded Anne, tears beginning to show themselves.

"My dear!" cried Mrs. Jenkinson, going over to the sofa where she sat and enfolding her in her arms.

"Now, Anne, there is no call to be blaming yourself," said Lady Catherine with some distaste. "Heaven knows, I am sure, we did everything. The lace round your neck tonight, and that locket…well, well. If only you could be a bit more animated…"

"I cannot be forward, Mama!" cried Anne, putting her fists to her eyes. "Some girls can but I cannot. Have you not taught me that forwardness was common, unladylike behavior? And common is just what I can never, never be."

"No, certainly not," answered her mother uncomfortably. "Well, there's nothing for it then. After church, on Easter Sunday, we shall ask Mr. Collins and the ladies to come to Rosings. They can come in the evening, you know, when Darcy and Fitzwilliam seem most to have the wish for company."

"We would have to invite them anyway, would we not?" asked Mrs. Jenkinson practically. "Mr. Collins is the clergyman and will have just given his Easter sermon that morning."

"Exactly so," nodded Lady Catherine. "It is a very proper attention indeed."

On the Easter Sunday evening, then, Mr. Collins, rather tired after his exertions, was pleased to spend his time looking over an album of horse engravings in Lady Catherine's best sitting-room. Mrs. Collins, showing herself to be truly well bred, sat between Miss de Bourgh and Mrs. Jenkinson, trying to converse, and admiring their bead-work.

Mr. Darcy and Col. Fitzwilliam were leaning over the pianoforte as Elizabeth played to them, so that their lively conversation was not audible, over the music, to the ladies seated across the room. Lady Catherine made one or two attempts to call out and ask what they were speaking of. She gave her opinions on her and her daughter's taste in music, with many instructions on how necessary practicing was to Darcy's sister. With each attempt, however, the conversation quickly moved away from her, to her displeasure, and nothing was heard in the intervals between songs but the intimate, congenial murmur of Elizabeth talking with the two young men.

There was something Lady Catherine did not like at all, in the intent way Darcy was looking down at Elizabeth, and when she heard Darcy's words "You have employed your time much better," she took alarm and called out once more to require them to tell the subject of their conversation. Elizabeth immediately began playing again. Lady Catherine tried some further remarks on Anne's taste, with expressive gesturings toward her daughter, but Darcy barely turned his head in their direction. Elizabeth, still playing, thought to herself that she saw no symptom of love in Mr. Darcy toward his cousin, nor any likelihood of their supposed marriage.

In a still more open attempt to remove her nephew from his absorption in Elizabeth, Lady Catherine rose to her feet, approached the piano, where she stood in state, and proceeded to take apart her performance.

"Do you not see, Miss Bennet, that your fingering is too heavy in that arpeggio? Cramer is meant to be played adagietto there. I fear you have not the light touch requisite for the classical form."

"I think Miss Bennet plays very well," said Fitzwilliam warmly. "The Scotch airs particularly. Won't you play us some more of those?"

"Yes, I think you are right, Fitzwilliam—simple, peasant music is best for such a beginner," said Lady Catherine condescendingly.

Mr. Darcy looked angry and shot a look at Fitzwilliam that would urge him to speak for both of them. "On the contrary,"

Fitzwilliam countered, "the lovely simplicity of the best Scottish songs takes confident playing, and great taste. Miss Bennet has them both. What would you like her to play, Darcy?"

"I liked those airs by Burns," he said reluctantly, and would say no more.

"Burns! Dreadful man," exclaimed Lady Catherine. "I wonder you can tolerate him, Darcy."

Col. Fitzwilliam's eyes twinkled. "I think my cousin would like you to play and sing 'My Love is like a Red, Red Rose,' Miss Bennet," he said. "Isn't that right, Darcy? Why, man, you are blushing as red as a rose yourself."

"Blush? Darcy? Surely not. I see nothing of it. What do you mean, Fitzwilliam?" rapped out Lady Catherine.

To forestall further comment, Elizabeth began to sing.

0, my love is like a red, red rose,
that's newly sprung in June.
0, my love is like a melody,
that's sweetly play'd in tune.
As fair thou art, my bonnie lass,
so deep in love am I,
And I will love thee still, my dear,
till a' the seas gang dry.

Her eyes caught and held Darcy's, in spite of herself. He was fathoms deep in love by this time, and moved forward, holding out his hand, with what gesture in mind no one could tell, for Lady Catherine at once intervened and said with asperity, "Well! We will have no more of that immoral ploughboy! Some instrumental music, Miss Bennet, if you please, and no more of that coarse singing. It is not at all the thing among the gentry, though you might be forgiven for not knowing that."

Mr. Darcy was moved to speak. "Aunt Catherine," he objected with some heat, "Miss Bennet, in my opinion, marries good breeding and good taste to perfection. You will oblige me to not speak of her in such a way."

Lady Catherine lost her temper. "I do not know what you mean in the least, Darcy. Miss Bennet has not a trace of the breeding and taste of Anne."

Mr. Collins heard the strident tones and hurried across the room, anxious to forestall trouble. "Perhaps my cousin has sung long enough, Lady Catherine," he said anxiously, "we do not wish to tire you, of all things. Shall I place the card tables? Would Miss Anne care for a game of Cassino?"

"Yes," came her faint voice from the sofa. "I should like that. Will you not play with me, Mr. Darcy?"

"Another time," he replied shortly, not turning around to look at her. "Now we are having the pleasure of listening to Miss Bennet. Will you play 'Ae Fond Kiss,' Miss Bennet? That is another favorite of mine."

She played the first few notes. "Who would have thought, Mr. Darcy," she said with an arch look, "that you would be a person of such romantic sensibility? You would think that Burns had a heart, after all. It is such a sad song."

Ae fond kiss, and then we sever;
Ae fareweel, and then for ever!
Deep in heart-wrung tears I'll pledge thee,
Warring sighs and groans I'll wage thee.

"Yes, a sad song, yet it makes me happy," he observed at its conclusion, low.

No one heard his words but Fitzwilliam, standing next to him, who looked surprised, but Lady Catherine saw or thought she saw enough to say tartly, "I consider that it is surely time for this evening to draw to an end. If you must have Robert Burns, Darcy, then let Miss Bennet sing Auld Lang Syne."

Charlotte Becomes Suspicious

by Monica Fairview

April 1, 1812

Why did Mr. Darcy come so often to the Parsonage? …He seldom appeared really animated. Mrs. Collins knew not what to make of him - Chapter 32

"Was that Mr. Darcy's voice I heard?" asked Maria as they entered the parsonage, taking off her bonnet.

Charlotte had not been paying attention, as she was thinking how best to inform Mr. Collins about something she had heard in the village. One of the tenants had complained that Lady Catherine had not sent a thatcher to repair a leaking roof as she had promised. Charlotte knew her husband would take offense at any suggestion of negligence on the part of his patroness. However, Charlotte believed it was his duty to remind Lady Catherine of anything to do with the parishioners' welfare. She had to find a way to suggest a gentle reminder would be appropriate without provoking a long lecture about Lady Catherine's generosity.

Maria's words, however, gave her pause. She listened intently but did not hear a man's voice. It was apparent that they *did* have visitors, since Elizabeth was not generally in the habit of talking to herself.

"I wonder what should bring Mr. Darcy to the parsonage. Very likely Lady Catherine has sent him with an invitation to dine at Rosings."

Charlotte hurried towards the parlor, worried that Mr. Darcy was awaiting her return impatiently and fearing that her absence may have caused offense. If she had learned anything from her association with Lady Catherine, it was that these fine folk were likely to be affronted at the slightest thing and that being around them was like walking on eggshells. It required a considerable amount of tact and patience. Charlotte felt as if she was spending her whole time trying to avoid one transgression or the other.

As they approached, they could hear Lizzy talking. Charlotte smiled at Lizzy's tone of voice. She knew what it signified, as they had known each other since childhood. It was the tone Lizzy used when she was trying her best to be polite even if she did not find the conversation very appealing.

"I enjoy walking amongst the apple trees," she was saying, with a smile on her lips, "but I am rather disappointed in Kent as it seems much like Hertfordshire. I had thought the "orchard of England" would have a great many more orchards than I have seen so far."

As soon as she stepped through the doorway, Charlotte halted, struck by the tableau in front of her. Mr. Darcy was seated in a chair opposite Lizzy. Intent on what she was saying, he had not noted Charlotte's and Maria's entrance. His gaze was glued to Lizzy's lips and he was listening as closely as if her words were divine intervention rather than humdrum polite conversation.

Ah. So that is the way the wind blows, she thought.

Just then Elizabeth turned to greet her. Mr. Darcy, registering Charlotte and her sister's presence, started and jumped up, his face losing all expression.

"Mr. Darcy, I am sorry to have kept you waiting," said Charlotte, hurrying to greet him. "I trust you left Lady Catherine in good health."

"Yes, thank you," said Mr. Darcy. "I—I was told the ladies were inside or I would never have intruded like this on Miss Bennet."

"My sister and I were out walking," said Charlotte, feeling a need to explain herself, though more out of awkwardness than to impart information.

They all sat down, with Mr. Darcy taking a seat in the corner as far from Elizabeth as he possibly could. He appeared even more uncomfortable than usual. Charlotte hastened to set him at ease.

"You plan to stay with your aunt for some time, Mr. Darcy?"

"I have not yet determined the date of my departure," said Darcy.

"Is the colonel enjoying his stay in Kent?" she said.

"Very much so," he replied.

A brief silence descended on the room in which the clock could be heard ticking. A crow cawed loudly outside the window. The four of them watched it as it spread its large wings and flew away.

"Did Miss Bennet offer you refreshments, Mr. Darcy?" said Charlotte, by and by.

"I require none. I will be leaving shortly," replied Darcy.

Silence settled over the small room once again. Darcy sat in the corner and contemplated the wall. Maria shifted her shawl and rearranged it around her shoulders. Lizzy began to drum her fingers against the arm of her chair. Mr. Darcy's gaze was immediately drawn to the movement. Lizzy, conscious of the scrutiny, stopped her drumming, throwing Charlotte a look of entreaty. Charlotte, accustomed to smoothing ruffled feathers around her husband, searched quickly for another topic of conversation.

"Miss de Bourgh appears to be in better spirits, now that she has so many people to keep her amused. It was very quiet at Rosings before everyone arrived."

"My cousin is accustomed to a quiet life," remarked Darcy.

Charlotte waited for him to elaborate, but he did not seem inclined to do so.

"But surely she is pleased to have company," said Elizabeth. "I cannot imagine she would prefer to be alone."

"*You* may not prefer to be alone, Miss Bennet. My cousin,

however, is sickly and does not care to exert herself too much," he said, giving Elizabeth a long glance. "Not everyone enjoys a lively temperament such as yours."

The words were spoken in such a manner it was impossible to tell if they were a compliment or a reproach, leaving Charlotte uncertain what to make of them.

Another silence fell on the group. Charlotte searched about for something to say, but she had exhausted the possibilities. Fortunately, there was always one topic that can be counted upon to draw everyone's attention and that was the weather. Charlotte fell back on that last resort.

"We are fortunate to have warm weather for Easter, are we not?" she said.

"Very fortunate," said Darcy.

There was a short pause. Elizabeth was looking down at her hands, her mouth curled in amusement. Charlotte hoped that Lizzy was not going to start laughing.

As if sensing the possibility, Darcy rose abruptly to his feet and the ladies followed.

"I must take my leave. My aunt…" said Darcy.

"Yes," said Charlotte. "I am certain she will be asking for you."

He turned to Lizzy and bowed stiffly. "Miss Bennet. I suppose I shall see you at church on Sunday."

Lizzy curtsied. "You shall indeed, Mr. Darcy. I would not miss it for the world." She gave one of her mischievous smiles. Charlotte could not be certain, but she thought his color deepened.

"Mrs. Collins. Miss Lucas." He bowed and walked stiffly away.

As the door shut behind him. Lizzy gave a sigh of relief and sank into her seat.

"I thought he would never leave."

"What can be the meaning of this?" said Charlotte, sitting down as well. "My dear Lizzy, he must be in love with you, or he would not have called on us in this familiar way."

"That is quite absurd, Charlotte, as you know very well. If I had listened to you, I would have believed that half the men in Meryton were in love with me," said Elizabeth.

"That is hardly true, Lizzy. I have never led you astray when it comes to such matters."

"Really?" said Elizabeth. "And what about the case of Mr. Hawker? Remember how you convinced me he cared about me when all along he was planning to marry Miss Kendall?"

"I still believe he cared nothing for Miss Kendall," said Charlotte. "He married her for her fortune."

"Let us suppose for a moment you are right, what evidence do you have? If Mr. Darcy has any regard for me, he has chosen a most peculiar way of expressing it. Before you entered, I was trying most desperately to maintain a civil conversation, yet all the while he stared at me in such a haughty manner I felt his goal must be to find fault with me. I am convinced he despises me."

"If, as you say, he despises you," said Charlotte, "then why seek out your company?"

"It was not my company he was after, it was ours. I do believe he comes here to escape from Rosings. I do not know how he can endure Lady Catherine's company for hours at a time."

Charlotte shook her head. She could not forget the expression on his face when she had first entered. He had seemed—she sought for a word—completely entranced.

"I believe you mistake the matter, my dear friend. I am certain he has formed an attachment."

Elizabeth laughed. "If you had been in the room with us earlier you would have realized how mistaken you are. He was far from happy when he found me here alone and his manner was so cold it was obvious that only civility prevented him from turning tail and leaving as soon as he arrived."

Charlotte thought this over. Could she have been mistaken? Had his rapt expression been nothing but a trick of the light?

"But are you certain, Lizzy? Could he not have been

embarrassed rather than displeased to catch you alone?"

"Embarrassed?" said Lizzy. "I would as soon call Lady Catherine shy! Have you not seen enough evidence of his arrogance and conceit, Charlotte? Have you forgotten Wickham's testimony regarding his character? You need only ask our neighbors in Meryton and they will all be in agreement in mentioning his pride and disregard for others. Tell me, Charlotte, since you are determined to redeem him, why he did not call on Jane in London to inquire about me if he is attached to me." Elizabeth came and sat next to Charlotte and took her hand. "I see what is happening, Charlotte. You are forced to live in close quarters with Lady Catherine as your patroness and so you are compelled to find the good in her. Now you wish to find the good in her nephew, too. There is a perfectly simple explanation, as you can see."

Charlotte reflected on this. It was true that she had found herself trying hard to justify Lady Catherine's often high-handed behavior. The Collins's were dependent on her for their livelihood and it was far easier to fall in with her husband's perception of their benefactress than to retain a critical attitude towards her. Elizabeth was right. She was now trying to do the same with the nephew.

She smiled at her own folly. "You know me too well, Elizabeth. I would like to believe the whole family kind and amiable."

"That is because you want to see the good in people, Charlotte, which is just as well or you would never have had me as a friend."

"I am not as blind as that," said Charlotte. "I know you are far from perfect. But you are my dearest friend and I would not have anyone say otherwise, including Mr. Darcy."

"You cannot truly wish Mr. Darcy upon me, Charlotte. Just think of his aunt. Think of the uproar there would be if he declared he wished to marry me! Supposing Lady Catherine were to take it in her head that it was your fault because you brought me to his attention?"

Charlotte shuddered and began to laugh as well. "Very well, Lizzy, you have cured me of such thoughts once and for all. Let us hope that nothing like this will ever come to pass!"

Darcy Plots to Accidentally Meet Elizabeth on Her Walks

by L. L. Diamond

April 2, 1812

Darcy peered anxiously about the edge of the orchard. Where could Elizabeth be?

As they drank tea after dinner, Elizabeth had indicated how she enjoyed the blush-colored, fluffy blooms of the cherry blossoms each spring. Indeed, Easter would not be the same without such a spectacle she had said.

How could he forget? Her fine eyes had twinkled as she spoke, the smile upon her perfect lips conveyed her joy at the prospect, and the slight tilt of her head was flirtatious. She was so beguiling that as she described the pleasure she took in the season, he instead, entertained visions of the lady walking amongst the pink bowers of flowers found all over England at this time of year.

It had been Fitzwilliam's boot painfully striking the toe of his shoe, which had brought him back to the conversation. He had cleared his throat and attempted to bring himself under good regulation, but his desire to make his fantasy a reality overrode his good sense. He made mention of this very grove in the hopes he could happen upon her.

After such a discussion, she had to come!

He leaned back against a wide oak near the river and folded his arms across his chest. One more peek around the trunk proved useless—she was not there.

A breeze wafted his great coat away from his body, and he pulled it back with haste. She could not know he had been waiting for her! The meeting *had* to be an accident since he could not arouse hopes in her that he might not fulfil, at least not yet.

He wanted to offer her marriage. But, no, he could never do such a thing. How could he forget the impropriety so often shown by her mother, her three younger sisters, and even her father. But, those relations could be ignored, could they not? He could pretend they did not exist and make the offer of his hand to Miss Elizabeth, despite her unfortunate connections.

He began to chew the nail of his thumb, but stopped for a moment to give another glance around the orchard. When not a glimpse of her was to be had, he began gnawing upon the poor, ragged fingernail once more.

Any lady with Miss Elizabeth's penchant for walking and preference for cherry blossoms would be eager to include such a prospect on their morning jaunt, would they not? She had to come!

A shaky hand removed the pocket watch from his coat, and he opened it to check the time. It was almost half nine! When at Netherfield, Miss Elizabeth had never departed later than eight for her morning walk. He had been waiting nigh on a half hour for her to arrive!

He groaned and shoved the watch back into its rightful place. What if she did not come? What if Mr. or Mrs. Collins detained her at the Parsonage? What if she had merely been making polite conversation? What if she were ill?

A sharp pain pierced the tip of his thumb, and he gave an abrupt inhale. He had to cease this biting of his fingernails! The habit was a new one—one he had adopted when Miss Elizabeth stayed at Netherfield with her sister.

London was supposed to solve his dilemma. His unfortunate thumb would heal and he would have the distance from Miss

Elizabeth that he required. Yet, the ploy had been unsuccessful. He was in a worse situation than before.

His hands covered his face as he suppressed a growl. She was irresistible, and he was in a sorry state indeed!

A crack, like that of a twig breaking, broke the silence of the grove. He removed his hands from his face, and tilted his head. Were those footsteps?

Careful not to make a sound, he turned to peer around the oak. A gasp escaped him at a glimpse of blue that moved behind the tree. He tiptoed around the trunk until she came into view. Miss Elizabeth *had* come!

Remaining out of her sight, he leaned upon the tree and stared as she brought down a bough to smell the blossoms. Laughter rang out like music when, upon releasing the limb, the blush-colored petals rained upon her head.

Her smile was radiant, her hair glowed in the sunlight permeating through the trees, and her delicate hands were before her as she caught the delicate flowers in her palms. She even giggled as she lifted her bonnet from her arm and strew the petals that had fallen inside.

Reality was better than he had imagined, but he still had yet to approach her. The point of waiting for so long was not only to view her as such, but also to speak with her!

His shoulders dropped. Unless he intended to propose marriage, he could not risk meeting her again under any circumstances. To do so would raise her hopes, and he would not do her the disservice. He had to decide once and for all!

She turned her back to him, and his chance had come. He darted without a sound behind a hedgerow. After a quick tug to his topcoat, he adjusted his great coat as he stepped from behind the bushes.

Miss Elizabeth, who turned in his direction when he emerged, startled.

He approached and bowed as she curtsied. "Miss Elizabeth,

how are you enjoying the grove? I do hope it meets with your expectations."

With a start, she glanced at her surroundings and back to him. "Cherry blossoms never disappoint, Mr. Darcy. But, I must confess I have been here before. It has become a favorite haunt of mine."

He stretched his arm before him, gesturing further into the trees. "Then, I hope you do not mind my intrusion. I have no pressing business and would be pleased to join you. The grove is particularly beautiful this year."

She bit her lip. Was she suppressing a smile? She was certain to be pleased at his attention!

As she fell into step at his side, he held back a sigh. This was as it ought to be. This was perfection! He had no other option but to beg Elizabeth to become his wife—no other woman would do!

Darcy's Discussions with Elizabeth About Her Staying at Rosings in the Future

by L. L. Diamond

April 3, 1812

Elizabeth tarried as she walked the well-worn path to the grove. What if Mr. Darcy appeared again? She was still bewildered by the perverseness of mischance that brought him to that particular spot less than a se'nnight ago. Why would he have appeared there when she had not seen a soul in that part of the park since her arrival?

As they had walked, she made a point to tell him the orchard was a favorite haunt of hers, but had he listened? No! Instead, the insufferable man appeared again two days later.

He had not appeared the day prior, but the weather had not been as fine. Perhaps he did not take his exercise if the sky was grey? Just as he might not walk if a light fog misted the grounds or the earth was damp after a light rain. Mr. Darcy was sullen and prideful enough for one to believe he possessed such an absurd notion.

Regardless, she had no wish to make idle conversation with Mr. Darcy! He was arrogant, condescending, and at times, he made the most inane prattle. His comment that day at the Parsonage about being settled too near her family. What could he have meant by it? Fifty miles was certainly not an easy distance, yet he insisted it a trifling thing if the roads were good. Fifty miles! The conversation was nonsensical; however, when had Mr. Darcy ever possessed good sense?

She rounded the bend, and her breath caught in her throat as it always did when she came upon the grove. Though the blossoms were nearly spent, the orchard was still magnificent. Clouds of blush-colored flowers shaded her from the morning sun whilst raindrops of rosy petals drifted from above with a gentle breeze.

Her fingers traced the rough bark of the first trunk as she left the trail to wend through the trees. A low branch ahead caught her eye, and she stretched to bring it down to her face, inhaling the sweet smell before it was gone for the season, not to return until next spring.

She released the limb, and to her delight, a shower of pink fluff rained upon her head. With a laugh, she shifted her bonnet, which hung from her arm, to strew the flowers that had landed inside.

This time of year was her favorite! Cherry blossoms bloomed around Meryton and Longbourn, but no grove like this one existed at home. She was fortunate to have discovered its presence so soon in her stay. What a dreadful prospect to have missed this beautiful sight!

With a turn, she headed towards another low branch on the far side of the orchard, but came to an abrupt halt when Mr. Darcy emerged without warning from a hedgerow, which bordered one side of the copse.

He bowed and she curtsied. "Miss Elizabeth, how are you enjoying the grove? I do hope it meets with your expectations."

With a start, she glanced at her surroundings and back to him. "Cherry blossoms never disappoint, Mr. Darcy. But, I must confess I have been here before, but it has become a favorite haunt of mine." Of course he already possessed such knowledge, yet it could not hurt to make mention of her preference again, would it?

He stretched his arm before him, gesturing further into the trees. "Then, I hope you do not mind my intrusion. I have no pressing business and would be pleased to join you. The blooms are particularly beautiful this year."

Elizabeth forced a smile as she stepped onto the path. "The

park is for all to enjoy, is it not?"

A bark of a laugh startled her. Mr. Darcy laughs?

"My aunt might disagree. She would insist the park is for herself, Anne, and any guests Rosings might entertain." His walking stick thudded against the ground between footfalls. "Though, I imagine you shall have many opportunities to take in the park when you visit again."

Visit again? Charlotte had not mentioned the possibility, but a future offer to visit would be welcome. Lady Catherine's company proved tedious, yet they did not have dinner at Rosings every evening. She could survive a few dinners in that lady's company.

"Should Charlotte extend the invitation, I see no reason why…
"

"Have you taken great pleasure in your solitary walks around Hunsford?" interjected Mr. Darcy

Were they not just speaking of her journeying to Hunsford in the future? She brushed a curl back from her eyes. "Kent is lovely. I have taken great delight in several walks around the area." This was one until his unfortunate appearance!

For a time he said naught, but continued to walk at her side until they stood by the side of the pond. He surveyed their surroundings before pointing to a path that followed the bank. "What do you think of Mr. and Mrs. Collins felicity in marriage?"

Her teeth gnawed at her lip. Did he not allude to this when he appeared at the parsonage over a week ago?

"I think Mr. Collins fortunate to be married to a woman of sense, and I believe Mrs. Collins pleased to have a home of her own. They find their own happiness in their situation."

She watched a flock of pheasants peck at the grass along the edge of the water, a bird singing a merry tune in a tree, a fish as it broke the calm of the pond. Anywhere but at Mr. Darcy! Would that he did not speak again until he departed.

"If you made frequent journeys to Rosings, you might view the cherry blossoms every spring. Would you not take great pleasure in visiting places to which you have taken such a fancy?"

Mr. Darcy must have nothing better to do but pester innocent females as they took the air. She clasped her hands, gripping them together tightly, as his random inquiries raced through her head—additional visits to Hunsford, her solitary walks, Mr. and Mrs. Collins happiness in marriage, frequent journeys to Rosings. Was Mr. Darcy in his cups this early in the morning? This conversation was as maddening as it was confusing!

"Would you not like to be a guest of Rosings Park?"

She glanced in the direction of the pond. Why would Lady Catherine request a visit from *her*? "A guest of Rosings? I would not flatter myself."

Could he be alluding to a connection between her and Colonel Fitzwilliam? No other reason could exist for her to be invited by Lady Catherine to stay at Rosings Park, yet she knew little of the colonel other than his amiable personality. She would not accept a man on such a slight acquaintance. She did not love him.

"You indicated you have enjoyed Kent?"

She wiped a few stray hairs from her forehead. "I find Kent to be a charming place, yet I know of no time when I will return to the area."

He remained silent until their circuit of the pond was complete. "I am certain you would find Rosings more comfortable than the parsonage."

Oh! Why had she not brought her parasol? One hit to his crown might knock some sense into him. Where did he get these absurd questions? He could not make ridiculous assumptions like these with a serious mind, could he?

"I would never suppose Lady Catherine to extend such an invitation. I am not family after all."

Mr. Darcy stopped, his head gave a slight jerk, and he swapped his walking stick to the other hand. After a few steps, she peered in his direction. His brow was furrowed as he stared at the ground before him. She did not dare speak or ask what occupied his thoughts, however, lest he feel the need to respond. Their discourse today was a puzzle in itself. His mind was a place she had no desire to visit! He could keep his further ideas to himself!

The scenery around them became of great import, and Elizabeth again took in each and every view it afforded until they reached the parsonage gates where Mr. Darcy turned.

"Thank you for the pleasure of your company. I should take my leave of you. I have been away for too long and must return to Rosings."

She pressed her lips together to prevent a smile. She could not be so rude as to appear joyful at the thought of his departure. "I am certain Charlotte shall be sorry you could not remain for tea."

"Yes, well…please give Mrs. Collins my apologies."

"Of course."

He bowed. "Good day, Miss Bennet."

She rose from her curtsy as he strode in the direction of Rosings. Thank goodness he was gone! Infuriating man!

Fitzwilliam and Darcy Visit the Parsonage Again

by Jack Caldwell

April 5, 1812

"Mr. Darcy and Colonel Fitzwilliam," the servant announced.

The party ensconced at the Hunsford Parsonage stood about the small parlor. Colonel Fitzwilliam quickly took in the scene: Mr. Collins, tall and stocky, was literally bowing from the waist.

Steady man, the colonel thought. *I am not my father, the earl.*

Mrs. Collins, plain and pleasant, stood next to her husband, her slight curtsey all that was correct for a woman of her station and that of her guests. Closest to the fireplace was Mrs. Collins's young and awestruck sister, Miss Lucas. By the table was her pretty friend, Miss Bennet.

"Mr. Darcy! Colonel Fitzwilliam! You honor us most acutely by your presence! That you would lower yourselves to once again enter this humble abode! Not that this house is so very humble, for what Parsonage in all of England could boast of the careful attentions, generosity, and taste of Lady Catherine de Bourgh! Such approbation! Such compassion to my relations! But who could expect less from the nephews of my most generous patroness?"

In this manner, Mr. Collins continued, and Fitzwilliam was hard pressed to hide his smile completely at the man's foolishness. He managed it by smiling as he greeted the ladies. In short order, he found himself seated at a small table with Miss Bennet, while the others attempted to attend to Darcy.

Darcy was behaving as he usually did, his cousin noted. Uncomfortable in any social situation away from his close friends and family, the man fell back into cold politeness and taciturn statements. Fitzwilliam was accustomed to it and hardly noticed, but the same could not be said for his fair companion.

"I am sorry all sport is done, Colonel," she said.

"I did not know that ladies paid any great attention to gentlemen's pursuits, Miss Bennet."

"Oh! You are severe on us!" Her smile took away any bite to her words. "We ladies do talk of things beside lace and finery. Gentlemen's activities are always of great interest to us, for it is said that a man grows ridiculous without an occupation, and the follies of our fellows are the very heart of gossip."

The colonel laughed heartily. "How well you know us! Indeed, sloth is abhorrent to me and my friend, too."

Miss Bennet's eyes darted to Darcy. "I have heard it said of your cousin that he dislikes quiet Sunday afternoons."

"I cannot say that is an accurate description of Darcy."

"I must bow to your superior knowledge, sir. But to defend myself, I was told by a very good source that there is no more awful object than that gentleman at his own house on a Sunday evening, when he has nothing to do."

Fitzwilliam laughed again. "Now that is true! Darcy always wants to do something useful, particularly for someone else. He has not accepted the idea that he must rest like us mere mortals!"

"Are people always dependent on his advice and efforts, then? He sounds very much like his aunt."

Fitzwilliam glanced about the room. It was a small, modest house, but Lady Catherine had seen to improvements. The furniture might be sparse, but it was of good quality, castoffs from the last redecoration of Rosings. The paint and wall coverings were relatively new and fresh, and Fitzwilliam could see his aunt's hand in the sensible arrangement of the furnishings.

Knowing my aunt's attention to detail, the Collinses are probably frightened out of their wits to move any of this more than an inch without prior approval!

"I would say that both my aunt and my cousin take a prodigious interest in the concerns of those under their care." *Although for dramatically different reasons! Darcy truly cares for his servants and tenants, like his father and mine, while Lady Catherine only desires to exercise control over the lower classes.*

Miss Bennet nodded to herself as if the colonel's words had reinforced a previously held opinion. She glanced again at Darcy, and Fitzwilliam could see that he was staring at her.

Darcy is showing unusual attention to my pretty companion. I believe there is some admiration in it. Is the lady's teasing a sign that she is aware of it and approves? I cannot tell. Her wit is so sharp I wonder if she means to tickle or wound.

Tea was then served, which gave Miss Lucas an excuse to join the pair. Mr. Darcy remained on the sofa, an unwilling recipient of Mr. Collins's insipid conversation.

Twenty minutes later the cousins were walking back to Rosings.

"Darcy," cried Fitzwilliam, "I know you can be reserved to a distressing degree, but if you insist on continuing to call on the Collinses, at least you could actually carry on a conversation with them."

Darcy shook his head. "I believe I talked as much as ever."

"You hardly talked at all!"

Darcy looked over at his friend. "Compared to you, anyone would seem struck dumb—" he paused dramatically, "save Mr. Collins!"

"Too true. There, you see! You do have a wit! You should show it if you mean—"

"Mean what?"

Fitzwilliam held his tongue. If Darcy was attracted to Miss Bennet, he would never admit it to anyone until he was ready. Besides, the colonel reminded himself that he might be mistaken.

"If you mean to show yourself to good advantage," Fitzwilliam finished lamely.

"Show myself to good advantage? To whom, Fitz? A foolish country parson, one who is suitable to no one save my overbearing aunt?"

"Darcy, that is harsh!" At Darcy's raised eyebrow, he added, "But true!"

They walked on for a little while. Upon beholding the front door of Rosings, Darcy blurted out, "We should visit the Parsonage again tomorrow if the weather holds."

Fitzwilliam grinned. *Well, I say! Darcy is lost to the charms of Miss Bennet!*

Colonel Fitzwilliam Meets Miss Elizabeth in the Woods

by Jack Caldwell

April 9, 1812

Colonel Fitzwilliam was not in the best of spirits as he left the main house. He loved Darcy like a brother, but there were times when his cousin's high-handedness drove the colonel to distraction. The reason for today's irritation? Darcy had hinted that he might extend his visit to Rosings. Again.

Blast and damnation! cursed the colonel. *I have little more than a month left to my leave, and then I must return to Spain. I had hoped to spend some of this time with my family and Georgiana. As fond as I am of Anne, I do not want to spend what little time I have in England trapped in Kent!*

Fitzwilliam brooded, trying to determine Darcy's real reasons for staying at Rosings, when he spied a likely motive. Miss Elizabeth Bennet was walking towards the house, perusing a letter in her hand. Fitzwilliam's countenance lightened as he began to contemplate the mystery of the level of acquaintance between Darcy and the lovely young lady from Hertfordshire.

Miss Elizabeth looked surprised when she glanced up and saw him. Putting away the letter immediately and a smile gracing her face, the lady shared the usual greetings with the gentleman.

She added, "I did not know before that you ever walked this way."

"I have been making the tour of the park," the colonel replied, "as I generally do every year, and intend to close it with a call at the

Parsonage. Are you going much farther?"

"No, I should have turned in a moment."

And accordingly she did turn, and they walked towards the Parsonage together. "Do you certainly leave Kent on Saturday?" said Miss Elizabeth.

"Yes, if Darcy does not put it off again. But I am at his disposal. He arranges the business just as he pleases." Fitz tried to hide any irritation he felt.

"And if not able to please himself in the arrangement, he has at least the great pleasure in the power of choice. I do not know anybody who seems more to enjoy the power of doing what he likes than Mr. Darcy."

"He likes to have his own way very well," replied Fitzwilliam. "But so we all do. It is only that he has better means of having it than many others because he is rich and many others are poor. I speak feelingly. A younger son, you know, must be inured to self-denial and dependence."

Miss Elizabeth's fine, mocking eyes flashed. "In my opinion, the younger son of an earl can know very little of either. Now, seriously, what have you ever known of self-denial and dependence? When have you been prevented by want of money from going wherever you chose or procuring anything you had a fancy for?"

Fitz was forced to grin. "These are home questions—and perhaps I cannot say that I have experienced many hardships of that nature. But in matters of greater weight, I may suffer from the want of money. Younger sons cannot marry where they like."

"Unless where they like women of fortune, which I think they very often do," the lady teased.

Fitzwilliam shrugged. "Our habits of expense make us too dependent, and there are not many in my rank of life who can afford to marry without some attention to money."

His companion colored at the idea, but recovering herself, said in a lively tone, "And pray, what is the usual price of an earl's younger son? Unless the elder brother is very sickly, I suppose you would not ask above fifty thousand pounds."

Fitzwilliam was surprised that she had mentioned the exact amount of Anne's fortune. *How could she have heard of it? Her cousin, the parson, perhaps? He knows all too much of my aunt's business.* He hid his disquiet well, however, answered her in the same style, and the subject was dropped.

After a period of quiet, Miss Bennet ventured, "I imagine your cousin brought you down with him chiefly for the sake of having somebody at his disposal. I wonder he does not marry to secure a lasting convenience of that kind. But perhaps his sister does as well for the present, and as she is under his sole care, he may do what he likes with her."

"No," said Colonel Fitzwilliam, "that is an advantage which he must divide with me. I am joined with him in the guardianship of Miss Darcy."

"Are you, indeed? And pray what sort of guardians do you make? Does your charge give you much trouble? Young ladies of her age are sometimes a little difficult to manage, and if she has the true Darcy spirit, she may like to have her own way."

The lady's playful speech alarmed Fitzwilliam. For an instant he wanted to shake her—make her tell him of what she had heard of Georgiana. *Had Wickham talked of Georgie? I will KILL him!*

He controlled his temper, however, but only barely. "I am curious as to why you suppose my cousin likely to give uneasiness to anyone."

"You need not be frightened," she directly replied. "I never heard any harm of her, and I daresay she is one of the most tractable creatures in the world."

Fitzwilliam relaxed as the lady continued. "She is a very great favorite with some ladies of my acquaintance—Mrs. Hurst and Miss Bingley. I think I have heard you say that you know them."

So relieved was Fitzwilliam that he did not mind his next words well. "I know them a little. Their brother is a pleasant, gentlemanlike man. He is a great friend of Darcy's."

"Oh, yes!" said Miss Elizabeth drily. "Mr. Darcy is uncommonly kind to Mr. Bingley and takes a prodigious deal of care of him."

"Care of him!" Fitz laughed. "Yes, I really believe Darcy *does* take care of him in those points where he most wants care. From something that he told me in our journey hither, I have reason to think Bingley very much indebted to him."

Suddenly, the colonel realized that he might have said too much. "But I ought to beg his pardon, for I have no right to suppose that Bingley was the person meant. It was all conjecture."

"What is it you mean?"

Fitz saw no harm in continuing. "It is a circumstance which Darcy, of course, would not wish to be generally known, because if it were to get round to the lady's family, it would be an unpleasant thing."

"You may depend upon my not mentioning it."

"And remember that I have not much reason for supposing it to be Bingley! What he told me was merely this: That he congratulated himself on having lately saved a friend from the inconveniences of a most imprudent marriage but without mentioning names or any other particulars, and I only suspected it to be Bingley from believing him the kind of young man to get into a scrape of that sort and from knowing them to have been together the whole of last summer."

"Did Mr. Darcy give you his reasons for this interference?"

In a gossipy tone, he said, "I understood that there were some very strong objections against the lady."

"And what arts did he use to separate them?"

"He did not talk to me of his own arts," said Fitzwilliam, smiling. "He only told me what I have now told you."

342

Miss Elizabeth made no answer and walked on. After watching her a little, Fitzwilliam asked her why she was so thoughtful.

"I am thinking of what you have been telling me. Your cousin's conduct does not suit my feelings. Why was he to be the judge?"

Fitzwilliam heard displeasure in her voice. "You are rather disposed to call his interference officious?"

"I do not see what right Mr. Darcy had to decide on the propriety of his friend's inclination, or why, upon his own judgment alone, he was to determine and direct in what manner that friend was to be happy!

"But," she continued, recollecting herself, "as we know none of the particulars, it is not fair to condemn him. It is not to be supposed that there was much affection in the case."

"That is not an unnatural surmise," said Fitzwilliam after a self-conscious chuckle, "but it is lessening the honor of my cousin's triumph very sadly!"

The lady did not seem to enjoy Fitzwilliam's jest, and therefore, abruptly changed the conversation. The two talked on indifferent matters till they reached the Parsonage, where the colonel took his leave.

As he returned to Rosings, he was uneasy. *Miss Elizabeth was decidedly unhappy. Could I have offended her?*

A ridiculous question! Of course not.

Darcy Plans His Proposal

by Susan Mason-Milks

April 9, 1812

Fitzwilliam Darcy was a man whose entire life was about responsibility and duty. Since boyhood, he had always done what people expected of him. His parents, his relations, and his friends all knew he would eventually marry a young lady from the highest circles. In addition to her beauty, she would have impeccable manners and breeding and would have been training all her life to fulfill the role of mistress of a great house like Pemberley. They would be the perfect couple in the eyes of the *ton*.

The longer he waited to select a wife, the more intensely society mothers competed to gain his attention for their daughters. His friends, acquaintances, and even strangers began to enter their bets in the book at White's as to when Fitzwilliam Darcy would finally decide to marry and who the fortunate young lady might be.

Darcy always believed he would follow the path set out for him since birth—then he met Miss Elizabeth Bennet. Last fall, she had taken him completely by surprise, upsetting his regulated, well-ordered world in ways he could never have imagined. She was unlike anyone he had ever met before. Though only the daughter of a country gentleman, she was enchanting, enticing... yes, even bewitching. Almost from the moment he met her, he began to comprehend he was in serious danger. The more time he had spent in her company, the deeper he fell under her spell. In order to keep his feelings under strict control, he had endeavored to limit his interactions with her, but the pull to be near her had sometimes proven more powerful than his resolve.

Unlike other women of his acquaintance, she never tried to gain his attention. Even more unusual, she appeared unimpressed by his wealth and social standing. At first, he thought her apparent lack of interest might be part of a game to attract him, but very quickly, he realized she was completely lacking in pretense. The more time he spent in her presence, the more difficult it became to resist her.

In spite of the ache he felt for her, he knew it was impossible to consider making her an offer of marriage. Because of her family's lack of connections, she would never be considered an appropriate wife for a man of his standing. A lifetime of training in duty and responsibility to his family name told him he must forget her. And so last fall, he had left Hertfordshire, certain he would never see her again.

During the winter months, she had haunted his dreams in spite of his diligent efforts to blot her from his memory and remove her from his heart. When he arrived at Rosings to spend Easter with his aunt, Lady Catherine de Bourgh, he was not prepared for the shock of finding Miss Elizabeth also in the neighborhood visiting with her friend Mrs. Collins. Was it chance or a cruel joke of the gods to put her in his path once again? Wrestling with his feelings every night, he found sleep elusive. Each morning he arose with dark smudges beneath his eyes and his patience in short supply.

A few nights ago over the pianoforte, his beautiful Elizabeth taken him to task, and at the same time, artfully let him know she understood his struggles to overcome his shyness in conversing with people. When she suggested he should practice the art of conversation, he hoped she was hinting she would be his tutor in this endeavor. He could see clearly how her natural charms would help him through those socially difficult situations in which he usually floundered. To this marriage, he would bring his social standing, old family name, and wealth, while she would bring her sincere and caring nature, her talent for witty conversation, and her innate understanding of people. Together, they would be a formidable couple. Logic was nothing compared to the desire he felt for her — he must have her as his wife.

After that encounter, Darcy knew he must act. Late at night, sitting alone in the library with only the tick of the mantle clock for company, he considered what to say in his marriage proposal to her. The problem was he was not practiced at expressing his admiration to young ladies. In fact, thus far, all of his efforts had involved finding ways to fend them off. As a result, he knew he must plan and rehearse his speech in advance because when he looked into her dark, expressive eyes, he invariably lost the ability to form a coherent sentence.

First, he would declare how ardently he admired and loved her. That seemed a good start. Then, he would add emphasis to the strength and depth of his feelings by describing his struggle to overcome the many objections and obstacles to their union. He would say, that in offering for her, he was going against the wishes of his family and friends, and in truth, against his own better judgment, but emphasize that where she was concerned logic had no place. The inferiority of her family's connections, which should be of concern to him, was unimportant when compared to the joy of having her as his wife.

Yes, this was the correct approach. His lovely Elizabeth had an intelligent mind and would appreciate knowing how he had struggled with this decision. She would understand that, in the end, reason and logic had given way to love.

Feeling satisfied with his plan, he retired for the evening. In a dream that night, he walked with her in the grove. He saw himself taking her hands in his and reciting his proposal. As he spoke, her eyes grew warmer, and she smiled up into his face. "Yes," she said, "I would be honored to marry you." Raising her hand to his lips, he kissed it softly. More kisses followed until they were suddenly at Pemberley in his room, in his bed.

Darcy awoke with a start in a tangle of linens, confused and disappointed to find he was still at Rosings. The delight of holding her soft form in his arms lingered, creating an aching need inside him. At least, he could take comfort that after today it would not be much longer until she was with him in reality, not just in a dream.

After dressing with great care, he left the house praying she had kept to her usual morning routine of walking in the grove. As he approached the area, he saw her, but she was not alone. She was walking with his cousin. Blast that Fitzwilliam for getting in his way again! His irritation grew as he thought about how often his charming cousin had monopolized Elizabeth's attentions in the past few weeks. Now he would have to find a way to speak to her later in the day. Frustrated, he turned on his heel and stalked back to the house feeling very put out that his plan had been thwarted.

Later that morning at the breakfast table, Darcy learned from his cousin Anne that the Hunsford party was coming early that evening to drink tea at Rosings. He hoped that at some point during their visit, he would be able to quietly ask Elizabeth for a private audience, either later that evening or the following day, but when the parson and his family arrived, Elizabeth was not with them. Darcy could barely refrain from rolling his eyes as the ridiculous Mr. Collins bowed and bobbed and begged Lady Catherine to accept the apologies of his cousin Elizabeth, who had stayed behind with a headache.

Frustrated, Darcy excused himself from the group and went into the library to rethink his plan. Was she truly suffering or could it be possible she had invented the headache in order to stay behind and create the opportunity for him to be alone with her? In either case, he must go to her immediately.

All the way to the Parsonage, he went over and over his speech. Upon arrival, he was pleased to discover she was in the parlor and could receive him. Entering the room, he was so distracted by the scent of lavender that he almost forgot to inquire after her health. When he did, her answer was polite but cool, and she seemed slightly uneasy. He brushed it off, confident he had been correct in his assumption she had invented a reason to stay behind in the hopes he would visit her.

When he looked into her lovely, expectant face, his resolve nearly failed. Sitting down, he took a moment to gather his thoughts and review what he planned to say. Then he rose, and taking a deep breath, he began, "In vain I have struggled. It will not do. My feelings will not be repressed. You must allow me to tell you how ardently I admire and love you."

After the Proposal

by Cassandra Grafton

April 9, 1812

Removing himself from the room with the remains of his dignity in place took all of Darcy's will power. He grabbed his hat and cane from the coat-stand in the hall and let himself out of the parsonage, thankful not to encounter any curious servants, and closed the door behind him with a resounding thud.

Then, he stood stock-still, the rigidity of his frame belying the incessant thoughts spinning around in his head. What, in the name of the *devil*, had just happened?

Be calm, Darcy cautioned himself as he inhaled deeply of the cool evening air, then stared about, striving to heed his own advice, but the rapid pounding of his heart and the raw anger filling his very being fought against him. How could the world look the same as when he had entered the parsonage, so determined, so fired up by his decision, so *excited* almost in his anticipation of claiming Elizabeth as his own? *Elizabeth.* Darcy could not bear to even think of her; *she,* who had ensnared his mind, his senses, and finally his heart. For longer than he cared to own, she had filled his thoughts...but now he must think of her no more. It was over; all over.

A momentary anguish gripped him, sweeping aside the wave of anger and disbelief that had carried him from the house. He must get away from this place, away from where Elizabeth remained but a few solid walls from him, an angered Elizabeth he did not recognise, speaking words he could never have imagined.

Somehow Darcy forced his body into action, at first his legs moving tentatively, as though they would not obey him, but then mechanically, rapidly, as his need to put space between himself and his recent humiliation increased. He strode quickly, his forgotten hat still clutched in one hand, but not fast enough to miss the chimes from Hunsford church as they chased after him.

Was it really only seven o'clock? Had all this—the utter destruction of his hopes and dreams, the defamation of his character at the hands of one woman—taken place in so little time?

Sufficient time, however, for it to have gone spectacularly wrong! Far from realising his dreams, the past half hour had unfolded into a nightmare of wretched proportions, and Darcy's mind reeled with the relentless sound of Elizabeth's voice and its cutting accusations.

"...*the last man in the world whom I could ever be prevailed on to marry.*"

Darcy willed her voice into silence, but failed to displace her image from moments earlier; her furious air and stony countenance smote him to his core, and he winced.

How could this be? *Rejected!* And what is more, rejected on every level: as a lover, as a gentleman, as a man of good character. Heat rose in his breast and stole into his cheeks as he strode along. Well, at least he had made it clear any affection he may have declared for her would soon be over. She would not believe him a love-sick pup, bemoaning his loss; she would understand the truth of it. What was it he had said?

"*I perfectly comprehend your feelings, and have now only to be ashamed of what my own have been.*"

Comprehend? He perfectly *comprehended* her feelings? *Never!* Never on this earth would he *ever* comprehend! But ashamed? He shied away from this thought. He did not wish to dwell upon what his feelings had been; they must be forgotten. Elizabeth Bennet did not deserve such honorable affections to be bestowed upon her, and certainly not from a gentleman of such standing...

"...had you behaved in a more gentlemanlike manner"

Darcy came to an abrupt halt. *Un-gentlemanlike?* How could his conduct be considered anything *but* that of a gentleman? Was he not of excellent character, family and social standing, acknowledged by all for his integrity and honesty in his dealings with the world?

Fitzwilliam Darcy, Gentleman: it was how he was known, had *been* known ever since his majority. It was everything about whom he believed himself to be. How could Elizabeth question it? How *dare* she?

Releasing a frustrated breath, Darcy stared around. How could everything be so benign, so *still*, when all within was in turmoil, raging and broiling like a fierce torrent? Why were the birds still singing softly in the trees? Why were the heavens not thick with black clouds the like of which filled his mind, why was thunder and lightning not raging about him?

His throat felt tight, and he tugged at his neck-cloth as his gaze fell upon Rosings, ahead of him through a break in the trees. How he despised it and all it represented. Yet slowly he began to move again, walking towards the house with no choice but to return, his eye fixed upon the stone edifice, desperate to settle upon something to calm him; all was in vain.

"...your arrogance, your conceit and your selfish disdain of the feelings of others..."

Ridiculous! Unfounded, totally erroneous accusations and, what is more, a slur on his character! His conduct was never questioned—*never*! What did *she* comprehend of his worth? Nothing!

A sudden memory touched him, words she had spoken at Netherfield, of seeking the illustration of his character, of trying to make it out, and Darcy was swept rapidly back to the previous autumn in Hertfordshire. Memories of Elizabeth flooded his mind and not even in his present anger towards her could he stem the relentless flow, nor taint the remembrance of his growing admiration for her back then. This interest in his character he had taken as affirmation of his being an object with her. It had stirred him beyond any expectation whilst simultaneously causing anguish

351

of mind as he had acknowledged the futility of his interest in *her*.

It was the recollection of this struggle, of his vain attempts to cease his fascination with her that roused his ire once more. His failure had been his downfall; *enough* with the lady! He swiped his cane angrily, decapitating wild grasses as he strode purposefully along, forcefully closing his mind to the past. The present, however, was less dutiful, and returned with a vengeance as once more Elizabeth's angry countenance appeared before him, her beautiful lips showering him in false accusation. How could he have admired and valued her refreshing opinions when this was hers of *him*? How could he have been so mistaken, and how the *devil* could she have so misconstrued him?

"Your character was unfolded in the recital which I received many months ago from Mr. Wickham."

A physical pain seared Darcy's chest. Elizabeth's championing of Wickham had cut him badly. Why had he not refuted her accusations, defended himself against whatever it was the cad had claimed? Why had no words come to save him in his hour of need, no words to prove his honor?

Stopping suddenly, Darcy caught his breath. Perhaps he should go back—demand a further audience and *make* Elizabeth see the truth, force her to listen to his side of the story? Yet before such a foolish notion could take firmer hold, more of the lady's words spun through his mind.

From the very beginning of their acquaintance, she had said. His actions as Elizabeth perceived them, towards her sister and Wickham, were merely contributory factors in building *"so immoveable a dislike."*

Darcy sighed heavily. Nothing could be achieved by trying to put his case to her, nor could he face more of her anger, her indignation and risk even further censure from the very woman in whom he had trusted and upon whom he had, but an hour earlier, pinned all his hopes and dreams. All his inner struggles had been for naught, swept ruthlessly away by such precious hands.

352

Striding down the path, Darcy emerged into the immediate grounds of Rosings and headed for the stone path leading to the front entrance of the house. It was bordered by flowering cherry trees, the spring blossom opulent and the scent over-powering. Would he ever acquaint it henceforth with his present feelings?

Wearily, he climbed the stone steps to the imposing entrance and then paused before lifting the latch to enter to glance over his shoulder at the parkland lying between the house and Hunsford. Dusk was settling upon the treetops, drawing down a mantle over his return, the day ending, much as his hopes had.

His eye was caught by the only brightness, a scattering of pale blossoms on the path along which he had just walked. It lay like petals from a bridal posy, mocking him, and with a feeling of disgust, Darcy turned his back and entered the house, intent upon seeking the solitude of his room.

He had barely made it to the third stair, however, when Colonel Fitzwilliam appeared in the hall.

"There you are, Darce! You were missed at tea. What was the pressing business? I assumed you would be sequestered in your room, up to your ears in papers, but I see now you have been out!"

Knowing he was in no humor for company, no humor for anyone, Darcy ignored him and continued to take the stairs two at a time. The sanctuary and solitude of his chamber was all he could think of, all he sought.

"*Darcy!*" The Colonel was not one to give up a chase, however, and he bounded up the stairs behind his cousin. "Good grief, man, whatever is wrong with you?"

Wrong with him? Darcy stopped outside his chamber door and swung around to face the Colonel's puzzled countenance. Bitterness seared through him as words almost fell from his tongue, sarcastic words, suggesting his cousin consult Miss Elizabeth Bennet. *She* would be able to enlighten him directly on all and everything at fault with Mr. Fitzwilliam Darcy. With difficulty, he bit down upon them.

"Forgive me, Richard. You must excuse me." Before his cousin could make any response, Darcy entered the room and quickly closed the door upon the Colonel's frowning face.

Darcy Writes a Letter

by Cassandra Grafton

April 9, 1812

Having dismissed his valet with the strict instruction he was not to be disturbed, Darcy had fallen wearily into a damask-covered armchair near one of the windows of his chamber. For some time, he simply stared ahead, but then his shoulders drooped, and his head dropped into his hands as he rested his elbows upon his knees. Thus he continued for some time, the passing of the hours making no impact upon him, nor the alteration in the light; he remarked neither the chimes from his mantel clock nor the falling dusk finally being consumed by the night.

The only disturbance to his introspection had been Colonel Fitzwilliam rapping on his door some time ago, but he had ignored him, closing his ears to the sound.

Gradually, Darcy had begun to acknowledge some of the content of Elizabeth's words. Her refusal had been a profound shock, but to learn of her dislike of him, her poor opinion of his character…the pain occasioned by such knowledge, accompanied by the devastation of all his hopes for the future, was almost more than Darcy could bear, and for a time, he had become lost in the depths of his own despair.

Struggling with a combination of disbelief and a dreadful sensation of sadness, of loss, Darcy found himself unable to remain calm, coolly assessing his situation, to assume an outward appearance of control, all things which had been ingrained in him since childhood—an edict from his father: one must always keep oneself under good and strict regulation.

But how to put this debacle behind him, how he was even to make a beginning was beyond him. His hands tightened on his aching head as he stared at the floor, conscious of a dull heaviness settling close to his heart. Despite his efforts to the contrary, he could focus on nothing but Elizabeth; over and over spun the facets of their meeting through his mind, the echo of her words, the memory of her countenance and her steadfast dismissal of him—his character and his hand—and her passionate defense of George Wickham.

Darcy stirred in his chair. Elizabeth's defense of that worthless bounder had cut him badly. His anger towards her had slowly been diminishing, but this recollection roused it quickly, his mind tormented by questions for which there were no answers.

What level of intimacy existed between them? Elizabeth had shown a surprising understanding of Wickham's present circumstances—or at least, whatever he had portrayed them to be. Clearly, he had informed her of the living, though no doubt he left out the pertinent fact of his taking a pecuniary benefit in its place. Raising his head slowly, Darcy leaned back in his seat, and then pressed a palm against his pounding forehead.

Was the lady's outrage on Wickham's behalf born of tender feelings for the scoundrel? If he had imposed himself upon her ... the ache within his breast intensified, and Darcy caught his breath. He knew not how he would bear it if it were so. He rose quickly from his chair and then peered into the gray light within his chamber, finally becoming conscious of the darkness. Then, he walked to the dresser against the far wall and lit a couple of lamps from which he also lit two candles. He stood for a moment, both candleholders in hand, staring at them as if unsure of their purpose, before walking over to place them on an ornate writing desk near one of the other windows. Then, he began to pace to and fro across the room.

Wickham was evil; he was degenerate and unworthy. That he had maligned Darcy's character to Elizabeth surprised him not; she would hardly be the first person to whom he had appealed, but to what extent had he imposed upon her open and generous nature? How was it that, in their brief acquaintance, Elizabeth had such a picture of him from Wickham? With a groan of frustration, Darcy turned on his heel and paced back across the room. Such thoughts were counterproductive; none of it signified. For even had Wickham not vilified his name, he had to accede that, in Elizabeth's eyes, his faults lay in more than one quarter.

Do you think any consideration would tempt me to accept the man, who has been the means of ruining, perhaps forever, the happiness of a most beloved sister?

How had she come to such a conclusion? Was it merely a supposition, an attempt to draw him out on the matter, to confess? Well, he had done as she wished; he had owned it openly, including his satisfaction over the outcome.

Darcy paused in his pacing as an uncomfortable notion filtered into his head. Could he have erred? Had the lady's affections been truly engaged as Elizabeth had implied?

No! He had the right of it! He had made sure to observe the lady closely and had thus done his friend a great service. How could Elizabeth doubt his good intentions? For heaven's sake, Jane Bennet and Bingley's acquaintance had lasted but two months from start to finish! *"As did yours with Elizabeth,"* whispered a voice in his ear.

Darcy sighed heavily. If only he had been strong enough to do the same for himself. He had tried, oh how he had tried, but all his efforts were proved worthless when the true test came. Had he not fallen at the first hurdle? From the moment he had learned of Elizabeth's presence in Hunsford, he was a doomed man.

Wearily, Darcy dropped into a chair adjacent to the desk and stared unseeingly at the window, oblivious to the darkness without and his pale and gaunt reflection flickering in the shadow of the candles.

Elizabeth's accusations haunted him, the discovery of her ill opinion consumed his every thought, and he could perceive no respite from it. Why had he not defended himself, spoken up to refute her allegations? *Why* did he not speak, challenge her words with the truth as he knew it to be?

He needed resolution, to defend himself and his character. But how? Her opinion of him was a matter of no little import, and if there was aught he could do so she despised him less, then do it he must.

Darcy's troubled gaze fell upon the writing instruments on the desk, and he studied them thoughtfully. A letter went quite against the form; moreover, in all likelihood she would refuse to accept it. Even should she do so, he had no guarantee she would read it with any intention of believing his word. It was hardly a foolproof plan; yet he had no other.

It was the only answer. Opening the drawer of the desk, Darcy retrieved a piece of parchment, selected a pen and flipped open the ink well. The letter must be written and without delay.

* * *

Dawn had risen over Rosings Park, the day beginning with the beauty of a sunrise quite lost upon the occupant of one dimly lit room where the fire had long smoldered in the grate and the candles had burned low in their holders.

Discarded sheets of parchment littered the desk and floor, testament to the struggle Darcy had faced in trying to put his case to Elizabeth. Forcing himself to recollect every memory of their discussion had stirred his anger once more, but as the night passed, his exhaustion dampened some of the fire in his belly. In its place, an ache had begun settling beneath his breast, at times gripping him with such intensity as he dwelled upon the words pouring from his pen that he had struggled to continue.

Then, as the clock on the mantel chimed eight in the morning, he began his final draft; within a half hour, it was done—all but the close.

Darcy dipped his quill into the inkwell one more time and then paused before placing the tip of the pen on the page. How *did* one close the most difficult letter one had ever had occasion to write?

He hesitated, then wrote, *I will only add, God bless you,* followed by his name. Blotting the words firmly, he then folded it precisely and reached for a roll of wax and one of the candles. It was done, and all he wanted was to rid himself of it, that he might shed once and for all his past hopes and dreams.

This thought propelled Darcy from his chair, and he strode over to the window. Having failed to close the shutters on the previous evening, the morning light poured into the room, and he narrowed his eyes against the glare. The day was fine. His only hope of passing his letter to Elizabeth was if he could encounter her in the park; a call upon her at the Parsonage was unfathomable on such a purpose.

With that in mind, he headed to the washstand, splashed some water over his face, and turned to survey the room where he had been closeted. It was time; he must dress without delay and find a way out of the building without being perceived.

Walking in the Grove

by Cassandra Grafton

April 10, 1812

Darcy strode firmly down the path, away from Rosings and towards Hunsford, half expecting a shout from behind him and for his cousin to come after him. Not finding Richard lying in wait for him outside his chamber on cautiously opening his door had been a relief. He had not relished the notion of using the servant's staircase instead.

Despite his desire to leave the house undetected, however, Darcy knew he must speak to the Colonel regarding one portion of his letter—that pertaining to Wickham. His pace eased a little once out of the immediate grounds, and he pushed aside any difficulty which may arise with his cousin. It was not his focus; for now, he must just keep walking, keep putting one foot in front of the other. Why was it his head knew his purpose, the only option for private delivery of his letter being to meet Elizabeth out on one of her walks. Yet his body showed such reluctance to retrace his steps from the previous day?

As he reached the parkland spanning the southern edge of the estate, he slowly came to a halt, his gaze scanning the trees and paths. Where might Elizabeth be on this fine morning? What if she had chosen *not* to walk for fear of encountering him?

What if he came across her, but she would not take the letter? Perhaps she might take it but never read it, consigning it to the grate in the way his first attempts were! How will he ever know if she permitted him the liberty of an explanation?

360

A sense of panic gripped Darcy, and he stopped abruptly. Had he seen his last of her already? Anguish almost overwhelmed him at the thought of never seeing her again, never hearing her voice.

"You fool," he muttered bitterly. "What possible good could come from seeing her again? She *despises* you; you heard it from her own lips."

After their heated exchange the previous day, the accusations leveled at him, her words still cut through Darcy like knives. He felt wounded—hurt and humiliated by her. With the stirring of his anger again, Darcy harnessed it. He needed to feel his outrage once more, to enable him to stay strong, to do this. Straightening his shoulders, he stared ahead, scanning the park for any sight of the lady; then, he set off towards the grove where he had most often encountered her.

Soon he passed beneath the outer trees of the grove, and for some time, Darcy paced to and fro under their canopy, his courage wavering one moment, his irritation drawing him back a moment later. Where was she? He flicked open his watch; he had been here nigh on twenty minutes. How much longer should he stay?

Perhaps this was how it was meant to be. Writing the letter could never be considered a sensible action; perhaps he was being saved from making an even bigger fool of himself. Darcy pulled the letter out and stared at it. Should he leave, consign *this* letter to the same grate as the other attempts?

The neatly written name, *Miss Elizabeth Bennet*, wavered before him, and he traced the lettering reverently with his finger. This would be the last time he would ever see those precious words upon the page.

With a rush of sensation, Darcy was consumed by the feelings he had repressed throughout his sleepless night. How was he to make his way forward in life and never lay eyes upon her again? Would he ever hear word of her, learn what life had lain before her?

What if...? What if Elizabeth had been likewise afflicted? Perhaps with a night of contemplation, she may have allowed him a hearing, may have thought carefully about all he had said and recognized she had made a mistake? Had she reflected upon their conversation, acknowledged she had erred in her judgment of him? Had she, even, reflected upon the offer of marriage she had spurned, of all that she was turning down? Perhaps...

Hope floated swiftly through him; for a moment, he truly believed it might be so. The heavy weight in his breast seemed lighter, the future—one he had imagined lately with so much pleasure—made a tentative gesture to return. Lost in such futile speculation, it was a moment before Darcy discerned a figure beyond the palings of the park, moving along the lane: *Elizabeth!* Swallowing hard upon his trepidation, he walked forward in the hope of meeting with her by the gate, but on glimpsing him, she turned away as though she would avoid him. A sense of despair gripped him, and he called her name, anxious to stall her escape lest this was his only chance.

"Miss Bennet!"

All was dashed in an instant as the lady stopped and turned to face him, her air and countenance proving her to be wishing herself anywhere but in his presence. With hindsight, he was thankful for it. It restored some measure of pride in him, encouraged him to say as little as could be whilst doing what must be done.

Darcy stepped forward quickly as Elizabeth, with palpable reluctance, walked to meet him by the gate. This reminder of how things truly stood, coupled with the wariness upon her pale countenance, struck him forcibly. There would be no second chance, no hope of her having repented her fierce condemnation of his character or her refusal of his hand.

Ignoring the pain gripping his chest anew, Darcy pulled his tattered dignity about him like a cloak, straightening his shoulders and raising his chin.

Presenting the letter to her, which Elizabeth instinctively took, he said in what he hoped was a measured tone, "I have been walking in the grove some time in the hope of meeting you. Will you do me the honor of reading that letter?"

Then, he bowed and turned away, walking as quickly as his pride would permit, even as his heart protested against leaving her.

Why oh why had he not brought his mount that he might be away from here more quickly? Increasing his stride, Darcy refused to give in to the urge of a backward glance; he strode on, trying in vain to banish the image of Elizabeth, pale and strained and reluctant—oh, so reluctant—to meet him. On and on he walked, his heart pounding almost as much as on the previous day, and before he knew it, the monstrosity of Rosings had risen before him.

"Darcy! There you are!"

Looking up quickly, Darcy saw his cousin walking briskly down the steps from the entrance to the house, bent upon joining him. The timing was opportune. He must make haste and enlighten his cousin—enlighten with much concealment—that he might be on his guard should an application be made to him during their final hours at Rosings.

"You are out early for a walk! I am off to the stables, such a fine morning warrants a gallop across the fields. Will you join me?" The Colonel peered more intently at him. "You look like you need one; you are pale as can be!"

"Cousin, I need you to do something for me."

The Colonel frowned. "I am well versed in taking orders, Darce, but not from such a source. What would you have me do?"

They turned to walk in step together towards the stable block, a silence falling as Darcy struggled to phrase what he wished to express as vaguely as possible. Silence, however, was not in the Colonel's nature.

"Well come on, out with it!" He threw his cousin a quizzing look. "Does this have anything to do with your rather odd behavior yesterday evening? Our aunt took some pacifying, I can tell you, when you did not show your face at all."

Darcy's pace slowed and perforce so did the Colonel's, and they came to a halt beside the mounting-block outside the stable. Drawing in a steadying breath, Darcy met his cousin's curious gaze.

"Something arose yesterday—a situation... I mean, a conversation." He halted as a vivid memory of his meeting with

Elizabeth seared through his mind. *That is what you call a "conversation,"* whispered the ever-present voice in his head, but he pushed it aside. "I have found it necessary to inform Miss Elizabeth Bennet..." Again, he stopped and swallowed hard on rising emotion as her name passed his lips. "I had to share with her the past history of our dealings with Wickham."

"What! Are you taken with madness?" The Colonel met Darcy's defiant gaze with incredulity. "No, Fitz," he shook his head, "surely not *everything?*"

"Yes. I am sorry, Richard; there was no alternative but to lay before her the connection between him and the Darcy estate in each and every aspect, both pecuniary and ... personal."

The Colonel grunted. "Am I to be told *why* you found it necessary? I assume you feel you can trust to her confidence? You have been in her acquaintance far longer than I."

Did he trust her? It was a question that had beleaguered Darcy throughout the penning of those parts of his letter. Before yesterday, he would have given an affirmative without hesitation, but after her damning condemnation of his character, did he retain any faith in her?

"Darce? Come on, Man! This is important!"

"Yes. Yes, forgive me, Cousin. I do trust her."

"Hmph. And pray, how did the lady receive such intelligence? I assume you are not going to enlighten me as to why you felt it necessary?"

"It *was* necessary. Please just accept my word that I would not have gone to such lengths had there been any other alternative." Darcy passed a weary hand across his forehead. "I do not know how she received it. I put it in a letter which I have just handed to her."

The Colonel for once seemed lost for words. He stared at Darcy wide eyed in surprise, his mouth slightly open, but then he seemed to rouse himself. "A letter? You addressed her by *letter?* You truly are losing it, Darcy! "

Darcy merely shook his head, but his cousin fixed him with a fierce stare. "I had no choice, Richard. Please just trust me in that." He could not handle an interrogation from his cousin at that moment, and he turned away. "You must excuse me; I will leave you to enjoy your ride."

"Wait!"

Darcy turned back warily, but his cousin's countenance was less forbidding now and more concerned.

"We must take our leave of the company at Hunsford, Darcy. Shall we go at once? I can defer my ride if you would rather get it over with."

Darcy paled. "Must we?"

The Colonel shook his head. "Really, Darcy. You know we must."

Why had he not thought of that? Darcy could feel trepidation rising at the thought of such a fraught occasion. Would Elizabeth have returned directly from her walk, or would she still be enjoying the beauty of the morning? He looked about frantically. What could he do, how could he deal with this?

Then, the Colonel grunted. "With hindsight, perhaps not; I suggest we make our calls separately."

Darcy blinked and then stared at his cousin. Separately?

"Why do you not run along now and do your duty, and I will call in an hour or so. Should Miss Bennet wish to approach me regarding any of the content of your letter, she is unlikely to do so in your presence, do you not think? I can easily suggest a turn in the gardens to give her ample chance to air any concern she may have."

A wave of relief rolled through Darcy and he nodded quickly, thankful for his cousin's level head. "Yes—yes, of course. That is best. I will go directly."

The Colonel hailed the stable boy to ready his mount, then turned back to Darcy and stayed him with his hand as he turned to leave.

"I will do as you ask, and I will do it willingly, but I am no fool, Darcy. I can see that there is something far beyond what you are revealing in all of this. Do not think you will get off this lightly when we are both returned. You owe me some answers."

With that he turned and strode toward the stable, and Darcy walked back down the path towards the lane to Hunsford. If this call must be paid, the sooner the better, and then let it be over. He hoped desperately, for both his and Elizabeth's sake, the lady had yet to return to the Parsonage, but regardless, he would spare them five minutes of his time and no more.

Beyond that, he did not care to think, for he was unlikely to fair *fare* any better on his return to Rosings. His cousin was a keen interrogator; he would not let him off lightly.

Elizabeth Reads Darcy's Letter

by Susan Mason-Milks

April 10, 1812

Elizabeth stood in the grove and watched Mr. Darcy walk away. In spite of how much she disliked him, she could not help but admire his fine figure and the way he carried himself. It was unfortunate that someone with so much to recommend him was also so decidedly unpleasant.

Looking at the letter in her hand, she was in conflict with herself. Even accepting the letter from him—from any man—was highly improper, but it had all transpired so quickly she had been unable to think of a polite way to refuse. Considering her biting words of the day before, perhaps she owed him at least the courtesy of reading whatever explanation he might wish to offer, although nothing he had to say could possibly take away the anger she felt—or the pain of receiving such an offensive marriage proposal.

Mr. Darcy's declaration had taken her completely by surprise yesterday. If only he had stopped after the part about how ardently he admired and loved her, she would have been able to refuse him politely, but he did not. He deemed it necessary to point out to her that he was asking for her hand even though it was against his better judgment to do so! He had continued to raise her ire by reciting a list of the objections against their union. In other words, he asked her to marry him, and then grossly insulted her!

She had been so disturbed by his words at the time that now looking back, she could scarcely remember how she had managed an intelligible response. Through the fog of emotion, she had a vague recollection of accusing him of not behaving in a gentleman-like manner, and then there was something about his being the last man in the world she would ever consider marrying. She could not feel sorry for what she said. He deserved every barb she shot his way.

Thinking back to when he handed her the letter, she remembered that for just a moment his mask of control seemed to slip, and she thought she saw sadness in his eyes. Was it real? Was she truly so important to him, or was it simply that his pride had been injured by her refusal? She did not imagine there were many times when Mr. Fitzwilliam Darcy did not get what he wanted.

Finally, opening the letter, she reluctantly began to read, and with each line she became more and more agitated. Several times she gasped audibly and was thankful no one was nearby to hear her exclamations. Her immediate response to each part was disbelief. Once she finished the letter—with some parts reviewed several times—she rose with the intention of walking, so she could mull over what she had just learned. After only a few steps, she wavered, her legs too uncertain to hold her up. Immediately, Elizabeth looked for a new place to rest. Then unfolding the pages, she read the letter yet again.

After studying it for some time, she accepted some parts with equanimity, while others reignited her feelings of anger and resentment. At first, she could not actually believe he thought Jane indifferent to Mr. Bingley's attentions, that her sister's heart remained untouched. Then, after reviewing the incidents she remembered, Elizabeth reluctantly allowed Mr. Darcy could have made an honest mistake because he did not know Jane well enough to recognize the indications of her feelings. Ironically, she remembered how Charlotte had warned her Jane should make it more clear to Mr. Bingley how she felt in order secure his affections. It added to the irony that Mr. Darcy had been no better at discerning her sister's feelings for Mr. Bingley than she herself had been at perceiving Darcy's for her.

At the references to her family's improprieties, her anger flared again, but even as she smoldered, she knew, sadly, most of it was

368

true. The boisterous, unbridled behavior of her mother and her younger sisters had been an embarrassment to Elizabeth since childhood. Many times she would see her mother ready to launch into another mortifying speech or action, but she was rarely able to stop it. Mrs. Bennet just did not know how to take a hint. For the most part, Elizabeth took the same attitude as her father by simply ignoring their silliness.

On the other hand, her family was certainly no worse than Lady Catherine, who was controlling, opinionated, and often, simply rude. Because she had an old family name and money, her behavior was tolerated. Elizabeth shifted uncomfortably as she remembered the evening Lady Catherine had offered to allow her to practice on the pianoforte in the room of her daughter's companion, as she would be "in nobody's way" in that part of the house. At the time, Elizabeth thought she had noticed Mr. Darcy cringing at his aunt's tactless statement, but she had not been sure. Now considering what she had learned about his attachment to her, she thought her impression had most likely been correct.

The new information about Wickham enveloped her in confusion and then left her dismayed. Darcy turned everything Wickham had told her on its head. Could it be true Darcy was the party who had been wronged and not the other way around? So much of what Wickham told her was almost the same as the events Darcy had related in his letter, but in each case, it appeared Wickham had twisted the facts just enough to make himself the victim who was deserving of her sympathy.

How could she have been so taken in—she who prided herself on being such a good judge of character? Why had she missed the signs that must have been so clearly before her from the beginning? When she overheard Mr. Darcy call her 'tolerable but not handsome enough to tempt him' on the first night they met, she had been both hurt and amused. Had his rude behavior in general and his insults to her personally made her predisposed to believe the worst of him? Although she liked to think of herself as more impartial than that, if she was completely honest with herself, she had to admit it could be true. Wickham must have sensed this weakness in her and taken advantage of it for his own purposes. Had he singled her out for attention because he sensed Darcy's interest in her and wished to hurt his old enemy in still another way? How could Wickham have detected something that had completely escaped her notice?

As she considered the situation, she chastised herself for missing from the very start the indications of Wickham's duplicity. She had not thought to question the impropriety of his sharing very personal information with her when she was little more to him than a new acquaintance. Over and over she had missed the clues of Wickham's subtle plot to undermine Darcy's credibility and character. For that grievous error, she reproached herself harshly. Most of all, Elizabeth flushed with embarrassment at having been taken in by Wickham's charms. How could she ever have been favorably impressed by him? What had happened to her good judgment?

The most shocking part of the letter dealt with Wickham's near seduction of poor Miss Darcy. Her heart went out to this innocent girl who was just about the same age as her own youngest sister, Lydia. Thankfully, Mr. Darcy had been able to avert disaster and save his sister's reputation before any damaging rumors could begin. The explanation of Miss Darcy's close escape and Wickham's part in it must be true, or Mr. Darcy would not have offered to have his cousin, Colonel Fitzwilliam, verify the story for her.

Could this be part of the sadness she had seen appear on Mr. Darcy's face from time to time when he thought no one was looking? If he was truly the honorable man reflected in this letter, then he must blame himself for his sister's situation. That would be a very heavy burden indeed to bear. It did not escape her notice that Mr. Darcy trusted her enough to tell her about Wickham's deception of his sister.

Elizabeth wandered the lane for almost two hours, reading and rereading the letter, walking as she turned the facts over and over in her mind. The emotion of this effort left her drained of energy, but she could not bring herself to face anyone yet. If she had only known Mr. Darcy would be here visiting his aunt at Easter, she would have arranged her visit for later in the spring. What an insufferable, arrogant, irritating man!

Finally, she realized if she did not return to the Parsonage soon, Charlotte might begin to worry. Reluctantly, she prepared for the inevitable challenge of looking calm when there was a storm raging inside her. If her friend knew how upset she was, she might ask questions Elizabeth would rather avoid having to answer.

After apologizing to Charlotte for any concern she might have caused by being away from the house for so long, Elizabeth excused herself to her room. Finally, exhausted, she lay down on the bed and fell asleep, awaking mid-afternoon. This short period of rest went a long way in helping her to regain her good humor. After splashing water on her face, she joined Charlotte in the parlor. Just as she knew it would, the topic eventually turned to Mr. Darcy.

"So what do you think about Mr. Darcy now, Lizzy? I still maintain he has taken a keen interest in you," said Charlotte.

Elizabeth turned red to the tips of her ears. "Oh, no, Charlotte, I cannot believe it. If Mr. Darcy truly had an interest in me, do you not think he would invent some excuse to extend his visit to Rosings?"

Charlotte considered this and then went back to her embroidery. Elizabeth hoped she had diverted her friend enough to allay her suspicions. Several times during the evening, Elizabeth found her thoughts turning to Mr. Darcy again. Whenever this happened, she put her hand in her pocket to touch the letter, as if to ensure it was real.

After staying up late that evening studying the letter, Elizabeth finally went to bed but slept very little in spite of being emotionally and physically exhausted. The next morning as she lay in bed, she heard a carriage pass by the house. Jumping up and running to the window, she saw the coach with the Darcy livery passing by headed in the direction of the main road. Elizabeth realized she felt both relieved and disappointed.

"It is over," she told herself. "I am grateful I will never have to face him again." At that thought, she sat down on the bed and cried.

Fitzwilliam Takes His Leave of the Parsonage

by Jack Caldwell

April 10, 1812

"Are you comfortable, Colonel?" asked Mrs. Collins.

"Perfectly, madam," he replied.

"Of course Colonel Fitzwilliam is comfortable, Mrs. Collins!" cried Mr. Collins. "Did not Lady Catherine de Bourgh herself pick out these very chairs? I assure you, my dear colonel, that your most excellent aunt arranged this room just in this manner, and we have taken pains so see that nothing is out of place, even by an inch! Surely, Lady Catherine's condescension knows no bounds!"

"Certainly you are right, Mr. Collins."

"Such a fine, fine lady. Always thoughtful and punctual. Unlike others—but I should hold my tongue…"

"Yes. Mr. Collins," said his wife. "Do you see Eliza yet?"

Colonel Fitzwilliam relaxed in his chair in the parlor of the Hunsford Parsonage. He was seated next to a window, and the morning sun felt good on his shoulders as he visited Mrs. Collins and Miss Lucas, all the time wondering where Miss Bennet could be. Mr. Collins apparently felt the same—he was staring out the window for the misplaced young lady, muttering apologies.

The colonel's calm demeanor and pleasant conversation gave the lie to the excitement at Rosings over the last eighteen hours. When Fitzwilliam walked out the day before and met Miss Bennet in the park, he had just come to terms of spending another week as a guest at Rosings. But a little while later at tea, an agitated Darcy stormed in late and announced that he was to quit Kent the next morning.

What an uproar that announcement caused! Lady Catherine raged and cajoled, and even Anne begged Darcy to stay, but it was to no avail. The man would not be moved. He was very sorry, but he was determined to return to Town.

"I hope you have enjoyed your stay, Colonel," said Mrs. Collins. "I am sorry that Mr. Darcy is unwell."

"I thank you for your concern, but do not distress yourself. A trifling headache will not lay my cousin low for long," Fitzwilliam assured her.

Later in Darcy's rooms, Fitzwilliam tried to learn the reason for Darcy's extraordinary demand. There were times his friend and cousin could be high-handed, but this behavior was well beyond anything Darcy had ever done before. By then his cousin had calmed down, but he refused to speak of it. Darcy apologized for the inconvenience, which took a bit of the sting out of Fitzwilliam's ill-treatment, but would say no more. He requested, politely but firmly, that he have some privacy for the rest of the evening.

Fitzwilliam had no recourse but to agree. He knew Darcy could be as stubborn as a mule when he put his mind to it.

"Colonel," said Miss Lucas timidly, "I have been meaning to ask you ... but—oh, it is silly."

Fitzwilliam smiled kindly. "What do you wish to know, Miss Lucas?"

The girl was nervous and blushing. Finally she declared, "Why do you not wear your uniform? All the officers back in Meryton are in uniform all the time!"

"But I am off duty," Fitz explained. "It is not right to wear one's uniform when one is off duty."

"But they are so handsome!" The girl blushed as she clamped her hands over her mouth. "Oh, I should not have said that!"

Fitzwilliam bit back a laugh. "I thank you for the compliment, Miss Lucas."

Darcy did something unusual again the next morning. Fitzwilliam was at table, eating his early breakfast, when Darcy came in—not from the passageway that led to the stairs, but from the front hall. The man had been outside, and at such an early hour! Fitzwilliam demanded to know the reason for it, but Darcy remained mute. He took coffee and very little else and requested that they take their leave of the Parsonage ere they departed from Kent.

Once there, they learned that Miss Bennet had yet to return from her morning walk. Fitzwilliam was disappointed; he had grown to like the pretty, rather impertinent young lady. But Darcy, who had already shown signs of tension, became downright distracted. He walked up and down the parlor for a moment, then to Fitzwilliam's bewilderment, paid the meanest of farewells to the Collinses and Miss Lucas before making for the door.

Fitzwilliam, of course, had to say something. "Darcy" he hissed in a low voice, "what are you about? This looks very bad."

"Forgive me … please," said his cousin, who to a person that knew him well, appeared distressed. "I must leave."

"Are you well? Have you a headache?"

He would not look at the colonel. "Make my apologies. I must return to Rosings. Do not hurry. We will leave when you are ready."

Fitzwilliam was so astonished at this incivility he said nothing as Darcy went away.

"More coffee, Colonel?"

Fitzwilliam waved her off. "No, thank you, Mrs. Collins. I should be off as I am sure my cousin is waiting for me. Allow me to take my leave of you."

Mr. Collins turned from the window, uncharacteristically with a scowl on his face. "Please accept my humble apologies for detaining you, my dear colonel! That you would grace my humble abode for such a length of time is condescension beyond even my noble—"

"Indeed you are correct, Mr. Collins," cut in his good wife, as she extended her hand to the colonel. "We have enjoyed meeting you, Colonel Fitzwilliam."

"It was an honor, ma'am."

"Oh, my dear, dear sir! It is we who are honored by your august presence!"

"Mr. Collins, this is too much—"

"But I do not know where my cousin has gotten to. I should speak to her upon her return."

"Pray do not, my good sir. The woods of Rosings are so delightful that one can hardly tear one's self from them. I do speak from experience."

"True, true—very true! Your most excellent aunt spends a prodigious amount on the care of them, does she not?"

"I cannot say. Good bye, Miss Lucas."

"Colonel," said she, blushing furiously. "I hope we should meet again."

Fitzwilliam felt regret about this. Apparently he had failed to guard his tongue around Mrs. Collins's young and impressionable sister. The lovesick look she bestowed on him made him guilty. He smiled and made his way out of the Parsonage as quickly as possible.

A Conversations between Cousins

by Cassandra Grafton

April 11, 1812

Darcy had filled the remainder of his final day at Rosings with activity, determined to exhaust both his mind and body and leave no room for thought or feeling. After a long ride, during which he tried not to think of Elizabeth, or of his cousin, who had been striding off to the parsonage even as Darcy walked his mount to the block, he returned physically fatigued but still fighting his memories and his despair.

The ensuing hours were spent sequestered in his chamber, burying his head in matters of business; matters he had ignored during his repeatedly extended stay in Kent, with correspondence from his steward at Pemberley, his legal advisors in London, and even his sister, abandoned as his fascination with Elizabeth had taken full hold and left him powerless to think of aught but her.

It was evening, therefore, before Darcy encountered any other person, where he endured, much as he had anticipated, a long lecture from his aunt over his absences in the past eight and forty hours. Dinner passed with Darcy contributing little to the conversation, but there was no escaping his cousin as he all but marched him from the room when the time came to separate, ignoring Lady Catherine's annoyance over the men withdrawing before the ladies.

"And so," said the Colonel, glancing over at Darcy as the two men approached the library, "here ends another visit to Kent and yet no proposal of marriage!"

Trepidation shot through Darcy, and he threw his cousin a frantic look. "I beg your pardon?"

They had reached the door, and the Colonel turned to face him. "Cousin Anne, old man. Aunt Catherine will now have to spend a further year attempting to draw you down to Kent at every turn."

Following his cousin into the room, Darcy berated himself for his foolish thoughts. Of course Richard was referring to Anne; he had no reason to think otherwise. Elizabeth would never have mentioned…she would not even have hinted at what had befallen her the previous evening…he gave an involuntary shudder as he came to a halt in the centre of the room.

"Are you well?" The Colonel frowned. "You look…"

Darcy raised a hand. "Be done with it, Richard." He had no desire to know how he looked.

With a shrug, Colonel Fitzwilliam closed the door and came to stand before him. "I regret to inform you I failed in my mission, Cousin."

Mission? Of course! "She would not believe you."

The Colonel shook his head and walked over to the sideboard where a tray of spirits glistened in their crystal decanters. "I had no chance to try her, Fitz. I waited beyond an hour, suffering all manner of foolishness from the hapless parson, but she did not return. I contemplated walking out to try and come across her, but the park is so vast and the lady, as well you know, a keen walker. It would have been akin to seeking a tack in a hay bale."

Taking the proffered glass from his cousin, Darcy walked over to the fireplace where he stood and stared into the flames. Why had Elizabeth stayed away so long? Was it an indication she had read his letter and needed time to consider it? Did she comprehend at last how faulty her judgment had been?

"Darce?"

With a start, Darcy glanced over at his cousin who was now seated in a fireside chair, watching him keenly.

"Sit down, man; you are making my neck ache standing there so stiffly!"

Darcy did as he was told, sinking into the opposite chair and placing his glass on a nearby table. "I appreciate your efforts. It was a foolish hope, that she might wish for clarification, might wish to at least consider the truth of my words."

Silence descended upon them, disturbed only by the crackling of the fire in the hearth. Darcy stared into the flames again; what might Elizabeth be doing at this moment? Had his letter made any difference at all, or had she consigned it to the grate? Was her disgust at his attempt to address her in such a manner so powerful, she had not permitted him the liberty?

Her face rose before him, dark eyes flashing and her lips speaking those cutting words, words that were in danger of haunting him forever:

"Had you behaved in a more gentleman-like manner…"

"It is a shame I did not know of your actions beforehand, Fitz."

Darcy started, his gaze flying to meet his cousin's. "How—how so?"

"I met Miss Bennet during my farewell tour of the park yesterday, and we continued in company." The Colonel frowned. "We spoke of you; it would have been the perfect opportunity to provide the authentication you sought from me."

Leaning forward slowly in his seat, torn between curiosity and trepidation, Darcy stared at his cousin. "You - you spoke of me?"

"Indeed," the Colonel picked up his empty glass and got to his feet, gesturing to his cousin to drink up. "Though she would likely have been in no humor to hear me out. My last memory of Miss Bennet is not of the pleasing good nature I had long associated with the lady. Her air and countenance were sufficient to guide me in her dissatisfaction with your actions."

"What in heaven's name were you speaking of?!" Darcy fixed his cousin with a fierce stare. "What did you say to cause her such... such *discontent* with me?"

The Colonel shrugged. "I merely advised her of your care for others, most particularly in saving a friend recently from an imprudent marriage. I mentioned no names, though I assumed it was Bingley. He is the most likely to get himself into a scrape of that sort, and you have spent an inordinate amount of time with him these past months."

Releasing a slow breath, Darcy sank back against the cushions of his seat. Elizabeth's understanding of his part in separating his friend from her sister was finally clear. Whatever her own suspicions may have been, this intelligence from his own cousin would have been sufficient to confirm her worst opinion of him. Though he saw now his suit would never have succeeded, he began to appreciate the significance of the timing of his cousin's revelation so close to his own call upon the lady.

Grabbing his glass, Darcy took a hefty swig, letting the liquid burn a trail down his throat. Then, he handed it to his cousin, who turned towards the drinks tray.

"Would you like to know what I think?"

"A rhetorical question, Cousin; you will tell me, regardless."

Colonel Fitzwilliam grunted. "You are inordinately troubled over the opinion of a young woman whose path will likely never cross with yours again."

Knowing he had looked his last upon Elizabeth was sufficient trial without his cousin reinforcing it. The tight band around Darcy's chest flexed itself, and he swallowed hard on a sudden constriction to this throat.

Taking his refreshed glass from his cousin, he tried to breath evenly to ease the tautness.

"I can well observe the matter is best left alone for the present." The Colonel raised his glass to Darcy. "Here is to the end of our captivity in Kent, be it by duty or otherwise."

Clearing his throat, Darcy nodded, thankful for the reprieve and raising his glass by return. "Indeed."

"Besides," The Colonel settled comfortably into his chair. "There will be ample time for further discourse on the way to Town on the morrow."

With that, he turned the conversation to Georgiana and the upcoming summer, and Darcy reluctantly followed his lead, unsure what unsettled him most: the notion of another endless night with no sleep and nothing but his disappointment and despair to console him or what his all too observant cousin may challenge him with as finally they left Kent, and Elizabeth Bennet, behind.

Lady Catherine's Company

by Diana Birchall

April 24, 1812

"I hope," sniffed Lady Catherine, "that those young ladies were sensible of the favor we bestowed upon them in the warmth of our farewells."

"Why, Lady Catherine, only you in your modesty could have any doubt in the matter!" enthused Mr. Collins. "How could they be anything but all gratitude? Your graciousness! I am sure my esteemed father-in-law would agree that there were few instances of anything like it, even at the Court."

Lady Catherine smiled benevolently. "But there was one thing—I did wonder, Anne, if you were not a little too warm, too over cordial, at the parting. Actually giving your hand to them both!"

Mr. Collins sighed with admiration. "Miss Anne's condescension was particularly well judging," he said. "As is everything she does. A Miss Anne of Rosings can do no wrong when it comes to manners. She is a perfect lesson-book of them. All young ladies can learn from the manners of the great. Do you not think so, my dear?"

Charlotte looked up from her stitching. She often brought a little piece of embroidery with her on their visits to Rosings. Nothing vulgar, like socks; but Lady Catherine did not object if it was something genteel. She sometimes went so far as to praise Charlotte's industry, though seldom without thinking of something else for her to do. A lace baby's-cap was the appropriate thing to embroider at Rosings; not too high, not too humble.

"I am sure Miss Anne did and said all that was polite," she agreed sedately, "and I know my sister and my friend were very grateful for the kind treatment they received here."

"Grateful!" exclaimed her husband. "I should say so! Nothing can be compared to it. The young ladies to be invited, again and again! Treated to the splendors of Rosings. Such dinners! And not least of all, admitted into the company of such fine gentlemen as Mr. Darcy and Colonel Fitzwilliam. It was a veritable coming-out for Maria; as good as being presented to the Queen."

"And Lizzy enjoyed herself," added Charlotte, more moderately, "she told me she had a very good time."

"Enjoyed herself! As who would not, on being admitted to the privilege of visiting at Rosings."

"I confess," admitted Lady Catherine, "that I feel myself a little dull tonight, without the young ladies, and my nephews. They all seemed to get on very well, I thought. I almost suspected, on one evening, that the dear Colonel admired Miss Bennet a little—but of course, I deceived myself. He is far too sensible."

"Oh surely not," bleated Mr. Collins. "Pray, do not let such a thought enter your head, Lady Catherine. "Our young guests know their place. Miss Elizabeth could never aspire to—that is, the Colonel was only treating her with the extreme graciousness that he shows all the world. A truly knightly spirit. Never was a man with such peculiarly warm, open manners!"

"He does form rather a contrast to Darcy, I admit," said Lady Catherine thoughtfully. "Darcy will sometimes sit for half-an-hour, staring at nothing. When Miss Bennet was playing those rather ill chosen Burns songs, he had his eye very firmly fixed upon the pianoforte, I saw."

"Oh no—oh no," Mr. Collins assured her, "do you not recollect, Lady Catherine, that Miss Anne was on the same side of the room as the piano—I am sure that his looking at the instrument was merely a pretext, so that we would not observe how intent he was in fixing his eyes upon *her*."

"I wish I could think so," said her ladyship, "but I was a trifle disappointed in Darcy, to say the truth. It is time he thought of settling down, you know, and Anne is ready, more than ready. I really thought that this time would be the charm."

"Of course he was charmed with her, never anybody more so, Lady Catherine—he could hardly tear his eyes away from her," assured Mrs. Jenkinson, leaning forward and adjusting Miss de Bourgh's pink headpiece with its silk rose. "I distinctly heard him say that pink was his favorite color, you know, and he had a great air of meaning as he said it, I do assure you."

Charlotte remembered that Elizabeth had worn pink, but she knew much better than to say so.

"Well. I hope you are right," said Lady Catherine. "The color did not affix him, but best not to speak of that. I do wish you had talked a bit more, Anne."

"I said everything that I could Mama," she protested, brushing aside Mrs. Jenkinson's tender consoling pats impatiently. "Did not you hear me ask Darcy how he liked going down to Ramsgate last summer, and if it was his favorite watering-place?"

"Yes, you did," Lady Catherine conceded, "and I was rejoiced, for that is a very promising topic, and well thought of. Darcy can be difficult to speak to, you know, with his singular reticence, the reticence of a gentleman; and he seems to require a lively— I thought you did very well, my dear. I was in hopes that he would talk of his knowledge of Weymouth and Worthing, but the subject of Ramsgate did not seem to interest him after all. And yet Georgiana was down there all last summer."

"I think he does not care for watering-places," Charlotte ventured to say. "He said as much, did he not? I thought I heard him."

"He did. He said he could not understand why the English people went to so much trouble to be at noisy sand-infested places

384

where they forgot their morals and were parted from a good deal of money," Anne told her.

"No, that does not sound as if he liked watering-place holidays, Anne, does it. I wonder you could venture upon the topic, if you knew it. Perhaps you had better not, another time," said her mother.

"No, Mama, I won't."

Lady Catherine brightened. "And do not forget, we will have another chance to see Darcy, next month, when we go to London."

"I remember you said you have business in London," Mr. Collins observed. "I hope not of any unpleasant sort."

"Oh no, nothing particular. We will be there only a week, so I can see my man of business, and settle my quarterly accounts. And we shall visit the best mantua-makers while we are in Town, to see about Anne's fall wardrobe. Oh, we have a great deal to do!"

"Will Mr. Darcy and Colonel Fitzwilliam also be in London?" asked Charlotte. "I do not know if Elizabeth and her sister Jane will be in Town then. They sometimes stay with my uncle's family."

"Oh! But of course we are not likely to meet— This is your uncle who lives in Cheap Street, is not he?"

"Cheapside. He is a very gentleman-like man however."

"But in trade, of course. And the Bennet girls visit him often, do they? I do not know if that is wise, as it will assuredly lessen their chances of meeting a better sort of company. Though, to be sure, they cannot aspire to moving in circles such as Darcy's, in London. Here in the country it is quite a different thing. People do not make those same sorts of distinctions in the country."

"True, true. Ten to one Miss Elizabeth and Maria may never have the honor and distinction of being noticed by your nephews again, Lady Catherine," Mr. Collins bowed toward her, "unless, indeed, that event takes place which we all expect, and the future Mrs. Darcy should be so kind as to invite the girls to Pemberley. But that is far too much to presume. I would think it the greatest privilege of my life, to be invited to see such a place myself; and the young ladies have not the advantage of our intimate acquaintance in your family."

"Indeed you may depend upon it, Mr. Collins," said Lady Catherine condescendingly, "that when my daughter is mistress of Pemberley, you and Mrs. Collins will be very welcome to pay a visit there."

"Thank her ladyship for the compliment, Charlotte! Thank her!" he urged in ecstasy, and Charlotte complied, but in a much more quiet and proper fashion.

"I think even when at Pemberley we should rejoice in having company," sighed Lady Catherine. "We certainly do feel its loss at present."

Darcy Cleanses His Palate

by Abigail Reynolds

April 25, 1812

Georgiana held out a leather-bound volume to him. "The bookseller thought I might enjoy this one."

Darcy took the book and turned the spine up. *The Cottagers of Glen Burnie* by Miss Elizabeth Hamilton. *Elizabeth*. He caught his breath as a stab of pain lanced through him. Could he not even put her from his mind for a few minutes while visiting a bookshop with Georgiana? Why did she have to haunt his every thought?

He knew he would forget her eventually, or at least stop remembering her a thousand times a day, but how long would it take? When his father had died, it had been months before he could go an hour without remembering his loss, but surely an acquaintance of a few months could in no way to compare to a beloved father. *Except that Elizabeth is still alive and thinks ill of you,* his conscience reminded him, *and she humiliated you, which your father never did. How many people has she told of your proposal, laughing all the time at your foolishness?* The familiar surge of sick anger was back until he remembered he was being unfair. She had humiliated him, yes, but he had never known her to mock someone when they were not present to defend themselves. How she had teased him during her stay at Netherfield, and how it had delighted him, never imagining there was bitterness behind her arch tones!

"Brother? Fitzwilliam, are you ill?"

He glanced down to see Georgiana's delicate hand balanced on his arm. Georgiana, who had also been taken in by that devil

Wickham! How delighted George Wickham would be if he knew his efforts had cost Darcy the woman he loved. Perhaps he already knew. Perhaps Elizabeth had not believed his letter and had confided in that scoundrel once more. Darcy cleared his throat. "I am quite well, dearest, merely lost in thought."

"You do not look well." Now even Georgiana was fretting over him, just like everyone else. His cousin Richard demanding to know what was bothering him. His aunt sweetly asking whether something was troubling him. His fencing instructor shouting at him in his heavy French accent *Non, Monsieur Darcy! What is wrong with you? That is an epee, not a pig-sticker!* Even his damned valet pestered him a dozen times a day whether there was not something else he required.

"Perhaps a little tired, but nothing more. I think Miss Hamilton's book will be an excellent choice for you. She is quite erudite; her *Letters on Education* made an excellent case for reforming the way we view education." Miss *Elizabeth* Hamilton. A woman of intelligence, integrity and decided opinions, just like his Elizabeth. Dear God, how could she have refused him? All those hundreds of times when he had imagined himself heroically overcoming his dangerous attraction to her, and when he finally gave in, she had refused *him*. And refused him cruelly—there had been no polite "thank you for the compliment of your attentions, but my heart is given elsewhere" for Elizabeth. No, she had to tell him he was the last man in the world she could be prevailed upon to marry. And she seemed to think *he* had been unkind to her! How hypocritical to accuse him of cruelty when she could give lessons on the subject!

Georgiana's face cleared. "I am a bit fatigued myself, since we returned home so late from the theatre last night. But what an amazing performance it was!"

Darcy could not have said for certain whether the play had been good or bad, or even if it had been in English. His mind had stopped paying attention when he saw the play's title. *The Hypocrite.* Yes, that was him, counseling Bingley against allying himself with Miss Bennet and then making an offer himself for her younger sister. Perhaps Elizabeth's refusal was his celestial punishment for hypocrisy. But damn it, he had been right to advise Bingley to forget Jane Bennet! The reason he deserved punishment was for forgetting to apply that lesson to himself. But oh, what a cruel punishment it had been! And then, after the play, he had gone home to his empty bed, the one he would never share with Elizabeth. Damn her for being so bewitching and so hard-hearted!

She had been so gentle and caring to her ill sister. Her playing and singing had a warmth that stirred his heart. He had seen her concern for others a dozen times. But to him she suddenly had become a virago, calling him proud, conceited, and selfish, when all he wanted was her smiles, her tenderness, her fine eyes shining at him. Elizabeth had not hidden any of her scorn for him. He flinched away from the thought that insisted on intruding, asking *why* she had felt that scorn.

She saw things differently than he did. She had claimed her sister was in love with Bingley; he would have sworn her sister indifferent to his friend. What did she see in *him* to make her decide he was insufferable? His head ached, and he longed for the comfort of his favorite leather chair in the quiet of his study, a glass of brandy beside him. No, that was a lie; what he longed for was Elizabeth, for her arms around him, soothing him, telling him she understood she had been mistaken, that she believed his explanations, that a future between them was still possible.

He realized Georgiana was looking at him oddly. "I will have them wrap this up. Would you like to stop at Gunter's on the way home for an ice?" It was her favorite treat; he needed to know he could at least make Georgiana happy.

She smiled shyly and put her arm through his. "I would like that very much, if you are not too tired."

"An ice is precisely what I need to refresh me," he said firmly. It was not true. Elizabeth was what he needed, but all that was available to him was a frozen sweet that would melt away to nothing in his mouth.

389

Lydia Bennet Has Something to Say!

by Susan Mason-Milks

May 8, 1812

Lydia Bennet's moods were as changeable as…well…changeable as the spring weather. In the vast experience of her fifteen years, if she had learned one thing, it was the wisdom of never dwelling too long on anything unpleasant. This time, however, she simply could not shake off the despair that came along with the latest gossip from Meryton. Two days ago, Lydia had learned the militia would be removing to Brighton in a few weeks, and she was absolutely convinced her whole world was coming to an end.

Walking along on her way to Meryton, she thought about how the winter months in Hertfordshire had been made exceedingly enjoyable by the presence of all the lively, young militia officers with their dashing red coats. Now they were ruining everything! She kicked a stone in the road to emphasize her disappointment. Who would she flirt with? Who would she tease? All the local young men were as dull as rocks, but the regiment was full of handsome, fun-loving officers like Lt. Denny, Lt. Kendall, Lt. Jameson, and of course, Lt. Wickham. The others were charming, but Wickham was… He was delicious. She grinned as she thought about him.

Ah, George Wickham! Just saying his name gave her a little thrill. When first he arrived last fall, Lydia's sister Elizabeth had caught his eye. Much to Lydia's delight, this spring with Lizzy away visiting Charlotte in Kent, he had turned more of his attentions her way. In her opinion, no one was as handsome or as clever as Wickham. No one was more elegant or lighter on his feet on the dance floor, and no one made her laugh as much as Wickham.

Today, she was on her way to visit with her dear friend Harriet Forster. Since Harriet's husband was the commander of the militia, she would be going to Brighton, too. It did not bear thinking about. In Harriet, Lydia had found a kindred spirit, someone who loved to laugh as much as she did. Lydia tried to find comfort that they would be able to enjoy a few more afternoons of lovely gossip before her friend left forever.

Knocking on the door of the Forsters' house, Lydia was admitted and shown into a small parlor. When Harriet saw her friend, she put aside her sewing. Immediately, they began sharing funny stories, talking about the attractive physical attributes of particular members of the regiment, all the while giggling as they always did when they were together.

"Oh, Lydia, my dear friend," said Harriet, wiping the tears of laughter from her eyes. "I am so pleased you are here. We always have such fun. How dull it is just sitting here and sewing. Truly, I was beginning to go mad with boredom. The most exciting thing I have done all day is choosing colors of thread. Is that not sad?" She held up the handkerchief she was embroidering and waved it in the air.

"Not as sad as the fact that very soon you will be gone, and I will never see you again. Oh, Harriet, I do not know how I will ever survive the loss! When you leave, Meryton will return to being the dreariest place in England." By now her smile had turned to a frown.

"Then I have news which should cheer you. We may not be parted so soon after all."

Lydia looked up hopefully at her friend. "Do not tease me."

"I told the Colonel I could not bear to be all alone in a new place with no friends around me." Harriet reached over and squeezed Lydia's arm. "He has given his permission for me to ask you to accompany us to Brighton for the summer as my special companion. Lydia, say you will come. We shall have such a grand time together!"

Throwing her arms around her friend, Lydia squealed, "Oh, dear Harriet, there is nothing in the whole entire world I would like more."

Then standing up, Lydia pulled Harriet to her feet, and they began to dance around the parlor chanting, "Oh, what joy! What joy! We are off to Brighton!"

Finally, out of breath, they collapsed back on the settee and started making plans. They talked at the same time, finished each other's sentences, and laughed about the grand time they would have together.

"You do think your parents will give their permission for you to come with us?" Harriet asked.

"Oh, la! Of course, they will," said Lydia with a wave of her hand. "My mother will think it a wonderful idea because it may help me catch a husband in a beautiful red coat." She grinned wickedly. "Mama has a partiality for red coats, you know."

"And your father? Will he approve?"

"Oh, do not worry about Papa. If he has any objections, Mama and I will wear him down quick enough. He is never able to resist a little pouting and a few tears."

The two friends spent the remainder of the afternoon dreaming of all the parties and balls they would attend in Brighton, and as they were nearly the same size, they talked of the gowns they would lend each other. Suddenly, there was so much to do—ribbons to buy, hats to decorate, and trunks to be packed.

On the walk back to Longbourn, Lydia's feet scarcely touched the ground. Her head overflowed with thoughts of all the handsome young officers she would flirt with and of one particular officer whom she liked best of all.

"I am going to Brighton! I am going to Brighton!" she chanted as she skipped along. How she would enjoy lording this special invitation over her sisters! Yes, things were looking up indeed.

What Was Wickham Thinking?

by Shannon Winslow

May 18, 1812

He was by no means discouraged. Mary King may have slipped through his fingers, but what did it matter? There were plenty more fish in the sea. And after all, it would have been selling himself pretty cheap to settle for a freckled face with only ten thousand pounds. He could...he would...do better in the end for being rid of her.

In the meantime, it might be entertaining to renew his flirtation with the intriguing Elizabeth Bennet. He'd had the girl fairly eating out of his hand before she went to Kent and, with any luck, absence had made that naïve young heart grow even fonder of him.

Marrying Miss Bennet was still out of the question, of course, but bedding her was not. In fact, it would be just the thing to cheer him. A little flattery, a few of his boyish smiles, charm skillfully and liberally applied, and she would be his. The juicy peach was clearly ripe for the picking, and who was better equipped to do it properly?

Such were George Wickham's contemplations upon learning that Elizabeth Bennet had returned to the neighborhood. But a fortnight later, after having been frequently in company together, precious little headway had he made with her despite all his varied and strenuous exertions.

Mr. Wickham was now to see Elizabeth for perhaps the final time. On the very last day of the regiment's remaining in Meryton, he dined with the others of the officers at Longbourn. Although he had nearly given up on the idea of an actual conquest (the time for that sort of thing running perilously short), he fully intended that Elizabeth should be excessively sorry to see him go all the same. And once he was away, she would no doubt repine, sorely regretting having kept him at arm's length.

After dinner, Mr. Wickham adeptly drew her aside and launched his closing campaign to win her over. By way of striking on a new topic—one which he hoped would cast him in a favorable light—he remarked, "You have become quite the traveler, Miss Bennet—now bound for the lake country and only just returned from Kent. Did your time pass agreeably in Hunsford?"

"Yes, it was very pleasant indeed to be reunited with my dear friend Charlotte."

"And Mr. Collins too?" He grinned conspiratorially. "I am thinking that, after a few days, the proportions and conversation of the Parsonage must have proved … a little confining, shall we say?" Surely, he thought, she could not help but appreciate the contrast with their own lively banter over the course of their acquaintance.

"Not at all, sir, since we were rarely restricted to the Parsonage. I am happy to report that we enjoyed a very frequent intercourse with the inhabitants of Rosings Park whilst I was there—a blessing of which very few could boast."

Wickham looked at Elizabeth quizzically. "Forgive me, but I would hardly have expected you to find Lady Catherine's conversation to your taste."

"Oh, but I do not refer to Lady Catherine alone. Did I not tell you that Mr. Darcy and Colonel Fitzwilliam were visiting there as well?"

Momentarily taken aback, Wickham recovered his composure soon enough. "No, I don't believe you mentioned that fact."

"Are you much acquainted with the colonel, Mr. Wickham?" Elizabeth continued with a glint in her eye. "I suppose you must have seen him very often at Pemberley as you were all growing up together."

"Quite true," he admitted, although he did not like the turn the conversation had taken…or the amused look on Miss Bennet's face. Could she possibly know something, he wondered. But then, with a moment's recollection and a returning smile, he replied, "I have not seen much of him in recent years, as you might well imagine. However, I believe him to be a very gentlemanly man. How did you like him?"

"Very much indeed! In fact, I believe I have rarely met with a man that I liked better, or whose sound judgment I could depend upon so completely. I found him to be kind, generous, and entirely trustworthy. He was designated Miss Georgiana Darcy's guardian, you know, and I think there can be no finer testimony to Colonel Fitzwilliam's character than that."

Wickham noticed that the room had suddenly grown overly warm. He could feel sweat beginning to bead on his forehead, and the collar of his military jacket drew curiously tighter and tighter around his throat. Affecting an air of indifference, he asked, "How long did you say that he was at Rosings?"

Her spirited report quite alarmed him. It sounded as if Miss Bennet had spent the better part of three weeks in the man's company, talking in depth about all manner of subjects. How near their conversations might have come to his own private concerns, Wickham could only guess. Elizabeth's way of speaking seemed intentionally designed to torment him with uncertainty, to leave him dangling on tenterhooks. Had she really learned all his secrets? He shuddered at the thought.

When Elizabeth's animated narrative moved on to Mr. Darcy and her improved opinion of him, Wickham's uneasiness only increased. There was something in her countenance which made him listen with an apprehensive and anxious attention.

How he answered her, Wickham hardly knew. Although deeply shaken, his self-command and polished manners did not desert him. He covered his embarrassment as well as he might and carried on, ending with an undeniably handsome speech:

"You, Miss Bennet, who so well know my feelings towards Mr. Darcy, will readily comprehend how sincerely I must rejoice that he is wise enough to assume even the appearance of what is right. His pride, in that direction, may be of service, if not to himself, to many others, for it must deter him from such foul misconduct as I have suffered by."

He was careful that the last words were accompanied by an appropriately sorrowful bearing and the slightest quavering of his voice. Yet these tried and true tactics proved singularly ineffectual on this occasion. Wickham could see at once that he had failed to excite the lady's sympathies over his longstanding grievances, as he had so effortlessly done in the past.

Clearly, Elizabeth had changed...towards himself anyway, and those she saw at Hunsford had the blame for it. That he should have lost the devotion of this prized pearl was something he could learn to live with. Knowing his defeat had apparently come at the hands of his old nemesis was quite another thing.

Wickham waited, but Elizabeth ignored the invitation to indulge in what had formerly been their favorite topic. Instead, by the curl of her lip and the way she tilted her head to one side, she seemed to be mocking him.

Enough! He refused to demean himself by lingering any longer only to be suspected and ridiculed by this impertinent chit, desirable as she might otherwise be. He excused himself from her presence at once and made no further attempt to distinguish her that night. If there were any justice in the world, the means to even the score would one day come his way. If so, he surely would not pass them by. Until such time, however, he very much hoped never to see Elizabeth Bennet's face again.

Elizabeth Remembers

by Shannon Winslow

May 20, 1812

Derbyshire. That one word brought it all flooding back to my mind, all that I had so studiously endeavored to put from it. My heart had been set on seeing The Lakes, but my aunt's letter two weeks ago not only put an end to that thrilling expectation, but replaced it with something like apprehension at the thought of diverting to Derbyshire instead. Even now, I am tormented by the idea.

I cannot think of Derbyshire without unhappy associations rising up in my mind. No doubt it is grand country, full of beauties that are not to be missed. But to me it can only ever mean one thing; I will be entering the county wherein resides the owner of Pemberley, a man I had fervently hoped never to meet with again in the whole course of my life. And I know he must feel the same. For proof of it, I have only to refer again to his letter.

Why I have kept it, I cannot rightly say. It is not normally in my nature to dwell on unpleasantness. But in this case, I make an exception. My culpability in the debacle with Mr. Darcy is something I dare not forget entirely, lest I should ever behave so badly again. How despicably I acted! How *dreadfully* I misjudged him! His written words at last taught me to properly know myself, and I have resolved to revisit them occasionally as a sort of penance.

Pulling the letter from its hiding place, I peruse its pages once more. The truth of his explanations concerning the two charges I so vehemently laid at his door, I have long since ceased to question. I need not read those sections again; I know them by heart.

Mr. Darcy's interference with Jane and Mr. Bingley is something I continue to lament most grievously for my sister's sake, although I can no longer bring myself to hate him for it. There was no malice in the case, only an error in judgment—a failing to which I proved similarly susceptible in the other matter. When I think what he and his sister suffered at the hands of Mr. Wickham, I believe I better understand some portion of his actions in Hertfordshire, some grounds for his distrustful reserve.

Although his careful explanations are most material in exonerating his character, it is always the beginning and the end of Mr. Darcy's letter that cut me to the quick. That is where my conscience seeks to punish me, for that is where the man himself and how I have injured him are most clearly revealed.

> *Be not alarmed, Madam, on receiving this letter, by the apprehension of its containing any repetition of those sentiments, or renewal of those offers, which were last night so disgusting to you. I write without any intention of paining you, or humbling myself, by dwelling on wishes, which, for the happiness of both, cannot be too soon forgotten...*

And then at the end ...

> *...If your abhorrence of me should make my assertions valueless, you cannot be prevented by the same cause from confiding in my cousin; and that there may be the possibility of consulting him, I shall endeavor to find some opportunity of putting this letter in your hands in the course of the morning. I will only add, God bless you.*
>
> *Fitzwilliam Darcy*

Oh, how these words have tortured me! If I still believed him to be a man without feeling, I could laugh at my own blindness well enough. Yet here is evidence that he has a heart after all, one capable of caring deeply... and being just as deeply wounded. Even should he one day find the charity to forgive how I have insulted him, I shall *never* forgive myself. But neither can I be content to wallow forever in self recriminations. I was not formed for unhappiness.

No, the only safe solution is that I never see Mr. Darcy again. He may get on with his life, well rid of me, and I will get on with mine, a little better for having known him. So there's an end to it. Now, if only I can tour Derbyshire without him crossing my path...

Lydia Enjoys Brighton

by Diana Birchall

May 21, 1812

Early on a bright morning in late May, a gay party left Meryton: the girls, Lydia and Mrs. Forster, with the latter's little maid, traveled all day in Colonel Forster's chaise, driven by a coachman, as the colonel rode with the regiment. By three o'clock they were on the high Downs, outside the Ramparts of Brighton, the sea a glittering line directly ahead.

Lydia, wild with excitement, hung halfway out the carriage window. "I can see it! I can see it!" she screamed. "'Tis the camp! I see the tents! Oh! Is it a parade, Harriet?"

Mrs. Forster peered around the bouncing Lydia, with the sedateness of a married woman who was seventeen to Lydia's sixteen, and the experience of one to whom Brighton was old hat, she having been there on her honey-moon, three months earlier.

"It is," she confirmed. "There is always something of the sort going on, marching or a review, on the Downs up to the racecourse. The whole town turns out every afternoon. See all the carriages?"

"I've never seen so many at once!" marveled Lydia. "What fine barouches—and landaulets. Why! There's even a fish cart. But the carriages are all getting in amongst the tents, and the ranks of men. How can they even march? What a confusion! How funny they look!"

"The spectators drive in as close as they can, so as to see better. It makes the officers wild, I can tell you."

Lydia's eyes were wide as saucers. "There are too many tents to count! I declare there must be hundreds. And the soldiers! Did you ever see so many soldiers in one place before, Harriet?"

"Why, there were almost as many, when we were here last. But to be sure there are more now," she smiled with a superior air.

"I think it is beautiful, quite beautiful," sighed the little maid, Sophy. "The red coats, oh! The handsome gentlemen."

"There must be two or three regiments at least," exclaimed Lydia, fanning herself, her eyes fluttering, quite overcome.

"Oh, yes, regulars and militia both," Mrs. Forster assured them, already an officer's wife. "Thousands of men."

"Thousands!" Lydia gasped.

"Remember they are not all officers," Mrs. Forster reminded her, "and it is only with officers we can have anything to do. Well, *you* could marry a trooper, Sophy—but I beg you not; I need your services for a while yet."

"Oh, I wouldn't never leave you, ma'am, it is too exciting," the girl breathed.

"There, Lydia, now we are turning toward the town. Brighton itself. You see the ladies and gentlemen walking on the Steine—that big grassy area - and the two Assembly rooms, opposite, the Castle and the Old Ship. Two! Not many towns have two Assemblies, I can tell you. And so elegant, with eating-rooms, and card-rooms, and dancing in the evening, you never saw any thing like it. We bathe in the morning—before seeing the officers assemble; and afterwards we promenade, and go to the libraries."

"The libraries?" Lydia's face fell. "I did not come to Brighton to read. I get enough of that at home, with my sisters telling me to mind my book."

"Silly," laughed Mrs. Forster, "the libraries are where ladies can play cards, and billiards, and oh! They are near the prettiest shops you ever saw in your life, Lydia. Such hats, and ribbons, and muslins, and chintzes! You will die. I hope you brought plenty of money, but it's no matter if you haven't, you may borrow of me."

The carriage turned into a narrow street lined with blue and buff houses. "We are not too near the Marine Parade. That is where the Prince lives," said Mrs. Forster importantly, "but then we are not the Prince's Regiment, and that makes a difference. That is for the aristocracy, but it is not nearly as much fun as our regiment. We are in a very genteel street however, and you will like our rooms."

Lydia did like their pretty lodgings in a green-painted hotel in the old cobbled Lanes. She dressed faster than the others and stood in the bow window, eagerly watching the promenaders in the street. Beyond, the vista led between the buildings to the yellow sands beyond and the sparkling sea. Flags waved, and white boats tossed on the water, but Lydia's eyes were on the officers and their ladies in their really smart finery.

Mrs. Forster came up beside her and passed her arm around her. "Do you like Brighton, then?" she inquired laughingly.

"Oh yes! Can we go out right away, and walk with all those people? They are so very fine. And when shall we see the officers?"

"Indeed we can promenade now, though I wish you had a prettier bonnet." Mrs. Forster tilted her head and eyed her friend critically. "That feather is impossible, nothing like it has been worn in three seasons, but what can you expect of Meryton. Never mind. I will undertake to find you a fine match before you've been here a month. What am I saying? You so handsome, and only turned of sixteen. Two weeks, and a colonel at least!"

"There are so very many officers, I believe I really could have my choice," Lydia breathed, her eyes shining. "Though it does seem a pity to have to settle for just one. What if you see a handsomer one afterwards?"

"You may marry as many as you like, or not marry them at all and play them off against each other, for all that I care, my dear. Look! Here comes Colonel Forster, with Denny, and all the others—they've come to take us to walk on the Steine, I know. I hope they've taken tickets for one of the Assemblies, or the theatre, for the evening. Have you got your lace shawl? Oh, what a dowdy thing that is, you'll have to get another."

402

"Yes, it belonged to my sister Jane. To be sure, I only ever rated hand-downs, that is how things are in my family. Never mind, it's so warm I'm sure I shan't need it. Harriet! All our very own set of officers—not only Denny, but Captain Carter and, yes! it is! I see Mr. Wickham, I do! Oh! He is the most beautiful of all! Could there ever be a handsomer man?" Out came her handkerchief and she jumped up and down, waving from the window.

Mrs. Forster was not the one to play propriety, and rather than attempting to restrain Lydia, she impatiently pulled her friend's hand, and they rushed through the door and out into the street, to waylay the officers.

The Gardiners Arrive at Longbourn Before Their Northern Tour

by Colette Saucier

July 21, 1812

A mixture of relief and gratitude flowed through Mrs. Gardiner as they neared the village of Longbourn. Even with so convenient a distance of twenty-four miles in a well-sprung carriage, the trip from London with four young children had tried her patience. Generally well-behaved, her two sons and two daughters—all under the age of nine—had begun the brief journey in quiet anticipation; but even the best behaved children could only remain enclosed in a carriage for so long before bouncing as much as the horses.

Mrs. Gardiner released a full breath and glanced at her husband, sitting with his typical stoic smile and his eyes fixed on The Times, seemingly impervious to the rambunctious antics of his offspring; but she suspected he used the newspaper as more of a shield than a diversion.

As the coachman brought the carriage to a halt in front of the Bennet household, she peeked out the window. Jane and Elizabeth stood awaiting their arrival, and Mrs. Bennet promptly emerged from the doorway with Mary and Kitty just behind. The moment the carriage door opened, the Gardiner children poured out and ran to Jane's open arms. Sweet Jane. Her attention to the children would allow Mrs. Gardiner's holiday to begin immediately.

Her husband alit from the carriage and offered her his hand, and she braced herself for the onslaught of her sister-in-law's grievances and nervous complaints. Comparing Mrs. Bennet—and

Mrs. Philips as well!—to her husband, she often marveled that they could be brother and sister, although on occasion she did wish her husband were not quite so complacent and avuncular.

In the cacophony of greetings that followed, Mrs. Gardiner kissed her nieces in succession then allowed Mrs. Bennet to whisk her into the parlor. Mrs. Bennet took her arm and ushered her to the sofa, where they sat down together. "Hill, Hill," she called out to the housekeeper. "Where are the tea things?"

Mrs. Gardiner turned to find her husband and glimpsed him disappearing with Mr. Bennet towards the library with a nod and a smile in her direction. Yes, they would enjoy a quiet glass of port whilst she succumbed to the tea and hospitality of her sister-in-law. No matter. She knew her sister Bennet would offer a glass of ratafia in short order, which would be a balm to both their nerves.

"Well, sister," said Mrs. Bennet in a confidential accent as their children milled about outside and in the vestibule. "What say you of my Jane? Do you see any change from last you saw her in Town?"

"I... I confess I could not form an opinion in the moments from the carriage to the house, but her face is as healthful and lovely as ever."

"Aye, her beauty has not diminished, but mark my words she still suffers greatly. Who would have thought Mr. Bingley could be so undeserving a young man! And she saw none of him in London?"

"No, but we live in so different a part of Town and share no connections, it was very improbable that they would meet."

"I do not suppose there is the least chance in the world of her getting him now. I told Lizzy and my sister Philips I am determined never to speak of it again!"

Mrs. Gardiner could not but doubt the reliability of that assertion, as she had thought they had thoroughly exhausted the topic of Jane's "sad business" when they were together at Christmas.

"I enquired of everyone likely to know," Mrs. Bennet continued, "and there is no talk of his coming to Netherfield this summer, and Lizzy does not believe he will ever live there anymore. Well, nobody wants him to come. But, however, I shall always say he used my daughter extremely ill. My only comfort is that she will die of a broken heart, and then he will be sorry for what he has done."

Unable to take comfort from such an expectation, Mrs. Gardiner made no answer.

"And when Lizzy stayed with you on her return from Kent, did she speak of how comfortable the Collinses live?"

"She did speak well of them and her delight in Kent but did not say much beyond that."

"Of course she could not say much before Maria Lucas. Oh, sister, that I came so close to having two daughters married! I cannot blame Jane, but Lizzy could even now be at Hunsford instead of Charlotte Lucas. I am sure the Collinses talk often between themselves of having Longbourn one day. I would be ashamed of having an estate not lawfully my own but only entailed on me."

The subject finally came to an end with the arrival of a maid carrying the tea things. Elizabeth and Kitty soon followed, and one poured as the other served.

"Aunt, I suppose you know Lydia is not at home," said Kitty, her tone as peevish as any of the Gardiner children's could be.

"Yes, Lizzy mentioned it in her letter. Lydia is gone to Brighton. Is that right?"

"It is not fair! I am two years older. Mrs. Forster should have invited me as well."

"Oh, quit your grumbling, Kitty," cried her mother. "You know Lydia is Mrs. Forster's particular friend. And if I had had my way, we would all be in Brighton for the summer, but your father has little compassion for my nerves. A little sea-bathing would set me up forever!"

"And you, Lizzy?" Mrs. Gardiner asked her niece. "Would you have preferred Brighton to a tour of the Peak District?"

"Indeed, I had much rather go North with you and Uncle, even if the militia was not encamped at Brighton, but I think we have had our fill of red coats."

Mrs. Bennet knitted her brow and puckered her lips. "Lizzy, what nonsense are you spouting on about? 'Our fill of redcoats' indeed!"

"What about Mr. Wickham?" Kitty asked Elizabeth. "Would not you like his company?"

"No, Kitty, not even Mr. Wickham."

"Mr. Wickham?" Mrs. Gardiner's eyes flitted from one niece to the other. "I thought we were soon to hear an announcement of his engagement to Miss King."

Elizabeth dropped her gaze to her teacup as color rose in her cheeks but said nothing.

"No, there is no danger of Wickham marrying Miss King now," said Kitty. "Her uncle took her to Liverpool two months past, so Wickham is safe."

As the conversation progressed from Mr. Wickham's failed engagement to the contents of Lydia's infrequent letters from Brighton, Mrs. Gardiner turned her attention again to Elizabeth. How odd she found it that her niece had not related this intelligence regarding Mr. Wickham and Mary King in any of her correspondence, particularly as the formation of that attachment had been the subject of much discourse between Elizabeth and herself. Mrs. Gardiner hoped that blush was not due to a renewal of her affection with Mr. Wickham, which she had warned her against; but neither did she want it to be a result of Lizzy being pained by his not renewing his addresses. She resolved to speak to Elizabeth as soon as possible.

That evening after dinner, Mrs. Gardiner sought Elizabeth, who was in her room preparing for their departure early the next day.

"Lizzy, may I help with your packing?"

Elizabeth smiled. "No, I thank you, but I have been instructed on the best method of packing by none other than Lady Catherine de Bourgh herself! There can be only one proper way of placing gowns in a trunk."

Happy to find her niece in good humor, she asked, "How has your time passed here since your return from Kent?"

"Soon after we returned, the impending departure of the militia incited almost universal dread and dejection throughout the neighborhood, and the lamentations of Kitty and Lydia could scarcely compete with those of my mother and her memories of a similar occasion some five and twenty years ago. Then the invitation to join Mrs. Forster in Brighton sent Lydia flying about the house in raptures and threw Kitty into misery and tears. For more than a fortnight after the regiment's departure, Jane and I were forced to listen to the constant repinings of my mother and Kitty, but the gloom and melancholy gave way once some of the families returned from London and summer engagements arose. Now Kitty can once again enter Meryton without tears, I have hope that perhaps, by Christmas, she might be able to go a full day without mentioning an officer."

Mrs. Gardiner laughed before turning serious again. "And how is Jane? Are her spirits much improved?"

"I fear she is still unhappy, although she represses those feelings to appear as cheerful as possible."

"I am exceedingly sorry to hear it. I had thought it reasonable to believe she might be recovered by now."

"With her disposition," said Elizabeth, "her affection must have greater steadiness than with most first attachments."

"Lizzy, I hope you were not excessively disappointed that your uncle's business requires that we curtail our tour."

"At first, perhaps, as I had my heart set on seeing the Lakes; but with all the beauties still to be seen—the rolling hills of the Peak, the river gorge in Dovedale—all was soon right again."

"I think you will find there is enough to be seen in Derbyshire." With the mention of that county, again her niece colored and occupied herself with her trunk, and Mrs. Gardiner chose to use this as an opening. "Of particular attraction to me, of course, is the town of Lambton where I spent some years growing up. That is in the very part of Derbyshire to which Mr. Wickham belonged. It is not five miles from Pemberley, where he spent much of his youth. He and I discussed it at great length when I met him here at Christmas."

"Yes, I recall you speaking of your acquaintance in common."

"I must own I was surprised to learn from Kitty that Mr. Wickham was no longer attached to Miss King. I wonder you did not mention it in your letters."

Elizabeth answered quickly, as if having anticipated the question. "Yes, I suppose, with the regiment soon to depart Meryton, I thought it of light importance."

Mrs. Gardiner still found the omission curious, especially with so little other news to report. "No doubt you saw him before they departed."

Elizabeth answered by a slight inclination of her head.

"Lizzy, you know I have nothing against him, but I do hope his new circumstance has not renewed an affection between you, which you know to be imprudent."

Elizabeth turned to her aunt with a genuine smile. "No, you have no cause for concern on that account."

"He did not disappoint you in his going?"

"Not at all. You must not fear I have been disappointed in love. He was as amiable as ever, he passed his last evening here at Longbourn with all the appearance of his usual cheerfulness, and we parted with mutual civility."

"I am very glad to hear it. But there was no return of his former partiality to you?"

"I would have discouraged it if there had been. Aunt, pray be well assured that my heart had not been touched by his attentions so much as my vanity."

With this answer, Mrs. Gardiner collected she must be content if not fully satisfied, as she could not help but wonder at Elizabeth's blushes. "I would not wish for you to be carrying any regret on our tour of Derbyshire."

"Indeed I have no reason to repine, and with you and Uncle as companions, I may reasonably hope to have all my expectations of pleasure realized. As I said before: What are men compared to rocks and mountains? I shall enter the county of Derbyshire in pursuit of novelty and amusement with little thought of that gentleman at all."

Jane's Heart

by Susan Mason-Milks

July 25, 1812

The last little face was washed, the bedtime stories told, and the Gardiner children finally all tucked in for the night. Jane closed the door and leaned against it with a sigh. She had forgotten just how exhausting it was to have four small children in the house. Although she had some assistance from Mary and Kitty, the primary responsibility to entertain and care for her nieces and nephews fell on Jane's capable, but weary, shoulders. Jane chuckled to herself reflecting that as usual Mrs. Bennet showed little interest in children who were too young to need her matchmaking advice.

Caring for the Gardiner children this summer was Jane's gift to her beloved sister. She wanted Lizzy to have the pleasure of seeing all the sights as she traveled north with the Gardiners to Derbyshire. Elizabeth always loved discovering new places and meeting new people. Over the years, Jane had realized that she herself was more comfortable at home. While she loved visiting with her aunt and uncle in London, she was perfectly content otherwise to be at Longbourn with her family and friends around her. The other reason she had for wishing to take responsibility for her nieces and nephews this summer was to try out what it would be like to be mother to a small brood of children.

Grabbing her shawl from a hook near the back door, she let herself out of the house, entered the garden, and navigated her way by the bright moonlight to her favorite bench. It was a nearly perfect summer night, the warm daytime weather having cooled into a pleasant, star-filled evening. As the sound of an occasional voice from the house or the clatter of pans from the kitchen drifted her way, she knew the servants were finishing the after dinner clean up and making initial preparations for tomorrow's meals. It was a never-ending cycle, one that usually brought her comfort and reassurance.

Whenever she was alone, her thoughts invariably turned to Charles Bingley, and tonight was no exception. What was he doing at that moment? Was he attending a ball or soiree in London this evening? Was he engaged to someone else? Each time she thought the pain of losing him was completely erased, the tear in her heart fully mended, she would suddenly find herself shaken with a fresh wave of grief. The pain of her loss had less pull than it had six months ago, but when it did rise up from time to time, she was never prepared for the way it nearly knocked her off her feet.

Last winter, when she had been forced to acknowledge that Charles Bingley was forever out of her reach, she had resolved to find a way to let their neighbor, Mr. Wyatt, know she might be receptive to his attentions. Mr. Wyatt was a widower, a good-looking gentleman in his early thirties. Although not as handsome or genial as Mr. Bingley, he was certainly kind and thoughtful. Shortly before the Bingleys had come to Netherfield last fall, Mr. Wyatt had begun venturing out into society again after completing the period of mourning for his wife who had died the previous year giving birth. It was no secret he was looking for a wife, a new mother for his children, but although he had frequently attended assemblies and parties, he seemed to be in no rush to make a choice. Jane had often danced and conversed with the widower, but Charles Bingley's arrival had so completely absorbed her that she had all but forgotten Mr. Wyatt.

One afternoon recently in Meryton with her sister Mary, Jane had encountered Mr. Wyatt in the apothecary shop. It was not too long after she and Lizzy had returned from London. Gathering up her courage, she had made a point of stopping to talk with him and inquire after his children. He, in turn, had asked if she had enjoyed her stay in Town. The exchange had been pleasant enough, and he definitely seemed pleased she had made a point of speaking to him.

Jane wondered about the relationship between the Wyatts. Whenever she had seen them together, they had seemed like a loving couple. Appearances could be deceiving, she knew. Was he as he appeared? Could she entrust her future happiness to a man she barely knew? And why was it that she continuously asked herself this question in relation to Mr. Wyatt? She had not known Charles Bingley all that well either but had never thought to ask these questions about him.

Although Mr. Wyatt did not give Jane the same flutters in her heart that she felt when she thought of Mr. Bingley, still the widower was a pleasant man. It was clear that he was interested in her, but was she ready to let go of her former love entirely? Was she truly mourning the loss of Mr. Bingley or was she just chasing the shadow of what might have been? Should she encourage the attentions of someone else? This might be her only chance to marry a decent man, as there were few eligible gentlemen in Hertfordshire.

Although Mr. Wyatt's estate, Willowwood, was about the same size as Longbourn, its owner was a better manager and landlord than her father, and so the income from the land was greater. If she married him, she would have a comfortable, secure life. Was it enough?

Last week, at the church fete, when her nieces and nephews were off playing, she had been presented with another opportunity to observe Mr. Wyatt with his two daughters and was pleased with what she saw. His behavior towards his children was much more like that of her uncle Gardiner than her own father. She admired the way he showed patience with the little girls, and the way his gaze tenderly followed their every move. He could easily have turned them over to their nanny, but he seemed to truly enjoy their company.

As Jane had watched them, it had occurred to her how natural it would be for her to walk past the little group, and casually engage the girls in conversation. Then Mr. Wyatt would undoubtedly ask her to join them for cake, and one thing would lead to another. She could almost hear him asking politely if he might call on her at Longbourn. Before she knew it, she would be engaged and then married to him. Her life and that of the rest of her family would be secure. Wasn't that what she wanted? What she needed? Then why had her feet stayed rooted to the ground? Why did she hesitate to take those first few steps toward a new future for herself?

Just then, a voice had interrupted her thoughts. "You seem very far away." It was Mary.

Jane gave a sharp intake of breath at being caught out.

"I was just thinking...thinking it is time for me to take my turn tending the refreshment table," she said with a false brightness.

"I do not believe anyone is required at the moment," Mary said looking around. "There is time enough for you to go talk to the Wyatts, if you wish. You may leave the other children to me for a few minutes."

"What makes you think that?" Jane began, looking at her sister in confusion.

"I could see by the look on your face what you were contemplating. Mr. Wyatt is a very nice man, and his daughters are charming little girls," Mary told her.

"Oh, I had no idea I was so transparent," she said, putting a hand on her sister's arm.

Mary smiled. "I know you think Lizzy is the only one who sees into your heart, but I know you, too. I have seen the shadow of pain that plays across your face in those moments when you think no one is looking. I have been worried about you."

Jane took both her sister's hands in hers. "I will be fine, Mary. Just fine." But they both knew that was not exactly true.

So this evening, sitting on the bench alone in the garden contemplating her situation, Jane felt a hard lump of emotion building in her throat and then the wetness on her cheeks. It was in that moment she knew with certainty that she had not forgotten Mr. Bingley. She still loved him even though she had not seen him in many months - even though she sometimes felt he had betrayed her. No matter how hard she had tried to erase him from her life, she had not been successful. There was no rational explanation for it; it was just true. Her head told her she could not grieve for him forever, but her heart would just not allow her to give up.

"Not yet," she whispered to herself. "Not yet."

Wickham's Scheme of Elopement

by Diana Birchall

July 29, 1812

About a month after Lydia's removal to Brighton, Mr. Wickham sauntered into a handsome suite attached to the Prince Regent's palatial quarters in Marine Parade. It was not where a young officer of a common militia regiment might expect to be admitted, but when he asked for Mrs. Younge, the servant girl dimpled at his handsome face, and admitted him.

The lady, an elegant slender creature between thirty and forty attired in fashionable muslin with crimped hair looked up from her delicate carved writing-desk, with recognition, but did not rise, though her eye-brows did.

"George Wickham! As I live and breathe. Well, this is a nice surprise, I don't think."

"I thought you might be glad to see me, Penelope," he said gracefully, in a warm tone, as if they had not parted long.

"What? After that fiasco? All our plans—ruined. I was out a pretty penny, I can tell you, and all came to nothing."

"There was always some risk, you knew that," he countered, with a gentle smile on his handsome face. "We were within only a few hours of Georgiana flying with me—and oh, what revenge upon Darcy it would have been, and what money would have been ours! She was worth at least thirty thousand pounds, and you know I always meant to divide it with you, Penelope."

"To be sure you did." She regarded him ironically. "It is easy to divide money we did not obtain. And who spoilt it all, pray, can you tell me that?"

"You know very well it was the girl herself. I could not control her entirely. I awakened her early love for me, yes, and thought it was enough; but she was cursed with a conscience."

"And now you have come to remind me of that unhappy episode?" she asked, taking up her pen again, her impatience starting to show itself.

"No. Not at all. I do not like to think of it myself, and I am most unhappy about the whole thing, and should like to forget it."

"What then?"

He sank into the velvet easy chair before her, and lounged, his hands in his pockets, a smile passing over his handsome features, as he looked about the room, at the gilding, and ormolu, and fine French paintings. "You seem to have done pretty well for yourself, Penelope. You do not appear to need Mr. Darcy's shekels. Attached to the Prince Regent, are you? Pretty preferment."

A little color came to her pale features. "Don't be absurd, Wickham. I am not His Royal Highness's mistress, and never was. He likes his bed-girls young, and I know where they are to be found."

Wickham raised his eyebrows. "Young. Like your name? A good advertisement."

"If you like. Brighton, however, is all a-boom, in the underworld trades; there is money to be made. It is the place to be. Why, not even counting the girls at the camp, in the tents—and each soldier seems to have his own, do not you?"

"We'll get to that," said Wickham, with a smile.

"There are at least three hundred superior Cyprians in this part of the town alone, in service to the men about the Prince. I am in charge of a good many of them," she finished complacently.

"So, you have landed on your feet, and got over the disappointment in Mr. Darcy's riches."

"I have," she answered. "It was always you who hated him and wanted revenge, and from the looks of things, I have done the better. What are you, a militia-man? Is that the best you could do?" She lifted a scornful eyebrow.

"Don't laugh at me, Pen. I remember when you were wearing a meek little black gown so as to pass yourself off as a learned governess, to be hired as Miss Georgiana Darcy's cicerone. There's embarrassment for you."

She shrugged. "It is past; I have forgotten it. Things are better with me now. And why do you seek me? We have not been engaged together in anything so successful that you would want me to remember."

"No," he agreed, "but I remember you were canny enough in the previous matter, and I have a bit of trouble of the same sort, again."

"I might have known, it would be a young lady," she sighed, rolling her great grey eyes resignedly. "Well, go ahead, tell me about it."

"It is this way. I am being monopolized by a young miss who is absolutely in love with me and will hear no refusal; she wants to run away with me."

"Does she? Well, let us get down to brass tacks. How much money does she have?"

"Nothing. That's the problem."

"That is a hopeless business then. Why do you come to ask me about it?"

"I thought I might bring her to you, and then when her family comes after her, there might be a thousand or two to make, and we could give her back to them."

"But why would they pay, when she can never be respectable again? She never will deserve a good name, if she has been your mistress."

Wickham twiddled uneasily with the frogging on his jacket. "They would pay if I promised to marry her, so we would get

418

something; but of course, I would not be so mad as to marry her."

"I should hope not! You must hold out for a girl of no less than ten thousand a year. You cannot afford to marry for less."

"If not more. I still hope to find her, but here's a thought—once I get the thousand or so I can screw out of her family, why, you can keep the girl."

"Me? What do I want with such a simpleton?" She thought a moment. "How old is she?"

"She was just sixteen a month ago."

"Is she handsome?"

"Quite. A tall, bonny lass, with blue eyes, yellow hair, and an easy temper."

"You think His Royal Highness would find her to his taste? Young, and a good figure, you say?"

"Oh yes. Stout and well grown."

"But then she's not a virgin. He likes virgins."

He waved his hand. "Never mind; I have broken her in and taught her something better. I'm sure you can get a pretty sum for her—you would know better than I."

"I have to admit there is something in your story. I may be a fool, but I will go for it. Do you remember that I keep a series of lodging-houses in London? Not far from Kensington Palace, for obvious reasons."

"Of course. Will I forget? So I shall take her there?"

"I think it best. I will go first, and meet you. She probably ought not be housed in my principal house in Edward-street, but I have other property available. When were you wanting to fly with her?"

"Almost at once. I have very pressing debts. The truth is, to be perfectly sincere, Penelope, I have made the town too hot to hold me."

"I have no reason to doubt that. Why would you change your colors? Well, you shall quit Brighton. Take the girl, if you will—have you money for a carriage? No? I thought not. I will give you some pocket-money. Let us meet in Green Street next week, and once we have settled up, I will take the girl and bring her back here."

"I knew I could count on you, Penelope."

"Well, you owe me something, you know, Wickham. By the way, what is the girl's name?"

"Lydia."

"Very well. Now be very sure, Wickham, that this goes better than last time."

"It will of course. What could go wrong?"

Wickham Tells Lydia He is Leaving

by Kara Louise

July 30, 1812

"George!" Lydia waved her hand excitedly. "Over here!" She placed both hands over her heart when she saw him look up and smile at her as he hurried to her side.

"Lydia! What brings you to the Steine? Is it the shops or the view of the sea?"

The young girl smiled and let out a laugh. "Both! You know I love looking out at the sea and shopping!" She gave a sideways glance at Mr. Wickham. "And what brings you here?"

"Do you really have to ask?" He raised a single brow. "I hoped to encounter a lovely young lady!"

Lydia giggled and looked at him coyly. "And did you find one?"

"I most certainly did!" Wickham bowed over her gloved hand and pressed his lips to the back of it.

"You are such a tease!"

Wickham smiled and leaned in close. "You have not come all this way without a chaperone, have you? I shall have to speak with Colonel Forster if you have."

Lydia waved a hand through the air. "Of course not. Harriet… Mrs. Forster is still in the tea shop. I prefer the millinery shops and am eager to go to the one down the road."

The teasing smile briefly vanished from Wickham's face, but it quickly returned. "Would you allow me to escort you?" He held out his arm to her.

Lydia dipped a rather deep curtsey. "I would be honored." She took his arm and they began walking.

"I think I could stay in Brighton forever!" Lydia said as she looked out at the sea. "On days like this when the weather is mild and the sky and water are so blue…" She paused and drew in a deep breath.

"Really?" A look of disappointment crossed Wickham's face.

"Why would I not? It is lovely here! There is nothing like it in Hertfordshire!"

"Ah, but there are so many other grand places to see." Wickham cast a sidelong glance at her. "In fact, I have big plans to see the world! I would much prefer to travel than remain in one place!"

Lydia smiled and let out a long sigh. "Oh, how I envy you! I only wish I could, as well!"

Wickham stopped and looked about him, before turning back to Lydia. "What is preventing you from doing so?"

Lydia shrugged. "I suppose I never really gave it much thought." She tilted her head and looked at him mournfully. "But I cannot travel alone, and there is no one who could accompany me."

Wickham leaned in. "Perhaps you can see the world with me!"

Lydia drew back with a look of surprise. She then gave him a playful smile. "Oh, you are teasing me again, George!"

"Me? Tease you? I am in all earnest!"

Lydia's heart began to pound and she felt a most delightful fluttering deep within. His eyes held hers with a piercing glint, and his smile assured her that his feelings were as deep as hers were for him.

"But how long must you wait before you are free to travel? How long must you serve in the Regiment?"

Wickham waved a hand through the air. "Being in the Regiment is not at all what I expected or hoped it would be. It has

422

become more tedious than I can bear. I plan to depart at midnight in two days."

Lydia tightened her arm about Wickham's. "You cannot leave! I cannot bear the thought!"

Again he smiled. "Oh, my dear Lydia, I would never leave you. Would you do me the honor of accompanying me? I can think of no one I would rather see the world with than you!" He gave her a pointed look. "Please say you will go with me!"

Lydia's breath caught. "Go with you?" The mere thought of departing with him brought upon a violent trembling—almost as if she were nervous, but no, these were certainly the pangs of true love! Finally, she stammered, "George, does this mean what I think it means?"

"Oh, my precious Lydia! Do you not even know me? Of course it does!" He leaned in to her. "What do you say? Will you make me the happiest man and join me on an adventure that will make every one of our acquaintances envious?"

Lydia began to slowly nod her head as she pondered this. Finally, with an emphatic nod, she cried, "Yes! Yes! Oh, George! I cannot wait! Must we even wait two days?"

"Yes, unfortunately we must. But can I trust that you will tell no one? Especially Mrs. Forster."

"Oh, I will try to keep it from her! But it shall be so hard! May I leave a letter? It will not be found until we are long gone." She drew in a deep breath. "Mrs. Forster and I have been quite at leisure in starting our day. She will sleep until ten o'clock if she has no appointments, sometimes later."

"If you feel you must, but remember, you cannot speak of it to anyone!"

"Oh, you know I will not!"

"Good. I will come for you precisely at midnight. Be ready with a small satchel. You will not need much." Wickham prodded her to begin walking again.

"But I must have some nice things!"

Wickham patted her hand and looked down at her. "Fear not, my dear. We shall have all we need."

"But will we go first to London? They have the best shops and then, I imagine, we shall head north to Gretna Greene. We shall…" Lydia was stopped at the sound of Mrs. Forster calling her name.

As Wickham and Lydia turned back to see her hurrying towards them, Wickham admonished Lydia again. "Remember do not mention this to anyone! This is our secret!"

"Yes!" Lydia concurred, her excitement building. "Our most wonderful secret!"

Lydia Elopes

by Diana Birchall

August 1, 1812

"Look here, Lydia," said Wickham, getting out of bed and standing by the window, watching red coated troops march by on their way to the Downs. "I have got to leave town."

Lydia sat up, clutching a bed-sheet to her bare shoulders. Her hair was tousled, her face flushed, her eyes bright.

"Darling Wickham! But why? What about your duty to your regiment?"

"Pish." He dismissed it with a contemptuous gesture. "It's nothing but the militia. I have no formal ties, they won't come after me."

"But Colonel Forster will be so disappointed, and all your friends. And you look so handsome in your uniform. Brighton is so gay, why must we go?"

"We?" He came and sat down beside her. "You aren't going anywhere. You go back to the Forsters' lodgings and go home with them to your mama and papa. But I've made the town too hot to hold me."

"What does that mean? And wherever you go, I'm coming with you, of course!"

"It means, my expensive little girl, that all this," he waved round the room at Lydia's brand new gowns and bandboxes strewn everywhere, "costs money. I've got into debt and the creditors won't stand it anymore. They'll come after me, and I've got to clear out before morning."

"Oh! You mean you don't have any money?"

"Curse it, that's just what I mean. Only enough left to get up to town and see if I have any friends there—or go to the money-lenders."

Lydia climbed out of bed and began scrabbling for the chemise and stays she had hurriedly thrown off the night before and flung to the floor. "I can be ready in ten minutes. Hand me those stockings, will you, my dearest Wickham?"

"But—you can't go, Lydia! It would be folly. I can't take care of you."

"You don't want to go alone, do you? All you have to do is get money from somewhere—perhaps my father would let you have some—and we can take a coach to Scotland and go to Gretna Green and be married!"

In spite of his haste to leave, Wickham stopped to laugh. "Oh, is that all? Go to Scotland, is it? As easy as go to breakfast. Well, well, I doubt we get that far. Do you still want to come?"

"I'm coming," she nodded. "What? Leave you to traipse all over the country alone?"

"I don't mind if you want to come, it's as good having a girl as not," he answered, "but you must know I can't promise you any thing. I can't afford to marry, and your family may raise the roof."

"Oh never mind them," she replied, busily stuffing her hats into their boxes. "I'm sure we shall be married some time. Come now, make haste. The coach leaves at seven, does not it? Just time to snatch a bun."

"If you wish it," said Wickham with a shrug. "Let's go then."

Jane Learns of Lydia's Elopement

by Kara Louise

August 2, 1812

Loud voices and repeated pounding awakened Jane from a deep sleep. It took her a few moments to realize that someone was knocking on the front door. She could distinguish someone speaking from outside as well as her mother's raised voice from inside the house.

Jane's heart pounded as she tried to comprehend what could be happening, but whatever it was, she was certain it was not good.

She peered out her bedroom door to see Kitty scurrying down the stairs. Mary followed close behind, saying, "This cannot be good. Someone coming to the door after midnight cannot be anything but bad news."

Jane trembled as she pondered what may have occurred. She put her ear to the door of the room in which the Gardiners' children were sleeping, and when she was assured they had not been awakened by the disturbance, she followed her sisters downstairs.

The door was closing as they arrived in the hall, and they watched their father hurriedly open the letter that had just come by express.

"Oh, Mr. Bennet! This can only be dreadful news! Something has happened to my brother and his wife and Elizabeth! I am certain of it!"

Jane felt a surge of dread at the thought that something may have happened to her dear sister. She held her breath, as did the others, while they watched and waited. It seemed an eternity as they awaited Mr. Bennet's account of the urgent letter or for some sign in his features that might reassure them nothing was dreadfully wrong.

Jane's heart pounded when she noticed his jaw tighten and face redden. It was a certain sign that he was more angry than grief-stricken. This left Jane somewhat reassured, but confused as to what news the letter contained.

He crumpled the letter in his hand. "Foolish Lydia! What was she thinking?"

Mrs. Bennet drew back. "Lydia? Oh, my heart!" she said, patting her chest. "What has happened to my dear, sweet Lydia!"

Mr. Bennet looked down at his wife. The glow from the candle Mrs. Bennet held painted his face with an eerie distortion. "It is not what happened to her, Mrs. Bennet! It is what she has done!"

"What is it, Papa?" Jane asked, feeling her heart begin to race.

"Imprudent girl! She has run off with Wickham! They stole away together at midnight, leaving behind only a note, which was discovered this morning." Mr. Bennet shook his head. "Colonel Forster is trying to determine if anyone knew about this. He believes they have gone to Scotland, but…"

"Oh, thank goodness," Mrs. Bennet clasped her hands together. "They plan to marry. He always liked Lydia so much. He was so attentive to her."

"My dear Mrs. Bennet, I am certain he has likely been most attentive to her, but I would not wish that sort of attention thrust upon any of my daughters!"

"I know Lydia must be delighted. He was always one of her favorites," Kitty said meekly.

Jane stepped back, remembering the discussion she and Elizabeth had about the man after Mr. Darcy informed her of his true nature. Her stomach churned as she considered the possibilities, none of which were reassuring. She stole a glance at Kitty, who did not at all seem surprised by the news.

"But certainly, if anything is amiss, the Forsters must be at fault for not protecting her. We must hold them accountable! They must ensure they marry!" Mrs. Bennet's hands began to shake, and Kitty reached over and took the candle from her.

"Until we know more details, I shall hold Lydia accountable!" Mr. Bennet waved everyone away. "There is nothing we can do about this now. Everyone go back to your beds and try to get some sleep."

"But how shall I sleep, not knowing what has happened to her?" Mrs. Bennet sobbed. "But they will marry! Certainly they shall marry!"

As they all turned to walk away, Kitty and Mary each took one of their mother's arms to help her back up to her room. Jane stayed back and took her father's hand. "Perhaps this is all a misunderstanding."

Mr. Bennet gave her a half-hearted smile. "Yes, or perhaps we shall all wake up in the morning and find out it was just a terrible dream!" He let out a huff. "But I doubt either of those will prove to be the case!"

Jane gave her father a quick hug and turned to climb the stairs, leaving her father alone. A short while later she heard his study door close.

A tear slipped down Jane's face as she walked into her room. "Oh, Lizzy!" Jane said in a fervent whisper. "How I wish you were here! There is no one I want by my side at this moment more than you!"

She sat down on the bed and saw the full moon shine onto the letter she had begun earlier to her sister. She rose and lit the candle on her desk and sat down. The next best thing to having Lizzy by her side to talk about all that had happened—all that might have happened—would be to put down her thoughts in a letter to her.

She began writing again, continuing where she left off earlier today...

Since writing the above, dearest Lizzy, something has occurred of a most unexpected and serious nature...

Denny Learns of Lydia's Elopement

by Jack Caldwell

August 2, 1812

Lieutenant Denny had just finished his breakfast when Lieutenant Chamberlayne walked in. "I say, have you seen Wickham? He seems to be missing."

Denny sat up. "Missing? Are you certain? Sometimes he sleeps in town."

At that moment, an angry Captain Carter walked in, followed by Lieutenant Pratt. "There is no doubt about it," he thundered without preamble. "Wickham has fled!"

"We just came from his tent," added Pratt, "and all his money and valuables are gone. He's lit out, the bastard! He owes me money!"

Chamberlayne paled. "He owes me money, too."

Denny felt a sinking feeling in his stomach. He knew that things were getting tight for George, almost desperate, his gambling debts being pressing, but surely he wouldn't just desert!

"Miss Bennet is missing, as well." Carter eyed Denny. "Colonel Forster wants to talk to you."

Denny just stared in horror at his captain. *George could not have done that! He could not have!*

* * *

Somehow, Denny made it to Colonel Forster's office without losing his breakfast. He stood at attention, watching his commander pace up and down the small space. Never had Denny seen the affable colonel in such a state.

"She's gone, she's gone, and I was responsible for her," he said over and over again. "How can I tell her father? I never should have let Harriet talk me into this foolishness!" He finally addressed Denny. "You are friends with George Wickham. Where the devil is he? Where did he go?"

"Sir, I do not know. Are you saying that Lieutenant Wickham absconded with Miss Bennet?"

"Yes, yes, we are certain of it. She left a note." He tossed a piece of paper in his direction. "Read it, if you like."

Denny picked it up and read.

My Dear Harriet, You will laugh when you know where I am gone, and I cannot help laughing myself at your surprise tomorrow morning, as soon as I am missed. I am going to Gretna Green, and if you cannot guess with who, I shall think you a simpleton, for there is but one man in the world I love, and he is an angel. I should never be happy without him, so think it no harm to be off. You need not send them word at Longbourn of my going, if you do not like it, for it will make the surprise the greater, when I write to them, and sign my name 'Lydia Wickham.' What a good joke it will be! I can hardly write for laughing…

There was more, but Denny had read enough. His disappointment, pain, and horror nearly brought him to his knees. Only his will kept him upright.

"Well?' the colonel demanded. "What do you know about this business?"

Denny's mind swirled with the possibilities. "Sir, I did not know that Wickham was going to desert. I was aware of his debts of honor as well as other financial difficulties, but I did not think him capable of this. Looking back, I suppose I should not be surprised that he left. I am disappointed in him.

"But I had no idea about Miss Bennet! Not a breath of this sort of action was ever hinted between us. I own myself shocked."

431

The colonel drew close. "You have called on Miss Bennet very regularly at my house, lieutenant. You had no suspicions of her attachment to Wickham?"

"None at all, sir!" Denny cried with more feeling than he intended. "I ... I knew that Miss Bennet liked George, but she showed him no especial attention. She was attentive to many of the officers." Including me was Denny's depressing thought.

Colonel Forster seemed to catch the level of Denny's disappointment. The interview became much less an interrogation. "So, you believe that the two are well on their way to Gretna Green?"

This was Denny's nightmare. "I am afraid, sir, that Wickham had often talked about his plans for the future. He has always held that marriage to an heiress was his goal." At Forster's look, he added, "For example, his courtship of Miss King in Meryton." Denny looked down at the note. "From this I can tell that Miss Lydia—Miss Bennet—believes that she and Wickham are eloping to Scotland. I have had many conversations with Wickham, sir, and I can categorically state that such a thing would be in opposition to all his long-term plans. Miss Bennet is not an heiress."

"Good God, do you know what you are saying?"

Denny came to attention. "Colonel, I do not know where Wickham has gotten to, but he would never willingly go to Gretna Green for anything less than ten thousand pounds."

Forster blanched and cursed. "Get Cater in here—now! I must find that bastard! There is not a moment to lose!" He glared at Denny. "As for you, you and the other officers are confined to quarters until I return! I will get to the bottom of this!"

* * *

Denny's mood darkened as he sat helplessly in his tent. He did not share his space, thanks to his seniority, so he could escape Pratt's grumblings and Chamberlayne's gossip. He had heard enough from the latter when he informed his comrades of their colonel's orders.

I am surprised Wickham made off with that Bennet girl. I thought sure he had his eye on Mrs. Forster! You have seen how she practically monopolized his attentions. Hah! Perhaps he was playing a double game! Who knows, maybe he had both of them at once!

How it was Denny did not break Chamberlayne's jaw for that, only the Good Lord knew.

Denny thought over his entire acquaintance with Lydia Bennet. Certainly she was a beautiful, young, spirited girl, but liveliness was no sin. Perhaps she was too young to be out in society. Denny conceded that she was, even though she looked and acted older than her years. However, there was no excuse for any officer to take advantage of a young lady, even one who was naïve and flirtatious. As a gentleman's daughter, Miss Lydia should have been protected from those who would harm her—even protected from her own mistakes. That was the duty of an officer and a gentleman.

I should have done more, Denny realized. *I should have protected her.*

Denny was infatuated with the lovely Lydia Bennet, and had she been older and had he more fortune, he would have offered for her. But marriage had been out of the question. At just fifteen, Miss Lydia was too young to marry, and as a lieutenant in the militia, Denny was too poor. In only two more months, he was to leave the regiment to join the regulars. Then, with three years of hard work and advancement, and the better pay that came with it, he would be fully able to support the daughter of a gentleman, and he intended to travel to Hertfordshire and court the then eighteen-year-old Miss Lydia.

Denny sighed. He thought the lady favored him as much as any man in the regiment. Now he saw that he had been a fool. Of course, she would fall in love with George Wickham—handsome, clever, witty George—not with poor, plain Archie Denny.

He recalled what he knew about Wickham. George was charming and affable—everyone's friend. Yes, sometimes he drank too much, and he certainly gambled too much, but Denny was sure there was not a wicked bone in Wickham's body. Foolish, boastful, and impulsive—yes. But evil? No.

433

George had suffered much misfortune in his life—losing his mother at a young age and later his father, the son of his godfather stealing George's inheritance, and that same Mr. Darcy interfering with George's courtship of Miss Darcy. George deserved Denny's pity and friendship.

Perhaps this misadventure was not George's idea? Mayhap Miss Lydia had learned of George's plans to desert and invited herself along. Could that be it?

There—that would explain it. Miss Lydia was in love with George and wanted to marry him. The only question that remained was would George marry her? George said he would only marry an heiress, but he said many things and did the opposite. Could this be another example of his unpredictability?

Archibald Denny was a man who strived to live above his station. He wanted one day to be a gentleman, so he taught himself to think and behave like one. Therefore, he tried to look at the world with a rational eye. But he was also a soldier, a good one. He had never been in combat, but he had taken to his training as a duck to water. If the time came to fight for his king, Denny expected that he would do his duty without hesitation.

He was a man of strong passions. Loyalty and trustworthiness were important to him. Wickham had been a good friend to him, so Denny would give him the benefit of the doubt. But Denny had spent time in London and had seen what happened to young girls who had been seduced and abandoned by their lovers. There was no way for them to earn their bread except on their back. It was horrible.

Denny wanted desperately to think well of George Wickham and Lydia Bennet, so he convinced himself that all would end well. Miss Lydia's charms and good humor would prove to be as irresistible to Wickham as they had been to himself, Denny was sure of it. They would marry, Wickham would somehow extract himself from this scrape, and they would settle quietly somewhere. Lydia would be as happy as she deserved.

Denny had to think that, for if George did Lydia wrong, if he abandoned her to the mercy of the streets, Denny knew he would hunt his friend down and kill him.

Midnight Express for Longbourn

by Shannon Winslow

August 2, 1812

The Bennet household had just settled down for the night after a day of industrious occupation. Mrs. Bennet had been to Meryton and argued not only with the butcher about her bill, but also with various ones of her neighbors who seemed to be circulating malicious rumors about that handsome officer she and her girls so much admired: Mr. Wickham. After exhausting herself in this manner, Mrs. Bennet had retired early, saying her head was very ill indeed.

Jane and Kitty had once again spent the entire day entertaining the lively Gardiner children whilst their parents were away to Derbyshire on holiday with Elizabeth Bennet in tow.

Mr. Bennet alone had been able to preserve himself from excessive exertion, and had thus found he was quite able to stay up late, reading once again his favorite of Shakespeare's plays (*Much Ado About Nothing*) and chuckling to himself at the silliness and absurdity he found there. Upon finishing, he thanked his lucky stars that his own household suffered no such dramas, and then he likewise retired to a gentle slumber.

Shortly after twelve, however, such a pounding came at the front door as would surely have awakened the dead. One by one, the Bennets tumbled out of their beds and down the stairs to see what the cause of all this unwelcome commotion was. It was an express, the contents of which turned out to be even more unwelcome.

Mr. Bennet, after paying the man and closing the door again, in silence read the letter, which was addressed to him:

My Dear Mr. Bennet,

It is with a heavy heart that I write to you with news that must bring you considerable distress. But I am afraid of alarming you. Be assured that your daughter is well, so far as it is within my power to judge. I am sorry to say that Miss Bennet last night removed herself from my house and from my protection. She has in fact eloped with one of my officers—Lieutenant George Wickham, whom you will remember.

From her own information—a brief letter left for my wife—we do at least know that she departed with him of her own accord and in very high spirits, stating that the couple's intention was to make for Gretna Green and there to wed. I have no real reason for doubting this, only a general uneasiness over the gentleman's character. He at first seemed to me to be as fine a young man as ever one could hope to meet with. On closer acquaintance, however, I have observed in him a worrying trend toward imprudence, this event being yet another evidence of it.

I feel myself in part responsible for what has occurred. You entrusted your daughter to my care, and I have failed to keep her safe from harm. I now pledge myself to do everything within my power to assist you in recovering her. I will closely question the men under my command, especially Wickham's particular friends, to see what is to be learned here. Then I plan to come to you directly at Longbourn, to offer whatever service I may render you. Till then, please extend my humble apology and sincere respects to all your family.

Yours, etc.

Colonel Forster

"Oh! What is it, Mr. Bennet?" cried his wife when he let his hand and the letter drop to his side. "Tell me at once. Have you no compassion for my nerves?" Thunderstruck and thoroughly incapable of speech, Mr. Bennet gave the letter to his wife, who in turn passed it on to her eldest daughter. "You read it to me, Jane. I am in too much of a tremble."

But hearing the letter only increased Mrs. Bennet's agitation. She was taken ill with hysterics immediately, and the whole house disintegrated into a state of utter confusion not soon to be recovered from. Moreover, there was nary a servant belonging to the business who did not know the whole of the story before the day was out. Within two more days the whole community knew of the Bennets' troubles. Half their neighbors then had the goodness to pity them their great misfortune, and the other half were only too proud to say they had always predicted such an unfavorable outcome for the family.

Colonel Forster Arrives at Longbourn

by C. Allyn Pierson

August 3, 1812

Colonel Forster left Brighton at first light, before the sun had actually appeared above the hump of Beachy Head to the east. The day was lovely, with a light mist filtering the sunlight and giving the trees along the highway an ethereal, mysterious beauty. But the colonel was oblivious to the wonders of nature as it awoke, and to the bird songs heralding the end of the dawn chorus; his thoughts were turned inwards to the reason for his ride.

Not two nights before, his wife's guest, Miss Lydia Bennet, had left their house with one of his men...to own the truth, with George Wickham. He could hardly believe it even now that one of his men would behave in such a scaly way towards a guest in his superior officer's house! Miss Bennet, of course, had gone willingly, and she had shown herself during her stay to have very little in the way of dignity or propriety. He had thought she would keep his wife happy while he pursued his duties, and, indeed, she had enjoyed having her friend stay...He shook his head to try to clear it of the tumbling thoughts roiling in it.

The two eldest Miss Bennets were lovely young women who always behaved like ladies. The two youngest girls, however, were the most unrestrained, rambunctious young women he had ever met. It was not long after the regiment moved to Brighton for the summer that he began having serious reservations about the influence Miss Lydia might have on his wife. His wife! He had married her for her good humor and her dowry of one thousand pounds, but she was twenty years younger than he. At first he had enjoyed her light heart and how young she made him feel, but the summer in Brighton with Miss Lydia had opened his eyes to the difference between youth and immaturity. Both girls (he could not call them ladies ... they were far too young) enjoyed flirting with the officers and he had often wished that his wife would behave more like a well-bred matron than like a feather-headed girl just out of the schoolroom. Several times he had had to restrain their exuberance for some scheme which threatened to hurt their reputations...and his.

What would he say to Mr. Bennet when he reached Longbourn? At least they would have received his express and he would not have to deal with the hysterics which he was positive had overcome Mrs. Bennet when the express had arrived.

He stopped at midday to bait his horse and to refresh himself with a tankard of ale and a light nuncheon of cold meat and bread before continuing on towards Hertfordshire. When he approached London he began making inquiries at the inns but could not trace the fugitives beyond Clapham. There they had, unfortunately, changed to a hackney coach and continued on the London road...and there the trail petered out. He could find no trace of them on the road they would have taken to Scotland. He finally gave up the search and found a small but comfortable inn along the road for the night (and not a very restful one) and set out very early again the next day. It was very fortunate that his horse was large and strong and that he rode very light, or the poor beast would have been done in by the exertion of the past days.

It was very late in the day when he finally arrived at Longbourn, covered in dirt and sweat from the long ride and wishing only for a glass of Madeira and a comfortable chair. Instead, he found himself in Mr. Bennet's library facing an angry father.

But it was not so bad as he had feared. Mr. Bennet placed the blame for Lydia's folly directly onto his daughter's shoulders and accepted the colonel's apologies...although without any lightening of his expression. He accepted Mr. Bennet's offer of dinner, (and a grim affair it was!) then set out for the return to Brighton, where he had engagements the next evening. As he left Longbourn he shook his head over the follies of youth and was glad his wife would no longer be influenced by Miss Lydia. She was stunned by the elopement of her friend…and shocked she had so misjudged her as to think her flirting was merely pretense, rather than a deep-seated lack of breeding. Perhaps, once this fiasco was over, his wife would start to settle down…certainly when they started a family it would give her something better to think about than parties and routs. The colonel managed a smile over that scenario as he cantered towards Brighton.

Lydia's Letter

by Shannon Winslow

This doesn't come here, should be some weeks later

~~August 3, 1812~~

My Dearest Harriet,

What adventures I have had since I saw you! I write to you now from Longbourn, where Wickham and I have just come to visit after our wedding in London. Yes, London! Are you not surprised? Or perhaps you have already heard that our plans changed after I left you in Brighton. My dear husband (for so he now is!) knew I should prefer London to Gretna Green, and I said I did not care where we went so long as we were to be married in the end.

There was a little delay of the wedding itself, and some horrid unpleasantness with my Aunt and Uncle Gardiner, but I will not take the space for such tediousness here. Only I must say that they were very ungenerous in their attentions to me in all respects. They could not be bothered to give one single party in my honor, to show me about the Town, or even to see to it that the church was tolerably filled with well-wishers and flowers for the wedding. My aunt only gave me some lilies from her garden to carry, and are not lilies more appropriate for funerals? Then there was some last minute business my uncle said he had to attend to, which vexed me greatly.

But at last we were at St. Clement's and there was Wickham waiting for me at the altar, looking vastly handsome. La! I thought I should have fainted for happiness, and what a good joke that would have been. However, I did not faint (for I have a very sturdy constitution), and my uncle gave me away. Then the rector talked on and on—about what, I have no idea, for I

442

was thinking only of my dear Wickham.

Now I will tell you a great secret, for I would not hide anything from you, my dear, and I know you are quite capable of keeping a confidence. Mr. Darcy was at my wedding! He came to stand up beside Wickham. What do you say to that? I never had any idea before that they were on such friendly terms, but my husband has since explained it, saying that Mr. Darcy has always had the greatest admiration for him. Now that is the kind of friend whom it is very well worth having, for Mr. Darcy is exceedingly rich and no doubt has many favors in his gift.

I could only wish that my sisters had been at St. Clement's to see me married. Since returning to Longbourn, however, I have at least had the satisfaction of observing how they all envy me. They try to hide it, of course, (excepting Kitty who freely admits it), looking grave and self-conscious, but I see that they are really embarrassed for having been outdone by myself, the youngest of them all. Jane had to give up her place to me, you know, since I am now a married woman. And Mary is sure to have noticed how hopeless her own situation is by comparison. But it is Elizabeth who suffers most acutely, I believe, for I daresay she wanted Wickham for herself. I did not mean to be cruel. I was just telling the story of showing off my ring to a neighbor I chanced to come across, when in fact Lizzy got so upset as to run out of the room!

Do not you think it a certain proof that she envies me? Well, I was as kind as I could be to her after that. But it is no wonder she and all the others are jealous, for my dear Wickham is the greatest catch in the world! He truly is the handsomest man that ever was seen, as well as being the boldest rider. Did not your own husband once say that he had the finest seat in the regiment? And tomorrow, when the shooting starts, I daresay Wickham will kill more birds than anybody else in the county. So I have told my sisters. They would be fortunate to have half my good luck in finding husbands. I have promised to help in that regard by putting them in the way of meeting some very smart officers when they come to visit me in Newcastle.

Poor Mama! She regrets my going so far away more than anybody else, but it cannot be helped. I am wife to a military man now, and I must follow by dear Wickham's side wherever his duty takes him. You understand these

443

things, Harriet, as my other friends cannot.

I hope that we may all meet again one day, but I hardly know when that may be—perhaps not these two or three years. In the meantime, you must write to me often. Wickham and I send our love to you and to Colonel Forster, and we shall remember to drink to your health, as I hope you may on occasion drink to ours.

Your most affectionate friend,
Lydia Wickham

Mrs. Reynolds Gives a Tour of Pemberley

by Susan Mason-Milks

August 4, 1812

To prepare for the arrival of the Darcys, Mrs. Reynolds mobilized the staff with all the efficiency of a military commander. Mr. Darcy would reach Pemberley tomorrow with Mr. Bingley and his family for a stay of at least a fortnight. Although Mrs. Reynolds was not looking forward to trying to please the ever temperamental Miss Bingley, as always, she would put forth her best effort. This was, after all, Pemberley, and there were certain standards to be maintained. It was part of her job to attempt the impossible and try to make each guest's stay a pleasant one.

This morning, Mrs. Reynolds, along with her assistant, Margie, was in the process of checking the linens, when Watkins, Pemberley's ancient and dignified butler, appeared at the door looking anxious. "Mrs. Reynolds, a group of three travelers has applied for a tour of the house. I know you are occupied today with preparations for the master's return. I was tempted to turn them away, but thought I should consult with you first before doing so."

Mrs. Reynolds hesitated, considering the long list of tasks ahead of her. As it was a point of pride for her to never turn visitors away, she would somehow have to make time for them. "No, Mr. Watkins, I will take them around," she said.

"I have shown them to the small visitor's room. Are you able to meet with them now or would you prefer to have them tour the grounds first?"

Mrs. Reynolds sighed and handed the record book to Margie. "I shall attend to them immediately. Margie, please carry on here, and also ... well, you know what to do," she said with a reassuring smile to her assistant.

Upon reaching the visitor's room, Mrs. Reynolds found a well-dressed couple, who had the look of people who lived in Town. They introduced themselves as Mr. and Mrs. Gardiner. The wide-eyed young lady with dark hair was their niece, Miss Elizabeth Bennet. At first, Mrs. Reynolds thought she might give them the abbreviated tour to save time. In all likelihood they would not be aware she was skipping certain rooms in order to move the group along more quickly. Later, reflecting back, she was glad she had taken time for the full tour.

"We have heard the family is away at this time," said Mr. Gardiner.

"Oh, yes, but we expect them tomorrow with a large party of friends," Mrs. Reynolds replied. At that, she heard the young lady take a quick, nervous breath.

After the tour, Mrs. Reynolds was just resuming her preparations for the arrival of Mr. Darcy's guests, when Margie came at a run to let her know Mr. Darcy had arrived home early and was in a somewhat agitated state. Hearing a commotion in the hallway outside, she arose and was startled to find herself face-to-face with the master himself.

"Mr. Darcy!" Her surprise was not only at seeing him there in her office but also at the condition of his person. He was dusty and disheveled, his face red from exertion, and he was out of breath as if he had run all the way from the stables.

"Welcome home, sir," she said trying to regain her usual calm demeanor. "I am sorry for not greeting you myself, but we did not expect you until tomorrow."

Waving off her apology he said quickly, "Yes, I rode ahead to meet with Mr. Jones on some estate business." He hesitated a moment taking time to wipe some sweat from his brow with his handkerchief.

Mrs. Reynolds waited patiently. She knew him well enough to be certain he had something else to say. "Mrs. Reynolds, I believe you gave a tour of the house to three people who are now viewing the grounds."

"Yes, sir, I did. The Gardiners and Miss Bennet." Sensing something was not right, she added, "I did not think my taking the time would be a problem, as our preparations for your arrival are nearly complete."

Sensing her concern he assured her, "No, no, I was not chastising you at all. In fact, I am well pleased you were able to show them the house. How do you think they liked it?"

Mrs. Reynolds furrowed her brow as she examined his face. This was an unusual question. Mr. Darcy rarely took an interest in people who came to tour the house. In fact, he always avoided them assiduously.

"What did she...what did they have to say? About Pemberley? Did they like it?" he asked looking at her with something more than his usual intensity.

"They seemed very well pleased with the house, but how could they not be?"

"Good. Good," he said nodding his head. "Tell me more about their visit."

Mrs. Reynolds began by recounting the time they had arrived and the rooms they had toured. "I believe they are from London, at least the Gardiners are from Town. I was not certain about Miss Bennet."

"Did Miss Bennet mention she and I are acquainted?" he asked hesitantly.

"Why, yes, sir. She did say she knew you slightly."

His dark eyes widened. "How did that come about?"

"I believe it was as we were looking at the miniatures on the mantelpiece. Mrs. Gardiner asked Miss Bennet how she liked the one of George Wickham. I told them he was the son of your father's steward."

"Did Miss Bennet make any comment about Mr. Wickham?"

"No, not a word. When I said he had gone into the army and turned out quite wild, she did not disagree."

"Please continue, Mrs. Reynolds."

"Then I pointed out the miniature of you. I think it was Mrs. Gardiner who said she had heard much about you. She said you had a handsome face and then turned to Miss Bennet to inquire if she thought it was a good likeness of you. That was when I realized Miss Bennet was acquainted with you."

"And?" he said impatiently.

Mrs. Reynolds thought back over the conversation. It was very unusual for him to interrogate her like this about visitors. Clearly, for some reason the opinion of this young lady was very important to him. "I asked her if she did, in fact, know you, and she said she was a little acquainted with you."

At this, Darcy gave a deep exhale as if he thought it might now be safe for him to breathe again.

"And then since she knew you, I asked if she thought you were a handsome gentleman," Mrs. Reynolds added with a smile.

At this, Darcy's eyes grew wide and he made a noise that resembled a stifled groan. "Mrs. Reynolds, I hope this is not something you regularly ask our visitors?"

Now it was Mrs. Reynolds turn to redden. "No, sir. I thought that since she knew you…," she trailed off. "I was simply making pleasant conversation. After all, they were very nice people."

Darcy sighed. "Yes, I am certain they were. Please tell me exactly what Miss Bennet said."

Mrs. Reynolds wrinkled her forehead. "Said about what, sir."

Darcy grimaced. He hesitated and then said very slowly, "What did Miss Bennet say of me?"

Mrs. Reynolds noticed that he was uncomfortably shifting his weight from one foot to the other. It was something he had done as a boy when he was called to account for his actions. Clearly, the mention of Miss Bennet was having the effect of disquieting Mr. Darcy.

"Oh, Miss Bennet agreed that you are," she answered softly. "Handsome, that is, sir."

At that, Mrs. Reynolds saw the corner of Darcy's mouth turn up in a slight smile. Yes, there was definitely more to this than he was willing to admit.

"Is there anything else they said about the house or…" Darcy hesitated putting a fist to his mouth as he cleared his throat. "Or about me?"

"I showed them the portrait of Miss Darcy, the one taken when she was just eight, and they inquired about her."

"What did you say about Georgiana?"

"When they asked me if she was as handsome as her brother, I told them she was the handsomest young lady that ever was and all about how she loves her music, playing all day sometimes. I showed them the new pianoforte you bought for her. I hope that was not wrong of me. Oh, it is so lovely. I know Miss Darcy will be thrilled when she sees it tomorrow."

Mrs. Reynolds blushed as she recalled the way she had praised Mr. Darcy for his kindness and good-temper, as well as his generosity to the people who depended upon him on the estate. Mr. Darcy was a modest man, and if he knew just how freely she had spoken about him, he might be upset.

"I believe you are not revealing all to me, Mrs. Reynolds. Did something else happen during their visit that you are reluctant to share? You may speak freely. I am not unhappy with you."

Now it was Mrs. Reynolds' turn to shift uncomfortably. "Mr. Gardiner inquired if you were much at Pemberley during the year, and I told them you spend nearly half the year here, although we always wish it were more. Then Mr. Gardiner suggested that if you were to marry perhaps we might see more of you."

Darcy raised an eyebrow.

"I agreed that was indeed possible, but I also said we had no idea when you would marry."

"Hmm…" He rubbed his chin thoughtfully.

"I think I might also have said I did not know who might be good enough for you," she confessed reluctantly.

Darcy groaned putting his fingers to his temple. "I am almost afraid to ask what Miss Bennet had to say about that."

"Miss Bennet said I was very fortunate to have such a master, and I told her if I were to go through the world, I could not meet a better."

Suddenly, Mrs. Reynolds found herself enveloped in a hug. "I thank you for your kind words, Mrs. Reynolds. You are too generous in your praise."

"I only speak as I see, Mr. Darcy. You are a good man, a very good man. Everyone who knows you says so."

Darcy mumbled something that sounded a bit like, "Not everyone."

"When I showed them the picture gallery, Miss Bennet did spend some time studying your portrait. Quite some time, in fact," said Mrs. Reynolds with a smile.

Suddenly, Darcy seemed to remember he had been in a hurry. "I believe I would like to show our guests around myself, but I must change my traveling clothes first. The road was very dusty. Who is taking them on the grounds tour?" he asked.

"I believe it is Mr. Eldridge, sir."

"Very good. Would you please send someone to speak with him? I would like him to go slowly—very slowly—so I may catch up with their group." Examining his dirty and rumpled shirt, he added, "Would you please send someone up to help me change. My valet is following later today with the baggage. And of course, I shall require some water although you do not need to take time to heat it."

Then before she could respond, he disappeared.

450

After following his instructions, Mrs. Reynolds took a moment to consider what had just transpired. Something was different about Mr. Darcy. What did this young woman mean to him? How had they met?

Although Mrs. Reynolds prided herself on not interfering in the Darcys' private business, her curiosity to understand the situation was just too much to resist. Unable to concentrate on the pile of papers on her desk, she kept returning to thoughts of the polite young lady with the expressive brown eyes. Finally, she gave up and went to stand at the window overlooking gardens at the back of the house. After a few minutes, she saw Mr. Darcy exit the house and stride off in the direction the visitors had taken, straightening his cravat as he hurried along. Turning back to her desk, she smiled. It did not escape her notice that Mr. Darcy was dressed in what she knew to be one of his favorite coats.

Darcy's Reaction to Finding Elizabeth at Pemberley

by L. L. Diamond

August 4, 1812

Darcy's gaze followed the carriage carrying Elizabeth Bennet as it wound its way around the lake. After the long journey, the afternoon in Miss Bennet's company was a welcome he had not expected, yet relished all the same.

Elizabeth's countenance revealed her shock at their initial meeting; she had not expected any of the family to be at home. Her expression when he joined the Gardiners and herself as they walked the grounds was no less surprised, but he could not ignore her presence as he did most visitors who toured the house. He had to prove to her that he had heeded her reproofs—that he had indeed changed.

Of course, their meeting was not without some awkwardness, and he did not miss the appearance of concern expressed in her fine eyes when he requested an introduction to the Gardiners. She was well aware of her relations' intelligence and manners, which meant her worry had been for his reaction. His heart ached at the remembrance of it.

Fortunately, the Gardiners, who could easily be mistaken for people of fashion, were indeed amiable, and Darcy found no great difficulty in conversing with such charming people. He had been in earnest when he invited Mr. Gardiner to fish in the stream. In fact, Darcy would happily show the man each and every spot he might find the best sport and bait his hooks if it meant he could change Elizabeth's feelings towards him.

Elizabeth's feelings! He had made such a misjudgment in Meryton, yet her unease in his company today was evident. His disquiet was no less acute. Had she understood the explanations contained within his letter?

In retrospect, the missive had been penned with such bitterness of spirit, a part of him hoped she had burned it. Her opinion of him was low enough without her perceiving a resentment that was not present, yet Mrs. Reynolds indicated Elizabeth found him handsome. Perhaps not all hope was lost!

He could not help but notice that at the mention of Mr. Bingley and his sisters, Elizabeth had become quiet. He had not had the opportunity, as of yet, to enlighten Bingley as to Miss Jane Bennet's feelings, but he had seldom been in company with the gentleman since Easter. Those few instances included Miss Bingley and Mrs. Hurst as well. He could not very well broach the subject in their presence. Could Elizabeth still harbor anger for his poor advice to his friend?

Yet, she had agreed to make the acquaintance of Georgiana! He had written to his sister of Miss Bennet, telling his younger sister of Elizabeth's intelligence and wit, and he anticipated their actual meeting. His sister required a friend who would not fawn and simper in order to gain her favor like Miss Bingley; no, she required someone with a touch of impertinence to draw her out of her timidity. Elizabeth's kindness and outgoing personality would suit well. Georgiana would arrive on the morrow and they would travel to Lambton straight away. His sister would love Elizabeth as much as he did!

The carriage would disappear from sight soon, into Pemberley woods on its way to Lambton, so he turned and began to stride toward the house. Pemberley was a beautiful place and he loved it with everything in him; however, he had often imagined Elizabeth walking the halls, inhabiting the mistress' suite, and laughing with him as he walked the gardens. His home was not the same as it had been prior to making her acquaintance; it now required her to be complete.

The time he spent denying his attraction and feelings for Elizabeth! This time matters would be different—he would not repeat his mistake. Whilst she was nearby, he would expend every effort to ensure she was aware of his affections and wishes. Those precious feelings had not changed since Hunsford, except this time, he would do everything within his power to gain a favorable response to the offer of his hand.

He glanced back just in time to view the back of the carriage as it disappeared into the trees. Miss Bennet may be leaving today, but one day she would return, never to be separated from him again.

Miss Darcy Meets Elizabeth Bennet

by C. Allyn Pierson

August 5, 1812

Miss Darcy alighted from the dusty carriage carefully; she did not want to soil her gown and embarrass her brother by appearing disheveled in front of his guests. After greeting Mrs. Reynolds, she retired to her room to change out of her traveling gown and freshen up. It was a delight to be alone after the long days of traveling with Mrs. Hurst and Miss Bingley. She knew her brother would not associate with unworthy or ill-bred people, but she had to admit she did not like Mr. Bingley's sisters. How her brother could tolerate Miss Bingley's odious fawning was beyond Georgiana's understanding, and Mrs. Hurst followed wherever Miss Bingley led in the matter of gossip.

Miss Bingley fawned over Georgiana, as well, but she could tell that the attention was all for her brother's ear. Miss Bingley constantly glanced at Mr. Darcy and made sure her affectionate conversation with Georgiana was carried on in his presence.

Before she had proceeded further in her ruminations, Georgiana heard a scratch on her door. Her maid admitted Mr. Darcy and then he sent her off. He pulled a chair up to Georgiana's dressing table, where she was seated, and took her hand.

"Georgiana, my dear, I know that you have just arrived and are probably needing a rest, but I wonder if you could do something for me?"

Georgiana was surprised, but responded immediately, "Of course, brother! What do you want me to do?"

He looked down at her hand as he caressed it soothingly, then, with a look of grim fortitude said, "I... I would like you to drive into Lambton with me. I want you to meet someone."

She stared at him in astonishment. "Who is it?"

He fidgeted with his cravat and straightened his cuffs. "It is Miss Elizabeth Bennet and her aunt and uncle. They visited Pemberley yesterday while touring Derbyshire, and I would like to introduce you. They are friends of Bingley's... and mine."

She was still more astonished! Her brother had never behaved so in her entire life! Obviously, this Miss Bennet was special to her brother in some way. She looked at him for a moment, then said, "Could they not come to Pemberley? Surely Mr. Bingley will want to see them also."

He flushed a little. "I do not wish to have you meet them in a crowd of people. I want Miss Bennet to be able to talk to you without being interrupted or without having to carry on several conversations at once." He smiled at his shy little sister. "I do not want you to be able to hide in the corner, my love."

His blush and his words gave her quite a different picture of her brother's motivations in this affair. Could he, perhaps, actually be in love with Miss Bennet? She answered the question in his eyes. "Of course, dear brother! I am ready to go at any time! But how will we leave without revealing our plans to the Bingleys?"

"I have the carriage waiting by the stables...we will leave through the kitchen. We will return before our guests even know we are gone."

They executed this plan, but it did not turn out quite the way they expected. When they came down the back stairs from Georgiana's room they ran into Bingley, who was looking for his man.

Darcy sighed quietly and gave in, explaining their errand to Lambton. Bingley insisted on accompanying them, even offering to wait downstairs until they had sought Miss Bennet's approbation for his visit. Darcy ordered tea for Miss Bingley and the Hursts when they came down, and the three of them sneaked out through the back door.

It did not take long to reach Lambton as it was only four or five miles from Pemberley. Darcy and Bingley kept up a light, effortless conversation during the first part of the drive, but as they approached the inn at Lambton Darcy fell silent. Bingley also seemed wrapped in his own thoughts and Georgiana could see tension in both the men's faces. How very odd!

When they stepped out of the carriage, Darcy and Georgiana went upstairs to the Gardiners' rooms and were announced by the innkeeper. Georgiana hardly heard her brother's introduction…Miss Bennet was lovely and had a beautiful, low-pitched voice. Georgiana curtseyed and spoke with her, while watching her brother out of the corner of her eyes. As Miss Bennet talked he seemed to relax his stiff stance, and he talked calmly with Mr. Gardiner, a genteel, well-dressed older man.

The visit went quickly, and Georgiana was not surprised when, while Bingley was renewing his acquaintance with Miss Bennet, her brother asked her to invite them to dine at Pemberley. She did so, rather awkwardly, but the Gardiners did not seem to see any flaws in her manner, so she was reassured.

They were all quiet on the ride back to Pemberley. Georgiana did not know what her brother and his friend were thinking, but she was very full of speculation. It seemed her brother had finally fallen in love…not surprising when Miss Bennet was so beautiful and kind. She would watch him carefully while the Gardiners and Miss Bennet dined with them!

Mrs. Gardiner and Elizabeth Visit Miss Darcy

by C. Allyn Pierson

August 6, 1812

After much thought during a fairly sleepless night, Mrs. Gardiner had come to no conclusions about her niece's relationship to Mr. Darcy. It was clear the handsome landowner had a soft spot in his heart for Lizzy, but his dignified reserve made it difficult to interpret his thoughts. Still, he could not take his eyes off Lizzy, and the extreme embarrassment evident between them was highly suspicious.

And then there was Mr. Darcy's visit with his sister, to introduce her to Lizzy, and coming when she had barely stepped out of her coach at Pemberley! Yes, Mr. Darcy loved Lizzy, but how did Lizzy feel? Her blushing and stammering when Mr. Darcy came upon them suddenly certainly suggested she cared about his opinion, but Mrs. Gardiner could not be sure if she liked him, or if she was merely embarrassed to be in a position where she must be polite to someone she disliked.

Elizabeth said virtually nothing the next morning while they breakfasted, so finally Mrs. Gardiner spoke. "Lizzy? Do you not think we should visit Pemberley this morning? I feel we should do something to return Mr. and Miss Darcy's exceeding politeness in waiting on us yesterday...and so soon after her arrival! Does that meet with your approbation?"

Elizabeth blushed, but answered in a calm voice, "Indeed, yes! I believe you are right. I would hate to seem rude to Miss Darcy. The poor girl is very shy, and I wouldn't want her to feel we did not appreciate her courtesy."

So it came about that they took their carriage to Pemberley to visit Miss Darcy. When they arrived they found Miss Darcy was in the saloon with her companion, Mrs. Annesley while Miss Bingley and her sister sat down in the room examining a bracelet Mrs. Hurst was wearing.

When Mrs. Gardiner and Lizzy were announced, Mrs. Annesley and Georgiana stood up to greet them, and Georgiana introduced them to her companion, briefly, then flushed with embarrassment. Mrs. Annesley smoothly took up the dangling conversation and invited the two visitors to sit. Mrs. Gardiner ended up nearest Miss Darcy with Lizzy across from Mrs. Annesley, and they carried on a conversation of little content, but great goodwill. Occasionally, Miss Darcy would whisper a contribution to the topic of conversation, but they were so quiet that her guests could not hear her.

Eventually, Mrs. Annesley, after several significant looks at Miss Darcy, induced her charge to ring for refreshments and the awkward behavior of everyone relaxed while they all selected some fruit and cake. While they were involved with the lovely trays of fruit the door of the saloon opened and Mr. Darcy entered, his eyes immediately going to his sister. It was clear to Mrs. Gardiner that he cared very much for his sister and for her comfort while entertaining the guests, and it seemed to her that he was very much aware of her niece and trying not to focus all his attention on her.

Mr. Darcy began several topics of conversation with his sister and Elizabeth immediately came to his aid and talked to Georgiana about some concerts she had attended while in Town. Things were going well until Miss Bingley suddenly piped up with a sarcastic comment to Elizabeth about the militia leaving Meryton, and how distressing that must be to the Bennets...especially having Mr. Wickham leave.

Elizabeth deflected the ill-natured comment, but Mrs. Gardiner was quite astonished at the reaction of Miss Darcy to it. She flushed to the roots of her hair and then went ghastly white, her lips compressed tightly. Mrs. Gardiner was afraid for a moment that the poor girl was going to swoon! Good heavens! What has come over the girl? Is she ill?

Her brother seems to not feel that she is ill...he is continuing to talk to Lizzy as if nothing is going on, although he gives Miss Bingley a withering look at the end of her little comment.

After a few minutes further conversation, Mrs. Gardiner felt it was time to go as they had already been there for a half hour. On the drive back to Lambton she chatted with her niece about all the non-essentials of Pemberley: the grounds, the fruit, the cake, the décor. What they did not discuss was what Mrs. Gardiner was most interested in: her niece's feelings toward Mr. Darcy, whom she clearly knew much better than her aunt and uncle had realized. She was disappointed, but did not feel she had the right to interrogate her niece over this matter...but still her curiosity was most frustrating!

Fishing at Pemberley

by Colette Saucier

August 6, 1812

That Mr. Gardiner could engage Mr. Hurst in lively conversation was a credit to the manners and breeding of the first gentleman. They spoke animatedly of common diversions in London; and Darcy did not remember another time in their acquaintance when Mr. Hurst had had so much to say, perhaps as the early hour had kept him from the port. When introduced to Miss Bingley and Mrs. Hurst, Mr. Gardiner was amiable without being obsequious and, if he noticed, did not acknowledge that each lady would only see him from the end of her nose.

Darcy, Bingley, Mr. Hurst, and Mr. Gardiner walked down to the trout stream with footmen following with tackle, rods, and bait, as well as refreshments for the anglers. They settled in on the bank in the warmth of the July day and talked genially for a while before falling into a companionable silence more conducive to fishing. Sitting next to Mr. Gardiner, Darcy struggled to remain still, not to prevent scaring the fish but because he feared all that might come pouring forth should he not maintain control.

Some time passed in the quiet of the sounds of nature before Mr. Gardiner, perhaps sensing the younger man's distress, spoke sotto voce to Darcy. "I cannot thank you enough for this invitation, sir. There truly is nothing quite so pleasant as fishing."

"You are most welcome any time."

"Yes, indeed, the ladies do not know what they are missing."

461

If possible, Darcy sat up straighter than before. "And what were Mrs. Gardiner and your niece planning for today?"

"Actually," he said, casting his line, "they planned to call on your sister."

A tingling sensation permeated Darcy's face as he held his expression in check. "Indeed? When did they plan to wait on her?"

Mr. Gardiner pulled his watch from his pocket. "Oh, I would say they should be there by now."

Darcy did not, dared not react nor even breathe. He stared out onto the stream, holding his rod steady.

Mr. Gardiner allowed several minutes to pass before speaking again. "You know, Mr. Darcy, I appreciate your hospitality, but I would not want to impose on your time. I know what a busy man you are. You must not feel compelled to remain here as host if you have any estate matters that require your attention."

Darcy glanced at his companion's profile and saw the slight turn of his lips as indication that Mr. Gardiner understood more than his words would suggest. "If you are certain, sir, there is an important matter I need to address," Darcy said, rising.

"Go to it, young man. Surely you will have more success in that quarter than you will fishing, seeing as you lost your bait some half hour   ago."

The Gardiners Reflect on Mr. Darcy

by Shannon Winslow

August 6, 1812

"What a day we have had!" exclaimed Mrs. Gardiner to her husband when they climbed into their bed at the inn that night. She had barely been able to contain herself until they were alone, until they could discuss the events of the day in private, but even now she had to be careful to keep her voice down lest her niece should overhear through the thin walls. "What say you about Mr. Darcy, my dear, now you have spent more time in his company?"

"I say he has some of the finest fishing in the country. I wish you had seen today's catch, my love—some of the best specimens I have ever had the pleasure of pulling in, I can tell you. There was one in particular that put up a heroic fight..."

Here Mrs. Gardiner impatiently interrupted, giving her husband's arm a vigorous shake for emphasis. "Not the fish! It is your opinion of *the man* I am far more interested in. What say you about your host, Mr. Darcy?"

"Oh! Well, my opinion of him is equally high, I should think. He is as fine a fellow as ever I have come across, and a great deal more civil than your average rich man."

"No false pride, then?"

"None that I could see. He is perhaps a little reserved, but he could not have been more accommodating and more obliging to me. That speaks well of his character, I think, especially when you consider that there could be nothing in it for him. There is no reason Mr. Darcy should have gone out of his way for somebody like me. I am in no position to do anything for him in return. I am certainly not his equal in wealth or position, and I have no influence or acquaintance that could possibly interest him. Yes, I thought it the most positive proof of his generous character. But you had opportunity to observe Mr. Darcy's behavior today as well, when he joined you and the other ladies. What is your own opinion?"

"Oh, I quite agree with you."

"Very well, then."

Mrs. Gardiner lay quietly for a moment, reviewing in her mind all she had seen and heard that afternoon. Her senses had instantly been called to high alert when Pemberley's handsome proprietor had unexpectedly entered the saloon, and it had been the same for all the others—Miss Georgiana, Elizabeth, Miss Bingley, Mrs. Hurst, and that agreeable, genteel Mrs. Annesley. Every female eye was drawn to Mr. Darcy at once, which was not surprising considering his fine tall person and commanding presence. She herself, Mrs. Gardiner recalled, had noticed an involuntary flutter within her own breast. Then the maneuvering had begun. Miss Bingley had clearly been eager to impress him, and even Miss Darcy. Yet, there was something else...

"I must beg to differ with you on one point, however," continued Mrs. Gardiner.

"Indeed? In what respect?"

"On your presumption of having no influence or acquaintance of value. I believe your niece may be of very particular interest to Mr. Darcy, in fact."

"Elizabeth? That hardly seems likely. Their past acquaintance was only trifling, and you know the decided dislike she has expressed for the man."

"First impressions are not always accurate, you must admit, and they are not always immutable either. I think a change may be at work here. Anybody who watched the two of them together this afternoon—how solicitous he was, how anxious to promote a friendship between his sister and our niece—must suspect there is more to the connection than Elizabeth has admitted."

"Perhaps you are right, my dear. Now that you mention it, Mr. Darcy could not get away from the river quick enough once I told him that you and Elizabeth were calling on his sister. That was the end of fishing! Clearly, what was going forward at the house was more pressing in his mind, the company there more intriguing."

"Imagine!" said Mrs. Gardiner, her hands raised to press against her cheeks and her eyes wide with wonder. "Our niece mistress of Pemberley!"

"Do not you think that may be leaping forward too far," cautioned her husband, "or at least too rapidly?"

"I am impatient to know the truth of it, if only Elizabeth would begin the subject. You noticed how she talked all round the idea of Mr. Darcy after we came away—his sister, his house, his grounds, and even his table—everything in favorable yet guarded terms. Not one word did she venture on the interesting person at the heart of it all, the man himself, though I could have sworn she was near to bursting out with it one time and then another. That must mean something."

"You seem a bit dazzled by the man yourself, my dear."

"Nonsense. He is an impressive gentleman, you must admit, and not in an off-putting way either, not now we have seen him for what he really is. I am thinking only of Elizabeth, though. I truly believe her happiness would be safe in Mr. Darcy's care. Yes, I would be very pleased to see her married to him as soon as may be. What a fine establishment it would make for her!"

"And what a fine thing for us if we should be welcome to visit her at Pemberley as much as we like thereafter. One cannot overlook that advantage to the match either," Mr. Gardiner, propped up on one elbow, said with a conspiratorial wink.

Mrs. Gardiner muffled a laugh and blew out the candle. "That is quite true," she whispered, nuzzling in close to her husband.

"Remember how we were forced to abbreviate our walking tour the other day, and I am sure I shall never be completely happy until I have been all the way round the park by some means or another."

"Ten miles, we were told! Perhaps next time a carriage of some sort—a phaeton with a pair of sturdy ponies."

"Oh, yes, my dear! That would be the very thing!"

Elizabeth Reflects

by L. L. Diamond

August 6, 1812

Elizabeth sat before the dressing table, idly fingering the bristles of her hairbrush as the lush grounds of Pemberley and the estate's master captivated her mind.

Were her feelings so different than what they were at Hunsford? Yes, they were; but had she changed or was Mr. Darcy truly so different? Perhaps by knowing him better, she understood him more?

His housekeeper's words echoed in her head. *He is the best landlord, and the best master that ever lived; not like the wild young men nowadays, who think of nothing but themselves. There is not one of his tenants or servants but what will give him a good name. Some people call him proud; but I am sure I never saw anything of it. To my fancy, it is only because he does not rattle away like other young men.*

Such a man of wealth and consequence had to be a good man indeed to be thought so well of by his servants. Even the gardener, who showed them the grounds, praised his master. In particular, how Mr. Darcy had paid for the apothecary when the loyal servant's wife was ill.

Mrs. Reynolds and the gardener were not alone in their praise. Not one person she and the Gardiners had come across since arriving in Lambton had an ill word to say of Mr. Darcy.

How could she have misread him so upon their first acquaintance?

Mr. Darcy's slight at the assembly had to be the culprit! He had wounded her pride and insulted her vanity, and she had never really forgiven him for it. She was accustomed to her mother disregarding her looks in comparison to Jane and Lydia, but not one of their neighbors had ever agreed or made a similar comment.

That evening at the assembly, the local gentlemen were all familiar, and held no interest. Mr. Bingley, whilst well-looking and amiable, did not stir her emotions in any manner other than friendship.

Mr. Darcy, on the other hand, had intrigued her, which was sure to be why she reacted as she did. Upon reflection, her first thought of him had been of his good looks and his appearance of intelligence. He did not seem a dullard or behave as one with little or no sense.

He himself had admitted, *"I certainly have not the talent which some people possess of conversing easily with those I have never seen before. I cannot catch their tone of conversation, or appear interested in their concerns, as I often see done."* Could that have played a role in his ill-humor?

Since they had happened upon one another on the grounds of Pemberley, he had been everything amiable and welcoming. The encounter had been awkward, and she had not expected him to make such a gallant attempt to put her at ease. His generous behavior towards her aunt and uncle, and his enquiries as to the health of her family, were a compassion he had never shown during their previous meetings.

After all, his manner and behavior in Meryton had been so aloof. He often stood, not speaking with anyone, whilst watching their local society with apparent disdain. His looks had shown particular distaste upon watching the antics of Kitty and Lydia, but his response to her mother's vulgarity was more pronounced—his entire body would stiffen when she spoke.

Whilst Mr. Darcy's behavior had altered since their last meeting, Elizabeth had also grown in understanding of the gentleman's character. Rather than merely thinking him handsome and learned, she had begun to consider him as one of the best men of her acquaintance.

He could have abused her abominably in the letter after their argument, but he did not. His explanation of the separation of Bingley and Jane rankled upon its first reading, but after further consideration, he had been justified in his concern. Charlotte herself had questioned Jane's feelings, so why should those emotions be evident to Mr. Darcy?

His explanation of Mr. Wickham illustrated his good character as well. Mr. Darcy paid the man's debts and honored his father's last wishes for his godson to the best of his ability when it was probable that Mr. Wickham did not deserve any sort of recompense for the living at all. Mr. Darcy could have claimed the sum for the debt Mr. Wickham owed him, but he did not.

Now that she recognized Mr. Darcy's worth, could she dare hope his feelings for her had remained constant? His gaze across the drawing room the night prior had left her heart pounding and her face burning. She now feared her heart might be touched. What if his intentions and wishes had altered since Hunsford?

She could not blame him after her intemperate refusal of his hand. His resentment of her would have been justified as well, yet his invitations to Pemberley and his recent generosity of spirit indicated no such feelings.

"Lizzy?" Her aunt placed a hand to her shoulder with an expression of concern upon her face. "Your uncle and I are to take our walk. Did you still wish to join us?"

"Oh! I apologize. You caught me wool-gathering."

Her aunt's smile bore a hint of mischief. "So I noticed, dear. Do go fetch your spencer and gloves, so we can depart."

With a quick nod, she gathered her outdoor garments, but upon her return, her aunt held two letters. "They were just delivered a moment ago. They are from Jane."

Darcy Cancels the Dinner at Pemberley

by Abigail Reynolds

August 7, 1812

After tearing himself away from Elizabeth at the Lambton Inn, Darcy had given free rein to both his horse and his temper. Galloping over the familiar countryside was the perfect situation for venting his rage at George Wickham, who once more had come between Darcy and his Elizabeth. Darcy wanted Wickham's blood. He would thrash him for ruining Lydia Bennet, then pummel him bloody for making Elizabeth cry. Darcy had never felt more helpless than when he had seen tears running down Elizabeth's lovely cheeks. He had longed to take her into his arms, to tell her that he would fix everything, that all would be well again, but all he could do was to offer her a glass of wine. He would have been happy to rip Wickham limb from limb.

By the time Darcy reached Pemberley, he had dismissed his fury and was once more a civilized man. If he wanted to help Elizabeth, he would have to render courtesy and no doubt a substantial sum of money to Wickham, rather than the beating he deserved. His love for Elizabeth and his responsibility as master of Pemberley left him no other choice.

Inside the house, Georgiana flew down the stairs to meet him, her face alight. "What did she say?" Then, as she took in his sober countenance, her smile vanished. "Oh, no. Did she refuse you? I am so sorry."

For a moment Darcy was taken aback by her question. "I did not ask her," he said shortly. "It was not the right time. She had just

470

received some bad news from home, and will be returning there immediately."

Georgiana hesitated. "I hope it is nothing too serious."

Darcy did not meet her eyes. "Some scandal concerning one of her sisters, nothing more. Hopefully it will come to nothing."

His sister looked puzzled by his vagueness, but did not question him.

Miss Bingley, of course, could not leave well enough alone when he announced that the Gardiners and Miss Bennet had sent their apologies and would not be dining with them that evening. "What a pity!" she cried with patent insincerity. "I had so looked forward to seeing dear Eliza again." Her attempt at civility annoyed Darcy as much as her insulting comments on Elizabeth's appearance had done the previous day.

"I say, Darcy," Bingley said. "Did they give any reason for their sudden departure? I had thought they planned to remain in the area for several more days."

"Just that they were returning home immediately," said Darcy. He had promised Elizabeth that he would hide the truth as long as he could, and with any luck, the whole matter of Lydia Bennet could be resolved before Bingley heard of it.

"No doubt one of the Gardiners' children has some trifling ailment," said Mrs. Hurst. Her tone suggested that such an ailment must have been deliberately planned by the child.

"Children seem to recover so quickly," said Miss Bingley, who apparently could not leave the subject of Elizabeth's family quickly enough. "Do you suppose tomorrow will be as fair a day as today? Perhaps we could take a drive through the grounds. I declare, there is no spot in England that can make the beauty of the park here!"

"I hope the weather will permit it, but you will have to excuse me. Some pressing business has arisen in Town that requires my personal attention, and I will be leaving early tomorrow morning." Darcy braced himself for the storm that was sure to follow his announcement.

It did not materialize, apart from an agonized look from Georgiana. Miss Bingley merely tightened her lips, and all conversation came to a halt until Mrs. Annesley displayed her good breeding by changing the subject.

Darcy let the discussion flow around him as his thoughts turned to his plans for locating George Wickham. He was not so preoccupied, though, that he did not notice Mrs. Hurst speaking urgently in her sister's ear. From their whispered conversation, he suspected that Miss Bingley had not missed the significance of his sudden change of plans immediately following Elizabeth's departure. Perhaps now she would finally stop pestering him with her obsequious attentions.

The image of Elizabeth's reddened eyes rose before him again. Damn George Wickham!

Lydia and Wickham in London

by Diana Birchall

Lydia's wedding

~~August 8, 1812~~

It was after breakfast that Mr. Gardiner was called away to consult with his man of business, Mr. Stone, and Lydia was wild with fear that he would take so long, that they would not reach St. Clement's by eleven o'clock, when the wedding was to take place.

Wait, they were forced to do, however; and Lydia in her agitation was changing her finery and tossing things into her satchel with such abandon that her tumbled undergarments were spilling out.

"Oh, Aunt! I declare I wanted to be married in blue, you know they say marry in blue your love's so true, but my blue muslin has that horrid nasty stain on it, one of the officers spilled something white…eggnog I believe, all over me and I could not stop to have it washed, though it was so sticky. This muslin gown is so limp it is positively insipid. I want to look beautiful for my dear Wickham, and I shan't. It is a shame."

"Lydia, I must talk to you," began her aunt with energy. "How can you think of your finery, rather than the wickedness of what you have done!"

"Oh Aunt, don't start that again," Lydia pleaded. "What have I done that thousands of girls have not. I'm getting married, any way, and I'm sure that is nothing to be ashamed of. Oh, if only I had some coral beads for this white thing. You wouldn't think white could fade, but this is absolutely dingy. Can't I borrow your corals?"

"The gown would remain white if you ever washed it Lydia," said Mrs. Gardiner with tight lips. "And I think I would never see my corals again if I lent them, for you are going home to Meryton from the church door."

"Yes, won't it be fun? I can't wait to show myself to my sisters, and Mama, and all the servants, as a married woman! Only think, me being married first, though I'm only sixteen, and the youngest. This makes old maids of all of them. Oh! What a joke."

"But Lydia, you must be brought to a sense of the shame you have given your whole family. Do you not know that it is wrong, it is wicked, to...to live with a man before you are wed? It makes you a fallen woman, and if Mr. Darcy and your uncle had not taken matters in hand, you would have remained one, for Mr. Wickham was in no hurry to marry you."

"What difference does it make?" Lydia shrugged carelessly. "I could wear my darling little red spencer jacket that I had made up at one of the shops in Brighton. I had no money for it, but Mrs. Forster lent me some. Just see what a compliment to the military it is! All corded, with braids, and frogging just like Wickham's, and see the gold tassels? I do think I ought to shake some gold tassels on my wedding-day, don't you?"

Mrs. Gardiner crossed the bedroom, took the spencer out of Lydia's hands, and put it firmly into Lydia's carpet-bag. "Certainly no gold tassels," she said with emphasis.

Lydia tossed her head. "Well, it isn't the colors of Wickham's new regiment anyhow," she said pertly. "I'm sorry he should lose his red uniform; that is why I always would have little touches of red about me, though it is too mean of you not to lend me your corals. But now he is to wear blue. To tell the truth, he will look handsomer than ever in blue." She thought a moment. "You do have jasper earrings, aunt; couldn't I borrow those."

"You may not," snapped Mrs. Gardiner. "Lydia, once and for all, I want you to understand that if Wickham had continued to refuse to marry you—and I believe he never intended such a thing—you would be, to speak plainly, ruined. Not only would you be ruined, but all your sisters! Do you not realize that? No one would ever marry Jane, or Elizabeth, or Mary, or Kitty. No decent gentleman would attach himself to the family, one of whose daughters was—"

"Never mind, Aunt, I will be married in half an hour, and then I will be quite as respectable as you," Lydia said pertly. "Hark! Do I not hear the gentlemen leaving the study?" She ran to the door. "It is them, uncle and the other gentlemen. Now we can go to the carriage. Do hurry, Aunt. If I can't have the jaspers, how about your blue silk handkerchief? Then I would have something blue. Oh! Wickham will look so handsome in blue. I cannot wait to see him! And only think, he will be waiting at the church, with Mr. Darcy, for me, his bride!"

"Lydia! Before we leave—do you, do you understand that you have broken God's commandments, and must repent? Even if you are to be married, if you are not penitent, you still carry the sin. Surely you regret the trouble and misery you have brought on your family. Mr. Darcy, a stranger, is having to pay for it all—"

"Well, and why should he not? He is very rich, and like a brother to Wickham, they say. Besides, you know, I think he likes Lizzy. When I asked which he thought prettiest, he got quite red. I said, I am sure you think Jane the best looking, and I teased him until he would answer, and he said, 'No, your next sister.' So there's for you, Aunt—unless Lizzy is a fool she will marry him and be rich. Though I don't think she will have as much fun as me. Mr. Darcy is such a stick, and not half as handsome as my dear Wickham."

Mrs. Gardiner blushed angrily in spite of herself. "Lydia, Lydia, you must not talk of such things. On your way to church to be married, you ought to think of sacred subjects, repent your sins, and vow that you will reform and lead a pure, quiet, useful, holy life."

"But I shan't," said Lydia with an impish grin. "How can you think it? Me and Wickham are going to have as much fun as possible. Indeed, we already have. He is so passionate!" She sighed and closed her eyes. "I don't suppose you know anything about passion, Aunt Gardiner, but I assure you it didn't take long for me to learn. And I think Lizzy knows, because she had quite a fancy for Wickham you know. Too bad! It's I who have him now!"

As Mr. Gardiner came to fetch them and the coachman picked up Lydia's satchel, Lydia put on her red gloves with complacency, and walked out to the carriage singing a camp song, which despite all Mrs. Gardener's efforts to get her to hush, she did not stop humming all the way to her wedding.

> *O ne'er shall I forget that night,*
> *The stars were bright above me,*
> *And gently lent their silvery light*
> *When first she vowed to love me.*
> *But now I'm bound to Brighton camp —*
> *Kind heaven then pray guide me,*
> *And send me safely back again,*
> *To the girl I left behind me..."*

Mrs. Gardiner Receives a Letter from her Husband

by C. Allyn Pierson

August 11, 1812

The Longbourn family had settled down into a routine, of sorts, after Mr. Gardiner left for London to help his brother-in-law look for Lydia and Wickham. The members of the family went about their usual activities—stitching and walking, discussing fashions and reading, with at least an appearance of calm. If Elizabeth or Jane spent more than their usual time staring at the same page of their book or went up to their rooms for a "rest" more than one would expect, Mary and Kitty did not seem much changed by the tension in the air.

Mrs. Gardiner spent a part of every day with Mrs. Bennet, hoping to bring her gently to a sense of resignation over the loss of her favorite daughter...or at least to the realization that it was a good idea to not pour every wild thought in her head into the ears of the servants. When she at last gave up, she would spend most of the day with her elder nieces, and her four children gave the elder sisters a source of entertainment and distraction which made the day go by more quickly.

After watching for the post avidly every day, the household was finally rewarded with a letter from Mr. Gardiner enumerating his efforts in the search for Lydia. Mrs. Gardiner shared the letter with her two eldest nieces:

My dear wife:

I write to you with a heavy heart. I found my brother Bennet at his hotel and convinced him to remove with me to Cheapside where we could at least be comfortable during our search. Unfortunately, Mr. Bennet's efforts for finding Lydia have been met with complete failure and we have not had a single clue to their whereabouts. He has spent much time since settling in London doing a systematic search of all the hotels that were likely to have sheltered the couple, but has heard nothing to the purpose.

I have heard from Colonel Forster, and it sounds as if he has spent considerable time interviewing Wickham's friends and acquaintances in Brighton, but he has found no one who has any idea where he could be. Apparently, he has said enough to make his fellow officers believe he has neither friends nor family outside the regiment who might be sheltering them. He has, however, left behind in Brighton considerable debts to many of the tradesmen and, worse yet, many debts of honor amongst his fellows. The men who earlier had found him a good fellow and ripe for any spree now curse him as a man who cannot be trusted to play and pay fairly."

Jane burst out at this point, "A gamester! This is wholly unexpected. I had not an idea of it!"

Mrs. Gardiner said soothingly, "I know, my dear, but surely it is all of a piece with his other behavior." She turned back to her letter:

Colonel Forster feels it will take at least one thousand pounds to clear Wickham's debts.

The one piece of good news I have for you is that I have finally convinced Mr. Bennet that he has done all he can for now and that his wife and remaining daughters need him. He will leave Town the day after you receive this and will be home before dinner. I fear it will be hopeless, but I will continue the search for the absconding couple without him, and I hope to have some success, but we must face the possibility that Lydia is lost to us forever.

I hope, my love, you will find yourself able to leave Longbourn to the care of Mr. Bennet and Jane and Elizabeth and will come home on the carriage that brings my brother to you. I miss you and the children;

the house is an empty shell without you, my dear. Share with my nieces and sister what you think appropriate from this letter, and I hope to see you soon.

Your loving, Edward

After Mrs. Gardiner shared the letter, they all sat for a few moments staring blankly at the trees visible through the window. Eventually, Elizabeth rose briskly and said, "Well, we cannot sit here and mope. Nothing has changed from what we believed before. I am going to go up and sit with my mother for a while. I will send Betsy to help you, aunt, as I am sure you will want to pack your portmanteaux and trunks for your journey tomorrow."

The three women embraced, then scattered to various parts of the house.

Darcy Calls on Mr. Gardiner

by Abigail Reynolds

August 15, 1812

Mr. Gardiner felt he deserved the luxury of spending the afternoon reading the book on fishing he had purchased during their visit to Oxford. He had been trying to finish it for days. He had started it in Lambton, but was interrupted by the urgent need to return to London. There had been no time to read on that chaotic journey, especially since all his energies had been devoted to consoling Elizabeth as best he could. When he finally reached London, he had to find Mr. Bennet's hotel; and once he had discovered his brother-in-law and brought him back to Gracechurch Street, there was no peace to be had. Mr. Bennet's disturbance of mind was evident.

He was fond of his brother-in-law, but on occasion Mr. Gardiner found Mr. Bennet's directionless behavior exasperating. By God, he did not intend to allow his own daughters to run wild simply because it was too much trouble to rein them in! For the last few days, Mr. Bennet had required his constant guidance in the search for Lydia. Although he would never have admitted it to anyone, Mr. Gardiner was glad to see Mr. Bennet depart.

He looked forward to seeing his dear wife and children again that evening, but he knew that their arrival would bring a happy chaos with it that would preclude time to himself. That was why he intended to make the most of this quiet time at home.

Mr. Gardiner had not even finished one chapter when he heard a sharp knock at the door. A minute later, his manservant appeared and handed him a calling card. Mr. Gardiner's eyebrows shot up when he read the name on it.

Why in the world would Mr. Darcy be calling on him here? Not only was their acquaintance slight, but Darcy was supposed to be at Pemberley, a full two days journey away. Mr. Gardiner chuckled to himself. Lizzy had been sly indeed! Apparently she and Darcy had far more of an understanding than she had admitted. But that still did not explain Darcy's appearance on his doorstep. Well, most likely he was in search of news of Lizzy, and did not want to interrupt the household at Longbourn during this crisis. That was fair enough. Mr. Gardiner instructed the servant to send Mr. Darcy in.

Mr. Darcy's face was marked with lines of tension, but he shook Mr. Gardiner's hand and exchanged cordial greetings. He did not hesitate in turning immediately to his business. "You have no doubt guessed that I am here to discuss your niece's situation."

"Well, that is good news! It is unfortunate you were not here yesterday, as Lizzy's father was still in Town then." So Darcy must be on the verge of making an offer—good news indeed!

The corners of Mr. Darcy's lips turned down and his brows drew together, then his expression cleared with understanding. "My apologies, sir; I should have been more precise. I am here regarding your niece Miss Lydia."

Now it was Mr. Gardiner's turn to be surprised. "I was not aware you had a particular connection to Lydia," he said cautiously.

"I do not. My connection—my unfortunate connection—is to Mr. Wickham. I feel a certain responsibility for failing to prevent the current situation, and having some knowledge of Wickham's confidantes, I felt I was in a good position to discover his present location."

"I will certainly be grateful for any information you can share with me. Our searches have been fruitless to date."

"I can do somewhat better than that, sir. I have already discovered them, and I believe the resolution is near to hand."

Stunned, Mr. Gardiner pushed himself half-way out of his chair. "You have seen them? Is Lydia well?"

Darcy hesitated. "Miss Lydia is in good health, but I am sorry to say that I was unable to persuade her to leave her present situation, even when I offered to assist her in returning her to her friends. She is absolutely resolved on remaining where she is, expecting they will be wed sooner or later. Under the circumstances, I felt my only option was to secure a marriage between them."

"Is Mr. Wickham agreeable to that?"

"He admitted marriage was not his design, but he has some very pressing debts of honor, and was therefore open to negotiation. He wanted more than he could get, of course, but in time we came to an agreement. He is now prepared to marry Miss Lydia, provided that certain conditions are met."

That was fast work indeed! Mr. Gardiner wondered just how expensive those conditions were. "Of course, the question is how to present this matter to her father. He is hardly likely to believe Wickham is marrying Miss Lydia for nothing more than her charms and her slight dowry."

"Indeed." Darcy looked out the window for a moment, as if gathering his courage. "This matter is my responsibility, and as such I will bear the financial burden. However, I would prefer that none of the Bennets be aware of my part in this."

Mr. Gardiner could not quite repress a smile at this. A secret from all the Bennets? Hardly likely; it was obvious that Lizzy must be party to this whole matter, since it was utterly ridiculous to think that Darcy had any responsibility of his own in this matter, regardless of what he might say. Still, if Darcy wished to pretend that it had nothing to do with Lizzy, that was his business. Clearly he would soon enough be a member of the family, and it would no longer matter. He could hardly wait to tell his wife!

But he only said, "Mr. Bennet is not a fool, and he has his pride. You would perhaps do better to allow him to pay some small part of what is required, allowing him to believe it to be the entire amount."

The corners of Darcy's mouth turned up in a slight smile. "Then perhaps we should discuss the details."

News of Lydia and Wickham

by Maria Grace

August 16, 1812

The narrow vestibule was far too quiet for comfort. An eerie hush had settled over Longbourn since the initial news of Lydia had arrived, punctuated only by moments of Mama's nervous episodes.

How nice it would be to be able to hide in her room, away from the work of the house, and indulge in unconstrained sensibility. But someone had to keep their home in order, and that task was much to Elizabeth's preference. So, to market she would go.

She squared her shoulders and tucked her basket under her arm. Jane tied her bonnet and fastened the buttons on her pelisse. Poor thing looked so pale and haggard. All these days waiting on news from London had taken their toll.

Mrs. Hill handed Elizabeth a list, a long one at that. Though she did not leave her rooms, apparently Mama was well able to organize her thoughts enough to manage a detailed market list. Best not dwell on that too much. Elizabeth tucked it in her basket and they left.

A gust of chill air caught the hem of her pelisse and tore her breath away. A storm was on its way. Had not mama yet learned the danger of sending daughters out in the rain?

She glanced at Jane, her face serene as always. But her eyes held silent notes of sadness. She never spoke of it—she bore it well. Still, the melancholy lingered and might never leave. Jane assured her that all was well, and she would rally in time. But with each passing day, it became more and more difficult to believe.

Who would have ever thought the Bennets of Longbourn would face such a situation? How much had they all learned—or had the opportunity to learn—over the last months.

The inconstancy of friends.

The flightiness of young gentlemen.

The dangers of leaving young ladies unchecked.

The fallibility of her own first impressions.

That was, perhaps, the most galling. How wrong she had been about both Mr. Darcy and Mr. Wickham. How much would that cost them? If only word of Lydia's folly might be contained.

Jane shaded her eyes and squinted into the distance. "Oh, look! I think I see Lady Lucas and Maria on the road ahead. Shall we try to catch them?"

"I think not. I do not fancy her company right now." In truth, there were few she less wanted to see.

"But why not? She has been so solicitous after Mama's comfort, calling on her nearly every day."

Dear, sweet, naïve Jane.

"Do you not see what a danger she is to our reputation?"

"What do you mean? The Lucases have been our friends these many years."

"Friends who have been quick to take advantage of any situation that they might turn to their advantage. You cannot deny—"

"Do not be so harsh, Lizzy. You refused Mr. Collins wholly and completely. Would anything have changed your mind?"

"No, but that is not the point." Elizabeth paused and bit her lip. It was not fair to use so harsh a tone with Jane. "Consider how quickly Charlotte became engaged to him, merely days. It is not difficult to believe a scheme must have been in place."

"A scheme? I cannot believe that. Even if that was the case, what possible scheme could they have now? Do you think Lady Lucas would have wished Mr. Wickham's attentions for Maria?"

"Hardly. Even she is not so desperate, especially when something far more subtle would serve her as well or even better. Consider, she has only to allow news of our misfortune to spread, and any attention that might have been offered to Kitty or Mary might very well turn away from them."

Just as Mr. Darcy turned away from her.

"And they will go to Maria instead? That is a far stretch of thought, is it not?"

"Perhaps, but perhaps not. In her mind though, I am sure it makes sense. Lady Lucas is so convinced in the scarcity of eligible men that I can easily see her counting distracting suitors away from our sisters as a victory for her own daughter. What's more, you cannot deny she has reveled in our misfortune and has not kept secret her own triumphs."

"You are determined to think ill of her." Jane turned to her with that look of admonishment that always inspired a flash of guilt.

"Lydia is not here for me to vent my spleen. It is only natural I should turn it somewhere."

"Please, Lizzy, let go of the vitriol. I am quite certain it is ill-founded. You will see. In Meryton, no one is giving this little upset any mind at all."

"I hope you are correct." Not that she believed it possible, but Jane would be so distraught if she offered any argument now.

The first drops of rain, cold and sharp, fell as they arrived at the baker's shop.

"Good day, Miss Bennet, Miss Elizabeth." Flour smudged the shop girl's face and apron. "What may I do for you today? Has not Mrs. Hill had her usual order delivered already?"

"Indeed she has." Jane said, "But there are a few dainties—"

"Ah, yes, for your mum, I suppose. I 'erd she were feeling poorly these days, take wholly to her bed, no? You ought to call Mr. Fischer. I know he ain't your regular apothecary, but he makes a fine tonic to set any woman's nerves to rights. Me mum's relied upon it for years. Here you go. Will these do?"

She held out a box with Savoy cakes, macaroni biscuits, and orange-flower biscuits.

"Yes...yes, that will be splendid." Jane's hand trembled as she pushed the box back toward the shop girl.

"How came you to the conclusion our mother has taken to her bed with her nerves?" The words hurt to push through her tight throat.

"Begging your pardon, miss, but under the circumstances, what else could it be?" She tied up the box with string and handed it to Jane.

Elizabeth bit her tongue and led the way into the bracing cold and rain.

"I know what you are going to say, Lizzy, but pray do not. Mama's nerves are a well know secret to one and all in Meryton. There is still no reason to suspect she knows more than what everyone in Meryton does."

She should have argued, but Jane's eyes pleaded so. This encounter did not bode well for the rest of their errand.

Elizabeth glanced over her shoulder, in the direction of Longbourn. "Perhaps we should—"

"No, no, I am certain it is not what you think. It will all be well yet."

Cold raindrops splashed their faces as they dodged the expanding puddles on their way to the chandler's. At least the rain remained soft and steady, not the torrential downpour that caught Jane on the way to Netherfield.

The spicy, dusty, sneezy smell of the chandler's shop tickled their noses and scratched their eyes as they entered.

"A dreary day." the chandler called. "Definitely calls for tea, does it not?"

"Indeed, sir, it does." Jane searched her basket. "You make a

487

particular tea blend for Mrs. Hill. She said it is quite calming." She handed him a paper with Hill's handwriting.

He straightened his spectacles and squinted at it. "Yes, yes, I recall this. I should have anticipated the order, what with all the bad news floating about."

"Bad news? What news, sir?"

Who knew Jane could sound so much like Mama.

His eyebrows shot up high over the rim of his spectacles. He opened his mouth.

Elizabeth glowered, borrowing an expression from Hill's repertoire.

"Oh nothing! There is always bad news about, what with Napoleon, no? Do not think me prone to gossip. No, not I. I make it a point never to listen to such drivel myself. I will mix this up for you and bring it right out." He trundled off.

Jane closed her eyes and clutched her temples. "Do not say it Lizzy. I will not hear it. He gives us no reason at all—"

"Please, see reason. It is quite clear—"

"No, it is not. I will not submit to your gloomy conclusions." Jane turned aside and examined a selection of candles on the counter.

Poor dear. The task of caring for Mama was surely compromising her own good sense. Elizabeth loathed to disquiet her, but was it kind or even responsible to aid and abet such self-deception?

The chandler shuffled back in. "Here you go, Miss Bennet. Please send my thanks to Mrs. Hill and my best wishes to the…ah recipient of my tea."

"Thank you." Jane took the box and tucked it into her basket, avoiding Elizabeth's gaze.

Truly? Was that necessary?

Jane's silent disapproval was far more distressing than Mama's shrill wailing might ever be. But it was not fair to punish her when none of this was her fault. She was just the bearer of bad news.

They did not speak the entire way to the apothecary's. Probably just as well. Elizabeth had little that was pleasant to say.

The rain turned heavier and the puddles harder to avoid. The nankeen of her half-boots turned dark with mud and rainwater, soaking into her stockings. How she hated cold, wet feet.

The flat-toned bell tied to the apothecary's door clanged as they entered. Like the chandler's shop, this one was filled with odd herbal scent. Sharper and medicinal, not warm and flavorful. Except for the scents of mint and ginger that wafted from two large confectionary jars on the counter. Colored glass bottles reflected light and cast bright shadows on the walls. The play of light and color had always fascinated Elizabeth as a little girl.

Mr. Scheer peered up from the counter and stared over his spectacles. "The Miss Bennets!" He scurried around the counter and met them halfway across the floor.

They curtsied.

"Pray tell, how is your dear mother? I can only imagine her delicate nerves have her in quite a state."

"At such a time?" Jane's voice was high and thin, pale as her cheeks.

"Forgive my indelicacy in bringing it up so freely, miss. I only wish to be as direct as possible in order to bring relief to your dear mother."

Jane's hand trembled and only a funny squeak came when she tried to respond.

"Thank you for your kindness, sir." Elizabeth stepped slightly in front of Jane. "We are indeed in need of my mother's tonic."

"Of course, of course. I shall have it for you in just a moment." He ducked behind his counter and appeared a moment later, two bottles in hand. I imagine an extra might be in order this time?"

"Yes, yes, thank you."

"I had thought to stop by Longbourn later this afternoon. Just to check up on the mistress, you know. Do you imagine she would be at home for my call?"

"I imagine she would welcome your solicitude." Jane managed a hoarse whisper.

"Forgive my boldness, but would you know, that is to say, is more bad news from London anticipated?"

Jane clutched Elizabeth's arm. Hard. Heaven's! Her fingernails were sharp.

"We cannot know the future, sir, but we are hopeful for good news soon." Elizabeth forced the words through gritted teeth.

The cheek of the man! Bad enough that the gossip had spread to such a degree, but for him to pry so. He might be Mama's apothecary, but surly there were limits as to what liberties that might permit.

Mr. Scheer inched back.

Apparently Hill's glare effectively cowed apothecaries as well as chandlers and scullery maids.

"I am pleased to hear it and I wish the best possible news for you to come very quickly," he stammered.

"Thank you." Elizabeth curtsied and led them out.

Cold damp wind slapped their faces with sharp rain drops as they stepped out into the street.

"Oh, how dare he! To be so forward, so personal!" Elizabeth yanked her pelisse tighter over her chest.

"What horrid, disagreeable weather." Jane adjusted her bonnet against the wind.

Poor dear. That would be as close as she could come to admitting her own distress over the circumstance.

Thunder rumbled over the rooftops. The sky flashed, and before she could draw breath, a violent crack followed. They yelped and ducked their heads into the next sharp gust. The falling drops, heavier and colder now, stung like slaps cross their cheeks.

Jane shivered, her eyes brimming.

Elizabeth grabbed her elbow. "Come, we should not stay out in this."

The post office was close. She dragged Jane inside.

"Frightful storm out there, ladies." The clerk at the desk barely looked up to acknowledge them.

"Indeed sir," Elizabeth brushed raindrops from her sleeves.

"Please, sit down and be welcome until the rain passes." He gestured toward a small bench in the corner.

"Thank you, sir, that is most generous."

"'Tis a shame I already sent out today's post. There were a letter to Longbourn posted from London. You might have had it to pass the time."

"There was?" Jane's teeth chattered. She clutched Elizabeth's hand.

"Indeed, a right thick one too, required extra postage."

"Oh, oh," Jane panted and fanned her face with her hand.

"I hope for all at Longbourn it is the good news you are looking for. I have found that such long letters often contain good news, especially when written by men."

Elizabeth stared at the clerk, head cocked.

"T'was a man's hand that wrote the direction, I would bet my position on it, seen so many in the post you know. No man wants to waffle on when news is bad, you now."

"I...I...suppose."

"We have little experience with male correspondence." Elizabeth forced a smile.

Surely he could not have intended such a vulgar implication. The Bennet sisters did not receive letters from men!

He jumped slightly and waved his hands, face coloring to match the sealing wax on the letters on his desk. "Of course, of course, I should have thought. Forgive me. I did not mean to offend."

491

"No offense taken, sir." Some of the tension left her shoulders.

"I only wish the best for you and your family. Longbourn is always kind to the folks of Meryton. If anyone be deserving of good news, it is you." The clerk smiled and nodded, returning to his work.

Jane squeezed her fingers tight enough to hurt. "It is good news. I can feel it. I am sure of it."

Elizabeth smiled. The post clerk had good point. If it was from Uncle Gardiner, a long letter might well bode better news.

But still, hope was a dangerous thing.

"Look, the clouds are parting." Jane pointed through the window.

More properly, a cloud thinned and the rain dwindled to light misty drops.

"Come, let us hurry home, perhaps the post has already arrived." Jane held the door for Elizabeth.

What point in arguing? The rain had subsided enough and whatever the news, best not wait for it.

Pray let it be good news.

Mrs. Bennet Comes Downstairs

by Mary Simonsen

August 17, 1812

The scene: Mr. Bennet's return to Longbourn after Lydia and Wickham's elopement

"Does your mother still keep to her room?" Mr. Bennet asked his eldest daughter.

As her father already knew the answer, a weary Jane merely nodded.

"Admirable! Truly admirable! If I thought I could get away with it, I should do the same. I would lie in bed in my dressing gown and nightcap and give as much trouble as I pleased."

"Mama no longer spends her day in bed, Papa. She is now in her chair."

"Truly! Mrs. Bennet has moved from bed to chair? Alert the town crier!"

Knowing there was little to be gained by continuing such a conversation, after returning her mother's breakfast tray to the kitchen, Jane went in search of Lizzy and found her in the garden. Since learning of Lydia's flight from Brighton to London with George Wickham, Lizzy had been downcast. She believed if she had succeeded in taking Wickham's true measure during his time in Hertfordshire, the elopement would not have happened.

They were in the garden but a short time when Mrs. Hill came in search of the two eldest Bennet daughters. "A post rider has come with a letter!" the servant announced, and Jane and Lizzy went running to their father's study.'

"What news, Papa?" the pair asked in breathless unison. After pointing to the letter on his desk, Lizzy was the first to reach it.

The paper, a letter from Uncle Gardiner, stated that Lydia and Wickham had been found in Town. After the meat of the letter had been digested, it was determined the couple had not married but would wed upon Mr. Bennet's agreement to settle on Lydia one hundred per year during his life and fifty a year after his death.

Although Jane was elated by the news, Lizzy and her father exchanged glances. How was it possible that Wickham could be induced to marry on so slight a temptation?

"I must tell Mama," Jane said and quickly departed.

Proof of the reception of the news that Lydia was to be wed came with Mrs. Bennet's hosannas seeping through the floorboards and settling, like dust, upon the inhabitants of the study below.

* * *

The news of the impending marriage brought about a miracle. After a two-week absence, the lady of the house took her seat at the dining-room table. As Mrs. Bennet made plans to rent various houses in the neighborhood for the newlyweds, her husband remained silent. But once the servants had departed, he informed his wife that if she wished to visit with the couple, she would have to make arrangements to do so somewhere other than at Longbourn as it was his intention to never welcome the pair into his home.

To that declaration, he added he would not advance so much as a guinea for wedding clothes. "Lydia may enter into marriage in the same way she came into this world—wearing nothing!"

"Oh, Mr. Bennet!"

After supper, Mrs. Bennet asked Lizzy to speak to her father. "It is our Christian duty to welcome the prodigal sheep back into the fold," Mama said, making a hash of the parable.

Lizzy was of a different mind. How dare Lydia mire her family in scandal! There was also the matter of Mr. Darcy. She was now heartily sorry to have acquainted the gentleman with her fears for her sister. Despite the resentment she felt toward her youngest sister, Lizzy understood the realities of village life. If her family were seen to have turned their backs on Lydia, everyone would do likewise. It would only serve to make a bad situation worse.

"What do you want me to say to Papa?" Lizzy asked.

"Oh, you will think of something," Mrs. Bennet said. "You are just like your father—never at a loss for words."

After initially rejecting Lizzy's argument for welcoming Mr. and Mrs. George Wickham into the bosom of the Bennet family, Mr. Bennet saw the wisdom of his daughter's argument.

"I know that tomorrow your mother will be in the village bragging—actually bragging—that she has a daughter well married at sixteen," Mr. Bennet said, shaking his head. "The fact that the man is a villain, a pirate, a scoundrel, will not enter into her thinking. But there will be no peace at Longbourn if I do otherwise than what she asks.

"Now that the matter is settled, do you have any words of joy for your father, Lizzy? Please tell me Mr. Bingley is hiding at Netherfield for the purpose of surprising Jane with an offer of marriage. Or that Mr. Collins has a friend who will marry Mary. Or that the apothecary's son has stopped flirting with Kitty and is moving the relationship forward."

"No, Papa. I have no news to cheer you." Nor would she. Lydia had seen to that.

Mrs. Bennet Persuades Mr. Bennet to Let the Wickhams Visit Longbourn

by Maria Grace

August 19, 1812

Mrs. Bennet's unique rap sounded at the study door just an hour after dinner.

Mr. Bennet leaned his head back into the soft wingback. Even if it was expected, he did not relish the call. She had only begun to come downstairs once again the day before yesterday. Could she not afford him just one more evening of peace?

"Come."

She bustled in, a hen with feathers ruffled, looking for someone to peck. "I would speak with you, sir."

"I assumed that is why you have come." He folded his hands on the desk.

"Then you will listen?" Her eyebrows rose.

"It does not appear I have a multitude of alternatives."

She blinked as though she did not understand.

"I am listening, Mrs. Bennet."

"Oh, very good, then." She pulled her shoulders back and nodded. "I insist you permit our dear Lydia to visit."

And so it began.

"I believe I have already made my position clear on that

matter."

"I recall you voicing your opinion." Her voice rose half a note, definitely off key.

"My decision." He rapped his knuckles on the desk.

"You have not heard my piece on the matter."

"You made your wishes quite clear on the issue. Clear, punctuated with great wailing and gnashing of teeth.

"But you have not heard my reasons."

Reasons! She wanted to argue reason?

"I do not see how that makes any difference."

"You go on and on about how you are such a rational, sensible creature whilst you declare I am not. No, no! Do not dismiss me with that look. You should then listen and hear me out, see if I cannot reason as well as you."

He pinched the bridge of his nose. What kind of travesty of thought would she lay at his feet? His stomach lurched. How disquieting would this be to his sense?

But, how disquieting would his refusal be to his sensibilities? Which was worse?

"Pray madam, tell me your reasons, but do be quick with it." Not that she was likely to abide by such a request.

She settled her feathers and clasped her hands before her like a school girl ready to recite her histories. "As you know, our youngest daughter has been recently married, and they will be on their way soon to the North."

He grunted. Why did she have to tempt him so?

"It is my firm belief that they should come, stay with us. Rather, they should be permitted to stay with us on journey north."

He clenched his hand tightly. "I beseech you, madam, make you point and do so with alacrity."

Little creases lined the sides of her eyes. "Yes, as to that, sir, my reasons for my petitions are first, the servants surely heard your declarations that they should not be welcome at Longbourn. You

497

know how the servants are apt to talk. No doubt the entire neighborhood will know, and what shall they think? More importantly, how will that reflect upon your other daughters? Surely you must see, we have more daughters who need husbands—"

"It seems our youngest had no difficulty in finding a worthless young man to marry her. I do not see why the others should have any difficulties. I cannot admit your reason, nor your initial implication that servant gossip should be any concern of mine."

She sniffed and straightened her shoulders. "I see, well then, my second reason—"

Actually it was her third reason—

"—is the impression you shall impart to your other daughters."

"I have no notion of your meaning, Mrs. Bennet."

"If the other girls see you rejecting your youngest daughter after her marriage, how will they think you will treat them after their own marriages? Consider Lizzy, your decided favorite. Why, if she fears the withdrawal of your affection, she might be reluctant to accept an otherwise acceptable offer of marriage."

He snorted into his hand. "An entirely ridiculous proposition on several counts. If my other daughters marry in such a way, they should very well expect paternal censure and well deserved at that. Lizzy is sensible enough to realize I would not shun her for marrying decently and in order. I will not listen to any more—" He braced his hands on the desk to rise.

"No, Mr. Bennet, you said you would hear me out, and I insist you do as you promised."

He clutched his temples. Unfortunately it would take far longer to win that argument than to simply hear her out. He waved her to continue. If only she would not don that smug expression.

"My third reason applies to your honor and sense of family. Recall that your cousin Collins came to us to mend the rift in your family. Should you now establish another?"

"I might remind you, he also visited during our time of uncertainty to suggest that we should turn our backs on her entirely

498

and never see her again."

"I...I...was not privy to that conversation. I am not entirely certain that was what he said as we only have the reports of the other girls to go by. He is not the kind of man who would contradict himself and I do not think well of you doing it, either."

He chewed his lower lip. In truth, admitting Lydia simply to vex Collins was the most tempting idea she had offered yet.

"Still, madam, you have not persuaded me. It seems no matter what course I take, I shall please Mr. Collins. If that is the case, then I do not see why I should not take the one most in accord with my own opinions."

"Must you take such delight in vexing me?"She stomped and her fists pumped at her sides. Exactly the same expression Lydia used.

"Perhaps I should remind you; it was you who came to me Mrs. Bennet. If you have exhausted—"

"No, no, not so fast, sir. I have one further reason."

"Then, pray, present it quickly that we may finish this conversation and peace may return to our abode."

Her face softened and the steel left her voice. "Are you aware, sir, of what today is?"

"Whatever do you mean?"

"The date, sir. Have you taken notice of the date?"

"No, I have not." He squinted and scratched his head. "Oh."

"Perhaps now you recall."

He removed his glasses. "Yes, Mrs. Bennet, I do."

"You might also recall, not everyone in your family was in support of our marriage. As I recall, your mother favored a young lady with a larger dowry. She did not welcome us at first."

"She never denied us entry to Longbourn."

"No, she did not. And yet," she bit her lip and turned her face aside.

A tear leaked from the corner of her eye.

She had been deeply wounded by his mother's initial rejection. Had that ever really healed?

"In honor of our anniversary, sir. I ask that you might permit their visit."

He threw back his head and dug his fingers into the back of his neck. What logic might he bring to bear to counter such a reason?

None but the most heartless. And he was not a heartless man.

He polished his glasses and sighed. "Alas, Mrs. Bennet, you have indeed overcome me with your reason. I see little alternative but to accede to your request. You may write to Lydia and ask when they shall visit Longbourn."

"Oh, Mr. Bennet." She whispered, dabbing her eyes with the end of her fichu. "You are the best of men."

She turned and looked at him with those same eyes that he fell in love with those many years ago. They were handsome in those days and had not changed that much in the ensuing decades. Yes, she had become silly and nervous, but those feelings had not entirely faded.

"Perhaps we might go upstairs and continue to reminisce over our wedding?" He offered her his arm

She slipped her hand into the crook of his elbow. "A capital suggestion, sir."

Lydia Prepares for her Wedding

by Diana Birchall

August 31, 1812

Mrs. Gardiner entered her husband's study quietly and glided across the room. Kissing him on the cheek, she pulled a chair up beside him and sat down. To her dismay, he looked even more tired and distracted than he had been for the past few weeks.

"Thank you for coming, my dear," he said.

"I am always looking for an excuse to spend more time with you, my love." She placed her hand on his thigh. Their eyes met and for a moment the world and all its problems seemed very far away. She saw the weariness return to his face much too quickly.

"I received a letter this morning from my brother Bennet." Mr. Gardiner rifled through the papers on his desk and finally came up with the one he had been looking for.

"He is not having second thoughts about the wedding, is he?" she asked.

"The letter contains mostly questions about the financial arrangements. He seems relieved he will not have to shoulder financing the majority of the arrangement, but I also detect a bit of guilt as if he feels he should be settling it all himself. I do hope this does not cause problems in the future for our friendship."

"I know it disturbs you Mr. Darcy is doing so much but insisting you take the credit. He has proven to be a most kind and considerate gentleman, not at all what we first thought."

"I have stopped trying to talk Darcy out of taking this all upon himself. He still refuses to hear of accepting any help. But that is not why I asked you to come speak with me. There is news of another sort in the letter which will undoubtedly affect the peace and tranquility in our household."

Mrs. Gardiner sat up. "Everyone is well at Longbourn, are they not?" She had been worried that the distress caused by Lydia's elopement might be too much for Mrs. Bennet's nerves. Everyone worried about Mrs. Bennet's nerves!

Mr. Gardiner patted her hand. "Have no fear. Everyone is well enough considering recent events. No, this concerns Lydia's request for funds to purchase wedding clothes."

"From the look on your face, I can see it is not good news."

He shook his head. "No, it is not. This is certain to send Lydia into one of her rants, but it cannot be helped. Bennet has decided not to send money for her."

"Oh, my," she said quietly.

Her husband looked at the letter again. "I believe his exact words were...yes, here it is: 'not a guinea.' Bennet has also said he does not wish Lydia to visit Longbourn after she is married. He is arranging to send all of her clothes from Longbourn, as well as the things she left behind at Brighton, but that is all. It appears he is washing his hands of her."

"She will not be happy with this news! Everyone will be able to hear her screaming all the way to Hertfordshire." Mrs. Gardiner rolled her eyes. She was a woman of good sense and great patience, but she was rapidly reaching her limit with her niece's antics.

"Surely, he will change his mind about allowing her to visit? Your sister will insist and as we know, she can be very persuasive."

"Yes, some things never change. My sister was always very good at getting her way with our father, and I am afraid her persuasive skills have only improved over time."

Her husband rubbed his thumb over the back of her hand in a soothing manner, as they sat in silence for a moment. She marveled at how different her husband was from his sister, as different as Lydia was from Jane and Elizabeth.

"I wanted to tell you first so you would be prepared," he said. "Frankly, I would almost rather face old Boney himself than give Lydia this news, but it must be done."

"I will tell her. You have enough other, more important things to worry about." Mrs. Gardiner squeezed her husband's hand and released it as she stood and smoothed out her skirts. There had not been much she could do to help Mr. Bennet and her husband in finding the errant couple, but at least this was something she could manage.

"Are you certain? We could do it together." Mrs. Gardiner saw the strain around his eyes and shook her head.

"No, I know you are behind with your work because of her, and the last thing you need is to listen to her whining and simpering again. It is enough that you must endure her at the table every evening." She turned to go, but stopped. "Speaking of supper, if she is too upset, I will suggest, no insist, that she have a tray in her room this evening. I am not certain I would be able to bear listening to her whining through another meal."

"Thank you, my dear," said Mr. Gardiner.

"Actually, I have an idea that might help soothe Lydia's ruffled feathers a bit. I have some leftover fabric in the attic, which should be enough for us to make up a couple of simple new gowns. Of course, we will all have to pitch in to get them done in time. What do you think of my plan?" she asked.

"Brilliant! Anything you wish to do within reason will be fine with me as long as you don't expect me to personally sew any buttons or lace." He laughed. "I will be so glad when this is over."

While the children were napping Mrs. Gardiner went in search of her niece. She found Lydia alone on the window bench in the sitting room, staring out at the street. The girl looked sullen instead of in her usual high spirits.

"Lydia, are you feeling well?"

"I am tired of waiting for the wedding. Why can't we be married immediately by special license? Surely, Mr. Darcy could arrange it."

503

"You know the cost of a special license is very dear, and there is no reason you cannot wait."

Just then a horrible thought occurred to her. "Lydia, there is no reason you must be married immediately, is there?"

Mrs. Gardiner held her breath while Lydia, never the brightest girl, worked out the meaning of her question.

"No reason except that I may die of boredom. I do not understand why we cannot go out to parties or balls. Surely, there are such events going on, even if it is not the season right now. This is London, after all."

Her niece's impatience and impertinence was astounding. Lydia appeared to have no idea of the seriousness of her escapades, and no concern that she had nearly ruined the chances of all her sisters to marry well. Even more disturbing, if she did understand, she did not care. Nothing seemed to matter except parties and balls, and of course, soldiers. How many times had they discussed her transgressions, and it still had not made any impression on the girl!

"You are here for one reason only and that is to be married, not for a ball or a party or any other entertainments. We are working to save your reputation and your family, something for which you seem to have no concern."

Lydia looked at her with wide-eyed innocence. "I have done nothing wrong."

Mrs. Gardiner took a seat next to her niece and put her hands on the girl's shoulders. She wanted to shake some sense into her but refrained as experience told her it would do no good.

"Nothing wrong? Oh, Lydia, what were you thinking?"

"I will be married first before all my sisters."

"That was why you ran off? Because you wished to be first? You are ruined and came just this close to not being married at all. Only your family's intervention saved you." Mrs. Gardner held her thumb and forefinger together in front of Lydia's face as she spoke.

"I knew we would be married sooner or later. It does not matter. I set out to catch a handsome officer as my husband, and I have succeeded. Why is everyone so upset?"

Only good breeding and years of training prevented Mrs. Gardiner's mouth from dropping open. This girl truly had no sense at all.

"My Wickham loves me," Lydia continued, "and I love him."

"That is a good thing since you may very well be married to that man for a long, long time," Mrs. Gardner muttered under her breath. Fortunately, her words did not seem to register with Lydia. Mrs. Gardiner sighed. Best just to change the subject. Trying to explain to Lydia what she had done wrong was like talking to a rock. The words just flowed past her.

"I came to tell you your uncle received a letter from your father this morning. I am afraid he has said he will not be able to send funds for wedding clothes for you."

"I do not believe it!" Lydia cried, jumping to her feet. "How could he do this to me?"

She stomped her foot and started glancing around the room as if looking for something to throw. It would not be the first time in her weeks at the Gardiners' house that she had damaged something fragile when in a temper. Just as Mrs. Gardiner saw the girl's eyes light on one of her favorite porcelain figurines, she decided she had had enough.

"Lydia, I will not tolerate your throwing things in my house. Where are your manners? Your behavior these past few weeks has been deplorable."

"I know this has to be a mistake. Mama wrote that I would have new gowns. It is only right as I am to be a bride." She crossed her arms over her chest defiantly.

"Your father does not have the funds at the moment. He has had to settle the debts Wickham left unpaid in Meryton."

That stopped Lydia, but only for a moment. "If Papa will not send money, then I will ask Uncle Gardiner."

"Lydia! You have done enough to upset your uncle. You will not bother him further with your petty complaints."

"But how can I get married if I have nothing to wear? This is absurd. Next you will be telling me I must be married in my shift," Lydia sputtered.

Mrs. Gardiner sighed. "You will not be wed in your shift. Of all the ridiculous things! Please stop your dramatics. Although your father will not allow you to purchase new things, he has at least arranged to send all your gowns and bonnets from Longbourn."

"What about the clothes I left in Brighton?" she asked.

"Yes, those, too."

"I wrote to Harriet and asked her to have Sally mend the great slit in my worked muslin gown before she packs them up. I do hope she remembers."

"That is all you have to say? You should be thankful to your father for making the arrangements."

Lydia sighed heavily and sank back onto the window seat. "Oh, yes, thank you, Papa. I am so grateful to have nothing but old rags to wear."

Should she just leave Lydia to stew? No, she could not be that cruel despite her niece's behavior. "You do not deserve it, but I have a plan. I have several different fabrics upstairs. It should be enough to make up a few new gowns if we work quickly."

Instead of smiling, Lydia's mouth turned down in a pout. "Oh, Aunt Gardiner, I am simply terrible with a needle. Couldn't we have someone else make the gowns?"

"There is no time or money for that. Even if my maid Mandy helps us, it will take the three of us the rest of the week to complete the gowns. You will simply have to apply yourself more diligently to sewing. It is fortunate I have some spare muslin lying around. That is not always the case, I assure you."

Mrs. Gardiner stood and went to her sewing basket to retrieve a measuring tape, pencil and paper. "Now stand up, Lydia, and we shall begin by taking your measurements."

Lydia stood, looking unhappy but resigned. Mrs. Gardiner thought she might have heard a slight thud of a foot stomp underneath the girl's skirt, but she ignored it and set to work.

Darcy Dines with the Gardiners

by Colette Saucier

September 1, 1812

> *They name thee before me,*
> *A knell to mine ear;*
> *A shudder comes o'er me —*
> *Why wert thou so dear?*
> *They know not I knew thee,*
> *Who knew thee too well: —*
> *Long, long shall I rue thee,*
> *Too deeply to tell.*

When We Two Parted, Lord George Gordon Byron

Soon after the wedding of Lydia to Wickham, Darcy stood between his solicitor and the Gardiners outside the house at Gracechurch Street watching the newlyweds' coach depart for Longbourn, and the last tenuous thread tying him to Elizabeth snapped. In a few hours, they would be with her, the woman he loved whom he would never see again.

Darcy knew scores of reasons he should decline the Gardiners' invitation to dinner, but he heeded only the one reason he had to accept: he could not yet cede all connection to Elizabeth. To himself he acknowledged that, a mere four months before, he would not have deigned to break bread with a family so far below his social strata; and now he could scarcely conceal his eagerness.

The house near Cheapside had defied his expectations. While certainly the furnishings were not comparable to his own in worth, unharnessed from the weight of generations of wealth, they bespoke a lightness, so fresh and new, which Darcy found appealing. The laughter and chatter of children contributed to the harmony that caused a bittersweet sensation to well within him. Here was a home the likes of which he would never know.

During the first courses, an implied moratorium on discussing the inhabitants of Longbourn hung over the dining room table, perhaps no one wanting the recent unpleasantness to spoil their meal. How Darcy craved, though, any word of Elizabeth—even to hear them pronounce her name. Instead, Darcy and Mrs. Gardiner spoke at length of Lambton and her childhood there and all the places in Derbyshire they knew in common.

Darcy then addressed Mr. Gardiner. "And you grew up in Meryton?" Edging ever so slightly closer to the one of whom he longed to hear.

"Yes, that is quite so, although I have not resided in Hertfordshire in over thirty years."

"How is it you came to London?"

"As you might know, my father was an attorney in Meryton, and he hoped I would join him in that profession; but I had my own idea of making it in the world. My father invested greatly in my education and sent me to Oxford for two years."

"Indeed!"

"Yes, but perhaps he erred in that. During breaks, I found myself coming to Town more often than going home to Hertfordshire until I had no notion of returning to Meryton at all. His clerk Mr. Philips took the position intended for me—and my sister, as well!"

Darcy smiled. "So it was you and two sisters, then, growing up?" Darcy could not reconcile this elegant man of good breeding with those vulgar women.

Mr. Gardiner gazed into his wine glass pensively before taking a sip. "You may have noticed that I am more than ten years older than Mrs. Philips and Mrs. Bennet—much like yourself and Miss Darcy. After I was born, my parents did not have any other children for quite some time, at least none that survived. Then my sisters came along not even a year apart, but my dear mother…well, she was not strong. I believe her passing broke my father's heart."

Mr. Gardiner cleared his throat as if the unpleasant memory had caught in his craw. "After raising a son for ten years, my father had no notion of what daughters were all about. Not having a wife to guide him, he left it to the housekeeper to raise the girls, but that was no parenting to speak of. I stayed busy with my studies and treated them like dolls when I paid them any attention at all. Then I went away to school, and I suppose they were left to their own devices, no guidance or discipline."

Darcy comprehended the intent of Mr. Gardiner's story as an apologie for his sisters, and he could not but be moved to sympathize with those motherless little girls—not so different from Georgiana in that regard, but denied the affection and structure his sister had been privileged to receive. He nodded at Mr. Gardiner in acknowledgment.

Darcy turned to Mrs. Gardiner, his patience nearing the end. "You are quite close to your nieces, yes?"

Mrs. Gardiner gave him a knowing smile. "Yes, particularly with Jane and Elizabeth." Elizabeth. "They lived here in Town with us for almost two years."

"Ah, so that must have been when Miss Bennet became acquainted with a young poet."

Mrs. Gardiner smiled. "Why, yes, in a manner of speaking. How did you know about that?"

"I recall hearing that his verse brought an end to the romance." Darcy had often wondered how the two eldest Bennet sisters could demonstrate a comportment unknown to the youngest, and now he recognized the influence of this refined couple. "How did they come to reside with you here?"

"I understand you have heard Elizabeth play the pianoforte, have you not?"

"Yes, I have had that honor." Now that the conversation had veered to his most desired topic, Darcy struggled to remember he was supposed to be eating.

"Elizabeth has a genius for the instrument and might have been quite the proficient. She came here to study with a master; but she and Jane were so close, so we invited them both to stay with us."

"You say she might have been a proficient. Did she stop working with the master?"

Mr. and Mrs. Gardiner passed a look between them as if silently discussing how much they should reveal. "I fear I am to blame," said Mr. Gardiner. "You see, I took Jane and Elizabeth to the British Museum. Elizabeth was fascinated with the Rosetta Stone, as if it unlocked a whole new world to her. With her avid curiosity, she became absorbed with the Ancient Egyptians. She began reading about them, which led to another subject and then another. She soon turned into such a voracious reader, she lost interest in music for the most part. At least she would not practice to the satisfaction of the master."

Darcy scowled in confusion. "Eli– Miss Bennet once insisted that she was not a great reader."

"Her mother believes she ought not spend so much time with her head in a book," said Mrs. Gardiner, "or at least not own it lest she be thought of as a bluestocking, which Mrs. Bennet considers a sure path to spinsterhood. A woman, especially, if she has the misfortune of knowing anything, should conceal it as well as she can."

Darcy marveled at all he was learning about his beloved and yet how clearly he could see how Elizabeth had become the only woman he could love. He smiled and glanced down and, reminded of the plate before him, pushed his food around. "I had been given to believe Mary Bennet the musician in the family."

"Elizabeth taught Mary how to play. We tried to bring her here to study with a master; but after two months, she declared London 'wicked' and returned to Longbourn."

Darcy smiled with his hosts. He recalled his time at Netherfield when he had joined Bingley's sisters in their ridicule of Elizabeth's relations, denigrating her uncle for being in trade without having ever met the man. Now he found he envied him: his light and happy home, his laughing children, his loving wife, all those things Darcy's wealth and status would never provide. Mostly, though, he envied him Elizabeth, that he would see her smiles and hear her play and enjoy her wit—all lost to Darcy.

His envy and consciousness of his own loss, however, did not dissuade Darcy from his next objective. Indeed, realizing the happiness he would be denied made him determined to undo his unconscionable actions so Bingley might have a chance at the joy that he himself would never know. Darcy hoped it not too late to make amends. Many months had passed—perhaps her heart, if ever it had been touched, had now turned against Bingley. Nevertheless, if Jane Bennet harbored any affection for his friend, Darcy must do all within his power to effect a reunion. If that meant he must face Elizabeth again, so be it.

Elizabeth's Letter to Aunt Gardiner

by Marilyn Brant

September 4, 1812

My Dear Aunt Gardiner,

Elizabeth paused in thought and worry. Not that this wasn't an appropriate beginning for a letter, but she was at odds with herself as to what the next line should be. Mentally, she tried out a few possibilities:

> *I have been meaning to ask you about some specifics regarding Lydia's wedding. Aside from you and Uncle Gardiner, the minister and the bride and groom, of course, who else was there?*

No, that made her query too open ended and it was, in fact, not what she desperately wished to know.

> *I'd heard some mention of Mr. Fitzwilliam Darcy being in attendance at my youngest sister's wedding. Could that be true?*

Better, but her aunt could merely confirm or deny his presence. Elizabeth needed to know WHY he was there.

> *Why on earth was Mr. Darcy—of all people!—at my sister Lydia's wedding?!! What possessed you to invite him? Or did he just barge into the ceremony? And for what reason? And for how long? What did he say or do? Tell me everything!*

Ah, that was exactly what Elizabeth wanted to write, but it sounded a bit, well, on the verge of hysterics…even just on paper.

Still, her curiosity on the subject was too powerful to be denied. What was the meaning of Mr. Darcy's attendance at the wedding? Her mind raced for a way to broach her inquiries with tact and

513

delicacy. But ten, twelve, fifteen entire seconds went by and she was no closer to finding the perfect phrasing and, let's face it, Elizabeth knew patience was hardly her strong suit.

She snatched the pen and hastily scribbled:

> *My sister Lydia had let slip that Mr. Darcy was gathered with you all at the wedding, but she likewise revealed that his attendance was not intended to be generally known. You may readily comprehend what my curiosity must be to know how a person unconnected with any of us, and (comparatively speaking) a stranger to our family, should have been amongst you at such a time. Pray write instantly and let me understand it—unless it is, for very cogent reasons, to remain in the secrecy which Lydia seems to think necessary; and then I must endeavor to be satisfied with ignorance.*

"Not that I shall, though," Elizabeth added to herself, as she quickly brought her note to a close. "And my dear aunt," she muttered, "if you do not tell me in an honorable manner, I shall certainly be reduced to tricks and stratagems to find out."

With that, she sealed her letter and called for Hill. She wanted this to be posted at once.

Then she just held her breath…waiting…

Mrs. Gardiner Receives a Surprising Letter

by Abigail Reynolds

September 5, 1812

The morning post brought a letter from Longbourn to Gracechurch Street. Mrs. Gardiner was delighted to recognize Lizzy's handwriting on the outside. Jane's letter reporting the arrival of the newlyweds at Longbourn had satisfied her basic curiosity on the subject, but she knew she could count on Lizzy to provide a more amusing version. She settled herself in her favorite chair to enjoy it.

She was disappointed to see how brief it was, but as she began to peruse it, those thoughts were replaced by astonishment. By the time she reached the last line, she was already on her feet and hurrying to her husband's study, where Mr. Gardiner peered at her over his ledger with an inquiring look.

Mrs. Gardiner waved the letter. "Oh, my dear, I have just received the most startling intelligence from Lizzy! It seems she had no knowledge of Mr. Darcy's involvement in Lydia's marriage, and she writes to me asking for an explanation after Lydia let something slip about his presence at the wedding."

Mr. Gardiner's brows drew together. "She was not aware of it? How can that be? She herself admitted in Lambton that she had told Darcy of their elopement. Of course, he never told me directly that she was aware of his involvement, but I would never have allowed him to act as he did but for the belief of her being a concerned party!"

"I know, my dear. Everything pointed to Lizzy's involvement—his ability to find our house in London, his detailed knowledge of the situation; and of course his admiration of her at Pemberley could not be denied!" She handed him the letter.

He scanned it with a frown. "I assumed that he would be a member of the family very soon. What must he have thought of me, to accept such a sum from a man wholly unconnected to us?"

Mrs. Gardiner laughed. "Do you suppose it would have made any difference, had you refused his assistance? I have never met any gentleman so determined on following his own course. If you had declined his offer, he would simply have gone ahead with it on his own."

"But why has he not made Lizzy an offer? Everything points in that direction."

"Perhaps he wished the matter of Lydia to be resolved before he spoke to her?" Mrs. Gardiner suggested.

"Perhaps so. After all, it would be better to allow this scandal to die down before tying the proud Darcy name to the Bennet family."

"Well, I for one hope he does not wait long! Poor Lizzy must be in such suspense. I will have to send her a reply without delay." She turned to go, then looked back over her shoulder with an arch smile. "Oh, how I will tease her about her great conquest!"

The Wickhams Depart Longbourn

by Maria Grace

September 10, 1812

Elizabeth stood with the rest of the family on Longbourn's front steps. The sun hung high in the sky as Lydia waved her final goodbyes. She edged back to allow Mama and Kitty better vantage.

The ten days of their visit could not have gone more slowly, and the final three had been the longest of all. Especially this morning when Lydia summoned all her sisters to help her pack, as though intending to leave just after dawn, then dawdled over breakfast with Mama until the rest of them left the breakfast room to follow their own pursuits.

Wickham handed her into the hired carriage that would carry them on the first leg of their journey to his regiment in the north. If Elizabeth had overheard correctly, Papa had been applied to for assistance in affording the equipage. Probably the first in a long line of such applications.

Mama waved her handkerchief at the departing forms, her sniffles dissolving into sobs.

"Come, Kitty, help me take Mama to her room." Jane slipped a hand under her mother's arm.

"Oh, Mr. Bennet! Whatever shall I do without my dearest girl?" Mama's voice climbed to a near shriek and she clutched her chest.

He rolled his eyes and glanced at Elizabeth. "You have two equally silly daughters available to take her place, madam. I think you shall do very well, indeed." He tipped his head and wandered inside, probably to his bookroom.

"How could he possibly understand? Replace Lydia? How could he suggest such a thing?!" Mama's hands flapped and her face grew flushed.

"Pay him no mind; you know he does not mean that. Come, Mama." Jane guided her inside, Kitty helping usher her along.

Mary, her expression nothing less than despondent, shrugged and followed them in.

Elizabeth sagged again the door frame. Her ears still rang with Lydia's constant chatter. That was familiar enough to be of relatively little bother, though. But the tension between her and her new brother, should it have grown any stronger, she might snap like an overtaxed rope.

Perhaps it had been a mistake to allow Wickham to know she thought better of Darcy and consequently less of him. But, what was she to do in the face of his insufferable insinuations and attempts to ingratiate himself?

Truly, it was too much to be borne. Particularly in light of what Lydia had let slip about Mr. Darcy and Aunt Gardiner's letter confirming it all as true.

She pressed her cool palms to her heated cheeks.

In all the commotion of the Wickham's visit, she had not yet begun to reconcile in herself Mr. Darcy's role in what happened or what it might mean. The opportunity to do so would probably not afford itself soon either. Not until the house settled back into some form of routine. There was little telling how long that would take.

Elizabeth slipped inside and picked up the sewing she had hastily tossed on the hall table when Lydia finally announced her imminent departure.

She was of no mind to continue sewing, but she should at least return the piece to her sewing basket hastily left in the parlor.

"Oh, Lizzy, I am glad you have joined us." Jane greeted her at the door, pulled her in and shut the door.

Kitty and Mary were already ensconced within, perhaps taking

518

shelter from Mama's nerves.

Jane gripped her arm tightly, almost as though seeking strength, with a hint of desperation.

So much for the welcome solitude of her own room. Ah well, she could seek that after Jane's equanimity was restored.

Jane guided Elizabeth to sit with her on the settee.

Kitty huffed and folded her arms across her chest. "I am so weary of Mama's vapors over Lydia's departure. And I fail to see what is all the great to-do. I think Lydia is quite lucky. She will be surrounded by officers and away from the dreadful dull of Meryton."

"Away yes, but with such a man." Elizabeth murmured under her breath.

Papa was not entirely wrong to consider Kitty every bit as silly as Lydia. But perhaps, without Lydia's constant example, she might be worked on for betterment. And without the regiment in town, it would be easier. Why did the notion weigh like a yoke across her shoulders?

"We must look at this in the best possible light. Lydia is safely married to him, so there has been no lasting harm done." Jane squeezed Elizabeth's arm a little harder.

Mary's jaw dropped, and she sprang to her feet. "No harm done? How can you say such a thing?" She threw up her hands and stalked toward the door.

"Mary?" The words fell from her lips before she knew they were there, far harsher than she would have intended.

"Do not rebuke me for I have done nothing. It is Lydia who is deserving of censure. Her loss of virtue, her wanton behavior, her complete disregard for the rules of decorum and propriety! Or perhaps you, too, consider that of no import."

Elizabeth winced.

Of course, Mary would feel the irony of Lydia's warm welcome so deeply. And not without reason.

"Of all people, Jane, you whose behavior has been called impeccable, I would have though you would find it in you to censure what she has done."

Jane slicked stray hairs back from her forehead. "What point is there in being so harsh, Mary? Truly—what is done, is done. Is it not better to make the best of it all and learn to live together in peace?"

"Indeed. Is it not our Christian duty to forgive her and welcome her back into the bosom of the family?" Elizabeth approached her, but Mary edged away.

"If she is repentant, yes. But I see nothing of repentance in her. Nothing! She is proud of what she has done. Do you not recall her offering to get husbands for us all?" Mary's voice rose, frighteningly like Mama's.

Kitty and Lydia were apt to sound like Mama, but Mary?

"Then you would agree with Mr. Collins, that we should consider her dead to us? What will that accomplish?" Matching Mary's tone was probably not the best way to calm her, but she was not the only one with a weary and bruised spirit.

Jane caught both their arms and urged them back to the settee. She crouched before them, her voice soft and tender. "Lydia will always be Mama's favorite, especially since she is now married. We must content ourselves, despite that truth, for nothing shall affect it."

Mary's eyes brimmed and she hid her face in her hands.

Jane was right, even after Lydia's capricious behavior, the rest of them would still not rise in their mother's esteem and might even fall since they remained unmarried.

Only if they married far and away better than Lydia had would they have any hope of rising in Mama's regard.

"It is not fair," Mary whispered.

"No, it is not." Jane slipped her arm around Mary's shoulder.

Not fair at all, especially considering it was Lydia's doing that would ultimately deny Elizabeth any hope of...Mr. Darcy.

But why then had he done so much for Lydia?

What could it all mean? Surely she could make some sense of it if she applied herself to understanding.

Beside her, Mary sobbed softly.

But that would have to wait.

Mary leaned into her shoulder, shuddering.

Perhaps for quite some time.

Darcy and Bingley Decide to Return to Netherfield

by Kara Louise

September 10, 1812

Darcy climbed the steps to the small town home Bingley had leased in London. He was grateful his friend was no longer residing with his sister and her husband, as this allowed them to visit without Miss Bingley hovering about them.

Bingley had been unsuccessful in locating a home in Town that suited him. Darcy believed there was more to his friend's apathy than just not finding anything to his liking; in fact, he was convinced it was due to him still yearning for Miss Jane Bennet.

Darcy stopped at the door and closed his eyes as he considered all that had happened in the past few months. The exultation of finding Elizabeth walking the grounds about Pemberley—despite the initial awkwardness—gave him hope for a second chance with her. He had watched in delight as she and Georgiana seemed to share an instant affection for each other. Suddenly those months of self-loathing after Rosings were erased from his thoughts.

But then there was Wickham. How dare he run off with Miss Lydia! It incensed him! He was furious with himself, however, for not being open about the man's character, but he was also grateful he had been able to salvage the situation for Elizabeth's benefit. He did it solely for her, knowing there was no guarantee that she would ever return his love.

Darcy had debated whether to encourage Bingley to return to Netherfield, for even though it would give his friend much delight in being united with Miss Bennet again, he would be thrown in Elizabeth's company. He doubted he would be able to endure another rejection from her.

But now he was ready. His friend had suffered too long, and he was determined to make things right. The thought still caused him turmoil as he considered seeing Elizabeth again. She had been most cordial to him and his sister while at Pemberley, but there was no guarantee that her feelings had changed since she had refused his offer. But at least his friend would be happy. He would do it for him.

He lowered his head and began to rub his jaw. Should he confess to Bingley that he had seen Miss Bennet in Town earlier this year? He slowly nodded his head. Yes, he would, but after they arrived in Hertfordshire. There was no sense getting Bingley's hopes up if Miss Bennet's heart was no longer inclined towards him.

"Darcy!"

Startled, Darcy looked up to see Bingley at the door.

"What are you doing here? Did you knock?" He turned to the butler. "Did you not hear him knock?"

Darcy put up his hand. "I had not yet knocked. You are on your way out. But pray, do you have a moment to talk?"

"For you, my friend, I will make time. I was just on my way to the Hursts. Please, come in."

Darcy gave his friend a nod of thanks and entered, walking past Bingley's outstretched arm. "This sounds important, Darcy. I hope nothing is wrong."

"Nothing is wrong, but I want to discuss something and hear your thoughts on the subject."

The two men walked to the sitting room and sat down. Would you like something to eat?"

Darcy waved his hand. "Thank you, but no." He sat erect with his elbows resting on the arms of the chair, his hands tightly clasped as his friend eyed him expectantly.

"I was wondering whether you ought to return to Netherfield."

Bingley reacted to his friend's words with a quick jerk of his head. "I still have possession of it for a few more months, but I did not feel that I should..." Bingley took in a deep breath and his brows lowered as he glanced down. "I do not think I should return."

Darcy unclasped his hands and dropped them to tap his fingers on his leg. Very softly, he asked, "Do you still love her? Do you still love Miss Bennet?"

Bingley shook his head several times before he spoke. "Oh, I have tried to forget her. I have tried desperately, but to no avail." He met Darcy's eyes. "I am in earnest, good friend. I know your thoughts on the matter, but I do still love her."

Darcy was silent for a moment and looked down at his hands. He deeply regretted what he had done and how much it had hurt Bingley. "I would suggest, then, that we return."

Bingley's eyes widened and his jaw dropped. "Do you really believe that I should?" Bingley's words tumbled over one another. "Do you think...do I dare hope...am I understanding you correctly? You want me to return to Netherfield?"

"Most definitely, and I will accompany you."

Bingley stood up and clapped his hands together. "When shall we leave? I can be ready by tomorrow morning."

Darcy put up his hand to stay him. "You ought to first send word to have the housekeeper prepare for your arrival. Send a message today and in a week's time we shall depart."

"Oh, yes! So good of you to give such wise advice!" He let out a satisfied huff. "I am going to Netherfield!" He looked back at Darcy. "Do you really believe this is best?"

"I cannot guarantee how events may transpire, but I hope that everything will work out for the best."

"Yes! I am certain it shall!"

The two men stood and Bingley approached his friend. "I could hug you, Darcy!"

Darcy laughed softly. "Please, do not. Save it for Miss Bennet... when it is appropriate for you to hug her."

"Yes, I shall! And I must get that missive sent to Netherfield directly!"

The two men said their goodbyes, and Darcy departed. He stepped out the door and drew in a deep breath. His friend was eager and confident that Miss Bennet would receive him as warmly as he hoped. He could only hope her sister would do the same for him!

Jane Ponders Bingley's Return

by Kara Louise

September 19, 1812

"Now," said she, "that this first meeting is over, I feel perfectly easy. I know my own strength, and I shall never be embarrassed again by his coming. I am glad he dines here on Tuesday. It will then be publicly seen that, on both sides, we meet only as common and indifferent acquaintance." - Chapter 54

Later that evening, Elizabeth peeked into Jane's room and saw her sister sitting quietly on her bed. "May I come in?" she asked.

Jane turned and smiled. "Please, do."

Elizabeth walked in and sat down next to Jane. "I thought Mr. Bingley looked well today."

"He looked just as I remembered him." Jane unwittingly trembled.

Elizabeth laughed softly. "Yes, he has aged quite well in the... ten months since you have seen him."

"Oh, Lizzy! One does not age in ten months! But it was good of him to come. And Mr. Darcy, as well."

"Oh, yes! I was rather surprised he accompanied his friend to pay us a visit." Elizabeth shook her head. "He was so silent and..." She took in an unsteady breath. "Actually, I think several of us were a little unsure of what to say." She smiled at Jane.

"Was I terribly quiet?" Jane asked. "At the time I thought I was speaking, but I fear most of my words were swirling about in my head." She cast a regretful glance at her sister. "Do you suppose he thought me terribly uncivil?"

Elizabeth patted Jane's hand. "No, I do not believe Mr. Bingley thought so. He was amiable enough for all of us."

"Yes," Jane sighed. "He is the most amiable man... I suppose the two men are paying calls to everyone in the neighborhood."

Elizabeth tilted her head and glanced at her sister. "That may be true, Jane, but I believe, that in the three days since they arrived, this is the very first call they have made."

Jane's eyes widened. "Do you truly think so, Lizzy?" She then furrowed her brows. "But we cannot be certain, and even if it was, we cannot assume there was any particular reason for them to visit us first."

"Perhaps not, but I noticed Mr. Bingley looked at you quite often."

"You must be imagining things, dear Lizzy. He and I both behaved as though we are merely good friends." Jane straightened her shoulders and gave Elizabeth a determined look. "I am quite certain I shall be perfectly at ease from now on when I see him."

Elizabeth took Jane's hand. "Yes, now that the two of you are merely good friends," she said with a teasing smile. "You just keep telling yourself that."

Jane looked down at their entwined hands, squeezed her sister's hand, and released it. "But that is all I can be assured of now." She stood up and folded her arms across her, and walked away from the bed. "I know what you are thinking, Lizzy, and I must ask that you not give me false hopes. It is bad enough that Mother constantly expresses all her aspirations, not to mention the speculative glances I receive from people in the neighborhood since his return." She spun around. "Promise me you will abide by my wishes. I need you to help me be sensible about what his feelings are for me."

Elizabeth stood up and walked over to Jane. "I will do anything for you. You will not hear me even mention that man's name again, and I promise not to look at you in any manner you might deem to be a teasing glance. My dearest Jane, you have my word!" She drew Jane into a hug, and as she looked over her sister's shoulder, she could not keep a half-hearted smile from appearing. She could certainly smile for Jane, but wondered whether she had the same assurance for herself. Did Mr. Darcy still possess the same affection for her?

Darcy and Bingley Dine at Longbourn

by Cassandra Grafton

September 22, 1812

Though the clock on the mantel had long chimed the hour, Darcy remained motionless at the window of his room at Netherfield. He knew he should present himself downstairs before he and his friend departed for Longbourn, yet he felt so little inclination for the evening ahead, he had yet to make any attempt at doing so.

It was but a few days since he and Bingley, newly returned to the neighborhood, had paid a call on the Bennet family; but what had it served? With a heavy sigh, Darcy turned away from the window. Bingley had seemed sufficiently satisfied; had he not been bounding about the house like a pup in need of exercise for the remainder of the day? It seemed a few minutes in the company of Miss Jane Bennet was all he required to raise his spirits and have him believe aught a possibility! Why could Darcy not harness some of that *joie de vivre*?

Because you were given naught of hope, whispered a voice in his head. Elizabeth's silence, her seeming reluctance to enter into conversation and the seriousness of her air and countenance had been sufficient discouragement. The marked change in her demeanor since last they met could be attributed to only one thing: Wickham!

Out of patience, Darcy pocketed his watch before walking out onto the landing. What did he expect? Their unanticipated re-acquaintance at Pemberley in the summer, though bearing its own awkwardness at first, had been untainted by the intelligence of the near ruin of Elizabeth's family. Had he not long suspected the lady would lay some blame for all that had happened at Darcy's door—after all, it was he who had chosen to conceal Wickham's true character from the populace of Meryton to ensure the protection of his sister, was it not?

Making his way swiftly down the stairs, Darcy forced away his regret. His interference may have achieved something—yes, the marriage had been a hushed up affair, but that it had taken place at all and the couple dispatched far off to the north, away from any gossiping acquaintance, would be certain to allow the Bennets to recover from such a stain sooner rather than later—but at what cost?

Wickham was now Elizabeth's brother. If there was a family ever in need of one, it was the Bennets—and yet he was *such* a man!

Was it any wonder the lady had shown such reluctance to speak to him? Darcy shook his head as he reached the entrance hall. No wonder at all.

* * *

Darcy's reluctance for the evening to begin paid him no service. He and Bingley were duly deposited at Longbourn by the coachman and before either of them could reach for the bell, the door was swept aside and they were ushered in to face Mrs Bennet, who was holding court in the entrance hall.

"Laying in wait for her prey," Darcy muttered under his breath as they handed their hats and canes to a servant.

"Mr *Bingley*! How delightful to see you again at Longbourn. You have become quite the regular visitor!" Bingley looked a little confused by this, but Darcy had no doubt the lady's raised voice and satisfied smile as she glanced regally about was aimed at anyone but themselves.

"And you have brought your friend," the smile had vanished, as had the unctuous voice.

Darcy bowed formally, spoke briefly to Mr Bennet who seemed to be drawing his habitual amusement from the scene, and stalked over to a nearby doorway whence came the sound of voices.

"Miss Elizabeth!" Bingley beamed at her as he joined Darcy, Jane Bennet already at his side. "May I say how *very* well you look this evening?"

Darcy almost rolled his eyes. Not only was his friend a master at stating the obvious, he had taken the very words Darcy himself had been summoning because, as usual, just the sight of Elizabeth had been enough to rob him of speech.

The lady curtseyed, her smiles all for Bingley other than the amused glance she cast in her sister's direction. "You are too kind, Mr Bingley, and far too generous with your praise, as I am certain all the ladies present will soon attest to."

Darcy almost laughed; Elizabeth remained as astute as ever.

It was a moment before he realised Bingley had gone, however, following in the wake of Jane Bennet, and he and Elizabeth stood alone, slightly removed from those guests still milling around in the hallway. Mrs Bennet, he noted briefly, had abandoned her position now her guest of honor had arrived, and was following Bingley into the room opposite with at least as much studied attention as he was giving her eldest daughter.

"Miss Elizabeth."

"Mr Darcy."

"I trust you are in good health?"

"As you see, sir."

"And your family? Are they also well?"

Elizabeth cocked her head on one side. "You would do well to ask them yourself, Mr Darcy; other than my youngest sister, my immediate family is all present."

"Of course. Forgive me."

"For what, sir? Displaying good manners?"

"No—no. I—er…"

With a smile, Elizabeth turned to greet a lady who just then presented herself and frustrated with his own ineptitude, Darcy bowed formally and walked reluctantly across the hall to join the other guests.

Two long hours later, whatever patience Darcy had managed to cling onto was wearing thinner than ever. He had anticipated the unwelcome obligation of being seated to one side of his hostess, but he had depended upon Bingley being on the other, and therefore the focus of all Mrs Bennet's attention.

Yet Bingley had quickly succumbed to Jane Bennet's charms and taken a seat beside her, and though his friend had sent him an apologetic look, he had looked far too satisfied with his choice. Conscious that Elizabeth had observed their silent exchange he had turned away and succumbed to the inevitable.

Never had time passed so slowly as he was presented with course after course—far more than was necessary for a small country dinner such as this—with naught to distract him. To his other side was a woman with whom he was not acquainted, and opposite sat Sir William Lucas, who bore with Mrs Bennet's constant twittering with far more grace than Darcy.

His glance was, more often than not, directed down the table to where Elizabeth sat—possibly almost as far distant as she could be, but clearly enjoying her dining companions—Bingley on one side and a young gentleman bearing a clerical collar with whom he was unfamiliar on the other. How he envied every word spoken to her.

His hostess, meanwhile, barely offered a word in his direction, for which he was entirely thankful. Her constant droning was an irritation he sought to ignore, but so vociferous was she in demanding her guests' comments on the fare put before them, it was almost beyond him.

Praise was sought for the soup and then for the venison, whether the guests had chanced to sample a morsel or not. As for the partridges, she had had the temerity to turn to him directly and demand his opinion, which he had given as succinctly as he could but clearly to her satisfaction, as she thereafter left him in peace.

With what feelings of relief did he finally observe Mrs Bennet indicating to the ladies to withdraw? Getting to his feet, Elizabeth finally looked in his direction, but her air and countenance were grave and with a slight inclination of her head, she turned to leave the room with her sister; he could take no encouragement from this. Then, he sat down heavily. What on earth of encouragement *could* he expect from her after her similarly solemn manner and uncharacteristic silence the other day?

However, the period of separation, which he had believed would stretch interminably before him, was over before Darcy was fully prepared. He had not stirred from his place at the table as the port was liberally passed, and Sir William, who seemed to think it would be discourteous to leave him in peace, had remained in his place opposite.

For the first time, Darcy appreciated the gentleman's propensity for inconsequential chatter; beyond uttering an occasional monosyllabic response, Sir William seemed content to prattle away, leaving Darcy to mull over Elizabeth. He had felt all the embarrassment of their meeting the other day, but had hoped this evening for...*what*? What had he hoped for?

Some indication, some encouragement, perhaps; any sign of some sort that their rapprochement at Pemberley could be reclaimed, that those tentative steps towards each other—which had teased him with the first soft tendrils of hope—were not lost forever.

The scraping of chairs was sufficient to rouse Darcy from his introspection, and he followed his host out of the room and along the hallway, uncertain as ever of how to proceed.

On entering the room, his eye was drawn immediately to the lady who held his heart. She and her sister made a charming picture, with Miss Bennet making tea and beside her, Elizabeth, pouring coffee. It took a mere second to acknowledge that there was nowhere near her to place a chair, and what might she think should he do so? A memory of the Netherfield Ball swept through him, and he sighed. Paying marked attention to Elizabeth was a leap into the unknown, and he was none the wiser today whether she would welcome the attention or regret it.

Bingley nudged him in the arm and nodded towards the ladies, and Darcy had no choice but to fall into step beside his friend. Barely had his eye met Elizabeth's however when a young lady nearby pulled her chair even closer and began whispering to her. With no other option but to take his cup of coffee and walk away, Darcy crossed to the opposite side of the room where both Bingley and Mr Bennet soon joined him.

They sipped their coffee in silence at first, their backs to the hearth and thus able to observe the room—though for Darcy, only one corner could hold his attention.

"And how does the air of Hertfordshire agree with you, sir, on your second acquaintance? Is it more fair or foul than before?"

Darcy's gaze fell upon Mrs Bennet, clucking away with a gaggle of women, the name of his friend liberally falling from her tongue. "I find the neighborhood little altered in the interim. Time moves on, yet human nature remains the same. "

"Good heavens, Darcy, I must beg to differ! It is all as delightful as ever, Mr Bennet," Bingley turned to his host, his genial smile widening. "I once declared I had never met with friendlier people than I did in Hertfordshire, and on my return I find them even *more* so!"

Mr Bennet grunted. "The removal of the Militia is an improvement, do you not agree, Mr Darcy?"

Darcy could do little but incline his head for fear of speaking too much and as he had little else to contribute, Mr Bennet turned his attention to Bingley. Draining his cup, Darcy glanced over at Elizabeth again; unless he was mistaken, she had at that very moment withdrawn her gaze from him. It was all the encouragement he needed to at least attempt a few words, and waving away a hovering servant, he walked slowly across the room to where Elizabeth remained with the coffee pot.

Before he had chance to speak, however, the lady turned to him with the first sign of animation since his return.

"Is your sister at Pemberley still?"

He nodded. "Yes, she will remain there till Christmas."

"And quite alone? Have all her friends left her?"

Darcy hesitated; he had no inclination to claim Bingley's sisters as friends of Georgiana. Then, he realised Elizabeth was looking at him expectantly, and he cleared his throat.

"Mrs Annesley is with her. The others have been gone on to Scarborough these three weeks."

Elizabeth said no more. Was it his turn to think of something? What should he say? Staring into Elizabeth's dark eyes, drinking in the charming sight of her, he could think of naught of any sense, as his feelings consumed him; if he *could* but speak, it would not be of inconsequential nothings.

The young lady seated beside Elizabeth had no such compunction, however; taking advantage of the silence, she began whispering once more to Elizabeth, and Darcy deposited his empty cup on the serving table and walked away.

The intolerable evening worsened. Mrs Bennet, on seeing him standing aloof, swept him into a place at a nearby table for a hand of whist, overriding any attempt he made at being excluded. Glancing over his shoulder with a sigh, he soon detected Elizabeth, seated across the room at a different table, after which he played appallingly, losing well—much to his hostesses' delight—and though he ought to have blamed Elizabeth, for it was she who drew his eye repeatedly, he could in all honesty blame no one but himself.

With what relief did he escape into Bingley's carriage, thankful it had been ordered ahead of the others, for Mrs Bennet was making noises about detaining them to supper after the other guests had departed. He could endure no more forced civility over a repast, even if in Elizabeth's presence. With such awkwardness between them, there was nothing of pleasure to be gained from extending the evening.

535

Declining Bingley's offer of a nightcap, Darcy took the stairs two at a time, closing his chamber door with relief, finally able to reflect on the success or otherwise of this brief return to Hertfordshire.

What had he achieved in coming here? His avowed purpose had been to see whether Jane Bennet retained her partiality for Bingley, as Elizabeth had long ago alleged, but he had no reservations in owning to himself that his *real* purpose had been to see Elizabeth again, to try and judge if he might ever hope to earn her regard, her affection.

Walking over to the window where he had stood earlier, he stared out into the darkness consuming the grounds. At first light, he would make a long overdue confession to his friend. Seeing Elizabeth had not answered for his hopes and dreams, but he could at least attest to having achieved one thing: he had been in error, as the lady had asserted to him in April. From his own acute observation, he saw now what he had blinded himself to last year, that Miss Bennet, despite her reserved manner, showed sufficient genuine admiration for his friend, and he was obliged to own his mistake and hope Bingley would hereafter forgive him his poor counsel.

On his own situation, he could not dwell at present. There would be more than sufficient time after his return to Town on the morrow, and beyond that, he refused to think.

Darcy Believes a Quiet Elizabeth Does Not Care

by L. L. Diamond

September 22, 1812

Darcy entered the carriage and glanced back at Longbourn while he waited for Bingley to join him. The outside of the house was quiet—as quiet as Elizabeth was when he called at Longbourn. Why had she been so distant? So aloof? Such qualities were simply not a part of her nature.

When he and Bingley called after their first arrival in Hertfordshire, he could not procure a seat near her—a mishap that prevented him from any sort of attempt at a private discourse. Not that one could have much of a private discussion with Mrs. Bennet in the room. That woman was on a mission and not even the presence of someone she disliked so vehemently would dissuade her. Mr. Bingley would wed Jane Bennet if she had to lock them in a room and hide the key!

God help Bingley should he purchase an estate near Meryton!

Bingley bounded into the equipage, and rapped his walking stick upon the ceiling.

Darcy pivoted and stared at the house. Perhaps Elizabeth would stand at the window—something, anything to give him some hope. Alas, she was not there. His chest constricted and prevented him from inhaling a deep breath.

Why had she been so quiet? During their initial call, Elizabeth appeared discomfited when they were shown into the room, but once they were seated, she concentrated so on her embroidery to the exclusion of most of the room. Even when he inquired of the Gardiners, she gave such a succinct answer. A trait he would never have ascribed to the Elizabeth Bennet with whom he was familiar.

"They were very well when we last heard from them, Mr. Darcy."

The words echoed in his mind and his stomach clenched.

She could have elaborated, could she not? He would have been pleased to speak of her aunt and uncle, any subject that might induce a conversation. But, she never responded with any more than what was polite before glancing at Bingley and Jane or returning to her needlework.

Elizabeth had even asked about Georgiana, but again, after he had responded, she bit her bottom lip, nodded, and returned to her sewing. Nothing further.

"Darcy!"

He started and looked at Bingley, whose head was tilted forward and amusement radiated from his features.

"Have you not heard a word I have said?"

He swallowed a frustrated exhale. "No. I apologise."

"Miss Bennet appeared well, do you not think?"

He pressed his lips together hard, holding back the growl that threatened to escape. He needed to consider Elizabeth's behavior and not her elder sister! Could Bingley not make a decision for himself just this once!

"She appeared very well and pleased to see you."

Bingley's countenance brightened. "Do you think so?"

"I do."

"Mrs. Bennet was certainly welcoming."

He bit back a snort. That woman would admit a complete stranger into her home if she discovered he was eligible.

But never mind Mrs. Bennet! Could he have been mistaken at Pemberley? Had Elizabeth merely forgiven him and been polite in company? If so, how could he have misread her behavior yet again?

She had not been comfortable in their company just now. That much was evident in her mannerisms during dinner. She shifted in her seat a number of times, her eyes widened in response to several of her mother's effusions, and she had difficulty maintaining eye contact with him—a problem she had never had in the past.

When the men had returned to the drawing room after dinner, Elizabeth had been pouring coffee with Miss Bennet. He could not have approached her then as the ladies had crowded around the table. She had not a single vacancy near her, and one lady had shifted particularly close for no reason he could fathom.

"Darcy?"

His head whipped around to where Bingley stared at him with his eyebrows knit together.

"Have you not heard a word I have said?"

Darcy exhaled. "My mind is elsewhere. Again, I apologise, but I have a great deal of work awaiting me. I am afraid it has dominated my thoughts since we departed Longbourn."

"You are always busy." Bingley shook his head as he faced forward. "You must remain at Netherfield for some shooting. After all, Mrs. Bennet offered the best of Mr. Bennet's covies when we have killed all of our own." Bingley wore a wide grin. "Very hospitable of him, is it not?"

Darcy's lips quirked upwards. "Quite neighborly."

Elizabeth had turned a brilliant shade of red when her mother made that statement. Her feelings towards her mother were clearer than her feelings towards him. How could he proceed without such knowledge? Another rejected proposal was more than he could tolerate. His heart could not be rent in two once again!

"Darcy!"

A footman stood at the open door of the carriage, and he looked out to find they had arrived at Netherfield.

"What has you at sixes and sevens? You are never so distracted."

"I would rather not speak of it at present, Bingley. I do hope you understand."

His friend's forehead was creased and his eyes narrowed. Bingley's concern did him credit, but Darcy would not reveal his heart so soon.

Bingley continued to natter on as they ascended the steps and entered, but other than hearing the noise, Darcy did not make out the words. As his valet helped him refresh himself and change, he replayed both visits to Longbourn.

When he took a seat at the desk in the library, he gave a heavy sigh. He had to have been mistaken at Pemberley. Elizabeth could not return his feelings and be so quiet in his company. She was never reserved. The only conclusion could be that she did not wish for his presence.

His chest pained him as he picked up the nearest piece of blank paper and his pen. He would return to London on the morrow. There was nothing left for him in Hertfordshire—not if Elizabeth lacked the tender feelings required for her to accept the offer of his hand.

He placed his pen to the paper and paused as an image of Elizabeth seated beside Georgiana at the pianoforte came to mind. Was he doomed to love her for the rest of his life while she carried on with her own, as she married and had children.

A wetness touched his finger and he flinched. A blot worthy of one of Bingley's missives stained the letter he had yet to pen. With a groan, he crumpled the page and tossed it into the grate.

This time he would write the correspondence. No more images of Elizabeth. He had to leave Hertfordshire. He could not remain and face the torture of another call where she was so grave and silent. He had to leave his beloved Elizabeth behind.

Bingley Hears Darcy's Confession

by Susan Mason-Milks

September 23, 1812

At first, Bingley was certain he had misheard his friend. Then his confusion turned to anger as he took in the implications of what Darcy was saying.

"I should plant you a facer right now." Bingley jumped to his feet, but instead of moving to hit Darcy, he began to pace.

Darcy sat up very straight in his chair and stared off across the room as if he could not bear to meet his friend's eyes. "I would not blame you at all if you wished to hit me."

"How could you? You knew I loved her!" Bingley, who never raised his voice, heard himself shouting. In an attempt to keep himself from carrying out his threat, he held his fisted hands at his side.

"Last autumn, I thought I was looking out for your best interests when I told you I did not think Miss Bennet held you in any special regard. I now believe I was wrong. I am sorry. Truly sorry."

Darcy's words stunned Bingley. This strong, confident man had never apologized to anyone for anything, not in the entire time Bingley had known him. Bingley wrinkled his brow as he digested this new information.

"What changed your mind? Is this based on something you learned or on your own observations?"

"The latter. In our two recent visits with the Bennets, I watched her closely. What I thought was indifference I now believe is her natural modesty."

"Yes, that is what I always believed, too, but you convinced me...and I..." Bingley's voice trailed off. He scrubbed his hand through his hair.

"I was mistaken about her in so many ways. I interpreted her calm manner as a sign of indifference, that she was only following her mother's instructions to trap a wealthy husband."

"She is not deceptive, just reserved."

Darcy nodded. "But even if I had been correct in my assessment, I was wrong to have interfered at all. You and you alone should have judged her interest. You spent time with her and were in a much better position to know her heart."

Bingley took a deep breath and closed his eyes to better envision the beautiful lady who was the subject of their discussion. He sighed. "Miss Bennet is an..."

"Yes, I know. She is an angel," Darcy said, managing a half smile.

Bingley felt his anger melting away at the mention of his favorite way of describing Miss Bennet. "Soon I hope she will be *my* angel. I must go see her immediately."

He was starting for the door when Darcy said, "Wait, there is one more thing I must tell you."

"Something else?" Bingley's smile turned to a frown.

Darcy hesitated as if what he wished to say was causing him actual pain. "I concealed something from you for which I am now heartily sorry."

"You had best just tell me," Bingley said, impatiently.

"Last winter, Miss Bennet was in Town for two months, staying with her aunt and uncle in Cheapside. Your sisters saw her and decided to keep it from you. They shared this intelligence with me and begged me not to tell you either. At the time, I thought it the best course of action."

Bingley felt his temper rekindling, and he resumed his pacing.

"Again, I know I overstepped. I should have told you what I knew and let you decide for yourself."

"She called on my sisters, and they did not tell me?" Bingley picked up a book and thought about throwing it. He had to find a way to get rid of this unfamiliar anger burning inside him. He slammed the heavy volume on the table and glowered at his friend. "You conspired with my sisters? How could you do that to me? You knew I was suffering terribly being separated from her."

Darcy looked resigned. "If you cannot forgive me, I will understand. My interference was inexcusable."

Seeing his friend so obviously suffering was not easy for Bingley. Slamming the book had helped a bit. Envisioning putting his arms around Jane and kissing her calmed him even more. He walked to the window and looked across the fields in the direction of Longbourn, just beyond the last visible rise.

Miss Bennet had never been out of his mind the entire time he had been away. Waking and sleeping, she had haunted him! Many a night he had restlessly walked his room while thinking of her. After hearing Darcy's confession, Bingley's first inclination had been to blame his friend and sisters for these months of misery and suffering, but he was beginning to recognize some of this was his own fault. Because he did not like conflict, he often gave in to others, especially his sisters, even when his own instincts told him otherwise. This was an important lesson to him that he should have more faith in his own judgment. At last, he felt calmer, more in control.

Turning away from the window, he saw Darcy was staring at the floor. Bingley walked over and put a hand on his friend's shoulder. "You cannot take all this on yourself. I am at least partly to blame. It is a mistake I will not make again."

This conversation seemed to mark a shift in the balance of their friendship. Bingley was always the one who looked up to Darcy almost as an older brother. He realized now he had been depending on his friend too much. If he was going to be the kind of man who deserved the love of someone like Miss Bennet, he was going to have to make more decisions on his own. She would be counting on him - that is, if she accepted his proposal.

"You are off to Town this morning?" Bingley asked.

"Yes, I have some business there."

"Do you know when you will return?" Bingley asked, shifting the conversation away from the topic that had become much too personal and uncomfortable. He was very careful to say "when" and not "if."

"So I would still be welcome here?" Darcy asked quietly.

"Of course. You are always welcome in my home." It was the best way Bingley knew to let Darcy know he was forgiven.

Mr. Bingley Proposes

by Susan Mason-Milks

September 26, 1812

Charles Bingley had never experienced such nervous anticipation in his life. Today was the day. No excuses. No delays. Today, he was going to ask Miss Jane Bennet to be his wife. He'd been looking into the mirror rehearsing what to say when James, his valet, interrupted him.

"Are you ready to dress for the day, Mr. Bingley?" the older man inquired politely as he entered the room.

Bingley's heart did a wild dance. Was he ready?

"I would like to look my very best today," he said nervously running a hand through his unruly hair.

James raised an eyebrow. "I do not believe, sir, that I have ever allowed you to leave your dressing room on any day looking anything less than your very best."

That brought a smile to Bingley's lips and some of his nervousness vanished. "Of course, you are completely correct. I trust your good taste implicitly. Now what have you planned for me today?"

When Bingley finally stood before the mirror to examine himself, he was very pleased with what he saw. Then James held out his pocket watch, brushed the back of his coat one more time, and pronounced him ready. Just as Bingley was almost to the door, the valet rushed after him.

"One more thing, sir," James said holding out a fresh handkerchief.

Bingley looked at him quizzically. "I believe you have already provided me with one of these."

"I was just thinking, that today of all days, you might wish to have another available. In the event that…" James' voice trailed off. He was clearly somewhat embarrassed.

"In the event that what?" Bingley repeated quizzically.

"If Miss Bennet…in case she is so happy that…well, you know women can be rather emotional in circumstances such as this," James explained.

Finally, Bingley understood. "How did you…?"

"Mr. Bingley, many years ago your father commissioned me with helping you learn to look and act like a true gentleman. In the course of the past ten years, I have come to know you, and well, I just had a feeling that today was the day."

Charles Bingley marveled at how James sometimes seemed to know his very thoughts before he himself was even aware of them. Bingley touched the pocket in his waist coat where he had tucked the ring he planned to give Jane when she accepted him.

"Wish me luck then."

"I do not believe luck will be required, sir. And let me add that your father would be very proud of you indeed."

Bingley decided to ride rather than take the carriage. The fresh air and exercise would be good for him. Darcy had returned to Town the day before and would be absent for more than a week leaving Bingley very much on his own. The conversation had been tense when Darcy had explained how he had withheld knowledge of Miss Bennet's presence in London last winter. Bingley had been shaken, but as he considered what that confession must have cost his friend in terms of pride, he found it easier to forgive him. The look of relief on Darcy's face had been genuine. For years, Darcy had been like an older brother to him. Finally, Bingley was seeing this complex man in a clearer light. Darcy was not infallible, and he had wisely acknowledged that deciding whom to marry was a choice only Bingley could make.

After just a short time in Hertfordshire, he knew he was more in love with Jane Bennet than ever. Most importantly, this time he was certain it was love and not just infatuation. Last fall, when he had talked to Jane, danced with her, courted her, he had been so in awe of her beauty that he had failed to fully appreciate her other qualities—qualities that in a wife were even more important than her elegant profile, porcelain skin and golden hair.

The long winter months had afforded him an abundance of time to contemplate what he had given up. When he compared Jane Bennet to the other ladies he met and to his own sisters, there was really no one quite like her. What he loved about Jane was how she always believed the best of people—even of him. She had been so quick to forgive him that he wondered daily what he had ever done to deserve her. He also loved how she never shared gossip of any kind. Every time he heard his sisters tittering and giggling, he knew it was at someone else's expense.

After reaching the decision to return to Hertfordshire, he had recognized it was time to assert himself with his sisters. He was, after all, the head of the family, and could no longer afford to have Caroline manipulate him. Bingley smiled as he thought back to that day in London when he had announced he would be traveling to Netherfield for some hunting. The ten-minute-long tirade from Caroline and Louisa about what a mistake he was making had been unpleasant and actually, rather boring. It did not matter to them that he had already heard their extensive list of objections numerous times before. Listening without saying a word, he had bubbled over inside with impatience. Prior to making the announcement, he had decided not to argue with them, as it would just prolong the confrontation. His mind was made up; nothing would change it.

During the entire conversation, Darcy, who happened to be visiting at the time, was curiously silent in spite of Caroline's efforts to solicit his help and take their side. "I expect Bingley knows what he is doing," was all Darcy would say.

When it reached the point at which Bingley thought his head might just pop off his neck and launch itself toward the ceiling, he finally did what he knew he should have done ages ago.

"Caroline! Louisa! Stop!"

Their shock was so profound at hearing their gentle brother raise his voice that they actually ceased speaking for a moment and sat with their mouths open in surprise.

"You are my dear sisters, and I would do almost anything to secure your happiness," he began, "but what I will not do is give up the one person who is so essential to my own happiness that I cannot imagine a life without her. I am going to Netherfield, and if I discern even the smallest sign that Jane Bennet still holds me in high regard, I plan to ask for her hand!"

"Dearest Charles, one would think you do not believe that your well-being is the most pressing and important concern in our lives. Of course, we want everything that is good for you. It is hurtful to think you do not believe we care," said Caroline with a pout and a barely audible sniffle.

Bingley opened his mouth to say what he usually said in these situations when Caroline managed to make him feel guilty, but this time was different. He stopped himself.

Very softly, he said, "And furthermore, I will not tolerate a single disparaging word from either of you about Miss Bennet or any other member of her family. They may soon become our family, and you will treat with them with the utmost respect — even Mrs. Bennet. Am I understood?"

When there was silence, he made his best effort to turn up the intensity of his glare and repeated, "Am I understood?"

Louisa had the good grace to nod and look a bit sheepish, but Caroline simply watched him with an air of studied boredom.

"Caroline? Should I take your silence to mean you wish to go live with Aunt Emmeline in Manchester until next spring?"

Suddenly, Caroline's eyes grew wide. Aunt Emmeline was the one person in the family who would brook no nonsense from her and had the potential to make her life a misery. Manchester in the winter? Cut off from the London season? Caroline would rather dress in burlap sacks!

She sighed heavily for effect before she spoke. "No, Charles, I promise I will do my very best to make the Bennet family feel welcome. May I ask when we leave for Netherfield?" Her voice suddenly turned sweet as honey.

"Darcy and I are leaving tomorrow. You and Louisa are staying in London until I send for you."

"But, Charles, dear, who will…," Caroline began.

Bingley stared at his truculent sister and mouthed one word— "Manchester"—causing Caroline to turn instantly white.

"Is there anything I may do to help you prepare for your journey?" she said brightly. He knew she was only pretending, but at least it was a start.

Once inside the carriage and on their way to dinner at their club, Bingley leaned back in satisfaction stretching out his legs and putting his hands behind his head. "I do not know about you, Darcy, but I am ravenous. I feel as if I could eat an entire cow at one sitting!"

Darcy gave his friend one of his rare smiles. "Standing up for yourself is very hungry work, Bingley. I congratulate you."

Now he was on his way to Longbourn, and despite everything that his family and friends had tried to tell him, he felt confident in the strength of Jane's affections. There was no artifice to Jane. No saying one thing and meaning something else as those coy young ladies he had met in London. Last fall, nearly a year ago now, when his sisters and Darcy had confronted him, his own lack of confidence had caused him to be swayed, and he had nearly lost her. For reasons he did not fully understand, but for which his heart rejoiced, Jane had forgiven him for abandoning her. That was a mistake he would never make again.

Later that evening when it was time for Bingley to retire, he found James waiting up for him in his dressing room. Before the valet could begin his work, Bingley asked him to pour a glass of brandy for each of them from the bottle he had requested be placed there. Darcy was gone, his family still in London, so there was no one else with whom he could share his elation.

"I hope you will drink a toast with me on this special occasion."

Picking up the glass, the valet looked at Bingley expectantly.

"A special occasion, sir?" he asked, although Bingley was certain the news of the engagement had already traveled from Longbourn to Netherfield earlier in the day.

Bingley could not stop himself from grinning. "This morning Miss Jane Bennet made me the happiest of men by accepting my hand in marriage."

James looked as pleased as Bingley had hoped he would be. "Congratulations, sir. That is indeed excellent news! If I may be so bold as to say, sir, you have made a wise choice. Miss Bennet is a lovely young lady, and I am certain you will be very happy together."

As they sipped the rich brandy, a strange awkwardness descended. Although a conversation such as this was not so unusual between them, for some reason, tonight, it felt odd. James seemed to sense his master's mood and began to ask about Bingley's activities for the following day so he would be able to plan his wardrobe. When the brandy was gone, the valet deftly took up his work. Once ready for bed, Bingley started toward his bedchamber but hesitated as he reached the door. So many things were running through his head, so many things he would like to say, but he realized that something important had shifted. Soon he would be a married man and head of the family in a way he had not been before. He would have to rely more on himself and on Jane. In the past, he might have said more, but tonight, he did not.

"Good-night and thank you," he said with simple sincerity, and then he waited for James' usual response.

"My pleasure, sir."

Bingley smiled to himself and headed off to bed.

Mr. Collins Shares Gossip with Lady Catherine

by Mary Simonsen

October 2, 1812

Charlotte Collins scanned the walls of the reception room of Rosings Park looking for something on which to fix her attention, her eyes settling on a magnificent Gobelin's tapestry of very large dogs bringing down a stag. Following hard on the heels of the mastiffs were riders with spears poised in preparation for finishing off the wounded beast. While Charlotte made a study of the grisly scene, her husband, the Reverend William Collins, studied the face of the tapestry's owner for some clue that she wished for him to begin a conversation. When Lady Catherine raised her teacup to her lips and pointed her extended small finger in his direction, he saw it as a sign that he might begin. Instead, the great lady spoke.

"I noted in your garden, Mr. Collins, that your vegetables are of a middling size. If the soil is not properly prepared in the spring, you will never achieve the size or volume of the vegetables produced here at Rosings."

"Yes, of course, Your Ladyship. But you may recall my early efforts yielded exceptionally large cucumbers and radishes. If the vegetables had not gone missing, I could have shown you a cucumber as long as—"

"Mr. Collins, you need not mention your cucumber every time you visit. As you are the only one who saw this gourd of mythical size, I am convinced it existed only in your mind."

I have seen it, Charlotte thought, and a slight smile crossed her lips.

Anne de Bourgh gave her mother a sideways glance. Mama knew very well that the cucumber was no illusion. Not only had she seen it with her own eyes, she had tasted it the very next day when, at dinner, cucumber sandwiches, garnished with sliced radishes, had been served at table.

"Your Ladyship, I can assure you—"

"Mrs. Collins, have you any news from Hertfordshire," Lady Catherine asked, turning the conversation away from the missing gourd. "Are your parents in good health?"

Charlotte informed Lady Catherine that all was well at Lucas Lodge and that there was no news to report. As Her Ladyship loved "news," Mrs. Collins statement earned a look of displeasure.

Noting the look of unhappiness on his patroness's face, Mr. Collins chimed in. "Although there is no news from Lucas Lodge, there is news from the neighborhood."

"Mr. Collins, why on earth would I care to hear stories about people who are not of my acquaintance?"

"Well, this particular bit of news concerns Mr. Charles Bingley, a friend of your nephew, Mr. Darcy."

Lady Catherine chewed on this revelation before declaring Mr. Collins could share the report.

"We have had a letter from Charlotte's sister, Maria, who, you will recall, visited us at the Parsonage last—"

"The news, Mr. Collins, the news!"

"Mr. Bingley is to be married to my cousin, Miss Jane Bennet of Longbourn Manor," the parson hurriedly said. "She is the sister of Miss Elizabeth Bennet, whom you met last April when she—"

"If this report is true, then Miss Bennet has made a most advantageous marriage," Lady Catherine said, interrupting—again. "Although Mr. Bingley is a man of inferior rank to my nephew, I understand he is very rich and a gentleman."

This declaration startled Anne. *Is Mama admitting that a man, not to the manor born, can be a gentleman? Is she actually shedding some of her prejudices?*

"Of course, Mr. Bingley must never come to Rosings Park. I do have standards," Lady Catherine added, and Anne sighed.

Encouraged by her responses about Mr. Bingley and Jane Bennet, Mr. Collins added that Maria's letter contained a bit of neighborhood gossip that might be of interest to Her Ladyship. A look of alarm appeared on Charlotte's face. In an attempt to warn her husband that he should not share that particular item of news, she coughed, twitched, and affected a fake sneeze before finally clinking her teacup with a tiny spoon. But all was for naught as Mr. Collins blurted out Maria's news.

"Apparently, during his time here in Kent, Mr. Darcy formed an attachment for my cousin, Miss Elizabeth Bennet. With Mr. Darcy's return to Netherfield Park, Mr. Bingley's home in Hertfordshire, there is speculation that an announcement of an engagement will be forthcoming. It is said—

"An engagement!" Lady Catherine rose up from her chair, and after growing to a prodigious height, she aimed a lightning bolt at Mr. Collins's heart before sentencing the parson to the heat of Hades where he would be purged of the sin of telling malicious falsehoods—or at least that is how Anne imagined it. Lady Catherine's actual response was only slightly less dramatic. In a screech that could be heard in the village, Her Ladyship called for her butler so that her carriage might be ordered.

"Your destination, milady?" the butler asked.

"Longbourn Manor, Hertfordshire!"

Lady Catherine Leaves Longbourn in a Dudgeon

by Diana Birchall

October 3, 1812

Lady Catherine de Bourgh sat very straight in her seat in the chaise. Her always formidable mouth was compressed into an angry, thin line, and there were patchy spots of red on her cheeks. The waiting-woman, Mrs. Dawson, a widow forced into service owing to her poverty, shrank back onto the other side of the seat. Since tersely directing the coachman to drive at all speed to Mr. Darcy's London residence, Lady Catherine had not opened her lips; and the speed and energy of the four post-horses she had hired, seemed to promise that they would reach their destination in a very few hours.

It was not until they were quite out of sight of Longbourn, Meryton, and anything connected with the vile Bennet family, and indeed fast approaching the Hertfordshire border as they pounded down the good, smooth turnpike road, that she spoke.

"I am excessively displeased," she said. "My journey has been for nothing."

Mrs. Dawson might have said that her employer's displeasure was evident, but she knew much better, and only murmured a sympathetic sound, inviting her Ladyship to say more.

"That girl. That pert, uncouth creature. I tell you, she intends to marry my nephew!"

"The Colonel, do you mean, my Lady? That will be too bad, won't it?"

"No!" Lady Catherine exploded. "Don't pretend ignorance, Dawson. That is as good as insolence and I shall not brook any such thing. You know very well I mean Darcy, and that Pemberley will be —rooo-hooo-ined!" At this point she gave a great glottal gulp and reached for her lace handkerchief.

If she knew nothing else, Mrs. Dawson knew how to deal with hysterical fits, in employers and their daughters alike; and she brought out a practiced technique in soothing. The smelling salts, the lavender-water bottle, the powder-puffs and the linen were all brought out of her handy well-stocked reticule, and applied over Lady Catherine's broad, red face, to the accompaniment of little mewing sounds and caresses. She straightened her Ladyship's lace head-piece, which resembled the figurehead on a ship's prow, and had slipped sideways with the bounce of the carriage, in a most undignified manner.

"I am very sorry to hear this, my dear Lady Catherine," she said apologetically. "No wonder you are distressed. I thought how it might be, when you did not direct coachman to take us to Lucas Lodge."

"What business had you to think at all, Dawson?" Lady Catherine expostulated. "Naturally I would not remain in the same county with that impertinent young woman for ten minutes longer than necessary. The Lucases do not deserve the honor of a visit from me. I am certain they have promoted this disgraceful match."

"Oh—but surely—they would not dare—"

"Speak only of what you know, Dawson. News of this wretched attachment came to me through their means, as they wrote to rejoice over the connection with their daughter, Mrs. Collins. Her stupid fool of a husband brought the tidings to me at once. They want the privilege of visiting at Pemberley, mark my words, and they completely forgot what they owe me."

"What—what do they owe you?" Mrs. Dawson ventured timidly.

"Loyalty!" Lady Catherine spat out. "And respect! After all the attentions I have bestowed upon them, and the great notice I have paid to their daughter. To promote my nephew's marriage with that girl, from a low, disgraced family, her sister no better than a—" She stopt and wiped her face.

"Perhaps it is not so bad as you fear," Mrs. Dawson consoled. "They are not actually engaged, are they?" "No," Lady Catherine conceded, "and I will take care of Darcy." She nodded. "Yes, I will remind him of what he owes the family, of the duty he owes to me, who have always loved him so tenderly and been a second mother to him."

"Indeed you have," breathed Mrs. Dawson, over the rattle of the carriage.

"I will represent to him," she continued, "every mutinous, insubordinate phrase that girl used. I remember them all. She pretended not to know what I came for—she dared to deny that she and her family and the Lucases have spread the report of the attachment themselves—and she refused to confess that she has used her arts and allurements to infatuate him!"

"Did she indeed," said Mrs. Dawson, not without a sympathetic pang for Elizabeth, "that was very bad."

"Bad! You may well say that. Even when I explained the nature of the engagement subsisting between Darcy and Anne, she utterly refused to promise not to marry him!"

"Poor Miss de Bourgh will be very sorry," agreed Mrs. Dawson, a little tactlessly. "It will be a great disappointment to her. I know she has always looked forward to being mistress of Pemberley."

Lady Catherine could sit it no longer. She reached out with her heavy, ham-like hand, made no lovelier by the delicate lace half-glove that draped it, and slapped Mrs. Dawson in the face. "Be silent!" she fumed. "It is not your place to say what your superiors think and feel."

"No, ma'am," muttered the poor woman, casting down her eyes to hide tears and rubbing her reddened cheek, where a handprint mark was swiftly forming.

"You are lucky I do not turn you out of this carriage, and dismiss you without a character. But I am ever celebrated for my extreme charity and tenderness of heart."

"To be sure, my Lady," replied Mrs. Dawson, as she knew she must.

"Where are we now? Coachman!" called Lady Catherine. "Can you tell us how many miles from London?"

"Tisn't that far now, your Ladyship," he bawled back, "we just passed the turnpike post sign, and it ain't more than a matter of another twenty mile or so."

Lady Catherine sat back with some satisfaction. "There. We should be with Darcy by dinner time. You may close your eyes if you like, Dawson; I am going to revolve in my mind what it is I will say to my nephew."

"Very good, your Ladyship," said the other woman obediently, and shut her eyes, exhausted. Before she could fall into a fitful doze, however, Lady Catherine spoke again. "I will tell him," she said, "that Miss Bennet is stubbornness itself; she has a nasty little spirit of independence, and obduracy, and contrary-ness, and she has told me herself that she is determined to have him."

"Did she?" asked Mrs. Dawson, opening her eyes.

"She as much as said so. I threatened her with all that would befall her, were she so foolish as to go through with her scheme; she should be shunned, and censured, and disgraced. You may well conceive, however, that she was only thinking of the advantages of being Darcy's wife. She cares for the man not at all, only the place. I pressed her hard, Dawson, very hard; but to all my representations, and importunings, she held to her position with a firmness that is positively uncanny in so young a woman. Mark my words, if Darcy does marry her, he will find himself tied to a termagant."

"I have no doubt," said Mrs. Dawson faintly.

"Yes. And that is what I am going to London to tell Darcy. Of the ambition, the calculation, the headstrong determination of this girl, who is bound to ruin him entirely."

"I daresay he will be very much concerned," said Mrs. Dawson.

"I mean he shall be," said Lady Catherine with some satisfaction. "You wait and see, I will open his eyes and show him what this young woman really is, a scheming creature; and we will have Anne at Pemberley at last, I am perfectly sure of that."

"I hope we will," echoed the waiting woman obediently.

Lady Catherine Calls on Darcy

by Abigail Reynolds

October 3, 1812

Darcy was not accustomed to having to make excuses. He had manufactured enough business to keep him in London for over a sennight, but now he had to make a decision: either return to Netherfield as he had told Bingley he would, or come up with another excuse for the delay. The logical option would be to return to Pemberley, but that would be intolerable. Georgiana was waiting there for him to return with news of his engagement to Elizabeth, news that would never come. Bad enough to be forced to live without the woman he loved; facing Georgiana's disappointment was more than he could bear.

His butler knocked on the study door. "Sir, Lady Catherine de Bourgh is here to see you. I told her you were not at home, but she insisted on coming in, so I asked her to wait in the sitting room."

Lady Catherine? She was the last woman in the world he wished to see at present. If she had come to press him about marrying his cousin Anne—and why else would she travel all this way?—he did not know if he could keep his countenance. Not now, when the memory of Elizabeth's quiet avoidance of him at Longbourn was still fresh in his mind.

Unfortunately, there was no choice but to see her. If he refused, she would force her way in, and he could not ask his servants to stop her. He capped the inkbottle and stood. "Very well, I will see her there. I assume she will expect refreshments."

"I have already ordered them, sir, and taken the liberty of telling her ladyship I believed you have an important dinner engagement."

"My thanks." Yet another excuse, and this one he was glad of.

In the sitting room, Lady Catherine had enthroned herself upon the chair Darcy's mother had always favored. The dust of the road still covered her skirts. "There you are, Darcy. You need to speak to your butler. He had the effrontery to tell me you were not at home."

Darcy bowed, although his aunt had not done him the courtesy of rising. "He was following my instructions."

"No doubt, but he should have known better than to think those instructions applied to me! As if I were not already vexed enough!"

He did not care if her vexation gave her an apoplexy, but the sooner she came to the point, the sooner she would be gone. "What has vexed you so?"

"That girl! That obstinate, headstrong girl! Completely unreasonable!"

So Anne must have finally told her mother she had no intention of marrying Darcy. It had taken her long enough. What precisely did Lady Catherine think he could do about it, even if he wished to? "No wonder you are vexed."

"She refuses to obey the claims of duty, honor, and gratitude, and is determined to ruin you in the opinion of all your friends, and make you the contempt of the world. I should not have believed it possible! Such a rude, impertinent, presumptuous girl!"

Something was wrong. Anne had many faults, but impertinence was not among them. "Are you speaking of my cousin, madam?"

"Of course not! Anne would never behave in such a despicable manner. That girl is perfectly ready to ruin all our plans for you and Anne!"

"Of what girl are you speaking?"

"Do not toy with me, Darcy! I speak of Miss Elizabeth Bennet, of course. Now what have you to say to that? She told me to my face that she was willing to drag you into disgrace!"

560

Darcy's hands clenched on the arms of the chair. "You have seen Miss Elizabeth Bennet?"

"Did I not just say as much? Of course I have. I called on her to demand that she have the report universally contradicted, and she dared to refuse! She refused *me*! And *this* was her gratitude for my attentions to her last spring!"

Leaning forward, Darcy said, "What report is this?"

"The report that not only was her sister was on the point of being most advantageously married, but that *she* would, in all likelihood, be soon afterwards united to *you*. My own nephew! Though I *knew* it must be a scandalous falsehood, though I would not injure you so much as to suppose the truth of it possible, I instantly resolved on setting off to make my sentiments known to her. But I had misjudged her; she is determined to snare you, Darcy. *You* must make it clear to her that you would never degrade yourself so far as to offer for her, and the best way to do it is to announce your engagement to Anne. You must send the notice to the newspapers tomorrow." She sat back with a triumphant expression.

Automatically he said, "I am not marrying Anne." But then her words sank in. Elizabeth had said she was determined to have him? Could it possibly be? "I pray you, what did Miss Elizabeth say?"

Lady Catherine tossed her head. "She said nonsense of every sort, even that she thought herself your equal because her father is a gentleman. As if he is your equal! And I do not begin to speak of the atrocity which is her mother's family, nor of her ruined sister. How could she believe you would ally yourself with Wickham's sister-in-law? She is quite mad!"

Darcy gritted his teeth and spoke very slowly. "What precisely did she say about me?"

"Well, there is no need for you to use that tone, nephew! Your mother taught you better manners than that."

Crossing his arms, Darcy silently glared at her. He could outwait her if needed, but he must know what Elizabeth had said!

Lady Catherine sniffed. "Not only would she not contradict the report that you were to be married, but she refused outright to promise me she would not enter into an engagement with you! Have you ever heard of such a thing?"

Had he heard correctly? Elizabeth would not agree to refuse to marry him? Why in heaven's name, if she truly did not want him, would she say such a thing? If she were firmly set against him, she would have said so, frankly and firmly. But that meant... An incredulous smile began to grow on his face.

"I can see, nephew, that you find it as difficult to believe as I do! But I assure you it is true. Her presumption knows no limits! You must take action at once before these rumors spread any further."

"Take action?" Darcy drummed his fingers lightly on his chair arm, more because he could not remain still rather than out of impatience. "I assure you, Lady Catherine, I will indeed take action, and immediately. Oh, yes, I will take action." Could he ride for Hertfordshire yet today? He glanced out the window. Blast it! It was almost dusk. He would have to wait for tomorrow. It was going to be a very long night.

"I knew you would do the proper thing, Darcy. You have never failed in your duty to your family."

Duty? He had a duty, true enough, but it was to make Elizabeth and Georgiana as happy as he could. He jumped to his feet. "I am most grateful to you for your timely intervention. I will make it my first priority. But now I must ask you to forgive me, as I have an urgent engagement tonight."

"Urgent? Hmmph. I am glad you at least understand you need to put an end to this nonsense with Miss Bennet."

"Indeed I do." Oh, yes, he would put an end to this nonsense. An end which would lead to the altar and his ring on Elizabeth's finger. It could not happen soon enough!

Mr. Bennet Hears from Mr. Collins

by Shannon Winslow

October 4, 1812

Mr. Bennet reposed in his library after breakfast, his feet propped up on a stool and a highly enjoyable book before his nose. With the most troublesome of his daughters permanently gone from the house and the most angelic one advantageously engaged, he had little left to wish for but that the peace of his household might last. He did not expect it to, however. Just as the little tyrant across the channel could not seem to behave himself for long, so too his own wife and at least one of his offspring were bound to soon involve him in another round of hostilities.

But the interruption that particular morning came from an entirely different source, and one not at all unwelcome. It was a letter—a letter from his cousin Mr. Collins.

In the months since the renewal of their acquaintance, Mr. Bennet had come to regard Mr. Collins's correspondence as a priceless source of amusement. He would by no means have given up the association on any grounds less consequential than the impediment that death itself would have constituted. So Mr. Bennet tossed his book aside; the newly arrived missive promised the finer entertainment.

He was not disappointed.

The absurdity of the letter's style—all affected humility and artificially formal language—was just what Mr. Bennet had come to expect. But the content was far beyond anything he had imagined.

It began predictably enough with an extravagant discourse in congratulations of the approaching nuptials of Mr. Bennet's eldest daughter.

…You may be assured, my dear sir, that Mrs. Collins and I send our very sincere felicitations to my cousin Jane and to you, her honored parent. What a triumph for you all—especially after that most regrettable affair with your youngest daughter—that your fortunes are so quickly on the rise again. I must confess that it has astonished me exceedingly. The thing speaks in credit to Mr. Bingley, I suppose, that he is so generous as to overlook what many certainly could not have—that is, your family's fatally tainted circumstances. He must be a gentleman of true worth, as well as being one of greater consequence than my cousin had any cause to hope for. I am sure you are all to be heartily congratulated on forming such a favorable alliance.

From these flattering and solicitous remarks, Mr. Collins moved on to his real purpose for writing, and to what was for Mr. Bennet the truly diverting portion of the letter. It seemed that the pompous clergyman had got it into his head that Mr. Darcy was violently in love with Elizabeth and meant to make her an offer.

"Oh, this is admirable!" Mr. Bennet told himself, laughing aloud after reading this delightful passage. "Mr. Darcy, of all men!"

Had Mr. Collins canvassed the whole world, he could not have hit upon a more ridiculous notion and a less plausible suitor for Mr. Bennet's favorite daughter. That Lizzy should be the romantic object of that proud, disagreeable man stretched the limits of credulity. Lizzy, who had been so outspoken in her pointed dislike of the man! Surely her true sentiments could not have escaped anybody's notice. Regardless of his high opinion of himself, Mr. Darcy could not be such a fool as to contemplate approaching her.

Mr. Bennet chuckled as he pictured the scene that might ensue if the man ever tried. No doubt his high-spirited daughter would make quick work of poor Mr. Darcy. She would probably hiss like an incensed feline at his first avowal of affection, and threaten to scratch his eyes out if he ventured anywhere nearer the question than that. It would certainly be a sight to behold, one Mr. Bennet would give a tidy sum to witness for himself.

The rest of the letter was pure Mr. Collins—his obsequious attentions to Lady Catherine de Bourgh's opinions in the matter (she disapproved, not surprisingly), his not-so-subtle hints of what was due that lady's opinion, and his intended kindness in warning the Bennets against crossing her. Then there was the bit about Charlotte's interesting situation, the expected young "olive-branch," which struck Mr. Bennet as being in poor taste to mention.

Finally Mr. Bennet could no longer keep these overpowering temptations to mirth for himself alone, not when his daughter would likewise appreciate the absurdities involved. Leaving the sanctuary of his library, Mr. Bennet ran straight into the person he sought.

"Lizzy," said he, "I was going to look for you; come into my room…"

Bingley Brings Darcy ~The (Second) Proposal ~Elizabeth Confides in Jane

by Colette Saucier

October 6, 1812

Mrs. Hill rushed up the path from Meryton to Longbourn, anxious to bring Cook the ducks and spices required for the elaborate dinner Mrs. Bennet had planned for Mr. Bingley that afternoon. If only Mrs. Philips had not detained her, begging that she pass the message to her sister that Miss Bennet's engagement had indeed hushed the gossip surrounding the elopement of Miss Lydia—er—Mrs. Wickham. Honestly! Has the woman not sense enough not to speak of such matters to the housekeeper? Even one who has been with the family four and twenty years. But Mrs. Philips and Mrs. Bennet both readily relied on the assistance of the servants to bring them news.

Mrs. Hill's thoughts were thus occupied when she noticed the approach of two young people. Assuming they to be Miss Bennet and her Mr. Bingley, she took a deep breath and adopted a smile to greet them; but within a few steps, the couple halted, and she realized it was not Mr. Bingley but his friend Mr. Darcy—and in close conversation with Miss Elizabeth!

Her polite smile faded as she stopped walking. They had not yet noticed her, quite seriously engaged and—Good gracious!—Mr. Darcy had taken Miss Elizabeth's hands in his! A genuine grin now spread across Mrs. Hill's face as she quietly slipped off the path into the sparsely wooded grove.

Mrs. Hill scurried towards Lucas Lodge then back on the path to Longbourn and entered the Bennet house through the kitchen where the cook and a housemaid were at work on the meal preparations.

"Thank heavens, Mrs. Hill!" cried Cook. "You are finally come. I hope you have my mace. It seems we are to have another guest at table today."

"Mr. Darcy?" Mrs. Hill responded with a sly smile.

"Aye, which means we must have mutton and veal." Cook stopped chopping the onion before her. "How d' you know?"

"I've just seen him on the path to Meryton—and with Miss Elizabeth."

"Was not Miss Bennet and her beau with 'em?"

Mrs. Hill shook her head. "I expect we shall be hearing of another engagement soon enough."

"D'ya mean it?" asked the maid. "Miss Elizabeth and that tall, handsome Mr. Darcy?"

"Aye, Katie, the very one—master of that grand estate, Pemberley!"

"But he is such a proud, unpleasant kind of man. Not nearly so pleasant as Mr. Wickham or Mr. Bingley. Oh! But he is very rich. Isn't he, Mrs. Hill?"

"Mind your work there, Katie," said Cook. "I suppose now he will be a daily visitor just as Mr. Bingley. The mistress says he has three French cooks!" She rammed the knife blade through an onion. "No rest for the weary, all I can say. We'll need plenty o' butter for the vegetables, Katie. And you got my pepper, Mrs. Hill, and my cloves?"

"Yes, yes, it's all there along with your ducks. Quite a heavy parcel, walking from Meryton," said Mrs. Hill. "I have found Mr. Darcy quite agreeable, if a bit shy. And, Katie, you watch yourself around that Mr. Wickham."

"Does this mean Mr. Collins won't turn us out of Longbourn?"

"No, Katie. The estate is just as entailed as ever, and that odious man is still to inherit, but with two such wealthy sons, my mistress is sure to keep her own household when the master passes and not have need to live at Netherfield, and she will require servants. We will be secure."

"Or mayhap I could be a maid at Netherfield—or Pemberley!"

"I'd not want to be goin' to Pemberley, I's you," said Cook. "Derbyshire is far north, away from everyone you know."

"You's not be goin' to Pemberley anyway, now would you," said Katie, "seeing as Mr. Darcy has three French cooks already."

Cook pulled back on the knife. "You mind your tongue there, Katie, or I might be of a mind to cut it out."

Their attention was soon captured by the sound of the front door closing and voices in the drawing room, and they were arrested in silence.

"Is that Miss Elizabeth come back?" Katie finally asked in a whisper.

They listened a moment before Mrs. Hill went out to the dining-parlor and called to the footman.

"Miz Hill, the mistress is asking after you," he said when he entered the kitchen.

"Who is just come in, Harold?"

"'Tis just Miss Bennet with Mr. Bingley." Then looking around at the six eyes gaping at him, he said, "What's all this? Why such a fuss?"

"Mrs. Hill thinks the gentleman from Derbyshire is gonna offer for Miss Elizabeth."

"Hush now, Katie," said Mrs. Hill.

"Do you, now?" Harold pulled out a cheroot. "S'pose then I won't be turned out when the master is kingdom come."

"Harold! You mustn't speak so! And don't you even think of smoking that in the house!"

"Right, Miz Hill. D' you s'pose that's why that gran' duchess called here for Miss Elizabeth?"

The three women gasped in unison.

"I hadn't thought of that," said Mrs. Hill. "Aye. Why else would her ladyship come? That seems the only probable motive for her calling."

"I'd not mind working in Mr. Darcy's household."

"You'd go to Derbyshire, Harold?" asked Katie.

"Pfft. A gentleman such as he is sure to have a house in Town. That's where I'll be. Miz Hill, don't be forgettin' you're wanted upstairs."

Mrs. Hill took the small bundle labeled British East India Company and sighed. "I better go on, then, before the mistress has a fit of nerves."

Mrs. Hill walked up the back stairs to the family wing and scratched at the door to Mrs. Bennet's apartment.

"Hill, Hill, is that you? Come."

Mrs. Hill entered to find Sarah attending to Mrs. Bennet's hair. "Yes, ma'am."

"My dear Hill, where have you been? Bless me, you know I cannot manage without you."

"I've been to Meryton, ma'am. I brung the tea."

"Do put it in the caddy," Mrs. Bennet said and handed her the key. "I cannot be bothered. Good gracious, if that disagreeable Mr. Darcy must always be coming here with our dear Bingley! No compassion for my poor nerves. What can he mean by being so tiresome as to disturb us with his constant company? But, however, he is very welcome if he likes, as he is a friend of Mr. Bingley."

With such a speech as this, Mrs. Hill could depend on her mistress having no intelligence on the understanding between a man of ten thousand a year and her second eldest daughter. "I met Mrs. Philips at the butcher, ma'am, and she sent a message to you. She says all of Meryton has pronounced the Bennets to be the luckiest family in the world." And soon to be thought luckier still!

"Aye, and why would they not, with two daughters well married? I am sure not a soul in all of Meryton would not want to be at Jane's wedding." Mrs. Bennet chose to entertain herself in this manner for some time while Mrs. Hill and Sarah assisted with her toilette.

As Sarah made to leave to help Miss Bennet, Mrs. Hill pulled her aside. "Now, Sarah, as soon as you are done with all the ladies, you make haste and hurry down to the kitchen. You understand?"

The young maid nodded and then left Mrs. Hill alone to listen to her mistress's repetitions of delights.

"Mr. Bingley is the handsomest young man that ever was seen. And with five or six thousand a year! Last year when he first came into Hertfordshire, as soon as I saw him I thought how likely it would be that they should come together. My dear Jane could not be so beautiful for nothing...."

Having heard this speech not less than incessantly for nigh ten days, Mrs. Hill knew when to offer the appropriate response without paying strict attention, allowing her thoughts to return to their previous meditations until such time as she could return to the kitchen.

"They're come back," said Harold when she arrived.

"Did you see Miss Elizabeth?" Katie asked her.

"I've been with Mrs. Bennet all this time. Has Sarah been down?" When they responded in the negative, she continued. "I asked her to come as soon as she has finished with the ladies' hair. She might have news then."

The sound of silver clanking coming from the butler's pantry then drew their notice, and Mrs. Hill called out to him. "Mr. Sloan, might I ask you into the kitchen a moment?"

The butler came to stand in the entryway to the kitchen. "Yes, Mrs. Hill?"

"Has Mr. Darcy requested a private audience with Mr. Bennet?"

"Mrs. Hill, surely you do not propose that I gossip about my master, and here in the kitchen?"

"Aye, that is precisely what I am asking you to do. This affects us all."

"And, pray, how are you entitled to any knowledge of Mr. Bennet's affairs?"

"I think Mr. Darcy intends to ask his consent to marry Miss Elizabeth."

"Indeed?" Mr. Sloan's eyebrows lifted at this. "The gentlemen are in my master's library, but Mr. Bingley is within as well."

"Is the door closed?"

"It was open, last I knew."

"Then go on, bring us a report," she said, urging him with a flap of her hands.

The butler opened his lips to protest but, perhaps anticipating an argument, sighed and withdrew. The others were fixed in wretched suspense, which was rewarded by his prompt return.

"My overhearings succeeded in nothing but lowering my own opinion of myself. They speak of nothing of consequence, merely speculating on the Tsar's response and if it might realign the coalition against Napoleon." His audience's disappointment was quite evident. "And how did you come upon this intelligence, Mrs. Hill, that another wedding is imminent?"

"I saw them walking together on my return from Meryton."

"That by no means equates to matrimony. Mr. Bingley had proposed they all go out when he and Mr. Darcy arrived, and Miss Catherine went as well."

"They may have all gone out together, but they did not return together, now. Did they? When I come upon them, they were quite alone, and they had stopped their walking. Mr. Darcy stood close to Miss Elizabeth and held her hands."

"And from this you make such inferences?"

"And that there duchess came to wait on Miss Elizabeth," offered Harold.

"Duchess?"

"He means Lady de Bourgh," said Mrs. Hill. "Have you not heard nor seen anything yourself?"

Mr. Sloan's countenance turned more solemn, as if considering his next words carefully. "Mr. Darcy, I think, has long admired Miss Elizabeth, as he looks on her a great deal; but his last visit before going away, when I brought in the tea things after dinner, I noticed Miss Elizabeth to be out of spirits, and her eyes never left him as he walked to the other side of the room."

"Lovers' quarrel," said Harold.

"Harold, you appear quite at your leisure. I believe the sideboard is in need of polishing."

"Yes, Mr. Sloan," he said while walking past.

"This may all come to nothing. Now, if we are done with this nasty business, I will go lay the table."

"You must contrive to have Miss Elizabeth sit beside Mr. Darcy at table," said Mrs. Hill.

"How might you propose I do that?"

"Oh, you will think of something."

Mr. Sloane quit the room but not before rolling his eyes and shaking his head. Mrs. Hill scarcely had time to talk over these new developments with Katie and Cook before Sarah arrived.

"You wanted to see me, Miz Hill?"

"Yes, Sarah. Were you just with Miss Bennet and Miss Elizabeth?" She answered in the affirmative. "Well? Did they say anything?"

"I don' take your meanin'. Say anything of what?"

"Miss Elizabeth's walk with Mr. Darcy."

Sarah hesitated, clearly uncomfortable under the scrutiny of the other women awaiting her reply. "When Miss Elizabeth came in, Miss Bennet asked where she'd been walkin' to for so long."

"And what did she say?"

"She said they wandered about until she was lost."

"Psst," said Cook. "Lost in his eyes, more likely. She could find her way across half of Hertfordshire on a moonless night."

"She said nothin' of Mr. Darcy?" asked Katie.

"None at all. Why would she?"

They then related all they knew and their conjectures as to the meaning of it.

"Mr. Durst was in the paddock when the duchess were here," said Sarah, "and he was right there on that side of the lawn when she spoke with Miss Elizabeth."

"Do we still have some plum cake left from breakfast? Katie, go fetch Mr. Durst. Say we have plum cake for him. Go on, make haste!"

Katie returned shortly with Mr. Durst, but Cook stopped him in the doorway.

"You are not bringing dirt all into my kitchen. Take off your shoes before you come in here."

Disinclined to do so, he said, "I don' need to come in. Jus' give me the cake and I'll eat it out here."

Mrs. Hill rushed to his side. "Now, now, don't be daft. Just knock the mud off your boots. That'll do well enough. Then come sit down."

He did as told, and Cook set the plum cake before him, but not in good humor, and the four women sat down around him.

"Now, Mr. Durst," began Mrs. Hill, "do you recall a few days ago when that chaise and four with the fine livery brought Lady de Bourgh."

"Well, 'course I recollect it. Was but three days ago. I'm not some cod's head." He looked up then and froze upon facing the expectant stares, his fork suspended in mid-air. "Right. What's all this about?"

"Were you there when Miss Elizabeth was with her ladyship?"

573

"I was goin' about my duties, but I happen by there a few times."

"What was her reason for coming? Did she have anything particular to say to Miss Elizabeth?"

His cheeks then overspread with the deepest blush, and he dropped his gaze down to his plate. "I don' think it'd be right for me to talk of it."

"You had better," said Cook, "or that will be the last piece of cake you'll ever have from me!"

He seemed to struggle to push past his discomposure before speaking. "Her ladyship was in high dudgeon. She accused Miss Elizabeth of trying to lure Mr. Darcy and draw him in to marrying her."

"I knew it! They are engaged!" declared Mrs. Hill.

"Now, jus' a minute. Her ladyship said that she being his closest relation, she would never allow it, and a marriage could never take place because he's engaged to her daughter." This pronouncement elicited a mixture of disappointed gasps and groans.

"So he did not offer for her."

Mr. Durst shook his head. "Her ladyship asked if she were engaged to her nephew, and Miss Elizabeth said no. Then her ladyship demanded a promise that she'd not accept if he asked."

"Hateful, hateful woman!"

"Then she stormed off and well-nigh jumped into her carriage before it bolted off."

The women were all discouraged and sorry. They were then forced to return to their duties without having gained any satisfactory information. Mrs. Hill relinquished any remaining hope when, during dinner, Harold came into the kitchen for the next remove and told her that Miss Elizabeth seemed quite agitated being seated beside Mr. Darcy and hadn't said a word, although the gentleman himself appeared quite at ease. Then Mrs. Hill was left to regret her part in this arrangement, which caused Miss Elizabeth

574

such embarrassment. Nothing more was said on the subject for the remainder of the afternoon.

That night, after seeing to Mrs. Bennet's needs and listening to her relate all the particulars of Mr. Bingley's visit, Mrs. Hill stepped out into the hall and, closing the door behind her, turned to find Sarah with her ear nearly pressed against Miss Bennet's door.

"Sarah," Mrs. Hill cried out in a harsh whisper, but Sarah waved for her to come near. They both leaned in to hear the muffled voices through the door.

"You are joking, Lizzy. This cannot be! Engaged to Mr. Darcy! No, no, you shall not deceive me. I know it to be impossible."

"This is a wretched beginning indeed! My sole dependence was on you; and I am sure nobody else will believe me, if you do not. Yet, indeed, I am in earnest. I speak nothing but the truth. He still loves me, and we are engaged."

At this, Sarah and Mrs. Hill gaped at each other with eyes as wide as their grins.

"Oh, Lizzy! It cannot be. I know how much you dislike him."

"You know nothing of the matter. That is all to be forgot. Perhaps I did not always love him so well as I do now. But in such cases as these, a good memory is unpardonable. This is the last time I shall ever remember it myself."

Mrs. Hill and Sarah quietly stepped back from the door and embraced.

"Mrs. Bennet must yet know nothing of it, or she would be in raptures! So you mustn't say a word to anyone in the family," said Mrs. Hill, to which Sarah readily agreed.

They then hurried away to the kitchen, eager to relate news which would give such pleasure to so many.

Darcy Talks to Mr. Bennet

by Maria Grace

October 7, 1812

Darcy paced the Netherfield library. The fool room was far too short and the threadbare carpet muffled what should have been a satisfying thud from his boots.

He had faced many intimidating men in his life. Men more educated than himself; men wealthier; men more powerful. None ever caused him a moment's anxiety. So why should an insignificant country gentlemen turn his insides into a wobbling mass of jelly?

None of those men ever had any power to deny him what he most desired.

Mr. Bennet did.

How was such a man to be worked on? Intractable and capricious, reason could not be trusted. But in order to survive life with his wife and silly younger daughters, he could hardly be susceptible to sensibility, either. What was left to him?

Appeals to status, perhaps?

Threats?

Gah!

Elizabeth insisted Bennet would present no obstacles. His nature was to seek his ease and what could be easier than consigning his daughter to a life as Mistress of Pemberley?

While that might be true, Elizabeth was Mr. Bennet's favorite child. Men could become unpredictable when their favorites were concerned.

Enough! This exercise was pointless and a waste of time. Time he could spend much better. He stomped out.

A gentleman should probably be seen to arrive on his horse, particularly if it were as fine an animal as his. But Netherfield's grooms were slow on the best of days and further delay would not bode well for anyone. He would walk.

Besides the journey might soothe his haggard spirit.

It did not.

The sun was too hot and somehow a burr had worked its way into his boot and lodged itself against his calf, just out of reach.

Excellent.

Longbourn rose in the distance. It was not a pretty vista. Apparently aesthetics were not something Bennet cared about either. But then, little was attractive this time of year.

In the shadow of the house, he lifted his hat and wiped the sweat from his brow. Father should really have prepared him for this sort of conversation as he had so many others. Then again, even if he tried, could he have ever foreseen a man such as Mr. Bennet. Or, a woman like his Elizabeth?

Elizabeth.

That is why he was here. She was the only thing that could inspire such an errand or make it worthwhile. For her and her alone he would see this through. Whatever it would take.

He rapped on the door and Hill admitted him with a satisfyingly alarmed expression.

"I need to speak to Mr. Bennet."

"Mr. Bennet, sir?"

"Did I not make myself clear?" He leveled a glare generally reserved for the impertinent of his own rank.

"Perfectly clear, sir." She dropped a nervous curtsey and beckoned him to follow.

Rarely had that glare been so effective as to cause a servant to forget to see if the master was home to a visitor. He could not complain.

Hill peeked into the open study door. Mr. Bennet sat at his desk, open ledgers before him, a quill in his hand.

"Mr. Darcy to see you, sir." Her voice quavered.

Mr. Bennet jumped and glowered. "Hill, I have told you…Mr. Darcy?" He removed his glasses and pushed to his feet.

Darcy stepped around Hill and took three steps into the room. "As you see, sir. I would speak with you."

"Close the door, Hill." Mr. Bennet came around the desk. "What business have you with Longbourn, sir?"

"Not with Longbourn, with you."

Mr. Bennet leaned back and cocked his head. "With me? Now I am intrigued."

"You have no idea why I have come?" Surely he could not be so thick.

"None at all."

And yet he was.

"I come on a matter of some urgency, a personal matter."

"An urgent and personal matter. You have me most intrigued, sir. What urgent, personal business could bring you to my doorstep?" Mr. Bennet folded his arms over his chest.

Darcy ground his teeth. *Mr. Bennet might find this baiting amusing, but at the best, it was ungentlemanly. And his attempts to be dominant must stop.*

"I come to discuss your daughter, Miss Elizabeth."

The color faded from Bennet's face and he sagged against the edge of his desk.

Darcy schooled his features into neutrality. Now was not the time to gloat.

"My Lizzy? What has she to do with you?"

"I have made her an offer of marriage, and she has accepted."

Mr. Bennet blinked and blinked again. "Surely that cannot be. My Lizzy? She accepted you? Impossible. That rumor was all an addle-pated notion from my cousin Collins."

"I rarely jest, sir, and never over matters so serious."

"My Lizzy? Who you have not looked at but to find blemish?"

"I have long considered her the handsomest woman of my acquaintance."

Mr. Bennet barked a harsh laugh. "I find that difficult to believe."

"Disguise is my abhorrence, sir. You may ask Mr. Bingley if you wish corroboration."

"Bingley? He is aware of your scheme?"

"I resent your implication, sir, but, yes, he is aware, and perhaps your eldest daughter as well."

Mr. Bennet raked his hair. "You are serious then?"

"Entirely."

Mr. Bennet paced to his window and stared through the spotty glass. "My Lizzy?"

"I have a settlement in mind that I believe you and she will find quite acceptable."

Generous in fact, but there was no need to bruise Mr. Bennet's pride just yet.

"And she has accepted?"

"Without hesitation."

Mr. Bennet slowly turned. "Why?"

What kind of question was that? No, it would not pay to take offense now. Elizabeth would want him to control his temper.

"Excuse me?"

"My Lizzy is a sensible girl. Why would she accept your offer?"

Because no sensible woman would refuse? No, that was not true. She refused him once. But then, no sensible woman should have accepted that offer.

"I have not seen the need to question my good fortune, sir. You shall have to ask her that yourself."

"I shall. You can be sure of it." Mr. Bennet's nostrils flared and his eyes widened.

"Have you any objections apart from the assurance of her approval?"

"I have no doubt you can provide for her adequately."

"Have you any objections?"

"Your reputation and your connections are excellent."

And so was his pedigree, but he was not a hound. He clenched his left hand into a tight fist.

"I insist on an answer, sir, will you refuse her permission to marry me?"

"She will be one and twenty soon enough. You could just wait—"

"She—and I—would prefer your blessing."

That seemed to cut off Mr. Bennet's next retort.

His shoulders slumped. "If she accepts you—truly accepts you—and I shall not force her to do that no matter what you claim—then I shall not offer any impediments."

Not offer an impediment? That was his response? Any other man would be congratulating himself on his good fortune. But not this quixotic gentleman.

Still it was enough.

"Thank you, sir. Shall I inform Miss Elizabeth, or do you prefer to do so?

"Tell Hill to send her to me. I might have a very long discussion with her."

Darcy bowed and pushed the door open, nearly knocking Hill to the ground. Her spying would disturb him far more had he not won his point.

"Send Miss Elizabeth to her father."

"I—I... Yes, sir." She curtsied and scurried away, nearly tripping in her haste.

Tension flowed away from him as the housekeeper disappeared.

Elizabeth would tell her father everything he needed to know, and they would have his blessing soon enough.

In the meantime he could see himself out.

Bingley and Jane Take a Walk

by Susan Mason-Milks

October 12, 1812

"Oh, Mr. Bingley," trilled Mrs. Bennet, "What a pleasant surprise! We were not expecting you back from London so soon."

"I hope I have not come at an inconvenient time, Mrs. Bennet," Bingley said politely.

"Oh, no! You are welcome here at any time. Our dear Jane will be so pleased to see you."

Mrs. Bennet took Mr. Bingley's arm and towed him down the hallway toward the sitting room all the while chattering to him about the wedding plans. When the door opened and he stepped inside, Jane looked up and gave him that sweet smile of hers causing his heart to do a little dance. Now that they were engaged, he experienced a particular thrill in knowing her special look was for him alone.

"Mr. Bingley," Jane said, setting aside her sewing, "you have returned early. I hope your business was successfully concluded."

"Doesn't our Jane look lovely today?" asked Mrs. Bennet urging him toward the chair next to Jane's.

All morning he had tried to think of a way to be alone with his angel but had not been able to come up with a better excuse than a walk.

"Miss Bennet, I was hoping we might walk out to take advantage of this fine weather."

"I will go fetch my pelisse and bonnet," she said without

hesitation. As she crossed the room, he thought, not for the first time, just how much her grace and beauty never failed to please him.

While waiting for Jane to return, Mrs. Bennet proceeded to carry on about all her plans for improvements to Netherfield. Trying to put an interested look on his face, he half-listened as she chattered on; finally, to his relief, Jane reappeared, and they were able to make their escape.

Once they had turned down a nearby lane and were out of sight of the house, Bingley stopped and turned to look into his fiancée's upturned face. Holding both of her hands in his, he said, "Oh, my angel! While I was in London, I could think of nothing but you. I concluded my business as quickly as possible so I could return. I hope you thought of me, too."

Jane smiled sweetly. "Of course I did, Mr. Bingley."

"I thought we had agreed you would use my first name, especially when we are on our own?"

At that, Jane blushed and fixed her eyes on the ground. Putting a crooked finger gently beneath her chin, he lifted her face up. Even one look into her clear, blue eyes was enough to tempt any man. After all, they were engaged now. Perhaps...

"When we are apart, you are never far from my mind, Charles," she admitted shyly.

The sound of his Christian name on her lips was too much. Unable to resist temptation, Bingley pulled her into his arms. Much to his delight, Jane responded by relaxing against him and laying her head gently on his shoulder. Her faintly lavender scent was intoxicating. Bingley could still scarcely believe his luck that after all those months apart she still loved him. He was forgiven for not returning to Netherfield last fall, and in just a short time, she would be his. He wanted nothing more than to kiss her, but discretion won out, and he decided they were too near the public road for any privacy. Still, once she was in his arms, it was difficult to let her go, and he was pleased to discover that she made no attempt to pull away. After enjoying the intimacy of their embrace for a few moments more, he reluctantly pushed back, took her hand, and tucked it safely in the crook of his arm.

"You cannot know how much I wish we could steal a few moments alone. Really alone," he confessed in a low voice.

"And you, sir, might be surprised to know that is exactly what I most wish for, also," she said very softly.

Bingley was so surprised by her comment that he was temporarily unsure if he had heard her correctly. Turning, he discovered she was watching him, and they shared an awkward, nervous laugh. Feeling his self-control slipping away at this revelation, he decided to change the subject to something less volatile.

"Your mother was telling me about her plans for improvements to Netherfield," he said lightly.

"You know you must not take her too seriously. She is always full of plans."

"I was just wondering how much of what she told me is her idea and how much is yours," he asked with some hesitation.

"There has been so much to do! I have not had time to turn my mind to that yet, although I have heard it said that it is best to live in a house for a while before making serious redecorating decisions. Do you also think that is true?"

Bingley breathed a sigh of relief.

As if reading his mind, she said, "Charles, although I have always tried to please my mother, you must know by now that she does not speak for me."

"I know, but I am pleased to hear you reaffirm it." He patted her hand as it rested on his arm. Although the temperature was cool, the sun was warm as they slowly strolled down the lane. He knew he was stalling but how to begin? The subject he really wished to discuss with her was delicate, and he had no experience of how to start such a conversation, but start it he must.

"You know I was able to renew the lease on Netherfield for another year without committing to a purchase."

584

"Yes, you have mentioned that."

"I have until next summer to decide whether or not we will settle here more...ah...permanently. Since the owner's ultimate goal is the sale of the estate, he has written certain terms into the lease agreement. As a result, I have just one more year in which to decide whether to buy Netherfield or look for a different property."

"Making such a significant purchase is an important decision," Jane said quietly.

"Darcy thinks the property would be an acceptable choice although some major improvements would be necessary if we stay. Netherfield is large enough to bring in a good income but not so large that I will not be able to learn to manage it with the help of my new steward. And of course, with Darcy's counsel, too."

"Yes, Mr. Darcy has been very helpful to you," Jane said.

"I have always thought you would want to live here in Hertfordshire to be near your parents. That started me wondering if I should begin negotiations with the seller now rather than wait for summer."

Jane looked up at him calmly. "As your wife, I will, of course, let you make an important decision such as that. I am certain you know what is best," she demurred.

Blast! Why couldn't this be easier, he thought.

"Yes, but I would like to hear what you think so that I may take that into consideration," he asked boldly.

"Oh, I see," she murmured. They walked on for a few minutes in silence.

"Of course, there are certainly advantages to being near family. When we have children, for example," she said.

Bingley could see that Jane's cheeks had reddened slightly at the mere mention of their children and found that his own face felt a bit warm, too.

"On the other hand, I shall miss Lizzy terribly," she added. "In fact, possibly more than I will miss my mother and father."

Bingley tried his best to puzzle out what she was not saying. Finally, he decided to be more direct.

"Do you mean you would prefer to live near your sister rather than your parents?"

"Lizzy and I have always been very close," she said. "Also, I confess I am not certain how I feel about the thought of my mother being able to drop in at any time she chooses." At this, her sweet smile turned into a slightly impish grin.

Although he had been thinking that very thing, to hear it from Jane was a great relief. It meant she was not as tied to her mother as he had feared. Although he was prepared to make the adjustments necessary to live in such close proximity to the Bennets, he had not exactly been relishing the idea. He only knew that he would do whatever made Jane happy.

"Apparently, your sister has had similar thoughts. Darcy recently offered to keep his eyes open for any possible leases in Derbyshire, but I was uncertain if I should tell him to go ahead."

"I would very much like to visit Derbyshire," Jane said brightly.

Bingley had a difficult time containing his excitement. "Then when we visit Pemberley, we will also make a tour of the area to see if it is to our liking," he said.

Jane squeezed his arm. "That would please me greatly."

They walked on for some time talking about small things. He told her funny stories about his childhood, and in turn, she shared some of her misadventures, although he noted that Elizabeth had generally been the one to instigate these escapades. Late afternoon arrived too quickly and the sun's warmth began to fade signaling time for their return. Reluctantly, they turned back. Not too far from Longbourn, they passed by a small wooded area very near the lane.

"This is a perfect spot for gathering pine cones," she said indicating the nearby stand of trees. "Will you assist me?"

When he gave her a questioning look, she grinned and taking his hand, gently pulled him away from the lane.

"Those woods look rather dense, Jane. We might lose sight of the road or become turned around."

"Oh, Charles, my dear, that was exactly what I was hoping for!" And blushing all over, she firmly led him toward the trees.

Suddenly, Bingley thought that gathering pine cones seemed like the best idea in the world.

Mrs. Bennet Plans the Wedding and Breakfast

by C. Allyn Pierson

October 12, 1812

"My dear sister! I am so delighted that I think I may have a spasm! I finally get to plan Jane and Lizzy's wedding!" Mrs. Bennet fanned herself with the bonnet she had just removed as she plopped down onto the settee in Mrs. Philips' saloon. "I was so afraid Mr. Darcy or Bingley's sisters would insist on St. George's Hanover Square, and, of course, I would have had to let my sister Gardiner assist me. As much as I love her and my brother, I must say they made a mess of Lydia's wedding—no guests, no flowers except a paltry little posy for Lydia to carry. I was ashamed of the niggardly arrangements. They did not even have a wedding breakfast afterwards!"

She breathed a deep sigh and allowed Mrs. Philips to pat her hand and nod consolingly before continuing. "That would not do at all for Jane and Lizzy! They are marrying into the *ton* and must have a wedding that will not embarrass their husbands by being miserly with the biggest event of my daughters' lives! And I think I will be able to convince Mr. Bennet to go along with my plans—after all, Lizzy is his favorite daughter. Surely he will wish to give her a lovely send off! I already have cook working on the menu for the wedding breakfast. I told her we want everything to be prime about it! Of course, I don't know how many guests there will be yet. I am sure Mr. Darcy's sister and Bingley's sisters will be here, but I am not sure about Darcy's cousin, Colonel Fitzwilliam and his parents. Darcy and Fitzwilliam are very good friends, from what Lizzy has told Jane about her visit in Kent, but his parents' estate is all of one hundred miles away...surely too far to travel for a wedding! Since the wedding is to be at Longbourn Church instead of at St. George's, I am afraid that not many of Mr. Darcy's and Bingley's friends will come to Hertfordshire...Oh, well, those that do will find Hertfordshire can put on a wedding just as well as London can!"

Mrs. Philips started to speak: "Yes my dear sister, indeed—" when Mrs. Bennet interrupted her. "And oh sister! Jane and Lizzy are in London right now, shopping for their wedding clothes with our sister Gardiner." She compressed her lips for a moment. "I wanted to go with them ... after all I am their mother, and I have shopped in London before! But Mr. Bennet said I was needed at Longbourn to plan the wedding, and he is quite right, of course. Jane has such exquisite taste that I have no compunction about letting her help her sister choose what is needed for their clothes...and, of course, Mrs. Gardiner lives in London and so knows all the warehouses. Mr. Bennet suggested to me that perhaps Mr. Gardiner could save some money by arranging for the girls to shop at the warehouses of some of his business acquaintances! It is not the thing to have a brother in trade, but perhaps he will turn his tradesman contacts to good use."

As she sipped her rapidly cooling tea she reviewed the plans she had made for the wedding. Mrs. Philips murmured on in the background of her thoughts, until Mrs. Bennet interrupted her again. "Oh! I will decorate the pews with ribbons and the girls' bouquets will be asters. There is not much selection of flowers this time of year, and we do not have a greenhouse to force flowers all year. Perhaps Mr. Gardiner could find orchids in London. They would be very expensive, but oh so elegant! I must have a new gown made for the wedding, too, as well as gowns for Mary and Kitty!" They must look their best. After all, there may be some wealthy single gentlemen who are friends of Bingley's. Would that not be fine, if Kitty would meet an eligible gentleman at her sisters' wedding! Ah me! It is all so exciting! I must go now...there are a thousand things to do before the 16th of November! It's been lovely talking to you, my dear sister!" She bustled out, her face flushed and her eyes brilliant, leaving Mrs. Philips with her mouth open.

Colonel Fitzwilliam Learns of Darcy's Engagement

by Jack Caldwell

October 20, 1812

On a cold November afternoon, Colonel the Honorable Richard Fitzwilliam jauntily ascended the steps of Darcy House in London. His knock on the door was swiftly answered.

"Ah, Thacker, has my cousin returned?"

The butler glanced at the door. The colonel was a constant and welcomed guest at Darcy House, but the knocker was not in evidence, a clear sign that the family was unavailable to visitors.

The colonel laughed. "Oh, do not bother, old man." He moved inside the vestibule. "I will just call on Miss Georgiana." He handed the imperturbable servant his hat and gloves and was removing his coat when a tall gentleman made his appearance.

"I thought I heard your voice, Richard," said a smiling Fitzwilliam Darcy, his hand extended in welcome.

"Darce! You have returned and looking exceedingly well, I might add. Now, where the devil have you been? What have you been up to?"

"Come into my study, Fitz. Your arrival is most timely if you mean to stay for dinner."

"Of course! You would not throw your poor cousin upon the mercy of the kitchens of Horse Guards, would you? The horses eat better!"

Darcy harrumphed. "I seriously doubt that the Crown's food is that deficient, but we will suffer your company. Thacker, be so good as to alert Cook that we have a guest for dinner." The butler nodded as the two gentlemen continued down the hall.

"You have not answered my question," Fitzwilliam pointed out. "You have been gone for a month. Did you return to Pemberley?"

Darcy's response was lost to posterity, for at that instant, a pretty young lady dashed from the music room.

"Richard," cried Georgiana Darcy. "Oh Richard, have you heard the news?" She leapt into an embrace with her cousin and guardian. "Brother is getting married!"

Fitzwilliam was dumbfounded. "Married?" His arms full of Georgiana, he peered over her head at Darcy. "To whom?"

Butter would not melt in Darcy's grinning mouth. "You are acquainted with the lady—Miss Elizabeth Bennet."

* * *

Thirty minutes later, the two gentlemen were comfortably ensconced in Darcy's study with cigars and wine, a roaring fire in the grate, and Georgiana was upstairs changing for dinner.

"Now that you have successfully distracted me with cigars and wine," said Fitzwilliam presently, "shall you tell me how things came to pass? Engaged to Miss Bennet? I am all astonishment!"

"I thought you had some wind of it. You must have seen evidence of my admiration in Kent."

"I thought I saw something, but to this degree? No. You have been very sly."

"Not in the least. I must wonder at your astonishment; surely my aunt spoke to the earl last month."

"I have not heard anything, and I would be surprised if I did. You know Father and Aunt Catherine hate each other. But why would—oh!" Fitzwilliam frowned. "She knew? You told Lady Catherine of your intentions and not me?"

"Peace, Cousin! It was not so much a matter of telling her as her finding out."

Mollified, the colonel sat back. "How did that come about? Anne?"

"No, I did not tell Anne, either." He imparted the story of Lady Catherine's journey to Longbourn, her confrontation with Elizabeth, and her attempt to warn Darcy off. By the time Darcy finished his tale, the colonel was excessively diverted.

"Ho, this is rich! The old bat thought she would have you bend to her will, but in all probability, she drove you right into Miss Bennet's arms! How Father will laugh when he learns of this!"

Darcy sat up. "Must you tell him?"

"Of course! I can keep nothing from him—especially if I wish to stay in his best books. My allowance depends upon it!" At Darcy's dark look, Fitzwilliam sobered and patted his cousin's knee. "It would be all for the best, Darce. You cannot think he will look kindly on your betrothal to a county lady of no note."

Darcy ground his teeth. "Elizabeth is a gentleman's daughter; we are equals."

"Do not be foolish! You know this will disrupt his plans for you. However, I can be of service. As much as he dislikes being thwarted, he enjoys thwarting Auntie Cathy more! The very fact that our aunt disapproves of Miss Bennet will raise her in my father's eyes."

Darcy was hardly mollified. "I will stand no disrespect for Elizabeth."

Fitzwilliam almost laughed at the image Darcy presented— glowering face, arms crossed over his chest. Why, if only he bit his lip, he would be the perfect picture of an angry, stubborn child. "Miss Elizabeth is charming. She will win over Father in no time, and Mother too, I have no doubt."

"And the viscount?"

Fitzwilliam's smile faded. "That will be a harder task. You know how much stock my *dear sister* Eugenie puts in appearances, and Andrew follows wherever she leads." The colonel's and the viscountess's mutual loathing was well-known within the family. "However, Father demands a unified public front in all things. Win his acceptance and the rest of the family will fall in line—including Lady Catherine."

Darcy relaxed. "My uncle is a reasonable man. I am satisfied. I shall write him presently. He is still in Derbyshire, I recall." He took a sip of his wine. "Shall you attend the wedding? If so, I would ask you to escort Georgiana."

Fitzwilliam nodded. "I shall be happy to if I am granted leave. After all, someone must represent the family. It certainly will not be Lady Catherine." He frowned. "I wish Anne could... but that is nonsense. Her health would not allow it, even if by some miracle our aunt gave permission."

The two sat for some time, drinking, the crackling fire the only sound in the room.

"Darcy," Fitzwilliam began again, "are you certain about this? Please understand I am only concerned with your happiness. Miss Bennet is all that is lovely and charming, but—"

Darcy held up a hand. "Fitz, I am certain. I shall not change my mind—I shall marry Elizabeth." He sighed. "It is hard for me to speak of this. In her presence, I feel—calm. Complete. At peace. I find she is as necessary to me as food and drink. I do not think I can now live without her, knowing I have finally won her tender affections."

"Have you?"

"She says I have, and I believe her." He chuckled. "I certainly know my fortune means little to her!"

Fitzwilliam frowned, the source of his misgivings now on the table. "Forgive me, Darce, but how do you know that?"

Darcy laughed out loud. "Because she turned me down at Rosings!"

"*What?*"

Darcy ignored his cousin's inelegant outburst and gave an abbreviated recounting of his misadventure in the parsonage at Easter. "So you see?" he concluded his tale. "If she were mercenary, she would have accepted my boorish proposal, and I never would have been the wiser until it was too late! But she had mercy on me and taught me a hard lesson on what it takes to please a woman worthy of being pleased."

"Apparently, you have learned this lesson."

"I will endeavor to put my better understanding to good use for the remainder of my days."

Normally, Fitzwilliam would have disregarded such a statement as mere hyperbole had it come from any other man. "She has bewitched you, has she not?"

"I am a better man for knowing her."

Fitzwilliam raised his glass and offered a toast. "Then I wish you joy with all my heart."

Darcy's eyes were suspiciously moist. "Thank you, Fitz. Your words mean more to me than I can say." He gathered himself and stood. "Shall we to dinner? Georgiana is surely waiting for us by now."

Fitzwilliam grinned, already relishing whatever arts Darcy's cook was to employ that evening. "Excellent! Lead the way, Cuz." *And if what you say about Miss Elizabeth is true, Darce, I shall love her as if she were my own sister,* he thought to himself.

Elizabeth Meets Darcy's Uncle

by Monica Fairview

November 2, 1812

The dreaded missive had arrived. Darcy stared at the elaborate seal for a while before the butler gave a discreet cough and Darcy realized that the poor fellow's arm must be hurting from holding out the silver salver holding the letter.

"Thank you," he said, taking the letter, although the last thing he felt was thankful. He wished the wretched thing had been lost. He would then have had an excuse not to deal with the situation.

Now that the letter was there, staring him in the face, there was no point in delaying the inevitable. He took up the letter opener and broke the seal.

The Honorable Mr. Fitzwilliam Darcy, Esq.

My dear nephew,

The fact that his uncle was using honorifics did not bode well.

News of a most alarming nature has reached me...

Darcy skimmed through the rest of the letter. It was just as he thought. The keywords sprang out at him: *duty, an ancient family, ancestors, status, rank in society* and some other words of similar meaning. These words were inevitably followed by: *degrade, throw away, penniless girl, a nobody* and other related terms.

The letter ended with a warning.

I shall be arriving post-haste in London and I shall expect you to provide me with an explanation for this untoward behavior. I shall also expect you to introduce me to the young lady in question. I am aware that sometimes strong passion can distort our perception of reality and that in a moment of folly we could destroy all hopes for future happiness. I would not be doing my duty if I did not do all I could to prevent you from taking such an unwise step.

Yours truly,

Matlock

This was followed by a formal listing of his uncle's titles—again, unusual enough to make it clear that it was a reminder of Darcy's own social situation.

Darcy put down the letter and sighed. It was all happening sooner than he had hoped. He had wanted to enjoy his engagement to Elizabeth without the pressure of family expectations, but now he was forced to introduce her to everyone and his uncle would not make things easy. Of course, it did not matter ultimately what his uncle might do. Darcy was steadfast in his intentions and his uncle could not prevent him from marrying, but in many ways, Darcy looked up to Lord Matlock as a father. He often consulted with him on matters regarding the estate and he trusted his judgment as well as feeling strong ties of affection for him. He would hate to lose all that, especially knowing that as head of the Fitzwilliam family, his uncle could influence how other members of the family would react to Elizabeth.

Darcy took out a paper and penned a response. Time had run out for him. He had to step out of the fairy tale and into the harsh light of day.

* * *

Two days later, as they stood at the bottom of the steps to the Matlock's elegant townhouse, Darcy slipped his fingers between Elizabeth's and gave her hand a quick squeeze.

"I am certain you will be a success," he murmured. "Just be true to yourself and my uncle will love you as I do."

"I hope he will not love me as you do," said Elizabeth, with a hint of mischief. "I have had enough difficulty determining your feelings. I hope I never have to deal with anyone else's."

Darcy laughed. "You are such a minx," he said, softly, his eyes wandering over her face and settling on her lips. "If it were not for the footman holding the carriage door open, I would plant a kiss on those tempting lips of yours right now."

"How very fortunate, then, that there is something to restrain you, Mr. Darcy," she replied, smiling, "or your uncle would witness a rather shocking scene."

She nodded in the direction of the grand door which had been flung open as a tall man clad in scarlet livery stepped out.

Darcy shuddered. "Heaven forbid. He is already more than willing to believe the worst of you."

Elizabeth shrugged. "Then we have nothing to lose," she said, beginning to ascend the steps.

"I cannot believe you are so calm about this encounter with my uncle," remarked Darcy admiringly. "I am far more anxious for you to make a good impression than you are."

"I do not know your uncle as you do, so perhaps I am making too light of it. I promise you I shall take the matter more seriously once I am face to face with him." She gently untangled her fingers. "Meanwhile, let us start with what is proper. The butler is watching us with a dour expression. We have already earned *his* disapproval. That is hardly a promising beginning."

How typical of Elizabeth to take that into consideration, thought Darcy. "You need not concern yourself with the butler's approval," he said. Then, when Elizabeth laughed, he turned to look at her. "Ah, I see. You were joking."

"Not entirely. I do believe winning over the servants is one of the best ways of winning over their masters, since the servants inevitably form an opinion and express it."

"Nevertheless," said Darcy, "the fact remains that my uncle is a great deal more powerful than a butler, and can sway the opinion of many—whether in your favor or against you," said Darcy.

Lizzy halted before the last step and turned to him. "Do you mean to frighten me, Mr. Darcy?" she said, looking at him quizzingly. "I have already met Lady Catherine. If her brother is anything like her, then I have nothing to fear. I am not daunted by their arrogance. They can only intimidate me if I allow it, and I have no intention of doing so."

Darcy felt a rush of pride warm him up inside. Elizabeth was so fearless, her spirit so free that he could almost believe her untouchable, but was it enough to overcome the prejudice she would inevitably encounter? What if they—the Earl and other members of their social ranks—set out to destroy their happiness? What if his uncle and aunt refused to accept her as part of the family? Would her wonderful confidence begin to decline?

He could not bear to think of that sparkling brightness fading in any way. He would do whatever was necessary to protect her.

* * *

They followed as the butler led the way, not upstairs to the parlor but to the library. So his uncle had decided that they would have to beard the lion in his den, then? Darcy's heart sank. The heavy mahogany furniture was oppressive at the best of times. Unobtrusively, Darcy crossed his fingers behind his back.

In an unusual show of ill-breeding, Lord Matlock did not rise as they entered. He remained behind his desk, fingers joined in a steeple, his sharp gray eyes fixed on Elizabeth.

"Good afternoon, uncle," said Darcy. "Allow me to present…"

"Yes, yes," said his uncle, waving his hand dismissively. "You may dispense with the introductions. I am aware that you have brought with you a certain Miss Elizabeth Bennet, daughter of Mr. George Bennet, of Longbourn Estate. You need not stand on ceremony. After all, if you plan to marry her, she is to be part of the family, is she not?"

There was nothing reassuring about his uncle's statement. In fact, the manner in which he made his declaration made him sound almost savage. Darcy looked towards Elizabeth uneasily, seeking to reassure her, but her gaze remained fixed on his uncle.

"So this is the young lady who has tempted you to defy family and tradition. Come closer, Miss Bennet. I cannot see you from this distance. I wish to determine what you look like." He raised his quizzing glass and fixed an engorged eye on Elizabeth.

Elizabeth drew a little closer and stood still, waiting patiently while he inspected her. To Darcy's astonishment, her lips twitched as his uncle looked her up and down.

"Could you turn around, please, Miss Bennet?" said Lord Matlock.

"I am not a piece of cattle at a village market to be prodded and probed to discover what price to settle on me," said Elizabeth.

Darcy winced. He wanted to warn her that his uncle would not take kindly to open defiance but since she was not looking at him, he could not think of a way to do so beyond clearing his throat loudly. She did not indicate that she had heard him.

Meanwhile, Lord Matlock's demeanor had turned frosty. Darcy knew that expression. It was the same one his uncle had when he had beaten him with a stick on a single memorable occasion. Darcy had broken the window of an old chapel by throwing a ball through one of the saint's halos in order to win a wager.

"No, you are certainly not," said Lord Matlock in clipped tones. "In fact, the shoe is rather on the other foot, I would think. It is Darcy who is to be bought and sold and I would prefer not to sell him too cheap."

Darcy had never seen his uncle quite so cold, quite so ruthless. In his imagination, he could suddenly see the ancestor they claimed was the original Fitzwilliam, the one who had been known as Aethelfrid the Fierce. Darcy had no objection to his uncle displaying some ancestral traits, but when it came to using them against Lizzy then it was another matter entirely.

"Now look here," said Darcy, a powerful instinct surfacing to protect the woman he loved from this ruthless attacker. "I will not allow you to speak to Miss Bennet in this manner."

F. Gwilliam is Norman,
Aethefrid Saxon.

600

"I shall speak to her as I please," said his uncle. "She is an upstart and a fortune hunter and I will not allow her to take advantage of a moment of weakness on your part."

"You consider love a moment of weakness, your lordship?" said Lizzy, her fine eyes flaring. "When it is one of the noblest emotions human beings are capable of? Poets have sung its glories from the earliest times—"

"I care nothing for poets," said Lord Matlock. "I deal with reality. The reality is, Darcy has little to gain while you have a great deal to gain from this marriage."

"I beg your pardon, Uncle," said Darcy, horrified at his uncle's bluntness. If he had known Lord Matlock would show so little civility, he would never have brought Elizabeth to meet him. "I believe *I* am the best judge of what I have to gain from this marriage."

"Your opinion is biased and is therefore beside the point," said Lord Matlock. "I wish to hear from this young lady what she thinks she has to bring to this marriage."

Darcy's agitation was growing so great he began to consider whether to plant his uncle a facer. He had never struck out in anger in since his early childhood when he did not know any better. His gentleman's code would not permit it. His uncle, however, had well and truly overstepped his limits. How dare he sit there so calmly and show Elizabeth so little of the respect she was due?

Elizabeth raised her chin and looked Lord Matlock straight in the eye. "Surely a person's worth is not measured only by how much land they own or how powerful a position they occupy. If that were the case, then the world's worst tyrants would be the most valuable people on earth, and I cannot accept that bleak view of humanity." Her gaze flicked towards Darcy then back again to his uncle. "I have a great deal to offer your nephew. I offer him companionship, affection, friendship and yes—the love that you seem to hold in so much contempt. I offer him something more valuable even than all these. I offer him happiness. I know I will do everything I can to ensure that he will be happy with me and that he will never regret his choice."

"But what of the friends he will lose? What of the opposition he will encounter? You will hardly make him happy if you cost him his seat in Parliament."

Darcy would have liked to protest that he would be pleased to be rid of that seat in Parliament. It meant nothing more than sitting through long, tedious sessions in which self-important men sought the attention of their peers. However, he had the feeling that at this moment whatever he said was irrelevant, that his uncle's attention was entirely centered on Elizabeth. As long as she was holding her own, he would not interfere, but the moment his uncle pressed too hard, Darcy would make it abundantly clear that if he had to choose between Elizabeth and his family, he would choose Elizabeth.

"Any friends who abandon him because he is marrying someone they do not approve of are not worthy of the name," said Elizabeth. "However, I am not so foolish as to think that we could find happiness if we lived in isolation. I mean to support my husband in his endeavors, not to destroy his ambitions. I will do everything within my power to mend any quarrels our marriage has caused."

She paused and took a step forward. "Which is why I will reach out to you, Lord Matlock, in the hopes that you will give Mr. Darcy your blessing. I know you have been like a father to him in many ways, and, while he does not require your approval, it will bring him great happiness to have it." She advanced to the desk and held out her hand. "Will you do it, Lord Matlock?"

Darcy held his breath. Elizabeth was smiling—*smiling* as if the encounter was nothing more than a routine afternoon call. Far from being cowed by his uncle, she was actually enjoying the situation.

For a long moment, Darcy thought Lord Matlock was going to snub her. Then suddenly, his uncle rose to his feet and with a swift movement, he took her hand and bowed over it.

"Miss Bennet, I have a strange feeling that if I do not, you will hound me until I agree. You certainly do not lack spirit."

Darcy let out the breath he did not realize he had been holding.

As if he had heard it, his uncle turned to address him. "I cannot pretend not to have misgivings, but I will give you my blessing. I can see that your young lady is quite capable of managing a grand estate and all that is required."

He paused and seemed for a moment lost in thought. "In fact, she reminds me of an incorrigible aunt of mine, Lady Amelia. Same fiery manner. Same brown eyes. She was quite exhausting to deal with."

Lord Matlock sank back into his chair and waved them away.

"Now go, before I change my mind. I shall have to think of a way of explaining my capitulation to Lady Matlock, who will be none too pleased…"

Charlotte Collins on Bonfire Night

by Abigail Reynolds

November 5, 1812

Across the clearing, sparks flew as the stuffed guy was engulfed in flames. Flickering yellow and orange tendrils shot up from the bonfire toward the sky. Charlotte remembered how huge and out of control the bonfires on Guy Fawkes Day had seemed to her as a child. She had always feared that the sparks would set a building alight, perhaps the result of all those years of stern cautions from her mother about taking care with candles, and her graphic descriptions of the possible consequences of carelessness. Now, of course, Charlotte did not give a second thought to the risk of the fire spreading. She could see the precautions the men were taking— the circle of stones to contain the fire, the buckets of water standing at regular intervals around the clearing.

It was a different kind of fire that Charlotte associated with Bonfire Night now. Had it only been a year ago that she had allowed Mr. Robinson to lead her off into the dark woods? That night had changed her life so completely, and none of it in the manner which she had expected. She was no longer an aging spinster, her future uncertain and dependent completely on her family, an easy target for a flattering seducer. Now she was Mrs. Collins, with a home of her own and security beyond any she could have expected.

Of course, that home of her own was precious little good at the moment, since she and Mr. Collins had fled the vicinity of Rosings Park. Lady Catherine de Bourgh's wrath over Mr. Darcy's engagement to Elizabeth Bennet, showing no sign of abating a

604

fortnight after receiving the news, had been enough to convince Mr. Collins that absence was his best defense. And so Charlotte, now a married woman, was back at Lucas Lodge on Bonfire Night, which had been when it all began.

Now there was to be another new beginning. Elizabeth would be marrying Mr. Darcy in less than a fortnight. Who would have thought it? Even she, who had seen Mr. Darcy's interest in Elizabeth before anyone else, had not believed it would lead to marriage. It made her wonder now whether Lizzy had been hoping for this all along, despite her early air of dislike for him.

Had that hope been what lay behind her friend's refusal to consider Mr. Collins's offer? Perhaps Charlotte was being too cynical, though. Lizzy had never had a practical thought in her head, so the benefits of marrying Mr. Collins would not have occurred to her—neither the financial benefits, nor the advantages of a husband who could be easily managed. Charlotte could not help smiling at the idea of any woman trying to manage Mr. Darcy! She hoped his attitude would not have too much of a detrimental effect on Lizzy's high spirits. Her friend was accustomed to making her own decisions, since her parents exercised so little authority. Marriage would be quite a change for Lizzy!

There seemed no question, though, that Lizzy loved him, and that he was overflowing with admiration for her. Charlotte did not envy Lizzy the riches and fine clothes she would have as Mrs. Darcy, but she could not help feeling a qualm when she considered that her husband would never look at her with that glow in his eyes. Not that she particularly wanted Mr. Collins to do so, but the idea of a husband who would love her so very much still drew something from her heart—a husband with whom she could share a marital bed without having to pretend he was someone else. Lizzy was fortunate in that regard.

Her husband came over to her then with a banal compliment for the festivities. As usual, she barely listened except to insert the occasional murmur of agreement which was all he expected of her. But she had no cause to complain. For all that he was not clever, witty, or well-mannered, her husband was a decent man who provided well for her and never beat her. And if he was not clever enough to notice that sometimes she would disappear for hours at a time with no particular excuse… well, all the better for her. Her lips curved as she thought about those secret hours and the man who shared them with her. Indeed, she was very fortunate, even if she would never have thought it a year ago.

Mr. Collins looked at Charlotte with great satisfaction, and congratulated himself on how much his wife had blossomed since he had chosen to marry her. She was indeed a fortunate woman to have attracted his interest last November!

Anne de Bourgh Sends Regrets

by Marilyn Brant

November 9, 1812

To Mr. Fitzwilliam Darcy of Pemberley
Sent on Behalf of Anne de Bourgh of Rosings by Mrs. Jenkinson

My Dear Cousin,

I have but a moment alone whilst my mother is attending to a number of decorative details at the Parsonage—you know how keenly she wishes to be of service to Mr. and Mrs. Collins—so I must endeavor to keep this note brief.

This morning, I happened upon my mother's letter to you in response to your kind wedding invitation. Indeed, she shared with me several passages from it and seemed, at times, rather feverish as she read it aloud. Although she may have presented to you my opinion on your upcoming nuptials in a somewhat different manner from what I, in fact, stated to her in private, I did want to assure you personally that I wish you and your bride the very best as you begin your life together.

Having had the pleasure of Miss Eliza Bennet's lively company at multiple dinners during her visits to Rosings, I could see clearly the attention the two of you paid to one another. Certainly, it was apparent to me (and, I daresay, even to my mother) that your interest in her was of a deep and - lasting nature. I was pleased to learn that Miss Bennet shared your affections. My only regret now is that I will not be able to make the journey to watch your exchange of vows from the nearest pew.

May the two of you pass many wonderful years together at Pemberley. I dearly hope to be able to congratulate you both in person before too long.

Fondly,

Anne de Bourgh

Lady Catherine Sends Regrets

by Marilyn Brant

November 9, 1812

My Very Own Nephew...

What have you done? I have no words.

The shades of Pemberley are darkening as I write this, and my speechlessness at your pointed betrayal of our family is equaled only by my shock. And after our recent conversation, too! We discussed this in London, Darcy!! You were standing but two feet in front of me. I know you heard my well-informed opinion of Miss Elizabeth Bennet and my report of her alarming behavior in Hertfordshire. I relayed it to you at length! You were neither asleep nor in some lamentable comatose state, which might have at least justified slightly your having not comprehended the full meaning of our discourse. But there is no excuse. You heard every sentence.

So, what could possibly have induced you to make an offer of marriage to that woman?!! I cannot account for such a frightening lapse in judgment.

I can only conclude that you must have been drugged at the time, perhaps by one of her many relatives. She seems to have an unlimited supply of sisters. Or you were otherwise induced by bribery or by the dark arts. Were some gypsies casting spells while you were dallying about in the wilderness? I am quite certain I saw a clan of them skittering along the side of the road when I visited that little place where she lives. Long...something. Out in the middle of nowhere fashionable. Not a high-class lady or gentleman to be found. Oh, Nephew, I am most seriously displeased.

Such stupidity in a marital choice might not be nearly as damaging to your young friend Bingley, as I have heard reports of his family's origins and, well, his reputation and place in society is not the equal of yours. But your foolishness in this matter is not to be borne!

Even if I were to overlook the grave insult in your having chosen a wife from amongst the ranks of virtual commoners, how could I possibly look the other way at your insensitive disregard for the dearest wishes of your mother, your cousin Anne and myself? My poor daughter is inconsolable. I know not how to express to you the pain you have willingly caused your nearest relations in the world. And for whom? For an upstart young woman of inferior birth, paltry connections and questionable taste?

It is unfathomable, Darcy.

I daresay, neither Anne nor I will attend such an event as your impending nuptials. I only pray you will have the good sense to call off such a scandalous engagement before it is too late.

Your Aunt,

Lady Catherine de Bourgh

A Sisterly Talk before the Wedding

by Maria Grace

November 10, 1812

The evening turned cold and the family retreated upstairs somewhat earlier than usual. Elizabeth and Jane withdrew to Jane's room. A warm fire crackled in the fireplace, and they sat together on the bed heaped high with pillows.

Elizabeth it removed the pins from Jane's hair and brushed it with the old silver hairbrush, a gift from Grandmother Gardiner so many years ago. Jane's hair was so beautiful, shining like molten gold under the brush, and always so well-behaved. Her silken locks submitted to the plait and pins as serenely as Jane herself walked through life, not like her own unruly locks.

She ran her fingers through Jane's hair. They did this so often, she would comb Jane's hair and Jane hers. How many more such moments would they share? Precious few. Life as Mrs. Darcy promised so much, but this she would miss.

"Have you become contemplative again, Lizzy?" Jane turned over her shoulder and caught her eyes. "You have. I can see it in the melancholy turn of your lips." Jane clasped Elizabeth's hands. "How can you be sad when so much joy awaits us? We have already made Mama so very happy."

"So she has said, countless times and to countless souls." Elizabeth laughed and slowly plaited Jane's hair. This might well be the last time she ever did this.

The door behind them squeaked and they both turned. Mary and Kitty, in their dressing gowns, peeked through the doorway as they and Lydia had done than when they were small, sneaking out of their beds to join their big sisters in clandestine gatherings.

"Come in, come in." Jane beckoned them in and slid toward the head of the bed.

Elizabeth patted the counterpane beside her. Mary and Kitty rushed in and piled on the feather bed, tucking their feet up underneath them.

"Do you remember how we used to do this after Mama would say goodnight?" Kitty giggled. "She would get so cross when she heard us laughing. She used to call us her 'little titter mice.'"

Jane wrapped her arms around her knees. "But she did not send us back to bed. I think maybe she and Aunt Philips did the same thing." She pulled her shoulders up around her ears and laughed softly.

Mary pulled her shoulders into a funny hunch and looked up like an old woman craning her neck. Her voice turned thin and brittle. "Remember how Lizzy would read us stories and do all the voices for the characters."

Elizabeth guffawed. "I had not thought of that in years." That would be another thing she missed. What would Mr. Darcy think of her—?

"You must promise to do that for your children," Mary said.

"And mine," Jane added, eyes sparkling.

"You shall have the most delightful children." Kitty clapped her hands softly.

Elizabeth rolled her eyes, not if any of Mama's predictions were correct. "Hardly, they will be all mischief and nonsense to be sure. Jane's, though, shall be angels, like her."

Jane's cheeks glowed. "Not if they resemble their father." She looked away.

What? Jane had never mentioned—

"Indeed?" Kitty scooted closer and pressed her chin on Jane's shoulder. "You must tell us, genteel Mr. Bingley is not as he seems? What secrets have you discovered about your betrothed?"

"Oh, Kitty, no!" Mary's hand flew to her mouth.

Jane laughed and turned back to her sisters. "No, no, nothing so outrageous as that. But he was a most high-spirited lad, or se he tells me."

"Nothing like your staid Mr. Darcy, I am sure." Kitty blinked with the same feigned innocence she often used on Mama.

Elizabeth smiled her brows lifted and cocked her head. There were those stories Colonel Fitzwilliam had told her in Kent.

"Oh, Lizzy!" Kitty gasped.

"What have you not told us?" Mary pressed her shoulder against Elizabeth's.

"How are his kisses, Lizzy? You seemed to like them very much." Kitty sing-songed.

Elizabeth gasped and traded looks with Jane. If her face burned any hotter, it would have burst into flame.

"That is not appropriate Kitty," Mary said softly.

"But I saw—" Kitty leaned back on her heels and pouted.

Elizabeth swallowed hard. "What do you think Charlotte's children will be like?"

Jane choked back laughter and hid her face in her knees. Mary and Kitty's jaws dropped.

"I am sure Lady Catherine will have to approve the child before he is born." Elizabeth peered down her nose and forced her voice into a staid, dignified tone. "Really, Mr. Collins, you must be certain to tell Mrs. Collins that the most proper time to be born is between three and four in the afternoon so as to allow the household to settle and have a proper dinner that evening." She pressed her fist to her mouth to contain her giggles.

Jane picked her head up and looked at Elizabeth, tears streaming down her cheeks. She fell onto her knees in helpless peals of laughter. Mary and Kitty dropped on each other's shoulders in breathless giggles. Elizabeth rocked back and forth, smiling broadly.

Mary wiped her eyes on her sleeve. Kitty pulled up the sheet and dragged it over her cheeks.

Only Jane had a handkerchief tucked up her sleeve. She blotted her eyes. "I shall dearly miss these times."

"I will too." Elizabeth's mirth faded away. How odd. Until now she had never contemplated the loneliness that might accompany her move to Derbyshire.

Kitty sniffled. "I cannot imagine what it will be like without both of you here."

"I have never imagined Longbourn without you." Mary blinked rapidly, her eyes bright.

Elizabeth patted Mary's arm and blinked back the burning in her eyes. "Well, never fear, unlike Lydia, I am quite certain I shall write so often you will quite tire of paying the post."

"You must, Lizzy, truly you must." Mary bit her lip. "Might we come to visit you?"

"Absolutely."

Jane clutched her breast exactly as Mama did. "After all, she might put you in the path of other rich men."

A fresh wave of laughter nearly choked them all. Few knew what a talented mimic Jane was, the most proficient of all of them. Did Mr. Bingley know yet? Doubtless, he would soon.

Elizabeth sighed. "I will need some time to settle into my role as mistress of Pemberley, but perhaps we might apply to Papa for you to visit during the summer."

"Really? You think Papa might agree?" Kitty clasped her hands below her chin.

"I do." The corners of Elizabeth's lips turned up. Pemberley would certainly not be like a trip to Brighton.

The glitter in Jane's eye confirmed their shared thought.

"You and Mr. Bingley too, if you would be free to come then."

"I am sure Mr. Bingley would appreciate the invitation. He speaks most fondly of Pemberley."

"Might we do this whilst at Pemberley?" Kitty asked in a very small voice.

"I am sure it can be arranged, it would not be a proper visit without an assembly of Mama's titter-mice."

Georgiana Arrives for the Wedding

by Monica Fairview

November 12, 1812

They changed horses at the Hart and Hounds Inn, their last stop before arriving at Netherfield.

"Almost there, now, Miss Darcy. It won't be long," said Mrs. Annesley, smiling as the carriage began its familiar sway and buck over the cobblestones leading out of the inn.

Everything suddenly became all too real. The thought of reaching her destination now filled Georgiana with apprehension. She shivered and drew her tippet closer around her.

Until this moment, it had all seemed like a fairy tale. She was so happy for her brother. Fitzwilliam was in love. There was a glow to him she'd never seen before, and that careworn look on his face that had been stamped there ever since their father had died was gone. His every footstep had a spring to it. There was such an eagerness to his face, such a sense of purpose and energy that it made her want to laugh and sing and play the piano as loudly as possible, which was really shocking because she'd always prided herself on the evenness of her playing.

Yes, she was very happy, not just for her brother, but for herself as well.

Her brother was to marry, and she was to have a sister. She had dreamed of having a sister for so long, someone to keep her company during the long days at Pemberley when Darcy was busy doing accounts or attending to the estate. Someone with whom she could sit and embroider. Someone who would look over fashion plates with her and discuss menus. Someone who would share with her all the female occupations which escaped her brother's interest. Then perhaps, too, if Darcy was married, he would spend more time at Pemberley, and she would not have to deal with long weeks of isolation in which she saw hardly anyone except for the five young ladies from neighboring families who occasionally came to call on her.

There were a thousand reasons to be happy, and none at all not to be. But still, there was that clenching feeling inside her, as if someone had tightened her stays too much. It made it hard for her to breathe. She felt guilty for feeling that way, but now that it had become rooted there was no getting rid of the anxiety.

She couldn't help being shy around strangers. It wasn't that she didn't meet enough people when she went down to London, but she wasn't always in London, and she was left to her own devices too often. The thing was, she had spent such a large part of her life alone. Her mother had died, then later her father, and Fitzwilliam— well Fitzwilliam was a young man and a young man with means and time at his disposal who wanted to see the world. It was only natural that he would spend large amounts of time away from Pemberley weeks at a time, even.

And then there was all that business with Wickham. Georgiana had made a terrible mistake. She had trusted Mrs. Younge, her governess, to keep her out of harm's way, never dreaming that there had been an agreement between Mrs. Younge and Wickham. She never could have imagined that Wickham was using her. Well, perhaps she had imagined it, just a little, because why else had she felt compelled to tell her brother about their secret plan to elope?

"Do you think Lady Catherine will be attending?" said Mrs. Annesley.

Oh, Lord. She hadn't thought at all of Lady Catherine. As if it wasn't enough to be meeting all those people without Lady Catherine there watching her like a hawk and telling her every minute to lift her chin and keep her back straight and stop simpering like a fool. She did not need constant reminders of how she needed to live up to the Darcy family name.

She sighed.

"I hope not, Mrs. Annesley," she said. "It will all be so much easier if she did not come."

"Don't you worry about her, Miss Darcy," said Betsy, Georgiana's maid, rousing out of her sleep. "She won't have much cause to chide you if the Master's there. You know how Mr. Darcy always puts a stop to it."

But Darcy would not always be there to protect her, especially when the ladies withdrew and left the men to their port. She would be alone in a room full of complete strangers and Lady Catherine would make her play the piano then issue instructions while she was playing and embarrass her in front of everybody.

She tried to reassure herself that there was nothing to worry about. After all, she already knew quite a few of those who would be there. She had met Elizabeth and the Gardiners in Pemberley, and she had seen them a few times when they came down to London, and of course she had known the Bingleys for years. Still, there was the whole Bennet family to meet as well as their friends.

Cousin Robert would be there. She had already met him in London. He was kind, and he had paid her some attention and told her stories about America, but she hardly knew him at all.

She would be an outsider.

Her only consolation was that all eyes would be on the wedding couples, and she would be left to her own devices.

"I do believe we've arrived," said Mrs. Annesley, as the carriage turned off the main road into a lane and through a large wrought-iron gate.

"I can hardly wait, Miss Darcy," said Betsy, her eyes shining. "You must be so excited."

Georgiana felt her throat go so dry she was afraid she wouldn't be able to say a word. It would be awful, not to be able to say anything at all.

Then the carriage stopped and a footman in red livery opened the door and helped her down the step.

There was the scent of lavender water; then Georgiana was gripped in a fierce hug. Elizabeth's laughing eyes met hers.

"There you are, Georgiana!" said Elizabeth. "What took you so long? We have been expecting you the last two hours, and your brother has been having dreadful thoughts of your carriage having overturned on some forsaken country lane."

Fitzwilliam was there behind Elizabeth, laughing, too.

Happiness soared inside Georgiana and she started to laugh with them. All was well. Darcy and Elizabeth would take care of her.

"Welcome to Netherfield, little sister," said Darcy.

The Musings of Mr. Collins Regarding His Cousin's Wedding

by Maria Grace

November 12, 1812

Breakfast should have been a quiet affair, but it seemed few meals were at Lucas Lodge. Mr. Collins squeezed his temples. So much banal chatter soured his stomach and ruined his appetite.

Mrs. Collins's brothers brought reports on new arrivals at Netherfield Park while her younger sister was brimming over with talk of lace and dresses. Collins could not bring himself to care about the brides' gowns and even less what the other ladies of their party would wear. How could Charlotte listen so patiently to all that blather? An uneasy shudder trailed down his back. How could Sir William and Lady Lucas fail to curb the exuberance of the young people at their table? Lady Catherine would never tolerate such ill-manners.

Thank heavens Mrs. Collins did not bring such manners with her into his home. Though she patiently listened and politely smiled thought the entire disgraceful display, she would certainly agree with his sentiment. She shared all his opinions, as a proper wife did. Without a doubt, young people should keep their trivial interests and conversations to themselves during meals. His children, when they came, would be taught properly.

Collins excused himself as quickly as could be, claiming a need for fresh air. Mrs. Collins smiled and encouraged him to go, noting that he must miss the time he usually spent in his garden and that a walk seemed necessary to his constitution.

A blast of chill wind buffeted his face as he stepped out. Though it burned the tips of his ears, he welcomed the discomfort to distract him from his own rising agitations. He pulled his hat down more snugly and tightened his scarf.

While Hertfordshire was pleasant enough and Lucas lodge offered many comforts, it was nothing to his Parsonage in Kent, the place he was currently unwelcome because of the thoughtless, headstrong actions of his *dear* cousin Elizabeth. His shoulders twitched at the thought.

How might he bear Lady Catherine's wrath. On his own count, he had never felt it, but now that his unruly and unrepentant cousin had crossed her ladyship, he felt its full fury. The hair on the back of his neck prickled. He rubbed it through his muffler though it did little to ease his discomfort.

Lady Catherine sounded just like his mother when in high dudgeon and her temper was much like his father's. How vexed her ladyship would be to be compared with such common folk. He chuckled, nonetheless. She would never hear that from him. Since both his parents had passed there was no chance Lady Catherine would ever notice the comparison.

His brisk steps crunched in the dry leaves underfoot. The sharp wind whipped dust around his feet and slapped small braches against his face. Bother! The gardener responsible for such unkempt paths should be fired, immediately. He grumbled under his breath and rubbed his chin. Bah. The barber's razor was going dull again. Did Meryton not have a decent tradesman in their midst? What other vexations were going to plague him now?

In the distance, he saw the tips of Longbourn's chimneys. Providence has smiled on him the day Cousin Elizabeth had so cruelly refused his offer of marriage. His bruised ego had not yet forgiven her, but her visit to Kent demonstrated her total lack of suitability. Collins winced. What a disaster it would have been to have brought her home to the Parsonage. Cousin Elizabeth would never have treated Lady Catherine with the proper deference and respect like his dear Mrs. Collins, with a bit of gentle coaching, did.

How was it that even now that hoyden still continued to plague him? How could she have such audacity as to marry Mr. Darcy? Did she not understand what she was doing to her father's heir? Even though she would not marry him, she owed him respect. Cold and unfeeling girl. It was her fault he was here in Hertfordshire, instead of enjoying the comforts, and quiet, of his own home in Kent.

There had to be some way to soothe Lady Catherine's ire and return to her good graces. He never failed to find a way to appease his volatile parents, so too, he would find a way to mollify his patroness.

He kicked a small rock out of his way. Letter after letter of apology had been sent but to no avail. More of the same would accomplish nothing. He needed a different tack.

How much easier his life would be now if not for his impudent, ill-mannered, ill-bred… There was a thought. The corners of his lips lifted. Yes, yes, there was nothing that soothed his father faster than to be agreed with. He rubbed his hands together.

He could quite look forward to writing his next letter—no letters. Ah, the pages and pages he could fill dedicated to the wrongs of his dear cousin. The critiques he could arrange for the pleasure of her ladyship would be most satisfying to write. What a gratifying change from finding another way to apologize for wrongs he never committed.

Surely he would return to her favor and on his way back to his own home soon. He ticked off the days in his mind. A fortnight should do it, perhaps a few days more. He turned back toward Lucas Lodge, his feet so light he nearly ran. He had letters to write.

Elizabeth Reflects on
Questionable Wedding Night Advice

by Shannon Winslow

November 13, 1812

I know that many brides go to the altar in complete ignorance—and consequently in great trepidation—of what will follow afterward. Neither Jane nor I shall suffer such an unfortunate fate, however. No, with our double wedding only a few days off, I expect we will both be supplied sufficient information on the topic in time. We shall have enough in quantity, at least. Considering the available sources, it is the quality of the information that is in doubt.

Months ago, Charlotte gave me the advantage of her wedded wisdom—painfully acquired, I fear—in the expectation that it would one day be of material benefit to me. I still remember what she told me then, and I have not withheld her penetrating insights from my dear sister Jane.

"The secret to connubial contentment," Charlotte had said, "is to organize one's life in such a way as to spend as little time as possible in one's husband's company. By day, any number of clever contrivances can be called into use. But at night, there is nothing so universally helpful in avoiding unwanted intimacy as a quarrel, and preferably separate bedchambers to go to afterward."

Amused, I responded with, "Dear Charlotte, you cannot possibly divine some fresh argument every night!"

"It is true that occasionally my resources fail me. I find, however, that being married to Mr. Collins is usually sufficient cause to put me in a very disagreeable humor by the end of the day."

This I could well believe. But such a philosophy will never do for me. I passionately long to spend more time, not less, with Mr. Darcy. And I secretly hope to find that the marriage bed is something mutually satisfying, not something to be avoided. Although Jane is too modest to speak of it, I suspect she feels the same. Perhaps, then, we should heed Lydia's candid opinion on the subject, as expressed in a recent letter addressed to us both:

"Oh, what a surprise you will each have on your wedding night!" she began. "I laugh to think of it. I daresay you will faint dead away, Jane, when your husband first approaches you. But Lizzy, I expect you to have a little more backbone. And you know there really is nothing to fear. Furthermore, I do not see why it should be only men who are allowed to admit taking pleasure in the physical act of love. In truth, it is often the only thing my dear Wickham and I can agree upon. So I find that, along with its other benefits, the conjugal act provides a very useful way of settling arguments."

Jane gasped when I read this part out to her in the privacy of her chamber. "Oh, my! What are we to think, Lizzy?" she asked, blushing furiously.

"A puzzling case, indeed. One friend says we are to use a quarrel to avoid the marriage bed, and another says the opposite— that we are instead to settle all our differences there."

"'Tis not sound, this advice!"

"I am quite of your opinion, Jane. If I love my husband, I must believe that his company will always—or at least almost always—be desirable. And temporary distraction is no way to settle disputes. No, we must hope to find more competent counsel elsewhere."

But where is this sage advice to come from? From our mother? Earlier today she dropped a hint that she wishes to have "a serious-minded discussion" with her two eldest daughters after dinner. She said this with a significant look that conveyed considerable embarrassment, leaving little doubt in my mind as to the intended topic of conversation. And alas, the time is now at hand.

623

"Lizzy, Jane, come with me," says Mama.

We rise and dutifully follow her from the dining room, leaving Papa and our two younger sisters behind. Papa gives me a pitying look, but I see that he is really amused.

Once in the sitting room, Mama closes the door. "We will not be disturbed here," says she with a wink. "Let us get comfortable by the fire, and then we can begin our little... our little chat. The wedding is almost here, girls, and it is my duty as your mother to prepare you in some measure for what comes afterward. You cannot, either one of you, have much idea of what goes on between a husband and wife behind closed doors, I suppose."

Jane and I look to each other for help, but neither one of us attempts an answer.

"Goodness!" continues Mama in some exasperation. "I never imagined this would be so very difficult. But it must be done, so I will speak as plainly as I can. You must surely know that there is a certain duty every wife owes to her marriage by way of procreation. If you are lucky, your husband may be patient and allow you a day or two to get used to the idea first. Sooner or later, however, he will insist on coming to your bed and having his way. I am afraid there is no avoiding it, my dears! You simply must each make up your mind to be brave about it."

Mama lets that somber tiding take its effect before continuing. "You have a right to know the truth, but I will give you a word of encouragement as well. Unpleasant as the business may seem in the beginning, it is part of the natural order of things and one tends to get used to it. Some women actually learn to enjoy it in time... or so I am told." Now it is Mama's turn to blush.

So what am I to conclude from the testimony of these three witnesses? I find little of their information to credit and even less to emulate. I believe I must take none of their advice too much to heart. Instead I resolve to keep an open mind. I trust Mr. Darcy and I will make our own way. And perhaps my own investigations into this matter will come to a much more gratifying conclusion. I fervently hope that shall be the case.

Mrs. Gardiner's Wedding Night Advice

by C. Allyn Pierson

November 15, 1812

Finally, after a busy and nerve-wracking day of wedding preparations, Jane and Elizabeth found themselves, limp and exhausted, in their shared bedroom preparing for bed. Elizabeth was just finishing tying her nightcap on, fluffing up a perky bow below her left ear and wondering what her wedding night would be like two nights hence. Her mother's "advice" to both girls, given earlier in the week in a private conference, had not relieved her nervousness over that important beginning to her marriage...no, not at all.

Jane was obviously thinking about the same subject, as she hesitantly said, "Um, Lizzy?"

"Yes, my dear?"

"Are you nervous about tomorrow?"

Lizzy pretended to misunderstand her, not quite sure how to answer. "Oh no, the wedding is all planned...nothing can go too terribly wrong...unless Lady Catherine decides to attend." Her attempt to soothe and reassure Jane elicited a weak smile from her beautiful sister.

"No, I am not nervous about the wedding itself... it is... it is the wedding night. All the advice we have received has my mind whirling...in fact, I feel...ill...quite ill." He voice dropped on the last two words so that Lizzy barely heard them. Before Lizzy could respond to her sister's fearful words and her ghastly white face, they heard a gentle tap on the door. Lizzy opened the door to her Aunt Gardiner.

"I hope I do not disturb you, my dear nieces, but I thought I would have a few words with you before bedtime." She paused and her face flushed. "I... I wanted to make sure that your mother talked to both of you about the wedding night."

Lizzy gave her a tremulous smile. "We were just talking about that subject... Mama's dissertation was not terribly...reassuring... nor was it...well, very informative. Poor Jane is feeling quite unwell, in fact."

Mrs. Gardiner sat on the edge of the bed between them and took their hands. "This is, of course, a rather embarrassing subject but I do not want either of you to marry without some idea of what to expect"

Lizzy gave a harsh laugh. "The problem is that we have been given far too much idea about what to expect ... and all of it contradictory!"

Her aunt smiled slightly. "I am not really surprised, my dears. Conjugal relations with your husband is a subject about which women have varying opinions. I believe that some of these variations are because of the common practice of marrying for family reasons, security, or wealth. If your husband regards you as a source of wealth, increased social status...or for passing your breeding onto his heirs, it is not surprising that he may not take care of either your heart or your body. I thank God you are both marrying for love... I am sure a marriage of convenience would be so much more difficult when it comes to physical intimacy. Well, to move on to the facts... the wedding night is a little frightening to a young girl, but it can be the beginning of a loving and fulfilling relationship with your husbands. Ummm...the first time you are ...with your husbands on your wedding night...you will, of course feel awkward...but you must realize this is the fulfillment of the relationship between a man and a woman who love each other."

She cleared her throat and continued, glancing at her nieces' pink faces. "God has designed men and women to fit perfectly together, but the first time is a little…difficult. Over time you will change and it will be easier, and you will find that you look forward to the private time you spend together."

Lizzy hemmed, then asked, "Do you have any advice for us, my dear aunt?"

"Try to relax and remember that this is the person you trust to care for you for the rest of your life. I am sure your husbands will be gentle and show you what to do…. I would suggest having a glass of wine together to relax and get comfortable with each other and then, go slowly. Although a gentleman would never discuss his previous experience in this area, I hope they have some… it makes things much easier if one of you is experienced, and you, naturally must depend on your husband for that knowledge, as you do not have it yourselves." She blushed even more, but had a determined look on her face as she dug in the pocket of her dressing gown. "My mother gave me this salve to use … down there. It can help ease things and also make you more comfortable the next day." She handed them each a small glass jar. "I guess my advice comes down to trusting your husband and trying to relax."

"Thank you, my dearest aunt." Both Bennet girls embraced their aunt before she left the room, then bustled around putting their clothes away, each tucking their little jar into the bottom of her going-away bag, before jumping into bed. Jane sighed and whispered in Lizzy's ear, "I hope she is right."

The Reflections of Thomas Bennet

by Maria Grace

November 15, 1812

Thomas Bennet was not by his nature a reflective man. Reflection tended to bring on discomfort and discontent, neither of which he favored. But his house—and his life—were in disarray on the cusp of his daughters' weddings and a little reflection could hardly make his discomfiture worse.

He picked his way around the trunks and boxes piled in the hall way. It was only a matter of time before Mrs. Bennet began demanding they be removed somewhere else lest the guests for the wedding breakfast see them. Thankfully Mr. Bingley had offered space at Netherfield for his daughters' things.

He slipped into the study and fell into his favorite chair. All the lumps and bumps in the seat matched his own. At least some things in his life would not change. He had had this old chair for decades and resisted all Mrs. Bennet's insistence that it be replaced.

But it seemed like everything else around him was changing, and he was certain he did not like it. Change brought disorder and distress. Change took away...

A lump rose in his throat. He pushed up from his chair and locked the door. A visit to the brandy decanter, and then he returned to his chair.

Lizzy told him Lady Catherine said a daughter was never of much consequence to a father, but the great lady was very, very wrong. He sipped his brandy and leaned his head back. Society told him he should want fine strapping sons—an heir and a spare to inherit his estate and carry on his name. But he did not.

Oh, he had intended to father a son, to be sure, but his heart had not been in it. Perhaps that was why Fanny only conceived daughters. That was what his father argued when he scolded his eldest son for not producing the required heir. As if a father's will could influence the choices of Providence. He shook his head and closed his eyes.

Though he would never say it aloud, it was best this way. After living with his father and a brother who was just like his sire, Bennet did not trust himself with sons. He could not shake the lingering fear that a son might be like his grandfather or like Collins's father. He shuddered. No, far better to have daughters.

Upon daughters, a man could dote. He could delight in them rather than try to shape them into the image of himself. He laced his fingers and rubbed his thumbs together. He was satisfied with his girls, the eldest two in particular, except for one thing, they were about to leave him.

True, he hardly missed Lydia, but she was her mother's daughter. Jane, and especially Lizzy were more his girls. Jane would sit and read to him. She had the most delightful reading voice. Lizzy was his chess partner and the one with whom he could discuss his interests.

Only yesterday he had bounced them on his knees, taught them to love the classics and to reason. Those days had flown so quickly. If only there was some way to recapture them.

He pulled his top lip down over his teeth. What we would give to turn back time and be with his little girls again. But that could never be. Perhaps the emptiness that kept threatening his consciousness would become a permanent fixture in his life. He stroked his chin.

On the other hand, he could tolerate Bingley's company with some equanimity, and, though he would not admit it aloud, Darcy's presence grew more and more tolerable as well. They girls had found fine men to be their partners in life. Well, Lydia had not.

Wickham was every bit as silly and banal as she.

If he could keep Fanny from alienating Jane with constant intrusions, they might remain welcome at Netherfield. In time, after Darcy's memory of Fanny's effusive praises had faded, they might even enjoy invitations to Pemberley. Then, if, no when, there were children, his grandchildren, he could be the grandfather his girls never had. Surely one among them would have Jane's disposition and another Lizzy's. He might be able to recapture those days after all.

He smiled, eyes a little moist. Sometimes a little reflection was indeed good for the soul.

Darcy Reflects on His Parents' Marriage

by Mary Simonsen

November 15, 1812

Tomorrow I am to be married, Darcy thought, as he enjoyed a glass of port in his bedchamber. Although delighted by the prospect of sharing his life with the woman he loved, his thoughts turned to another couple—that of his parents, George Darcy and Lady Anne Fitzwilliam.

As a child, it seemed as if his mother was always going somewhere—a card party, a reception, a ball, the theater, each requiring that she be swathed in layers of clothing. Before each event, the young Darcy visited her suite and watched as her lady's maid powdered her hair. That exercise was followed by the insertion of elaborate hair accoutrements: feathers, strands of tiny pearls, and, on at least one occasion, a songbird. Only when everything was just so did Lady Anne descend the stairs, and in his impressionable, young mind, she appeared to float above them. At the bottom of the stairway, his father waited for his bride in a sky blue jacket, matching satin breeches, and shoes with jeweled buckles. In addition to his finest clothes, he wore his best wig—the queue tied with a satin ribbon to match the color of Mama's gown. All this Fitzwilliam observed whilst holding tightly to the hand of his nurse or governess. Once his parents had left Pemberley or Darcy House, depending upon the season, he would be whisked back to the nursery for lessons or a bedtime story.

Darcy was at Cambridge when he had been called into the headmaster's room. It was there that he had learned of his mother's death following a brief illness and that his father was sending a carriage for him.

Although his dear Papa's grief was real and sustained, so much of his parents' lives had been spent apart. Whilst Mama preferred London or visiting with her brother, the Earl of _____, and her sister, Lady Catherine de Bourgh, his father was happiest when working on improvements at Pemberley—his mother frequently teasing her husband that every time she returned to Derbyshire, it was necessary for her to have a tour of the house and its gardens as nothing would be the same as when she had left it. *An exaggeration, of course*, but it was evidence of their lengthy separations.

With his mother's death, all improvements at Pemberley had ceased, and the elder Darcy turned his attention to making the estate as profitable as possible. To that end, he leased land to a pottery and timber concern and doubled the size of the grist mill. In Lambton, he subsidized the building of a new assembly hall and the expansion of the town hall, a place where, as Lord of the Manor, he served as magistrate in connection with minor disputes. Observing the flurry of activity, Fitzwilliam understood that with his mother gone, his father had lost the only admirer that mattered for the vast improvements he had made at Pemberley.

Darcy shook his head at the memory. Although he loved and admired his parents, their type of relationship was not what he wanted in his marriage with Elizabeth.

After walking to the window, his eyes followed the tree-line that would eventually lead him to Longbourn where his bride would spend her last day as Miss Elizabeth Bennet. Tomorrow night, they would share the same bed—something his parents rarely did—or at least something he was unaware of. In the morning, when the children were sent for, Lady Anne could be found propped up on pillows in her own chamber—alone. After gently tapping the satin covers, Fitzwilliam and little Georgiana ran towards the bed and climbed in beside their mother who regaled them with stories of her time in London.

Thinking of the children Elizabeth and he would have, he smiled, but swore that when his children came into their mother's suite, they would find their father there as well.

"I want the first person I see every morning to be Elizabeth and that she will be a part of every day of my life, and I want to be a part of hers," he said aloud. "Of course, that does not mean I shall meddle with the menus or discuss household purchases nor will she accompany me when I meet with my steward. But in all other matters, I want Elizabeth by my side. Ours will be a very different marriage from that of my parents. Tomorrow, when the parson declares that two have become one, it will be a statement of fact not some lofty ideal. And why should it not be," Darcy continued. "I have found the perfect wife. I am determined to be the best husband I can be."

A Conversation between Jane and Elizabeth on the Eve of their Weddings

by Jane Odiwe

November 15, 1812

Elizabeth watched Jane take the pins from her hair as she sat before the looking glass on the dressing table. She noted, as if for the first time, Jane's nimble fingers following the nightly ritual Lizzy had witnessed for years. With swift strokes, Jane brushed her hair back from the crown and the sides before inclining her head to reach underneath the tresses at her nape. Lustrous curls tumbled about her shoulders and cascaded down the back of her nightgown. In candlelight, her sister thought she'd never looked more beautiful.

Jane sat up to meet Elizabeth's eyes in the mirror.

"Oh, Lizzy, do you realize this is the last night we shall spend together? I've been so caught up in wedding preparations that I am not certain I have fully comprehended the fact until now."

"Do you mean to tell me that you have only just understood our mother's timely advice that we shall be expected to share our husband's beds?" quipped Lizzy. "Or, that you've not fully grasped that implicit in her motherly counsel was a pearl of a reminder that in future we should be 'slaves to our masters' in order to warrant connubial felicity for all eternity!"

Jane laughed, delighting in her sister's humor. "I have never been so embarrassed in all my life. From Aunt Gardiner such advice is so well-meaning, so tactfully done, but our mother could not have made a more uncomfortable speech."

"Lizzy! Don't snigger!" mimicked Elizabeth in imitation of her mama. "How do you think your father and I have enjoyed such a happy marriage for so long? It isn't by the efficacy of separate sleeping arrangements such as the Longs and the Lucases have adopted, except, I daresay, if I had produced an heir I might have befallen such a fate myself. Though, truth to tell, Mr. Bennet has never made a secret of the fact that he still finds me irresistible and if you can still say the same after twenty four years of marriage, you will be doing well!"

"Please stop, Lizzy, my sides are aching with laughter."

"Oh, Jane, I shall miss our evening conversations." Elizabeth sat down nudging her sister further along the seat.

"And all our confidences," said her sister. "How shall I do without you? Mr. Darcy is to have all your good humor and share all your secrets besides the attention of your 'fine eyes', which look as pretty tonight as I ever saw them."

"You'll do very well, I am sure, when you're lying in the arms of Mr. Bingley. I never saw a couple so well suited, so made to have confidences in one another. There are few people who become a superior entity together than are able to work as two halves but I sincerely believe that you and Charles are the exception. You were made for one another. Besides, you will not have time to think about me. As mistress of Netherfield, you will be a very busy lady."

"But, will I be mistress of Netherfield, Lizzy? I am sure Caroline Bingley will have very firm ideas about who is in charge, and I cannot think she will take kindly to me attempting to step into her shoes."

"If anyone can deal with Miss Bingley, it is you, sweet Jane, and I believe you will achieve your ends with grace and charm. In any case, I am certain that Charles will make it clear from the start that you have precedence. He may be the most obliging, complying gentleman that has ever lived, and he loves you with all his heart. Your happiness will be his own, and if that means he has to speak sternly to his sister, I am certain he will be your champion."

"As I am sure Mr. Darcy will be, too, when it comes to his aunt, Lizzy."

"Goodness, Lady Catherine, I hadn't given her a thought! Well, I doubt we shall ever see her. After all, from tomorrow the shades of Pemberley will be thoroughly polluted!"

"I would not be so sure, dearest Elizabeth. Curiosity may well get the better of her. She may be planning a visit as we speak."

"Now, you are teasing, Jane. At least we are spared her glowering presence at the wedding."

"The wedding! Lizzy, can you believe it? We are getting married tomorrow."

Elizabeth took her sister's hands in her own. "My love, I can believe it, and I know we shall both be very happy. And, even if we shall be apart for a while, as we have never been before, I know our husbands will not let us suffer."

"No, it will be difficult enough for both of them to be apart. They have become so like brothers!"

"You and Charles shall come to Pemberley as soon as Christmas if you would like it, and I shall persuade you both to look at houses whilst you are there. I have one in mind that Mr. Darcy tells me is very suitable and only just over the border in the next county. If I have my way, we will not be separated for long."

Jane threw her arms around her sister, hugging her tightly. "You will write to me, won't you?"

"Every day, I promise."

Though not sentimental by nature, Elizabeth felt the tears prick at her eyelids. In her heart she knew life would never be quite the same and that tomorrow they would face new lives, not as the young girls they'd been at Longbourn House but as married women with all the excitement and challenges that would bring.

"Oh look, Jane," she said, turning her face to the window to hide her emotions, "it is snowing!"

Whirling through the night sky, snowflakes plummeted, settling like swan feathers against the casement window. A robin flashing his scarlet breast flew into the tree whose branches tapped at the glass. Beyond, the fields formed a patchwork across the Hertfordshire countryside. Familiar scenes and sounds, and a lifetime of reminiscences were wrapped around the sisters in that moment like the arms that clasped them so tightly.

The Longbourn Ladies Dress for the Wedding

by Susan Mason-Milks

November 16, 1812

Elizabeth stood behind Jane carefully pinning her hair up and patiently winding ribbons though the curls.

"This is the last time we will do this, you know," said Lizzy. "From now on your maid Molly will be fixing your hair."

"Lizzy, don't be a goose. We can do this again when we visit," Jane replied trying to cheer her sister.

"But it will not be the same." Lizzy and Jane's eyes met in the mirror and they shared a knowing look.

Just then, Kitty and Mary swept in, giggling as they gathered around.

"What do you think of our new dresses?" asked Kitty, twirling in a circle to display her new pink gown to its fullest advantage. "Mary, show them the beautiful lace on yours."

Mary was usually the last one to be looked at or admired, and so when her sisters turned to look at her dress, the attention made her blush. Then they realized that something was different about her.

"Mary, you look lovely!" Jane exclaimed. And in fact, she did. Her hair was done more softly around her face making her look less severe. Lavender-colored ribbons, the same color as the flowers on her muslin dress, were wound artfully into her hair.

"I fixed her hair," cried Kitty. "Did I not do a splendid job of it? For once she did not insist that I pull it back so tightly. I think it does wonders for her face. Why…"

"Please stop talking about me as if I were not here," Mary said, clearly embarrassed at the compliments she was receiving.

"But, Mary, you look wonderful. In fact, I have never seen you look better." Impulsively, Elizabeth pulled her blushing sister into a hug.

"I think entirely too much is made of how young ladies look. It is our more substantive qualities and accomplishments that are most important," Mary pronounced.

"Yes, however, it does not hurt if the outside is just as lovely, too," Jane said, putting a reassuring hand on Mary's arm.

"We should be talking about you and Lizzy today. After all, it is your wedding day," said Mary, clearly trying to deflect the conversation away from herself.

"What do you think of what I have done with Jane's hair?" Elizabeth asked, returning to the subject at hand.

"I think you should add more ribbons," Kitty suggested.

"And I think it is perfect as it is," said Mary with a rare smile. "She does not need more ribbons to enhance her natural beauty."

"Thank you, Mary, dear. Now enough fussing about me; it is your turn, Lizzy." Jane stood up and offered the seat to her sister.

"Yes, we should all help with Lizzy's hair!" At that, Kitty nudged her sister into the chair and picked up the brush.

As Kitty worked diligently over Elizabeth's dark locks, her sisters giggled with excitement, sometimes all talking at the same time.

"Are you anxious about tonight?" Kitty asked nonchalantly. They all looked at her with wide eyes. "Well, it is what we are all thinking about, is it not?"

The response was more nervous giggles and blushes all around.

"You know that is not a proper topic of discussion for unmarried ladies," Mary scolded.

"Oh, do not be such a bore, Mary. When Lydia was here after her wedding, she told me all about it—how terrifying the marital bed is and all the indelicate things a husband…well, expects," Kitty said with a gulp.

Jane and Elizabeth looked at each other with their eyebrows raised.

"Although I am certain that Mr. Darcy and Mr. Bingley would never behave in such a manner," she quickly added.

There was another awkward silence.

"Oh, heavens, Kitty! You surely did not believe everything she told you," Elizabeth exclaimed.

"Why not? She is now a married woman and knows all about the conjugal mysteries we are not even allowed to think about," Kitty told them.

After a moment of silence, Lizzy spoke. "I cannot go into details, but Jane and I had a letter from Lydia sharing her 'married woman' wisdom. I am certain what she said had at least some elements of truth to it, but it was certainly nothing at all like what Aunt Gardiner has told us to expect. The words 'terrifying' and 'indelicate' were never mentioned at all."

Another moment of complete silence followed during which all of the Bennet girls considered the situation. First, Lizzy started to laugh, then Jane and Mary and finally, Kitty. They laughed until tears rolled down their cheeks, and they were holding their sides. Mary and Kitty leaned on each other for support just to stand. Mary pulled out her handkerchief and patted her eyes.

When at last they were able to be coherent again, Mary said, "You know Lydia is in Newcastle right this moment laughing even harder than we are at the little joke she thinks she has played on you, Kitty."

"I was under the distinct impression you believed her, too, Mary," Kitty replied a little indignantly.

Mary frowned. "I did not."

"Oh, at moment like this, I do wish Lydia was here with us," said Jane wiping away the last of her tears with the back of her hand.

"Yes, so I could get my hands around her little neck," said Kitty, stifling another giggle. "In spite of everything, I do miss her sometimes though."

"Do you also miss chasing men in red coats or running wild at parties so that we are all mortified with shame?" Mary asked.

Kitty turned serious. "No, Mary, my eyes are wide open now. It has become very clear to me that I was following the wrong sister. I only hope Lizzy and Jane will allow me to spend more time with them. I would prefer to learn to be a lady—just as they are." Her eyes began to twinkle with mischief. "Then, perhaps, I will catch a rich husband, too."

Jane was the first to put an arm around Kitty, and then Elizabeth joined them. After Mary was waved over, she finally came and put her arms around her sisters.

"This is more like it—true sisterly affection. I love all of you very much, and you will always be welcome at Pemberley," said Elizabeth. Then she added with a note of humor in her voice, "That is, as soon as I actually manage to learn my way around my new home. It is so large that I know I shall be in constant terror of becoming lost. Why, the house has so many hallways and stairways that I might need to use a ball of thread like Theseus in the Minotaur's Labyrinth. It would be too embarrassing if Mr. Darcy had to send out the footmen or maids looking for me."

"It might be much more fun if Mr. Darcy went looking for you himself," Kitty said with a giggle.

"Kitty! Where do you get these ideas? "Elizabeth cried as she broke into laughter again and her sisters joined her.

"Oh, look at the time! We must hurry! We have only a few minutes before we leave for the church, and there is still so much to do!" Jane told them.

Suddenly, tears formed in Mary's eyes.

"What is it, my dear Mary? This is not like you. Are you unwell?" asked Jane moving quickly to put an arm around her sister.

Mary tried looking at the floor to hide the tears and shook her head. Jane put a gentle finger under Mary's chin and lifted it. The watery pools that were forming seemed to magnify and distort her golden brown eyes. Instead of pulling away, as she normally did in a situation such as this, Mary smiled through the tears as Jane used a linen handkerchief to blot her sister's eyes.

"I am so very happy for you, but after today, you will belong more to your husbands than to us. It will all be so different," Mary told them between sniffles.

"We have talked about this before. We are sisters — forever and always. That is something that no wedding can change."

"I know that."

"Then what is it?" Elizabeth asked. "Are you afraid that you will never fall in love and get married?"

"Oh, romance is for other people, not for me," Mary said, trying to sound serious.

"That does not have to be true, sweetheart, but for love to have a chance, you must open your heart and see the possibilities. If I had not taken the time to get to know Mr. Darcy, I might never have discovered all of his fine qualities. He would have passed out of my life as an enigmatic figure, a puzzle never to be solved, and I would be the poorer for it," Elizabeth told her.

Mary managed a smile. "I shall remember your advice."

"Come here, Mary, let me fix your face so those tears do not show. We cannot have all of Meryton saying that the brides' sisters were crying even before the wedding. They might think you are not happy for us."

"I am happy for you. Truly." Mary hugged Jane.

Then in the distance, they heard their mother's shrill voice calling, "Girls, girls! The carriages are here. You must come at once!"

Scrambling, they picked up bonnets, gloves and other little accoutrements. Jane, Kitty, and Mary rushed off leaving Elizabeth as the last one out. After a brief look around the room, she smiled and closed the door on this part of her life.

The Wedding

by C. Allyn Pierson

November 16, 1812

Jane's and Lizzy's wedding day finally arrives...

Elizabeth glanced at Darcy from the corner of her eye. She still could not believe that they were married, even though they had been man and wife for several hours. When they left Longbourn in Darcy's carriage after the wedding breakfast they sat with rigid propriety as they drove through Hertfordshire, where they were both known. Only their clasped hands, resting on Elizabeth's lap and hidden from the avid stares of the local inhabitants, demonstrated their affection.

As they met the toll road and turned north, Darcy reached across her and closed the velvet curtains halfway, hiding them from the other travelers around them. He reached for her and drew her towards him, holding her as they continued towards their first stop on the way to Pemberley. When they were not kissing or touching each other, Elizabeth thought back on their wedding day, which already seemed almost a dream.

That morning, when they reached the church, Elizabeth stepped carefully from the carriage, making sure that her gown and veil did not catch on the latch of the door or drag on the ground. After surviving the pandemonium of the Bennet household that morning, she did not want her or her sister's wedding gown to be damaged right at the church door. Her father, his lips compressed as they did when he was trying to suppress an emotion, held her hand

and steadied her as her sisters straightened the train and smoothed her veil, then Lizzy stepped to the church door while he similarly helped Jane down.

Mary attempted to look indifferent at such material conceits as wedding gowns and flowers, but her eyes were almost as bright as Kitty's. Kitty felt that attending her sisters at their wedding was a fair repayment for the previous suffering caused by their sister Lydia. Lydia might have married before her sisters, but her marriage had barely given her respectability after her infamous elopement, and Kitty now felt justified and revenged for the rudeness she had had to endure when Lydia had been invited to Brighton without her.

When they were finally ready, the organist started playing, and Papa offered Jane and Lizzy each an arm. The usher flung open the double doors of the church and they began their procession. Lizzy glanced at the guests on either side—a little confused by the many faces of their friends and family smiling at the two brides. Well, all were smiling except for Miss Bingley, who looked like she had had curdled milk in her tea that morning. Lizzy suppressed a smile and looked towards the altar as they had approached it. Suddenly, she felt herself tremble. There was Mr. Darcy, his expression serious but his eyes warm as he watched his bride approach. Mr. Bingley stood next to him, a wide grin on his friendly face and his eyes glued to her sister's face.

When they reached the front Lizzy hardly heard the minister as their father solemnly handed each of them over to their husbands; she saw her papa's eyes were moist, and she found herself blinking away a few tears herself in spite of her happiness. Papa would miss both of them so. She wanted to throw her arms around him and reassure him about the happiness of both his daughters, but her hand was already in Mr. Darcy's and, once her eyes met his, she forgot about Papa, about her mother...about anything but Darcy.

The ceremony seemed to only take the blink of an eye, and when it finished, and the two couples signed the church register, there was no time to think of how lonely Papa would be as they kissed or shook hands with the guests as they left the church, before all bundled into carriages for the ride back to Longbourn for the wedding breakfast.

When they were all seated for the breakfast, Lizzy finally had time to attend to something besides her husband's hand in hers. Her parents welcomed the guests with tears sparkling unheeded on their cheeks and Lizzy reached over to squeeze her sister's hand. "Congratulations," she whispered in her ear, "All the happiness in the world my dearest Jane." They embraced each other; then each turned to her husband with a smile to face the future together

Mrs. Bennet's Wedding Reflections

by Jane Odiwe

November 16, 1812

Happy for all her maternal feelings was the day on which Mrs. Bennet got rid of her two most deserving daughters. With what delighted pride she reflected on the day's events as she and Mr. Bennet sat amongst the detritus left from the celebrations in the dining-parlor.

"Mr. Bennet, did you ever attend such a wedding? What a remarkable day! I think it all passed off exceptionally well. I am excessively pleased with everything. Everyone behaved prettily, and I never saw so many onlookers gawping at the church gate. Mrs. Long's nieces seemed enraptured, in particular. Of course, those poor girls will probably never see a wedding of their own. They cannot help being so very plain but I like them well enough for it. Plainer even than Charlotte Lucas—not that I think her exceptionally so, but then she is such a cherished friend. Next to Jane, anyone would be at a disadvantage. I said to Lady Lucas and Mrs. Long, 'Did you ever see a more radiant bride?' and, of course, they concurred."

"How could they do anything else, my dear?"

"And I know you are not fond of discussing lace, Mr. Bennet, but our girls' lace marked them out with distinction. Elizabeth's veil has been in the Darcy family since the time of good old Henry, I believe. I daresay Anne Boleyn herself saw it grace some noble head."

"More than likely. And before she lost her own, I presume."

"Mr. Bennet! Nothing you say will vex me today."

"I am glad to hear it!"

Smiles decked the face of Mrs. Bennet. "And dear Bingley is so good-looking and everything a gentleman should be even if he has not quite the consequence of dear Darcy."

"Dear Darcy, is it?" Mr. Bennet smirked and picked up a newspaper before settling himself in a chair by the fire.

"I have always thought so. Dear, dear, Darcy! Did he not look a picture in his black coat? I cannot even think that a red one could improve him, you know, despite my partiality for a uniform. Such a tall and handsome man! Always obliging! So charming! And, so rich!"

"He is generous too, for which we are exceedingly grateful—for more weddings than this one," added Mr. Bennet (under his breath) from behind the paper.

"Well, who else should have done it? Mr. Darcy would not notice if he settled an amount on twenty weddings! The money is a pin-prick on my best gown, a mere drop in the ocean, a single star in the heavens! Though I have to say despite Darcy's generosity, my Lydia did not have the best of it. Her nuptials were a poor affair but I have lately forgiven my son-in-law for he is helping dear Wickham rise in his profession."

"I am certain Darcy would be delighted if only he knew how magnanimous you are towards him, Mrs. Bennet."

"To him I could not be anything else. I only hope that Lizzy has a true appreciation of his worth and does not go letting her tongue run away with her, as she is wont to do. I cannot help thinking that Jane with all her sweet ways might not have been a better match for him, but then Lizzy could never have suited Bingley. Yet, I should have thought she might be more capable of keeping Miss Caroline Bingley in her place. What a delight to see my Jane take precedence over her. Did you see her countenance as they left the church?"

"Whose countenance?" Mr. Bennet's own peered around the edge of the newspaper.

"Why, Miss Bingley, of course! She will have to give way to Jane on everything now. I do not suppose Miss High and Mighty will relish playing second fiddle. If only we could get her married off and then she would have to leave Netherfield. Colonel Fitzwilliam might do if he did not seem so keen to marry Miss Georgiana, or Mr. Hurst's brother, if he were perhaps taller. But, then Miss Bingley would be too close to Netherfield and I feel sure she would be better placed far away."

"I daresay, Jane and Miss Bingley will get along until such time as a suitor comes to call."

"Well, if anyone can make that sly cat purr, it will be my Jane. And talking of purring cats, it brings to mind the bowls of golden cream served at our wonderful wedding breakfast!"

"Yes, it was a very satisfactory meal, my dear."

"Satisfactory! Hill outdid herself, I'm sure Mr. Darcy's three French cooks could not have done more! Such sweet ham! The tongue so pink, the cake such a confection! And all a hundred times better than what we endured at Charlotte Lucas's wedding. I never saw a more paltry lack of victuals in my life—stale bread rolls, the cream curdled and a piece of pound cake I would not give to a beggar. Lady Lucas keeps a very poor table, and I keep an excellent one if I say so myself. But, I do not trust my own partiality, it is what everybody says."

"I am sure they do, my dear, Mrs. Bennet."

"Anyway, it is all over and now all I have got left to think on is that three of my dear girls have left me, though it is a comfort for me to know that Jane is so near when my dearest Lydia is so very far away. It is no surprise that Lizzy is gone off to the Peak—nothing she might do would be a revelation! No doubt, Kitty and Mary will move to Scotland and have done with it! Jane will follow when she wants a home close to her sister and I shall be left, a poor widow all on my own at the mercy of Mr. Collins and his wife!"

"I am glad to see you have plans for me at any rate, Mrs. Bennet. But, I hope you will not put me into too early a grave and deny me the pleasure of knowing my grandchildren."

"Oh, Mr. Bennet, what a happy thought! Lord bless me! Good gracious! After today, I daresay we shall not have to wait too long for such an announcement!"

Mr. Bennet shook his head and disappeared once more behind the news of the day.

Caroline's Wedding Reflections

by Shannon Winslow

November 16, 1812

"How thrilling!" a woman in the pew behind said in hushed excitement. "A double wedding!"

Caroline Bingley rolled her eyes heavenward and leant closer to her sister. "Double disaster, more like," she whispered. Although she had no choice but to attend this farce, she did not have to make believe she liked it.

Her brother's choice of bride was truly a disaster. He might have married a girl from one of the best families, someone who would have enhanced the prestige of the Bingley name... and perhaps added to the family's fortune as well. What had they all been working for, after all, if not to raise themselves to where nobody would ever remember their humble origins again? Louisa had done her part, at great person sacrifice. But Charles! He was this minute throwing his one chance away on a nobody, and there was nothing she could do about it.

Caroline could not bear to watch her brother disgracing himself, but she did hazard a glance in Mr. Darcy's direction...and a sigh. Were there any justice in the world, she would have been the one standing up beside him now, the one he was regarding so tenderly, the one to whom he plighted his highly covetable troth. It was unaccountable—and patently unfair—that after all her efforts, all her attentiveness, he should also prefer a Miss Bennet! It was not to be borne!

Had Darcy determined to marry Miss de Bourgh over herself,

she might have understood, for then she would have been beaten by the undeniable claims of a noble bloodline and a superior fortune. But what did Miss Eliza Bennet have to boast of... except for those notorious "fine eyes"?

It was indeed a harsh blow, and one that was not to be recovered from anytime soon.

Charlotte's Wedding Reflections

by Abigail Reynolds

November 16, 1812

For at least the third time, Charlotte Collins felt an elbow poke itself into her ribs. Her sister Maria was beside herself with excitement at attending Lizzy and Jane's wedding. Her parents were puffed up with pride as well, and her mother was no doubt taking note of every detail so that she could report on it later to her friends. Most of their neighbors were green with jealousy since only family members had been invited to the ceremony. Charlotte felt a distinct sense of satisfaction at knowing her family's invitation was owing to her connection to the Bennets, not because of her father's position.

It had been a revelation for her to return to Meryton as the future mistress of Longbourn. People who had little time for her in the past made an effort to ask her opinion on various matters. After years of being viewed as nothing more than the plain spinster daughter of the former mayor, now she had a position of her own in society and an enviable future. She had never realized before the extent to which she had been disregarded by many people. This was a definite improvement.

Of course, if the change in her status had been a shock to her, it was nothing to what Lizzy must be experiencing. In a few short minutes, she would be Mrs. Darcy of Pemberley. No longer would she be Mrs. Bennet's least favorite daughter, the one whose liveliness had more than once caused people to whisper behind their hands that no man would ever take up with the likes of Lizzy Bennet. Now she would be the one they would go to, hat in hand, to beg a favor, that she put a word in the right ear, that she use her influence for this or for that. It was fortunate that Lizzy was not the gloating sort.

No, Lizzy was the generous sort, and so apparently was her husband to be. A few days ago Lizzy had taken Charlotte aside and told her that Mr. Darcy hoped she would contact them if there were to be any serious difficulties between her husband and Lady Catherine as a result of their marriage. Since Charlotte's great worry these days was that Lady Catherine might make life in Hunsford intolerable for them, she was greatly relieved by her friend's words. It would hopefully be many years before Mr. Bennet departed the earth, leaving Longbourn to Mr. Collins, and in the meantime, they needed a place to live. Charlotte had no desire to leave Hunsford; she was fond of her home and had made friends in the area, but it was good to know they would not be forced to remain in an unpleasant situation if Lady Catherine continued in her fit of pique.

And there was Lizzy now, being escorted in by her father, with Jane on his other arm. Lizzy's gown of white silk gleamed in the morning light that shone in through the windows, set off with fine lace and a gold sash. The necklace of sapphires around her neck, a gift from Mr. Darcy, marked her future status even more clearly than her elegant dress. Charlotte would never own a dress so lovely, nor jewelry a tenth as expensive, but that was just as well. Lizzy in her finery looked like a rose in bloom; Charlotte would have merely looked overdressed and gaudy. She would not have enjoyed some of the duties Lizzy would face, either. Charlotte was just as glad not to be part of the *ton*, however often her father might speak of his presentation at the court of St. James.

As Lizzy reached Mr. Darcy's side, Charlotte sent her silent best wishes to her dearest friend that her marriage would bring her all the joy she deserved.

Lady Catherine, Alone at Rosings

by Diana Birchall

November 16, 1812

Rosings! Poor, poor Rosings. No longer allied with Pemberley, no longer a shining crown in the Darcy panoply of great houses, Rosings now stood alone and forlorn. There would be no more visits from the young men with whom Lady Catherine had been so proud to be connected. Mr. Darcy would never come to Rosings now, and Colonel Fitzwilliam, shamefully loyal to his cousin rather than to his aunt, would not pay his respects to her there either. The new Mrs. Darcy, and the deluded Miss Darcy alike, would be henceforth dead to the mistress of Rosings. For Lady Catherine de Bourgh had cut them all off at one stroke: her abusive letter regarding Darcy's disgraceful marriage had been decisive.

Not that Lady Catherine would admit to administering anything more than a mere corrective, though admittedly it was rather like whipping a horse's empty stall, after the beast itself had jumped its traces and escaped. Never mind; she had given her opinion, and stated what she felt to be right, no matter how unpleasant the consequences might be to her personally. But that was her character, for which she was so justly famed. She would brook no compromise. It would be the young men who were the losers, no longer having the entree to the superior society of Rosings.

At Rosings, then, Lady Catherine sat alone in splendid solitude, with nothing but the satisfaction that she had been right: as she always was. No, not quite alone; for there was Anne, to be sure, and her companion Mrs. Jenkinson. Even to a mother's eye, disposed to be prejudiced until inevitable disappointment set in, it was plain that Anne was not the sort of company to satisfy a woman of the world, with education, fortune, and wisdom such as Lady Catherine's. A lifetime of maternal homilies had been directed toward making Anne such another as herself, and by extension, the perfect wife for Mr. Darcy of Pemberley. What was her chagrin, then, to have a daughter who would hardly ever speak, and silently put sickliness up as a wall between herself and everything her mother required her to do.

Lady Catherine occasionally had an uncomfortable inkling that it was her own incessant decrees that had rendered Anne silent; but no, that was impossible. It had all had been done with the best intentions; who could have been a better mother than herself? No one could say where she had failed. Lady Catherine could hardly suppose such a thing. Had not her instructions always been calculated to bring Anne out, to develop her powers of attention, of conversation? No, it was Anne's ill health, unquestionably, that prevented her from attaining the character, the reputation, of the great lady she should not have failed to be. And now she would be an old maid, unless another man like her father, Sir Lewis de Bourgh, could be found for her. Lady Catherine shuddered. She knew that there was not another Mr. Darcy.

At Rosings, apart from Anne, who was there? Jenkinson was an inferior, a distant connection, a widow fallen on destitute times; and most praiseworthy it had been of Lady Catherine to take her in and give her occupation. However, in accepting her condescending charity, the woman had become no more than a servant, and a lady of Lady Catherine's degree could not treat such a one as an equal.

There were other families of fortune in the neighborhood, but none of a lineage to compare with Lady Catherine's own, and what with long standing feuds, and insulting instances of patronage, and intolerable neglect, and bitter enmities that never could be wiped away, there were few families of quality who had anything to do with her any more. All the blame was on the side of these upstart families, of course, for Lady Catherine chose to connect herself only with the best, and there was precious little of that in this sad part of Kent.

It was not surprising, then, that she had placed such great importance on the sort of clergyman who should come to Hunsford. As he would necessarily become an important intimate of her household, he must be someone she could at least endure, if not respect. Mr. Collins had been recommended to her by chance; and when summoned for the all-important interview, he had shown himself most properly respectful of all her benefits. So, she smiled graciously upon this gentleman, and in due course, accepted his wife. Mrs. Collins was a very proper, sensible, submissive sort of body, and not unladylike; good enough for him, and already well instructed in what her position in the parish must be.

But where were these tame Collinses now? Gone; and most humiliatingly, they had followed her own aristocratic relations. That is human nature, she thought vengefully. The Collinses—how had she ever thought them biddable? They had seemed to know their station so well! Yet it was they who had promoted the marriage between Mrs. Collins's pretty friend and her own nephew, and baser betrayal had never been seen and could not be borne. A pity one could not sack a clergyman, thought Lady Catherine, grinding her teeth; just as one might a thieving bailiff.

Anne had retired to bed, and Mrs. Jenkinson had scuttled off somewhere to hide. Lady Catherine was left alone, in the principal parlor at Rosings, as the sparkling December day outside, pale sun shining on crisp snow, began early to darken into twilight. She irritably removed to the long dining-table to eat her roasted beef and vegetable ragout in silence, before calling for a fire. No venison, no plump little birds shot and killed by the young men, and kept for a winter's evening to be enjoyed, she thought bitterly; her meat now was bought at the butcher's.

The evening sky outside was a velvety indigo, with a sweeping of little twinkling white stars in such profusion as had never been seen in the heavens before; but Lady Catherine would not look out a window to see such vulgar omens. She knew very well, with

657

astronomical exactitude, what tonight was. It was the wedding night of Darcy and Elizabeth. And she was spending it alone.

Resolutely, she picked up the nearest book, but it was Fordyce's Sermons, and she felt she required something more entertaining. No comfortable game of cassino for her, however, no light diverting novel left by an animated young visitor. It came to her, of a sudden, that she was unhappy, and a strange sound emerged from her corseted, iron midsection, that a listener might have thought was almost a wrenching sob. But there were no listeners.

Then, from some remote place long dead within her, arose a memory, of what she had endured from Sir Lewis de Bourgh, so many years ago now. She had not thought of it—oh, almost since it happened. She had firmly suppressed the memory, as one must press down such unsuitable things.

It had been a very proper, approved match, for the de Bourghs were both a rich and ancient family, and Lady Catherine had retained all the rights to be her own mistress, as a strong minded heiress, rising thirty. She intended from the beginning to rule the roost; and Sir Lewis, timid in temperament and frail in health as his only surviving daughter would be, was not the man to gainsay her. Still, there had once been a wedding night, and for what reasons she could not say, with her back to the dark window, gazing at a low glowing fire, Lady Catherine thought of it now. Images rose up in her mind, unbidden.

Sir Lewis had emerged from the closet, his knees knobbly in his nightshirt, and he clambered onto the cold satin sheets. Lady Catherine lay stolidly in the center of the bed and did not move. "My dear, will you make room for me?" he bleated timorously. "Certainly not," she answered. "That is not the proper method of proceeding, at all. Do not you know that a gentleman never approaches his lady on the wedding night, or indeed, ever, until and unless he is invited? And I do not recollect giving you the invitation."

Sir Lewis had meekly gone into another bedchamber, his white shirt pale in the darkness like a ghost. And that was that, until, several years later, her own brother, then Viscount Fitzwilliam, came to visit at Rosings, bringing his lady and their little boys. He had expressed himself surprised at his sister's childlessness, and a few shrewd questions to his brother-in-law had ascertained the state of affairs. A walk in the shrubbery; a hint to Lady Catherine that if Sir Lewis died with the marriage incomplete, unknown heirs might appear to challenge her widow's possession of Rosings.

So she had reluctantly, and with infinite distaste, allowed Sir Lewis to have his fumbling way; the puling sickly Anne had been the result; and the father had faded away soon after, like a gentleman spider eaten by his lady, and not regretted by her in the slightest.

As a full, majestic, bright jubilant winter moon rose at midnight over Pemberley, it rose over Rosings too; but it only gleamed in on a widow in her own majestically caparisoned bed, which reflected white in the moonshine, like a galleon. Lying awake, Lady Catherine allowed her thoughts to drift to her benighted nephew and his bride. Would the new Mrs. Darcy be likely to know how a lady managed her husband on the wedding night? Humph! she thought. That coarse girl, how could a knowledge of proper behavior be expected from her? Why, they were probably behaving like barnyard animals at this very moment...

No. She would not think about such things. Resolutely she turned over, away from the window, and closed her eyes, to sleep the dreamless and undisturbed sleep of the just.

The Wedding Night of Charles and Jane Bingley

by Susan Mason-Milks

November 16, 1812

The decision where to spend their wedding night had not been an easy one for the Bingleys. Clearly, staying at Netherfield would have been more familiar and comfortable for Jane, but after a few hints from Mrs. Bennet that she might need to "check" on her darling daughter, the bride-to-be decided that London seemed infinitely more attractive.

Although moving to Bingleys' home in Town meant traveling on the day of the wedding, they would have more privacy and the potential for both spending time alone and enjoying the delights of London. Caroline and the Hursts would have to choose between staying at Netherfield and moving to Hursts' family townhouse. This option also had the distinct advantage of installing Caroline, who had so far been maintaining a thin civility toward her future relatives, in another household. Bingley secretly hoped it might set a precedent. Perhaps, she would continue to spend more of her time with the Hursts and less with her brother and his new wife although he knew in all probability that was a futile hope.

The Bingleys arrived at the townhouse early in the evening on the day of the wedding. During the long carriage ride, the groom had refrained from ravishing his bride more from sheer exhaustion than any sense of propriety, although a sleeping Jane snuggled against him had proven to be more than a small temptation. Once at the townhouse, he used up what was left of his self-control to prevent himself from seizing her and rushing up the stairs to their rooms. Although he was always concerned he might alarm Jane with his ardor, he was delighted to find she seemed equally as eager as he to be alone.

Once they had settled in, a light meal was served, but neither the bride nor the groom had much appetite for food. Bingley fed small bites to Jane urging her to keep up her strength, but both were too anxious to even taste the fine fare prepared especially for them. Finally, although slightly embarrassed at the early hour, they decided to retire for the evening and let the servants think what they will.

In Bingley's dressing room, his valet, James, helped him untie his cravat and ease off his coat. After giving his master a quick shave, the valet assisted Bingley into a dark blue velvet dressing gown over his breeches and an open-necked linen shirt. Then James disappeared to check on Mrs. Bingley's progress.

"Molly tells me Mrs. Bingley has completed her bath and will be ready to receive you in her bed chamber in about a quarter hour," James reported upon his return. "Perhaps you would like another glass of brandy or some other refreshment while you wait?"

"No, but you did arrange for the champagne to be put in Mrs. Bingley's room?"

"Oh, yes, sir, just as you requested."

"Hmm...very good," Bingley answered distractedly, his thoughts already wandering into the next room.

Tugging anxiously at the belt of his dressing gown, he checked his appearance in the mirror for at least the tenth time. "How long do you think it has been?" he asked.

James gravely consulted the clock. "I believe approximately four minutes have passed since I returned, sir. Is there anything else I may do for you this evening before you retire?" the valet inquired patiently.

Bingley's groan was almost audible. If he had not been so busy being mortified, he would have noticed James stifling a smile. Then

Bingley smiled and thought, what man would not be impatient to be with the most wonderful woman in the world who by some miracle had just become his wife?

"Perhaps I will have a small brandy after all," he replied, fidgeting yet again with his belt while Molly helped the new Mrs. Bingley into a gossamer, blue silk nightdress and matching dressing gown. Seated at the dressing table, Jane glanced in the mirror, nervously checking to make sure the neckline of the new garment revealed just the right amount of pale, delicate skin. It is rather low, she thought wondering what her husband would think. One corner of her mouth turned up as she realized he would probably be delighted. Fingering the fabric, she reveled in the soft feel of it and marveled again at how well the color of the gown set off the warm blue of her eyes. Although everyone, especially her mother, always told her how beautiful she was, she was not, in truth, overly vain or obsessed with her looks. To her, it was only important that Charles thought she was beautiful.

"Would you like me to plait your hair, Mrs. Bingley?" Molly asked politely.

"I think not this evening," Jane replied as she combed through her long hair with her fingers.

Jane's new ladies' maid was a sweet, highly competent young woman whom she had selected after a half dozen interviews conducted during their recent trip to London. At first, Jane had resisted Charles's suggestions that she engage a maid for herself. Practical country girl that she was, she thought it seemed wasteful to have someone who was wholly devoted to taking care of the needs of just one individual. After all, she had shared a maid with her sisters all her life. Neither was she comfortable with the idea of always having someone fluttering around her. Finally, Charles had persuaded her she needed someone to attend her, not because it was the done thing for proper ladies, but for more practical reasons.

"You do not have your sisters to help you anymore, and while I plan to be an attentive husband, I cannot be there for you at all times." He grinned. "Who will do up those tiny buttons at the back of your dress if I am not around?"

Jane looked down to hide the fact that she was blushing and said, "Very well, I suppose I will adjust to the idea."

"Caroline has graciously offered to help you conduct the interviews," she heard him reply.

For an instant, Jane's heart sank. Then glancing up, she realized Charles was looking at her with the most impish grin on his face. Playfully, she pushed at his shoulder.

"I am sorry, sweetheart, but you are so easy to tease that I cannot resist sometimes. Would you prefer it if I—," he began, but she stopped him with a quick kiss.

Pulling back to read his face, she was delighted to see she had taken him completely by surprise.

"If you think a kiss is going to discourage me from teasing you, then you are quite mistaken. In fact, I can assure you it will have the opposite effect."

Jane had only smiled and reached out to him again.

After dismissing Molly for the evening, she was alone and a little anxious as she waited for her husband to come to her room. Glancing at herself in the mirror yet again, she decided that something was missing. After opening the flat velvet jewelry box on her dressing table, she lovingly examined the double-strand pearl necklace Charles had given her the day before their wedding. The clasp was simply decorated with a sparkling cluster of sapphires shaped like a small, delicate flower. "Sapphires to match your eyes," he had told her. After fastening the strands around her neck again, she rechecked her appearance in the mirror and decided the effect was perfect. The lustrous pearls lay gracefully along her collarbones setting off the creamy white of her skin.

Fingering the beads, she thought about how much finer they were than anything she had ever owned. In fact, they might just be the most beautiful thing she had ever seen. Along with the necklace, he had also given her a matching bracelet, as well as pearl combs for her hair. Other women might desire flashier jewelry, but this gift was simply perfect. His choice showed just how well he knew her.

Jane picked up her brush and began to move it slowly through her hair, just as she had done hundreds of times before. Only this was different. In a few minutes, Charles — her husband — would come to her room, and they would begin their life together as man and wife. She was not scared, just a bit uncertain, if truth be told. With all the advice she had received from her family, she had some idea of what was ahead of her, but even armed with all that information, she could still feel her stomach doing a country-dance.

She only knew that every time Charles took her in his arms, her heart beat so loudly she was positive everyone could hear it in the next county. And when he kissed her—well, when he kissed her, she was never certain her legs would continue to hold her up. If that day in the little woods when she had feigned interest in gathering pinecones was a sample of the physical pleasures that were to come as husband and wife, then all would be well tonight. It had certainly been an enlightening experience to realize she could be so wholly taken over by passions she had not even known she possessed. "Trust your husband," her aunt Gardiner had told her, and she planned to do just that.

In spite of expecting his arrival, when she heard his knock at the open door to her dressing room, she almost jumped.

"Come in." Jane hoped she sounded more confident than she actually was.

Charles came and stood behind her putting his hands gently on her shoulders. Her heartbeat quickened as she felt the heat of his hands warming her skin.

"I know I should have waited in your bed chamber rather than come to your dressing room, but I was anxious to see you," he told her.

When their eyes met in the mirror, she saw the kindness and love that was there–kindness and love, but also a deep well of emotion. Yes, she was right to have waited all those months for him.

She was as certain as she had ever been of anything in her life that they were meant to be together.

"You are still wearing your pearls."

Her fingers brushed the strands again. "I love them so much that I wanted to wear them for just a little longer."

He smiled. "Every time I looked at you today, it was all I could do to keep myself from doing this," he said giving a demonstration.

She shivered as his finger moved lightly along the pearls against her skin. Closing her eyes, she relished the new sensations. "I know it was just a silly whim of mine to put them on again. You may unclasp them now for me, and I will put them away," she said, reaching for the velvet box.

"Leave them on."

"You want me to...?" She gave him a puzzled look.

"Yes, leave them on."

Will I soon be wearing nothing but my necklace, she wondered. Just the anticipation of what that might be like caused her to turn a rosy pink from the top of her dressing gown to the roots of her hair. She certainly hoped he could not read her mind.

"May I do that?" he asked, indicating the brush still in her hand. Moving tentatively at first, he gained confidence with each stroke. "Your hair is like a beautiful shining halo."

"No wonder you mistook me for an angel when we first met," said Jane with a twinkle in her eyes.

Charles smiled, but then turned more serious. Laying the brush aside, he set his hands gently on her shoulders again.

"It was not a mistake. You are an angel." He kissed the top of her head and inhaled the scent of fresh lemons with a hint of lavender layered in.

"I am not so perfect as you might think," Jane said softly.

Pushing her hair to one side, he exposed the delicate skin of her neck and kissed the hollow just behind her ear. Jane sighed at the touch of his lips.

"To me, you are perfect," he whispered. The feel of his breath against her ear sent a shudder rippling through her body. Then as if overwhelmed by the intensity of the moment, he suddenly changed the subject. "Shall we have some champagne? I thought it might help us both to relax."

Charles poured a glass and handed it to her. After her first sip of champagne, Jane giggled as the bubbles tickled her nose. Flashing her eyes at her husband over the top of the glass, she was thrilled at the reaction she evoked in him.

"I am the most fortunate man in the world. And to think I nearly lost you through my own foolishness. Sometimes, I still cannot believe you have forgiven me," he told her.

"There was nothing to forgive," she said, meaning every word.

"You are too good. Why is it you only ever see the best in me?"

"I am not too good," she said, "and I see what is really important in you—your kindness, your gentleness. I know I can entrust myself to you completely, and you will always take care of me."

Taking the glass from her hand, he set it aside.

"I can hardly believe you are mine." Raising her to her feet, he pulled her into his arms. Jane reached around his waist and pressed her forehead against his chest.

"You are not afraid, are you?" he whispered in her ear.

Jane shook her head and mumbled against the fabric of his dressing gown. "Only a little."

"Someone in your family told you what to expect tonight?"

She nodded.

"You can trust me, you know," he said.

"Always."

Leading her by the hand, Charles walked slowly into the bedchamber. Upon reaching the bed, he sat on the edge and pulled her close until she stood with his legs bracketing either side of her body. Taking her face in his hands, he placed soft kisses on her forehead, her cheeks, her eyes, her nose. Each kiss brought a tiny shiver that only encouraged him more.

"You remember how it was a few weeks ago when we were gathering pinecones?" he said.

"Oh, yes, I do. I confess I have thought of little else of late." She reached up to run her fingers though his curly locks.

Charles groaned softly, and taking her face in his hands again, he kissed her lips. After dreaming of this moment for so long and wondering if he would somehow be disappointed when holding and kissing her this way finally became a reality, he realized he need not have worried. Although he knew Jane to be an innocent, she seemed to know instinctively how to respond. Some of his married friends at the club had warned him wives could be merely passive and submissive on their wedding nights, but that was certainly not the case with his Jane.

"Oh, my dearest angel," he whispered. "How I love you!"

First, he lightly traced along the pearl necklace again and moving down, let his fingers follow the lacy outline at the top of her dressing gown.

Looking into the depths of her husband's blue-green eyes, Jane imagined she was standing on a cliff, his eyes a swelling ocean that she was in danger of drowning in. When she felt Charles impatiently pulling her mouth to his again, she let herself fall.

What followed was beyond heavenly—more exploration, soft touches, and intense kisses along with much fumbling with buttons and ribbons. Finally, both her new dressing gown and nightdress were reduced to a puddle at her feet. With almost no self-consciousness at all, and just as she had imagined, Jane went to her marriage bed wearing nothing more than the golden halo of her hair and her double strand of pearls.

Starting the Rest of Their Lives

by Maria Grace

November 16, 1812

The wedding breakfast had been everything it was supposed to be. Loud, crowded, a table well-set, and a house full of flowers. A gushing mother, a satisfied—or was it relieved—father, and a blushing bride, surrounded by her dearest connections. But now it was over and time to start the rest of his life—their lives—together.

Most of her trunks had been sent on ahead, but the two that were to accompany them today were waiting, already loaded on the luggage wagon with his. How well they looked together

It was a ridiculous thought to be sure. One of many he had begun to entertain since regularly keeping company with Elizabeth.

Darcy waited for her near the carriage. He had already taken his leave from the Bennets and the Gardiners. The latter, they would meet again soon in London—a dinner had already been set at the Gardiners' house for a fortnight hence. Was it ridiculous to be pleased to have connections he could truly look forward to seeing in London, not just the ones he tolerated for the sake of civility?

A light snow began to fall. Not the kind that would impede their travel, but the gentle sort one could hear falling if one was quiet enough. The kind that would dust the countryside in a veil of white, much like the one Elizabeth wore this morning.

The front door swung open creaking in complaint at being pressed into service. Mr. Bennet and Elizabeth emerged. He walked her to the coach, his eyes suspiciously bright.

"So the time has finally come for you to take my Lizzy from me. I cannot delay you any longer." He patted Elizabeth's hand tucked into the crook of his elbow. "Take good care of her—you are taking the brightest light from Meryton."

"Oh, Papa." She leaned up on tiptoes and kissed her father's cheek.

"I shall, sir." He took Elizabeth's hand, helped her into the carriage and climbed in after her.

Mr. Bennet shut the door behind him and waved the driver on.

The carriage lurched, forcing him back into the buttery leather squabs beside her.

Elizabeth straightened her bonnet and peered out of the side glass, waving until the road turned and Longbourn was out of view. Her smile faded for just a moment, but returned when she glanced at him.

He slipped his arm over her shoulders and she settled in against him.

Was it the warm bricks heating the coach or her nearness that brought the perspiration to his forehead?

Her cheeks glowed—did she feel it, too?

The glint in her eye and the mischievous turn of her lips suggested she did.

"So Mr. Darcy, now you are an old married man—"

"I am indeed a man, and now I am married, but I am hardly old." His eyebrow rose and he cocked his head.

She batted her eyes, beaming. "That is a most inappropriate expression, Mr. Darcy."

The way her eyes sparkled when she smiled, such a wholly appealing and desirable—and kissable expression.

What was a man—a married man to do? He kissed her, slow and gentle, relishing each moment.

"I hardly expect that would be considered appropriate, either," she whispered in his ear, her breath tickling the side of his neck just so.

She was trying to drive him mad.

"Now you are concerned with what is appropriate? My dearest Elizabeth, if you give it any real consideration, propriety has not been something amply present in our relationship from the start."

She drew in a deep breath and pressed her hand to her chest. "What are you saying, sir? Are you accusing me—"

Darcy "You consider scampering about the countryside alone and unchaperoned highly appropriate behavior for a young woman?" He schooled his features into something quite severe—or at least he hoped they were.

Eliz "And meeting said young woman to walk alone and unchaperoned is equally inappropriate for a gentleman is not? In fact, I seem to recall a certain gentleman calling upon said young woman her and discovering she was alone in the house. Yet, he did not leave, but stayed and insisted upon speaking with her alone."

Darcy "Have you forgotten, an offer of marriage is traditionally offered in a private audience?"

She harrumphed playfully, "Perhaps that is true, but an appropriate man does not make suggestive comments about the figures of the ladies in his company as they take a walk about the room."

He was only remarking upon the figure of one of those ladies that day.

Elizabeth looked too smug.

Darcy "And it is fully appropriate to accept a letter from an unrelated man and then read said letter? Multiple times?"

Eliz "No less appropriate than the gentleman who writes such a letter. Besides how would you know how many times the letter was read?"

The high color in her face confirmed what he suspected—it had been many times indeed.

670

"So then you fully agree, propriety has perhaps not been the primary characteristic of our courtship."

"Perhaps you are correct, sir. Now I am an old married woman, I shall see to it all matters of propriety are carefully attended to." She folded her hands in her lap and lifted her chin, just so.

"I said nothing of the sort." He tugged the ribbon on her bonnet and the knot fell away. A gentle touch and the bonnet slipped back to reveal her lovely hair, done up with ribbons and pearls. The gauzy white veil, pooled over her shoulder like a dusting of snow.

"I have no intention of being proper for at least a fortnight."

Her eyes grew wide, a touch of genuine surprise in them. "A fortnight, sir? Will not the servants talk?"

"Perhaps you have a point. I will restrain myself to just five days—and to be entirely certain no untoward talk circulates, there will be no servants."

"You cannot be serious, sir—how will the house run with no staff?"

He pressed his lips together. She would not appreciate being laughed at just now, but her bewilderment was entirely amusing.

"I said nothing about the house. You have not asked me our destination."

"We are not to Darcy house?"

"We are, but by way of my friend Wingrave's cottage."

She cocked her head, a faraway look in her eye—her thinking expression the he enjoyed so much. "Is he not the baronet whose seat is—"

"But five miles from here? Yes, he is. He and his family are to be away for the Christmastide season. He has a cottage on his property and has offered us the use of it. The housekeeper will attend us in the mornings and evenings—so I suppose we shall have to maintain some minimal propriety whilst we are there."

"What are you saying, sir?"

671

"Only that I intend to spend the next five days being entirely inappropriate with you, Mrs. Darcy. I am going to remark on your figure and how it is shown to its best advantage, no less than—what say you, five times a day?"

"Only five?" The mischief returned to her eyes.

Yes, she was pleased!

"Will there be time for more? I expect you will be scampering about the countryside, unchaperoned in the company of a man a great deal."

"Will that man write me letters?"

"Will he need to when he is left alone to converse with you as much as he might like?"

"And about what will he converse?"

She ran her tongue over her lips.

He leaned in to kiss those lips.

The carriage rolled to a stop. "Lavender Cottage," the driver called.

He grumbled under his breath.

She laid a finger on his lips. "A show of temper is highly inappropriate, sir."

"I will show you inappropriate, Mrs. Darcy." He helped her down from the carriage and swept her off her feet, carrying her into the waiting cottage.

Hours later, he gazed at her sleeping face, the blush had not faded from her cheeks and the smile had not faded from her lips. It seemed his Elizabeth relished impropriety as much as he.

Darcy and Elizabeth Arrive at Pemberley

by Jane Odiwe

November 21, 1812

Elizabeth Darcy looked out of the carriage window as they crossed the ancient stone bridge on the road into Lambton village, instantly recognizing the clutch of stone cottages, the church, and several handsome buildings that formed the landscape. She remembered the first time she had seen this very countryside when touring Derbyshire with her Aunt and Uncle Gardiner and how she had dreaded the thought of being so close to Pemberley. Last August the trees had been dressed in their finest emerald leaves, but now winter was on its way and fingers of pale sunlight slanted through bare branches, lighting up the leaves scattered on the ground in tones of amber and gold. Elizabeth recalled her mixed emotions about visiting Pemberley, dreading that Darcy might be there, but also overcome by a curiosity to see the house where he lived. Remembering her feelings of mortification as if it had been yesterday, she could not help smiling at the memory of bumping into him in the grounds. After all, there could have been a very different ending to their story if she hadn't been persuaded to visit the house by her uncle and aunt.

"Penny for your thoughts, my darling?" Darcy took her hand, raising it to his lips.

"I was just remembering last summer, and the first time I came to Pemberley. How different were my feelings then."

Fitzwilliam Darcy studied Elizabeth's countenance, noting her amused expression.

"Are you talking of your feelings for *me*?" Darcy kept his gaze steady upon Lizzy's eyes. "I think you must have despised me when you first arrived."

Mrs. Darcy's eyes flew wide open in horror. "Oh, do not say such a thing. I did not ~~exactly~~ despise you… I did not know what to think. You were the first person in my life whom I could not puzzle out. Everything I thought I knew about you seemed to be contradicted one way or another. And the truth was even when I thought you were the most odious man that ever walked the earth, a small part of me was fascinated by you."

"And what did you think when you first saw me walking towards you that afternoon?"

"If I could have reversed time and spent an extra day with Mr. Collins for my sins, I would have done it. I was so embarrassed, I think you must have seen how dreadfully uncomfortable I felt."

"But I was too busy being mortified myself. And yet, I could not help thinking how very beautiful you looked and how perfectly you fitted into the Derbyshire landscape."

"You always say the loveliest things, my darling, even if I am sure you must have been thinking what a nerve I had to show my face. It was all quite a blur, but I do remember thinking how very different you looked in your own setting, how you seemed more at ease in your surroundings. A thousand thoughts crossed my mind in those seconds. Your countenance wore none of its usual strain or pride, I remember, and you instantly made me feel less awkward. I was made to reflect a little on your housekeeper's words. She had told us how kind you were as a master and I could not help thinking I had misjudged you. Her description of you as the sweetest-tempered, most generous-hearted boy in the world came from the heart and from that very moment my mind was quite changed about your character."

"*Your* housekeeper...Mrs. Reynolds is *your* housekeeper now." Darcy squeezed her hand. 'I know she is looking forward to serving her new mistress."

Elizabeth took a deep breath. The enormity of her new situation in the Pemberley household was beginning to strike home. "And I am looking forward to working with *our* housekeeper and learning how to run a great house."

Mrs. Darcy turned her face towards her husband and hoped he could only see the part of her that was thrilled and ready to face her new challenges. She was excited by the prospect of her new life with the man she adored, and yet at this moment Lizzy felt unequal to the task. She wanted to be the perfect wife and mistress of Pemberley, and wished Jane were there to reassure her that everything would turn out for the best in the end.

They were entering the village and turning into the high street when Elizabeth cried out in surprise, for lining both sides of the road it seemed the entire population of Lambton had turned out to greet them. Caps and hats were thrown into the air as deafening cheers and enthusiastic applause rang out from every side. The faces of the villagers, young and old, peered into the carriage as it trundled past, and the same wishes of joy were heard over and over again.

"God bless you, Mr. Darcy, and God bless you, Mrs. Darcy. Welcome to Derbyshire! Three cheers for the lady!"

"Oh, how delightful," Elizabeth cried. "What a turnout! Look at the children running alongside, it is easy to see how everyone loves and adores you."

"I do not think they are in the least bit interested in me," said Darcy who nonetheless felt very touched by the scene. "Pemberley's new bride is the object of their curiosity and their good wishes, and I know you do not disappoint them. You look a picture, my dearest."

Elizabeth gripped her husband's hand tighter as they passed through the village on the last leg of their journey. The landscape rose on every side, the Derbyshire hills majestic in their setting, and when the familiar wooded slopes came into view, Lizzy's heart somersaulted. The park seemed larger than she remembered, and as the carriage climbed up through beautiful woodland, Elizabeth was reminded of her visit last August once more. When they arrived at the top of a considerable eminence where the wood ceased, she remembered with great anticipation the remarkable sight, which would next come into view. Pemberley House, situated on the opposite side of the valley, looked more magnificent than any memory she could recall. She couldn't help feeling excited and when she met the gaze of her adoring husband Lizzy knew she was about to embark on the happiest time of her life.

"Welcome my dearest, Elizabeth; welcome to Pemberley, and to your new home," said Darcy, planting a sweet kiss on her cheek.

They descended the hill, crossed the bridge and drove to the door, where Lizzy could see a reception party waiting for them. Georgiana Darcy, looking rather nervous, stood at the front with her governess Mrs. Annesley and waved when she saw them. Elizabeth hoped above all things that they would continue to get along together as they had on their first meetings in the summer.

"Dearest Mrs. Darcy, I have been waiting so long to call you by that name. I am delighted to welcome you to Pemberley," Georgiana said, rushing forward and curtseying before Elizabeth as she stepped down from the coach. Mrs. Annesley was introduced next, and then Mrs. Reynolds stepped forward to offer her very best wishes on the occasion.

"Thank you for such a wonderful reception, you are all very kind," Elizabeth said, and turning to Georgiana, she added, "I hope you will be so good as to teach me all I need to know about Pemberley, Miss Darcy. I am quite relying on you to show me the ropes."

"It will be a pleasure, my dear sister, and please, let us not stand on ceremony. I hope you will call me Georgiana."

"And you must call me Lizzy, as all my other sisters do. Isn't this exciting? I admit, I felt rather nervous before we arrived, but having you here makes me feel completely at home."

Darcy stared after them aware that he seemed to have been totally forgotten, but secretly pleased to see that all his schemes and plans to gain the heart of the woman he loved and getting her under his roof had finally come to fruition.

Antony Fitzwilliam Visits the Bride and Groom

by Mary Simonsen

November 22, 1812

Arm-in-arm, Mr. and Mrs. Fitzwilliam Darcy walked the gardens on their first full day at Pemberley. The previous day, they had arrived at the manor house just as the sun was dipping below the horizon. Nearly exhausted from the wedding breakfast and their travels, the pair had dined on a light supper before retiring for the night. After making love, they were quickly asleep in each other's arms.

Since Lizzy's first visit to Pemberley in August, the gardens had been completely transformed, with vivid yellows, oranges, and reds replacing the softer pastels of a warmer season. There was also another difference. When Lizzy had first admired the gardens, she did so as Elizabeth Bennet, a woman contemplating the very real prospect of spinsterhood after having rejected the marriage proposal of Fitzwilliam Darcy. Instead, she had returned—triumphantly—as the Mistress of Pemberley.

As they walked the gravel paths, Lizzy's role as the mistress of such a great estate was much on her mind. Her husband was attempting to reassure her that she was more than equal to the task when they heard the sound of a carriage coming down the drive. From the noise it was making, they knew the conveyance was substantial, and Lizzy wondered aloud who their visitor might be.

"Good grief!" Darcy said as he caught site of the carriage with its two matched pairs of white stallions. With that exasperated exclamation, Lizzy knew who their visitor was: William's cousin, Antony Fitzwilliam, Earl of _____, the black sheep of the Fitzwilliam clan, an unrepentant reprobate and willing fodder for London's scandal sheets.

Through gritted teeth, Darcy declared he was not ready to return to the house. "Antony can amuse himself," his face a mask of scorn. "It is so easily done."

Pulling Elizabeth by her hand, he turned in a direction away from the manor.

"William, I know you are unhappy with your cousin's unexpected arrival, but, really, it is our responsibility to make him welcome," Lizzy said, trying to keep up with her husband.

"But he is NOT welcome. He has come for one of two reasons: to make sport at my expense because I am newly married or to find relief from his creditors by hiding in Derbyshire. In the first instance, he shall fail because I am happy to be married. As for the second reason, he knows better than to ask for money."

There was a third possibility. His wife, a woman he referred to as the Evil Eleanor, had prevailed—again—in one of their epic rows, and he had to run for his life.

"William, is it not possible he has come to wish us joy?"

"If that were his purpose, then he should have attended the wedding breakfast. Although I did not invite him, I know that you did!"

In the whole of England, there were few who could get a rise out of Fitzwilliam Darcy, but one of those people was now moving his considerable luggage into a guest chamber at Pemberley.

* * *

"You can stay the night, but that is it," Darcy said by way of greeting his cousin.

"I am very happy to see you, too, my dearest Fitzwilliam," Antony said, chuckling. After taking Elizabeth's hand, he pressed it against his lips and allowed them to linger.

679

"Enchanted."

"If you were so keen to see us, why did you not go to the wedding breakfast?" Darcy barked. "And please remove your lips from my wife's hand."

"The reason I did not attend the wedding was because it is the height of rudeness to outshine the bride," Antony said in a serious voice. "Or so I was told by my wife on our wedding day."

In an age of men's fashion dictated by the immaculate Beau Brummel, Antony Fitzwilliam, wearing an embroidered coat, hose, and high-heeled shoes with jeweled buckles, much preferred the more ornate dress of his father's generation. For the earl, "fitting in" was never a desired outcome.

"William, Antony, shall we continue this conversation in a room where there are chairs and away from the ears of the servants?" Lizzy asked, leading the men from the foyer to the drawing room.

"Elizabeth, if you don't mind, I would like to speak to my cousin in private."

"Well, I mind," Antony immediately answered. "If you leave, my dear, I shall be subjected to one of William's sermons, and I get preached to on Sunday."

"Nonsense!" William answered, his voice nearly a shout. "The last time you were in a church, it was struck by lightning." It also happened to be Antony's wedding day.

"I shall see to the refreshments," Lizzy said, backing out of the room, leaving the two bulls to lock horns.

"Antony, you cannot stay here. I have no intention of beginning my married life with Elizabeth with you making mischief at every opportunity."

"William, William, William," Antony tsked. "I am not moving in. I am merely paying a call to wish you and your delightful bride connubial bliss."

"I would be more likely to believe you if you did not travel with enough baggage to furnish the court at Windsor," Darcy harrumphed. "And the length of this visit will be...?"

"As my host, that depends entirely on you."

"How much do I need to pay to make you go away?" When Antony told him the amount required to satisfy his most pressing creditors, Darcy agreed to advance him the sum. "When do you leave?"

"Another twenty pounds and I shall be gone by first light."

"Done."

Taking Tea with Mrs. Darcy

by Maria Grace

November 23, 1812

Elizabeth checked her hair in the looking glass and straightened her dress for the third time. There was no reason for such anxiety, none at all. It was not as if she were going to be presented at court.

In many ways, though, that would be far less demanding. At court, she would only have to make her curtsey and remember all the steps and lines for her performance and nothing more. But here...

She smoothed the hairs on the back of her neck.

Darcy assured her she had nothing to fear from Mrs. Reynolds. Little did he understand the complex and dynamic relationship between the mistress of the house and her housekeeper. No doubt Mrs. Reynolds was well aware that she had not been raised to manage an estate the size of Pemberley. Mama had taught her well, but Longbourn was naught to the vast manor and thriving village that now looked to her to oversee, provide, nurture, and educate...

How could she ever undertake such a task? Why did Darcy ever think her up to the challenge? He believed in her, insisted she was capable of anything she set her mind to, a little like Papa. But perhaps, this once, his confidence was misplaced.

The clock chimed. Like it or not, it was time. Mrs. Reynolds would be waiting in her office, and she was nothing if not punctual.

Elizabeth wove her way to the back of the house. At least she had learned enough of the house's layout not to require directions to move from one room to another. The accomplishment felt far more impressive than it actually was. After all, even the lowest scullery maid managed the same task with little effort. What a grand achievement with which to begin her career as Mrs. Darcy.

The housekeeper's office, tucked at the back of the house near the kitchen, looked like Mrs. Reynolds herself: tiny, tidy, and treasured. Along one wall, shelves held stacks of neatly folded linens, on another, rows and rows of sparkling china and crystal. A perfectly clean window held sharp winter breezes at bay while a small fire warmed the room to cheeriness. A little plate of Elizabeth's favorite biscuits invited her to the table where Mrs. Reynolds presided. Several sheets of paper lay spread on the desk before her. She squinted through her spectacles and hummed a little tune under her breath as she checked items off a list.

"Mrs. Darcy." Mrs. Reynolds looked up from the table piled high with journals and ledgers. She rose and curtsied.

"Good morning, Mrs. Reynolds." Her voice sounded far more confident than she felt, but that probably was not a difficult thing at the moment.

Mama had always said the better part of confidence was in one's voice. If one sounded confident, they were half way to being believed competent. That might work for most people, but somehow it did not seem that Mrs. Reynolds would be so easily persuaded.

Elizabeth sat at the table, across from Mrs. Reynolds. A cool sunbeam shone over her shoulder and on to the intimidating pile of paper. "Where do you recommend we begin this morning?"

"Where do you prefer?" She opened several books and laid them out along the table, tapping each one in turn. "Menus are needed for the coming weeks. Laundry is planned for next week—you might wish to review our ways to ensure they meet your satisfaction. Perhaps you would care to go over the newly revised inventory of the larder. We have meats just out of the smokehouse and hams curing. The maids are getting ready to change out the curtains for the winter. Would you care to inspect their efforts?"

Gracious heavens! So many books and lists.

Elizabeth rubbed her temples. "I have no idea where to begin."

Mrs. Reynolds pressed her lips and nodded. "It is a lot to manage, is it not? The late Mrs. Darcy found it quite daunting, especially during the visiting months when company would fill the house. Oh, she loved the house parties, but between you and me, ma'am, the work would overwhelm her sometimes."

"Indeed?"

"Absolutely. I kept a ready supply of willow bark for her headaches and mint for her digestion. She found her brother, now the Earl of Matlock and sister, Lady Catherine, particularly challenging guests."

"Mr. Darcy has never mentioned it."

"His late mother never showed a sign of distress to her family or her company. She faced the trials with every imaginable grace, but make no mistake, it weren't easy for her."

"Oh." It was not the most original of responses, to be sure. But when one received intelligence that changed everything they believed about the world, more creative replies were out of the question. "Many have gone out of their way to tell me of what an excellent mistress she was."

"You never saw a more attentive mistress than Mrs. Darcy. She was well loved, indeed. Except by those who tried to take advantage of her. They found her rather disagreeable, I would think. She did not suffer such things lightly. I don't expect you would either." She cocked her head and lifted an eyebrow.

Elizabeth chuckled. "I suppose you are right."

"Pemberley has run for a long time now without the hand of a mistress. The estate, she needs one. I done the best I could, but it ain't the same."

"No one criticizes your service, at least not to me."

"Of course not, I would box their ears if I heard of it!" Mrs. Reynolds threw her head back and laughed.

How delightful that the servants here could laugh. A house needed laughter to truly be a home.

"Still, it's good for a mistress to preside here again. The master, he knows the land and the tenants, but the house—that has always been a mystery to him."

"I fear it may be a bit of a mystery to me as well." Elizabeth shrugged.

Mama would scold her for revealing so much uncertainty to her staff, even though she regularly confided in Hill. But then, Mama had Hill's respect. Would she ever have Mrs. Reynolds'?

"A clever girl like you will have it figured out in no time at all. I have no doubts." She caught Elizabeth's gaze, though it was entirely improper for her to be so bold.

The dear woman believed every word she said.

"I appreciate your confidence."

"I know the master well enough. He could not tolerate a stupid woman. Only a very clever one would make him as happy as he is now. You have nothing to worry about, Mrs. Darcy. It will come to you. All you need is a little time."

Elizabeth swallowed hard. The approval of a servant, even an old trusted one like Mrs. Reynolds should not be so meaningful. But it was.

"I have just the place to start." Mrs. Reynolds ambled around the desk to a plain cabinet under the window. "Here it is!" She returned with a worn, red journal and handed it to Elizabeth.

She opened the cover and was greeted by elegant, flourished handwriting. "Whose?"

"I think she would want you to have it. It is the late Mrs. Darcy's common place book."

Elizabeth stroked the fine lettering. Darcy's mother had written this. She flipped through the pages. Receipts, garden plans, directions for her favorite washballs... "Oh!"

Mrs. Reynolds leaned over her shoulder. "Mrs. Darcy made

lovely sketches, did she not? We have quite a number of them framed in the house. I will point them out to you when you wish. That one," she tapped the page, "that is the master when he was just five years old. Such a serious little boy he was, but so kindhearted even then. See here. She says it herself."

Such a boy! Fitzwilliam is the dearest of souls. He picked flowers for me this morning. I did not have the heart to tell him that he pillaged my kitchen garden. Cook will be happy to know that she will have far fewer courgettes to deal with this year. She considers them a most disagreeable vegetable.

Elizabeth giggled. A young Darcy's earnest eyes peered out from the page at her. He had not changed very much.

"It's good to hear you laugh, ma'am." Mrs. Reynolds smiled a maternal smile. "Take it and get acquainted with Pemberley through her eyes. Tomorrow is soon enough for the menus."

"Thank you, I shall." Elizabeth gathered the book and pressed it to her chest.

How many times had she wished she could have gotten to know Darcy's mother, and through her, know him just a little better. Perhaps now she could.

"I shall be in my dressing room."

"Shall I send a tea tray up for you and Mrs. Darcy?"

"That would be lovely … and perhaps send this plate of biscuits as well?" Elizabeth picked up a biscuit and nibbled it.

"Those were her favorite as well. I will see to it." Mrs. Reynolds trundled out, probably to get water heating for tea.

Elizabeth made her way back to her dressing room. How pleasant it would be to spend the rest of the morning taking tea with Mrs. Darcy. Perhaps with the guidance of Pemberley's former mistress, she would be able do the role justice after all.

Darcy and Elizabeth in the Library at Pemberley

by Diana Birchall

November 24, 1812

The maid pulled apart the curtains, and left the tea tray. As soon as she had withdrawn, Elizabeth opened her eyes and lifted her head from the feather pillow. Darcy, in his nightshirt, was beginning his ablutions with water-pitcher and bowl.

"Oh, Darcy," she fairly wailed, "only look at the rain!" He turned from his splashing and smiled at her warmly.

"Derbyshire can be damp in winter, I believe I neglected to warn you when making my proposals," he said teasingly, and turned back to his mirror. "No; I remember mentioning the rain on neither occasion."

"Damp! My dear, it is pelting down sheets. Just look at the window-pane. And we were to have a long walk in the hanging-wood, which we did not reach yesterday. I have always wanted to see it."

"Where is your philosophy, Elizabeth? You have a whole lifetime, and many summers, I hope, to inspect our hanging-woods. Today we shall enjoy ourselves indoors. There is still more for you to explore within Pemberley House, I do assure you."

Elizabeth got out of bed, wrapping herself in her white baptiste peignoir and went over to him. They embraced warmly and some silent moments passed, ending with Elizabeth's low laugh.

"Heavens! You are as damp as it is outside."

"Never mind, I am only happy that your ardor precluded your waiting until I was dry."

Elizabeth blushed and she changed the subject. "Well, and what have you in mind for entertainment indoors? It is true I have seen over the entire house now, but I have been so busy with arrangements, and learning where everything is and who everyone is, I have not become as tolerably familiar with my new home as I ought to be."

"What do you say to the library?" Darcy suggested. "I have always meant to show you its contents, and have never yet achieved that."

Elizabeth brightened at once. "Oh, yes! Let us go to the library immediately after breakfast."

He gave her a last hug. "We will. Dress warmly, and I will tell them to build a fire in there. The damp does get into one's bones."

An hour later, they pushed the great library doors open and were greeted by a noble fire roaring in the handsome fireplace. Elizabeth looked about, glad of more leisure to study the room, which must, she thought, surely be one of the most beautiful in all England. The library faced north, the long windows framing the green hills and woods rising behind the house, a magnificent landscape. Comfortable seats and alcoves were scattered throughout the long, large room, with paintings interspersed between the tall standings of books, dark red, dark blue, and golden in their ancient bindings.

"How beautiful," she breathed.

"Is it not? I confess it is my favorite room in the house. The Darcys have always been reading men, and the collection holds some very fine books of great antiquity."

"Which is the oldest?" she asked.

"I believe our edition of Erasmus, the *Moriae Encomium*, from 1523. There are several other sixteenth century works, and a beautiful edition of Chaucer—here it is, the antique Speght edition

688

of 1598. It is not the one I read, myself; too rare and fragile, I read a more modern copy."

"Do you like Chaucer, and read him regularly?" Elizabeth asked in wonderment.

"Indeed I do, he is an old favorite, and I venture that you feel the same, for you are a student of human nature, and he is the best."

"Oh yes! I learned to love to read Chaucer because he is my father's favorite, too. He would always laugh to himself about the Wife of Bath. I ought not to say so, it is not respectful, but I believe she reminded him of my mother."

Their eyes met and they laughed. "I am glad your father has such good friends to keep him company," Mr. Darcy told her warmly.

"Yes. And you have many of our other favorites too, I see— Peregrine Pickle and Gulliver's Travels, and oh, all of Johnson. I have never yet read his Tour of the Hebrides, and have longed to do so, but my father did not have it."

"Do you like to read travels? We have many such—over here," and her husband led her to shelves packed with gentlemen's travels through several centuries.

"Oh, yes, I have been reading Miss - Miss Wollstonecraft's letters from Sweden, which are so peculiarly interesting. However, I think it was a writer of fiction, Mrs. Radcliffe, who has most made me want to visit Italy; reading her *Udolpho* and *The Italian*, I quite felt I was there. And some of the descriptions in *Corinne* were sublime, though I don't like Madame de Stael's writing as well."

"I have been hoping," Darcy said diffidently, "not to read travels with you, but to take you a-journeying on the Continent. Should you like to go to Italy in the spring, Elizabeth?"

"Would I!" she gasped, and could not keep from clapping her hands.

He nodded. "Then we will. I shall delight in showing you its beauties—and Italy, your beauties, my beloved Elizabeth."

"I never dreamed of such a thing in my life!" she exclaimed. "The Lakes were my farthest aspirations."

"We shall see them too," he smiled. "But meanwhile, we have this rainy day to get through, and probably a good many of them, until we go to London for the Season, after Christmas."

She looked at him with sparkling eyes. "I do not think we will ever grow tired of being at home together in Pemberley, do you, Darcy? And it will take a long lifetime to read even a portion of so many thousands of books!"

"That is what I have been thinking. It will be an autumn and winter such as I have never experienced at Pemberley, with you here, my Elizabeth. We shall read together—and what luxury, if you will read to me!"

"To be sure. I shall read you some of my favorite novels, Miss Burney and Miss Edgeworth and Miss Austen—"

"Why, I have read them all! Many times, too."

"Have you? I imagined you amused yourself with classical scholarship. It looks like it, if these shelves are any evidence," and she indicated the volumes of Herodotus and Horace, Euripides and Virgil."

"Certainly, any gentleman who has had a classical education finds perennial pleasure in the oldest authors. Do I collect that you feel the miss of such an education yourself? Will you like me to be your instructor?"

He had seated himself on a peculiarly carved wooden chair by the fire, and without more ado, confident enough to be familiar, Elizabeth climbed onto his lap. He caressed her, and the subject of books was forgotten for a few moments.

"I do hope that our marriage will give me some more solid education than I received in rummaging through my father's much smaller library, and by patronizing the lending-library of Meryton," she told him, abstractedly smoothing his hair.

"We will revel together in books, Elizabeth. I can hardly comprehend the pleasure it will be."

690

"Nor I. But Darcy!" she exclaimed, "Whatever is this thing you are sitting upon?"

"Oh, this? It is quite a clever device, the chair turns into a library stair—get up, and I'll show you."

He demonstrated how, by opening up the wooden frame, a solid set of stairs to reach the highest shelves might be formed.

"Will the wonders of Pemberley ever cease?" she marveled.

"I hope not. Do you know what I should like, Elizabeth? If you would read to me from the Arabian Nights. I suspect it would be something, to hear those stories told in the voice of my own lovely Scheherazade."

"Oh, if you wish, I will. My father never would let me read it; now I shall find out why. But oh, Darcy, look! It is clearing up—so suddenly too. There is the sunshine, positively streaming down from out of those silvery clouds."

"You are right. By afternoon it may be dry enough for our walk, after all. We have just time for one story. Come and sit with me on the sofa. It is much softer than that hard chair, and I can put my arms about you."

He took her hand and they reclined together on the pretty striped satin sofa, the Arabian Nights on their knees.

Darcy Shows Elizabeth the Grounds at Pemberley

by Jane Odiwe

November 25, 1812

There had been little time for exploring Pemberley's grounds, what with adjusting to her new position as mistress, generally finding her way round such a large house, and being busy receiving callers eager to greet the new bride, so when Mr. Darcy announced he was taking a few days off from estate business to please her every whim, Lizzy knew exactly what might please her fancy.

Wrapping up warmly against the cold weather, they set off across the formal gardens where nature was at its most restrained. Frost mired the stone planters on the balustrade, which in the summer had been filled with a riot of blooms, and Darcy gripped Lizzy's arm tightly as they descended the stone steps and walked along the path that led to the wilder scenery beyond.

"Have a care, dear, I would hate you to slip on the ice."

Lizzy gazed up at her husband. He was so protective and always thinking about her welfare, but the last thing she wanted was to be kept permanently wrapped up like an ancient porcelain figurine or constrained in any way.

"Do not worry, my love. I have my stout boots on, and I am known for my excellent walking skills," she retorted, and easing her arm out of his firm grip, she broke into a trot and ran on ahead down the path before he realized she had escaped. "Catch me if you can!"

Elizabeth's laughter rang across the gardens. She looked behind her to see that her husband had taken up the challenge and was bearing down on her fast, which made her laugh even harder. Spurred on to run like the wind, she pelted hard through the iron gates at the end that separated the gardens from the park. Lizzy entered a beautiful stretch of land by the side of the stream, every step bringing a nobler fall of ground or a finer reach of the woods into view. Frost glittered on every blade of grass and sparkled like diamonds on the rocky outcrops in the distance, silvering the distant hills like shimmering mist. He was closing in on her as they entered the woods, and running past the water glinting in the winter's sunshine, they ascended some of the higher grounds; where they were rewarded by sublime views of the valley and the opposite hills. Elizabeth spurred on ahead through the hanging woods before skipping and running down to the edge of the water. She knew he was almost upon her when she saw the bridge, which Lizzy remembered from her walk last August, and the glen with room only for the stream and a narrow walk amidst the rough coppice-wood. Elizabeth longed to explore; and leading her husband on, sped swiftly along the winding path.

Finally, with her heart beating so hard she felt it might burst, Lizzy was forced to stop and catch her breath. Within seconds Darcy caught her and had her trapped in his arms. Gasping for air, and laughing so much she felt she might explode Lizzy surrendered at last.

"I knew you could not catch me," she said with a grin.

"And I made sure I did not. I enjoyed the chase, quite as much as when I was courting you."

"Whatever do you mean? You cannot be telling me that you were always in pursuit of me."

"For longer than I think either of us were aware. And you must admit, we had some sport with one another."

"We did, indeed, though it has to be said I oft had the upper hand," Lizzy said, smiling coquettishly.

"On that subject, I shall be silent as a gentleman should be. The lady must have her way."

Lizzy pummeled him with her fists. "Oh, arrogant boy! I might know you would try and have the last word."

"I haven't been along here since I was a child," said Darcy, ignoring her comments and looking about him, "though I do not recall it looking quite so lovely as it does today."

"I daresay you were intent on chasing rabbits or some such sport," said Elizabeth, still panting for breath but aware that her husband's eyes were observing her carefully. "I do not think small boys are still long enough to appreciate the beauty around them."

"No, you are probably right, but I certainly acknowledge it now." Darcy twisted a curl at her throat around his finger. "These woods with you at their heart have never looked finer."

"Flattery will not prevent my running away again," Elizabeth teased and looked away with a toss of her curls.

"I have you now, and I am never letting you go again," Darcy whispered tenderly into her hair.

"I am happy to submit for the time being, kind sir, if only to get my breath back for a moment."

Darcy threw back his head of unruly dark curls and laughed. "You won't escape me another time."

"And that sounds like a challenge, dear husband."

Fitzwilliam Darcy gazed into the fine eyes of the woman he adored. "I am ready for you, Mrs. Darcy. Let us see if you dare to run this time."

He tightened his grip, bringing her closer until there was no space between them, backing her up against a twisted oak tree. Elizabeth felt the weight of his body pressed against her, and his lips on her cheek, peppering her face with kisses. Passions rising, Darcy found her mouth with the lightest touch, but then she felt him hesitate before he stepped back away from her. He looked solemn and grave as Elizabeth stared back into his dark eyes, black as slate in the dim woodland light and watched their breath making wisps of smoke on the cold air, the sound magnified in the quiet space, redolent with the scents of earth and moss. She saw him staring, drinking in every feature but boldly never left his gaze. She willed him to kiss her, hoping he would not take long.

"This is your kingdom, Mrs. Darcy, I do hope you like it," he said at last. "These woods and all you survey are ours to share."

'I simply adore it, and with you at my side, I truly must be the luckiest creature in the world.'

"I love you, Mrs. Darcy with every last breath in my body, and I know all of Derbyshire and Pemberley will soon love you just as much."

Elizabeth's laughter broke the stillness of the air. "Oh, my darling Darcy, how did it take me so long to know how much I love you too?"

Stepping closer once more, he ran his fingers along her cheek, cupped her chin in his hand, tilting it towards him. Closing her eyes, she felt his fingers in her hair and his lips on her own. It was a slow and tender kiss, and Elizabeth felt herself sinking under the spell he cast so easily. She pulled him closer, willing it to last forever. They neither spoke again; both feeling that time in such a sacred place was so precious that words alone could not do justice to their feelings. Wrapped in each other's arms, Pemberley's woods seemed to embrace them in a moment never to be forgotten.

Mr. and Mrs. Darcy at Home at Pemberley

by Susan Mason-Milks

November 30, 1812

Elizabeth awoke slightly disoriented but then quickly remembered where she was—the big bed in Darcy's room. The past few days—and nights—had been perfection. Their first night together, their afternoon nap, dinner by candlelight, and then more nights of new experiences and revelations—this kind of intimacy in a relationship was so much more than she had ever dreamed of. At last, she was truly his wife and although her face reddened at the thought of what transpired between them, her body tingled and her heart rejoiced.

As she lay quietly taking time to enjoy becoming more fully awake, she sensed she was alone in the big bed. It seemed strange to her that Darcy could have arisen without waking her, and she began to wonder how late she had slept. The clock told her it was only eight in the morning, not so late as she had first thought. Reaching her arms above her head, she stretched out fully and thought about her plans for the day.

Just as she started to sit up, she realized she was missing something very important—her nightdress. In the rush to be together last night, Darcy had pulled it off and tossed it into the air. It must have landed somewhere on the floor near the bed. Scanning the room, she saw it was now neatly draped across a chair along with her dressing gown. She groaned. Two things came to her mind—how did it get there and more importantly, how was she going to retrieve it.

It was a long way from the big bed to the chair. Reclaiming her nightclothes would necessitate walking eight to ten feet across the room completely unclothed. She would die of embarrassment if one of the servants should choose that exact moment to come into the room! Or what if Darcy returned? It was one thing to be with him under the covers, but it would be something different altogether to be caught out in the open. Just thinking about it made her face warm.

Finally, acknowledging she might be forced to wait for a long time if she did not brave the walk, she took a deep breath and made a dash for the chair. She had just slipped the gown over her head and was starting to reach for the robe when there was a knock on the door. Startled into action, she dashed back to the bed and leaped in pulling the covers up around her.

The door swung open, and Darcy entered carrying a tray with coffee and scones. "I have brought your breakfast, Mrs. Darcy. Ah, I see you have been up already," he said, nodding toward the chair.

"Did you...," she trailed off, waving her hand anxiously in that direction.

"No, your things were there when I awoke."

"So someone came in while we were asleep and..." her voice trailed off again. Elizabeth groaned and pulled the covers over her head. Darcy laughed as he set the tray down on the bed. Gently, he uncovered her face and kissed her forehead.

"Most likely, it was your maid Margaret since your dressing gown was on the chair as well," he said as he began pouring coffee into the delicate china cups.

"I do not think I shall ever become accustomed to having servants around me all the time. Does it never disturb you? Sometimes, I feel as if I am never alone."

Darcy shrugged. "I do not think about it. Their presence is just a fact of life. Of course, there are times when I wish to be alone.

Everyone knows not to come into my study without knocking, and usually no one enters my bedchamber in the morning until I ring. Perhaps, you might tell your maid the same."

"I am not sure if I shall ever be completely comfortable. They must know everything we do."

He raised an eyebrow. "Well, not everything." Darcy added milk and sugar to the cup before handing it to her. Reaching up, he fingered a stray lock of her hair and watched her intently. She blushed under his gaze.

"My love, if you are going to turn red every time I look at you...," he began as he stroked her cheek with his thumb. She leaned her head against his hand.

"I cannot control it. It just happens," she told him.

He gave a short laugh. "Strange, isn't it that this is the one sort of situation in which you are the one who is shy and instead of me."

"Do not tease." She set her coffee aside. "Now I feel very much in need of hearing again that you love me."

At that, he smiled. "Lizzy, sweetheart, you must know you are my whole world. I do not think I truly lived until I met you." Starting just below her ear and working his way down to her shoulder, he placed light kisses on her sensitive skin.

She shivered. Tipping her head back slightly, she closed her eyes, lost in the sensations.

When he reached the obstacle of the strap of her nightdress, he gently slid it off her shoulder. "Lizzy?"

"Hmm?" Dreamily she opened her eyes and found him watching her.

"I love you," he said softly.

Putting her arms around his neck, she pulled him down to her. Slowly, taking his time, he made sure his lips communicated exactly the extent of his regard.

Lady Catherine Condescends to Inspect the Happiness at Pemberley

by Diana Birchall

April
December 16, 1812 1813

The approach to Pemberley was on a giant scale—the wide valley, the great house, the vast garden before and forested land rising behind. The inmates of the house, the owner and his family and servants alike, could see from very far off, across the valley, when carriages approached; and they had their choice of windows to watch from, as Pemberley numbered them in the hundreds.

Darcy and Elizabeth both paused for a moment in their busy lives to gaze out the long windows of the library at the bridge that crossed the river. A carriage and six were crossing at a rapid clip, and Darcy was able to identify the arms even from that distance.

"Yes, it's Aunt Catherine." He did not sigh, and his small philosophical shrug was barely noticeable.

Elizabeth peered out apprehensively. "You can't possibly see the de Bourgh arms from this distance, without the eyes of an eagle," she argued. "I do see that the coach is painted purple. I thought only royalty could have carriages that color."

Mary, who was on a visit and always spent all her time at Pemberley in the library, shut her book. "That is true," she said, "Lady Catherine is breaking with protocol if she has painted her carriage purple. A magistrate for her county ought to know better."

699

Darcy did not appear to hear her, and took out his watch. "From where she is, it will take just under ten minutes until she is handed out of her carriage. If we know what is good for us, we had better not fail to be standing in the portico to welcome her."

"Yes, indeed," said Elizabeth, following him swiftly out of the room. "And we had better give the signal to Mrs. Reynolds."

"She already knows," Mr. Darcy said with a slight smile, "don't you suppose the intelligence has traveled to her offices as swiftly as to us?"

"Oh, yes. And the whole kitchen staff has been working so hard these two days. The pies are like nothing ever seen outside of France before, I am told. Is it not a pity that the menu is likely to be judged a failure, and myself to blame?"

"My dear," he protested, "you would invite her! It was you who over-persuaded me. I should not, on my own judgment, have ever invited Aunt Catherine here again, after the things she said about you."

"Never mind," she said hastily, putting her hand gently on his lips. "I mean to make a fresh start with her, and forgive the past—if she will allow me."

"Always generous Elizabeth," he murmured, taking her hand and kissing it.

The carriage was drawn up, the appropriate servants opened and shut the doors, and Lady Catherine herself was standing in the hall. She looked from Darcy to his wife with sharp, disapproving eyes, and gave her head a small sententious shake, which made her high feathers quiver, bird like. Darcy bowed, and Elizabeth made a respectful curtsey.

"Welcome, Aunt," he said politely. "My wife and I are glad to see you at Pemberley again."

"Your wife! She at least has never seen me at Pemberley before," said Lady Catherine scornfully, turning a cold face toward Elizabeth. "But sometimes we live to see things that we never expected to countenance."

"You must be tired, Lady Catherine," said Elizabeth civilly. "Your room has been made ready, perhaps you may like to rest."

"Rest!" Lady Catherine thumped her silver-topped stick. "I have only driven from Bakewell this morning, and I am not so old for such a drive to completely overset me. I will take some tea. In Lady Anne's green Empress Catherine service, if you please. Our father—the Earl you know," she enunciated for Elizabeth's benefit, "brought it home from his Russian trip."

She turned back to Darcy. "I am glad to see at least, that the drive has not been altered, nor the beeches cut down."

Darcy's eyebrows lifted. "Cut down? Who would cut down such a noble line of trees? What could give you such an idea, Aunt?"

"I have heard of a great many shocking alterations," she said sourly. "It is common talk all over the countryside."

Darcy and Elizabeth wisely ignored this, as they walked through the grand saloon at a pace that accommodated Lady Catherine, who stopped every few steps to peer sharply at some object or inspect some vista.

"There! This is not the original Turkey carpet, I know. And the crystals on your mother's fine French chandeliers—they look peculiarly dark and muddy. It breaks my heart to see them so." She cast an accusing eye at Elizabeth. "I knew the new wife would not be able to manage a large staff properly," she declared contemptuously. "How could it be expected, coming from such a family? She has not been brought up to it."

"I had the Turkish carpet moved into my room, when making some improvements before our wedding," Darcy informed her coolly. "I feared too many pairs of feet trod over it here. A good many visitors come to tour round Pemberley during the year, you know, Aunt."

She was only partly mollified. "Certainly, you have the right, as Master of Pemberley. But I am not sure the dear old house is properly cleaned." She ran a finger over the pink Italian marble fireplace at the head of the saloon. "I suppose your wife has sacked half the staff, and brought in her own favorites. Flibbertigibbets not trained properly in the art of dusting, no doubt. For it is an art, you know," she nodded significantly.

The staff is exactly as it was before our marriage," Darcy told her calmly, "not one change, except a new lady's maid for my wife." He and Elizabeth smiled into each other's eyes.

"And I know Reynolds has the chandelier crystals dipped in lemon water quite regularly," Elizabeth spoke up, "she told me so."

"Silence! No true lady speaks of her housekeeping. And if you have hired only one new lady's maid, then who, may I ask, will be attending me?"

"Did you not bring your maid?" asked Darcy, surprised. "I was sure I saw someone with you in the carriage."

"And we were hoping to see Miss de Bourgh," added Elizabeth, "and Mrs. Jenkinson."

"You speak of my daughter? You, who have taken her appointed, nay sacred, place— I do not know how you can dare—"

"Aunt Catherine," said Darcy firmly, with a look in his eye that succeeded in quelling her, "this is not the way to speak to Mrs. Darcy. Is Anne unwell, that she could not come?"

"Yes," answered Lady Catherine ungraciously, "she did not want—that is, she has a weak throat, and I fear quinsy, so I left her at home with her companion. I am here with Akers only. Where is she? Where is that fool woman? I want her to take my tippet. You keep it stiflingly hot in here. What is the use of a great fire in this hall, in April too, if we are not to sit here? I hope this does not mean there is a new regime of extravagance abroad at Pemberley."

"Mrs. Akers has been brought to the servant's hall for a hot drink and some victuals," explained Elizabeth. "I will pull the draw, and one of our maids will attend to you. And I thought we might take our tea upstairs in Georgiana's sitting-room, it is more comfortable than these great state-rooms."

"Humph! I can see the whole ordering of the place is in complete disarray," said Lady Catherine with disgust. Before she had

702

finished speaking, a maid had entered, and was quietly helping her off with her ermine-tipped outer coat.

They mounted the stairs, about which Lady Catherine had much to say about proper care of hardwoods, the need to air marble, and the ill advisement of ever permitting a cat to enter a house. The lobby above merited only a brief catalogue of complaints about the placing of its portraits, which had not been changed, though Lady Catherine was sure that they had; but at last they reached Georgiana's pretty sitting-room. The young lady rose to greet her aunt and be kissed by her.

All were soon seated by the fire, and tea was brought in, as Lady Catherine surveyed Georgiana's appearance. "You look well enough," she said grudgingly, "I hope that the sad demotion from your proper place as mistress of Pemberley has not made you ill."

Georgiana was shy, unwilling to speak at the best of times, and more frightened of her aunt than of most people, but she could not let this pass. "Oh no, Aunt! I am so happy with my new sister. I do love Elizabeth dearly, and there could be no better mistress of Pemberley."

"You put a good face on it," said Lady Catherine dryly, "but I suppose you must, or risk her temper. There may be no end to the petty ways in which such a termagant will torment you when I am gone."

Georgiana continued to earnestly protest her love for her sister, and Elizabeth did not lift up her eyes, as she wanted to do, but only went on composedly pouring tea.

Mr. Darcy instructed the butler to invite their other guests to join them, if they desired, and in a few minutes Mr. and Mrs. Gardiner entered. With a true ladylike air, Mrs. Gardiner seated herself by Lady Catherine and helped Elizabeth and Georgiana to play hostess, as Elizabeth was uncharacteristically quiet and Georgiana made no more attempt to speak at all.

Lady Catherine seemed not displeased to meet the new lady, who was fashionably dressed and well spoken, and she unbent enough to give her, unasked, all the details of her journey, the dirtiness of the roads between Kent and Derbyshire, the discomforts of the inns, and her apprehension that the fabled luxuries of Pemberley might have diminished, through having a mistress who did not know its ways. "I was quite prepared for it having fallen to the condition of a veritable forlorn old ruin," she lamented.

"Oh, no," Mrs. Gardiner assured her with a smile. "We have been staying here some weeks, and I can tell you we have never been more comfortable in our lives. The beds you know are excellent—such fine old linen, all laid up in lavender—and the dinners deserve their wide fame. Why, John, tell Lady Catherine about the fine haunch of venison that was presented last night. I never saw such a one."

"The finest I have ever seen," her husband beamed, "shot by Darcy and Fitzwilliam, and cooked to such a turn! No French chef, I think, could."

"It will be on the sideboard tonight," said Elizabeth, "and there is a fresh turkey, as well as some astonishing pies."

Lady Catherine drew her heavy eyebrows together and tapped her cane. "Talking of your bill of fare. No lady does that. You will disgrace yourself before these elegant people. I knew how it would be," she sighed. "A constant series of shame."

Elizabeth's eyes sparkled. "I am endeavoring to learn the ways of the great," she said solemnly.

Darcy turned to his aunt and said earnestly, "Aunt Catherine, I believe your prejudices will be gradually removed, as you observe that not only is Pemberley quite unharmed, but the heart of its owner has been made completely happy by marriage—much in the way of my friends the Gardiners, I believe." He bowed to them in his friendliest manner.

"Hey? What is the name? I did not catch it."

"These are Mr. and Mrs. Gardiner—my wife's aunt and uncle."

Lady Catherine flushed a deep red. "Oh, indeed! Not the Cheapside people! Impossible!"

"Yes, our home is there, near my husband's business you know," said Mrs. Gardiner briskly, "we are most comfortably settled."

"Bless me! I had no idea any gentlefolk lived in such a place," exclaimed Lady Catherine, lifting her lace-mitted hands in alarm, "no wonder that— You must be very pleased with Pemberley, as I do not know who is not."

Darcy looked ashamed of his aunt's rudeness, but Mrs. Gardiner responded cheerfully. "The country is always a great refreshment to those who live in the city, indeed Lady Catherine," she said, "the contrast is what is delightful."

"Well, you do seem to have lived among your betters," Lady Catherine observed. "How large a house have you. How many children?"

Mrs. Gardiner submitted to answering a series of impertinent questions quietly, and Darcy looked impatient. But Lady Catherine's conclusions were, on the whole, of a positive nature.

"I see, Mr. Gardiner, that despite your connections in trade, you have married a lady. Your wife is a treasure. I was in fear that my nephew might have involved himself in a complete mesalliance, and those, you know, always turn out badly. Still, it may be that your wife's teachings will make up for the deficiencies of the bride's own mother. I hope so."

"We may hope for a good dinner at least," said Mr. Gardiner jovially, trying to turn the subject.

"Yes; and it is time to go in." Darcy rose and gave his arm to his aunt rather unwillingly, while Elizabeth walked behind with Georgiana, into the dining-salon, lit by hundreds of wax tapers that made the glass glitter. The finest victuals were laid out, in all their appointments, from the pigeon pies to the turkey, and all the removes were accompanied by such very fine wines, that Lady Catherine gradually unbent.

"I must say, this turkey is cooked to a turn," she conceded, "I never had a better dinner at Pemberley, even in the old days. And we have nothing like this wine at Rosings. Darcy's cellar was always famous."

Elizabeth exchanged relieved glances with Darcy.

"Speaking of Kent, we have not asked after Mr. and Mrs. Collins," Elizabeth ventured.

"I hardly ever see them, I assure you. Mrs. Collins is far too busy with her new baby to wait upon me and consider my needs," was the displeased reply. "Her selfishness is now thoroughly manifest. And that odious Mr. Collins—"

"Why, I thought you approved of him," exclaimed Elizabeth.

"Approve of a gossiping clergyman, and his endorsement of infamy!"

"Surely you don't mean our marriage?" asked Mr. Darcy. "Aunt Catherine, that is really the last time you can be allowed to speak disparagingly of our union. That is, if you wish—"

He said no more, but Lady Catherine knew he was referring to visiting rights, and she capitulated. "Very well. I can say that you seem to be happy. And Pemberley has not materially suffered."

"Damned good of her," Mr. Gardiner could not resist murmuring softly to his wife.

"But now tell me, truthfully now, Darcy, for I shall know if you dissemble. How has the county received you? Is Mrs. Darcy welcome in all the great houses? Surely you have had no invitation from Rowlands—or from Tilden Court. Only the very highest quality are admitted as visitors there."

"We made wedding-visits to all the houses round," he answered quietly, "including those you mention; and were kindly received everywhere. Now that I am not a single man, I daresay I am less sought after, but these days I am happiest at home, you see."

"And it is so much pleasanter for me, Aunt Catherine, to have my sister here," spoke up Georgiana diffidently. "We have such good times walking and reading together."

"Oh, indeed? And what do you two read?" asked Lady Catherine incredulously. "A book of manners would be useful," she said pointedly, with a look at Elizabeth.

"We have been reading The Wanderer, and some of the modern poets."

"Not that dreadful Byron," she said with a sniff. "Stuff and nonsense!"

"No; Scott's *Marmion*, Aunt," said Georgiana.

"I do wish they would read Dr. Johnson," put in Mary fretfully.

"Hm! And who is this young lady to give her opinion? Is she one of her sisters?"

"She is. My next sister, Mary," Elizabeth answered concisely.

"And better educated than most of you, I collect."

Mr. Darcy looked askance but Elizabeth hastened to answer, "Mary has always been a very great reader, ma'am."

"But not as good-looking as you and your eldest sister. Well, she looks sensible, at any rate, and if you like her to return to Rosings with me, she may pay us a visit, and make herself useful. Perhaps we will find somebody—Mr. Collins may have an acceptable friend, I suppose."

Elizabeth could barely restrain a shudder, but Mary looked interested, and so Elizabeth civilly accepted the invitation for her, as she saw she wanted her to do.

It was settled, with Lady Catherine stating her purpose to make her usual tour of the house and grounds, and then in two or three days to return to Rosings, bringing Mary with her. If Darcy said "two birds with one stone," it was not in any one's direct hearing, and Elizabeth ignored what she guessed of it.

The dinner, to the relief of many, was at an end. But as the ladies prepared to withdraw, Lady Catherine remained seated. "I wish," she announced, "to have a private word with my nephew."

Mr. Gardiner was plainly relieved to follow his wife and the other ladies, and aunt and nephew were left to themselves.

"It is time," she told Darcy, "that you explain what made you so forget yourself as to contract this marriage. Oh, do not agitate yourself; I say nothing more against the lady. What's done is done. She is pretty, and she is clever, and does not seem entirely without some acceptable connections. I confess I am relieved to see Pemberley still being run as it ought. More or less," she amended.

"Then I hope you are beginning to discover what my Elizabeth really is," Darcy replied.

She shrugged. "You must know that my astonishment and dismay were not roused by the lady individually, Darcy. No, it is that you, descended from noblemen on your mother's side, and from an ancient, respectable family on your father's, should so forget what you owe to your family, and to their shades. To think that you should so forget your pride!"

"Ah, my pride," said Darcy, leaning back in his throne-like dinner chair. "Yes. You have judged rightly, Aunt Catherine. It is to my great benefit, that I have loosened the bonds of my pride. This, I acknowledge, I owe entirely to Elizabeth."

A smile overspread his face, making it really handsome. "I fail to see," said Lady Catherine indignantly, "what there is to smile about in such a situation. Your dear, late mother, I know, would be grieved to the heart."

"Not so, aunt," he said earnestly. "I loved my dear mother, and she and my father were all that was good; but you know, they lived in another age, and ideas have changed with the times."

"Heaven and earth! I hope not so," exclaimed Lady Catherine, falling back in her seat, and indicating with gestures that she wanted more brandy.

Darcy duly poured, and then leaned forward to explain. "Yes. In their day, and earlier, it was considered as truth that some sets of people were better than others; that noble folk, in particular, were intrinsically superior to others."

"What kind of Revolutionary talk is this?" demanded Lady Catherine. "Have you been corrupted by emissaries from France?

Have you become a Leveler? Good God, Darcy, whatever would become of England, if everybody thought like you!"

"But England is what I am thinking of, aunt," he said seriously. "God knows I love and will defend my house, my village, my country, with all my heart and strength and might. But England is not perfect. You must know this to be true—only look, yourself, at all you try to do to improve her."

Lady Catherine was silent, not wanting to contradict that she did a great deal.

"Yes. Even in your parish, there are many poor, who would work if they could; and some people live in great palaces while others are out in the cold."

"True. But that is the way of the world. 'The rich man in his castle, the poor man at his gate,' you know, Darcy. That is how things are ordered. If not so, there would be chaos."

"But we who have feeling hearts, and comfortable lives, have a duty to try to make the world better, Aunt Catherine."

"This is not telling me why you married that girl," she said ironically.

"It does. By Elizabeth I was taught that there are not such differences between people; and it is wicked to perceive yourself as something superior, when we are all God's children."

"Not superior? But, naturally we are superior, Darcy. What can you mean? We are the masters, made to rule, and lead, and others are made to follow and serve."

"Well, I do not wish to debate philosophy with you," he said, with a tone of finality in his voice, "only to make you see that, being brought up to think as you do, had the tendency to make me highly arrogant and indeed obnoxious; and it took a very superior woman to teach me my real place in the world—and hers."

"I see," Lady Catherine sneered, "you will be wound round your wife's apron-strings. She has you right where she intended you to be, from the start."

"Oh, Aunt Catherine, if you only knew! Elizabeth did not even wish to marry me. I assure you, she refused me at first, so strenuously, I can hardly be glad enough that I was able to win her in the end."

His aunt looked skeptical, and sipped at her brandy. "Really, there are no limits to what a scheming woman can make a man believe," she observed, "and she is one of the cleverest women in the world, to make you think what you do. If you could only have seen her, when I had my interview with her; she was positively obstinate in her insistence on having you. Clever, indeed."

"If you wish to think so, aunt, there is no use trying to convince you otherwise. But I believe that if you were able to watch us for the long lifetime we hope will be ours, you would see a couple who bid fair to be the happiest pair in the world."

He rose, and she followed. "Stay," she said, laying her hand on his arm. "You must know, Darcy, that I love you tenderly, and indeed I do wish you every happiness."

He smiled down at her, and his eyes sparkled. "I hoped you could feel so, dear aunt."

They joined the others in the sitting-room again, and Lady Catherine went over to Elizabeth, who looked alarmed.

"Mrs. Darcy," said Lady Catherine, addressing her so for the first time, "I am not a fool, and can accept facts as I see them. My natural discernment was always remarkable; and while many people of my age refuse to acknowledge change, my mind has a singular penetration. I am ready to believe that you may become a good wife to my nephew, and fit chatelaine of Pemberley, on one condition."

"And what is that?" asked Elizabeth, with more curiosity than trepidation.

"Have the patience to let me explain myself. You know that I was own sister to Darcy's mother, and I suffered bitterly when she died. I loved the lad as my own; and all that I have said and done since he was drawn in by your allurements, was only for his own good."

"Yes, I can understand that," said Elizabeth quietly.

"I must and shall continue to have an interest in all his concerns, and I will grant you that he at least looks well and happy—at present."

"That is very good of you."

"Silence, if you please! Impertinence is uncalled-for, when I am conceding so much as this. You know that my brother, the Earl, is provided for in his line. The de Bourgh line continues in another branch, and I still have hopes that my Anne may marry, though if she does her husband must take her name." She fell into reverie.

Elizabeth, and the rest of the company, waited patiently for her to resume.

"The Darcy line is not my own by blood, yet I have respect for it, honoring my beloved sister's marriage as I do. So I would give a great deal to see the succession of Darcy's house ensured." She paused, with a meaningful look.

"Aunt Catherine, that is none of your business," Darcy exploded, really annoyed at last. "You are not entitled to know such personal concerns of ours! We have not been married a six-month."

Elizabeth looked at him fondly. "My dear—may I speak?"

He looked surprised. "Why—if you will. It is your own choice."

Immediately, though with some natural shyness, and hesitancy of manner, she gave his aunt, and all the party, to understand that there was reason to expect that the coming autumn would bring a new small shade to Pemberley.

To say that Lady Catherine was pleased, is only to speak the truth, for she was very eager that all connected with her should prosper grandly, and for Darcy to have a son and heir would tend to the well being of his house. If she nursed a hope that the young mother might not survive the process, and a second wife of a better class of society be required, she at least brought herself to a tolerable enough state of politeness enough not to say so.

Georgiana, and the Gardiners, were truly and unfeignedly delighted, and the rest of the evening was not enough for all their expressions of happiness.

As they mounted the stairs at night, after seeing their guests off to their respective bedrooms, Mr. and Mrs. Darcy were much relieved, and well content.

"The old Gorgon, she was positively civil at last," Darcy said with relief.

"I thought she might be, when she heard all."

"Did you? I confess, I feared she might go into one of her rages, and I could not tolerate your being exposed to such unpleasantness."

Elizabeth smiled a secret smile. "You need not have worried. I have been matched with Lady Catherine before, and you see I did not lose the battle."

Darcy looked amused. "Very true. Though I don't like thinking of myself as the prize in spoils of war. You are the prize, my Elizabeth, and our little one to be."

"And you are mine. Ours," she declared, placing her candle by the bedside, and loosening her dark tresses so they fell down along her white nightgown and the satin counterpane. "Though some might say that the prize is Pemberley."

Pemberley - 1845

by Abigail Reynolds

With satisfaction, Darcy scanned the crowd of friends and family gathered in the Pemberley dining room. It had been a good day. Darcy approved of the young lady of good family to whom Thomas was now safely married. Her impertinence sometimes dismayed him, but she reminded him of his Elizabeth when he had first met her, before he knew the warm heart that lay under her teasing. But it was good that Thomas' bride had spirit; even as a baby, he had been the most energetic of their four children, the one who always spotted trouble and managed to find the messiest part of it. The army had settled Thomas a little, but still, his wife would have her work cut out for her.

The wedding breakfast was proceeding without a hitch. The new housekeeper whom Elizabeth had hired seemed to know her job, although it was odd to have a housekeeper who was younger than he himself was. He still missed old Mrs. Reynolds, who had retired not long after Elizabeth found her feet as Mistress of Pemberley. It had not been an easy transition for his own bride; several times in the first months of their marriage he had found her in tears of frustration over learning some aspect of the work she was required to oversee. Of course, she had mastered the complex role as quickly as anyone could expect, but then again he had known she would. Those few servants who had been foolish enough to question that when the new Mrs. Darcy arrived had found themselves rapidly replaced by Mrs. Reynolds, who allowed no criticism of his choice of bride.

He shifted as close to Elizabeth as her voluminous skirts would permit, thinking for the thousandth time how much he wished for a return of the fashions of their youth. Girls might look pretty enough in these modern dresses with their bell-shaped skirts buoyed out by masses of petticoats and their waists constricted to an unnaturally tiny size, but he missed those high-waisted gowns that had fallen so naturally along Elizabeth's form. How he had loved watching her in them, the thin muslin clinging to her shapely body, the translucent fabric exposing just a hint of the shape of her legs. He pitied the young men of today, condemned never to catch a glimpse of a woman's true shape except in the most intimate moments. Thank heaven Elizabeth had never adopted the full modern regalia. Her public dresses were fashionable, but she managed to look lovely despite keeping her corset comfortably loose, and, knowing his preferences, she often dispensed with some of the petticoats when they sat together in the privacy of their rooms. And she *was* still lovely, after all these years, with four children grown and a world changed beyond recognition.

How unimaginable all of this would have been to him in those early days! Had the world ever before altered so much in the course of one generation? Theirs had begun in a bucolic world, and now they were surrounded by the new industrial age. The huge factories in Manchester and Birmingham, the ugly railroads that were springing up everywhere, the influx of the poor into the cities where they became poorer still, forced to endure terrible conditions until they were near collapse from exhaustion. Oh, he could admit that it was pleasant to be able to reach London from Pemberley in a day, forgoing the jolting ride of carriages over rutted roads for two or three days at a time, and not having to worry about changing the horses or the quality of the coaching inns. Still, he did not like being locked up in the noisy box of a train car, even the elegant first class ones. He likely would never have boarded one in the first place had it not been for Elizabeth's urging. She loved new experiences, and he loved to give her the pleasure of them. Giving her pleasure was still one of his greatest joys.

Of course, he had not always been able to protect her from unhappiness. The tears and depression that had followed the death of little Emma, just three months old, had seemed to last forever, and he had not known how to help her, just when she had needed him the most. But life had gone on, and another disaster had brought them together again - that cursed year of 1816, when they had to work together for the sake of Pemberley, through famine and a smallpox epidemic. The Irish Disease had come close on its heels, carrying off many of their servants, and for a time they had feared for Georgiana's life. Thank God they had managed somehow to keep the tenants of Pemberley fed when the harvests had failed! That was when he congratulated himself on choosing such an intelligent and capable wife whom he could depend on as a helpmate rather than a society miss without a thought in her head.

He chuckled at the idea that he had *chosen* to marry Elizabeth - his need for her in the early days had been more like a force of nature - causing his wife to give him a quizzical glance. Patting her hand to assure her all was well, he smiled into her eyes that were every bit as fine as when they had first met. Her hair might be threaded with silver now, but he could still see the laughing, teasing, bewitching girl he had married all those years ago when she tilted her head in that special way of hers, an arch curve to her lips. When she had first accepted his hand, he had believed that no man could ever love a woman more than he did at that moment, but he had been a callow youth. Passion and fascination were powerful, but they were nothing to the love that grew over the years, improving like brandy with age.

So much had changed, but some things never would. He leaned close to her and said softly, "In vain have I struggled. It will not do. You must allow me to tell you how ardently I admire and love you." Her eyes lit up, and he felt the power of their bond, which had survived misunderstandings, great joy and equally great pain. She was, indeed, a woman well worth pleasing.

Table of Contents

Author Index

Acknowledgements

The authors would like to thank the readers of the Jane Austen Variations website (austenvariations.com) for their support and encouragement, and Deborah Fortin for her invaluable assistance in proofreading the manuscript.

About the Authors

This book was written by 15 authors of Austen-inspired fiction who are part of the Jane Austen Variations group blog. Our books include both Regency-set and modern novels, sequels, variations, retellings, and mash-ups.

If you'd like to more about our authors, please visit our web site at **http://www.austenvariations.com**.

Authors' Websites

Austen Variations
www.austenvariations.com

Diana Birchall
www.lightbrightandsparkling.blogspot.com

Marilyn Brant
www.marilynbrant.com

Jack Caldwell
www.cajuncheesehead.com

Cassandra Grafton
https://cassandragrafton.com/

Monica Fairview
www.monicafairview.com

Maria Grace
www.RandomBitsofFascination.com

Kara Louise
www.karalouise.net

Leslie Diamond
https://lldiamondwrites.com

Susan Mason-Milks
www.austen-whatif-stories.com

Jane Odiwe
www.janeaustensequels.blogspot.com

C. Allyn Pierson
www.callynpierson.wordpress.com

Abigail Reynolds
www.pemberleyvariations.com

Colette Saucier
www.colettesaucier.com

Mary Lydon Simonsen
www.austenvariations.com

Shannon Winslow
www.shannonwinslow.com

17984729R00403

Printed in Great Britain
by Amazon